Praise for Cole Alpaugh

THE SPY'S LITTLE ZONBI

"Forget James Bond. I'd much rather spend my time with Chase Allen, the idealistic journalist-turned-government spook at the center of Cole Alpaugh's outlandishly entertaining new novel, *The Spy's Little Zonbi*."

—Josh McAuliffe, *The Scranton Times-Tribune*

"Imaginative. Funny. 3D Characters that come to life on the page and leave you wanting more. *The Spy's Little Zonbi* is Cole Alpaugh's best work to date!"

—Michelle Hessling, Publisher, *The Wayne Independent*

"*The Spy's Little Zonbi* defied my expectations. It is at times gruesome. It is at times heartless. Cole Alpaugh's use of dark humor and timing is impeccable .... Part T*he Girl with a Dragon Tattoo* and part *The World According to Garp*, Alpaugh's latest offering is an exhilarating read that I highly recommend."

—Ann Schmidt, MLS, The Public Library of Cincinnati and Hamilton County

"*The Spy's Little Zonbi* is a clever and sometimes sad novel about the lunacy of the modern world. It is a vivid, emotional, and imaginative read."

—Olivia Patel, Redbridge Central Library, London

THE TURTLE-GIRL FROM EAST PUKAPUKA

Finalist, 2013 Next Generation Indie Book Awards
Finalist, 2013 ForeWord Magazine Book of the Year Award

The book is playful and comic in its creation of... misunderstandings and coincidences. As their stories unfold and intersect, one comes to believe the island is indeed paradise, as Jesus plays a heroic role and the cannibal, Albino Paul, the shark god, and the birds play out a finale resounding with echoes of myth."

—ForeWord Magazine

"Dr. Doolittle meets LOST ... interesting and colorful cast of zany characters on a crash course with fate."

—Michelle Hessling, Publisher, *The Wayne Independent*

"Teeming with outlandish scenarios and bizarre yet deeply compelling characters, *The Turtle-Girl from East Pukapuka* is a veritable feast for lovers of playfully absurd fiction. Who knew cannibalism could be this much fun?"

—Josh McAuliffe, *The Scranton Times-Tribune*

"Would a god really eat his own boogers? He might in this wonderful, crazy, non-linear novel filled with a cast of characters floating in and out of a literary universe peopled with pirates, South Sea Islanders named Dante, Jesus, and Butter, and a Loggerhead turtle with cosmic consciousness. Controlled craziness at its best, this novel dazzles with its stylistic inventiveness. "

—Jack Remick, author of *Blood* and The California Quartet series

"Lyrical and yet wonderfully warped, if *The Lord of the Flies* had been written by Kurt Vonnegut, you would have some idea of what to expect from Alpaugh's second novel. Heavily outfitted with wry humor and cutting sarcasm, this unique tale doesn't pause for a breath. You are swept into *The Turtle-Girl from East Pukapuka* with the same energy as the tsunami that sparks the critical events leading the reader across the vast South Pacific and at breakneck speeds along a downhill race course, all headed to a place in the afterlife known as Happa Now .... A highly entertaining read."

—Hua Lin, MLS, Los Angeles Public Library

"Butter is a six-year-old Pacific Islander who cares for wounded creatures; Dante is a hot-shot downhill racer; Jesus Dobby runs a scavenging barge; Ratu & Jope are pirates and Abilone is a cannibal. All these characters meet and while it is not always pretty, it is pretty entertaining. I quite enjoyed the ride. Alpaugh reminds me of James Morrow with more gore and explosions. He has created a fairy tale with mythic figures and classic characters; and an assumptive logic to the cosmos that allows him to end the story without tying everything up with a bow. *The Turtle Girl from East Pukapuka* made me laugh and made me cringe, but most importantly it made me think about the world order and how to spend the time we are here."

—Uncle Barb's Blog

"Alpaugh's words dance in the mind and tug on the heart."

—Regan Leigh, writer/blogger

"In Alpaugh's world, flaws are beautiful, no hero is perfect, and every person—no matter how strange or depraved—has a purpose. And, of course, there's always hope."

—Rhiannon Ellis, author of *Bonded in Brazil*

THE BEAR IN A MUDDY TUTU

'There's a story inside, both charming and heartbreaking."

—Alex Adams, author of *White Horse* (Atria Books/Simon & Schuster)

"If you enjoy fast-paced, quirky reads filled with offbeat, colorful characters and a touch of sorrow draped in the colorful striping of a circus tent, I think you'll enjoy *The Bear in a Muddy Tutu*."

—Damien Walters Grintalis, author of *Ink*

"Pick up *The Bear in a Muddy Tutu* if you enjoy taking a literary journey that is twisted, peopled by characters who are social misfits, caught up in events that range from bizarrely tragic to merely sad. Reminded me in a way of *A Confederacy of Dunces*."

—Molly Rodgers, Library Director, Wayne County Public Library

"I'd recommend it if you want a charming, bizarre tale with a satisfying, fate-driven ending. It reads a little like Christopher Moore but with more heart. It's fanciful, beautiful, and escapist to the core."

—Mercedes M. Yardley, author of *Beautiful Sorrows*

"A delightful read full of wonderfully twisted characters trying to muddle through this thing we call life ... a must-read."

—LK Gardner-Griffie, author of the two-time Pearson Prize Teen Choice Award-winning Misfit McCabe series

"If you are looking for a 'big top' read with lots of heart and laughs, and characters you can sit down with to listen to their story for a spell, magic, whimsy, and dancing bears, then look no further than Cole Alpaugh's *The Bear in a Muddy Tutu*."

—Shannon Yarbrough, author of *Stealing Wishes*

"From the first page to the last Cole Alpaugh had my attention. His zany and colorful characters and style of writing puts me in mind of one of my favorite authors, John Irving. I suspect that I have now found my next new favorite author."

—Michelle Hessling, Publisher, *The Wayne Independent*

THE SPY'S LITTLE ZONBI

THE SPY'S LITTLE ZONBI

Cole Alpaugh

coffeetownpress

Seattle, WA

coffeetownpress

Coffeetown Press
PO Box 70515
Seattle, WA 98127

For more information go to: www.coffeetownpress.com
www.colealpaugh.com

Cover design by Sabrina Sun

THE SPY'S LITTLE ZONBI
Copyright © 2014 by Cole Alpaugh

ISBN: 978-1-60381-184-2 (Trade Paper)
ISBN: 978-1-60381-185-9 (eBook)

10 9 8 7 6 5 4 3 2 1
Library of Congress Control Number: 2013943292
Printed in the United States of America

For Sydney Fahrenbach,

who continues to inspire

Acknowledgments

M Y THANKS TO Gary Ruckwarger for leading the way to the best firefights, and to the night clerk at the Panama City hotel who surely saved my life. Thanks to the Montage Mountain Ski Team coaching staff for sharing their incredible skills. My gratitude to Bryan Records for letting me tag along inside burning buildings at all hours of the night, and to Ivan for keeping my Kat happy and safe. To Kristine Baney for her lovely notes, and Regan Leigh for her inspiring words. And special thanks to Catherine Treadgold, the most talented editor on this sometimes volatile world.

Also by the Author ...

The Turtle-Girl from East Pukapuka

The Bear in a Muddy Tutu

Chapter 1

THE LEPERS SHUFFLED in from the dirt street and took their regular position as cheerleaders. Seven women lined up shoulder to shoulder along the far sideline to murmur and hoot, each shrouded in U.S. Army surplus blankets despite the tropical heat. They were olive drab shadows and glimpses of leathery flesh who celebrated high scoring games no matter which side was winning.

Chase Allen eyed his assistant coach, worried about another bad scene. When the lepers first appeared at the soccer field each day, Stoney's behavior was unpredictable. It was probably because the drugs from the night before never had a chance to clear out of his system. His latest kick had been from cocaine and some sort of animal tranquilizer.

On the defensive, Stoney returned his best friend's look. "It was the sudden moves, they freaked me out," he said from behind crooked sunglasses.

"They move in slow motion. They are physically incapable of sudden moves."

"I was having a bad day." Stoney kicked at the dirt field with the toe of an old Converse. "Everything about this place is bad."

Chase blew his whistle and the ball was kicked. He glanced at his wrist from habit, but saw only a pale band of skin starting to turn pink. His watch had gone to that place everything went when you weren't looking.

"Keep your elbows down!" Chase grabbed his own arm, pointing, wagging a finger. They were too rough when they were still filled with energy, one bad shove from a free-for-all. "Dude, how do you say 'elbow'?"

"Elbow." Stoney was rubbing his temples, grimacing from the noise and bright light.

"Funny, thanks." At least Stoney was keeping his cool. Better hung-over than any more Captain Bizarro shit.

It was on an equally hot afternoon that Chase had been forced to corral his friend, trapping Stoney inside one of the goal nets before anyone had gotten hurt. He'd pinned him to the searing dirt, shouting his name and reassuring him it was safe, that whatever he'd been swatting away from his head was gone. Stoney had later sworn that hundreds of bats had flapped out of the lepers' blankets and come straight for him. The boys who'd gathered to play soccer had screamed in laughter, loved every second. One had even tried pulling Stoney free, wanting the show to go on. Craziness was nothing to kids with lives this shitty. No chance one would run for the cops. The cops were the bad guys and these goofy *blancs* were good entertainment.

Chase had every right to be pissed at Stoney. He'd put their fifteen credits for school in jeopardy and risked making the drudgery already endured through the first half of spring semester pointless.

Haiti was a thousand times worse than they'd imagined. Hot and dry until the rains brought the rank mud that flowed through the streets like lava. Chase didn't understand the buzzing carpet of flies coating the muck until realizing it was run-off from open sewers. When they'd had time to explore, they hadn't found any hidden gems. They didn't exist. Back from an evening drug purchase, Stoney had wandered into their room at the orphanage on wobbly legs, face ashen, unable to stop shaking his head.

"Shit, man, if you see a dog scratching at the dirt trying to dig something up, walk away real fast," he said, then pulled a little square of paper from his pocket and swallowed whatever was folded inside. Stoney had reluctantly agreed to keep his best friend company in a complete hellhole, sticking it out despite having an open return ticket. It was tough to blame Stoney for all the drugs, but Chase worried. Scoring animal tranquilizers from a street dealer in this frigging place was pushing his luck with a sharp pitchfork.

The eight week mission was to design and run a youth camp in the main city of Port-au-Prince. It was one of the international aid programs rotating among departments of their college in Northern Virginia. During each term, professors could draft a unique curriculum to suit specific studies. Chase had applied through his journalism professor, then vouched for Stoney, promising to keep him out of trouble. Stoney's grades and reputation were irrelevant because no other students had applied for this semester's project in Haiti.

Chase's campus paper didn't cover international politics, but someone was always leaving a *Washington Post* strewn across the office, comic strips cut out and taped to office doors. The news from Haiti scared them all away, or maybe it just scared the tuition-paying parents. There had been gun battles and coup attempts, headlines with the words *unrest* and *anarchy*. To Chase, it was a road trip away from the classrooms and the bullshit check-passing ceremonies filling the newspaper's assignment board. To Stoney, it was a road trip with his buddy, clinging to the false hope that there would be bikinis and beach volleyball. It was an island in the Caribbean, after all, and he had every intention of nailing a hula dancer or two.

Chase blew the whistle, jogged to a small boy who'd had his legs kicked out from behind. He lay face down in the dirt holding back sobs, clutching his knee.

"*Nou bezwen yon dokte*," said one of the older players, and they laughed and high-fived. Chase recognized the word for doctor, shook his head and motioned for them to back off.

A thin line of blood trickled down the boy's cut shin when Chase helped him up. He was maybe eight years old, still fighting the tears, chest heaving. His skin was rough, small raised scars all over his arms and back. The boy slapped at Chase's hands when he tried to lead him off the field.

"*Dan bounda ou*," said the boy, his watery eyes narrow and suspicious. Chase knew he'd told him to shove it up his ass, or something close. It was a common phrase for the kids. Chase had also come to understand that any insult not involving violent sex acts and your mother wasn't meant to be particularly hurtful.

"Okay, okay," Chase told him, trying not to smile. He headed back to the sideline with his whistle. "You keep playing, tough guy."

From ten to four in the afternoon, Chase and Stoney were in charge of two dozen boys who, like the lepers, seemed to appear out of nowhere on the soccer field just as church bells chimed the hour. Only a few they recognized from the orphanage. Even the two adult helpers who delivered sack lunches came and went with just a nod of their heads. They were tall, thin men who wore large gold crosses that bounced and swung over button-down shirts. Both were overly serious, making snarling warnings at any clowning around. The men never introduced themselves to the Americans and didn't seem to speak English, although Stoney had begun calling one Tricky Dick and the other Agnew. They looked like they must have some double-secret plot brewing or were saving up for a new underground torture chamber.

The local agency working with the college had provided Chase and Stoney with a nylon bag stuffed with eight completely flat balls, some faded orange cones, and a dented metal whistle. It had taken two days to find a working air pump. They'd also arranged for cots to be crammed in a room adjacent to the kitchen of the nearby orphanage, where they were served breakfast and dinner. Aside from being chaperoned from the airport, the sweaty round man in a fedora who represented the agency had disappeared in the same way the kids did at four o'clock. Chase decided the lack of supervision was fortunate, considering all of Stoney's drugs.

Without supervision or any direction, they mostly played soccer and bullshitted in the shade. Good old fashioned boy stuff, especially since it was always so goddamned hot.

"Imagine how awesome they'd look with real uniforms," Stoney said, as they watched the ball being moved from end to end in a dusty, barefoot scrum. "Or colored pinnies so they knew who to pass to."

Stoney relied on Chase to teach them soccer, or football as the kids called it. Chase had played in high school and had started at center midfield for George Mason University his first two years. Stoney had only shown up to watch his friend play when the cheerleaders were around, actual pink girls, smelling of perfume with all their body parts intact.

Chase whistled for halftime when the boys, exhausted and thirsty, started bending over and grabbing their pants at the knees. Tricky Dick and Agnew shouted angry Creole at a few of the nearest players before stalking off toward a soda vendor who'd staked out a spot beyond the field. The boys sprinted to a mound of plastic bottles of murky water kept in the shade from the concrete wall surrounding the field on three sides. There weren't enough, so the smaller boys stood waiting, dripping sweat.

"Hey, boss, I'm gonna score two goals next half." The boy, maybe fourteen, had come up next to where Chase sat with Stoney and leaned against the scratchy wall with the other older boys.

"Not boss. Boss is for work and coach is for sports," Chase said. But the kid knew far more English than he knew Creole.

Stoney had tried to share what he'd picked up from the language, but phrases for where to score porn and dope were useless. Chase's coaching had been left to teaching by example, which worked just fine. He'd been on a travel squad with foreign players who hadn't needed to learn a new language. Soccer was a dance you taught or learned by leading with tempo and motion, not words.

"This is the only good work in Haiti," the boy said, making a sweeping gesture across the field. He was tall and gangly with knobby knees and long narrow feet. All the boys were shirtless and wore raggedy slacks torn away above their shins. "My father played on the national team against Brazil. I saw him score the winning goal in the big stadium. I'm gonna be a hero like him. You'll see, boss."

The boy jogged out into the sun at midfield and began juggling the old ball with his bare feet. Chase struggled through the alphabet and came up with the name Henri.

"Good job, Henri," he called out. "Real good job."

"His dad was a ship captain yesterday." Stoney pulled off his sunglasses to rub bloodshot eyes, curly blonde hair matted to his head. "And something like a general the day before."

"It doesn't matter."

"You think any of these kids even knew their fathers?"

"Hey, they keep coming back and they love soccer. That's all I care about." Chase grabbed the bottle of water Henri had left behind. Holding it up to the sky, he could just make out tiny moving creatures. "I bet it wouldn't be hard to raise money for some real gear when we get back to school."

"Yeah?" Stoney took a minute, rubbed his scruffy chin and seemed to give the idea some thought. "We could have a kegger. Five bucks a head, easy. And doin' something like that for poor kids would definitely score us some sorority pussy."

"It wouldn't take a lot to make a big difference."

"We'd have to find somebody to trust down here, though. The round dude who runs this program is totally sketchy.

And these guys are from some other fucking planet." Stoney nodded his chin toward the two Haitian helpers across the field. "Those dudes are grim fucking reapers."

"This is a fake charity," Chase said, as they watched Henri showing off, the ball never touching the dirt. A few others had begun to make their way out onto the field. "That guy who picked us up at the airport is pocketing all the money. He was at Mason to accept one of those big, poster-size checks from the school. There was a picture in the paper. You see five thousand dollars worth of anything around here?"

"No way, you think?" Stoney looked around the field. They'd spent their own money to buy sacks of flour to line the field by hand, using paper cups and getting sore backs.

"All that cash woulda bought a truckload of shoes. And just look at this shit they have to drink." Chase was holding the bottle out to Stoney when an angry male voice barked orders from where most of the boys still sat huddled.

"What the hell?" Stoney asked as they both scrambled to their feet. They'd taken a few steps toward the cluster of boys when Chase saw a rifle lift above the head of a uniformed man then crash down with a heavy grunt. Chase froze in disbelief, a hand out in front of his friend. He'd heard the impact from twenty yards, but didn't see what had been struck until the group of boys sprinted away from the dead child. One side of the boy's head had been completely caved, a dark seeping liquid blooming out in the hot dirt.

"Holy fuck." Stoney's voice was a hiss in Chase's ear. "Holy fucking shit."

The soldier wore mirrored sunglasses across a jet black face. His lips were tightly pursed when he brought the gory rifle butt up and tucked it into his armpit. He spoke more words, his voice muffled by the wood stock, but Chase didn't think they were meant for the running boys. The words seemed perverse, sexual, and Chase imagined they were the same words the soldier—or whatever he was—uttered at the moment of release while mounting a local prostitute, hands squeezing her throat.

More soldiers appeared around the field, some clambering down from the cement wall, some camouflage demons seeming to rise from the dust. Each man was leveling a rifle at a target, their fatigues recognizable from the G.I. Joe collection stuffed away in Chase's old bedroom.

The two smallest boys were cut down first, bodies bounding in different directions as they were shot from opposite sides of the field, like pinballs caught in a tight corner. Four boys who Chase recognized as his fullbacks made a break for the road nearest the midfield stripe. The lepers took cover in their blankets as they were hurdled by the sprinting boys. Bullet after bullet slammed the boys' backs. They were struck with slapping thuds that sent them sprawling headfirst into the ground, puffs of chalky dust enshrouding their sudden stillness. The cheerleaders held their ground, quivering and silent, as if waiting for the storm to end, seeming to understand that this time they weren't the targets.

As Chase helplessly watched the slaughter, he realized the stories were true. This was the government's unofficial extermination, the thinning of the homeless boy population. The boys hadn't bothered pleading with the soldiers, as when they were caught out on the streets swiping fruit. They had known right away to run or die because they'd all witnessed this before. Had he heard the boys joke about being caught together? Hadn't the older boys warned the younger ones that they risked being shot by the bosses if they were found playing in a group? Maybe, but his Creole was just too weak to be certain.

With nowhere to hide and no cover, Chase and Stoney stood frozen in place as the slaughter continued. Bullets whizzed by and crashed into the cement behind them, pricking their bare skin with tiny shards. The soldiers fired single rounds, either to save ammunition or provide better sport.

"Oh, god, no." Chase was watching the fourteen-year-old boy

who planned to score against Brazil like his father. Henri was probably last to be targeted because he wasn't running, wasn't trying to get away. Instead, the boy was dribbling through imaginary defenders, the black and white soccer ball at his huge bare feet. Henri crossed the eighteen yard mark into the penalty area, doing a step-over move to fake out one pretend defender, just like Chase had shown him. Six rifles followed the boy's graceful movements, as he cut left and then right, an attempt at drawing the goalie away from the net. It made for a more difficult angle but Henri was executing the play perfectly.

With the goalie off his line, Henri took his chance. Instead of a booming power shot, he flicked an artful chip, lofting the ball softly over the charging invisible goalie toward the far corner of the net. It was one of those moments in soccer that is excruciating for the defense and exquisite for the attackers. The ball lifted in a slow arc, just beyond unseen fingertips.

Before the ball crossed the goal line, a single gunshot rang out. The sharp crack echoed from the cement walls as Henri fell in a heap, one arm stretched out above his head as if in celebration.

The soldiers retreated, their jobs apparently done. What remained was the smell of gunpowder and the hush of death. Across the field, the cheerleaders began their slow motion exit of lurching blankets. Chase and Stoney looked from body to body. Movement of any kind might have forced them to do something. Chase stood listening to his own heartbeat raging in his ears, as if he were deep underwater. A single siren announced the approach of an emergency vehicle, and within minutes two policemen were casually taking statements from the American students as if they'd witnessed a fender bender in a mall parking lot.

One of the policemen used his radio to summon a group of blue-shirted men who climbed out of an old truck and began dragging the dead boys to midfield. Chase watched over the shoulder of the officer conducting the interview in broken English as the bodies were piled up. Henri was last, swung by his ankles and wrists, thrown on top. Chase looked at all the holes that weren't seeping blood, knowing that's what happened when the heart stopped pumping. All these boys had dead hearts. He wanted to count his soccer players, but it was too hard because they were piled in a mound of black skin and shiny gore. He could only guess, like those contests where a store would fill a jar with jellybeans and challenge customers to come up with the right number in exchange for a gift certificate.

"They'll get a good cemetery spot," the policeman assured Chase, but that wasn't what was about to happen. They weren't being piled up like that to be loaded into trucks, but Chase knew any argument was useless. And dogs just dug things up anyway.

The policemen drove Chase and Stoney back to the orphanage. They were told to pack quickly, that the last plane was leaving in less than an hour. They stuffed their backpacks, grabbed the few cheap souvenirs they'd collected, and jogged back out to where the officers waited.

Chase watched the column of black smoke rising from the soccer field as they turned onto the highway.

"Twenty-four," Chase said out the window. "I think there were twenty-four boys."

Chapter 2

———

THEY WERE DRIVING fast in a convertible, the wind too loud to follow the Allman Brothers' song.

Thump. A brief pause, then one more thump as the speeding car bounced over yet another object in the road.

"What the hell?" It was the pretty girl in the back seat. She leaned forward to hand over the joint rolled with strawberry paper.

"Chickens," Chase shouted over his shoulder, then drew a massive hit, his body lurching to hold in the smoke. It took a mighty sick bastard to booby trap an entire highway with chickens. Where would you get so many chickens? And how did you keep them from running away? Chase imagined little chains and leg irons then had to cut the wheel after drifting toward the muddy ditch. "There's a lot of them," he added, and coughed hard.

Thump.

"My tongue!"

"Sorry." Chase's knuckles went white on the wheel, trying to keep it together, the remains of the joint a glowing orange nub between his lips.

Chase watched Stoney inspect the girl's tongue in the rearview mirror. They'd been dry-humping ever since Bob Marley.

"Could you stop running over fucking chickens, dude?"

Thump-thump.

Chase took the last hit and chewed up the roach. "They're everywhere, man. It's a real bad scene up here," he said, then broke into guilty laughter, giggling from the good pot. He started to ask for a beer to be passed up from the cooler, but they'd be coming up on Salisbury soon. Better to straighten up a little until they hit the far side. Chase drained the last of a can of flat orange soda plucked from the cup holder. It tasted like heaven.

The pretty girl wore an American flag bikini and had a peace sign tattoo just below her right collarbone. Her long hair had tangled into a crazy whirl since they'd dropped the Mustang rag-top back at the dorm lot in Fairfax. With Memorial Day weeks away, traffic was light. Final papers had yet to be written and the ocean was still winter-cold despite these first hot days.

They caught up to the lumbering chicken hauler, a squat truck filled with crated birds surrounded by rusting wire. The chickens had found a hole big enough to squeeze through, and were lining up to make their escape. It was disappointing to solve the mystery.

As Chase watched through the smudged windshield, another chicken popped through the narrow gap in the wire, launched like a champagne cork. The bird made no attempt to flap its wings, simply freefalling away from the only life it had ever known. Chase imagined that for one fleeting moment, the chicken gloried in its freedom, uncrowded, unpecked, and breathing in fresh cut grass and wild flowers instead of the heavy ammonia of droppings. Why would it waste time trying to fly when this instant was so perfect? It exploded in the Mustang's front grill, a violent blast of white feathers and pink gore. The girl in the back seat spit out one of the feathers and mouthed a single word into the mirror: *killer*.

"Fuck, dude, it was better when you were just running them over," Stoney said.

Pulling past the old truck, the girl returned to chain-smoking menthol cigarettes, while Stoney went back to work chewing on her ears and feeling her up.

They were on a four-hour trek to Ocean City, Maryland. Occasionally she caught Chase's eye, staring him down in the rearview mirror, maybe daring him to say something, or maybe flirting despite what he'd been doing to the chickens. Girls who hung with Stoney were hard to figure because they were usually in it for the good drugs. Stoney performed magic with drugs. He rarely wore more than ratty old cut-offs, but a flick of the wrist produced a tightly rolled baggie of Columbian Gold the size and weight of a big dog turd. From behind an ear he could snatch a tab of blotter acid. And he always knew where the keg tap was, just in time.

Stoney's girl would raise her right arm every few minutes, extending her cigarette into the strongest current of wind, a line of firefly-like embers bursting from the tip. Chase found it impossible not to watch her tuft of black armpit hair, also caught in the wind, a dancing nest of spiders. She was bigger than Stoney, long arms and legs painted at their ends. Stoney had climbed into her lap to work on a hickey or something. She kept her eyes half shut, either from pleasure or the hot wind.

As they slid past a steel milk-tanker that reflected their wavering image, Stoney slipped one bikini top strap over her round shoulder, prompting the driver to pull the air horn chain. The flag's white stars folded into the blue sky and a pink nipple rose like a full moon in the middle of her jiggling breast. *Yes*, Chase thought, *God bless America for these small treats*. Again, she stared at the mirror, daring him, but he kept silent, just listened to the wind and the Allman Brothers.

They were alone again on Route 50, flanked by bean fields,

the smell of unseen cows and the swirling heat of the black highway. The ride was much smoother now that they were out in front of all those chickens.

Chase focused on the road, trying to keep the crappy debates he'd been forced to endure from harshing his buzz. His journalism professor, a man who claimed not to own a tie but whose flowing beard would cover most of it anyway, was ready to sign off on the fifteen credits of work study in Haiti. The department chair, however, wasn't having any of it. Doctor Wrinkled Bitch had grave concerns with regard to rewarding students for incomplete work. The fact that the school had tossed wads of cash at a bogus charity for god knows how many years wasn't much of an issue. The fact that Chase and Stoney had nearly been shot to pieces was discussed with the same casualness as their lunch order.

Stoney had been little help during the two tedious meetings in the crammed office. Both times he'd burst through the door wreaking like old bong water and beer, causing Doctor Wrinkle Bitch to bury her nose in a hanky. Both times he'd fallen asleep right before it was his turn to speak. Startled awake, he'd excused himself, fleeing the room for the toilet down the hall.

"It's going around," Chase said weakly, but he knew it was probably for the best after seeing the cartoonish drawing Stoney planned to enter as evidence. It had stick-figure soldiers shooting guns at stick-figure children and was captioned with words like *bang*, *ouch*, and *help me*.

Chase had dreaded walking inside that room, too. The flight of stairs had been a mountain climb. The carpeted hallway was quicksand. He'd wanted to turn and run downhill, but he had no place to go. He'd practiced calling home to announce he was quitting school, but only when he was good and drunk. He'd even held a beer bottle to his ear because he was too chicken shit to get that close to a real phone. Not with that sort of news.

Chase had become the Golden Child of his family after their dad had caught his older sister Amanda diddling the dog. "A violation of nature," was how the former U.S. Army Staff Sergeant and current plant foreman described the incident to his wife.

If he only knew.

Chase was eleven when he'd woken in the dead of night to Amanda pressing the barrel of one of their father's guns to the center of his forehead. He'd looked up at her cross-eyed at first, the glow from a Flintstones night light enough for him to take stock of his circumstances. With great stealth, she'd mounted his chest, straddled him in his sleep, and with her left hand pressed the cold and impossibly hard metal of the .45-Caliber revolver to within millimeters of his brain. Her other hand had been shoved down inside her white panties, which were decorated with little blue dancing hippos in skirts. That hand, just inches above his belly button, had been making small circles he vaguely understood to be a girl's version of jerking off. Frozen in fear of his lunatic sibling, he could feel the circular motion of her right hand transferring all the way up through the barrel of the gun. He'd wanted to cry because he was so scared and because she was so sick.

Maybe because of the long strand of drool reaching for him from the corner of her pursed lips, he had been certain she was going to eat him.

But after she'd finished, she'd pulled the gun away and leaned down to bestow a quick, sisterly kiss on the bulls-eye mark the gun had left. She brushed away the spittle and disappeared from his room.

Chase had tried falling asleep as fast as possible to escape.

By the time he'd entered high school and Amanda had been caught violating their German Sheppard, she had made her own escape to Upstate New York with a woman she'd described as her Venetian Love Goddess. The family knew her general whereabouts from the postmarks on the homemade pornographic postcards that would arrive in their mailbox. The Post Office would intercept some and they'd be delivered in official-looking brown envelopes also containing dire-sounding form letters regarding federal mail crimes. But more often than not, the five-by-seven inch close-up photos she'd lovingly and carefully mounted on white cardboard would arrive directly. The slightly out of focus images of what appeared to be her vagina filled with things you'd find around the house on the front; little hand written notes on the back.

"Wish you were here!" and "Thinking of you!"

The mostly out of focus pictures could have been of the Grand Canyon, or maybe Fidel Castro's beard. A stainless putty knife protruded in one, a battery operated stud finder in another. She and her Venetian Love Goddess might have been doing home renovations.

Chase could not go home a failure. Maybe it would have finally killed his father. More likely, his father would have killed him. He had no choice but to ascend the stairs and brave the precarious hallway to beg for his credits.

"Can we stop?"

The sharp female voice in Chase's ear nearly made him crash into a camo-painted pickup they were flying past at eighty miles per hour. He eased off the gas pedal.

"I really have to pee." The bikini girl reinserted her breast into the flag top.

"We're almost in Salisbury."

"Cool," she said, and Chase felt a fingernail run along the back of his neck in an elliptical pattern. "You know who you look like?"

Chase shook his head. He couldn't see her in the mirror, just felt that sliver of a touch.

"If you had round glasses and cooler hair, you'd look like John Lennon," she said, and then her fingernail was gone.

Near the middle of the last leg of their journey Chase stopped at the 7-Eleven where he found the local newspaper. He opened the crisp edition and spread it on top of all the other bigger papers, which included *The Post*, *The Sun*, and *The Inquirer*. Each were huge and important papers carrying news from their grand and considerable cities, as well as from around the world. *The Daily Times* was skinny by comparison— skeletal, actually. But Chase sensed every front page story was important to the people in these parts, from grain prices to a new parking meter proposal. Inside *The Times* was a section listing who was expected to have dinner at a neighbor's house, right next to a grainy photo of a migrant worker wanted in connection with a shooting. Chase had learned in class how a newspaper was supposed to hold a mirror up to its community. And here was a perfect mirror, however thin and irrelevant it might seem to outsiders.

These weren't stories about egocentric professors who held the ultimate power of grades over frightened eighteen-year-olds. Narcissistic, bullshit-laden blathering about recent sabbaticals to their homeland or wherever. These were real human beings, real people. This was real life. And on the front of the second section was a picture of an old man in even older clothes. In glorious black and white he was kneeling on wet grass, with long wild hair, and his tears were caught by the camera streaming down his face. In his bony arms were three dead cats he'd apparently scooped up for the photographer. There had just been a fire and these were the victims. They were his only family, the caption explained.

Chase refolded the paper and dropped the twenty-five cent issue on the counter with the rest of his drink and candy bar breakfast order, while his passengers climbed over the car doors. It was hard not to watch the girl in the tiny bikini pull off this gymnastic move, not the least bit modest, with an unchecked wedgie exposing most of her lovely rear end.

The clerk, who was observing Stoney tickle the writhing girl just outside the big glass storefront, was having a hard time making change with his ancient black fingers.

"Daz one fine use of Ole Glory," the man said under his breath, his yellow eyes flashing.

"Can you give me directions?" Chase pointed at the newspaper.

Climbing behind the hard plastic steering wheel, Chase was careful not to spill his gigantic cup of raspberry slush.

"I wanna check something out," he told his passengers, but they were oblivious, again busy groping and slurping one another. The *Times* was just two quick right turns off the highway, according to the clerk, and he wanted a fast look before heading back toward the ocean. Among the sandy towels and boogie boards in the trunk was a batch of cover letters, a few résumés, and sets of student newspaper clippings left over from his summer internship applications. Why not hit this place?

After three years of covering the who, what, where, when, how, and whys of grade-cheating scandals and anti-Iran marches on the Capital, Chase had been rejected by all the big-time papers and attracted only the mild interest of crappy little rags that wouldn't do much for a post-graduation résumé. The crappy rags were just looking for convenient ways to get coverage while their regular reporters were on vacation during the typically slow summer months in non-resort towns.

The Daily Times' lot was nearly full of reporters and photographers meeting deadlines, as Chase backed into a visitor's spot to sit comfortably and get a good look at the heartbeat of the town. Stoney and the pretty girl continued their softcore sex acts. It sounded like someone was eating a ripe peach behind Chase's head.

The sprawling one-story brick building was squat and ugly under the glare of the hot sun, and yet Chase's stomach churned with envy as an old blue Honda Accord sped into the lot on squealing bald tires. There was an awful, metal-on-pavement thud as it bottomed out, screeching to a halt in the last open spot directly in front of the employee entrance. The thirty-something-year-old guy jumped out of the driver's seat and raced to the building, fumbling with a set of keys, the car door banging open on its hinges and slamming shut behind him. Chase saw the yellow pencil behind one ear and in the back left pocket of his corduroy pants the narrow white reporters' notebook, curved from being sat upon for the hurried ride to make this deadline. Chase had burned through dozens of the same brand of notebook for the school paper, not one filled with anything of real consequence.

Seconds later, the scene was over. The heavy door slammed behind the harried reporter, leaving only the ticking sound of his cooling Honda.

Had there been a fire? Was he coming from the courthouse where a murderer had been brought in for a first appearance? Were the words scribbled in his notebook less than an hour away from becoming some huge banner headline announcing a suspect arrested for a string of sexual assaults? Chase's hands were cramped from clenching his own grooved steering wheel.

"Wow." He relaxed his grip and looked up into the rearview mirror, where Stoney had his right hand casually cupped under the girl's bikini top. She'd turned her face up to catch the rays, a small bead of sweat drawing a line from one temple, oblivious or not caring who saw her getting felt up in the back of a convertible.

"That dude really had to take a dump," Stoney announced, struggling with a pack of matches to light a joint one-handed.

"Yeah, maybe." Chase climbed out to rummage through the trunk for his résumé. His heart was pounding.

Chapter 3

▬

THERE WAS A coin flip that decided an awful lot.

The quarter spun through the haze of bong smoke, parting the molecules with ease, then clacked off the ceiling and was lost among the empty beer bottles and dirty laundry that had overrun every square inch of floor space.

"Shit," Chase said, blinking hard to try and clear his vision.

Stoney laughed, flicked the Bic lighter, and added more pot smoke to the blue haze in the second floor dorm room.

"You dumbass," Stoney said, then choked back another hit, spiraling tendrils of smoke rising from the corners of his mouth and out his nose. Chase thought Stoney looked like a curly haired blond wizard when that happened. Not the Wizard of Oz kind of wizard, but the Merlin Gandolf Frodo Baggins kind.

Chase's brain was as foggy as the room. He was a bobble head doll with gigantic cheeks that he touched with his warm fingers. He needed to shave at some point and would kill for a bag of Fritos with their salty, crunchy goodness, oh, my. The cafeteria was closed, but there was a vending machine in the student center. If only he had a quarter.

"I need to find a quarter."

"You lost your quarter." Stoney pointed at the ceiling and Chase followed the wobbly finger down to the mess on the floor.

Yes, right, there was a quarter down there, he thought, surveying the immediate area for some silvery glint off Washington's face or an eagle's chest. The bits of trash and colored dirty clothing—combined with a dozen or so bong hits—made the floor a kaleidoscope of amazing textures and earthy hues.

"I have to focus." Chase rubbed his face, then swallowed a shot of some harsh, clear alcohol his roommate shoved toward him. "This is really freaking important. This is my future."

Stoney handed him the bong with its bowl packed tight. He flicked the lighter.

"Okay, last one." Chase prepared by shaking his upper body and taking a few deep breaths.

"Heads," Chase was accepting the summer journalism internship the *Salisbury Daily Times* had offered; "tales," he was applying for a lifeguard job at a local community pool to work, party, and scam on bikini-clad girls until fall semester. David Eugene "Stoney" Steinmetz, his roommate for nearly three chaotic and often stoned years, was his connection for the lifeguard job. Stoney had miraculously risen through the ranks of lifeguard hierarchy, charged with training new guards and keeping children and adults safe for the last two summers, despite spending much of the time quietly sleeping in his perched chair behind mirrored sunglasses and an oversized umbrella. He'd fallen out of his chair at least a half dozen times, right onto the concrete deck. Luckily, he was always still drunk enough not to get hurt trying to break his fall.

Remembering he was on a mission, Chase handed back the spent bong and exhaled the smoke.

"I gotta find the quarter." But Stoney's latest stash of Columbian Gold had rendered him a spastic marionette.

Pinocchio, he thought and tried to spell it while rolling off his cluttered twin bed to the cluttered floor. He was as careful as circumstances would permit to search while still preserving the outcome of the flipped coin. "This is vitally important to my current life situation."

"You're gonna fry your ass, son," Stoney said, referring to the maze of stereo and hot plate wires. Their appliances all came from various trash days, and even the slummiest frat houses tossed out anything with cords frayed this badly. One day they were really going to come through on the threat of buying some electrical tape and making these things as good as new.

Chase paused to replay the coin's arc, path, and last-known coordinates in his head. Under or behind his desk was the most likely spot.

Who had tossed used fucking condoms under here?

Oh, yeah. He should try calling that chick. Anna? Mary Ann? Ann Marie? If he could find this quarter he'd definitely call her. She smelled great and didn't wear panties.

"The RA's are gone, so I'm crankin' this up." Stoney brought Pink Floyd's "Dark Side of the Moon" to life, which was distracting because it was the music Chase had used to nail that chick. Or was it? Maybe it had been Zeppelin. That chick smelled great. She drank a half gallon of sugary sangria and chased it with a pint of gin. She had the finest blond hair on her legs. She probably didn't have to shave them, but her pit hair wasn't cool. Next time, Chase thought, he was just gonna leave her shirt on. Problem solved.

"I think I found your driver's license." But the music and bubbles from the bong Stoney was hitting were too loud. He shouldn't be driving anyway. Some ice cold sangria would sure hit the spot.

Chase found the dog-eared copy of last year's February issue of *Hustler* Magazine.

"Picture of the World's Grossest Sex Freaks!" announced the cover. And, "How to Buy Life Insurance."

Chase tried flipping to the centerfold but most of the pages were stuck together. Fucking Stoney. Always the same shit. One of the guys from down the hall had left a pack of family vacation photos his mom had sent him on Chase's desk while stopping by to score a few joints from Stoney. The guy—what's his name?—remembered to get them the next day only to find them stuck together, tight as a brick. Stoney had defiled pictures of the guy's mom and little sister, Minnie Mouse and Cinderella.

"Snow White is hotter than Betty Boop," Stoney had quietly announced late that night before passing out with a smoldering joint in the corner of his mouth.

What the hell was he looking for down here? That chick's number!

"Hey, Chase!" Stoney shouted from above. Side one of the album was already down to the last song, "The Great Gig in the Sky." Had he really been down here that long? "I see it!" Stoney called.

Reaching forward to push himself back from under the desk, Chase accidentally grabbed the frayed stereo wires, which turned out to be an awful lot like being hit in the head with a shovel. He involuntarily jerked sideways, slamming his already stunned head into the side of the desk, splintering the wood and making the needle bounce across the record.

"What the fuck?" Stoney bumped him with his knees while lunging toward the turntable, as Chase made a feeble effort to simultaneously unclench his jaws, hands, and toes. "Dude, you just scratched the shit out of my record."

Was that burning hair Chase smelled? Was that sizzling sound his head on fire?

From somewhere deep inside, Stoney's lifeguard training kicked in and he rescued Chase from under the desk, pulling him out by his leather belt. "Dude, you musta touched the wire. I told you not to touch the wires. They're totally electrified."

Chase's jaw was starting to ache like crazy, the record

skipping to what sounded like a crackling heartbeat.

Shhh-thu-bump … shhh-thu-bump …

Getting no reaction, Stoney began chest compressions and Chase nearly threw up—which indeed could have been fatal at that point if he had aspirated it—as he began prying open his mouth to begin ventilation. The relief his molars felt from the unhinging was immediately tempered by that first dry, cotton-mouth kiss.

Chase recalled the old images of the long, sloppy wet kiss Stoney had given the CPR doll as a joke when he smuggled her back to their room one night. Chase never saw him hump it, but if ever there was a sure thing …

Stoney's own head bumped the desk and the tall bong he'd abandoned to rescue Chase tipped over. The pungent brown water cascaded over the back of Chase's head, soaking his hair and both their shirts. Wow, that bong need to be cleaned, Chase thought. The record needle found a groove, killing the heartbeat and setting free Roger Water's beseeching vocals.

"C'mon, you gotta come back to me, Dude." Stoney huffed, pumping Chase's chest and wiping nasty white spittle from his mouth, working like a true professional, despite the fact that neither Chase's heart nor breathing had ever stopped.

"That's it, walk to the light!" Stoney shouted, now thumping the patient's chest with a closed fist. "Go toward the light!"

And from the panic in his eyes—was he also crying?—Chase knew just how good a friend Stoney was. He could sense how much he cared, despite being stunned and barely conscious from the 120 volts. Chase knew Stoney loved him as a brother despite the fact that he was pretty much beating him to death.

"Aaaaaaccckkkk," Chase finally managed after Stoney removed his lips from a long, chest-expanding ventilation. Stoney grabbed him by his dank shirt and hugged, shaking and rocking him in a trembling embrace.

"Oh, man, oh, man," Stoney repeated, as they settled that way for a while, swaying slowly to the Pink Floyd. Chase suddenly remembered it really had been this album he'd screwed that girl to.

Chase wanted to tell him, but then decided it wasn't important.

"I'm really gonna miss you this summer, you motherfucker," Stoney whispered in his ear. Despite the bong hits and the blow to the head, Chase realized his friend had seen the quarter and it was heads.

Chapter 4

———

"PHOTOGRAPHY INTERNSHIP?" CHASE was trying to keep pace with his new boss, who was jogging from copy editor desk to the press room and back again. The man in charge of his summer internship was a sweating flurry of cusses and thrown papers. Managing Editor Mack Butterfish's once crisp white button-down shirt was streaked with black printer's ink after clearing paper from a jammed gear in the press. His navy dress slacks had a six-inch split down the butt seam. It was apparently all hands on deck when something got in the way of the morning run. Even Chase's palms were black.

"You called it a photo internship," Chase tried again.

"It's all journalism." Butterfish coughed and spat as they bounded down a hallway and through a set of double-doors to the loading dock. Hundreds of heavy stacks of newspapers, all tied in neat bundles with thin kite string, were waiting on the wood platform. "You're the kid from Mason, right?"

"Yeah, but ..." Chase stopped, realizing he'd be completely screwed if he turned down the only spot available. He'd taken pictures for the school paper with the point and shoot. They sucked and were slightly out of focus, but only because he hadn't really tried. With a foot in the door he could always talk his way into writing instead of shooting.

"You see that?" Butterfish pointed at the pavement below the loading dock. "You see those thirteen trucks lined up right there?"

Chase shook his head. It was barely dawn and he'd only slept three hours. Should he be seeing trucks?

"I have thirty thousand papers not being loaded into the backs of trucks at this very moment, but do you know what the real problem is?"

Again, Chase shook his head, taking a step back to avoid Butterfish's jabbing finger.

"I have forty goddamn business owners who paid to have their ads tossed into the front yards of thirty thousand goddamn subscribers." Butterfish was nearly yelling. "And not one of my goddamn drivers is here!"

Butterfish hiked his black framed glasses with the knuckle of his right middle finger, probably to avoid smudging them with ink. The overhead lights gave his round face a yellow sheen. Butterfish opened his mouth as if to continue the rant, but spun on his heels instead. He kicked back through the double doors so hard that a square pane of glass cracked and fell out of its heavy frame. Chase followed at a safe distance.

Butterfish stormed into the newsroom, grabbed a phone from the nearest reporter's desk and began yelling at the receiver. When the phone rang on the adjacent desk, he added it to his other ear and kept up the unbroken tirade. With deadline long past, the room was otherwise barren except for one old guy a few computer terminals down a narrow isle. The man appeared to be trying to hide from the commotion, pecking lightly at his keyboard as a meandering wire of cigarette smoke drifted from an overflowing ashtray toward the bank of fluorescents above his desk. His eyes darted from the screen to Butterfish and back.

Chase sat on the corner of a metal desk and inspected

his stained hands while Butterfish continued his rant to the phones about the missing drivers.

The old guy coughed and cleared his throat. He held up his phone's handset and pointed at it to get Butterfish's attention. "Call on four, boss."

"This better be somebody with one hell of a good explanation." He dropped one phone and jammed the number four button down with a stubby index finger. "Butterfish here!"

There was an almost deafening pause, silence except for the ticking of the AP photo transmitter across the room and the hum of the lights. As he watched the transformation of Butterfish's expression, Chase imagined these might be the sounds familiar to a professional bomb diffuser. It went from angry, to puzzled, to horrible realization.

"Is it about the funeral procession, boss?" The old guy at the computer rubbed out his cigarette.

"This didn't happen." Butterfish let both phones drop from his hands. They clanked off the desks and hit the floor. Butterfish went for the men's room door.

Chase looked at the old man and shrugged his shoulders to ask if he knew what had happened. The man eyed the bathroom door and motioned for Chase.

"Mack was supposed to send a whole team to cover a funeral and then the procession." The man lit another cigarette, took a deep drag, and checked his watch. "The show's probably wrapping up right now."

"What's it got to do with the delivery trucks?"

"It's one of their boys that's dead. He was supposed to be loaded up at the funeral parlor and shipped to the graveyard in the first truck. Real sad story. And Mack had forked over enough cash to paint up all the trucks for a photo op. Not something a tightwad like him would do unless he had bigger plans."

The man paused and cocked his head. It sounded like

Butterfish had turned all the faucets in the restroom on full blast.

"Dead kid was kind of a moron," the man finally said, then loaded his lungs with more smoke. "Not a run of the mill retard, just gullible and dumb as a shingle. Name was Clayton Butterfish, same as Mack. An old family name, there's tons of 'em here on the shore. Some are good and some are mean as snakes. This one was too dumb to be either. Don't matter, though, after you're dead. People mostly forget what degree of shitheel you were on two feet."

"But why such a big deal?"

"Mack had two reporters work up a real nice feature on the kid. Then he ran the raw copy past one of the girls who'd move on over to the *Washington Post* from this shithole. She loved it, saw all the possibilities for a real tearjerker. She was here for two days and talked to everybody under the sun."

Chase's entire body tingled at the idea of going from a newsroom like this to the most important newspaper in the world.

"Mack convinced the *Post* editors to leave everything up to him. This is his territory, after all, so their reporter was sharing a byline with our guys. Mack screwed up something fierce this morning. I'm surprised he isn't on the horn trying to get the kid dug back up for a redo."

"Wouldn't at least one reporter have gone to the funeral without being assigned?"

"Nah, it just doesn't work that way around these parts." The man tapped his cigarette into the overflowing ashtray. "You're either on the clock or off it. And you just don't see a whole lot of mixing among drivers and reporters. Two different bars after quitting time. No, Mack let a big fish get away. Today's front page should have had a four-column shot of those shiny *Times* trucks coming across the bridge over the Wicomico, the sun rising up from behind. But now the weekly cross town has first crack. Instead of interviewing our drivers, they'll talk to the half-wit's nutty aunt about how Little Clayton had gotten his life turned around after setting fire to a litter of kittens. Kid was dumb enough to take Polaroids to show his teacher."

"Jesus."

"Wasn't really the kid's fault." The man used the stub of his cigarette to light a fresh one. "And, speaking of Jesus, he found Christ and gave up heroin while at a camp for young offenders up in Delaware. You get the picture?"

"So what was the good angle for a story on him?"

The old man's fingers clattered across his keyboard. "C'mere and read for yourself. Here's the copy the *Post* girl turned in. It might run like this in her big city paper, but it needs a hard massage for our readers."

Chase came around behind his desk, fanning away smoke with one hand. He leaned over the man and scrolled down with the arrow key.

LEON TOOMAN DIDN'T particularly like people. The girl who'd asked him a bunch of questions about Clayton had a decent enough rack, but her ass lacked any sort of real beef to hold his interest. You give a woman a steady diet of fried soft shells and beer and that problem tends to go away. And having to talk about the dead nitwit choked him up bad. He hadn't wanted to tell how he'd helped kill the boy, but feared losing his job by refusing to talk.

Clayton Butterfish had been drawn to Leon mostly just because he didn't go out of his way to cause him any extra pain. Didn't make fun of him and didn't flick cigarette butts at him when he walked past. At least that was the theory Leon had come up with. Leon had been put in charge of training the idiot kid to handle a delivery route in one of the *Daily Times* trucks. Kid drove just fine, never got a case of road rage, and never showed up any drunker than anyone else. The real pain in the ass was hanging around the dock with the CB turned on because, after dropping the last bundle, the boy would just pull the damn truck over to the side of the road and sit there like he was waitin' for a big ol' train to go by. It was the damndest thing, like the kid had some sort of switch problem inside his brain. Leon would click down to channel three and shout himself hoarse getting Clayton to pick up the damn microphone and answer. If he couldn't get him on the horn, Leon would have to go track him down and fetch him back.

Two hours after every other man had gone home, Leon might finally get an answer. "This is Clayton Butterfish," he'd say real slow and drawn out.

"I know who the hell you are," Leon would shout. "What in the name of Christ is wrong with you, boy? Get your ass back here!"

But Leon knew exactly what was wrong with him. Clayton had spilled his guts in his never ending gum-flapping way that would have driven just about every other human to the nut house. Not that Leon Tooman cared or was all that interested in anything the boy went on about. Leon helped Clayton load every morning, then went over his route time and again. All the while, the noise just kept coming out of the half-wit's pie hole.

But Leon caught enough to understand. School was tough on a kid so slow and stupid. It had meant arm punches, Indian burns, and ears flicked so hard they turned blood red and eventually stayed that way.

"You see?" Clayton had said, turning his head sideways and showing off his ears. Boy had ears just like those wrestlers who didn't wear head gear. Cauliflower ears, they called them, all lumpy and wrong looking.

The noise out of Clayton didn't bother Leon any more than when the knob came off the radio in truck six and for a solid three weeks he'd had to listen to some preacher yap about fire and hailstorms. For certain, it would be one perfectly shitty way for most people to start their day, but not so much for

Leon. Nope, he just tuned it out like he'd tuned out his three ex-wives and he was good to go—no harm, no foul. Also, the boy never once asked to borrow a ten spot 'til payday, a major improvement over all the other bundle jockeys.

Clayton had claimed the open road had been calling him ever since he was a little kid. He had dreams of finally passing the test for his Class A commercial license and buying his own big rig for cross country hauls.

It was right before Clayton died and the two men were sitting on the loading dock waiting for a downpour to let up. The rain beat down like a fist and Leon was sour knowing the window was rolled down in his pickup.

"You ever see that movie called *Duel*?" Clayton asked, but Leon said he hadn't.

"My daddy took me up to Dover when I was 'bout ten. Told me it was the only time he ever went inside a movie theater. Can you picture that?"

"Uh-huh."

"Momma didn't wanna go 'cause her eyes were all blacked up. I think she was just happy to be home alone for a while."

Leon remembered thinking how odd it was that the kid couldn't find his way back across town and had to have someone else count his bundles when they got past twenty. But talking about his rotten old man somehow put focus into his scatter brain.

"I never saw my daddy ever say goodbye to so much cold hard cash except at the Liquor Mart." Clayton sat back with his arms stretched out behind. He lifted his legs into the rain until his jeans went dark.

"Uh-huh."

"I didn't get no popcorn, but I was happy enough just smellin' it. You like popcorn, Leon?"

"I like it just fine," Leon said, watching the purple thunderheads build over the western half of the city. His goddamn truck seat was gonna be drenched. Lucky his floorboards were rusted out so there wouldn't be a pond.

"Then came this big truck trying to run down a car. On the movie screen, I'm sayin'. The rig driver starts having a chase up and down the mountains with this asshole businessman. It was like when Danny flipped off that kid from the college for tailgating, then pulled over and got his ass whooped."

"Yeah, I recall."

" 'Git 'im,' my daddy yells. And I watched how happy he was when the car starts overheating and losing distance on a steep hill. Daddy was cheering the rig drive on even with all these people telling him to shut his trap. That's when I knew I was gonna be a driver. That was when I seen myself high up behind a big steering wheel, head rockin' side to side with the bumps in the road. No teacher woulda dared call me stupid again, no sir. Jeb and Donny Brooks wouldn't flick my ears no more. Daddy woulda loved me for real and not hit me no more."

"Dads can be hard on a boy."

"You know what my daddy said right there in the movie theater?"

"Nope."

"He leaned over to me and whispered 'That's a Peterbilt Two-Eighty-One.' I never heard my daddy whisper nothing in his whole life. And later on he whispered 'Them's snakeskin boots!' "

"Uh-huh."

They sat watching the rain and Leon was pretty sure the kid had lost his train of thought when he started up again.

"The movie ended real bad when the rig went over the side of a mountain and crashed. But my daddy took it pretty good. He fired up one of them skinny cigars with the plastic tip and had Hank Williams turned up loud in the one good speaker. And he was laughin' at me 'cause I had my own steering wheel in my hands. I was running through gears, mowin' down every rotten kid who ever once pulled my ears."

"Sounds like a good time with your pa."

"You wanna know how I got to be a retard?"

"No, not really."

"Back when I was a little baby, my daddy used the toilet to keep me quiet. Least that's what my momma told me. Whenever I'd get howlin' over something, he'd grab my ass up from wherever I was and head straight for the john. Momma said my head would get banged up along the way, but she said it was probably bein' dunked under water that made me stupid."

"That's a sorry thing to do to a baby."

But Leon knew it wasn't the boy's father who had eventually killed him. It wasn't even the awful case of head lice that had practically driven Clayton crazy with the nonstop itching and burning, his scalp a moonscape of scabs and open sores.

No, it was Leon who killed the dumb halfwit and on the slow drive to the cemetery in the lead truck he was riddled with guilt. Leon drove with manic tears streaming down his stubbly face, the body of the poor bastard boxed up not four feet behind him. Each small pothole made the untethered coffin jump and Leon was sure he could hear Clayton's body making a second, echoing bump from inside. Leon didn't have a mean bone in his body and was usually the one telling the other drivers to quit pickin' on the nitwit.

Leon wished he'd never become a driver in the first place. He wished he'd never met Clayton Butterfish and had never been put in a position where the kid trusted what he had to say. The middle-aged Leon was too lanky for being a driver in the first place. He should have listened to his aching back. He was always cracking an elbow or knobby knee climbing in and around the trucks. Now he was killing people.

With an ever-present spattered painter's cap and a thermos alternately filled with coffee or Southern Comfort, Leon would never work another day in his life if booze and fishing rods were free. The booze kept his bones from hurting, and he was drunk and clumsy enough to snap more rods than was really fair. And now he was a stone cold killer.

As the procession crested the mid-span of the Wicomico River Bridge, Leon nearly lost the last bit of control. It was right down there on the bank where Clayton's charred upper torso had been discovered by a young boy with a fishing pole and a brimming cup of night crawlers. Clayton had come down here by the water's edge to carry out Leon's suggestion to douse his skull in gasoline.

"Yeah, Clayton, only way to get them buggers gone is with high test gasoline," Leon had told him during a morning load up. "Just fill a bucket and give yourself a good dunk and you're good to go."

Leon should have known the dumb-as-mud Butterfish was never without a stub of cigarette dangling from his chapped lips, the long glowing ash curling down, just looking to spark anything remotely flammable.

Another bump and Leon let out a little scream, then promised to get the dead moron to his grave if it was the last thing he did on God's green Earth.

"Lord Jesus knows I got ya kilt," Leon sobbed, the guilty waterworks just going and going. "But I'm gonna get you home, boy. Leon's gonna get ya to the Promised Land, you poor dumb bastard."

MACK BUTTERFISH TWISTED the restroom faucets hard, but water kept dripping. Why hadn't his goddamn city editor reminded him in this morning's meeting? There was gonna be heavy shit flying tomorrow morning, and some serious hell to pay. He'd put the fear of god into a couple of editors and a few lazy-ass reporters who couldn't find City Hall unless someone there had just made a doughnut run. Get your butt canned from this place and see where you landed. There wasn't much further down to go from here, except rags like that piece of shit cross-town weekly.

Lord knew he caught his share from the publisher and the ad

manager. Newspapers, run by people who only cared about the
bottom line, were dying a slow death. Editorial content came
halfway down the list of priorities, just ahead of the assignment
of parking spaces. In a recent meeting the ad manager had
the balls to suggest his reps take over the spots nearest the
employee entrance so they could get to their daily rounds on
time. To hell with covering fires and car wrecks, let's make sure
his people max out their monthly commissions.

Mack had considered punching the ad manager in the
nose when he'd demanded he kill a story about the local
Junior Chamber of Commerce president being charged with
embezzlement because it would cast an ugly light on the entire
downtown business community. Mack saw their publisher
quietly nodding off across the table. But Mack was an expert
when it came to knowing what kind of newspaper you landed
at when you got your ass fired from a place like the *Daily
Times*. He'd sat through the last twenty minutes of the meeting
thinking about next Sunday's fishing trip out of Pocomoke
City.

Butterfish punched the silver knob to dry his hands in hot air.
He calmed down a little. It was always better to have someone
else to blame. As he tucked in his shirt, he wondered how it had
gotten so filthy. He hoped he'd left his tie draped over his office
chair instead of inside the greasy printing machinery. His wife
had taken pains to let him know she'd gone to the ends of the
Earth to find the perfect sixtieth birthday gift. God knows a
man's life wasn't complete without a closet full of striped ties.
But if it was lost, then so be it. Just like the *Post* was going to
have to live without a feature package and sunrise procession
photos of his dead driver.

Butterfish emerged from the men's room feeling cool and
collected, half of the chewing out speech to his city editor
already written in his head. Calling the *Post* with an apology
could wait an hour or two. Happy to kick the can down the
road a bit, he decided to wait for them to call him.

"You were asking about the photo internship, right?" Mack peeked beyond his new intern into his glass-walled office. His tie was nowhere to be seen.

"I'm supposed to start today." Chase had left the night editor's desk and approached Butterfish like he was a strange dog who might bite. Mack liked being feared and the edge that came with it. Once the fear was gone, the bullshit had a way of creeping in and things didn't get done on time.

"Limp's our chief photographer and he'll show you the ropes. You'll go out with him for a week and then you're on your own. Work fast and keep people in focus. That's all I need, nothing fancy." Mack motioned for the kid to come with him. "There's plenty of old gear to get you started."

The kid followed Butterfish to a locked closet outside the darkroom as he pawed through his ring of keys. He wondered if this kid would survive a summer of Limp's nonsense. Before shoving the key into the lock, he took a good look at his new intern. You just never knew these days. When Mack had recruited spies, he looked for crew cuts and football player shoulders. This one looked like he was about to pick up a guitar and sing "Hey, Jude." But he'd been wrong before. Maybe the kid would make the cut.

Chapter 5

A FAT MAN in a thong became Chase's mentor.
Times Chief photographer Limp Shockley went out of his way to make people uncomfortable. One of the descriptions circulating the newsroom was that Limp could make a rabid timber wolf feel awkward and slink off to the other side of the ponderosa until the coast was clear. Limp mostly sported striped seersucker slacks with vivid thong panties he flashed at inappropriate moments. His recent marriage to an eighty-five-year-old woman forty years his senior seemed to provide a treasure trove of new material. He was quick to show off honeymoon snapshots to anyone brave enough or too slow to get away—images of Speedos, thongs, and horribly wrinkled skin.

"Lord have mercy, you're the spittin' image of that sixties boy-band leader." It was the first thing he said to Chase. "My name's Limp, but it sure ain't floppy, you know what I mean?" Then came the pucker of lips and fast wink.

Chase sat in the passenger seat of Limp's beat-up Honda Accord. They both had old Nikon FE cameras with 24mm lenses in their laps. Limp said it was all any news photographer

THE SPY'S LITTLE ZONBI   39

worth a damn needed. If something happened far away, you strolled in closer. If you were too close, then you stepped back. A motor drive was made for wasting film and creating more work in the darkroom.

"One at a time," Limp said. "You squeeze 'em off real slow, one at a time, just like ripe pimples."

The odometer read 299,962 miles and Limp claimed to have a bottle of Cold Duck in the back hatch to celebrate the 300K mark.

As they cruised the shaded road along Salisbury City Park, he said, "I sure do like breaking in the new boys."

Chase could hear the peacocks and other exotic birds echoing up from the small Salisbury Zoo, which took up most of the land adjacent and east of the city park. The zoo and park were sliced in half by Beaverdam Creek, where the slow-moving water was layered with feathers from black-necked swans, great blue herons, pigeons, bald eagles, and seagulls. Gulls were so ubiquitous that one had been named the mascot of the local college sports teams at Salisbury State. The maroon and gold were led onto the various sporting fields and courts by a trotting Sammy the Seagull.

As a gentle breeze spun the feathers on the muddy creek in slow circles, Limp pulled up to a spot in front of an ivy shrouded split-rail fence. The small parking area divided the city park from the zoo. Limp explained it was his old standby spot for easy feature pictures.

"Just like a good fishin' hole when you were a tan and frisky ten-year-old boy. You knew right where to go when the mood struck you for some twelve-inchers."

They sat and took in the view of the late-morning visitors coming and going from the park and zoo. Baby strollers, ten-speeds led by the handlebars, and dogs tugging on their leashes—all possibilities, Limp explained, but not interesting enough unless he was on a tight deadline and needed to fill space quickly.

"I use a special rating system." Limp sat back in the driver's seat and adjusted the camera in his lap. "Feature pictures run from one to three, like you were giving stars for a restaurant critique. One would be a kid throwing a Frisbee. Nothing more than some little honey pie with a nice expression. I'll get his name, age, and town, then write up a caption back at my desk. Mack might complain but run it anyway. If I get a shot of the kid being hit in his little angel face with the Frisbee, I might rate it a two—if you can still see his expression and all."

"So what makes a three?"

Limp paused to add something to the scene. "That's when the boy's dog is chasing the Frisbee and runs into him just as the disc bounces off his precious noggin'. If I captured the mid-air collision, eyes wide and scared, with the dog, boy and Frisbee in the frame, then bingo, that's definitely a three."

Limp continued, "But if the boy gets hurt, then you might be screwed. A shot of a kid getting hurt is no good, although you might be back at square one with a news photo. A kid being loaded on a stretcher next to an ambulance is a one news photo. Now, if the kid dies from getting hit, then you may have a three, but they may not run the picture at all. This is a small town. Displaying pictures of dead children is frowned upon by local advertisers."

"So we have to come up with a front page feature photo every day?" Chase fiddled with the camera in his lap, still trying to grasp the f-stop versus shutter speed conundrum. "One per day and it may or may not get bumped to section two if there's spot news?"

But Limp had apparently decided he'd covered enough details. He closed his eyes and held an index finger to his lips for Chase to be quiet then adjusted the seat for a nap. Chase rolled down his window and felt the cool air trapped in this shady ravine. The air smelled like a circus, with hay and animals and something sweet like cotton candy. There were happy screams and gentle conversations as people milled about. The half dozen picnic tables just outside the zoo entrance were crammed with families.

Limp began to snore so, camera in hand, Chase carefully escaped the Accord and found a spot on a long log converted into a bench.

One little boy, maybe three years old, dropped and retrieved his popsicle, meticulously picking away bits of dirt and dry leaves. A couple lay tangled on a blanket in a narrow spot of sunshine. Using his belly as a pillow, she read a book, while he faced the passing clouds. An old man fed squirrels from a baggie, but they kept returning to empty peanut shells, apparently spoiled by other treats.

Chase figured Limp would rate these all a one as far as feature pictures went. Then he heard the sounds of some commotion—urgent voices—coming from the direction of the zoo entrance. Families from the picnic tables paused to look up. Chase was preparing to investigate the racket when he recognized laughter mixed in with the angry shouts. He held his ground when he realized the ruckus was coming toward him.

The laughter and screams came from fifteen or so children moving in an excited group. They half-surrounded an elderly zoo volunteer carrying a whisk broom, attempting to herd an uncooperative litter of pink piglets back to the enclosure they'd apparently escaped from.

The litter of ten moved in unison, with fish school precision. They brazenly rushed the frustrated woman, nipping at her boot toes, then wheeled about toward the children, who backed into one another with shrill screams. The wall of kids would re-form as the woman steered the litter with the broom, and the little pigs again found her boots interesting, possibly edible.

Chase crept toward the scene, set his exposure to automatic, and manually advanced to a new frame. He knelt ten feet from the woman, who was trying to brush the piglets in a new direction they didn't want to go. He squeezed off a frame, advanced, and took another. The woman's monogrammed zoo cap was askew, and she wielded the broom with no sense of menace. The background of these images was the smiling faces, the pointing fingers of the children. Chase took frame after frame, shifting to stay at a distance, kneeling for a better perspective. Then from back inside the zoo came a loud grunt and two high-pitched squeals, as the mother pig apparently had woken alone. The tiny herd immediately altered course and sped full throttle in retreat. The spectacle was over. All that was left was frozen, Chase hoped, among the millions of light-sensitive silver halide crystals that made up the film in his camera.

Chase caught up to the woman before she could disappear back into the zoo, and she was happy to give him her name and confirm she lived here in town. She'd been volunteering at the zoo since losing her husband to cancer in the summer of seventy-five. "You better have gotten my good side," she said before marching back to work.

Chase's hands were shaking. He hadn't realized how much of a rush this could be. If Chase hadn't captured it, the little scene would never have been remembered, except perhaps by the woman and the children who had watched. Like grain prices and proposed parking meters, it would mean something to this community. He'd anticipated being nervous photographing strangers, but it wasn't like that. Even if you got as close as you needed to be with such a wide-angle lens, you were still hidden—both voyeur and intruder. Chase tucked away his small pencil and the thin reporter's notebook in his back pocket and settled on the log bench to savor the emotions before Limp woke.

"WILL I GET a scanner?" Chase asked when they were back on the road.

"Yeah, sure, you'll get your very own," Limp said, and Chase noticed his was switched off.

"Yours is off."

"It makes too much noise."

"But what if there's a fire?"

"It's a small town, Sugar Pie. Anything happens, I'll find out."

The slim Radio Shack police and fire scanner was a burden to Limp, who preferred cruising for photos of playing children and artsy images reflected in puddles and ponds. Spot news was an interruption of his day, although he did seem to love unnerving cops protecting their yellow police lines.

"I bet you tie your wife up with this stuff," Limp said to a bored cop during their first week of training, adding a lascivious wink. Their press passes allowed the photojournalists to duck under the bright yellow tape for shots at a garage fire. Limp took care to flash that day's pink whale-tail underpants as he bent under the fluttering barrier. The cop continued to look bored, nodding them in the direction of the Fire Chief.

THE ODOMETER FLIPPED to 299,970 as Limp turned them south on Route 13, past the college on the right and away from Salisbury. A few miles later and they were rushing through Fruitland. On the outskirts of Eden they hit 299,980.

"Where are we headed?"

"Just cruisin', Pie." The noonday sun snuck behind tall thunderheads, which regularly built over the Chesapeake in the heat of the day and then raced across the peninsula toward the Atlantic. The storm's wake would leave millions of fat night crawlers miserable and dying, flooded from their holes and trapped on the steaming pavement.

Limp raked a comb one-handed through his greased-back hair, and when he wasn't talking you saw the hint of Elvis. "Southern Queer," was how Limp once described himself.

"I love you," he said to break the silence, tucking the comb in his shirt pocket.

"What?"

"See how that is?"

"How what is?"

"Tell someone you don't know very well that you love them," Limp said. "And they look at you like you called them the N word."

"I took a picture, Limp." Chase fumbled the notebook out of his back pocket. "Back when you were sleeping."

"Power napping, Pie." Chase saw him glance down as the numbers rolled to 299,982. "So what'd you shoot? Something that might let us knock off for an early dinner?"

"Maybe, if it's in focus."

"Shootin' that wide angle lens makes it hard to screw up focus. Did your manly fingers switch over to automatic exposure?"

"Yeah, but it all happened so fast."

"Well, rewind the spool now and a little later in the dark we'll see if you got lucky."

The clouds roiled overhead, dropping low and dark, and Limp flipped on the head lights. The first giant drops hit hard, almost hail-like, and he had to fight the steering wheel against the buffeting wind. Limp threw a quick glance over at Chase, making a funny face and shrugging his shoulders to acknowledge the awesome display.

"Mother Nature's pissed 'bout somethin'," he said in a fake southern drawl, and Chase went to fasten his non-existent seatbelt. Instead, he clutched his camera tighter.

A nearly blinding sheet of rain cut their pace in half as Limp switched the wipers to their fastest setting. The mileage rolled to 299,985 as he craned forward to see the right turn that would take them due west, through the little towns marked Venton and Monie, and directly into the buffeting storm.

Chase kept quiet and let him drive, partly because the rain was so loud. He'd found that sometimes you needed to take a break from talking to Limp.

The clouds continued to lower over the little blue Accord, deep puddles yanking hard at its narrow tires. Giant plumes of water splashed up over the hood from brand new rivers rushing across the pavement. They hit 299,990 and lightning cracked directly overhead. Green leaves tore from swaying limbs, a few plastering themselves to the windshield before the wipers broke their veiny grip. Limp leaned forward and smeared fog from his vision.

"It's like drivin' a submarine!" he shouted. "I'm 'bout gonna have you send up the periscope and have a look around to see what ocean we're lost in."

They defied the wind into Dames Quarter at 299,994, then 95, 96, and 97. Chase had read about this unwelcoming plot of land once known as The Damned Quarters—a stretch of whipping marsh grasses possibly hiding the buried loot of eighteenth century pirates who'd pillaged trade ships en route to Baltimore.

Passing through Chance, they saw whitecaps dancing in the harbor below the Deal Island Bridge. The small car rocked from the exposure as they crept up and over the long, narrow span onto the three-mile island nestled against Tangier Sound. A sign announced that this spot was home to annual skipjack races each Labor Day.

Enormous rusting crab pots were stacked against ancient wood shacks, as violent waves slapped the bulkhead, erupting in milky foam that was whisked away on the wind like tumbling birds.

Limp's odometer came to a rest at 299,999 and probably nine-tenths. All six numbers had rolled upward and were impossible to read if you hadn't been keeping track. He frowned down at them as they sat in the public boat launch, empty except for two pickups and trailers of boaters possibly caught in the storm.

They sat, not talking, listening to the wind and rain, watching a loose roof section of one of the crab shacks rise and fall, as if the building were finally able to talk. Maybe Limp was thinking about trying for the Cold Duck in the back hatch, if the bottle really existed.

Chase would come back to this spot twenty times over the next two months to shoot kids flying kites in the ever-present breeze. He'd return to photograph the oyster yawls returning, silhouetted against the setting sun and to capture images of the tourists who came for a glimpse at a life completely different from their own. The heart of Deal Island was being lost to time, though. The once thousand-strong fleet of skipjacks that had worked these waters was down to the last couple dozen, Limp had explained. Many rested at the bottom of the bay, some rotted in shallow guts off the feeding rivers and coves. Others were cut to pieces and nailed into the seafood shacks that sold the freshest soft shell crabs anywhere. The watermen who Chase stopped to photograph were eager to tell their stories. Maybe they saw it as an opportunity to keep their way of life from dying out.

The sky over the boat launch was brightening. The rage had gone out of the rain, leaving just a steady drumbeat on the metal roof. Limp sat sideways against the driver door and looked across at Chase, who again tightened his grip on the camera in his lap when Limp seemed about to speak. Their breath and body heat had fogged the windows the way lovers' did and Chase knew Limp wouldn't pass on this opportunity to spout something truly depraved.

Limp finally spoke. "Do you think you could kill a person and not get all crazy about it?"

Chapter 6

CRASHING THROUGH THE briars and sticker bushes, Chase beat a path in the direction of the voices of police and firemen and the smell of a decomposing body.

Limp was swearing behind him, swatting at dive-bombing deer flies with karate chops. His soft felt fedora, snatched from his head by a low branch, was now the victim of his unwillingness to backtrack. It was hot, with the humidity that comes with stagnant air trapped between the Chesapeake and the Atlantic, and Limp continued his rueful monologue over having acknowledged his friggin' pager in the first place.

Chase had overheard Limp's side of the conversation after they'd pulled up to the 7-Eleven payphone.

"No."

"Absolutely not."

"You can't order me."

"Okay, so you can order me, but it doesn't mean I'm doing it."

"I don't care."

"You are such a bitch, Mack."

"You can't call me that."

"You will not."

"I'm not going."

Slamming the payphone receiver, Limp bumped past Chase in an angry flourish of Old Spice. "Dead people smell gets all over your clothes. I hate it. Get in the damned car."

"A dead body?"

"Mack said it came across the scanner as a possible suicide. But it was called in as a black male, so you never know."

"Never know what?"

"Sometimes the Klan boys get carried away in that particular neighborhood. And this one's hanging from a tree."

"Jesus."

"Alcohol and rednecks are a bad mix, Pie, even though they keep finding each other."

"I'm hoping that when you asked if I could kill someone and not get all crazy about it has nothing to do with this."

"You reckon the Klan has expanded its membership ranks to include wonderfully refined and sexually omnivorous men such as myself? I'd look like a fat ghost in Klan sheets. Imagine the Halloween fun."

"Sexually omnivorous?"

Limp barely drove forty on the highway out to the small town of Hebron. Loaded Purdue trucks blasted by, leaving tiny white feathers like snow flurries in their wake.

Limp's complaints stopped as they parted the last of the underbrush to find a group of uniformed men chatting quietly among themselves, heads mostly tilted upward.

"Well, look there." Limp gasped for breath, pointing up to the slowly rotating corpse at the end of what appeared to be the type of nylon rope used for hanging laundry. The suicide—or whatever this was—explained the underpants and t-shirts scattered around the yard they'd cut through.

"Doesn't look right," Chase whispered to Limp as they joined a semicircle of a dozen police and firemen. They were apparently waiting for a hardy volunteer to climb up and cut the man down. The tree was nearly as dead as the dangling man, and there was no chance of maneuvering a ladder truck back through the dense woods. The man's naked toes were maybe fifteen feet off the ground.

"It's because he's filled up with gas," said one of the town cops, who stood next to Chase scribbling in a small black notebook with a pencil nub. "Makes his features all out of whack."

"See how he's bloated?" Limp's breath was hot in Chase's ear. Radios crackled around them, competing with the noise of buzzing flies. "You think it smells bad now, wait until they pop him." A fireman nodded in agreement.

As if on cue, a young fireman in rubber boots and turnout gear tromped through the brush toward the group, hauling an eight-foot fireman's hook. It was the kind of tool used to pull ceiling material down to get at hot spots.

"Here ya go, Chief." He turned the hook over to the commander of the volunteer department.

"Piñata," Limp whispered, nodding his head. "No candy, though."

The chief walked toward the tree, careful not to stand directly under the body since the limb holding the twisting corps was bent hard under the weight. It looked as though the limb would snap at any second. The man had apparently climbed the dead tree, thrown the cord out over the branch, tied it off in a slip knot and then attached himself to the other end. The final step was just letting go of the trunk and swinging out, quickly choking to death.

The rope was out of reach of any of the fire department ladders, so the chief decided to attack from below.

"Jimmy!" he shouted, and the tallest of his men shuffled forward from the semicircle. The chief handed him the hook. "Try to get him by the belt."

"Turn around and face me, Pie." Limp checked the settings of his camera. "Hold your left hand up like this, like you're dangling a piece of string." He demonstrated with his own hand. "Pretend like you're holding a mouse by the tail."

Behind them, Jimmy hooked the victim's belt and pulled down with most of his weight, but neither the tree limb nor the rope budged. Chase watched over his shoulder as the tall fireman secured his grip higher on the hook bar, increasing the pressure until his own boots were a few inches off the ground.

"Hearns!" the chief shouted. Jimmy and the corpse were now both slowly rotating. "Give him a hand, for Christ's sake!"

The new fireman stepped up behind Jimmy, looping his arms under Jimmy's armpits and mounting him from behind to add weight. Small sharp warning cracks came from the heavy limb as the dead man's feet tap-danced on Jimmy's yellow helmet, his milky eyes bulging to the size of golf balls.

"Almost," said the chief. "Somebody grab a body bag. I want him zipped up as soon as he's down."

"Smile." Limp framed Chase in the foreground, with the optical illusion of his pinched fingers holding the top end of the nylon cord and three men.

Chase smiled.

"This doesn't seem right, Limp." But the chief photographer was busy firing away, bending and dipping to line up the shot just right. Sweat was pouring down his face, and his shirt was plastered to his thick body.

"Chin up a little to the left. Good. Perfect. Hold that."

The branch snapped like a gunshot, echoing through the woods, the body crashing down on the two firemen in a heap. The twenty-foot limb missed hitting the firemen, but slammed down on the head and back of the dead man, pinning all three in a spider web of white rope.

"Oh, God!" moaned one of firemen from under the rapidly deflating corpse, which had become a gigantic whoopee-cushion of evil-smelling gases. The long, fart-like blatting sound drew sniggers from the on-looking cops and firemen until the odor reached them. They backed up a few steps, their emergency response training stuck in neutral.

"Help!" But the more Jimmy flailed to escape the body, the more entangled he and the other fireman became, thrashing under the dead weight and tree branch.

"That tall boy's gonna have nightmares," Limp said, motioning with his chin.

"Hold the fuck still!" The second fireman, who was on the bottom of the pile, tried digging his heels in to push out from under the mess.

"There's shit!" screamed Jimmy. "Oh, Lord, there's shit everywhere!"

Limp slowly rewound the spool of film. "I can't wait to turn these in to Mack," he said. "You might want to grab a quick photo once they get him all tucked into the body bag. Then help me find my hat."

ON THE RIDE back to Salisbury Limp's car stank with the odor of dead body.

"So what do you think?" Limp adjusted his fedora in the rearview mirror, the black satin band puckered from the thorns he'd carefully removed.

"About?"

"Could you kill someone who rightly deserved it? Make him or her just as dead as that poor colored boy up in the tree? It isn't against your religion, is it?"

"I don't have a religion."

"You smell that?" Limp took his eyes off the road to stick his nose into his right armpit. "The smell clings to the hair in your nose."

"I could protect my family and friends."

"I think you'd make a good secret agent," he said.

"They get all the girls, right?"

"That's just in the movies. Most of our spy work keeps you too busy for the poontang."

"What have you been spying on, Limp?" Chase asked, but

Limp was busy trying to squeeze back into the slow lane to make the next exit. "We aren't going back to the paper?"

"As much as I adore beating around bushes, I believe the time has come to have us a serious powwow." Limp maneuvered through traffic on West Main, before turning into the parking lot next to the boat docks off Fitzwater. Chase had concluded that Eastern Shore people seemed to do most of their talking either on board boats or while sitting and looking at them.

"I recruit spies for a division of the Central Intelligence Agency," Limp said after switching off the ignition. The car faced expensive boats bobbing in their slips.

"No you don't."

"The Data Base Six, or what you'll come to call DB6, is an organization that mostly does information gathering." Limp mopped his forehead with a shiny teal handkerchief. "They pose as journalists in foreign countries, working as support for the real CIA spies."

"You're full of it."

"Even our closest allies have thick dossiers on every one of our highly paid, full-time agents. The CIA jobs are coveted spots, filled with glory and decent pay, but all that limelight kills any chance for double-agent work."

"Mack's expecting us back," Chase said. He was tired and smelled like the dead guy.

"When a CIA regular stepped off a plane in Tehran during the Shah's rule, he or she would be listened to, photographed, and followed around by at least ten SAVAK guys every minute of their visit." Limp's voice had changed. It was deeper, with less southern drawl. "It happened all the time. And Iranian, Chinese, and Soviet agents made the same casual visits to America on a regular basis. The point of the trips was classified, but it could be assumed they were nothing more than a way to say howdy, we're still around and haven't forgotten about you."

Limp paused, reaching behind his seat to rummage in his camera bag for a bottle of what had to be hot water. He took a long drink and offered it to Chase, who shook his head.

"Yeah, I'm listening."

"Aside from the monitoring, the agents were left alone to sightsee and do a little whore-mongering, as long as they didn't seem to be doing any real spying. Every once in a while, a spy would be picked up, interrogated, beaten a little, and have his camera and film analyzed. They'd stick him on a plane headed home, his face full of ice packs. That would require a swift and comparable response from the violated spy's country, but nobody was really interested in turning these things into some kind of Hatfield and McCoy feud. The host countries would mostly tolerate the visits and use them as a chance to update the photographs in the enemy spy's fat dossiers. You following?"

"You're crazy."

"Ingrid Bergman crazy, or Bette Davis crazy?"

"What does that mean?"

"I can't deal with Mack right now," Limp said, and his voice had returned to flaming gay mode, which was somehow comforting. "I could go for some fancy egg blossoms and hollandaise sauce. Maybe lime instead of lemon? How's that sound to you, Pie? I know just the place."

"I wanna believe you aren't screwing with me."

"Well, maybe I am trying to screw with you in a few different ways." Limp reached across and squeezed Chase's left thigh, just above the knee. "But lying to you, I am not. I knew you had all sorts of potential the minute I saw those blue eyes."

Limp steered them away from the boat launch and slips, over the river, then through busy traffic out onto Route 13. They slowly headed north, through a dozen traffic lights, toward the Delaware border.

"YOU'LL BE GIVEN photo or story assignments just like any

foreign journalist," Limp began over a huge, rank smelling plate of crab eggs benedict. The combined odors of Old Bay Seasoning, eggs, and dead body left Chase glad he'd stuck with coffee and a muffin. They sat in a booth at the Delmar Diner, a little brick building just below the Delaware state line. "Your work won't be much different from any regular journalist's."

"So what's the spying part? Is there anything dangerous?"

"Nah, you get the fluff. You just do the interviews and take the pictures, just like what's on the assignment sheets at the *Times*." Limp sopped up yellow hollandaise sauce with his muffin and stuffed it in his mouth.

"Okay." Chase still wasn't clear what made it espionage. "So what happens to the stories and pictures I take?"

"You might never know." Limp dipped his napkin in water to dab sticky sauce and greasy flecks of crabmeat from his fingers and chin. "God this is so scrumptious but I can just feel my ass getting fatter. Honey, like any good woman, you just do what you're told and you'll get to travel to some exotic places. Do you know how many countries there are where you can buy actual living, breathing human beings?"

"So why do you recruit people instead of doing these assignments yourself?"

"Oh, gosh, I did, for years and years. But my stomach just couldn't take the travel and God-awful food. I'd get the most terrible bouts of Montezuma's revenge." Limp sat back and polished his bulbous stomach with both hands. "It was absolute misery. Just imagine running down some third-world sidewalk with your belly churning and your butt cheeks clamped together, and not a single clean toilet within five miles. But you're young and tough and are probably more careful about what you put inside your body, if you know what I mean."

"You're telling the truth, aren't you?"

"Look, you'll work and have a regular job for AP doing local stories most of the time. That'll be your cover. You'll be a legitimate journalist and you'd survive the most thorough background check. But then you'll get a special assignment and drop everything. Easy as that."

"But you asked if I could kill someone."

"Yeah, well, sometimes plans don't go perfectly. But don't worry about it too much. We all have to kill one or two bad men here and there, but you can't let it upset you. Ever hear of something called autoerotic asphyxiation?"

Limp leaned across the table and spoke in a low voice. "We call it chokin' off. You have to be careful not to go too far, though. Get right up to that special time and cut off the air. Makes me stir up just talking about it, Pie. You see stars and flashes of light, and you shoot off like there's no tomorrow, oh my. It kinda gave me a head start in learnin' how to kill a man."

"You were taught how to kill?"

"Taught? Nah, somebody will show you how to cock a pistol if it might be needed. But I already know quite a bit about you."

"From my résumé?"

"That's a good one, Pie. I believe your daddy was regular Army and your sister lives with a lesbian activist in Syracuse, New York. I can name the seven years you had both bow and shotgun deer licenses. I know you're an above average snow skier and can kick a soccer ball. I know your grade point average in Spanish class and that you did more than a little experimenting with various narcotics, mostly under the tutelage of your best friend Stoney."

"How's my sister, by the way?"

"Still a very strange young woman, judging by her photography shows. You think about it, Sugar. Sometimes we all gotta chase some wild geese here and there. That's what wild geese are for." Limp sat up and wiggled the fingers on his right hand for the waitress and pecan pie for two. "You have the summer to mull it over. In the meantime, Mack has been persuaded to give you a hard news assignment that might be worthy of some pretty boy capable of shooting a big front-page picture so early in his photojournalism career."

"I'd be dropping out of school?"

"I believe a family just isn't complete without skeletons. My dearest momma clean bit off my daddy's nose right around the time they divorced."

"I can't leave school," Chase said, looking out the big diner window.

"We aren't still on that subject," Limp said sharply. "Some time back, I was taking pictures of the writer Erica Jong when she was speaking over at the college. My goodness what a powerful specimen—with those huge, strong hands and that gravelly voice. I sat there practically forgettin' where I was and what I was 'sposed to be doin'. Just watchin' those big, delicious fingers all filled up with antique rings. I wanted to climb up on that stage and just bury my face in her gorgeous bosom while she talked all hard and deep in my ear."

Chase looked down at the brown pie. "Erica Jong?"

"Okay, so then she says something real simple, which maybe you should carry around for a bit. Erica says in her deep voice, 'If you don't risk anything, you risk even more,'" Limp repeated in what Chase assumed was an imitation of Ms. Jong's voice. "Think about it."

And it did give Chase something to think about in the coming weeks—those long, hot summer nights when there was nothing good on the radio while he ironed his new Klan sheets.

Chapter 7

———

CHICKEN CRAP WAS everywhere during Chase's summer on the Delmarva Peninsula. Caught in the soles of farmers' boots, little geometric shapes sprinkled in Hansel and Gretel-like trails up grocery store aisles and down dark-colored movie theater carpets. It was smeared into his car's floor mats and was responsible for the main stink coming from the dirty laundry basket in his crammed downtown one-bedroom.

Sunday night through Friday afternoon, most of what Chase listened to was cops going out of service for lunch and fire dispatchers making alarm checks.

"Everybody, toss a shovel of dirt at me on three," Chase would say by day and sometimes dream at night. Coverage of ground-breaking ceremonies and check-passing affairs kept advertisers and new business owners happy.

But when the week ended and the bars opened, the possibilities became endless, as the city and county streets quickly filled with drunk drivers, jealous gun owners, and a host of others whose decisions were fueled by alcohol.

Chase counted on the eight little red light bulbs at the top of his Radio Shack portable scanner to make all the grip and grins tolerable. Each bulb was the indicator light for an emergency frequency, and they lit up, one after the other, in quick succession, searching for a transmission. Salisbury City Police on channel one, Salisbury Fire on two and three, Wicomico County PD on four, then the larger volunteer fire companies on the remaining channels.

"Come check this out!" A youngish cop led Chase to the far side of a wrecked Chevy, oil and coolant seeping toward the darkness at the edge of the road.

"My god, look at that." The cop's voice was hushed as he pointed down through the gutted remains of a customized '72 Nova. Its polished intake manifold was spattered with blood and its twisted right front quarter-panel was torn back to expose an engine block clean enough to eat off. Except now there was gore splashed from the passenger's upper torso.

The call came in as a "ten forty-two" (traffic accident) "and ten thirty-eight" (ambulance needed), "Route 50 at Powellville Road, all units respond." The first officer had arrived a few minutes later and the call came in to "slow the ten thirty-eight and please ten twenty-one" (call by landline). Chase had learned that meant the accident was fatal and the details would be shared by telephone, depriving the civilians with scanners the macabre details.

It was a certain detail the young cop wanted to share with Chase in the glare of the emergency spotlight along Route 50, just east of Salisbury, the road he and his friends traveled to reach the ocean.

"I never seen anything like this." The cop squatted just above the black pavement. "Ain't that something?"

Chase leaned over the cop's broad shoulder and squinted into the maze of car parts to follow his line of sight. Next to a wiper blade and a large chunk of windshield was the steering wheel, still connected to a foot-long piece of steering column. Propped up by the spidery remains of glass, it still had both of the driver's hands attached, neatly sliced away just below each wrist. The white-knuckled appendages gripped the wheel at the proper ten and two o'clock positions.

"Talk about a death grip." The officer stood to stretch his legs and start writing his report. In what seemed like an afterthought, the cop asked for a favor. "Get a picture of that, would ya? But don't show nobody, all right?"

An hour later, both lanes were open, the wreck had been towed on a flatbed and the glass swept away, leaving the scene as if nothing had happened. As if a car hadn't lost control at a hundred or so miles per hour chasing a friend's Camaro, glancing off a tree just a few feet from the shoulder, then bouncing and rolling down the slow lane until it came to a stop, hissing, with a turn signal blinking and one tire still spinning.

Alive one minute and dead the next could have been the official Delmarva bumper sticker on summer weekends.

Chase was scrubbing the developing trays and preparing to mix fresh chemicals when Limp barged through the large revolving door that kept the darkroom light-safe. An old radio was wired to a rooftop antenna to pull in an Ocean City station that played decent music at night. Eurythmics, Boy George, and Eddie Grant were big that summer. Prince and the dispatcher from the Salisbury City Police kept Chase company as he performed his own cleaning up after a car wreck.

"We gotta talk, Pie." Limp sat with hands clasped behind his head and legs stretched out in front.

"What brings you out in the dark?" Chase rinsed his hands with warm water and grabbed an old dishtowel.

"Mack and I have been talking 'bout you finally gettin' your crack at a special story," he said in his extra slow Southern way. "You been chasin' ambulances and robbers and gettin' along just fine. He agrees with my line of thought that all the noise those crazy Klan boys been makin' deserves a little more notice from the likes of our news pages."

"An investigative story on the Klan? Really?"

Limp pursed his lips and nodded.

Over the previous weeks, local chapters of neo-Nazis and the Ku Klux Klan had a public relations battle heating up. It began when Klan members broke up their weekly Saturday night meeting in a marshy field near Princess Anne, climbing fully hooded and robed into the backs of Ford F-150 pickup trucks, loaded with six-packs and softball bats.

Not one of the half dozen pickups made it out of the field without ejecting at least one fat man in a white sheet, but the trucks eventually hit the pavement with bald tires screaming. Information came from press room workers who didn't mind shooting their mouths off unless it was to a cop or some dipshit reporter. Most didn't give a darn about the news, didn't care about the stories folded and wrapped up inside the thick bundles. They only gave a damn that there were bundles to be made and shipped out.

The Klan group was big on softball bats as weapons because they also fielded a fast pitch team that traveled to tournaments around the Eastern Shore. They were not so cryptically named the White Knights and were tolerated as long as they kept their language in check around the women and children. Their record was just four wins and thirteen losses so far this season, but they expected to pick things up when their clean-up hitter was paroled in early-August.

The first night Chase showed up decked out in a crisply ironed cotton bed sheet—which Limp had helped sew together—he was welcomed without any questions. His only immediate regret was not reinforcing the hood with some sort of cardboard cone, since it kept leaning way over to one side. The point could easily have put someone's eye out.

Chase pulled his Mustang right up to the regular spots they used in a field outside Princess Anne and joined the activities.

"Take a six-pack," had been Limp's advice. "None of those boys ever turned away anybody cartin' suds. That's all the greetin' card y'all be needing."

Limp had been right about that.

Chase was welcomed with pats on the back of his sheet and then mostly ignored by the sixty or so beer-gutted revelers in their own dirty robes. All went about their business of lighting burn-barrels and hoisting a cross made from two by fours cinched with nylon rope. The wood stank of gasoline and was set ablaze after two kegs were tapped and bottle rockets were ceremonially fired up into the mosquito-infested night sky. Short speeches were offered by two officers, but most of what they said was impossible to understand because of their hoods and thick watermen accents.

Chase discovered that the only things separating a KKK meeting and a night at the local bowling alley were the robes and the ten pins. There was lots of swearing and racist jokes, and plenty of griping about politics and Jew bosses. The night's activities culminated in some mailbox baseball, where the boys all headed off in different directions to destroy mailboxes owned by black and probably Jewish families. The caravan of old pickups, belching thick exhaust and having to rev engines hard with the heavy payloads weighing them down, streamed out into the steamy hot July air. It was the driver's job to zero in on mailboxes with the names Lincoln and Sapp, Washington and Blades.

"We're huntin' Katz!" someone shouted and everyone in the pickup laughed.

They took their chances with Bozmans and Bivens and Perkins, since they could have been white, but decided it didn't really matter; they were drunk as shit.

Chase had climbed up into the back of a rusty Dodge Ram with an ominous wide grill and one headlight. Stuffed with some of the fattest Klansmen, it couldn't go fast enough to flip over—or so he figured—but their tires were spinning as they hit dry pavement, a one-eyed roaring monster careening into the darkness.

"Cliffy, up on yer left!"

"I see it!"

Amos held the Louisville Slugger in his left hand while using his right to battle wind that was trying to rip his hood off. A lefty hitter, Amos wasn't getting as much action as righty Tiny Simms. Chase sat with his back to the cab, thumping up and down on his rear, trying to hang on in a churning ocean of half crushed beer cans.

"Cliffy, heads up on the right!" shrieked the four-hundred pound Tiny Simms, who'd already lost his hood a dozen mailboxes back. Simms, a right-handed hitter who was three-for-three tonight and hitting a respectable .400 in the league games the *Times* sometimes covered, took a few practice cuts, then got ready for the next mailbox coming at him at fifty miles per hour. With a slight uppercut, Simms sent the green metal box soaring into the front yard of a double-wide.

"Home run!"

"C'mon, Cliffy, you shit!" Amos complained from the opposite side of the truck bed, as they barreled on, coughing smoke and shedding empty beer cans. "It's my turn to hit!"

The party went on like that until the gas tank got down toward empty and nobody had the guts to work the pump in a Klan sheet. They headed back to the field in Princess Anne and everyone drove off with the look of impending hangovers.

Late the next morning, the phone in Chase's apartment rang with a tip about an arrest. Jimmy Ray Jones had been hauled in after being overheard bragging to one of the girls behind the Salisbury Dunkin Donuts counter. Chase was allowed to sit in on the interrogation as Jones confessed to the mailbox bashings, as well as a few other crimes they'd committed. Jimmy Ray had been driving one of the other trucks that had been responsible for five smashed car windows and a dumpster fire behind the elementary school. The group obviously had no respect for the rules of mailbox baseball.

When both the *Times* and the *Delaware State News* up in Dover ran front page photos of the mailbox and property destruction, a Delaware neo-Nazi chapter didn't take it too well. In fact, it turned out they were jealous of all the Klan's attention, according to one of the *Times* delivery drivers who had friends in both groups. These little crime sprees were good for attracting new members, and new members meant more guys pitching in for beer, Leon Tooman had told Chase in exchange for a pack of smokes.

The Nazi chapter called their organization the White Armed Warriors for America, or WAWA for short, not to be confused with the convenience store.

The WAWAs decided to make their statement on a grander, more historic scale, Tooman warned Chase. It wasn't a new plan, by any means, since retired exterminator Elkins "Pinkie" Gunder had been just bugging the heck out of his Nazi buddies to use some of his hoarded poisons for years.

"Now they've had a kick in the pants," Tooman whispered through a puff of menthol smoke, "and they got a boy with some bad know-how."

Among piles of unlabeled, noxious chemicals, the Nazis stored pounds of Gunder's thallium in Maxwell House coffee cans in their meeting hall basement. Chase had researched thallium in microfilm files at the city library, discovering it had once been used as a rat and ant poison but was eventually banned because of high toxicity and human cancer risk. One of the earlier uses of thallium was as a hair remover, according to a ten-year-old *Baltimore Sun* story. It said the CIA had come up with a plot to have it applied to Fidel Castro's shoes while they were being polished. The plan wasn't to assassinate him, an informant had told the *Sun* reporter, but to emasculate him by making him as beardless and bald as a baby.

The plan hatched by the Nazis, according to Tooman, was to assassinate a poultry house full of chickens owned by old Abraham Greenberg, a local Jew who had fired more than one of the WAWAs over the years for not showing up for work. Those who did show up were stinking drunk from the night before.

CHASE PARKED HIS car near Greenberg's irrigation pond and killed the engine, eyes adjusting to the light from a three-quarter moon. Twenty minutes later an old Ford pickup rolled past the farm with its headlights off. Chase watched three WAWA boys dressed in blackface paint jog across a bean field toward the sleeping chicken houses. The one taking up the rear had a Styrofoam cooler Tooman had said was filled with a mix of soy chicken feed and thallium shavings.

Chase slid out, clicked the door shut, and made his way to one end of the building the trio was trying to enter. The heavy ammonia smell seeped through the vents and made his eyes burn.

"Man alive, this shit does stink," he heard one of the WAWAs say over the hum of the circulations fans, as they found the door latch and stepped into the coop. "I never knew anything could smell so fuggin' bad."

"Will you shut the hell up!" another nearly shouted, and there was a murmur from stirring chickens. Chase saw the three silhouettes take careful strides through the mass of chickens toward the center feeding trays.

"Smells like somebody poured ammonia on dog turds."

"Breath in an out yer mouth, dumbass."

"Feels like it's burning the nose off my face." Chase could see the lead man hike his shirt out of his pants to use as a filter mask as they squished across the thick layer of chicken shit.

The man with the cooler dumped some of the lethal contents into the steel tray and they slowly retreated as birds began to feed. One house done, they slipped back out and proceeded to poison the other three coops in an easy and terrible crime.

With every fiber of his being, Chase wanted to yell out from the moment he saw the first poison being poured, but there was more to this assignment than covering a story. His job was to take control of an event, to work under the cover of a journalist while producing results as a spy.

Their mission accomplished, three black-clad figures ran from the last chicken house toward their truck, one tripping over a garden rake and falling headfirst.

Reaching into his pocket, Chase pulled out a thick black marker and looked for a flat surface to write.

THE SLAUGHTER OF thirty-seven thousand chickens made newspaper headlines and was the lead story on both local TV news stations. You didn't mess with chickens on Delmarva.

But it wasn't the poultry industry that had Chase feeling as though he no longer possessed a soul when he returned to the scene of the crime later that morning on a spot news assignment. He spent two miserable hours wandering among lifeless white lumps, shooting a few frames of old Abraham Greenberg comforting his wife. He was careful with his exposure inside the chicken house, where hours earlier he'd used a thick marker to rob credit from the WAWAs. He'd drawn three large Ks over the door frame and matching crosses on each side.

According to Tooman, the Klan was nervous about accepting responsibility for the massacre even though it had been Jew chickens.

"They were talking about wanting to turn in who done it," Tooman told Chase on the loading dock after his rounds later in the week. "None of the boys are ready fess up and for good reason. Ain't nobody supposed to be killin' chickens. Kill somebody's momma and a family wants revenge. Kill chickens and the whole Eastern Shore grabs the hangin' rope."

Chase was called into Mack's glass-walled office and sat next to a man who introduced himself as an FBI agent.

"Seems we have a hornets' nest stirred up." The agent, in a gray suit with tan work boots, had tracked little rectangles of chicken shit into the small office. Chase could smell it.

"We know the poison belonged to a group of boys up in Delaware," said the agent. "But somebody used a Klan autograph on the job and stole their credit."

The look Chase gave Mack was as innocent as possible. Then he glanced down at the place on his right hand, where he'd had to scrub a spot of indelible ink with the rough soap they used in the press room.

"Those boys get to drinking and some dangerous ideas get thrown around," the agent said.

"Like poisoning a chicken farm," said Mack.

"That's right," said the agent. "And we're thinking that everyone in the media should take a little more care to double-check their locks at night and keep an eye on their pets."

DURING THE SECOND week of August, just as the temperature and humidity started evening out in the low nineties on the Eastern Shore, WAWA Captain Early Wayne nervously dropped coins into a gas station payphone and began to dial.

"City desk." The voice on the other end was tired, disinterested.

Wayne reached into left front pocket for the handful of marbles he'd stolen from his little boy's collection. He shoved them into his mouth and worked them into his cheeks.

"We have Shockley," Wayne said into the phone. From the video store he'd rented and watched all four movies that involved kidnapping. "You have twenty-four hours to come up with fifty thousand dollars in small, unmarked bills."

"What?"

"Or Shockley dies!"

"Buddy," said the older male voice on the other end. "Spit out the marbles and try again. I can't understand a word you're sayin.'"

Wayne nearly dropped the receiver. His heart thundered in his chest and his hands shook as he scanned the parking lot for cop cars. Was he being watched? How did the guy know he just jammed his mouth with a handful of marbles? Kidnapping, extortion, and they surely knew all about the animal porn. He'd never see his family again. But no SWAT team came swooping in with weapons pointed. Not a single blue light turned circles in the parking lot of the Exxon station that was about to close for the night. It began to dawn on Wayne that he probably just sounded like he had marbles in his mouth. His heart slowed as he dropped his chin and let the little glass orbs spill out, bouncing off his work boots. He cleared his throat.

"We want fifty grand or Shockley dies," Wayne told the man.

"Fifty grand, huh?"

Emboldened, Wayne strayed from his notes for added effect. "Or this time tomorrow he'll be swimmin' with the fishes."

There was a pause and Wayne was sure he could hear the man lighting a cigarette and taking a deep drag. That was a good sign. He had him shaken. Wayne patted his pockets for his own pack.

"Look, buddy, I don't know what bar you're callin' from, but Shockley's right here. Hold on."

It wasn't possible. He'd left Shockley hogtied back in the basement of the WAWA meeting hall not fifteen minutes ago.

There was a click on the other end of the phone. "Limp here," said the voice. "I work for chocolate, so you better be sweet."

Early Wayne ran for his idling pickup, the receiver still swinging at the end of its metal cord. In eight minutes he was taking the meeting hall basement stairs three at a time.

"Where's the fire, Early?" Some of the guys were playing poker around a folding card table as Wayne darted past. He knocked over half the empties, breaking a couple on the concrete floor.

Wayne pulled up in front of their captive in the dim end of the basement, hands on his knees, gasping for breath. Limp Shockley was tied every which way and hadn't budged from the old wooden chair.

"What's got into you, Early? Everything's been quiet as could be."

Wayne reached out for the Agway corn sack covering Shockley's head and slowly lifted it up. The duct tape over his mouth had turned into a weird, robot-like smile and the man's hair was wet and all crazy. His nose dripped snot and his eyes were bloodshot and fearful.

"When's the money comin', Early? We're outta beer."

Wayne pulled the newspaper clipping out of his breast pocket and unfolded the small byline photo of Shockley. He held it out and squinted in the bad light. Same fat cheeks, same eyes, same everything. Wayne switched hands with the clipping and took hold of the duct tape. Slow didn't work, so he put one palm on Shockley's sweaty forehead and gave it one big rip just as a flash grenade burst through one of the high narrow windows and exploded at his feet.

Temporarily blind and partially deafened, Wayne hurled himself to the floor and tried crawling on the dirty concrete. His boots kicked out behind him, searching for traction, but snapped one of the wood chair legs and brought a screaming body falling over him. He was pinned. Wayne thought he heard someone shout FBI and he was half certain he heard someone call out the name *Mrs.* Shockley.

Wayne felt the hogtied body inch higher up on his torso, pushing air out of his lungs. Hot breath was on his neck and in his ear. Wayne, helpless as the mouth hungrily probed his cheek, was repulsed by the great looming blur. Early Wayne knew he was never going home again and it caused him to surrender. The boots stomping down the stairs were coming to carry him away and that left nothing to fight for. The pain of Mrs. Shockley biting off his nose was somehow comforting.

"THEY SHOULD COIN a phrase for this kind of journalism." Chase was packing away prints and negatives he wanted to keep from the summer while Limp sat eating a peach over a napkin. Limp's slurping was accompanied by the darkroom radio playing classic rock.

"You saved my mother's life."

"How do you figure?"

"The Feds would never have tapped those boys' phones to know what they were planning."

"They kidnapped your mother—well, they thought it was you—because I stole their credit."

"Yeah, there's that." Limp hadn't shown any real emotion over his mother's abduction. She'd suffered a sore hip but had refused a trip to the hospital and was more upset over missing an afternoon of soap operas. "She's a tough broad."

"My mom would be under psychiatric care."

"My mother scares psychiatrists," Limp said, folding the peach pit into the napkin. "You aren't having any second thoughts?"

Chase stacked three empty photo paper boxes on the counter and began filling them with five by seven prints he'd made over the last eight weeks. Many were over- or under-exposed discards, but some were duplicates he'd made of his best work. There were a few good feature pictures, but most were spot news, the parade of weekend fires and car wrecks.

"I'm dropping out as soon as I get back to campus." Chase flipped through a new stack of black and whites. Limp had told him to expect a letter with instructions on where and when to report for a two week training and orientation session. "I don't know if I could sit through classes even if I wanted."

Limp tossed his pit in the trash and stood over his shoulder. "You never showed me this one."

Chase held the accident scene photo of the severed hands still attached to the steering wheel—the one the cop had asked him to shoot. "I don't know why I took it," he lied.

"You'll do just fine in your new job," Limp said, reaching for the photo. "You see the beauty in such awful circumstances. That's a rare gift that'll come in handy."

"I'm going to miss my friends," Chase said, meaning Stoney and the dopey girls they both managed to bring back to their dorm.

"I'm going to surely miss you, too, Pie." Limp embraced him from behind, his head in the nape of Chase's neck, his right hand still clutching the photo. "It needs a name, don't you think? How about Driving with Severed Hands?"

"That's fine." Chase tried wriggling out of the bear hug that reeked of Old Spice and sweat.

"You keep yourself safe. There's going to be places where they cut off more than just hands."

Limp's tears dripped down the back of Chase's shirt.

Chapter 8

———

STONEY WASN'T TAKING Chase's new plan well.

"Where the fuck are you really going?" Stoney was following him across campus toward the registrar's office, shirtless to show off his deep tan, wearing mirror sunglasses and cut-off jeans. "You're full of shit. No way you're going home."

"I got a job and I have to go to a training program." It was the truth, but the letter Limp had advised was coming had warned Chase about the dangers of friendship. In his new career, Chase would put Stoney in danger if a foreign country identified him as a spy. Chase was less worried about his family.

They wound around the banks of Mason Pond, through the Student Union, where Stoney bought a can of Coke from a machine. He punched buttons hard enough to send a few coeds scurrying away. They dodged Frisbees in front of the library as Stoney continued his rant.

"Bullshit. You don't drop out of school like this. A cult! Did some bitch lure you into joining a cult? I read about stuff like that. That shit never turns out cool."

"It's not a cult."

"Jonestown, man. Think about the purple Kool-Aid." He put a hand on Chase's shoulder and slowed their pace across the short cropped lawn. "They'll draw you in by giving you like ten wives, dude, all bangin' you at the same time and making grilled cheeses and shit."

"It's not like that."

"Then the crazy leader will decide some asteroid is a spaceship coming for you, and he'll pray it up and shit and make everybody drink poison. Porking ten chicks always has a downside."

"It's not a cult."

"All you poor bastards." Stoney seemed absolutely convinced he had it right. "I should tie you up in our room and have that chick you banged from last semester deprogram your fucked-up head."

"Okay, I joined the Army," Chase lied.

"That would be worse. The Army is just like prison, man. You'll get ass-raped and then forced to do push-ups. Stop bullshitting and tell me why you're leaving me. I followed you all the way to that open sewer to watch a bunch of kids get killed."

They were nearing the building housing the registrar's office.

"I know, man. I dream about it all the time." There had been nightmares. They came less and less frequently over the summer, but Chase learned that falling asleep stoned made them come back vivid and hard. He'd even woken Stoney last night.

"It's friendship treason."

"It's a chance to do something big, Stoney, you just have to understand." Chase escaped at the doorstep of the registrar's office. No shirts, no shoes, no service. Stoney had to wait outside while Chase withdrew his student status.

STONEY DROVE TOO fast. Chase's Mustang wasn't meant for speeding down gravel roads at high speeds with a drunken kid in aviator sunglasses at the wheel. Chase knew Stoney wanted to squeeze out their last hours together and didn't complain about the long drive out toward Shenandoah National Park. They'd come twice before with girls and a trunk full of beer and ice.

Stoney made the last turn onto a closed road, the wooden barriers with no trespassing signs knocked to the side long ago. They parked in a turn-around spot, each grabbing a backpack with a few cans of beer and a towel. It was buggy and hot and it took Chase a while to realize they'd made the entire trip in silence, no music and no talking.

The narrow, overgrown path was a straight line to the flooded quarry. They climbed down the least steep wall, one careful step at a time, to a small patch of crushed stone. They drank the beer then swam the fifty yards across the deep, dark water to the side where people came to climb and jump.

Every splash was echoed from the soaring rock walls. Some stories said the water was a hundred feet deep, others claimed it was a thousand.

They emerged from the cold water and found the best climbing line to begin the ascent. The face was nearly vertical, but had easy hand- and footholds. You could turn and jump from five or twenty-five feet, or go all the way to the top for a hundred foot freefall.

Chase followed Stoney, but stopped at a small ledge where kids had scratched curse words, names, and the height—they'd guessed it at twenty-five feet. He edged sideways then turned, his back to the wall, hands flat against the cool stone. It was a beautiful, postcard-kind of view, but he closed his eyes.

Chase listened as Stoney climbed higher and higher, slipping and catching himself. He could hear his close calls, his swearing, and his determined grunts. If you started falling, you were supposed to push off backwards, away from the outcropping, hoping not to clip anything on the way down.

"I made it," he called from almost directly overhead. Chase craned his neck and could barely see him leaning over the edge. "It's really high, man."

"You're crazy, Stoney." But Chase was really just in awe of him. Stoney always went farther, to places Chase was afraid of, and that wasn't crazy at all. Stoney wasn't afraid of anything.

"You see that?" His words echoed, were carried back by the stone walls and the water below. "Look!"

It was a hawk, or some other large bird of prey, making a fast, banked turn around the perimeter of the water's edge, maybe seventy feet off the surface. With a slight angling of its wings, it gained altitude and headed out over the middle of the water, then dropped into a dive bomb at an incredible rate, reaching its talons out at the last instant to pluck a small, shiny fish from just below the surface. It beat its wing against the warm air and rose up and out of sight of the manmade cavern.

And then it was Stoney's turn to soar. Chase watched as he pushed off the ledge with a mighty howl, arching his back like a skydiver, arms reaching forward. He fell silent and fast, a blurry swoosh just a few feet in front of Chase, before slamming into the surface of the water fists and head first. Kids never jumped head first from the top ledge. Never. It seemed forever before Stoney came back to the surface. Most of the white bubbles had already disappeared.

STONEY DROVE CHASE to the airport two days later. Right up to the international terminal, but Stoney pretended not to notice. Again there was no talk and no music, just the sound of the wind on the highway, then the roar of big engines when they arrived.

"I'm sorry," Chase tried. He couldn't see past Stoney's mirror lenses.

Chase grabbed his backpack and new camera bag from the

back seat. Stoney hadn't moved from behind the wheel, the Mustang idling at the loading zone curb. A cop was strolling up to keep people moving along and Chase didn't want Stoney hassled for all the empties visible with the top down.

"The pink slip is in the glove compartment. I signed it over."

"Christmas present?" It was Stoney's first words.

"Take care of it."

Stoney let go of the steering wheel and draped his right arm over the seat to look at Chase. "I'm the one who jumps, not you."

"Maybe it's my turn."

The cop was standing next to Chase and seemed interested in the collection of bottles and cans strewn across the back seat and the piled on the floorboards.

"Yeah, but you ain't got my style." Stoney revved the engine and popped the clutch. The tires spun and smoked as the startled cop jumped back and lost his balance, nearly falling on his ass. Chase held his ground because he knew Stoney and was in awe of how he kept the powerful old car under control, probably hitting eighty miles an hour by the time he reached the interstate.

Chapter 9

——

IN THE AIRPLANE window seat Chase was feeling like a little kid, nose pressed to the acrylic surface, circles of moisture appearing and disappearing. They banked hard right on approach and he searched every inch of the exotic view. The green hills spreading out below were hazy with smoke from dozens of what seemed to be small fires. The towns, built from dirt and stone instead of wood and steel, were earth colored. And Chase was here to help kill their president.

The tires touched down with a screech and the stewardess reminded him three times to stay seated until they'd reached the terminal and come to a complete stop. With just his camera bag, one backpack, and a suit bag containing a rented tuxedo, Chase zipped through the special line at customs reserved for journalists.

He checked into the Hotel Intercontinental and left his gear in the room. The concierge confirmed the address of the Palacio Nacional and promised a number of taxis would be waiting outside the hotel tomorrow night. Everything was falling into place, but he couldn't be boxed in. His adrenaline was pumping and he needed to find the pool, maybe take a long walk. He checked his watch every ten minutes even though the formal state dinner was twenty-six hours away.

A bite to eat then a second swim before collapsing into the queen-sized bed, where he just stared at the ceiling. Chase checked his watch a dozen more times before falling into the usual dream about the bloody day on the soccer field. In the dark he groped for a drink of water, the thick crystal glass shaking in his hand.

The envelope had come to his dorm room, seeming to appear from nowhere like any good spy message should. It made it real for the first time. Inside was a passport, visa, plane tickets, and instructions detailing how he was to aid in a presidential assassination during the formal dinner.

Chase went back to bed as the sun began to rise. He slept with it bright in his face until a little past noon, when the maid knocked. He had two bites of a room service sandwich, then went down to swim laps. Kids sat along the edge, feet kicking the chlorinated water as he lumbered past. Mothers in one-pieces with gold jewelry and full makeup were seated at round tables sipping fruit-filled drinks. Chase looked at his watch then tried knocking the water from his ears until realizing they weren't clogged. Something other than the pool was making his head feel underwater. He did two more laps and grabbed his towel.

Chase dressed an hour before cocktails were to be served. His pants were an inch too long and the shoulders were too tight. It didn't matter. James Bond he was not. His hair was too long and he'd lost his soccer-honed muscle tone. He pulled the press pass over his head and checked the bag of brand new Nikon gear, which had also magically appeared in his dorm. The same cameras the big city shooters used, but these didn't have nicks from stumbling and falling over fire hoses. No worn metal edges from throwing two camera bodies over the same shoulder to run toward a paramedic performing CPR. He splashed cold water on his face and wondered if he would

feel different after taking part in a murder. He looked at his
wet face, the face of a soon-to-be assassin. Would he be racked
with guilt? Would he be so overcome he'd need to confess his
crime?

"I can kill someone without getting all crazy," he told the
mirror. He wasn't confident.

The Palacio Nacional was an impressive structure that drove
his sense of apprehension even deeper. The complex could have
been lifted right up out of Washington, D.C., and planted here
among the earthquake-condemned cathedrals and abandoned
office buildings. Sixteen massive columns held up the front of
the square structure, lights reflecting on the low clouds from
what was probably a central courtyard. Dozens of bats soared
and swooped, dancing for food. Silent beggars lined the street
in front, their reaching hands waiving like a cluster of sea
anemones. Chase paid the driver in blue and red money and
followed an elegant couple through a wrought-iron gate and
into the arched entryway. After a quick security search Chase
was directed down a wide marble hallway toward the dinner
hall.

President Daniel Ortega had been all over the news in
recent weeks, his army mired in an ongoing war against the
U.S. funded Contras in the north. Most media accounts held
that Ronald Reagan wanted military bases built within the
strategically located Central American country to keep an eye
on Cuba. And the U.S. President had been accused by many
political pundits of employing the CIA in an assassination
campaign.

Ortega was fresh off a trip to New York. He'd stood in front
of the U.N. General Assembly and given a rambling, personal
account of his twin brother's death at the hands of the CIA.
He claimed to have proof that the American spy agency had
recruited a prostitute because of her uncanny resemblance to a
much younger version of his wife, Nicaragua's First Lady. The
prostitute had been purposely infected with syphilis and put in

place at an exclusive brothel a CIA informant claimed Ortega frequented on a weekly basis.

The plan went off perfectly, except for the fact that it was Ortega's brother with the taste for whores and expensive Champagne. And it wasn't even the syphilis he'd contracted from the hooker that had killed him. It had been the man's wife, the president's sister-in-law, who had caused the untimely death when she'd hacked off her sleeping husband's afflicted member with a steak knife.

The president's brother had bled to death in his own coffee fields trying to chase her down and recover his penis. But it had been easy to outrun a man with such recently inflicted damage. The ultimate revenge had been clenched tightly in her right fist. Mrs. Ortega danced into the night, screaming and laughing, sometimes pausing to talk to the penis in a mocking tone.

"Look at me!" she commanded the penis in Spanish, holding it firmly in front of her as if admonishing a naughty puppy who'd soiled the carpet. "You were bad, very bad. Bad, bad penis!"

Mrs. Ortega then held it high over her head, making the sounds of a revving engine. According to the peasant workers' statements to investigators, she had eventually skipped off into the darkness like a child pretending to fly a toy airplane. Ortega's speech writers had a field day when preparing El Presidente for his pleas in front of the U.N. for help defending against America.

The dinner at the Palacio Nacional was a morale booster for the upper crust, the industry leaders and spiritual advisors of the masses. Journalists were invited and encouraged to spread the word.

The sound of a single violin mingled with the polite chatter as Chase approached the banquet hall. An armed guard nodded at the open double doors and Chase was led to his seat by a waitress. He nudged his camera bag under his chair and surveyed the vast room. There were maybe a dozen guards and an army of servants in crisp black and white, wearing linen gloves.

"The main course will be corvine from the Tipi Tapa River," the waitress serving Chase's section announced in English. The sixty people surrounding the long table were assigned by occupation. Chase recognized *News Core* commentator Hugh McManny and ABC's Geraldo Lopez. Two women on either side of Lopez were introduced as local television news anchors. The journalists were seated mid-table, perhaps to soak in the night's positive energy despite the ongoing guerilla war waged by Reagan's rag tag Contras.

The first course was served ninety minutes before Chase's sharpshooter would be in place. He surreptitiously checked his watch and picked at his salad. There were eleven people between him and the president, and he could sometimes hear the man's laughter. He watched as Ortega took a glass of wine from a waiter's gloved hand and raised it to toast the people nearest him. A stunning young woman in a black evening dress who sat to his left seemed to be interpreting his words. After he finished speaking, Ortega drained the glass, made a bitter face, and reached for a sip of water. A moment later he used a napkin to wipe sweat from his forehead and from under his huge, black framed glasses. From where Chase sat, the president looked suddenly pale, brown cheeks having gone ashen. His crystal wine glass was definitely shaking. Was he somehow sensing his own mortality, his impending death? Chase peeked at his watch, wondering if the CIA shooter was taking a position on the distant rooftop.

GERALDO LOPEZ TOOK his seat among the journalists, morose over his recent run of lousy luck and resentful of the phony pomp and circumstances.

His first foreign assignment was a ridiculous public relations fiasco masquerading as a state dinner. Who the hell cared what happened in a Third World shithole such as this? These Frito Banditos probably didn't have a working helicopter, let alone anything dangerous, like a nuke or a flamethrower. A small fleet of unarmed UPS drivers could hold them off at the Texas border if the shit really hit the fan. A real foreign assignment meant safari and flak jackets, tracer missiles being fired in the background of hunched over stand-ups. His cameraman had been ushered off with his fellow lowlifes to eat in a separate room, probably one that could be hosed down easily.

Geraldo had begun the year with a formidable contract deal at the network, getting him away from the grind in San Diego and onto the national desk. The managing editor had made a hundred promises about his future, explaining the path he'd take doing serious interviews and then getting a full thirty minute slot at 6:30 within the year. He was even provided a tutor to work on his accent, to add some color by juicing it up a little. Within the first few weeks, he could roll his Rs and artfully pause to decide on the most appropriate English word while in pressure situations, as if he hadn't been born and raised in Gary, Indiana. He had been surprised to learn there was more than one N in the Spanish alphabet.

Geraldo had suddenly found himself in a Manhattan apartment with a doorman, an around-the-clock concierge, and a great tip for an extremely discreet escort service. What more could a single guy still on the right side of forty want?

Then, six weeks ago, a call had been put through to his tiny but smart office with a peek-a-boo view down West 66th Street. It had been some shady ass lawyer from San Diego, saying he was willing to work something out on behalf of his client and her baby she claimed was his. Impossible, he'd told the lawyer. A sixteen-year-old virgin, the lawyer had countered. Virgin, that was, until becoming a statutory rape victim of a famous news personality.

Geraldo remembered her vaguely at first, then the details

had come back. She'd been a piece of work, a real stalker type from the get go. She'd first appeared with a little pen and pad outside the KGTV front doors, begging for an autograph, big wide eyes and pouty lips working on a Ring Pop. Then she'd shown up at his favorite lunch spot with a little plastic camera and wearing some kind of cotton candy perfume. That's when Geraldo had noticed the long legs and white cotton panties. How the fuck was he supposed to know she was sixteen? Was he a fucking bartender? Where the hell were her parents when he was balling her on his brand new waterbed?

"What about an abortion?" he'd asked the attorney long distance.

"We're all way beyond that, now, aren't we?"

"Adoption?"

"She's a loving mother of your two-year-old son, Mr. Lopez. And I'm sure the age of my client is an important consideration for you in how we proceed from here."

Geraldo had slumped in his expensive, ergonomically designed office chair and ran fingers through his gelled hair.

"My client and I also understand the importance of keeping the name Antonio Vespucci out of any headlines."

"Jesus Christ." Antonio Vespucci was Geraldo's real name, one he'd abandoned as a college junior, believing that a Hispanic would stand a better chance at being hired over an Italian. A journalism professor he'd slept with and trusted had convinced him.

Geraldo Lopez had known at that moment that the financing of his concierge service was in serious jeopardy. A phone call from a second attorney claiming to represent yet another young woman came three weeks later, sealing the fate of his dry cleaning delivery and one-touch restaurant reservations. He had once again slumped in his office chair, chin on his chest, shaking his head at his treasonous crotch.

Geraldo became distracted in his new job, spending far too much time calculating his remaining salary against the dueling acts of blackmail. His tension was building unabated now that he could no longer afford the two thousand dollar a pop escorts. He'd stumbled through assignments, endured a mortifying live studio interview with Oscar winner Sam Waterston from *The Killing Fields*. So what if he hadn't seen the damn movie? His life had become depressing enough that he didn't want to sit through two hours of bloody Cambodian poverty.

A whiney male voice startled him back to his present circumstances. Geraldo adjusted his cuffs and wiped his nose with the back of a knuckle.

"This is my wife, Margie," the voice repeated. It came from a fat old man who was introducing some old hag for whatever reason. Lost in his miserable thoughts, Geraldo didn't recognize his surroundings at first. He'd been fantasizing about hiring a hit man, but had to start counting on two hands the number of people who needed to be hit. Right before this god forsaken assignment, he'd had to move to New Jersey and begin taking the Path train into the city. New Jersey smelled like everything he'd imagined and then some. He knew every tattered garbage bag along the highways and train tracks contained mobster body parts. Having abandoned his Italian ancestry, which included not calling his parents for over ten years, he was all the more chilled by the idea of being exposed as a fraudulent Mexican. And he'd be mortified the first time some wiseass called him Tony around the newsroom. It would be worse than knocking up the girls. They were both eighteen now, so it wasn't even a crime anymore, right?

"Geraldo Lopez is an up and comer over at ABC, honey." Geraldo looked into the milky eyes of Hugh McManny, then took his wife's wrinkled hand across the table. Her grip was hard and ice cold. He immediately wanted his hand back.

"Nice meeting you."

Geraldo waited for the old lady to settle into her chair before flagging one of the serving girls and motioning to his empty wine glass. The girl looked familiar and it took him a minute to place her face. He'd last seen it in profile, pinned to his bed after he'd taken her back to his room on his first night in this lousy country. She was a waitress in his hotel restaurant.

"Did you play baseball, Geraldo?" It was McManny again, leaning forward, elbows on the table, great folds of neck skin erupting from his tux collar.

"Yeah, a little, I suppose." The server girl had nodded and disappeared without showing any sign of recognition. He'd left her a fifty dollar bill on the pillow before heading out for a swim and then wandering the gift shop. He'd given her plenty of time to gather herself up and clear out of his room.

"When I was a kid, players had names like Babe Ruth and Lou Gehrig. Isn't it funny how these days there seems to be one team all named Rodriguez and another named Lopez? And all the players seem to have full mustaches."

"Are you joking?" Geraldo kept his eyes glued to the door that led to wherever they kept the wine bottles chilled.

"You know, that reminds me of a joke a man on the subway once told me."

Geraldo was relieved when the girl appeared with a full glass of wine, but disheartened to see her intercepted by one of the male servers. The prick snatched the glass from her hands despite her protests and hurried toward the head of the table. Geraldo watched President Ortega lift the glass to his immediate neighbors and mouth a toast from behind his bushy mustache. Then the bastard drank his wine.

"Geraldo, what do you call a Mexican with a new car?"

Lopez looked at his neighbors on both sides, but they were turned away, already involved in conversations. He looked for the server girl he'd recently screwed, but she'd vanished. He desperately needed a drink and was about to be assailed with off color jokes by the old *News Core* has-been.

"A felon. Ha! Isn't that just wonderful? You know, it's funny because it rings so true. One more?" McManny emptied his wine glass despite his wife trying to pin his arm to the table, whispering harshly in his hairy ear. "What do you get when you cross a Mexican with an octopus?" he said.

Geraldo sat silently.

"I don't know either, but it can sure pick lettuce."

"You have to stop drinking this moment." Geraldo heard McManny's wife beg.

"Why doesn't Mexico have an Olympic team?"

Geraldo shook his head.

"Because if they can run, jump, or swim they're in the U.S."

And just then, a set of arms clad in a white tuxedo shirt surrounded McManny and locked at the wrist. McManny and his chair began to slowly elevate above the elegant table settings. Geraldo could see the old man's bent knees and the linen napkin spread across his wide lap. He was suddenly looking up the man's nose, white clumps of wiry hair sprouting in ten directions, as McManny was lifted and tilted backward, arms pin-wheeling for balance.

"Help!" McManny's voice whined as he began grabbing at the sides of his chair and Geraldo got a glimpse of the culprit.

"Hugh!" His wife reached for him, the loose sleeves of her pale blue dinner dress flapping, but the Mexican Secretariat of Tourism had an iron grip. Geraldo had met and interviewed the man. He couldn't recall his name, but knew he'd attended college in Canada and then gone to Harvard. Was it Tony? Geraldo thought it might have been.

McManny, whose voice had turned shrill, began reciting jokes without finishing the punch lines. "What do you call a Mexican without a lawn mower? How do you get fifty Mexicans into a phone booth? How many Mexicans does it take to change a light bulb?"

Before security could intervene, one of the guests managed to intercept the Mexican Cabinet member who seemed to be attempting to leave the dinner hall with McManny still seated in his chair, as if taking out the trash. To Geraldo, the guest looked like some sort of John Lennon hippie, which meant he was probably a lowly newspaper or magazine photographer.

In the commotion, Geraldo reached across the table, snatched up Margie McManny's glass of wine and drained it. He took some tiny measure of comfort in the fact that although he might live in New Jersey, at least he wasn't a news photographer.

"GENTLEMEN!" CHASE KICKED back his chair and nearly stumbled over his camera bag. A commotion like this could wreck the operation. He lunged past an elderly woman in a blue dress and grabbed the shoulder of the man carrying a chair load of the old *News Core* commentator, who was wildly spouting off one-liners at the top of his lungs. Chase tried slowing them down, but the man doing the carrying had gained momentum, heading for the double doors. Instead of stopping them, Chase sprinted ahead and kicked open the one door and cleared the path down the marble hallway. Several members of the security detail bumped past him, the sound of running boots echoing down the long chamber and competing with the obnoxious rants of the man in the chair.

"Have you ever wondered where all the heroes have gone?" the voice seemed to ask the soaring walls. McManny's companion in the blue dress was hurrying after, her heels click-clacking.

Chase stepped back into the stunned dinner hall, cleared his throat and straightened his tuxedo jacket. All eyes were on him, including Ortega's and the remaining bodyguards. The photo op had been prearranged through the Associated Press and the President's public relations office, so he decided to push forward. "Perhaps this is a good time for a very brief photograph of our host?"

Ortega nodded to his young translator, who had to help him to his feet. The President's face was pale, drops of sweat pooling at his chin, as Chase leaned down and pulled a Nikon from his bag. Attached was a 24mm lens, the length Limp had taught him to rely upon.

"Señor Presidente, perhaps in front of this beautiful window?"

Ortega stood shakily, looking like hell. A bodyguard had retrieved a glass of ice water, held it out to him. Ortega's bronze skin was white, his lips tinted blue, and he'd removed his jacket to expose a dress shirt that was practically translucent, drenched in sweat. He looked up at Chase with bloodshot eyes.

"Sí, por supuesto," Ortega groaned. "Sería un placer."

"Yes, of course. It would be my pleasure." His translator's strong voice was an odd contrast to Ortega's.

Chase had a recurring fantasy of Ortega taking the sharpshooter's bullet, collapsing forward with a red bloom forming at the breast of his shirt, his wife coming to sweep his head from the hard floor. Chase knew the Pulitzer committee would be overwhelmed by the First Lady's pleading eyes, begging God not to take her husband.

It's show time, Chase thought giddily, one simple mission to change the course of history. Books would be written, encyclopedias would need to be changed. The murder of a dangerous Central American leader was about to happen right in front of his eyes. And he was going to be responsible, it being his job to arrange the man in front of the thick glass panes of the hall's enormous windows.

With the bodyguard's help, Ortega took shuffling steps toward where Chase was motioning. There was silence in the room as everyone stopped to watch the president's struggle to walk, hobbled by pain or drink. He was about two-thirds of the way when he stumbled and barely caught himself on the back of a chair. Chase took a step toward Ortega, grimacing, his arms out as if to catch a phantom, willing Ortega not to collapse and ruin the mission. The bodyguard managed to right Ortega, tried speaking in his ear, but was shrugged off and pushed away. Ortega took a few deep breaths, smiled wanly, and gathered his strength to make it the rest of the way under his own steam.

Faint gongs began to echo down the marble and granite corridors from what sounded like grandfather clocks in distant rooms. Chase could hear his own pulse as Ortega finally arrived at the window radiating feverish heat. He sensed the sniper off in the night tracking Ortega, waiting for the target to be lined up.

With great difficulty, Ortega accepted his tuxedo jacket from the bodyguard, straightened the collar, and flattened the lapels. He wiped his brow with a swipe of one sleeve, took another strained breath, lifted his chin and said, "*Ahora.*"

"Now," repeated the translator from behind Chase.

Chase fumbled with his Nikon, hands clammy with nervous sweat and burgeoning paranoia. Journalists were everywhere and one had to recognize the huge mistake of putting the subject in front of a reflective window for a flash photo. It was more than a rookie mistake. Chase looked around at the waiting eyes that were filled with suspicion. Fraud, someone was about to shout. A murder plot!

Ortega flattened the hair across his forehead, teetering on his heels. When he tried licking his lips, Chase saw that his tongue was swollen.

The clocks all began to chime in earnest when Chase brought his camera to eye level and turned the focusing ring. Chase vaguely wondered if the high-powered round would pass through Ortega and also hit him.

Too late; this was it. Was that tiny speck of light off in the night a glint of moonlight reflecting from a powerful shooting scope?

Chase blinked to clear his eyes and braced for impact, just as the clocks around the palatial building mostly agreed the hour had come.

Chase fingered the shutter release button just as the distant sniper must have begun squeezing the last bit of pressure on his trigger. As the bullet struck the window, Ortega lurched forward out of its way, projectile-vomited all over the front of Chase's tuxedo, and collapsed at his shiny rented shoes. Frantic bodyguards rushed to Ortega's convulsing body on the marble floor as the beautiful translator lay dying from a single gunshot wound.

Chase turned and took her picture.

Chapter 10

CHASE STOOD IN line at customs, the backpack propped against his shins weighing a ton from all the newspaper clippings. He'd hit every newsstand and vending box, stealing more than half because he needed the last of his cash for an airport taxi. It was hard to feel bad about the blown assignment after the Associated Press had distributed his series of Ortega's near-miss across the world. It would have been much better if Ortega had taken the bullet, but the death of the twenty-three-year-old beauty seemed to strike a chord.

Someone had poisoned Ortega. At least that was the official line fed to journalists. Residue of a common rat poison had supposedly been found in his wine glass. Chase figured the CIA had been covering all bases, but who knew? Maybe it was an inside job, or just a pissed off servant whose family had lost a farm. Instead of being under suspicion for leading Ortega to the assassin's crosshairs at the window, Chase was credited with saving the president by getting him up and moving. He might have just keeled over and died on the white tablecloth had he not been enticed to walk across the room and puke on the photographer.

Photo by Chase Allen. *El Nuevo Diario*, Nicaragua's national newspaper, used thirteen pictures in an assassination attempt special issue. *The LA Times, Dallas Morning News, Seattle Post-Intelligencer*, and *Chicago Sun-Times* all ran Chase's photos, most above the fold on page one.

It was ten at night when he hailed a cab outside the Philly terminal. His new address was in the letter he'd received at school, along with a single key he assumed was for the front door. The city was still hot, but the air changed as they headed north to a part of New Jersey that was thick with woods. Chase wanted to show off one of the newspapers, but what would this guy care? The cab was dark and there was a baseball game on the radio. The man's name might have been Haitian, or maybe he was French. His skin was as black as that of the boys Chase had coached, but that didn't mean anything.

Signs on the apartment complex indicated it was near Trenton and Princeton. He handed over his last thirty dollars and lugged his two bags up concrete steps to a peeling front door. He was up another flight, over an apartment with low music and cigarette smoke. It was like checking into a budget motel, with the same sort of furniture. Everything was brown, even the TV with long rabbit ears.

Chase dropped his camera bag and backpack on a cushioned chair.

"Hello?" It was empty, of course, and he didn't expect an answer. He switched on lights as he explored the long hallway that led to a bedroom and yellow tiled bathroom.

There was a new towel draped over a bar by the toilet and Chase leaned into the shower to twist the knobs. He'd abandoned all his clothes to make space for the newspapers and realized he probably had nothing left in the world except what was on his back. He was incredibly tired from the long trip and couldn't decide if he cared.

He washed his hair with soap and wore his dirty boxers out to the kitchen. There was an envelope on the counter just like the one back in his dorm. This one was stuffed with twenty dollar bills and a plane ticket to Panama.

Chase picked up the phone and dialed information for a pizza joint, but everything was closed.

Chapter 11

CHASE FOLDED THE newspaper with the headline announcing Bush's million dollar reward for the capture of Panamanian President Manuel Noriega. The taxi driver had stopped again, confused by the lack of street signs in the posh neighborhood. He seemed ready to give up before pointing to a number partially obscured by tall shrubs.

"*Aqui*." The driver pulled to the curb in front of one of the many compounds purportedly owned by Noriega.

"*Gracias*." Chase paid him and jumped out.

With indictments for cocaine trafficking, racketeering, and money laundering secured, twenty-seven thousand U.S. troops walked, boated, and flew into Panama and quickly beat down Noriega's Panama Defense Force. When Noriega wasn't in any of the obvious places, the invasion became a manhunt around the mostly middle-class capital city.

The envelope left on Chase's kitchen counter had given this upscale address, with instructions to keep an eye on the place and alert a CIA contact if Noriega or anything suspicious turned up. It also said the CIA wanted Noriega before the Army Rangers got hold of him.

Noriega's house was the only one surrounded by a low cement wall, topped by strands of dangerous concertina wire. Chase imagined that the neighbors were happy to have a de facto military dictator on the block, but pissed off at the walls and wire, which were ugly and a drag on property values.

Chase looked both ways then draped his jacket over the wire and hopped easily inside the compound. He circled to the back of the two-story Mediterranean-style villa, with its white walls and red-tiled roof. Its small backyard was packed with dozens of water fountains, crammed tightly around a meandering cement pathway. Tall shrubs grew well above the wall and wire, making the space private except for a narrow metal service gate. Chase shook it to make sure it was locked.

The power was on. A little cherub stood peeing in one stone bowl while Atlas struggled to hold four tiers of cascading pools. There were flying angels and diving dolphins, as well as Neptune rising from the sea. Chase walked the path, read the placards. The largest fountain was a replica of the Naiad Fountain in the Piazza della Repubblica in Rome. Its four naked bronze nymphs had caused a scandal at their unveiling in 1901, read the small sign.

Chase headed for the back door of the villa and knocked. What could it hurt? He had press credentials and his camera bag. Noriega's top officers were cooperating with the U.S. military and his bodyguards would probably be lying low until things settled down. A maid with a frying pan might be the worst Chase would have to deal with.

A tangle of red, green, and black wires erupting from a small security pad indicated that the alarm system had been disabled, probably during a Ranger sweep. It was a good bit of luck, since Chase had to use his elbow to break out a pane of glass.

If it had been the Rangers, they left a big mess. Every drawer was opened and tossed. Chairs kicked over, trash dumped. And from the look of the pile of empties in the kitchen, Noriega wasn't hiding at the bottom of a beer can either.

In the great room, VHS tapes were spilled from glass cases around a big screen television, and every book in the adjoining library had been taken from the shelves and piled haphazardly. Lids on toilet tanks had been removed and shampoo bottles pulled from under sinks.

Just off the kitchen and through swinging doors was a walk-in pantry. Two large freestanding freezers had bags of vegetables and white paper wrapped meats collecting layers of frost. Their lids had been left gaping, like an open coffin viewing at a funeral home. Bags of ice were strewn across the floor, melting.

There was nobody upstairs. Just more mess in the study, two smaller bedrooms, and a huge master suite. Chase stashed his camera bag in the bathroom off the master and took a sip of water from the gold plated tap. He decided the best vantage point to wait for Noriega was the top of the dual staircase, which rose from both ends of the black and white checkered marble first floor, meeting at a large hardwood second floor landing. Before him was a view of the driveway entrance gate through a grand window beyond a chandelier; behind him was a smaller window overlooking the backyard fountain collection and service entrance gate. There was a small powder room at the top of the nearest set of stairs; no toilet, but a sink and a spot to hide should he need to take cover.

The first outdoor floodlights came on—either by timer or solar sensor—about an hour later. Then, one by one, small colored lights illuminated each fountain, producing a cheerful scene below as Chase leaned against the wall next to the back window. The air was cool in the still house and he was certain he'd catch any sounds of entry should anyone jump the wall out of view and come in through an unseen door.

The hours passed and adrenaline rushes kicked in and out as car lights occasionally swept across the large iron front gate. But the cars didn't stop. Only a tiny sliver of moon rose over the palm trees as his watch ticked toward midnight.

Chase yawned, stretched his back and neck, and then watched the back service gate slowly swing open. A huddled dark figure made its way along the winding pathway amid all the colorful water and fancy sculptures. Chase realized he hadn't planned for getting to a phone. At some point he'd decided that if Noriega appeared, he was going to take him down alone. Even though he hadn't personally botched Nicaragua, the mission had been a failure. He'd been on enough lousy teams to know how much he hated losing. Noriega was a shot at redemption.

Keys jingled and a door on the main floor opened. The echoing footsteps puzzled Chase because the sound they made wasn't the clomp of combat boots or the squeak of sneakers on the marble. Some sort of healed shoe—a woman's shoe—made its slow, tapping way into the main foyer, then unsteadily up the stairway to his right.

Chase had long since adjusted to the finite lighting, but the approaching figure, taking one step at a time while grasping the railing for support, was silhouetted by the glow coming in the large front window.

Chase melted back into the dark powder room, assuming the figure would make a left toward the main bedroom. He could easily take her down from behind. As the figure crested the final step, Chase caught a glimpse of a flash of metal and what looked like the snub nose of a nickel-plated .38 Special right out of a TV cop show. Now on his level, the woman was revealed to have a stocky build, with narrow shoulders and short legs. Her hair was black and piled in an uneven mess. She wore a light blue house dress, something you'd imagine a maid wearing in a fancy neighborhood like this. The heels were low, and she bent forward and held the railing and her gun with one hand, pulling off her shoes with the other.

A distinctly masculine voice uttered a sigh of relief.

Chase's heart raced and he clenched his fists, poised in the darkness. Noriega adjusted his wig, wiped his brow, and gripped the .38 in his outstretched right hand.

As Chase had anticipated, the disguised dictator turned left toward the master bedroom, his aching feet now bare on the hardwood floor. Chase let him get two full strides beyond the stairs before stepping out of the powder room darkness, making his move. But Noriega had left his shoes behind, with their various straps and tangled laces, and just as Chase reached out, he tripped on the shoes and fell to his knees.

Noriega screamed, fired three shots blindly over his left shoulder and ran into the master bedroom, slamming the door behind him.

"Dammit," Chase hissed, getting to his feet, ears ringing from the shots. He was more angry than frightened. Chase glared at the door. Noriega had no exit, but had at least two or three remaining rounds, depending on the make of the revolver and whether he'd tucked away additional bullets in his bra. Deciding to stay on the offensive, Chase did what he imagined Stoney would have done. He strode up to the bedroom door and kicked it in. The intricately detailed knob and bolt action exploded into brass shards and loose screws, as the wood splintered easily. The door slammed open, exposing Noriega standing on top of the king-size bed across the room, his back against the wall for support as he took aim.

Blam! Blam! Click. Click. Click. Click.

His two remaining bullets nearly parted Chase's hair, harmlessly smacking gaping holes into a door at the far end of the upstairs hall.

Noriega wound up like a baseball pitcher on top of the bed and hurled the small gun, but was low and outside for a ball. His tight-fitting house dress was bunched up high on his chubby thighs, exposing olive drab underwear.

I see London, I see France, I see a crazy dictator's underpants! Chase's thoughts raced.

Noriega stood with legs spread for balance on the soft bed, his wild wig askew and his bright red lipstick smeared into an

ugly clown face. He feinted right, then jumped off the left side
of the bed, running directly at Chase as he tore off the wig and
tried to jam it in his face as he lumbered by. Chase ducked the
fistful of hair and tripped the president as he passed. Noriega
dove headfirst into the door jam, like a base runner trying to
bowl over the catcher during a close play at the plate.

Again Noriega screamed out, this time in pain, as his
right shoulder connected with the door frame, but he was
immediately back up and scrambling into the hall. Chase was
right on his heels.

"*Hola, Señor Presidente.*" Chase kicked Noriega's ankles out
from under him before he could get to the stairs. His body
took a mid-air spin, thudding to the floor.

"*Por favor, no más,*" Noriega cried, face down on the floor,
trying to cover his head with his arms. "*Soy dolido, soy dolido.*
I am hurt."

"Fight me and you die, *entiende*?" Chase ordered, putting a
knee in the small of his back as he imagined Stoney would have
done. He reached for one of the discarded shoes, untangled a
long strap, and ripped it free. Chase cinched Noriega's wrists
behind his back.

"*Soy dolido,*" Noriega whimpered.

"I'm not going to fuck around with you." Chase's voice was
clear, business-like, and he spoke directly into the man's ear.
"I'm taking you downstairs and I'm making a phone call."

"Your family is dead." Noriega's voice was a growl, his cheek
pressed into the wood floor.

"Get up."

"There's money in the bed." Noriega's tone had changed to
sleazy businessman and it pissed Chase off. He'd threatened his
family and then shifted his tactics so easily to offering a bribe.
Chase grabbed Noriega by the collar of the dress and slammed
his head into the floor.

"Ouch! You fucker!"

"How much you got?" Chase had the man with both hands

around his neck. Could he kill someone without getting all crazy? He was starting to think it would be pretty easy.

"I'll have their heads cut off."

"Ten thousand? Twenty? How much money to let you walk out of here and start cutting off people's heads?"

"Two million dollars."

"Bullshit." Chase began to squeeze.

"The money is all right there," Noriega croaked, jerking his chin toward the bedroom despite being choked. Chase turned to his right, loosened his hands.

"You take half and we both win," said the dictator.

Chase stood up, spun the little man around on his belly, and dragged him by the dress collar back into the bedroom. Noriega yelped as his body bounced over the slightly raised threshold.

"*Donde*?" Chase demanded, and Noriega motioned with his chin at the heavy wood frame of the right side of the bed. "There's a compartment?"

"We have a deal," Noriega said from the floor.

"I don't need money." Chase was intent on finding the secret latch to open the hidden compartment in the side of the bed. He fished in the darkness, running his hands all along the dark wood, aware that there might be a booby trap, but Noriega didn't seem to be cowering away, so he figured it was safe.

"Everyone needs money."

Chase's fingers found the latch and a three foot section of bed frame came open in his hands. He brought one of the small bedside lamps down and ripped a pillow case off to smother most of the light as he twisted the switch. Inside the compartment were a metal briefcase and an interesting looking antique box. It had a small, inscribed plate on top that read "Adolph Hitler, Walther PPK."

"No fucking way." Chase turned to ask Noriega if it was real, but the floor was deserted. "Shit!" Chase closed the wood hatch and scrambled for the door.

Noriega was mincing barefooted, midway down the stairs, hands still bound behind his back, his dress fully up to his hips. "Stop!" Chase shouted and Noriega took a great misstep, tumbling forward, head over heels down the tall staircase. The president made at least five full forward revolutions, his head finally breaking his momentum against a large terra-cotta pot at the base of the stairs, creating a zigzag lightning bolt crack down one side of the planter.

Just as the unconscious dictator came to a sprawling rest, the front entryway became awash in bright headlights of what might have been a U.S. military Humvee just outside the front gate. A soldier jumped out of the passenger side door carrying long handled bolt cutters. While his silhouette worked the chained gate in front of Chase, his enormous shadow worked behind him on the wall.

"Shit." Chase gathered Noriega over one shoulder in a fireman's carry and headed away from the front door. He considered a rear-exit escape, but if it was the Rangers, they'd definitely have that side covered. Were they back on the reports of shots fired or just to re-sweep the house? Losing Noriega to the Rangers would be the second screw-up in two missions.

Chase jogged the dictator into the kitchen and did one quick rotation. The oven? The dishwasher? Then he spied the swinging doors to the pantry and banged through them, using Noriega's ass for a battering ram. After scooping out a bunch of bags of Birdseye frozen vegetables, Chase dumped Noriega's warm body into the nearest freezer. It was a tight squeeze, but Chase got the lid closed and turned the tiny silver key in the lock.

As an afterthought, he reached back and kicked the plug out of the wall for both freezers. The low drone went silent. How long would Noriega have before hypothermia killed him? Before lack of air suffocated him?

Chase ran back through the kitchen and out to the foyer, then took the stairs four at a time. After reaching down to toss

Noriega's shoes into the powder room, he sprinted into the master bedroom.

He lay back on the wonderfully soft duvet, letting his respiration settle, taking deep, even breaths, knowing this was going to be impossible to explain. How long did Noriega have? Thirty minutes? Twenty?

A single Humvee rumbled down the short drive, shifting into park with its lights still on, just outside the front door. The heavy idle was menacing and the house was almost in daylight from the bank of spotlights high over the windshield. Chase couldn't make out what they were saying over the engine noise, but the language was English and not Spanish—a comforting fact. Definitely a U.S. Humvee.

When the front door was shaken and not kicked in Chase knew there was hope, that it was probably just a quick perimeter check and not an investigation of shots fired. Besides, shots fired at one of Noriega's compounds would surely have brought out half the Army.

Moments later, the soldiers jumped back in the truck and the driver revved the engine and spun the tires. Chase crept off the bed and out the door for a look. The soldiers had apparently decided the coast was clear and it was time for some off-roading in the president's yard. There was yahooing and yeehawing as the Humvee spun doughnuts on the manicured lawn. The engine got loud, then quiet, then loud again. They seemed intent on leaving no blade of grass unscathed.

Chase lost sight of the headlights and the engine sound changed as the powerful Humvee sped around the side of the house. The motor revved as they made the turn, entering the backyard at what sounded like a pretty good rate of speed. And then worn brakes squealed too late as a series of metal on concrete cracking noises went off like shotgun shells. One water fountain after another was mowed down and the hullabaloo ended with one great gong, which had to be the Humvee bumper striking the naked bronze nymphs.

The engine died and the headlights were extinguished.

Chase edged down the hall to the nearest window.

"We're in some serious shit, Larry."

"Fuck if we ain't."

"Try and turn it over but don't give her too much gas."

The dead starter clicked and clicked, but stayed dead. There was the noise of a popped hood.

"Fucking starter's fried. It ain't goin' nowhere."

"Got any ideas?"

"We gotta report it was stolen."

"And having our ride hijacked will save our asses in what way?"

There was the sound of concrete being moved, grunts from heavy lifting.

"Both front tires are flat."

"What is all this shit, anyway? Come check this out. Looks like you ran over a nekked broad."

"It's some kinda statue."

"Well, no shit. Hit the lights and help me pull her out."

There were grunts and low cussing as they worked under Chase's window. Chase had expected the police to investigate the backyard crash, but they might have been told to stand down from their regular duties during the manhunt.

"You think she's gold?"

"Do I look like I'd know if she's gold?"

"You're in a shit mood."

"We just totaled our ride. What kind of fucking mood should I be in?"

"Look, maybe we say we had a runner. You ordered him to stop, but he took off around the house and we followed. Then, bam, this shit was all over the place."

"What about all them doughnuts you done on the front lawn? How we gonna explain that? Was the guy runnin' in circles when we chased him?"

"Fuck me."

"I ain't takin' the heat for this, no way. We gotta report it stolen. Ain't no other way."

"Okay, grab the weapons and my sunglasses from the ashtray. And come help me with this nekked broad. I'll get her by the legs."

"You really think she's gold?"

Chase slipped away from the window as the soldiers banged through the back servant gate. The sky had turned purple as Chase grabbed his camera bag from the powder room and went for the secret compartment in the bed. He pulled out the cash-filled briefcase and box containing Hitler's gun. In the kitchen, he twisted the oven broiler to high and spilled the cash onto the top rack. The electric elements glowed orange.

Chase set the antique box on the granite counter and went to fetch Noriega, who was nearly white from the cold, lips an astonishing shade of blue. But he was still alive and shivering like a wind-up toy. He let Chase smooth out his dress and lead him back out into the kitchen, where he sat in a chair with his hands still tied behind him. Noriega's makeup was a total mess and a big purple knot from cracking the terra-cotta planter was blooming on his forehead.

With the smell of burning money filling the first floor, Chase used the phone on a small table in the front hallway to call his CIA contact to come pick up the target. The agent's excited tone was instantly muted when Chase identified himself as DB6 instead of CIA. A lowly part-timer had nabbed the bad guy.

"You would have been rich and I could have been free." Noriega spoke slowly, his teeth chattering. He was watching the fire behind the glass oven door.

"There are more important things than money."

Noriega's eyes were closed and his head lolled from side to side. "Like what?"

"Like climbing to the top of a cliff," Chase said, searching the mess in the great room next to the kitchen. He picked through broken picture frames that had been ripped down from a wall filled with tiny nails. "And then diving head first."

"Suicide?"

"You could never understand." Chase dumped broken glass from the picture he'd hoped to find—one that Noriega claimed in interviews to have a hundred copies of. It was of a younger Noriega seated on a couch next to the current U.S. President. Everyone was smiling for the *Newsweek* photographer. At the time the photo was taken, George Bush had been the Director of the CIA and integral in recruiting and training Noriega for covert work on America's behalf. Chase propped the photo in Noriega's lap and went to his camera bag. He wondered what kind of rating Limp would give his idea. Was the shot of a drug trafficking dictator nabbed in a dress already a three? Would the irony of the added picture of Noriega's one-time CIA boss register with readers?

Noriega leaned forward to look at the picture displayed against his belly and shook his head. "Times change."

Chase's flash lit up the messy kitchen.

Chapter 12

IT WAS THE same airport in the same city. Again it was late when Chase stepped out to the curb and climbed inside a yellow taxi. He needed to sleep, but couldn't remember his address. He'd have to point the way once they got close. Or was this the same driver who might remember?

It was Friday night and the pizza joint was still delivering. Chase wandered the apartment, tried ignoring the new envelope. A baseball game on TV had gone into the ninth.

Chase wanted to call someone else. That his mom and dad were asleep was just an excuse. His dad would wake up and talk. Would ask him what the hell he was thinking when he quit school. Lying would just make him feel worse.

Would Stoney even be coherent at this hour? It would have been a good three hours of drinking and bong hits. And what if Stoney was honest? What if Stoney asked what kind of friend up and bolts like that?

Maybe he could handle that later. Right now he was too tired, too close to the edge. There'd been no fifteen minutes of fame on this trip, even though it had gone better than any of his bosses could have imagined. No credit lines, just a nod from a couple of CIA guys in expensive suits and dark sunglasses. They'd flashed their IDs and carted off the prisoner.

Chase pulled the wood display box containing Hitler's gun out of his backpack. Christ, had he just flown through two airports armed? He supposed he would have thought fast. He would've said how embarrassed he was, admitted what a dumb thing he had done. He'd found the counterfeit gun in a small shop, paid forty bucks, or something. It was a novelty and he should have declared it, or done whatever you do when travelling with such an item. He was just a journalist, after all, the type of person who avoids any type of real gun.

Chase broke open the case and felt the weapon's weight, pointed it at the television then out the window. The side of the short barrel was marked Walther Model PPK 7.65mm. The grip was rough plastic. It wasn't much heavier than a water pistol, but it had changed the world, or at least deprived it of satisfaction when Hitler put it to his head and pulled the trigger in the Berlin bunker.

Chase held the gun to his temple, closed his eyes and tried imagining how it must feel. But instead of Hitler, Chase was flooded with visions of his sister that night in his bed. He began to squeeze the trigger, but then wondered if it was loaded. Chase dropped the gun on the couch next to the pizza box and went to find the new envelope.

Chapter 13

A NARROW, WINDING road led onto the school grounds. Small palm trees leaned inward, their heavy leaves brushing the dirt as a slight breeze stirred the heat. The sinuous lane was meant for bicycles and motor bikes, and for people in no great hurry. A few shacks lined the road. Burned garbage smoldered in piles where you might find mail boxes in a different country. A naked, mud-caked child poked a short stick at one mound, trying to stir up the flames.

Thailand was a land of kings and queens, of ghosts and monks, in which a young woman from Massachusetts had apparently come to spread peace but had gotten mixed up in something bad.

Chase's assignment was to write and photograph a general interest Peace Corps feature story for the Associated Press to be distributed among all member papers. For DB6, he was only provided a cryptic mention of a mysterious "Bat Girl" in the envelope left on his kitchen counter. It told him to *secure* her, but he didn't know what that meant. Protect her? Could it have meant to kill her?

Beth Flanagan didn't just shake Chase's hand when her

principal introduced him as the American journalist who had traveled so far. She shook his whole body in a giant bear-hug, and he could no longer imagine a possible scenario in which he'd have to kill her, if indeed she was the Bat Girl and it turned out she'd somehow gotten on the wrong side of the CIA.

Beth was tall and confident and her gentle touch seemed all over you, if you were anywhere near her. Chase later discovered this might be the Thai children's influence on her, since they bonded so immediately with light-skinned people from the West. Being light skinned meant you didn't toil in hard-labor, you must be wealthy. Beth wore no makeup and just a simple green dress, a gift from a student's parent. Her pale skin and piercing blue eyes were framed by a long shock of messy, sandy blonde hair. Chase came to find that when she wasn't laughing, she was either just smiling really big, or pretending to be disappointed in a misbehaving student.

Beth was from a large Irish-Catholic family, the fourth-oldest of six children. Her father, Patrick, had been teaching phys-ed for thirty years at a small high school in Western Massachusetts, where he also coached three sports. Her mom was a middle school teacher.

For more than a year, Beth had been teaching English to junior high aged school children in rural Thailand, about two hours northeast of Bangkok.

"Teaching English for the Peace Corps is difficult for a number of reasons." Beth led Chase from the main school building to a series of tiny, raised faculty homes, where she lived with a cat. Chase took notes. "You never really see the good you are accomplishing. I'm always asking myself, 'so what if they learn to speak English in this part of the country? Is it for them to run away to work at the tourist resorts?' Those are my down times, my bad days. But the Peace Corps is about sharing cultures, trying to help people understand the way others in faraway places live."

Wat Prachamimitr School was in the Bua Yai district, two

kilometers from a town of the same name and surrounded by thousands of acres of rice paddies. The school, built with World Bank money, was meticulously kept. The swept pathways were lined with tropical red-flowering bushes. Clusters of ferns and other plants grew at each intersection along the meandering walkways. The dorm and school buildings were long, two-story structures, with dark, gleaming wood floors that the children polished daily with coconut shells. Student uniforms were white collar shirts; boys in brown shorts and girls in matching skirts.

Three hundred students, ages twelve to fifteen, were taught by two dozen teachers. They also had a small group of younger kids on campus living in a dormitory room lined with bunk beds. The orphanage meant additional government aid for the school. Tuition was the equivalent of sixty cents per week, plus a kilo of family rice. Beth was one of three English teachers, but the only *farang*, or foreigner. This school would be the last formal education for most of these kids, she explained. For hundreds of years, the children had worked on family farms, eventually taking them over. The farms consisted of small houses, several buffalo, and plots of land to grow rice. The school was a relatively new and not entirely welcome addition to the culture. Some saw the new opportunities made possible for the children as an infringement upon their tradition, Beth explained.

Chase continued scribbling pages of notes and took a few photos with his Nikon. He shot Beth seated cross-legged in the middle of her main living area, a black cat making slow laps around her, as she smiled and talked and waved her long arms for punctuation. This was the infamous Bat Girl?

"There's no air conditioning anywhere." Beth dug through her clean laundry for a cotton rag she held out for Chase to wipe his face. The heat was overwhelming. "Classrooms have window vents and the doors are left open. The sun may bother them, but not the heat. They try to avoid the sun, but it'll be ninety degrees and some of the girls will complain about a chilly breeze. In my first lesson plan I tried teaching them about the snowstorms back home, about frozen rivers and night skiing at Mount Tom. But parents complained to my principal I was giving the kids nightmares." Beth laughed and stroked her cat.

Just how long Chase was to endure this heat and question-filled mission wasn't clear. The school had readily offered one of the unoccupied single-room houses near Beth's, where an elderly teacher had died in bed two years earlier. Nobody on staff had wanted to test the waters regarding his ghost, so a new *farang* was a welcome guinea pig.

Chase couldn't imagine what this young American could have gotten herself into. Or was she just a link to the Bat Girl, an innocent connection?

The morning classes had been canceled so that Buddhist Monks from a nearby temple could speak to the children about rebirth. Disruptions such as this weren't uncommon, for the monks made at least twice-monthly visits for various reasons. Just last week, Beth told Chase, they'd come to explain the importance of not playing doctor, following a discovery of children performing medical exams on one another in the closed, one-room infirmary.

"The monk missed the point, though. He lectured about playing with expensive medical equipment."

The three hundred kids sat packed tightly together on a concrete floor in the auditorium, while the faculty occupied wooden chairs along one wall. The monks, Beth explained in a hushed play-by-play translation, told the children that death wasn't the end of life, but the passing of one living stage to another. The dead are reborn into other life forms. The new life depends on how much merit was gained in a previous life. Good deeds are cumulative and one can be reborn each time into a wealthier, happier life. If enough merit is accumulated, the person will reach Nirvana, a place of no suffering. One of the simplest ways to gain merit, they explained, was to make offerings to the monks. Every morning, the monks walked the streets of the towns and cities with canisters for people to fill with rice and other foods.

As Beth whispered in Chase's ear, he searched the faculty from face to face, looking for clues to the Bat Girl mystery, but each teacher had the same look of interest or was trying to get the attention of a child who'd begun to fidget.

After the monks led a final prayer, the students filed out for lunch, stopping to hunt for shoes among an enormous pile left on the front steps. They laughed and giggled, trying to match shoes that all looked exactly alike.

"It's an amazingly spiritual society," Beth told Chase as the casual interview continued. "Many Thais believe in ghosts. Next to almost every house is a small spirit house on a pole. When a family builds a home, they displace the spirit that was living in the space. To maintain harmony, they put up these small, elaborate houses for the spirits to live in so they won't haunt the new owners."

"I thought they were bird houses."

"Ha, every visitor thinks that," she said, laughing. "People are always asking if Americans believe in ghosts. I tell them it's the same as here, that some people do and others don't. But for the believers here, it's more spiritual, more a way of life. They arrange their lives to be, I don't know … at one with the spirits. To get along with them, you know? Like our Native Americans. I wish I'd read more about the Navajos and Hopis. My folks are sending me some books."

"Is the fear of ghosts mostly with the older generation?"

"Not fear, really. Respect would be a better way to describe it. The children here are much more innocent than back home, more curious and less cynical. When I first got here, I would be walking down the street and a child would reach out and touch me as we passed."

Chase had already experienced this twice on the narrow pathways.

"So what are the tall, skinny boxes next to the spirit houses?" Oddly shaped structures on tall poles rose parallel to those of the spirit houses. They sat talking on the front porch of her home, and at least a half dozen of these narrow boxes were on this pathway alone.

"Oh, those are bat houses," she explained, and for the first time Chase detected a troubled note in her voice. "Peace Corps volunteers have what's called a crossover specialty. Like English teacher and farming. Or English teacher and well digger. Here, they needed help keeping the mosquito population under control since many of the limestone bat caves have been destroyed. It's unsafe and just not possible to chemically treat thousands of acres of rice paddies. An outbreak of malaria killed dozens of villagers the year before I arrived. Without a healthy bat population, it's just a matter of time before everyone becomes sick."

"There are bat caves around here?" Chase knew he was closing in on the Bat Girl.

"Yes. And there are some caves with more than ten million bats. A single colony will eat hundreds of tons of insects each year. There are over a hundred sacred Buddhist caves in Thailand where the bats are protected. A key part of the religion recognizes that to understand human nature, one must be immersed in nature. Caves had awesome acoustics for chanting, and they were a peaceful receptacle of spiritual energy during meditation."

"Like singing in the shower?"

"Yes, right, a combination of harmony and meditation, as well as being places for birth and rebirth. They were the gates into the subterranean world where both demons and angels lived."

Beth reached out and corralled her skinny black cat, giving it long strokes down its arched back with her fingernails. The cat purred deeply, collapsing in her lap as she rubbed behind its ears and under its chin. But something had changed. Her smile and energy were gone.

"These days, when a monk is living in a particular cave, a yellow cloth is hung at the entrance. He'll meditate and sleep in the cave, only leaving for alms-round, which is when they collect food from villagers. The monk may live there for a few days or even a few years. The caves are either part of a monastery, or are pretty close to one."

"I don't know much about bats, but my grandmother's horse farm had a barn attic that would pile up with bat droppings."

"Well, they spend a lot of time cleaning guano from the rows of Buddha statues as part of their workday. And it's definitely heads-up at sunset when the bats stir and leave to feed. There's a particular cave west of Bangkok that's pretty big with tourists. Some German researchers counted a hundred million bats. Every day, starting at dusk, they leave the cave in a steady stream. It takes three hours before the last one is out."

Chase had stopped taking notes beyond her description of building the bat houses for the school. She went on to describe Thailand as having thousands of these caves, created by the mixture of limestone mountain ranges that are carved by the tropical monsoons.

Chase knew he'd found the Bat Girl.

A bell was rung from the main school building to signal lunch and Beth set her cat down to lead the way.

"Can you eat Thai food?" the smiling principal asked Chase, as a female student served the faculty table at the front of the cafeteria. Chase had quickly learned that foreigners were given proper warning about the insanely spicy food.

Chase was blinking back tears from smelling his lunch when a young serving girl set a plate piled with colorfully dangerous foods in front of him, then quickly reached between his legs and jammed something against his crotch.

"What the hell?" he almost said aloud, but she was gone in a flash and hadn't done any damage. Then he felt the gun and slid the small weapon into the deep front pocket of his khakis.

The girl students lingered over their lunches, chattering away in their singsong language. The boys rushed through the meal to have more time on what Beth called the takraw court. Takraw was a combination of volleyball, soccer, and acrobatics played in an area similar to a volleyball court. Players used heads, knees, and feet to get the ball over the net.

"Have you seen it played?" Beth led him to a spot along the sideline. "It has to be the least likely sport to ever be embraced by America, but it's so much fun."

The non-takraw playing boys headed for the concrete basketball court, where a game of tackle basketball broke out. That game, a combo of rugby and basketball, would definitely work in America. Several boys were quick to acquire bloody lips and knees. Thai boys appeared quite durable, despite their small size. They would sit dazed from near-concussion blows to the head, but only for a moment, as they were mercilessly teased by their tacklers into rejoining the melee at the other end of the court. Pens and coins jolted from their pockets remained scattered behind. Chase finished shooting his fifth roll of film and scribbled more notes.

Chase tagged along when Beth carried a banana bunch to her afternoon English class. She was a favorite among the children and they often stopped by her house to visit, Beth told him. She cringed when she described the whippings administered by her coworkers at the school, a popular method of Thai discipline.

"A rough translation of an old Thai saying goes, 'If you love your buffalo, you beat him; if you love your child, you beat him. Respect comes from fear.' " Beth rolled her eyes.

"The kids know they can get away with anything with me, and I have a few boys in my class who do. They aren't interested in learning English. The stereotypical Thai boy goofs around while the girl studies. When they grow up, the men womanize and the women stay at home."

Beth explained how she'd lost the respect of some colleagues who found it eccentric that she and her students would pal around. Refusing to use a whip was disrespectful to the culture. She didn't care.

After writing exercises, Beth brought out the bananas, placing them on chairs at the front of the class. The children took turns pretending to be at an American market to buy the fruit with broken-English transactions. Beth made notations on the chalkboard as she maneuvered around a sleeping dog named Pete.

"They remember this stuff," Beth explained, taking frequent breaks from her lesson to keep Chase filled in. He sat to one side of the class, trying not to be a distraction but failing. A group of girls had their desks huddled together and were giggling as they spied on him over their textbooks. "I'm the wacky, white-skinned teacher to them, but I really don't do anything much different from any teacher in America."

Beth was treated as special from the beginning of her stay, as the principal took her around to the surrounding communities to recruit students. "I was a novelty, a way for him to sell the idea of the school to the farmers. It's probably best that my Thai wasn't all that great at the time. I felt like a sideshow freak, the main attraction for kids to come to our school. I resented it then, but I understand it better now."

As the school day was winding down, Beth asked the class, "What time is it?" in English. She held a cardboard clock, the hands displaying six-thirty.

"Nine o'clock," a boy offered from the middle of the room, and two other boys agreed.

"No," Beth said. "Now, what number is this?" She pointed at the six.

"Twelve!" several children shouted.

"Six," a quiet, shy looking girl in the front row finally said. A boy behind her muttered something, perhaps an insult.

"So what time is it?" Beth asked the class again.

"Half past six thirty," was the best guess.

With the school day over, Beth borrowed a scooter to give Chase a tour of the surrounding countryside. He climbed on behind her and she zigzagged around the lush rectangular fields through a maze of rice paddy dikes. The rice was a velvety green carpet above the water and mud; the air finally cooling an hour or so before sunset. A few farmers trudged behind their buffalo through the heavy muck on their way home, and an old woman yelled and slapped the ground with a walking stick because the scooter agitated her own lumbering beast. To Chase it seemed one heavy downpour would simply submerge this part of the world.

Beth stopped the scooter at the edge of a wide, muddy lake. Children were swimming and diving from the banks. A man walked neck-deep, about fifty feet from shore, dragging fishing nets. In the distance was a Buddhist Temple built on pilings. Monks bathed in the setting sun, crouched in the water, still wearing bright orange robes.

As Beth stepped off the little scooter, the children flocked to her. Most were young, pre-school age. They were the children of these farmers, still too young to work in the fields. A tiny girl haltingly made her way up to Beth, who crouched so the girl could stroke her cheek and feel her white skin. It was easy to tell which children hadn't seen Beth before.

"This is my special place," Beth told Chase, as he snapped a few photos even though the light level had dropped too low. The first stars had broken through the purple sky as dusk engulfed the flat land, the sun sinking toward the horizon as though into quicksand.

"Every once in a while I need to get away, and it's so beautiful and peaceful here," she said, the sounds of belly-flops and unseen chickens close by.

As Beth talked to the group of children nearest her scooter, Chase found a patch of grass on the bank with the least amount of Buffalo dung and lay back on his elbows. The long trip and exotically passive scenery had him off guard and suddenly sleepy. His stomach, working on the burning food, seemed the only restless part of his body.

But the sudden sleepiness was tinged with something else. There was a swirling, narcotic sensation taking Chase beyond just tired. He tried sitting up but couldn't. His arms and legs weren't cooperating. He turned to Beth, tried to focus. She looked back at him with sympathy. Chase was certain she knew what was happening.

He had found the Bat Girl and now he was poisoned. The two thoughts were crystal clear. Now what?

Was that popcorn he smelled? Chase imagined he was in a theater for a movie. The darkness swept aside like a giant curtain that opened to intense action. He could almost feel the wind from a giant helicopter swooping in. His body might have been plastered with spraying water and stinging dust. The noise was too much, too loud. Three soldiers hopped out of the chopper carrying a red backboard, black straps flapping violently in the downdraft. They rolled Chase on his side, slipped the stretcher underneath, then carried him back to the hovering craft. He felt the chopper dip slightly from the weight as they climbed aboard.

Then the Bat Girl was kneeling over him, her pale face vibrating close, as the chopper powered up, surging forward and away from the swirling dust and spray. He tried to ask for her help, but the poison was closing his throat. He struggled to keep his eyes open and focused as Beth was pushed away. One man tore at Chase's shirt and attached blurry electrode patches. Another grabbed a handful of hair and forced his head back while jamming a turkey baster into his dry throat. The soldier squeezed the bulb, emptying the contents. When it was removed, Chase tasted oil and then leaned to one side and vomited.

His toes and fingers, which had moments ago been in some other distant room, were now back—cold, and tingling. He tried pulling against the straps with no success, so he concentrated on breathing the good air, watching the helicopter ceiling.

Chase's pulse was checked and other vital signs were shouted in some unrecognizable language. His world again wavered, shifting from gray to black, as they climbed higher into the night sky, rotors screaming, beating down the thick air and taking them from one alien tropical place to another.

"Good night," Chase whispered with a smile to anyone nearby.

Chapter 14

B ETH FLANAGAN WAS famously known as the Bat Girl in this rugged land where the helicopter touched down. She and Chase were roughly disembarked and deposited in a harshly lit subterranean room, which may or may not have originally been a cave.

Chase would soon find that the entire structure was carved into a mountainside by rainwater and by machinery, thousands of square feet of chambers and connecting tunnels. Unleashed from the backboard, he had woken with the driest mouth possible and a rolling nausea from the poison. He sat up from the army-style cot and gingerly dropped his legs over the side. Nearly palpable waves of blackness threatened consciousness then slowly retreated.

"Sorry about the poison." Beth was perched cross-legged on an olive green blanket spread over the concrete floor. And here again with her were small children, although these were more subdued. The three young, barely school-aged girls lay across Beth in different directions, all holding one of her hands and nuzzling at her lap and belly. "I promise it wasn't my idea. It's just their way of bringing certain visitors up here while keeping the location a secret."

"No blindfolds in this part of Thailand?" Chase rubbed his forehead and eyes with his palms.

"I'm sorry."

"You're Bat Girl."

"I didn't mean to be Bat Girl." She slowly stroked the hair of each girl, one after the other. They nuzzled closer in their sleep, like a litter of kittens.

There was just a single desk with a blank yellow legal pad, a pen, and a paper cup on top. Next to the desk was an empty, dust-covered water cooler and a vinyl chair covered in duct tape patches. The cold light emanated from long, fluorescent light tubes. About half were flickering. The door was solid wood and Chase assumed it was locked. There were no mirrors, and he didn't see anything that might be a video camera or listening device.

"It doesn't make a great first impression, does it?" She followed his gaze around the room, but probably meant the drugging and kidnapping. This was the second time he'd heard her voice with the joy gone, sullen and tired. "The first time they brought me here the same way. I think they like the theater of it. You missed the high-fiving."

"So what's this about? What is this place?" Chase stretched his muscles, but wasn't ready to test his legs. "Have I been kidnapped? What do they want from me? What did they want from you?"

The mountain complex rose above a network of limestone caves west of the Ubonrat Reservoir, south of Nong Bua Lamphu. If he'd been conscious during the flight, he'd have enjoyed a scenic thirty minute ride. Beth explained the important central location of this place when it came to its bat population.

"It's all about the bats. It's why I'm here, and why you're here. It's why they brought the girls here."

"Go on."

"This is where bats are being collected and stored by induced hibernation," she said. "There are cold storage units for more than a half million bats."

She paused, looking down at the small brown children who were now sound asleep in her lap. She continued to stroke their hair. They wore what looked like old uniforms, just slightly different than those of Beth's school.

"These guys are the jihadists of Lukman Lima," she finally said, almost in a whisper. "Do you know what a jihad is?"

"A holy war."

"Yes, right, a jihad is a holy war." Beth spoke the word jihad as if it tasted bad. "And these are called PULO, which stands for the Patani United Liberation Organization. These soldiers are the fighting wing, the New PULO fighters, or something. Their goal is to create an independent Muslim state out of the southern Thai provinces. Down where all the tourist spots are."

"I've seen stories about them in the papers."

"They demand a free and independent Patani," Beth continued quietly, almost wistfully. "No matter whom they hurt." She was having a hard time looking at Chase.

According to Associated Press reports, PULO fighters were being trained in al Qaeda camps in Pakistan and Afghanistan, then returning to Thailand to set off roadside bombs and commit drive-by shootings. Their targets were mainly groups of Buddhist monks wandering the southern countryside to receive alms.

Most people in Thailand viewed the roaming monks as a calming, stabilizing influence, the stories had said. They'd always been welcomed and were constantly posing for pictures with chubby-kneed tourists in Bermuda shorts. Mostly offerings of food, the alms allowed mere mortals to forge a symbolic, spiritual connection to what the monks represented. But the monks' bright orange robes were like great bulls-eyes to PULO. The targeting of the monks caused trepidation among the villagers, who had always welcomed the roaming religious men in the past. Some villagers blamed the Buddhists when their own village people were killed or injured in the attacks.

"The Thai government began cracking down on PULO in the south," Beth continued. "Lima put out a call to all Islamic nations for help. It's pretty clear that when an Islamic fighter cries persecution in a non-Islamic country, money pours in from Arab nations."

"I couldn't place the language in the helicopter," Chase said. "I knew it wasn't Thai."

"This was once a limestone quarry, but Lima used the Arab money under the guise of a bogus corporation to buy it for a training camp two years ago. There are natural barriers because of the terrain, so the only way in is by helicopter or by foot."

"How many jihadists are here?"

"Four hundred, maybe."

"Why are you helping them? And why do they call you Bat Girl?"

"I'm not helping anymore," she said defensively, and pulled the girls tighter into her lap. "When the first commanders tried to use some of the deeper, more elaborate caves as their headquarters, they had soldiers try get rid of the bats. They used smoke bombs and fire and finally hoses to flood some of the chambers. Nothing worked. Bats are like rats and cockroaches in that way. They even tried machine-gunning the streams of bats as they left the caves at dusk, but they'd just kill a few hundred out of millions and were left to clean up a disgusting mess of dead and dying bats. They had this great, geographically secure location for training, but were being driven off by bats. Imagine a commander sending that message back to his leaders."

"So what did they do?"

"About six months ago, Lima came up with a crazy idea to use the bats instead of trying to exterminate them."

"Use them how?" Chase was getting to the heart of Bat Girl's involvement.

"The first idea was to have them carry a biological weapon, something like anthrax. But setting anthrax-contaminated bats free in urban areas didn't do much killing. The bats would fly into the building crevices and die. That's when one of the commanders in charge of explosives training came up with the idea of attaching small bombs to the bats."

"And it worked?" Chase already knew it had.

"Yes, it worked better than they could have imagined. They netted a few dozen Wrinkle-lipped Free Tailed bats, which are the main species here, tied miniature hand grenades to them, pulled the pins and set the bats free. In four seconds, the delay material burns up, igniting the contents in the detonator and the whole thing explodes."

"Who would've thought?"

"Well, it wasn't perfect, because they needed a longer delay, and the bats could only carry a tiny amount of weight. But it was enough to convince the people with lots of money that they were on to something good. Or something really bad."

"So why did they need you?"

And she reminded Chase of her reputation as the bat expert of Bua Yai. She was the white American bat expert who had helped save a town from malaria by using her ingenuity to revitalize the bat population. Beth had been proud of her success, sending home the original copies of lovely thank you notes from the grateful mayor of Bua Yai, along with letters from rice farmers. There were also the adoring portraits of her, drawn by peasant children who had been told of this white woman's magical power over the bats. In many of these pictures she had wings. Not the rounded, sweeping wings of an angel, but leathery, stretched membranous wings, usually including details like the thumb and three small fingers. Despite the creepiness, Beth considered these especially touching because so much time and effort had gone into them. They were drawings of the Bat Girl.

"The entire story had reached all the city papers in Bangkok and they did what jihadists do." Tears filled her eyes, spilling out and splashing down on the sleeping children. "They came to my school at night and kidnapped me and three girls from the orphans' dorm."

And Chase realized this was just a young Irish-Catholic woman from a town in Western Massachusetts who had been dealing with all this subterfuge alone, the weight of the world on her shoulders. The weight of knowing she was, in a fairly direct way, helping fashion a terrorist attack that could kill thousands of people.

"The kids are scared but okay." She softly stroked the sleeping children. "It's amazing what children will adapt to. They're locked in a room all day, have to ask for a bucket to relieve themselves, and are fed only rice and water, yet they laugh and play and argue. They forget they're in prison. Half a year to you and me is nearly a lifetime to a child, you know?"

"Why these kids?"

"The jihadists are evil but not stupid," Beth said, showering the girls with more tears. "They stole orphans because they knew the school would only search for so long. There wouldn't be parents holding vigils, drumming up outrage until they got answers. They took the children to hold me hostage to their demands."

"And the principal doesn't want any trouble," Chase said. "Not from bad guys and not from the government."

"That's right. The principal is a good man at heart. He wants what's best for the kids and the school. When I was brought back and released, I was told to explain the soldiers and helicopters were from the Thai government. That it was all part of the search for the girls."

"He knew that wasn't true."

"I don't know, but he allowed me go on teaching. I look him

in the eye, maybe for help, maybe to have him tell me what to do. But he looks away."

"And these guys let you return to the school because a missing American girl would get our government involved?"

"Yes, exactly, they let me go until they were ready, until the bats were collected and set to go. Bua Yai is isolated, but government welfare trucks come through with supplies every couple of months or so."

The same notoriety that got her kidnapped had also kept her alive. A famous American Peace Corps volunteer being killed by Islamic jihadists would bring the entire Thai military into the region, followed closely by the U.S. State Department and the world press corps.

Instead of taking the risk of locating and importing a bat expert, the insurgents found their own in Beth, who knew enough from her Peace Corps training to be useful. She'd been taught how to induce an artificial hibernation that would allow for the safe examination of a specimen—an important step in collecting and storing enough bats to create havoc in the Thai capital.

Lukman Lima had read the wonderful *Bangkok Post* article about the magic *farang*, and ordered her capture.

After explaining to the reporter how she and the villagers had constructed dozens of new bat houses from wood bravely salvaged from homes occupied solely by ghosts, she'd gone on to describe how they were able to examine and even tag some of the pregnant females.

"Bats can easily be induced into an artificial hibernation," she explained to the *Post* reporter, who had traveled to the Wat Prachamimitr School to meet the American Bat Girl. "And as the body temperature is lowered and the heart-rate is slowed, a bat can survive on only a few grams of stored fat during a six-month hibernation. We experimented and put the caged bats in the school kitchen refrigerator and, sure enough, they entered a deep sleep from which we later woke them. All our bats survived and were returned to their roosts, tagged and perfectly healthy."

"Hear that droning noise?" Beth asked. "If you listen closely, you can hear the generators running the freezers from anywhere in the mountain."

Chase could feel the humming in the metal edge of the cot he was sitting on, could hear them over the gentle snoring of the three children.

"So why did they grab me?" He hoped it had something to do with his job as a journalist and not as a DB6 agent. He was really concerned about receiving the gun, that at least one student had been trusted with the knowledge that he might be more than just a reporter.

"You were in the wrong place at the wrong time, I suppose. They're getting ready for the final phase of this plan, just as an important American journalist arrives to do a story on the school. It was their good fortune that you came at this time."

Did they really believe he was just there by coincidence? What about the gun they'd found and taken from him while he was unconscious? Whatever was about to happen, his role would be much easier if they didn't suspect he could cause them any problems.

"So if not anthrax or tiny hand grenades, how are they arming the bats?" Chase got up to stretch his legs.

"They tried a whole bunch of different things while I was back at school. The girls told me a lot of scary stories about burning and exploding bats, things that gave them a lot of nightmares. Some of the bats took off like rockets. I believe the formula they decided on came from a Pakistani bomb expert. Tiny hearing aid batteries are wired to blasting caps. The electrical charge is temporarily interrupted by insulation at a point where it's tightly wrapped around the hibernating bat's leg. Once the bat is released, it comes out of its sleep pretty quickly and its first instinct is to find shelter in some high-up crevice."

"It wakes up and finds a place to hide."

"Yes," she said. "Once in a safe spot, the bat would begin to gnaw at the foreign object, chewing away at the insulation and freeing the electrical charge into the blasting cap. That would detonate the small casing packed with plastique C-8 explosive. They'll also explode if they hit something hard enough to rip the insulation, so it's no place to be when they wake up."

"Each ounce of C-8 would create a one meter blast radius."

"You know about explosives?"

"Things I've read. I know a lot of people would to die from half a million bat bombs."

Just then, the door banged open and an armed soldier in the same uniform as those on the chopper strode toward Chase and stuck an AK-47 in his face. It was apparently time to find out exactly what they wanted.

Beth and the children were left behind, as he was prodded down a carved natural stone corridor lit at intervals by mesh-encased light bulbs. It was cool and damp, as water dripped here and there into small black pools. The passageway opened into a large cavern, maybe thirty feet high and twice that at its widest. It was a little more festive looking in here, as they'd strung hundreds of feet of the white Christmas lights designed to resemble twinkling icicles around the highest perimeter. It was a merry little cave—if you ignored the row of coffin-like freezer chests chock full of sleeping bats.

The floor of this space was crammed with seven large Maytags, side by side, with narrow passages on either side. A great tangle of extension cords came together in a heaped mass, like an exhausted rubber-band ball at the far end of the room. The wires disappeared through a small round cut in the stone, which had to lead to the generators.

"This is one of five such rooms," came a man's voice from behind. Chase was greeted by the head jihadist himself, Lukman Lima, with a clasped-hand bow of the local custom. "Lukman Lima." He reached out to shake Chase's hand Western-style, his Domke camera bag slung over his left shoulder.

"Chase Allen, Associated Press." They shook hands. "Now that you've poisoned and kidnapped me, what can I do for you, Mr. Lima?"

Lima handed over his camera bag, which must have been snatched up by one of the helicopter pilots. He motioned for them to continue out of the cavern and down a narrow corridor. Despite the friendly greeting, the rifle muzzle never left the small of Chase's back. They turned left into what was apparently Lima's cave headquarters.

Maps on walls, radio equipment, and laptop computers made for an interesting juxtaposition to the clump of bats hanging from the farthest corner of the ceiling. They were like a bunch of fuzzy gray bananas, there as if to say, "You humans may have taken over our home, but we're sticking around over here in one nasty, throbbing ball, just so you know it's not over." They'd left a dark cone of guano beneath them.

"They are beautiful." Lima smiled toward the huddled, throbbing mass. It was a statement, not a question. He stepped behind his compact desk covered in more maps and notes written in elegant Arabic, and took a seat in a swiveling red vinyl office chair, which rolled noisily on the stone floor. "Please have a seat, my dear Mr. Allen."

"It seems you're interested in a reporter for an upcoming exclusive." Chase rummaged through his bag, pulled out a pen and a reporter's notebook. His passport and other credentials were gone.

"Miss Flanagan has provided you with the background of our situation, am I right?"

"You plan to attack the government and people of Thailand with bomb-laden bats."

"We are a peaceful people of the Nation of Islam." Lima removed his wire-rimmed glasses, wiped them on the coarse material of his untucked uniform. He wore a plain black Muslim prayer cap and the same olive drab uniform of all the other soldiers Chase had seen. There were no decorations on his chest or arms, no bars or brass on his collar. In this army, you were either in charge or not in charge.

"It is the oppressive Thai regime that has forced our hand." Lima replaced his glasses, an unimposing jihadist leader, with thick jowls and a complexion ruined by too many hours in the sun.

"And when will you be releasing the bats?"

Lima smiled. "In two days time, Mr. Allen, on the fifth of May."

"Coronation Day," Chase added. The papers had been filled with stories and photos of the upcoming anniversary of King Bhumibol Adulyadej's coronation.

"I've been told that American journalists would sell their souls for an exclusive story. Would that be a fair assessment, Mr. Allen?"

Yeah, well, of course it was true, Chase thought. "Yes, Mr. Lima, that's a fair statement. So how are you getting the bats to Bangkok?"

"Shortly before daybreak on the morning of the coronation, twelve helicopters carrying seven freezers each will be dispatched to their targets," Lima gleefully explained. "Each of your very well constructed American appliances holds roughly six thousand explosive devises. *Allahu Akbar!*"

Chase did the quick math in his head.

"Here is my offer to you." Lima paused for effect, again removing and wiping his glasses on his dusty uniform. "Would you like a ride on our thirteenth helicopter?"

Chase smiled and reached across to shake his hand, saying, "I would rather not refer to it as selling my soul."

"Terrific news. *Allahu Akbar!*" Lima rose, still clenching Chase's hand, pumping away. "I knew you would be interested in bringing news of this great victory to the world."

"My job as a journalist is to reflect events as they happen. The teacher and three girls will be set free?"

"Of course, of course they will." His face split into a wide jowly smile. "They'll receive their freedom at the conclusion of our successful mission, *Allahu Akbar*!" He lowered his voice. "Our mission is perfect. It is a mission of Allah and there can be no flaws in His will. You will join me and my generals for dinner tomorrow tonight when they arrive from Patani. I'm sure you have many more questions."

And Chase did. Like, how to blow up this mountain in the next day or two, while rescuing Beth and her kids, and still get his own ass out alive.

"I'll hold you to your word to set them free. I'll write this story and see that the entire world understands your views, but not at the expense of innocent children or the teacher."

"You think Muslim children are not innocent? This entire operation is to ensure the future of my children and my people against the repression and suffering inflicted by this country's illegal regime."

"I'm a journalist here in this country doing a story about a peace mission. I'm just asking that Beth and her kids survive your successful mission and are set free."

"Our mission is one of peace as well." Lima signaled his men to take Chase away. "It is in the hands of God."

The soldier with the AK-47 pushed Chase into the hall. Lima's radio crackled and the hanging clump of bats screeched a response.

It was all hands on deck for Lima's four hundred men to arm the remaining bats with their small packs of explosives in order to be ready for Friday's coronation. Each passing hour brought more shouting and running soldiers, hurrying to respond to various orders of more wire, more detonators, and more straw to tuck between the bats.

Beth played tea party with the captive girls, sipping pretend cups and telling them stories about her family back in Massachusetts. They laughed to tears when she explained the name of her dog, Flea Bag. They sat in silent awe when she described Christmas at the Flanagan house, and how a fat jolly elf flew a reindeer-driven sleigh across the sky to bring presents down the chimney. The girls fingered the small pieces of loose gravel on the floor as she described packing icy-cold snowballs and they laughed again as she told how she'd scored a direct hit, right between her older brother's eyes. The little girls tried hard to picture a tree inside a house, strung with electric lights and colored glass balls. They asked question after question about the presents and where they came from, and how Santa Clause knew what to get each child. A list? This magic man knew when children were bad and when they were good?

"Why doesn't Santa Claus come to Thailand?" asked the youngest.

Orders were barked just outside their cave-like room. The hurried pace of the footsteps became more frenetic, as Chase's watch ticked past midnight.

Probably because no soldier could be spared, the three children were left in Beth's care, and there was no reason to return her to Bua Yai. Let them send a message of the missing American girl to Peace Corps headquarters in Bangkok; it was far too late for them to cause any trouble. Just after one in the morning, two soldiers banged open their door with another army cot and a filthy, twin-size mattress, returning a few minutes later with bowls and pots of soup and rice.

When the soldiers were gone and the girls were asleep again, Chase asked Beth to draw a diagram in the dust on the floor of every detail she could remember of the mountain compound. Each detail she could recall about the other four freezer chambers, the bunkrooms housing the soldiers, and the generator room. And what passageway connected to the room where the helicopters were fueled and ready to go.

"It's getting close, isn't it?" Beth asked, working on her dirt diagram.

He checked his watch again. "Yeah, it's Wednesday morning,

now. They lift off with the bats before daybreak on Friday."

"For Bangkok? For the ceremonies?"

"Yes, the anniversary of the coronation."

"There will be a million people. The morning ceremony is at the Royal Grand Palace and the King arrives in a long procession from his home at Chitralada Palace. It's a sea of people." Beth shook her head and held her face in her hands.

"This is the only exit you know of?" Chase pointed toward her diagram to where a main passage emptied at the base of the mountain. She'd marked off spaces to show the helicopter landing pads.

"Yes. It slopes down from here maybe forty feet, but it's hard to say for sure."

"No other exits? Nothing here to the left of us?"

"Not that I know of. The deepest part of the cave goes directly in from the base of the mountain. That's where we collected at least half of the bats. I've never been to the end of the cave, but it has to be a dead end. Even with the helicopter blades spinning and all the noise right at the mouth of the cave, the bats always exit through this opening.

"It's not passable anyway," she continued. "The deeper you get into the cave, the deeper the guano is. It starts out shin deep; then it's like walking through a waist-high snow drift. Twenty feet later and we had to bring in ladders and wood planks, or you'd sink in over your head. That far into the cave it always sounds like it's sleeting from the defecating bats."

"What's this room?" Chase pointed to a circle she'd indicated off one of the passageways.

"It's the latrine. It's out our door to the right, then a cut out on the right side. It's fairly large, maybe twenty feet square."

"Where does the waste go?"

When Beth said she didn't know, Chase decided to see for himself. Plus, he had to take a leak. Their door wasn't locked, but when he stepped into the hallway he was immediately bowled over by a soldier jogging blindly behind a box of plastique explosives. The soldier fell over Chase, the unarmed explosives tumbling out and spilling everywhere.

The soldier cursed in Arabic, but was more relieved not to have blown up than angry. He was grateful for Chase's help finding every last piece. He thanked him then, praising Allah before rushing onward.

Chase followed and then turned into the alcove housing a series of eight traditional squat toilets. Instead of porcelain bowls, these had simple wooden platforms, with holes in the middle for the user to squat over. They were like good old American outhouse stations, but directly on the floor. The fifty-gallon drum half-filled with water and smaller bucket meant they didn't work like an outhouse, though. An outhouse would require lime, or something else to kill the smell. The smell in here was no worse than an airport bathroom. The water bucket meant the waste was being flushed to somewhere.

After taking a long, relieving piss down the hole, he carefully pried up one of the two-foot by two-foot wood platforms. The hole was pitch black, but was definitely bored out with a drill at about a fifty-degree angle outward, away from the hallway. He poured half a bucket of water and carefully listened, but there was no splash-down, just fast moving water, which disappeared in the dark as the sound trailed off. The direction of the angle was encouraging, away from the center of the mountain.

He replaced the platform, trying to come up with an idea for a better test, but a group of sweating, harried soldiers burst into the latrine, noisily griping about some stupid-ass order or the lousy food. It was always the same, no matter what army you hung out with.

The soldiers ignored Chase as they started dropping trousers. He headed back to Beth and the sleeping girls.

If Beth was right and they were forty feet above ground level, where would the latrine holes lead? At a fifty-degree angle, the usual angle of a stepladder, the hole would be a little over sixty feet long, which meant a forty-foot drop. Math gave

Chase headaches in school. What if he got this wrong? What if instead of climbing into the toilet holes and sliding safely out of the mountain, they slid into a large natural pool chamber, somewhere in the dark guts of the mountain? There would be no way to climb back up, for sure. And how deep had four hundred soldiers made the cesspool over the last six months?

"What did you find out?" Beth whispered over the sleeping girls.

"That I'd sure like to find a better way out of here. Have you seen the generators?"

"Yes, a while ago." She was gently rubbing the backs of the sleeping girls.

"What do they look like? How big and do they have wheels?"

Beth closed her eyes to picture them. "Most of them are the same brand, or at least look alike. I'd guess there are eight, maybe ten at most. They're red, with a bar that runs around them like a bumper. They have two wheels in back, away from where the wires plug in. That's pretty much it." She opened her eyes.

"Okay, so these are small, portable generators, probably four-stroke engines," he said. "Fifty-five hundred watts each would be enough to keep all the freezers running on their lowest setting and still power the lights."

"But if you manage to shut them down, the top layers of bats will be awake within a few hours. They'll start blowing up."

"How long for the bats to wake up if the freezers are open an inch or so?"

"Thirty minutes, maybe? But I've seen the bats wake up and just crawl deeper into the freezer to hide. They end up back to sleep in a cold pocket."

"We just need to knock out one generator. Portable generators run on fuel, like unleaded gas or diesel. They probably top off the tanks every five or six hours. They might not notice one that's stalled. At least long enough for us get out. It's gotta be noisy as hell in there. Did

the exhaust?"

"No, they weren't even tu

to me. How are we going to

"Wake the girls quietly," h

make a game out of this. The

cords that run from the free

bet. But we won't fit." He mot

"What do you think?"

"Sugar in the gas tank?"

"Something like that. More like dust in the oil intake. It'll score the pistons and chambers, and the engine should seize without a lot of smoke. Anything in the gas tank might hit the filter and not work for us."

Beth cooed and snuggled the girls slowly awake, then led them down to the toilet, where she stood guard at the door. Soldiers continued their march up and down the passageway, bringing more loads of explosives and detonators to the freezer chambers. The mountain continued to hum with energy, as Beth quietly returned with the girls and closed the door behind.

"Tell them they have to listen to everything we tell them," he began, and Beth translated. The girls huddled on the mattress around her as Chase knelt on the floor facing them. The youngest was five and the other two were eight. "It's almost time for you to go home, but we have to do something that may seem really hard when I explain it."

Beth again translated and the girls stared at her and nodded.

"My name is Chase. Can you say that?" After Beth's translation, they all gave it a whispered try. "And your names are?"

Beth helped the shy girls. "Sunee, Kama, and Mali."

"I know that you miss your friends at school and I know that you are very brave girls. And I am trying to guess which

s it you?" Chase asked, motioning to the
rank into Beth.

der girls, Mali, sat up tall and told Beth that she
avest. She had been regularly stealing food for the
trio, late at night.

Do you know the sound of the motors, Mali?" Chase asked, and they all nodded. "The motors make electricity for the lights and for other things. If I can teach Mali how to make the motor of one stop, then we'll be able to run away from here and go back to your friends."

Mali protested to Beth that she didn't know anything about motors except that they were noisy, and the only one she'd ever seen was attached to the bicycle Beth sometimes drove back home.

"Mali, you don't have to know about motors." He reached down to scoop a handful of dust. "You just have to know what makes motors stop working."

Chase shrugged his shoulders and held out the scoop of dirt for all to see.

"This is it," he explained. "A brave girl who turned a small screw on the side of a motor and fed it a handful of sand would be a hero, wouldn't she?"

All three girls sat staring at him, sizing him up. In the dust Chase drew a cartoonish picture of the generator, showing the round cap to be removed when adding oil or, in this case, dirt. He made a twisting motion to the left with his wrist, then mimicked pouring the dirt in. Since they couldn't know how much dirt would be available in that room, Mali would have to bring her own. And they'd just have to be sure to have her follow the freezer cords that matched up to the generator she was disabling.

"And there's another job that two girls who are also very brave can do. Do you want to know what that is?"

The girls looked at each other then nodded their heads while he reached for a few small rocks that had been swept to the edges of the room.

"Do you know the refrigerator in the kitchen at school? There are things just like the refrigerator at school, only they are lying down. They make things cold, right?"

The girls nodded.

"Well, we want to let some of the cold air out. So Sunee and Kama will open the refrigerators and put a few stones in the doors so they won't close back up. And Miss Beth and I will help you do this, okay? Easy?"

The girls again sat quietly staring, thinking.

"It's almost time to go home, Mali," Chase said to the bravest girl, and she nodded her head before saying something to the others in Thai.

All three girls climbed off the mattress and began scooping thin handfuls of fine dirt and collecting the small stones from the perimeter of the room, gathering the treasure in their shirts. Mali had the idea to remove their socks and use them to store and carry the dirt and stones.

"They'll have wired this place to blow up," Chase told Beth, while the girls worked. "You and the girls aren't needed. The longer we wait, the better the chance they'll walk in here and kill you. You're still alive because Lima wants me to do the story. But nothing's stopping him from taking you all out of my sight and just being done with you."

"How do we get out?"

"Easy," Chase said. "Right down the crapper, just like Alice down the rabbit hole."

"What are we waiting for?" she asked with a smile.

When Mali had enough dirt and the other two had collected all the loose stones from the room, Chase had them huddle with Beth while casually opening the door. Every few minutes, one or two soldiers hustled by, oblivious to their cave room or anything going on inside.

"Come," Chase hissed, a finger pressed to his lips for silence.

They snuck into the corridor, Chase in the lead and Beth taking up the rear. The cavern holding the freezers stocked with armed bats was about forty feet dead ahead. The noise from the large appliances seemed louder than ever. They stepped down into this room and Chase led Mali along the skinny pathway to the mess of wires and the small hole in the wall, while Beth and the other two went to work propping the freezer doors open with pebbles. Sunee, the other eight-year-old, had no problem breaking the cold suction, but the youngest struggled against the weight of the door.

Chase picked out a particular heavy-gauge wire and indicated to Mali that this was the one to follow. She crawled into the low archway and disappeared without a word into the darkness, dragging her sock full of fine dirt along with her.

Beth and the girls plucked a few more stones from the floor of this room and finished with the last freezer doors before crawling over to where Chase waited for Mali to reappear.

Minutes passed and there was no change in the drone of the engines somewhere at the other end of the dark hole. Chase checked his watch and tried to decide on a time limit for her return. Even if she was caught, he might still be able to get the others out. They'd have a limited number of soldiers to waste on a hunt.

When four minutes had passed, Chase motioned for Beth to stay put. He stood, lifted the lid of the nearest chest enough to reach inside and carefully remove one of the armed bats, then knelt back down. Beth replaced most of the stones he'd knocked free. Kama's eyes grew large at the terrifying creature and Sunee put her hand over the little girl's mouth to stifle a scream.

"It's asleep," Beth said quietly in Thai, putting her hands to the side of her head to mime sleep.

As a backup plan, Chase slipped the bat into the crook of the wood pallet the freezer was resting on. Just as he was about to recheck his watch, two soldiers burst into the room carrying more boxes filled with explosives. The four squeezed between humming freezers, Chase's shoulders painfully pinched. One soldier threw open a door without noticing it was already ajar or the small rocks that fell to his feet.

The soldier barked an order just as Mali emerged from the hole. Beth reached down and grabbed the bat Chase had stowed and hurled it across the room as a diversion. It tumbled through the air just over the heads of the soldiers, who instinctively ducked, probably from months of casually dodging low flying bats in these caves. Beth grabbed Mali and pulled her down between the freezers with them. The bat bounded off the far wall without exploding and came to a rest a few feet from the soldiers.

The men looked at each other then scanned the room with wide eyes. They stepped over to the fallen bat, one prodding it with the toe of his combat boot. Both used the same phrase in Arabic, which sounded like it would translate loosely into English as "Holy fuck!"

From the deep shadows, Chase could see them look at each other, then down at the armed bat, as if trying to figure out what to do next. One finally took charge and gave an order, which might have been "Pick it up and put it back."

The other soldier vigorously shook his head, stepping away from the crumpled bat. Cursing, the soldier in charge shoved the other away and plucked the bat with fingertips. He jerked open a freezer door and tossed the bat bomb inside.

They grabbed their boxes of explosives and hurried back into the corridor, seemingly perfectly happy to forget what had almost happened.

The five un-squeezed their way back out from between the freezers and Mali excitedly told Beth she'd killed the machine. The other girls screeched in delight, which brought a simultaneous "Shhhhh!" from Beth and Chase.

"Let's go." Chase led them back down the corridor toward the latrine, which was mercifully empty. Beth stood at the door as the three girls watched Chase pry the wood seat loose and lean it against the wall.

He pointed down the hole and said, "Go!"

To which the three girls replied, "No!"

Beth turned and came into the room and dropped to the floor, dangling her legs into the open hole. She said "I love you" to the girls in Thai, crossed herself, and slid into the darkness. The girls looked at each other, unconvinced, until the first explosion nearly knocked them off their feet. Bits of dust and small pieces of limestone rained down, and the lights danced off and on.

"Come!" Chase shouted to Kama, reaching for her tiny body. He snatched her up and dropped her over the edge of the hole, where she too disappeared out of sight, a blood-curdling scream trailing behind.

Then the fireworks really went off, explosion after explosion, along with the sound of wings beating against air and against the walls in the corridors, as more and more bats poured out of the freezers. It went black after the next explosion brought down a huge chunk of ceiling and there were shouts and orders from running soldiers. As the entire mountain began to shake and sway, Chase found one of the older girls on the ground and dragged her to the edge of the hole, where she managed to fall inside.

Another detonation slammed down the hallway tunnel, the blast lighting the room in a yellow flash. Chase saw Mali sitting with her back against the far wall, pinned against the fifty-gallon drum of water, shielding her face.

"Mali!" he shouted into the blackness and thick dust, as more bats began to beat their way into the room, squealing and confused. He took a few steps toward the cringing girl as another bright blast just outside the room blew out the wall and a ton of debris slammed down on them in small chunks. Again in darkness, his face cut and burning, Chase reached blindly for the brave little girl.

"Mali!" He found her desperate hand in a pile of jagged stone. Two more blasts from farther down the hall rocked the floor and sent him sprawling over the girl, but he was able to push piles of limestone rocks off and dragged her back to where the hole must be.

Another blast and then another, and a deep rumbling began that Chase knew would never stop. It was the roll of thunder, the approach of a freight train, which began to shift the entire room to a new angle. He crawled over what had been the ceiling and found the still unblocked hole. Chase stuffed the limp Mali into the opening and she slid away as he gagged and choked on the dust that had replaced the last of the air. One more monstrous explosion and the rest of the latrine ceiling collapsed, just as Chase dove into the crapper.

"Geronimo!" he yelled, knowing Stoney would be proud.

Chapter 15

———

AN OLD MACAQUE monkey had the perfect view of the commotion in the valley. He was far enough away that the exploding bird-things didn't feel threatening. He'd brought two handfuls of sweet berries to his favorite spot on the knoll and was enjoying the warmth of the sun on his fur and munching away when the shit-covered humans were spit from a hole at the bottom of the mountain. It was an odd surprise added to the other ruckus and he wanted to hoot and cheer, but his back had been aching, so he stayed still and sniffed the wind. The nasty smell reached him on the breeze that blew harder when the big metal things with spinning wings caught fire. The monkey put the berries down in a little pile, careful that none rolled away. *Maybe later*, he thought.

The monkey liked most humans. They left food cans outside their homes for his family to rummage through in the morning sun. Some yelled and threw sticks, but were slow and didn't bite. Humans were mostly harmless.

The exploding bird-things were something the monkey had never seen. They had flown into the belly of the giant metal creatures then bounced around all crazy and upset, trying to get back out. Then, boom, boom! The noise was exciting and there was a time when the monkey would have jumped up and down and yelled boom right back. But not now. He watched and his mind wandered.

The monkey picked a beetle from the back of his pink ear and chewed. He thought maybe the bird-things might be food makers inside the mountain. They acted the same as the big swarm he'd found inside a tree a long time ago. He'd followed the sweetest scent ever up the rotten wood, stuck his hand inside the hole with all the flying bugs. He'd pulled out a sticky treat that tasted like ripe bananas and warm flowers. But then the bugs began biting. First one and then a dozen had hurt him, tormented him with their angry buzzing and chased him to the ground. They'd come from every direction, biting at his ass, shoulders, and even his tail. He had run screaming for his family.

These exploding bird-things brought the memories of the awful bugs flooding back. It had hurt to lie in his nest, to sleep, to be scratched. He'd been miserable for days. Watching the hubbub continue to unfold, he scratched at the small lump on his right butt cheek, a spot the biting bugs had made bleed, that had become hot and throbbing even as he had crouched in the river. He leaned over and snatched a small stone to keep next to the berry pile, just in case.

Orange flames seemed to eat the big metal creatures, made them fall over dead and hollow. That the bird-things didn't seem to want to hurt the humans was very curious and gave the monkey an idea. Could it be because the humans knew to rub shit over themselves? Was the secret to stealing sweet treats from biting bugs and exploding bird-things as simple as making yourself smelly?

Once the booming died down and the pretty fires had turned to ugly black smoke, the monkey began to lose interest. It was about lunchtime, anyway. No use trying to beg a candy bar or piece of sandwich from these humans. They were coated in nasty human stink and seemed in a hurry to get somewhere else; they were already halfway to where the river began. The monkey took a last look, picked a beetle from his crotch and rubbed his belly. He scooped his berries, turned and headed back into the forest, where his family had been napping in the shade. Maybe he'd find some poop and see if the human trick really worked.

TWO MONTHS AFTER escaping the bat cave—and the unsettling glare of a solitary monkey on an adjacent knoll, absently masturbating with one hand and scratching his Buddha-belly with the other—Chase dipped another ranch-flavored Doritos chip in a jar of onion dip, sprinkling a few more crumbs between couch cushions.

Chase's one-bedroom New Jersey apartment was near the Delaware River, just north of the capital, Trenton. The magically appearing envelopes had been replaced by emails on a laptop left on the counter while he was grocery shopping. A checking account debit card with a three thousand dollar balance had arrived in the mail. The key to a leased Ford Taurus parked out front had been slipped under his door.

His email instructions were to keep an eye on a group of Iranians who'd rented a house in Trenton. Chase was to log their evening activities, which turned out to be drunken videogames in their living room and trips to one of two dance clubs frequented by local college kids.

If the Iranians were planning to blow up the New Jersey Capital, they were taking their time and doing absolutely nothing suspicious. They weren't buying fertilizer by the ton or sneaking gallons of chemicals into a basement lab. And they'd fallen into a clockwork routine of visiting food joints every night, then clubbing at City Gardens on Fridays and a place up across the river in New Hope every Saturday.

The young, six member cell had undergone a rapid

Americanization. They'd started with *Miami Vice*-era sport coats and sneakers, and evolved to black jeans, collared shirts, and Doc Martens. The only item they hadn't given up were ZZ Top sunglasses, despite how often they bumped into things in dark clubs. They were living in what was once one of the higher priced neighborhoods along the river, now a mixture of middle class families and crack houses. Chase thought that anyone doing morning or afternoon surveillance better have a good book. None of the group ever woke before lunch, as far as he could tell.

City Gardens, resembling an old high school gym on the outside, was split into two sections on the inside. Quiet smaller bar area to the left; main bar, stage and dance floor to the right. The walls were painted flat black under a high ceiling. There was a giant mirror ball, single video screen showing black and white cartoons, and various colored strobes for lighting. Posters of past shows by Nirvana and The Ramones lined the hallway entrance.

The Iranians became drunker and more obnoxious as the weeks passed. They seemed to be less and less a terrorist risk than a danger to the club kids and even themselves. It was a Friday night that the six men surrounded a girl on the dance floor. Chase, nursing a vodka tonic in a plastic cup, leaned against a wall near the stage. It was still early and the girl was dancing alone when she was accosted, trapped in a circle. They were hooting, drunk and macho, beer bottles waving over their heads. The four bouncers, huge black guys from the neighborhood, stepped out of the shadows, and Chase watched them looking at each other, deciding if it was time to pounce.

The Iranian men danced by, throwing out their hips and making little hops that rained down foamy beer. The circle tightened and it took them a while to realize the girl had somehow escaped, slipping through their gyrating gauntlet.

"I'm Mitra." She was next to Chase, a drink in her hand.

"Chase."

"I don't like the early music, anyway," she said, and Chase watched her lean against the wall, arms folded in front, eyeing the Iranians. She was tiny, with dark hair and pale skin. "But it's nice to have your own space, you know?"

The Iranians spotted her and Chase could see the cheated looks.

The song changed, was faster and louder. "Hey Man, Nice Shot" began to play as the group of drunk, pissed-off Iranians came for the girl who'd gotten away.

"I love this song," Mitra shouted, not budging.

"They look mad."

"Can you believe one grabbed my ass?"

"It looked like all six were grabbing your ass," Chase said over the thumping music that had enough bass to vibrate the air. The men stopped their march a few feet from where Chase and the girl stood. "Maybe they came to apologize for being born complete douche bags."

Mitra had shimmied closer, her right arm and thigh brushing up against him. She smelled like heaven. Chase took a long sip as one of the men shouted what was probably a terrific insult in Farsi. They were huffing, out of breath, slicked hair all messed and pointed spikes. The tallest came to Chase's chin.

"Sorry, I can't hear you," Chase answered, shrugging his shoulders, pointing at one ear. The group hadn't noticed the gargantuan bouncers who'd come up behind them.

"I think he asked you to dance," Mitra said, laughing, her head touching Chase's shoulder when she leaned sideways.

"Bastard!" one of the Iranians shouted. He lunged at Chase but was immediately plucked backward as if on a bungee cord. His accomplices turned to see what had happened and they too suffered the same, neck jarring event. The entire Iranian cell was carted to the exit by the bouncers, leaving nothing behind but a few beer bottles spinning on the floor.

"You're a total troublemaker, aren't you?" Chase looked down at her almond eyes, breathed her in. For the first time in two months he didn't care where the idiots from Iran were. Let them kidnap the governor and set fire to the gold-domed State House. She had tiny freckles and soft lips. There was a new song and she took the cup from his hand and emptied it in one long swallow.

"I bring out the worst in people," she said and left him to dance alone, before the mob of college kids began to descend.

He let her go for now.

Chapter 16

CHASE FELL IN love with the little dancer. He fell fast and hard and did everything possible to convince her to feel the same way. It was a take-no-prisoners approach, with scenic small plane rides out of the Princeton Airport, slaved-over candle-lit dinners, and lovemaking matched to the music.

It took two weeks for things to even out. Under the ugly glow of yellow streetlights outside the club, she said she loved him back and kissed him in a different way.

"You're beautiful," she had whispered later, swaying to the gentle music coming from the speakers next to the bed. She had sung the lyrics of some New Age lullaby in his ear and it seemed different, too. "You are the light, the dark, the fire, and all the rain." She repeated these same lyrics as her wedding vows a few months later, eloping in a living room ceremony at the home of the local mayor. Their witness was the mayor's niece. Chase couldn't call Stoney, and Mitra's plan was to break the news to her father after the fact, when it was too late.

Mitra had no idea of his real work. There was no spy manual to use for reference, but Chase had been warned away from close friendships. He was a journalist and had the news clippings as proof. What a great story it would have been to tell, the coincidence of a group of half-assed Iranian terrorists bringing them together. He imagined her father would have laughed heartily, pounded the table and complained how typical it was of the men charged with securing his nation, his former homeland. But Chase kept his secret for now, maybe forever.

According to what had always been a cloudy recounting of her recent family history, Mitra's father had fled the politics that had overrun any ability to teach at the University of Tehran. He had arrived in America on Thanksgiving Day, 1979, just a few weeks after a group of Islamic revolutionaries stormed the U.S. Embassy in Tehran and took hostages.

Doctor Bamdad Hami, who repeated this story each time Mitra had taken Chase for visits, could tolerate just so many interruptions in and around his classroom. There had been smoke everywhere and the constant stench of gasoline being sloshed around in jars to be used as propellants. His classroom stank like an auto repair garage, and by the end of his lectures his students were in an oxygen deprived buzz. There had been smoke from burning American flags and Jimmy Carter effigies. Then there had been smoke from the clothes of the protesters who caught themselves on fire while lighting the effigies. It was all more than the doctor could tolerate.

"I can tolerate this no further!" Doctor Bam, as he preferred to be addressed, claimed to have shouted at his cowering secretary. "Pack my dugong, I'm out of here."

Doctor Bam's secretary had a lot of work ahead of her if she was going to pack the dugong all by herself. Even though it was dead and therefore not moving, it was nearly three meters long and over three-hundred kilograms. Plus, there would be all that ice to keep it from rotting and stinking like only a blubbery dugong could rot and stink.

"I'll bring you over to the college and you can have a picture taken with the famous dugong," Mitra had told Chase, teasing her father.

The death of the dugong had been something of a tragedy, a victim of scientific exploration mixed with alcohol. Dugongs had been having a tough time trying to peacefully subsist on Persian Gulf sea grass since humans were constantly spilling oil, Doctor Bam had explained in his story. These great mammals were a nearly extinct version of sea cow, with paddle-like forelimbs and fluked, dolphin-like tails. Furthermore, they liked to hang out and play just under the surface of the water, a practice that put them in constant danger of getting struck by boats.

Doctor Bam admitted to nudging along the extinction process by accidentally killing this particular dugong with a thirty-foot outboard motorboat. He'd struck the poor creature while, ironically, helping a coworker gather data on the critically endangered hawksbill turtle. Truth be told, the pair of professors had been doing more drinking than data gathering just prior to the accident, but they blamed that mostly on the stress from all the burning effigies everywhere they looked.

"The young people in my country burn everything," he'd said, shaking his head wistfully.

The two Iranian doctors of education would take kabob koobideh and bottles of Russian vodka, then motor around the Persian Gulf oil tankers while blasting Aerosmith from a Chinese-made boom box.

A drunken Doctor Bam would sing snatches of "Sweet Emotion" in his thick accent at the dinner table—the part about a big woman with a man's face—raising his glass of clear liquor to the light. "The lyrics prove Steven Tyler knew many Iranian women!"

Bamdad Hami was a short man, with a thick head of black hair, a perennial five-o'clock shadow no matter how often he shaved, and the growing belly of someone who loved his vodka and kabob.

Doctor Bam explained he hadn't needed to sneak out of Iran under the cover of darkness. Nor did he have to purchase fake credentials or slip through secret border crossings to find his way onto an America-bound airplane. In fact, the university board members were both delighted and relieved to help him secure a special visa and all the accompanying paperwork for a one-way trip to the United States. His habit of throwing open his classroom window and shouting at the revolutionary protesters that Saddam Hussein should gas their mothers made the regents nervous.

"*Awaladi kus mashk*!" the doctor would proudly scream at the protesters, which he claimed translated to something like "son of a woman with a gigantic vagina."

When Doctor Bam became distracted with his collection of vinyl records during their visits, Mitra would tell the part of the story about the young girl caught up in Doctor Bamdad's madness. Without a mother, little Mitra was something of a mascot around the University of Tehran science wing. She spent so many hours in the building that one of the secretaries brought in a mattress so she could nap in one corner of the doctor's office. Most of the child's toys were fashioned from scientific instruments. Her tea sets were test tubes and beakers. Her erector sets were really DNA and molecular models. Her stuffed animals were actual stuffed animals. The ingenious little girl would set up various jars of aborted and preserved fetuses all around, then read them to sleep from lab manuals.

Her favorite pet was an old anatomical display labeled Common House Cat, in which the tabby had gone through a preservation process prior to being cut in half the long way and placed under a glass frame. The wonderful teaching tool was turned into an even better pull toy after Doctor Bam attached small wheels and the string from a discarded lab coat.

What had become of the girl's mother was never discussed by her father.

"The subject was taboo. Late at night, when Dad would

tuck me into the bed in his office, I'd sometimes ask about my mother. I remember being snuggled in with my pet frog safely sealed in a jar of formaldehyde, looking up at his huge hairy face. 'I am your mother,' he would always tell me. 'I made you from an experiment. Go to sleep now and may your dreams be sweet, my little sugar plum.' "

Doctor Bam and his little girl arrived in New York City on November twenty-second, his frozen dugong following two weeks later on a cargo ship. All took up residence in the Trenton State College science department for the spring semester of 1980. The nearly extinct dugong went from a crate of ice to an enormous tank of its own formaldehyde, while the good doctor and his nine-year-old girl found their very own house in Newtown, Pennsylvania, an easy commute to the college.

"Dad's never gotten used to these winding country roads. He runs over animals all the time and feels just terrible. Like with the dugong. And he always stops, always picks them up and rolls them into a newspaper and brings them home. The refrigerator freezer is packed. You should see the freezer chest in the garage."

"What does he do with them?" Chase asked, and Mitra frowned while looking at her father pulling records from sleeves to blow away dust.

"Dinner parties for his Intro to Biology sections," she said. "The vegetarian kids get off easy."

"No kidding? He eats them off the road?"

"I loved the parties when I was little. I helped marinate the squirrels and things. We wore lab coats for aprons, pan-frying pigeon hash with diced onions and garlic. He taught me how to make fried chipmunk cakes. Each patty needed the meat from at least a dozen squashed rodents."

"They are the delicacies of our new homeland!" Bamdad cried out happily from beneath the record player, a half-empty bottle of vodka perched next to the turntable.

"Yes, Dad, your students loved every bite," she said, then

lowered her voice. "I was allowed to play dress-up for his students. Colorful silk Persian robes I imagined my mom had worn."

Mitra described her castoff scientific toys as she eyed the eighteen and nineteen-year-old students from various dark corners, Steven Tyler's "Uncle Salty" blaring in the background.

To little Mitra, all the commotion in the house was wonderful. Such was the life of a girl born on a microscope slide, cultivated in a test tube, and raised in a series of Petri dishes before being set free to walk on two legs. She loved her strange father like any child of a strange father would.

"I never knew anything different."

Mitra had no remnants of an accent, and not a single family photo album or any other artifacts from her past, besides her toys. It was as if she'd been born and raised in a reasonably sterile laboratory. She seemed to exist just as a twenty-seven-year-old biochemist, with dancing as her only diversion.

As with her father, the line between Mitra's work and personal life was blurred. She had a bed in her laboratory break room. Some people crow about being workaholics, with their seventy or eighty hour work-weeks. Mitra explained that before meeting Chase, she'd quietly spent a hundred or more hours each week at her lab in a cancer research center. Other than her dance nights, she didn't have anything particularly interesting to go home to, especially since her dad had stolen a mattress out of an unoccupied dorm room and delivered it as a gift to his hard-working sugar plum.

She found time for her real passion, the one thing she claimed made her feel alive. It usually came sometime around midnight on the vibrating air in front of banks of speakers. It was the frantic bedlam that moved her body from the inside, and the pounding bass that took her breath away. Nine Inch Nails, Depeche Mode, OMD, and Ministry were some of her favorites. And the passion she felt for them was the reason she had always danced alone. A partner, she said, got in the way of the magnificent feeling she got from the fusion of sound and light.

"And then I danced with you," she told Chase on the way home from breaking the news of their marriage, and he loved her more than ever.

They danced and made love, while Chase still tried to keep an eye on the Iranians. But they'd apparently been especially frightened by their City Gardens encounter with the bouncers. They were playing more living room videogames than ever. *Fine*, thought Chase.

EVERYTHING HAD BEEN falling into place until an email assignment landed in Chase's inbox. It was a feature story on a Haitian pot farmer who was raising money for a run at the presidency.

Mitra's dad had insisted on going with them to the Philadelphia airport, scooting them along in his little pickup down Route 95 with Chase's stuffed backpack bouncing around in the back bed. Doctor Bam worried about Mitra's ability to drive because she'd been crying steadily ever since Chase agreed to the assignment.

"You have to come back," she managed to say from the middle of the front seat. Chase's shirt was wet from her tears. "You can't go there and get killed. We just got married."

"I promise I'll be fine."

"Haiti is a shit place, lousy murderers running around everywhere," Doctor Bam announced, which made his daughter cry more. They bounded down the highway in relative silence, past the Betsy Ross and Benjamin Franklin Bridges, past the baseball stadium and the Naval Shipyard, and on to the airport exit.

In the terminal Doctor Bam shook Chase's hand, then gave the couple room to say their goodbyes. He went to poke around at a postcard display, while Mitra crushed Chase with a long, last hug.

"You have to come back. Promise you'll come back to me."

Chase's plane was called for boarding as he promised to return in one piece and gave her a final kiss. He hoisted his backpack over one shoulder and headed for the gate.

"I love you," she said from behind.

"I love you, too."

"If he doesn't come back, you can marry a scientist," Chase heard her dad say.

Chapter 17

———

THE BULLETS FIRED in his dream left the black steel rifle barrels in slow motion. They worked like heat-seeking missiles, able to change course while tracking the running boys. Chase held a clipboard, the pencil in his right hand checking off each child's name as they were struck dead. Stoney was arguing with him, something about wanting to add new players to replace the ones being slaughtered.

"There are thousands of boys," Stoney was saying. "We'll never run out. We can keep getting more."

Chase had finally relented, allowing Stoney to blow the dented whistle to bring on reinforcements, little black boys screaming and darting in blind hysteria. But the bullets never missed, not even the boys who'd slithered into nooks among the growing piles of dead flesh. Stoney kept blowing and blowing, and the soldiers kept firing.

"I don't know their names!" Chase had begun panicking, willing to make up names because it was suddenly important that they didn't die anonymously. Stoney would keep blowing the whistle until Chase woke up, right hand cramped from squeezing an invisible pencil. A stewardess brought Chase a plastic cup of water without being asked.

During his junior year of college, Chase had raided the campus library for every book on Haiti, quickly earning a reputation as the jerk who left deserted coffee cups everywhere. This opportunity to create a recreation program for Haitian kids was too good to be true, the perfect escape for an entire semester. He remembered thinking what a breeze it would be. He'd abandoned the smoldering bong in his dorm and pored over every relevant book. He'd even learned to use the microfilm machine to filter through *Washington Post* stories. The application to his Department Chair was going to be so compelling that it would overshadow the slacker reputation he had earned by association with his roommate.

Stoney had ridden shotgun to a D.C. bookstore that sold international newspapers and maps from around the world. Chase had boned up on Haiti's past and present politics, the diseases and the long, crazy history of voodoo. Stoney had bought a stack of zombie comic books from a shop in Georgetown for his own research. The trip with Stoney had begun with powerful emotions. It was filled with hope and charity, until the first shot. Chase's return was lonely and disorienting. His row was empty, no reek of hash oil or spilled gin wafting off a trusted friend.

WHEN CHASE'S PLANE rolled into the terminal, nothing was familiar. His first trip—the one that ended with boys being exterminated like a pack of rabid dogs, then the rush to the airport in a police Jeep—might have happened in a movie. The walkway carpet was clean and new, bright orange. People were in a hurry but smiling. Voices were loud but not shouting.

Chase had spent hours reading through the file emailed from DB6. He also had to retrieve a small package crucial to the assignment at the Post Office. According to the file, the ranch owner had political aspirations with plans to overthrow the current government led by René Garcia Préval. The rancher, who was being referred to more and more as a rebel leader—a dangerous moniker to have in any country—wished to make an official statement to the world with an exclusive interview provided to the Associated Press. But first the winter marijuana crop on his mountain farm needed to be fully dried, packed, and distributed to his small army of dealers from Port-au-Prince to Santo Domingo.

The file made no mention of Jean Luc Moreau's motive in risking a thriving drug business, other than the usual hunger for power. President Préval still had the authority to order farms such as his raided and burned, so it was assumed Moreau was offering the government the usual payoffs and profit-sharing. Any income would surely be welcome because of the heavy-handed sanctions imposed on Haiti by the U.S.

The geopolitical section of Chase's file included a rehash of what he'd learned his junior year. Nothing seemed to have changed. Maybe it had gotten worse. Deforestation was nearly complete—a few clumps of pines in the mountains and mangroves in the swamps remained. The forests were dying at the hands of the poor, who pillaged wood and sold it for charcoal. Once cleared of trees, rains began carrying the soil, the lifeblood of Haiti, into the sea at the rate of fifteen thousand acres each year. All the native animals had been hunted to extinction except for a few stray caiman and flamingos. An outbreak of swine fever had killed the pigs, leaving farmers to scratch out an existence in dead soil, raising sugarcane, coffee, and sickly cotton plants.

The humans hadn't fared much better than the native animals, with ninety percent of the population living in poverty. Expanding neighborhoods of cardboard shelters were built around growing mounds of human feces. And with brutal dictator after brutal dictator, it was no wonder so many Haitians grew up wielding machetes on their way to a voodoo-injected version of the Roman Catholic Church. The file read like a depressing novel, only with no surprises.

Moreau's plantation on Montagne Terrible, north of Port-au-Prince, thrived because he could afford to import tons of Mexican bat guano, rich in nitrogen and perfect for early vegetative growth.

Roughly translated, an old Haitian voodoo saying refers to the native soil as being as "dead as a zombie at a salt lick." Salt was the only known cure in Haiti for anyone unlucky enough to be turned into a zombie by a local *bokor*, or voodoo sorcerer. Pot farmers, according to the DB6 file, were infamous for using zombies to protect their crops from poachers. The file claimed Moreau had created and posted hundreds of zombies to protect the perimeter of his ranch, an actual crime under Article 249 of the Haitian Penal Code.

Chase had pored over the zombie literature in the campus library, sharing the best parts with Stoney. He'd used it to keep his roommate from backing out at the last minute. The books described how a living person could be turned into a zombie by the introduction of two special powders, usually through an open wound. The first powder, a toxin called terodotoxin, was found in the puffer fish and left the victim in a near-death state, barely breathing and seemingly without vital signs. The second powder, composed of datura, removed free-will and allowed the *bokor* to take charge of the new zombie.

Terodotoxin worked by blocking the sodium channels to the muscle and nerve cells. Once salt was introduced to the subject, the zombie was said to simply drop dead. Thus, the "dead as a zombie at a salt lick" saying. Stoney had proposed they make t-shirts.

"The entire George Mason University cheerleading squad," Stoney had said. "Imagine the possibilities."

The books had described the most brutal former Haitian dictator of all, Papa Doc Duvalier, who was believed to have had a secret zombie army called Tonton Macoutes. A devout voodooist, Duvalier had promised to come back from the dead to rule Haiti forever, which is why, after his fatal heart attack in 1971, authorities posted a guard outside his tomb. It was believed that his son, the ousted dictator who had assumed his father's rule, grabbed his father's still dead corpse before fleeing to the South of France fifteen years later. All that was left of his grave in Port-au-Prince was a jumble of white bricks and a shattered tomb.

"We have to go!" Stoney had said. "I gotta have one of those bricks."

Chase missed Stoney more than ever. This new destination was a ranch of swaying green marijuana fields on a plateau of Montagne Terrible, a place his friend would have surely braved the zombies to see. Chase was met at the airport by two of Moreau's men, loaded into the back seat of a freshly washed and waxed green Jeep Wrangler, and whisked north, into the hazy afternoon sun. He was traveling light, carrying just the one backpack loaded with two camera bodies, lenses, film, notebooks, microcassette recorder, several sets of socks and underwear, and a few shirts. The top was rolled down and he leaned back to enjoy the fresh wind, but buckled up tightly as the Jeep sped along the blacktop, passing buses and slow-moving trucks even on blind curves. The driver was either feeling invincible or suicidal. Happy and in love, Chase was also feeling pretty invincible.

The only tricky part of this job—which included killing Moreau and ending the coup plans that would completely destabilize the nation—would be slipping out of the country. Aside from authentic papers, Chase had a hidden pouch sewn into his pack that contained a clean passport under a different name, as well as three separate plane tickets to Puerto Rico departing on consecutive days. Even if things got hot, he'd still have a good shot at getting back out through the main airport. A secondary plan was to sneak across into the Dominican Republic, but recent reports said those roads were currently controlled by machete wielding bandits.

The most critical item in Chase's backpack was from the package picked up at the Post Office. It was a can of Planters Mixed Nuts that had been tampered with by the CIA lab people. This particular can, with a smiling Mr. Peanut tipping his top hat, contained an extra type of nut beyond the normal six—Moreau's favorite, Macadamia nuts. Five average-sized Macadamias, each containing a lethal dose of LSD, were positioned at the top of the nut pile. The container was then resealed with the original aluminum protective top. Chase had been assured that no acid would leech into the other nuts, so it would be safe for him to munch a few pecans should Moreau insist on sharing the reporter's gift.

The lysergic acid diethylamide, according to the DB6 file, was chosen for Chase's safety because it would mimic the more mild poisoning symptoms of the voodoo potions already in use at the pot ranch. They'd include rampant hallucinations, but have a more measurable dosage because it was a synthesized drug. LSD is one of the most potent drugs available; a typical dose is equal to one-tenth the mass of a grain of sand. Chase's Macadamia nuts each held two hundred times the normal dose, but in various time-release coatings. Moreau would start with a euphoric acid trip lasting a few minutes. The file described how his hallucinations would intensify, ramping up in stages, likely resulting in seizures before death. The plan was to make Moreau's death look accidental, or like an inside job because of the drug's similar properties to those his people were already using.

Leaving the highway near a town called Riobe, they turned west toward the sun, climbing in elevation on a pitted dirt road. It had recently rained, making progress slow, as the driver shifted into the lowest gear to ford rushing streams and test the depth of flooded potholes.

Thirty minutes of four-wheeling brought them to the edge of Moreau's ranch and the first zombie guards. The four bodies were buried to their hips, two on each side, with backs turned to the muddy road. They were naked, emaciated men, with curved spines and leathery skin so black it shone blue. Their arms were posed unnaturally in front of them, and a large hand-painted sign nailed to a post on the left side of the road read, "Y AP MANJE."

"They are eating," the driver translated over his shoulder in a hushed tone, possibly not wishing to further disturb the undead. For real? Chase had flashbacks to the haunted hay rides his parents took them to as kids at Halloween time. The campy idea of posing corpses with signs saying they were eating trespassers or lost children was amusing, except that these were real dead bodies, according to the file.

A mile or so farther up the mountain, Moreau's men jumped out of the Jeep to unlock and push open a swinging gate. They followed the road to the right, along a ridgeline and into the shadows of Montagne Terrible's lone peak. In a few hundred yards they passed another collection of zombies in more stark and threatening poses. Some were upright, wielding machetes, while others were stretched on the ground with arms forward at the very edge of the road, crawling into passing traffic. These hands might have been crushed by the Jeep's tires, had the driver not been careful to maneuver just beyond the probing fingertips.

These were dead bodies. Or real zombies.

Most disturbing were the zombies scattered among the remaining dead trees, barely visible. Rotting faces peeked around decaying trunks, watching over the road from a distance.

They bounced along the rutted road in silence until approaching a two story, open-sided concrete building, where a half dozen or so of Moreau's workers were busy employing their *bokor* magic.

This was the zombie-making factory.

"Gardyen yo." The driver pointed to a row of sewn together

human remains just outside the structure, probably the finished products, perhaps mismatched by size, color, and sex on purpose. The Jeep stopped a few yards from the wide open building, likely on Moreau's orders, to give the journalist the full effect of this plantation. Chase gasped. The rancid stench came and went in palpable waves that seemed to be heated contractions in the air.

The driver and his coworker pulled the bottoms of their shirts up over their faces, trying to filter out the smell that apparently no longer fazed the workers inside the factory. This had to be absolute proof a person could get used to the smell of anything.

The smell transported Chase back to his summer at the *Daily Times*. There was the hanging corpse, and then another body right before Labor Day. A suicidal man had used a short length of rope to suspend a boat anchor from his neck; he had then stepped off the end of a dock into the Wicomico River. After a few weeks of late-summer heat, his body gasses had built up enough so that he was floating upside down in eight feet of water. A gray, comically bloated bare foot—waving gently to and fro under the surface—was eventually spotted by a family from their pontoon boat bow.

Chase had arrived at the river's edge just as cops used a hook and rope to haul in the body. The dragging hook had pierced the bloated corpse, which excreted a gas one of the officers described as "heated rot."

This Haitian building was erupting with the same heated rot smell, as *bokors* busily went about their grim duties. Bodies were stacked high at each end, sandbag-fashion. The upstairs loft held at least fifty more cadavers. The brown, unsteady clumps on open wounds and gashes, Chase realized, were huge clusters of feeding flies.

The jeans-clad men were shirtless, coated in blood and gore from sawing appendages and then reattaching them to other bodies for maximum scarecrow effect. There was an old black man with the arms of a younger white woman; a child with two heads; a small body with four arms instead of any legs. The Mister Potato Head options were endless.

The left side of the building appeared to be for deconstructing the corpses, with a series of five autopsy tables equipped with saws and curved recesses to catch fluids. The middle area comprised four heavier wooden tables stacked high with arms, legs, torsos, and heads. Large white metal buckets sat below these tables, filled with assortments of smaller items, such as noses and ears, feet and hands. Some buckets were just for hair and scalps. These buckets drew by far the most flies.

The right side of the building was where the intricate work of reassembly was performed on a half-dozen surgical tables. A man sat on the gory floor, trying to untangle a mass of what might be fishing line, while others continued sewing above him. The finished zombie guards were lined up just in front of the Jeep, ready for deployment.

"*Gardyen yo*," Chase said, repeating what the one escort had called them. Both guards were trying to smoke unfiltered cigarettes through their shirts.

"Guardians," the other escort said in English. "These are the guards being made."

"*Zonbies*," added the other man, who retched and began coughing and choking on the smoke or the smell. After catching his breath and holding his gorge, he waved for the driver to get going. "*Prese prese!*" he pleaded through the material of his uniform shirt.

Beyond the barn was a shock of rich deep green, so totally out of place as to seem even more unreal than the zombie factory in the foreground. Healthy young marijuana plants stood knee high, like early Kansas corn, in a field that stretched out in a carpet down the mountain, disappearing from view. This had to be Moreau's summer crop.

The driver shifted the Jeep into gear and they slowly headed into the middle of a complex of low concrete and tin buildings.

The main house was the largest, painted yellow with grated steel vents instead of windows. The style was a combination of Haitian and Spanish, with a low-pitched roof, stucco siding, and an archway over the front door. Missing were palm trees, or any live trees for that matter. The few living, low-growing tropical plants anywhere in the dusty shade of this part of the mountain needed water or just to be mowed down and put out of their misery.

Chase grabbed his backpack and jumped down from the Jeep just as Moreau burst through the front door to greet them. Chase watched closely as the driver left the keys in the ignition and climbed out, shouldering an old twenty-two caliber rifle that had been stashed between his seat and door.

"Welcome, welcome, my friend!" The squat, bulldog of a man charged forward, hand open for a lusty grasp. His accent was unidentifiable—not French, not Creole and not exactly American. Moreau proudly sported the pot belly of a successful Haitian man. His hands were strangely dainty and his head was roughly the size, color, and shape of a twelve-pound Brunswick bowling ball—only with the holes arranged differently.

His two men disappeared into the house, as Moreau embraced Chase and asked his first impression.

"I'll be honest and say there's no place else on Earth just like this."

Moreau laughed knowingly as he led them up the red brick path to his front door.

"This is a labor of love, my new friend. That God has blessed our soil to raise such beautiful and productive crops is validation of the vital importance of our pursuits."

Chase thought the shiploads of bat guano sure seemed to be helping the soil, too.

The floors of Moreau's home were polished tan tile, and each hallway and all visible rooms were crowned with the same Spanish-style archways. Somewhere, a generator droned on, taxed by the enormous, ancient window-model air-conditioning unit that valiantly attempted to do its job, despite there being no glass on the windows to trap the cool air.

Moreau gestured for Chase to sit across from him in the great room, while the passenger seat chaperone from the Jeep appeared, lugging a tripod, a bright orange extension cord, and a hard plastic video camera case. He set up the older model VHS camcorder to record over Chase's shoulder, behind the couch, screwing it onto the tripod and then flipping on the small, intense light. After making a few noisy adjustments, he cursed under his breath in French or Creole and disappeared, apparently in search of a fresh videotape. Moreau sat patiently, lips pursed, legs crossed, hands clasped together with fingers entwined on his bent knee.

"Pardon the wait," Moreau said. "I'm sure the historians will be interested in a video recording of my rise to power, don't you agree? A documentary could be of great inspiration to my people. But at this stage in my political career, there is only a small circle of men to safely rely upon, if you understand my situation."

"I totally understand." Chase set his microcassette recorder on the coffee table between them. "I appreciate just how careful anyone must be to challenge a man like Préval. I've read some of the stories describing the atrocities his soldiers have committed. Opposing him is dangerous business."

Chase crafted his words to present himself as a sympathetic ear to Moreau's plan. Journalists are trained not to take sides, not to have a point of view, but to hold a mirror up to unfolding events and give a clear and accurate reflection of what is occurring. But Chase had discovered the gray area when it came to stroking someone he was interviewing, especially off camera. Not that DB6 had journalistic standards—they could just as easily jam a .45 revolver in the left ear of an uncooperative politician—but Chase was in character and following the plan.

As Moreau's cameraman returned with a fresh tape, a

servant—who had to be at least a hundred years old—ambled into the room with two tall glasses of warm ice tea on a shaking sterling platter. She settled the glasses on cloth coasters in front of them, splashing a few drops under the glare of her boss and the bright, cold video light. The woman was a black skeleton under a plain blue dress. Bare-footed, she wore a brightly colored silk scarf over her sparse gray hair. She never looked up from the floor, flinching ever so slightly at each of Moreau's movements, like a dog with a long history of unjust beatings.

After she pattered away, Moreau leaned forward, stressing the buttons and material of the tight-fitting, light yellow dress shirt he wore un-tucked in the fashion of the tropics. Sweat had made his matching, thin cotton pants see-through in spots. Replacing his glass on the coaster, he got down to business.

"I need you to deliver a message to the world, my friend. I contacted your bosses at the venerable Associated Press in New York City for an exclusive announcement that will change the course of history for my country. It will open wonderful new opportunities between America and the humble people of this great nation."

"We were very grateful." Chase wasn't lying. He happened to know Moreau had also contacted *Time*, *Newsweek*, *US News & World Report*, and at least ten other news organizations for this exclusive, for which he was told to submit a press release containing no more than five-hundred words. If he could attach a small headshot, that'd be great, too. As for the broadcast media he'd contacted, CNN and ABC had referred him back to the local Haitian stations, claiming any such breaking news would begin with a live local feed.

In other words, Moreau had been discounted by the world press. Shrugged off as some non-lethal threat, just one more wealthy farmer wanting to use airtime and news holes to announce he was about to take over the Haitian government. His current rise to power had been too peaceful thus far for the likes of *Time Magazine*. If he wanted attention, he needed to start with a gun battle or two. He lacked a good news hook, to this point.

DB6 and the CIA recognized the threat.

Another element dragging down his newsworthiness was his caveat of not releasing the story until "all the final touches were in place." Nobody told the press when and how they were going to release news. But his unusual conditions seemed to have piqued the interest of Chase's bosses at DB6. It added credibility to his threat that he was getting properly bankrolled for a sufficient number of soldiers-for-hire from the proceeds of the recent pot shipments. These guns for hire would be ready to storm the National Palace just as his message was being released by international news outlets.

This wasn't a bad idea, Chase knew. More than a few times, various Haitian rebels had toppled the government, only to have the power grid blown up. By the time the television and radio stations were back on the air, the deposed leader had regrouped enough loyal soldiers to retake the National Palace. Without at least one working radio station to deliver the great news, nobody had come to rally in the streets behind the rebel leader and join the cause, so it was as if nothing significant had occurred. Just another Wednesday evening gun battle to make the coffin-makers work overtime.

Moreau was banking on the neighboring Dominican radio stations to relay news of the siege. The overthrow of an evil dictatorship broadcast to the battery-powered transistor radios in Haitian shops and coffee houses around the capitol and surrounding towns. The shaky part of his plan, which Chase did not point out to him, was that ninety-nine percent of Dominican radio stations broadcast in Spanish, which might as well be Martian to almost one-hundred percent of the Creole-speaking Haitians he wanted to reach.

"My message is that the corrupt and godless Préval government is being overthrown by the starving and deserved masses. The righteous people of the great nation of Haiti are rising up from the ashes of their murdered forefathers to seize power over the oppressors." Moreau paused for a quick breath and to wipe his brow with a small handkerchief pulled from his back pocket. "The brave sons and daughters of Haiti are on the doorstep of Mr. Préval at this very moment, and they have chosen me, Jean Luc Moreau, to stand up and represent their needs and wishes. I am a servant to the will of our people."

Acting the role of dedicated reporter, Chase fretted to keep up, scribbling line after line in his reporter's notebook, as Moreau shifted into high gear in this speech he'd evidently practiced quite a bit. His oddly accented voice echoed in the sparsely furnished room. The couch on which Chase sat, along with two reclining chairs and a long coffee table, were the only pieces, except for a pair of tall, freestanding lamps. Above the brightly tiled fireplace was a huge portrait of a Spanish Andalusian horse, head cocked toward the artist and its right foreleg bent in stride. Chase knew the type of horse because a large silver plaque attached to the frame named it "Majestic Spanish Andalusian Horse".

Chase's attention returned to Moreau, who hadn't broken stride, when the reporter started to notice something familiar about this speech.

"We refuse to believe the bank of justice is bankrupt. We refuse to believe there are insufficient funds in the great vaults of opportunity of this nation," Moreau, the zombie-making pot farmer intoned earnestly, and Chase recognized bits of Martin Luther King's "I Have a Dream" speech. "And so, we've come to cash this check, a check that will give us upon demand the riches of freedom and security of justice."

Chase continued with his furious notes, even as Moreau paused for a long swig of tea. Chase also began to recognize hints of a Brooklyn accent. He was sure he'd heard "we've come ta cash dis check," among other tiny clues. Chase was suddenly a lot more interested in this crazy man he was about to kill.

Setting the empty glass on the coffee table, Moreau rose. He cleared his throat to continue, but his cameraman stepped on the extension cord powering the camera while trying to keep his boss in frame. The man nearly toppled the tripod and did manage to momentarily extinguish the video light.

"Sorry, boss," he whimpered, fumbling and prodding until finally fitting the plug back into the underside of the camera. Light returned and Moreau took a deep breath.

"Duty, honor, country: those three hallowed words reverently dictate what you ought to be, what you can be, what you will be," Moreau said, eloquently plagiarizing U.S. General Douglas MacArthur, despite pronouncing the last part "wut yooz will be."

"They are your rallying points: to build courage when courage seems to fail; to regain faith when there seems to be little cause for faith; to create hope when hope becomes forlorn."

Finally Moreau was silent, shaking his head wistfully, dramatically, coming—Chase hoped—to a conclusion. His hand had begun to cramp and he really needed to take a leak.

"I ask my brudders and sisters to entrust in me their faith as their new leader in this hour of turmoil. Faith must be enforced by reason. When faith becomes blind it dies." Moreau clasped his dainty hands in front of his chin and closed his eyes tightly. "But I firmly believe that any man's finest hour, his greatest fulfillment of all he holds dear, is the moment when he has worked his heart out in good cause and lies exhausted on the field of battle—victorious."

Mahatma Gandhi, Vince Lombardi, and Jean Luc Moreau all rolled into one.

Moreau opened his eyes slowly, head nodding in a satisfied manner. He waited for applause, or maybe for Chase to dab his eyes, perhaps forgetting for a moment that he was just a journalist with pen and pad. Picking up the cue, Moreau's cameraman did start clapping, but Chase continued his scribbling.

He finished jotting the last line and closed his notebook.

"We done now, boss?" Moreau's cameraman asked from over the reporter's shoulder.

"*Oui*! I believe my message is clear like a bell. Make a copy for our guest to take with him."

"That would be fantastic." Chase packed away his notebook and recorder. "May I use your bathroom?"

Instead of answering, Moreau barked for one of his workers in some other room to fetch his driving gloves. His cameraman had begun the intricate task of unscrewing the camera from the tripod.

"Come, time for a tour of my humble ranch." He pulled on velvety kid-leather gloves brought to him by the man who'd driven Chase to the ranch. "You need pictures of me and I have a wonderful spot which will be perfect. It will be a photo of me with *fanmi mwen*, my family."

Moreau led them back to the Jeep and Chase climbed into the front passenger seat, carefully stowing the backpack between his legs. Moreau had donned a white Panama hat and the kind of oversized wrap-around sunglasses usually found on slow-driving retired folks in Florida. He seemed somewhat entranced following his successful interview-turned-rallying-cry, soon to be delivered to the masses. Chase had to piss like crazy, but still needed to know about this accent.

"Where did you learn to speak English so brilliantly?"

Moreau paused before popping the Jeep into reverse. He struggled to pull a new, larger handkerchief from his back pocket. He removed the Panama with his left hand and rubbed tight circles all around his sweaty, black bald head with his right.

"As a young boy, my father took me away to the New York borough of Brooklyn. It was in 1963, I believe. My wonderful father was a proud man, with no fear of speaking his mind. But unfairness followed him because of his brave words. Sadly, my mother was coerced to stay behind, as the criminal Duvalier forced our exodus."

Chase took from this that his father was booted from the country and the boy was taken along because his mother didn't want to go.

"It was in a small restaurant in Brooklyn that my father toiled as a waiter. It was during these years that he taught me the value of hard work. And it was during this period that another Haitian ex-patriot began working side by side with Papa. But this was an evil man who did not believe in the brotherhood of men and families forced from the homeland. Instead, he stole my father's tips. And when he stole the tips of other waiters, he blamed my father."

Chase interpreted this to mean Moreau's father was a thief.

They sat in the idling Jeep, the rancher's gloved hands locked on the steering wheel as he stared off into the hazy sky.

"The restaurant owner confronted my father with the weakest of evidence, nothing more than the words of a lying turncoat pig. And my father defended his honor mightily. When the owner tried taking my father's life with a kitchen knife, Papa had no choice but to kill him."

Moreau's father murdered the restaurant owner when he tried firing him, Chase concluded.

"And do you know who the treacherous thief was?"

Having long ago read excerpts of Préval's biography, Chase recalled that he'd been a waiter in Brooklyn for five years before returning to Haiti. "President Préval?"

"Yes, *oui, oui!*" Moreau shouted gleefully, fully reinvigorated to his post-speech state. "My journalist friend, you are very smart to know what kind of man Rene Préval is. He is a dog! *Yon chyen!*"

Moreau jammed the gear shift into reverse, spinning tires, and Chase almost smashed the windshield with his forehead. Back in forward motion, he led them in the opposite direction from which he'd arrived, and that was fine with Chase. He was curious about a better escape route, one that didn't lead past the zombie factory. The driveway was narrow at that point and some of the workers were armed. Chase wasn't worried about the zombies, but sure didn't want to provide spare parts for any of those lunatic undead dollmakers.

The Jeep bumped down the rutted drive, jolting Chase's bursting bladder, as Moreau happily gestured toward the panorama of marijuana plants.

"You know your first American president was rich because of his marijuana crops," Moreau shouted over the engine noise and splashing puddles. "It is a plant that brings joy and not the suffering of tobacco."

"Yes, I read that George Washington grew marijuana." Chase clutched the door handle and dashboard to keep from flying out. Moreau was going much too fast and nearly ran over a few of the half-buried zombies that lined the road as they made their way down the mountain, away from the ranch. Chase wouldn't have been surprised if Moreau credited Lincoln with using zombies as scarecrows to help emancipate the slaves.

Moreau brought the Jeep to a skidding halt and a cloud of dust caught up and consumed them. Here was a clutch of small concrete buildings, ten in all, neat but with a haze of cooking fires and a heavy stench of raw sewage. They were just beyond the far edge of Moreau's fields, in a dry ravine, maybe a half-mile from the main house. Chase was disappointed at the dead end. No escape route here.

"*Fanmi mwen!*" Moreau proudly declared, rising on the Jeep's floorboard, knees against the steering wheel. He made a sweeping gesture with his Panama hat to bundles of native blankets huddled in the open doorways of most of the buildings. As Moreau dismounted, the bundles began to lurch toward them, crawling, limping, or dragging themselves in a slow-moving rush.

Some of the blankets began to fall away, getting caught on this or that or abandoned to get to Moreau faster. Chase saw that Moreau's family members were lepers, maybe thirty souls inflicted with Hansen's Disease, all making their way toward their smiling benefactor.

"Such a terrible, terrible disease." Moreau seemed genuinely distraught. "This is the suffering of my people which goes ignored. They are shunned by Préval and his followers and so are shunned by everyone out of respect and fear of that thieving pig."

As the sorrowful, ragtag mob reached Moreau, Chase backed up to the Jeep, dug out his Nikon and quickly took a light reading off his palm. Those able to hobble over first now sat resting with the others at Moreau's feet. All had their hands outstretched, begging in Haitian Creole, but Chase couldn't believe even a native would understand all the excited wheezing and hissing; most were missing noses and lips. The disease, which flourished in the cooler oral and nasal membranes, had rotted the flesh and opened nasal cavities.

Moreau removed a clear plastic bag of jerky from his pocket and gave each one a small piece. Those with no arms he fed directly, like baby birds, but Chase noticed Moreau kept his driving gloves on. He used his twenty-four millimeter lens for these photos—the wide-angle lens Limp had once recommended because of its great depth of field—giving the scene a "You are there" quality. A lot of work in dangerous countries requires long telephotos for most pictures, but Chase was ignored here. There was food in Moreau's hands and these people didn't seem to see much of it on a regular basis. Nobody cared or even noticed they were being photographed, except Moreau, of course. He was puffing his chest, chin held high over his loyal family, offering the camera his best side.

"A society will be judged by how it treats its weakest members," Moreau proclaimed over his shoulder. Was that Truman?

"There is a change coming, my journalist friend." Moreau removed his gloves and placed them inside the empty food bag. He handed the gift to an old man with milky gray eyes who seemed to have most of his fingers intact. The leper tried tasting the gloves before realizing what they were. He stuffed them down his shredded pants and crawled away.

With the food gone, the rest of the lepers began their struggle to return to their own doorways. Chase had to piss that very second and told Moreau so.

"Please go back up the hill to the field." He gestured toward the lush growth, smiling broadly. "The plants love the urine of humans. Then we'll have some more photographs."

As Chase climbed over a small rock wall that delineated the edge of the pot field, he was startled by yet another bundle of twitching rags and blankets. It was an elderly woman, also a leper, but in a more advanced stage of the disease than the others. Much too debilitated to have crawled over the low wall for the jerky treats, Chase wondered how she'd found herself on this side of the barrier.

She sat propped against the jagged stones. "*Blanc, blanc*," she whispered hoarsely, her tongue extending out beyond her teeth to make the sound. No lips, no nose, and only one remaining eye. But the fact that she called him a *blanc*—a white—meant she could still see through the gray, cloudy glop. A filthy scarf covered seeping sores on her head. Gigantic flies swarmed her lazily, in no particular rush, as if they knew they couldn't be swatted.

"Hello." Chase paused, didn't know what else to say. His bladder cramping, he shifted from foot to foot.

"*Blanc*," she repeated and, with what seemed like great effort and pain, began fishing with one hand inside the clump of rags she wore. She nearly toppled, but finally came up with what she was searching for.

Chase couldn't wait. "I'm sorry, I'll be right back." He held up one finger, gesturing that he needed a minute. He jogged about thirty feet into the low mass of pungent pot plants, unzipped his fly and peed in an almost never-ending stream. His eyes teared as he soaked a dozen plants, spraying an arc that rained down three rows up the hill. Through blurry eyes he saw two sweat-slick black laborers about fifty yards across the field, spreading what might be fertilizer by hand from large packs on their backs. Ever-present machetes dangling from their belts, they paid no mind to the pissing *blanc*.

With the pain drained away and leaves dripping all around as if from a spring shower, he turned and made his way back to the old woman, careful not to crush any little plants.

"*Blanc.*" The women nodded down at her hand, reaching up toward him. She held out a small object wrapped in dirty cloth, offering it to Chase as some sort of gift. Her hand began shaking violently and he bent down to accept the item, mostly to stop the awful shaking. He feared her hand might break off.

Then, his blood froze as she spoke in perfectly clear English, "Take me with you, *blanc*. Take me with you."

He was about to return the small shrouded object when a loud racket broke out somewhere back in the leper compound. First screams, then angry shouting. He turned from the woman, jumped across the wall and ran back to where he'd left Moreau.

The first thing Chase noticed as he came past the Jeep was his backpack, open, on the passenger seat. He reached in and saw the can of poisoned nuts was missing. *Shit!* There was no immediate sign of Moreau or any of the lepers, but Chase assumed the rancher had noticed the can in the open bag and decided to continue spreading more good will to his family.

Shit! Shit! Shit!

He jogged to the nearest building and peered into the dark, only to see a frightened bundle cowering in the farthest corner. Chase turned, went to the next doorway and found a similar scene, just in a different corner.

He hurried back out to the shared fire circle in the center of small buildings and called out. "Mister Moreau? Hello?"

Chase was finally answered with more hissing screams just

ahead, coming from the building farthest from the Jeep. He ran toward it, very aware that he had no weapon. And then he noticed the trail of nuts under his feet, leading the way like Hansel and Gretel. Instead of bread, it was a pecan here and a hazelnut there. *Shit! Shit! Shit!*

"*Diable!*" The accusation came from inside, the voice joined by others shouting the same word. "Demon!" He stopped just before the threshold, taking some cover at the side of the door frame, and sneaked a peek inside, his hands craving a weapon, his heart hammering.

Inside, Moreau was naked from the waist down, his pants actually still attached at one ankle where they didn't get over his shoe, trailing him like a kite tail. His Panama hat was gone, as were his old man sunglasses. He was pinning down one of the bundles, grotesquely trying to work his small, erect penis inside one of the lepers. His black body was shaking and pouring sweat down on the hapless pile of rags and bones, whose pencil thin legs were exposed and spread apart like toothpicks poking from a raisin.

"Ggggrrrrr!" Moreau struggled to position himself over what might have been a very old woman. It was hard to be certain in the low light, but she didn't appear to have arms and was unable to defend herself in any way. She seemed to be arching her back, head lolling from side to side on a long, narrow neck, small grunts and moans escaping her that could have been interpreted as pleasure. Moreau was panting like a dog, drool spilling from his mouth, fumbling from the high dosage of acid pummeling his brain. His coordination was a frantic mess, trying to match movement to electric brain commands being interrupted and skewered by the LSD.

Bearing witness from the sides of the room, ten or more lepers shouted at the bizarre scene, "*Diable! Diable!*" And then chants of some sort, or prayers, followed by more shouts of "*Diable!*" They were hurling these words at Moreau like stones.

Before Chase could intervene he was knocked into the room

from behind, sent sprawling to the ground within a few feet of Moreau's humping, dog-like motions. Chase saw his face. It was clear he was long gone, lost to some crazed train of thoughts and actions, maybe some brutal fantasy sent to the surface, which his body was performing.

In that instant, Chase had the perfect angle to see Moreau's little purple member finding purchase in the helpless leper. The success encouraged what was once Moreau's mind and he doubled the piston action, head bobbing from side to side, giant veins threatening to burst through the skin of his neck. Moreau's lips drew back and his eyes widened fantastically, which momentarily froze the two men who had slammed past Chase, machetes clutched in sweaty black hands. These were the men who had been spreading fertilizer in the field.

The shorter, more muscular of the two machete-wielding men looked from the coupling mess on the floor to the chanting lepers surrounding them. He just happened to be the closer of the two to Moreau when they'd crashed past Chase and burst into the room, and seemed to accept charge of the immediate game plan.

"Ggggrrrrr!" Moreau repeated, perhaps at his ejaculation, but the sound was cut short as the razor-sharp blade of the machete swooped down and separated Moreau's head from his body with a *whump*.

The head of the man who would be the next president of Haiti rolled up next to Chase and he was glad it stopped face down in the dirt. Moreau's body spasmed once, then collapsed on the poor leper, pinning her under the emptying flow of gore.

At first there were orders from the two machete-armed men, but none of the lepers lining the walls budged an inch. The men yelled at the leper under Moreau, but she wasn't going anywhere either. Finally the shorter man walked past the prone couple and grabbed a handful of Moreau's pants to drag him off the cowering leper and out the doorway. With a grimace, the taller man used his boot to nudge Moreau's head out the door, like a lopsided soccer ball, sending it over to its body with a nicely placed short pass. He wiped his shoe in the dirt.

Chase slowly climbed to his feet, brushed dust from his hands and stepped out of the building, trying to feign the same sort of incredulous fear the lepers were showing at the sudden appearance and execution of a real demon. He didn't want to be associated with the demon or anything that had caused Moreau to become one.

"*Diable*?" Chase asked the two men, motioning down at Moreau, and they both followed his gaze and nodded heads in agreement.

"*Diable*," one croaked.

But now that the adrenaline of the moment had been flushed away, fear began to flood in on these men. It is the type of fear exclusive to Haiti, where possessions and demons and witches and the undead are part of everyday life. Any type of anger or sense of duty was replaced by this growing knowledge of having just struck down an actual demon. And no regular run-of-the-mill demon, but one who happened to be the Boss Demon of the zombies in these parts.

It was a fast and curious transformation for the machete men who, in the ensuing calm, were suddenly reduced to frightened children. They began backing away from the head and body, machetes held out in front of them for protection rather than any sort of threat. Their eyes darted from doorway to doorway as they stumbled backwards, shoulder to shoulder, crushing some of the mixed nuts under heavy black boots.

They screamed out as they blindly backed into Moreau's Jeep. The shorter man scrambled around and tore open the driver's side door, fumbling at the steering column for the keys. No luck. He shouted at his companion, who opened the passenger door and upended Chase's backpack on the seat. He tossed Chase's things one by one to the ground, including the rest of his camera gear, while the other man searched under the visor and in all the compartments.

The possibility of food being among the discarded items emboldened some of the braver lepers, who began their torturous journey back to the Jeep. The site of the small converging legion of diseased outcasts was the last straw for the two men. They gave up their search, turned to the poison village, crossed themselves in unison, and then broke into a sprint back out into the field of green.

The men far out of sight, Chase bent down and plucked the keys from Moreau's front pants' pocket. He made his way past the lepers, who were stuffing his t-shirts and underwear into their clothes as consolation prizes for not finding food. Chase checked to be sure the hidden pouch holding his passport and plane tickets was untouched, then started the Jeep and began the long, bumpy trip through what was suddenly a deserted pot ranch. Deserted, except for those half-buried zombies.

Chase's plane rose and sharply banked across the Windward Passage that separates Haiti from Cuba, then settled at cruising altitude for the short hop to San Juan, Puerto Rico. It was night and he was exhausted. He thought about catching a bit of sleep and was getting comfortable in his seat when he noticed the small lump in his left shirt pocket.

When he pulled out the dirty rolled-up rag, he realized it was the gift from the leper he'd encountered near the stone wall, just before Moreau went berserk. He slowly unraveled the musky treasure, encased by a material which may have once been a flowered scarf. The artifact seemed fragile and he gave each turn a great deal of care. Finally, out dropped a small brown object into his lap. He picked it up and turned it over and around, examining the brown, leather human finger.

"Take me with you, *blanc*," she'd asked.

And so he did.

Chapter 18

———

LIFE FOR CHASE and Mitra turned routine when the Iranian terrorist cell jumped to their deaths from a cliff in Acapulco.

The Iranians had cashed in credit card points for airline miles and taken the party south of the border, to the new heart of the sunny Aztec Empire in Mexico. They missed their return flight and a local DB6 operative—who was also a stringer for *Acapulco Today*—retraced their fateful final night of mixing booze and illegal cliff-diving. Chase was forwarded an email with the last known details.

"Hotel security was dispatched to the subjects' Fiesta Americana Villas room just after midnight on Christmas Eve in response to guest complaints of loud music, people urinating from the balcony, and thick smoke described as smelling like burning hair. The encounter resulted in the six subjects being ordered to immediately vacate the premises. One security guard reported being assaulted with an object described as a plastic penis pump, which subsequently required twenty seven stitches to the guard's head. Subjects' rental car was found overturned and abandoned on the fourth fairway of the Club de Golf, east of the hotel on Costera Miguel Aleman. Acapulco Police located the vehicle following the resident groundskeeper's complaint of a gang of banditos burying a body on the front nine. Upon further investigation, police determined from the pattern of divots and the collection of fishing gear left behind in the car that the shovels the men were seen carrying had been used to dig for night crawlers. Subjects contacted a taxi company to pick them up on the fairway, but instead agreed to meet in the parking lot next to the club swimming pool. The cab dispatcher described the caller as drunk and belligerent, and that only his unusual accent made him conclude he was not American. Police arrived at the golf course minutes after subjects escaped in the taxi. Police reported the locked pool gate had been pried open with a shovel, as had a liquor storage cabinet behind a pool-side bar. An unknown quantity of bottles was missing, although several were recovered empty from the pool's shallow end. Subjects were taken eight kilometers across town after demanding to witness the famed La Quebrada Cliff Divers. When the driver suggested three a.m. was much too late for the show, one subject brandished a garden shovel. The driver, fearful that his poor English had caused the upset, delivered the subjects to their last known whereabouts. Two additional empty bottles of locally produced tequila, one empty salt shaker with cocaine residue, and six pairs of men's shoes were found atop the unlit, forty-meter cliff-diving platform. Acapulco Police have left the case open until bodies are recovered."

Chase and Mitra also disappeared, buying a small chalet-style home in the Pocono Mountains of Northeast Pennsylvania. The move was only three hours from the apartment, but night and day when it came to the congestion of traffic and people. Chase didn't ask permission from DB6, mostly because he wasn't sure how. He responded to an earlier incoming email that he had a new address and was leaving the key on top of the television set, like you might do at a hotel. The email bounced and they finished packing.

Mitra had left her science lab to work as the director of a small community library tucked inside a former church parsonage, while Chase wrote newspaper feature stories for a weekly and skied most winter days. His DB6 email account remained empty.

On New Year's Day, Chase dug the vibrating phone from his Spyder jacket. He'd just hopped on the North Face chairlift at Montage Mountain, a dilapidated ski resort overlooking Scranton-area rooftops. Despite the natural beauty of the Northern Poconos—and the Endless Mountain Range just to the north—Scranton had long been the butt of snobby jokes having to do with its proliferation of the bowling alley industry. When Hollywood arrived in Scranton to shoot on location, it was a good bet that beer and bowling were key elements of the storyline.

"I think it's time." Mitra's voice was breathless at the other end. She was back at their new home, a half hour from the ski hill parking lot. Chase had left her on her own after she'd promised not to have the baby while he was off skiing.

"Time for what?" He reached forward to loosen his boot buckles. The Phoebe Snow lift ran up the steeper North Face slopes and was painfully slow at the poorly funded county-owned resort. Montage's unusual layout was split in two: the easier slopes at the top and the more difficult black diamonds at the bottom. The vast gravel parking lot was in the middle plateau, right where the Phoebe Snow lift deposited skiers. Getting off the lift, you either turned right, left, or went to your car.

"The baby is coming," Mitra answered, and Chase dropped his phone thirty or so feet, just where the snowmaking runoff created frozen waterfalls over the terraced boulders below. The phone shattered amid the litter of chewing tobacco tins and lone gloves.

"Uh, hey, excuse me?" Chase leaned forward against the retention bar to face his fellow passenger, a guy with high-end gear he remembered zipping past on the diamonds. "Do you have a cellphone?"

The man looked down between his expensive Volkl skis in the general vicinity of where Chase's phone lay shattered.

"Not one with a parachute."

"I'm having a baby," Chase pleaded.

"No you're not."

"My wife is having a baby at this very moment."

"And you're off skiing?"

"The baby is early," Chase lied. The baby was right on time, but the man didn't need to know that. Mitra had promised to wait. He was only going to be gone for two hours, maybe three. A few quick runs and right back to her side, ready for fatherhood.

"There's a payphone in the lodge." The man pulled up the collar on his shiny Obermeyer one-piece ski suit for privacy.

Chase hummed nervously, pulling off his glove to check his watch as the lift stopped three excruciating times, the minutes trudging by.

"You really having a baby?" The man handed over his phone.

Tylea Rain Allen was born the next morning, weighing in at six-pounds, one ounce. She was seventeen inches long.

"Is there always so much blood?" Chase had asked the nurse, who assured him everything was fine. "Why does she look purple? What's all the crusty stuff? Do other babies cry like that?"

"She doesn't look purple."

"What if she stops breathing?"

The hospital sent mother and child home a day and a half later despite Chase's concerns.

"It's seems too soon," Chase told Mitra, who appeared confident in the belief that all this stuff was natural. Nothing got to her and it was frustrating. It didn't make sense. Having a seed planted inside her, then having it grow to the size of a melon, didn't begin to faze his wife. Having it turn out to be a human whose care you would be in charge of for decades to follow, after painfully squeezing it out a too-small opening was something she seemed to relish. And what if the child turned out more like him than her? There was no re-do in childbirth, according to the pamphlets Chase read.

Doctor Bam's Toyota sat idling in their driveway, tinny stereo speakers blasting an AC/DC tune, his round head bobbing in heavy-metal fashion. Chase pulled past his truck and up to the house with their brand new family.

"Please check if she's breathing," Chase begged Mitra. Nothing was moving in the baby carrier over his shoulder. Dead silence, just a still pile of fuzzy pink and blue blankets, surely now just a cold mass of sorrow and tragedy. And they'd even given her a name! No matter what the books promised, he could not trust Tylea to breathe without being watched. He knew life was filled with regrets because you let your guard down in one of its fleeting moments. Every second, every breath, had become an opportunity for catastrophe. Fatherhood was already overwhelming.

"The new baby girl!" Doctor Bam hooted, flinging open the rear car door to examine his granddaughter up close, while also grabbing Mitra to give her a kiss. Chase opened the door on his side and slid over to try and figure out the seat belt and how it was connected to this thing. He knew he was useless, that the carrier was now permanently attached.

"What do you think, Dad?" Mitra carefully rearranged the soft cotton hat on the baby's miniature head. Chase had read details regarding the soft spot under those little caps and still could not fathom why they weren't made of metal, like helmets. There must be an enormous untapped market for Kevlar bonnets.

With three adults hovering, Tylea opened her mouth into a great, straining oval, either yawning or making a silent cry for help. She reminded Chase of a hungry baby bird whose mother had returned to the nest, ready to regurgitate berries and worms.

"I think she looks like a scientist." Doctor Bam spoke in a low, almost reverent voice. "Young man, after you bring in the baby, there are toys in the back of my truck."

Tylea Rain Allen's first toy was a pickled fetal pig.

Chapter 19

———

WHILE GOVERNMENT INTELLIGENCE agencies around the world looked to shore up likely marks, terrorists and rogue nations searched for soft targets.

Ali Saleh had never wanted to kill anyone. All the shouting about death to Americans, infidels, and Jews from his young friends hurt his ears. Why the al Qaeda elders had chosen him to leave his mother for strange lands was far beyond his comprehension. Ali wanted quiet peace and for Layla to allow him to touch her bare hand. Killing was for soldiers and people who believed in change. Ali just wanted to make chicken mansaf and baba ghanouj because he knew Layla loved eggplant and the smell of toasted almonds. In the kitchen Ali would be a warrior!

Except now he was supposed to kill himself. Al Qaeda had intended to use the world stage of the 2006 Turin Winter Olympics to blow up a medal ceremony with heavily favored American Bode Miller standing on the podium. Miller had been a favorite to medal in all five disciplines, giving a Saudi terrorist plenty of opportunities.

Early on in his assignment, Ali had tried to be a cheerful

helper in the wax room and sponsor offices. He'd been a gofer all his life, in fact, doing a similar job at his hometown mosque in Madinah, where he'd mopped down the prayer halls and kept the foot bath water fresh. But Ali, the soon–to-be martyr, was instructed to stick close to Miller whenever possible. It meant that after a ten hour day of picking up granola bar wrappers these people couldn't manage to put in the trash bin, he had to squeeze into the shadows of hellish bars and nightclubs until all hours of the morning.

Ali missed prayer at least three times a day and almost never knew the direction of Mecca.

What was an Italian nightclub like for a meek servant of Allah? A boy who simply wanted to close his eyes and blow up an infidel as quickly as possible to collect his ticket to Paradise for seventy-two black-eyed virgins? Almost exactly like the time a bomb factory accidentally blew up in his old neighborhood. The noise was similar, as were all the flashing lights and screaming people. He truly needed to get to Paradise fast. Or home to Layla and her lovely soft hands.

A roaming bar girl was shouting foreign words, an inquisition, at the humble Ali. He was cowering in a corner of the club, where he'd followed the famous Bode Miller and his entourage. Ali had done his best to tolerate all the frightening women on the streets exposing themselves to the sea of lecherous men. The elders would condemn such female exhibitionists as disloyal to Allah, ignorant of the Legends of Punishment. They'd order them put to death and then shrouded in the very burkas they ignored. Ali suffered terrible nightmares in which he was ordered to slaughter these women. Two razor-sharp shafra daggers would grow from his fists, glimmering metal extensions of his own body. He would slash his way down busy sidewalks, forced to mete out justice on these shameless women while offering tearful apologies.

Ali would awaken and switch on his hotplate. He'd stir a cube of chicken bouillon into a cup of water, a pathetic substitute for a true kitchen warrior.

In the chaotic, Zionist hellhole, Ali was trapped against one wall by a set of gigantic breasts. Herded like the sheep he'd become, afraid of moving. He shaded his eyes from the flashing lights, a hand over one ear to protect it from the buffeting music. The bar girl was making demands he could not understand. Lips and eyes painted unnatural colors, she towered over him even though he was standing. Ali could see glimpses of her pink tongue behind white teeth, but his eyes were drawn downward. Her breasts were less than a meter from his face, encased in pink triangles of glistening material. There were strings holding the material in place and he recognized that one tug might unleash her bosom like a collapsed dam.

"Please, Allah, please go away." Ali shook, his words in useless Arabic, as he tried dissolving into the pulsating wall behind, unable to take his eyes off her chest, knowing Allah was surely going to punish him for his weakness. He was also dimly aware that he'd lost track of the infidel he was told not to lose track of.

More words and impatient gestures from the bar girl's free hand; the other held a tray of drinks she could easily convert to a weapon.

All the basic Italian phrases Ali had learned—such as, which way to the toilet—had vaporized. He suddenly feared she might have discovered his mission and was demanding his papers. The al Qaeda elders would have him skinned alive and then stoned. Ali's mind raced with all the worst thoughts of a failed mission. Never again would he see Layla's bare hand, her long, delicate fingers. With panic setting in, it was fortunate for everyone inside the club he wasn't wearing his suicide vest. He had started to dig through his shirt for the detonator, mumbling "*Allahu Akbar, Allahu Akbar.*" Allah is great.

Ali's inquisitor tapped her foot while balancing the tray near her shoulder, Ali furiously patting himself down while trying to dissolve into the wall behind. She was surely aware he hadn't taken his eyes off her chest for a second, but it didn't seem to affect her in the least. She thrust them out farther, as though they were weapons. *Yes*, Ali almost cried, *they are weapons. They are dangerous, dangerous weapons and I submit. Please, take them away and leave me alone. Layla, forgive my sins!*

Ali was sick to his stomach, the soft fleshy cushions of motherhood willing themselves closer, growing rounder and fatter with each breath sucked through her red lips. "I beg you, please," Ali whimpered in Arabic.

The woman uttered a few short words and snapped her chewing gum. She abandoned her interrogation, turned and stalked away, tray held high as if making an offering to whatever god she might have. Ali watched the material covering the round lumps of her buttocks and nearly collapsed with relief. When he felt he could walk, he ran out of the bar.

It would only get worse for Ali.

Each failed race during the day had Bode Miller spending even more time in these churning pits. Ali drifted into a deep depression, losing faith that his mission would succeed. It had started well enough, with the famous American skier just a tiny fraction of a second off the podium in the first event. But the next race was a heartbreaker for Bode and the would-be martyr. Bode had led the first portion of the race by nearly a third of a second and was the hands-down favorite going into what were called slalom runs. But Ali, who watched the races on a huge projection screen near the finish line, heard the cries of disappointment as Bode's skis straddled a gate and he was disqualified.

That night, the martyr broke Shariah law and sipped from an abandoned glass of alcohol left on a cluttered table next to the dance floor. He told himself it was to aid his mission by dulling some of the pain caused by this pounding music and bomb-flash lighting. Across the frightful, exploding room, he watched the infidel tossing back colorful shots while crowded by a herd of half-naked females. Ali began emptying more leftover glasses. The pain was too deep.

Over the next days and nights, Ali's depression blossomed and he was tired beyond belief. How did this infidel expect to compete in a ski race if Ali could hardly push a broom down a hallway without rushing for a toilet? Ali could barely guide the wash bucket down a flat corridor, so how could the American expect to stay upright and make proper turns around such skinny poles?

An event called the Super G was another disaster. Ali had snuck away from his duties to watch him cross the finish line in first place. Something bad had happened up on the mountain and the famous racer never even made it to the bottom. And two days later, Bode finished sixth in an event called the giant slalom—another total failure for all radical Muslims across the world. All the talk around the wax room was that Bode had no chance in hell of finishing the two-run slalom race scheduled in five days—also his last event—and Ali's gloom grew blacker.

Following Bode into a nightclub on the eve of the final event, Ali had strapped on his bomb vest. It appeared there would be no world stage under the glare of international television cameras, so he was contemplating a preemptive strike. How many black-eyed virgins he'd receive for killing a hundred or so infidels outside of the spotlight, he didn't know. But since he himself was a virgin, he would praise Allah and be happy to have just one, even if it couldn't be his dear Layla. The virgin didn't even have to be very pretty. And he decided he could live with the fact that she wasn't even a virgin.

Ali was considering all his options when one of the young females who swarmed Bode insect-like grabbed his arm, pulling him over to join them for tiny glasses of orange alcohol. Ali raised the glass shoved in his hand as the American racer seemed to be thanking the Italians for their hospitality. Ali raised another when Bode seemed to thank the Italians for producing such beautiful women, touching the front of the females' shirts as if he were their husband. The wobbling Saudi terrorist cheered an agreement in Arabic, and everyone laughed as another round was poured. Drunk as a jihadist skunk, the humble martyr was now searching the room for those two big boobies from the other night, even though they'd been in some other bar. Females were touching his shoulders and hands, and he felt the serpent in his pants again turn to stone and point upward accusingly. Allah's mighty dagger, he'd heard the old men from his mosque call it. Was it pointing at him? Ali tossed back another glass of stinging liquid and the room began to spin out of control as his mission's last thread unraveled.

The heat from the mass of gyrating bodies—and all the packs of explosives duct-taped to his sweating belly—was too much. Ali clawed through the revelers, trying to find the exit, screaming in Arabic as the panic tightened its grip. He ripped at his clothes as he pushed wide-eyed people out onto the street in front of him, then fumbled at the detonator button to end his misery.

The button didn't work. Ali plunged it over and over until his thumb ached, but it failed to do anything but make little clicking sounds as a crowd of onlookers began to close in. He was aware that he was crying, crumpled on the sidewalk like a homeless beggar, cold from having torn his shirt. What must have been a popular song began to play inside the club and the people lost interest, hurried back in to dance and drink some more.

Ali shed the suicide vest as he rose and stumbled away from the club. Two blocks later, he paused to retch against a parked car and then wiped his chin. When the sensation of the turning world released its grip, he resumed his march along the dimly lit pavement. The night grew quieter and his mood began to lift. If he was not to be a martyr, then he would surely be alone in heaven when Layla's time came. Maybe he wouldn't know her touch in this life, but perhaps it wasn't too late. He marched as he imagined a good warrior might, down one street and then the next. He caught sight of the snowcapped peaks in the distance, the mountains shrouded with purity. There was one thing to do, he decided, and put street after street behind him. The mountains grew larger and the snow brighter, as Ali left the outskirts of town on shoes with widening holes, his torn shirt flapping behind.

The first banks of snow were plowed and dirty, so up the road he went, his breath coming harder, big puffs of steam in front of his face like a mighty dragon. The moon was full and high in the sky as Ali searched and finally spotted the perfect blanket of white in what might be a meadow in springtime.

Ali dropped onto his back in the snow and worked his legs and feet in sweeping arcs. He made his first ever snow angel, like one he'd seen created by children on a television soda commercial. He craned his neck to admire his work. An angel, he thought, just like his far away Layla. Ali began to pull snow up over his legs and torso, scooping the frozen crystals with bare hands. He covered as much of his body as he could in white, then settled back and allowed himself to relax every tired muscle. He watched the stars and the moon, and the traces of meandering lights he thought must be airplanes. Warmth spread from his heart, some kind of magic produced from the sense of tranquility. He wasn't cold, being mostly buried in the snow on the side of the mountain. Not with all he had to look forward to. Ali pretended his wings were real, flapped them to rise from his bed of white. He began following one of the moving lights above as he drifted into the most peaceful sleep of his short life.

"HI, TYLEA."

"Daddy!" The phone crashed to the floor and Chase could

hear her fumble with the long cord and then the click of the kitchen light switch. "Guess what just happened?"

"Why are you still awake?" His current assignment for DB6 was to keep tabs on a ski racer and his technician, who were involved in another Iranian plot. The duo had been hopping back and forth from USSA Masters races in Colorado and Vermont.

"Mommy fell asleep on the couch reading. When are you coming home?"

"I'm flying home after the morning race."

"Is it a slalom?"

"Yes, it's a slalom, honey." Chase knew what was coming next.

"Then you can come home after the first run," she teased, meaning he wouldn't survive a full first run down the steep, icy course of single gate slalom poles. The slalom event was almost impossible for skiers still low on the learning curve. Chase had skied since he was a kid, but his only races had been in two dollar a run timed events set up on gentle intermediate slopes. Masters racing was open to anyone who purchased a license, and the competition was filled with entry-level racers all the way up to former national team members who weren't quite ready to give up their adrenaline addiction. Masters courses were set on expert slopes and had a seemingly endless number of gates that left legs burning, ready to give out before the finish was in sight.

Because these races were sanctioned by the International Ski Federation, the fastest skiers could earn a qualifying point ranking for the Olympics. Ski racing was dangerous enough that any person with desire and a bankroll couldn't simply declare residency in a country and compete in the Olympics. A racer had to earn admission.

"That's not being very supportive." Chase gave the expected response. He enjoyed this little comedy routine he had with his daughter. As her soccer coach, he teased her about skipping games and going to a movie instead of the soccer field. As his ski racing psychologist, she teased back hard. And midway through her first season on the Montage Mountain Development Race Team, she'd now had more formal race training than her father.

"Try to look three gates ahead," she'd advised, "and sing a fun song out loud. It relaxes you. And, Dad?"

"Yes?"

Tylea's voice had turned serious. "You have to smile. Coach Steph says smiling makes you faster. It's very important."

Coach Steph was the woman at Montage in charge of what was nicknamed the Skittle Patrol, a group of a dozen or so future ski racing stars she led across every inch of the mountain, often in a snake-like formation of follow-the-leader.

"I'll try to smile," he'd promised, "but I'm not as brave as you."

Chase was also playing follow the leader, keeping tabs on former Austrian National racer Bernie Resch. Iranian President Ahmadinejad's people had hired Resch, funding his tune-ups in USSA Masters races for a crack at the Americans in the 2010 Games. No vest bomber martyrs needed, just a series of armed assassins, recruited from the growing radical Islamic population in Canada. Exporting a little Hezbollah-style terror—as he'd done in Syria and Lebanon—into the Olympic Games would showcase his enormous reach. Ahmadinejad's plan was to have a veteran skier in charge, with a technician as second in command.

CIA operatives in Tehran documented Ahmadinejad's obsessive following of al Qaeda plots, even the ones that had failed.

The plot to blow up Bode Miller in front of millions of television viewers had been unraveled by Italian police after it had fizzled on its own. They'd put the pieces together after being called to investigate what turned out to be an abandoned bomb vest with bad wiring and the body of a dead

Saudi national who'd apparently committed suicide in a snow bank. Al Qaeda had easily infiltrated Bode's main sponsoring company by having their martyr fill out a job application for a flunky position, where for five Euros an hour he'd push a broom and get sandwiches and cold beer for the wax room guys.

Ahmadinejad vowed not to make the same mistake, repeatedly stating that the great flaw in al Qaeda's plan was to rely on a single untrained martyr. That Ahmadinejad finally chose former Austrian National Ski Team member Bernhard Resch to command the operation for the 2010 Games wasn't much of a surprise. Not to the CIA spies in Tehran, or to anyone receiving the report back home. Not after you'd read through Resch's bio, which was what Chase was doing in his hotel room once again the night before his slalom race in Copper Mountain, Colorado.

"Smile," was what Chase's little coach had instructed over the phone, her mom sleeping on the couch, a half-finished book no doubt lying open on her chest. With her dad away, it was a perfect chance for Tylea to catch up on late night cartoons, which she certainly deserved. Her teacher had suggested her for the gifted program and Tylea had loved the new attention. Outside of school or the library, she was shy and introverted. While in her element, she ruled with confidence. She'd become the library's unofficial mascot just as her mom had been the mascot of the science department at the University of Tehran. Every day Tylea carefully crossed the street from her elementary school to hang out among the narrow passageways between the tall book stacks. By the end of first grade, she was checking patrons in and out and reshelving returned books. By second grade, she was helping elderly patrons connect to the Internet on the public computers and showing them how to sign up and use a Hotmail address to keep in touch with distant family.

Chase once listened to their little girl explaining antipodal points to a woman at the copier machine. He'd overheard her quizzing a school board member as to why classrooms only had one computer and no Internet access. Didn't he know the encyclopedias were outdated and plenty of grants were available? She offered to help write the grant form, just as she'd helped her mom write them for the library. She backed up her request with items she'd learned while on the library computers.

"Did you know that if you got on a spaceship and traveled near the speed of light to a distant star, then turned around and came back, you might only be one year older, but your goldfish might be two-hundred years old?" She clutched her favorite Einstein book she'd had her mom order from Amazon, tapping the cover for the board member to consider the possibilities. "You can't really go the speed of light, though. Know why not?"

It was also pretty common for a patron to stumble over the sleeping little girl if they weren't watching where they walked among the rows of book stacks.

And just as Mitra had taken to science, Tylea took to the books that surrounded her childhood. Her parents weren't sure if they should punish her for sneaking home a copy of Kurt Vonnegut's *Breakfast of Champions* to read to her favorite bear.

"I wanted to show Brownz all the pictures," she'd explained. "I didn't read him any of the bad words."

They let it go, of course.

Chase smiled when he was on the race course because Tylea had told him to. She had been solemn in her belief and he couldn't have stopped smiling if he'd tried.

Chase had met Resch the night before the first Masters race. Though his file said the forty-one-year-old former Olympian hadn't been on skis in a decade, he immediately took his place at the top of this group. Everyone gravitated toward Bernie, both in the race start area and the restaurants and bars after events. Waiting for some advice that never came, Bernie simply recommended they ski faster. Most just wanted to be next to a guy who could do things they'd only dreamed of—from marching into a stadium during opening ceremonies of the Olympics, to having the balls to hit on every woman in the room.

Bernie was entertaining and bought rounds of drinks. Chase didn't particularly dislike the man, even though he planned to lead an Iranian mass murder plot at the 2010 Vancouver Olympics. But the heavy Austrian accent made him difficult to understand, and Chase found his wry sense of humor off-putting.

"There is a mostly undetectable poison in those sausages." Bernie had pointed to the warming tray in the breakfast buffet line, and it didn't sound like he was kidding.

"The blood has clotted in my right foot from these boots. I am beginning to fear the need to amputate my small toe," Resch had complained to Chase while riding the lift, tapping a ski pole on his right boot. Were you supposed to empathize or laugh?

But the guy was so damn fast on skis. Not powerful through the turns. Not the brutal, American-style of trying to load and unload the ski's energy, blasting out and forward at the end of the arc. Bernie's style was grace. He had very little upper body movement and ever so slightly tipped his skis from turn to turn, always on the correct, high line. He skied with no wasted energy, had the handful of former U.S. Ski Team members shaking their heads in the finish corral. There was little doubt he could get his FIS points down to qualify for Vancouver.

Bernie Resch had spent most of his six-year Austrian race career crashing out of too many races. He'd had tremendous potential, but had a self-described problem with losing proper focus at critical moments. Namely, the parts of race courses where straight-aways became tight turns, as well as those tricky blind entries over steep headwalls.

Chase had read the files describing Resch's likely motives.

What drove Resch to sign on with the Iranians to help murder Americans had a lot to do with what had occurred during his tenure on the World Cup. Skiing was a way of life in Austria, not just a sport. The world converged on places like Kitzbuhel for the running of the famous Hahnenkamm downhill, which was revered as the most dangerous and historic of the World Cup speed events. But during Resch's years on the Austrian team, it was an American who collected all of the fame and trophies.

While Austrian legend Franz Klammer was coming toward the end of his career, American Phil Mahre was dominating the world with three consecutive Overall titles. Mahre was from a country where next to nobody gave a damn about alpine ski racing, while the Austrian press hounded its young racers, who were getting shown up.

Resch had complained in interviews, and the CIA had collected many of the clippings to present to their profilers. Psychological studies were done to identify his strengths and weaknesses.

Books describing the once proud and invincible Austrians, and how they had been brought to their knees, had been written and published by just as many American sportswriters as Austrians. And while the American book versions had been filled with cheerful reflections on great moments in ski racing history, the Austrian versions were filled with dark indignation and angry speculation regarding the future of skiing as it was then known.

Resch had taken losing hard and had made no secret of his loathing of Phil Mahre, Bill Johnson, and everything else American. He had been vocal enough about his hatred to make a lasting impression on Iranian ski coach Issa Saveh Shemshaki, who would be approached nearly a quarter-century later by men from President Ahmadinejad's office in search of a suitable recruit. Shemshaki had eagerly offered up Resch's name in a transcript Chase had read of the meeting, recorded by a CIA operative in Tehran.

Resch was a short, skinny man, with a booming voice common among Austrians, especially former downhillers. Chase first saw him in person as he was drunkenly toasting the bartender in their hotel restaurant. The bartender didn't seem to mind, since Resch had been tipping twenty dollar bills.

"To the most beautiful breasts in America!" Bernie drained his tall beer glass in a single gulp.

For a retired downhiller, Resch could bash Break-A-Way slalom gates like a pro. He could carve a giant slalom course like nobody else on the Masters circuit. Bernie did not lose one race—or even a single run—through the first eight events of his premier Masters season, outclassing his American counterparts while knocking the ten years of rust from his edges with ease.

Bernie was also fast to earn a reputation for his time spent with the female racers, as well as female family members of other skiers. When caught in compromising situations, he would escape by blaming cultural differences and the language barrier. There were rumors, but these paled in comparison to Bernie's descriptive storytelling. He was caught in a hot tub with the eighteen-year-old daughter of a woman in Bernie's age class, after a mid-season Super G. Sharing the Sheraton Hotel's fitness center hot tub would have been almost acceptable, had it not been for his growing reputation. It was also problematic that the young woman had been straddling Bernie's lap when her mother happened in.

"The mother asked if I was wearing a bathing suit. Who wears a bathing suit to have sex in a hot tub?"

"You're going to get shot," one of the men at the bar had said.

"There are worse ways to die," said Bernie. "I told the mother I had seen her in a speed suit on the race course and that she had a fine big ass."

"No you didn't," another guy said.

"Yes, I said to her that I would like to make a sandwich with them. That's how you say it, right? It was very hot in the tub and I was very aroused. It was time for a sex sandwich."

"What'd she do?" Chase asked.

"Well, the young daughter was not interested. She stopped hiding in my armpit and climbed out of the tub. She ran off to the ladies toilet room. That was very disappointing because I was not finished, if you know what I mean. It is very frustrating for a man to be interrupted, am I right?"

"This had to be Anna Collins," said one of the men next to Bernie. "She blew out of the hotel after dinner. I know her girl, Bernie, she's gotta be six feet tall."

"The mother helped my condition very much," Bernie said, signaling to get the attention of the bartender. He bought a round of drinks for their group, and Chase saw the bartender slip a scrap of paper into Bernie's hand when he tipped her.

Much later that night, Chase had discovered Bernie behind an artificial bamboo tree next to the snack machines, sleeping off the Kranbitter gin he couldn't seem to stop drinking once he'd started.

"What's your secret?" Chase asked, after untangling him from the plastic leaves and getting him to his wobbly feet.

"I'm going to kill Americans," Bernie said, his head lolling.

"I mean what's your secret with women."

Resch clung to Chase in the cramped elevator, attached like a pet monkey. His arms wrapped around Chase's neck and his legs entwined around his left leg. Chase prayed the elevator wouldn't stop for more passengers; the sniggers from the young couple trapped behind them had been bad enough.

"Do not confuse secrets with talents," Resch replied in Chase's ear, his breath moist. "Do you want to see my best talent?"

Chase was pretty certain what Bernie considered to be his best talent was pressed up against his left pants pocket, but Bernie let go of his neck and dismounted. Apparently also curious, the young couple stopped sniggering. Bernie took a wide stance, battling the heavy seas of the rising elevator before plunging his right hand deep into his front pocket. Pitching and swaying, he withdrew his hand. It held a wallet-sized laminated photo, which he waved triumphantly over his head.

"My secret weapon!" He showed it to Chase, who recognized Bernie's late wife. Chase had a copy of this same photo in a CIA file. "You fucking Americans would never understand."

Chase had a vested interest in keeping Bernie from being drowned in a hot tub or choked to death by a jealous husband. As the race series passed the halfway mark in the season, exactly two years remained until the Olympics. That gave Bernie thirty weekends' worth of opportunities to seduce the wrong female, prematurely blowing both of their chances at a big time public relations coup. The CIA wanted the Iranian plan disrupted at the last possible moment, under the spotlight of the Olympics. Their motive was to show the world the true evil empire, perhaps getting some meaningful U.N. sanctions in place.

The Iranians simply wanted mayhem and death.

Chapter 20

MASTERS SKI RACING began a late season swing at East Coast resorts—four consecutive weekends in Vermont. Chase skipped the first two, spending ten days at home, the longest stretch since November. He'd gone to his daughter's races instead, joining the throng of noisy parents lining the slopes and ringing cow bells. Mitra stood at his side with the video camera. Tylea wore a bubblegum pink speed suit, and he was sure he could see her smiling as she conquered the tricky flush gates and icy headwalls.

"Go, go, go," he shouted, heart in his throat until she was safely in the finish corral.

Then Chase packed and headed for Vermont. Three days at Killington, then a final weekend up the road at Sugarbush. After arriving at his hotel Friday evening, he'd been trying to reach Mitra, getting only the machine. He wondered if she might be on the road with Tylea for a surprise visit, but knew that was unlikely. Both Mitra's Saturday library volunteers had called out, and his daughter wouldn't want to miss ski team practice even to come see her dad race. He didn't mind her priorities one bit. It would soon be spring and time for soccer.

Chase skipped the late dinner and drinks with other racers. He waited by the phone, calling every twenty minutes and getting nothing but Tylea's recorded voice. By midnight he knew something was terribly wrong. He sat in the padded vinyl chair, elbows propped on the round table of the musty room.

Chase gave up, grabbed his ski jacket, headed downstairs to his Jeep in the frigid air. His tank was full and he had every intention of driving through the night, pulling into their driveway as the sun was coming up. He detoured instead, driving to Bernie's townhouse rental through a steady snowfall. Parked in a recently plowed space was Mitra's little red car with Pennsylvania plates and its "I Love Libraries" bumper sticker. Somehow he'd known it would be in that exact spot. In the back of his mind he heard Limp's voice asking if he could kill someone without getting all crazy.

Chase felt the blood drain out of him as his Jeep headlights washed over the back of her car, his right foot pressing down on the brake pedal, the left on the clutch. He hadn't needed the wipers because the fluffy snowflakes simply blew off the glass. He sat there frozen, idling in the cold night, staring at the license plate, reading the letters and numbers one by one. He remembered watching Mitra attach the yellow and white bumper sticker, teasing her because it was crooked. The snow fell straight down in clumps, slowly cocooning his Jeep. He had never in his life felt more alone.

He switched off the ignition and killed the headlights. Chase reached under the driver's seat for his gun—Hitler's PPK—and slipped it inside his ski jacket next to a small plastic container of race wax.

Chase decided this must be the reason Bernie had disappeared for five days last month, passing up bigger Masters events in the Rockies. Chase's cover had been blown and Bernie had done what all spy agencies had been doing since the beginning of spying: he'd gone for the loved ones, the family. But instead of kidnapping or killing, Bernie had attacked with his best weapon, his strong point.

Chase slipped on his calfskin gloves, pushed open the Jeep door and stepped out into the icy air. The townhomes were all dark, too expensive for the college partiers. Killington had dozens of neighborhoods of townhouses spread across its hills and valleys. Each group of two hundred or so homes formed a maze of entryways and stacks of protected firewood. The complexes were designed to create the appearance of privacy. White exteriors matched the white interiors. Floor plans were mostly the same, depending on the number of bedrooms, but Chase knew where he'd find Bernie this time of night, knew where he'd take Mitra.

Chase forced himself to slow down and be deliberate, not to break into a jog. Resch's front door was locked, so he popped out a single pane of the closest window with his elbow, just above the locking mechanism. The window slid up smoothly and he stepped over the low threshold.

Depeche Mode blasting from the living room stereo had covered the sound of breaking glass. He allowed his eyes to adjust, taking in the dark room. The final glowing embers in the fireplace provided most of the light. The disheveled blanket in front of the brass-trimmed hearth was where they had screwed the first time. Chase had listened to enough of Bernie's stories to know how he worked. He got their attention with his accent and his swagger. Bernie had explained that the key to seduction was the art of the balancing act. You had to appear as though whatever might happen didn't matter, while making her feel more desired than anyone else in the world. It was a skill not easily mastered, according to Bernie, but once perfected, deadly.

And now Bernie was about to be dead.

A used condom, like some piece of gore from a gutted trout, screamed at Chase from the stones in front of the fireplace. Along with a hunk of yellow cheese and a few red grapes, it lay crumpled on a plate left on the hearth, the firelight reflecting off its latex skin. His heart raced and raced.

Chase knew everything. He could hear Bernie's voice telling the story of how he had manipulated a lonely wife who had come to one of the races here in Vermont. The super fast racer with the exotic accent set the hook with a single unexpected compliment. After the nightly awards ceremony, in which he'd accepted the first place trophy—a little boyishly embarrassed by all the over-the-top praise from the announcer—he'd catch her eye and smile in a way that made her flushed and curious. He'd hold her gaze for an extra second or two. It was always the same when it came to wives and girlfriends.

Bernie would make sure these women knew that their secret was absolutely safe, despite his reputation. He'd come up behind them a little later and gently touch their waists in a non-threatening way. That was the first touch. And the fact that it lasted only a moment and was quickly withdrawn built some measure of trust. It let the wife or girlfriend know he was aware of a boundary to be respected in public. Then Bernie would pick a time to lean close in a friendly, playful way and say how much he wanted to make love to her—just one time.

"I knew I must do it since I first saw your beautiful eyes," he'd say in a low voice, milking his Austrian accent. "Don't say no right away."

They rarely said no. Mitra hadn't.

Chase looked up from the plate full of evidence toward a light glowing down the second floor hallway. He was drawn to the short flight of wide oak stairs and took slow, deliberate steps toward the master suite's open doorway. As each step brought him closer, he was able to see the bed, lit bright as a movie set, with disheveled silk sheets and a twisted down comforter in the middle. His heart pounded as he recognized his wife's soft black hair. Her legs were entwined in the sheets, naked, almost the same ivory color as the silky fabric. He couldn't hear what she was saying because of the music, but she laughed and raised herself up on her elbows, looking toward the far corner of the bedroom. She was so happy in that instant. He couldn't hear words, but he could hear the laughter.

The last inch or two of a candlestick flickered in the bright room. As he crept closer—within a few feet of the open bedroom door—he could see Bernie, a towel wrapped around his waist, using a second one to dry his hair and upper body.

Hot tears bubbled to the surface, but there was too much pressure. He wouldn't have been able to let a word escape, let alone tears. The music was swallowed in that unbearable pressure, like diving down into the deepest end of a pool. His temples throbbed, about to explode.

Chase stood watching a silent movie scene and was surprised when he noticed the gun extended in front of him. It was his gun and his hand and arm. And then he realized it was aimed at Bernie's naked chest. The PPK was smooth and hard, and still cold in his palm after being stored in his frigid Jeep. His focus went from the center of Bernie's chest back to the two small sighting nubs at each end of the sliding barrel.

Bernie stood at the far side of the large bed and let the towel slowly slip from around his waist to expose his flaccid penis to Mitra. He had a hair brush in his right hand and reached up to run it across his head as Chase's aim moved with it. Chase picked a spot directly in the center of Bernie's forehead.

He pulled the trigger.

Chase didn't hear the shot, but a tiny wisp of smoke escaped the un-silenced barrel and momentarily blurred his view. Then he saw a small dark spot appear in the middle of Bernie's forehead, and time and sound suddenly returned to normal. Bernie's head snapped back and hit the wall as if he'd been punched in the nose. His body slid to the left and down to the floor, creating a giant bloody comma on white paint.

Not in a million years could Chase have predicted what happened next, after Mitra turned to look back over her shoulder to see him lowering the smoking gun.

"We'll have to clean this up," she told him in a matter of fact tone, swinging her legs off the bed and looking to find her shoes. "I'll tell you everything that happened and why, but not right now."

"What are you talking about?" His voice seemed to come from far away. Red drips formed on the comma.

"Get in here and help me clean this up. Now!" Mitra shouted. "We'll talk later."

Chase stepped into the room. What else was he going to do? He looked down at the dead, naked Bernie and his wife rummaging the bedroom closet and then the master bathroom. She was finding towels. He hadn't planned on cleaning up this mess. He hadn't planned on anything.

"Think about Tylea!" Mitra threw an armload of towels down from a high shelf, the lovely muscles of her calves dancing beneath the skin. She was wearing a pair of Adidas running pants rolled up to Capri-length, and a thin, bright yellow sweater. Had he thought she was naked? Bernie had sure been naked, so he assumed she was, too, since she was on his bed, mixed up in the sheets.

Bernie's wound was seeping dark stuff onto the hardwood floor.

"Jesus Christ, wake up!" she yelled, as he knelt down next to the body. Was she talking to him or Bernie? "You have to think about Tylea, right now. If we don't get this cleaned up, you'll end up in a jail cell and you'll lose her. You got that?"

"What have you done to us?" Chase asked, not in anger. All emotion had been drained away. He hadn't really expected committing murder to have such an odd effect. It had sapped away all his rage and passion and somehow plunged his wife into a crazy cleaning mode.

Then she slapped him across the face, hard.

"I need your help right now!" His face was numb, although it should have been hot and stinging. "We need him on the bed and all the blood wiped off the floor and the wall."

"What did you do?" He fingered his cheek.

"I hit you." It was her calm voice, and then she smiled and almost giggled. Mitra took his face in her hands. "This isn't what you think. I'll explain it all later, but I didn't have sex with him."

"Why …" Chase started to get up, but she pushed him back down next to Bernie.

"He was crazy." She pointed down at Bernie with her palm up. Chase watched her slender fingers. "He thought you were some kind of spy and that you were after him. He thought you were going to kill him."

"I don't understand? Why are you here? Where's Tylea?"

"I came because he was going to hurt you, and she's fine, she's at my dad's house."

"But …"

"I know how it looks." She reached down and grabbed hold of Bernie's ankles, jerking her head in the direction of the skier's head so that Chase would grab him from the other end. They swung his limp body onto the bed.

He knew from his drunken night in the elevator, hanging off Chase like a monkey, that Bernie was light as a feather. Plus, he was now missing a gallon of blood. Mitra began scooping up all that blood with bath towels and draping them across Bernie's body. She had apparently set about to create a wickedly gruesome piece of art. Chase admired the stark contrast of shapes and colors.

"Did you put your gloves on before you broke in?" she asked, and he looked at his hands and started to pull off the soft gloves. "Don't!"

"Right." And he was the spy? "Yes, I put them on outside and didn't touch anything at all."

Mitra left him with Bernie and padded down the hall. He heard cabinets open and close, then bottles clanking. She returned wearing cartoonish looking yellow dishwashing gloves—which kept hands soft and sexy—and carrying a load of whiskey bottles.

"Here." She foisted a half dozen various whiskeys at him. "Just soak the bed and the body. Leave about an inch in each bottle and put the caps back on tight."

It was no longer Bernie? Just a body? Chase was more than fine with that. He unscrewed caps and did as he was told while Mitra emptied the remaining bottles on the body formerly known as Bernie.

"Leave all the bottles on the bed. I'll be right back."

"You're telling me the truth, aren't you?"

"I wasn't here to sleep with him."

She returned with a small brown rectangle he recognized as a fire starting brick, pulling at the plastic wrapper. The funny gloves were making it difficult.

"Do you have your keys?"

"In the Jeep," he said.

"Okay, you leave through the front door, slow and casual, like you just had a nice little neighborly visit and are heading home. Pull your jacket collar up and if someone's walking their dog, just say something about how cold it is, nothing memorable, no stupid jokes. I'll be at your hotel five minutes after you. Park in the back lot and wait for me in your Jeep. Got it?"

"I'm not leaving you here," he said with no authority whatsoever.

"You're leaving right now if you ever want to see your child again," she told him in a voice colder than anything outside these walls. "One more thing."

"Yes?"

"Try not to back into anyone's car on the way out."

He imagined she lit the fire starter when the sound of his Jeep faded into the night. He never asked for details. He assumed she left the lit kerosene-based brick on a paperback book. It would provide a little extra time between her exit and the raging fire, which would engulf Bernie and all the alcohol soaked bedding.

She probably anticipated having some explaining to do. How she knew Bernie was feeling threatened by Chase. But once the truth came out, he was the one who had filled their lives with lies. That Bernie *was* being stalked by Chase. That a pretty good chunk of their life together was grounded in one whopper of a lie, and he was actually serving their country by maintaining surveillance on Bernie. Killing him prematurely was sort of a fuckup on his part, but what assignment ever goes down without a few glitches?

Mitra turned the murder scene into a tragic accident. Depending on the extent of the fire and subsequent damage to the body that had once been Bernie, the sheriff or fire inspector up here in Vermont might request an autopsy. It probably came down to whether they noticed the bullet hole, but the little Austrian ski racer had left a two-thousand mile trail of scorned women and enough pissed-off husbands and boyfriends to keep any investigators occupied right through the summer.

Mitra and Chase made love later that night in his hotel room. They did not talk.

The phone jarred Chase out of a bad dream while the room was still dark. It was a message that the morning's race had been cancelled. There had been a fire and one of the racers had died. They were all encouraged to meet at breakfast and talk about the rest of the weekend; they could help plan services and perhaps hold a race on Sunday in Bernie's honor.

Chase wasn't sure why they made love so often over the next few days. Maybe it was to replace talking. Maybe it was because they sensed some sort of end was near. And a very strange thing happened between them, as each passing moment made it easier for Chase not to tell her everything, especially since she didn't ask. And he never pressed her on how she knew Bernie thought he was a spy out to kill him.

Escaping Vermont, her little red car followed him west through Rutland, across the state line into New York, and then due south. They wound their way down to New Jersey and across the icy Delaware into Pennsylvania, to where their little girl was waiting.

Tylea had a whole new bag full of interesting toys and stories about how each one had died. Chase listened to every word, holding her close, feeling her mom's breath on his neck, wishing it would get warm soon.

Chapter 21

TYLEA'S BARE KNEES were scabbed from rough soccer practices and games with the bigger girls, some three grades ahead. It was the middle of soccer season and Mitra's father insisted on celebrating his birthday by attending one of her games. Chase argued the risks of her potentially volcanic father, but Mitra had been firm.

"Grandpa eats people's pets." Tylea was in the back seat of Mitra's car, Chase at the wheel, as the three made the long round trip journey to pick up Doctor Bam.

"No, he doesn't," Mitra said and turned to Chase with a brow-furrowed look that said she wasn't in the mood, that she wanted today to be as normal as possible.

"Why do you think so?" Chase asked and shrugged his shoulders at his wife.

Tylea folded shut the book she'd been reading, something about vampires and good looking teenagers. "The packages in his freezer all have names written on them. Names of pets, like Princess and Buster."

"That's just Grandpa's sense of humor, honey," her mother said.

"Grandpa said that we could solve a lot of the world's problems if we considered cats and dogs edible. Like the neighbor's dog who goes to the bathroom in his flower garden. And know what else?"

"Grandpa doesn't really think that," Mitra interrupted, but Chase knew it was true. The man loved animals, wouldn't hurt a fly until it dug up his prized marigolds. That's when the gloves came off.

"He says that people should be made into food after we die. He says that dead people don't need to take up so much room and that the planet only has so much space."

Chase stifled a laugh, but Mitra was obviously upset. Chase knew it must bring back troubling memories, ones she'd rather their daughter not have to deal with.

"My teacher says we go to heaven when we die, but Grandpa says … well, he called it a bad word having to do with cow poop. He said if it were true, heaven would be just about the scariest place ever, a bunch of dead people walking around. I sure don't wanna go to heaven."

"Your teacher meant to say that she believes a person's *soul* goes to heaven," Mitra explained. "Not their whole body."

"I wouldn't want to eat dead people, anyway. What if you found out it was your uncle? How come you don't have brothers and sisters, Mom?"

"Because your grandfather only wanted one little girl," Mitra told her. "I was his one and only sugar plum."

"He says he made you in an experiment." Tylea opened her hardcover book and hunted for her place. She scooted down to put her knees against the back of her mother's seat. "But I saw pictures of your mom before she died. Grandpa keeps them in a drawer next to where I sleep at his house. She looks just like you."

Chase took his eyes from the narrow country road that had cost the lives of so many wandering pets. Mitra's head was turned away from him, her hands clenched into fists in her lap. Her mother had been the original taboo subject of their marriage. If her knuckles hadn't been so white he might have dared ask again what she really knew of her mother's fate.

As soon as they pulled into the shaded driveway, Doctor Bam's front door burst open. They were greeted by loud rock music and a short, stocky man hoisting a lumpy sack with a dark stain at the bottom.

"I'll ride in back with the star footballer!" Doctor Bam squeezed past Mitra. He wore a new lab coat, was recently shaved, and looked to have attempted maneuvering a comb through his wiry hair.

"We call it *soccer*, Grandpa. Football is a different sport."

"Do you know, young lady, what my country does to its soccer players who do not win?"

"Dad, please."

Chase had backed out of the driveway, taking extra care over the speed bumps installed in front of Doctor Bam's house. He suspected the township had targeted this stretch in particular because of the doctor's notoriously erratic driving habits.

"I'll tell you what they cut off when your mother is not listening. Here, have a cookie."

"She can't have sweets before a game." Mitra's tone was stern and supposedly meant for her daughter, but Chase knew it was more to protect Tylea from having to reject the offer. Tylea was aware of the risk of taking food from her grandfather.

"Then turn on the radio," Doctor Bam ordered, and Chase heard the sound of the cookie being shoved back into the dirty plastic sack. "What are athletics without music? What is life without music?"

Chase rubbed his left temple with his thumb, relieved to have Mitra's father singing along behind him instead of talking. "It's just one game," Mitra had promised. And so much better than an afternoon spent inside his house, surrounded by peculiar smells and the same scratchy records played too loud while brown things were served in deep bowls.

Chase began to relax as he settled in for the drive. The spring and summer had flown by, his secure email account remaining empty. Not a peep from DB6 or anyone at the CIA, which was fine with him. He welcomed their silence, as he welcomed it from Mitra when it came to Bernie. Even as a newlywed, he'd been anxious between assignments, worried that the jobs would dry up, each passing day more certain he'd been replaced. But now he dreaded that an assignment would take him away from what he needed most in his life—an uninterrupted season on the soccer field with fourteen girls in crisp new uniforms, a season with his Tylea.

As moms and dads pulled into the community park fifteen minutes before practice, Coach Chase was already placing corner flags and laying out obstacle courses of orange and yellow cones.

"Devon's here," Tylea would say, as she helped arrange the small cones in an arc around the goal mouth for a new drill he had planned.

"Claudia's here." She announced each arrival of her friends, her teammates.

During her first three seasons, Tylea had been happy picking clover and testing buttercups rather than running after the ball. She'd been one of the kids who Chase was just happy to see leave the sidelines and her mom's lap, tears barely held back. Players started in the Under 6 division, four and five-year-olds herded up and down miniature fields by coaches in what looked like a rugby scrum, the black and white ball somewhere in the middle.

As seasons passed, the players would learn about making and using space; then the games took the shape of real soccer. Chase kept the set of cones in his Jeep to mark off fields at the empty school playground down the road from the library. They could practice there, even if it was just for a half-hour between errands. When the other kids were playing t-ball and little league, Tylea was juggling and dribbling, building her skills.

As soon as the snow disappeared in April, a few of her friends would take the after-school bus to her mother's library, change into shorts and old t-shirts in the bathroom, then cleat up, grab their water bottles and balls and hike to the field. They'd cross the busy county road, then cut through the town's water company with its snarling guard dog. They continued on through backyards and out into the park where Chase would set up a short field and scrimmage for two hours before it was time for dinner and homework. Every week a few more girls joined. Soccer was co-ed in their part of the state until the kids turned ten—much too old in his opinion—so they made their own niche for the girls to play among themselves. They started with eight girls and ended with more than twenty.

When league play began in late-summer, Chase moved Tylea up an age level to compete on an all-girl team he'd volunteered to coach. But she wasn't sure about leaving the co-ed team and playing against older girls.

As they sat in his Jeep before sign-ups, she said, "You worry about me getting knocked down by the boys."

"That's true. It happens a lot."

"I get back up."

"You'll play on all-girl teams when you're older, anyway."

"I'll miss playing with Max and Ryan. And even Harrison."

"I'll miss coaching them. But the kick-arounds have been fun, right?"

"I like walking to the field from the library. I like playing with the girls."

"This whole season will be just like that."

"Will I be a captain?" Chase had handed out little felt patches in the shape of the letter C for a parent to sew onto the shoulder of three of his players each season. His captains were chosen for hustle and for gathering cones at the end of practice. It was the captains who the referee called out to midfield for pre-game coin flips. While giving last-minute pep-talks to his huddled team, he'd observe his three captains out of the corner of his eye as they trotted out, listened to instructions, and watched the coin being tossed. They'd decide on a goal to defend, shake hands, then jog back for their "One, two, three, team!" chant.

"I'll need someone to show the new girls all the things we've been learning."

"Like Cruyff turns and shielding?"

"Right."

"I can show them, but some are already in middle school. They won't listen."

"A captain figures out a way to make her team pay attention," he told her. "Being a captain still means picking up cones, but it's also about being a leader, especially now that you're older."

"You'll help me figure it out?"

"Yup, that's what a coach is for. Some of the girls on this new team haven't played much soccer before. I need a couple of girls who aren't afraid to get up in front of everyone and demonstrate moves."

"But don't act like a know-it-all, right?"

"That's a good starting point."

"When I nutmegged that kid last year he got mad and knocked me down." She'd worked hard to learn to dribble the ball between a defenders legs and then sprint around them to receive her own pass. It left the defender embarrassed, sometimes even angry.

"Well, if you nutmeg an older girl, she might get mad and knock you down, too."

"But I'll still try and nutmeg them, right?"

Chase made Tylea a captain the season after he murdered Bernie. Mitra had sewn a captain's C on the left shoulder of her uniform. The extra responsibility seemed to boost her confidence. She treated soccer less as a sport than a math problem—something she knew she could solve.

"That girl always dribbles to her left, Dad." And he'd see

she was right. "Number four always back-pedals and doesn't challenge. I could take her deep for a cross to Sarah."

And she would.

Despite his uncertain future and whatever DB6 had in store, the worries disappeared on Saturdays. All Chase's concerns hovered around the best way to keep his center forward from being trapped offside, although he now had a potentially volatile Iranian scientist along for the ride. Chase had witnessed his father-in-law's version of cutthroat Monopoly with his granddaughter, had seen him hurl a vase at Vanna White for refusing to expose letters he was certain were correct.

"The sky looks as though it is having a nightmare." Doctor Bam was leaning forward between the front seats as Chase pulled into the entrance road of the other team's field complex. Dark clouds rolled across the treetops, but the forecast only mentioned light showers. It had rained on and off all week and the field would be muddy.

Before Chase switched off the engine, he turned to prepare Doctor Bam for the team the girls would be facing. "We're playing what's called a 'select team' today. Our parents know to be extra supportive of the girls because it's a program that has cuts, more like an all-star team."

"So we will make them fall hard in miserable defeat," Doctor Bam said. "It will be an even greater victory!"

"Courtney's here," Tylea said, pulling on her shin guards and folding her socks down over them.

"There's no misery and no great victories. This is a chance for our girls to play their very best," Chase tried. "Our league schedules matches like these to give them an opportunity to improve by playing over their heads. It isn't about winning or losing in any of the games, and especially not today."

"Nonsense. Today will be triumph!"

"Brianna's here."

Chase saw flashes of yellow behind their car, knew his entire team was arriving.

"You have to behave," Mitra warned, taking his hairy hand in hers. "Promise you'll cheer nicely? This is about the girls having fun."

"That one in the enemy uniform looks like Saddam Hussein," Doctor Bam said, wagging a finger, but at least his voice was low.

During warm-ups, Chase smiled at his wife, who had blown him a kiss from the far sideline. Her father was still clutching the dirty sack, making what looked to be friendly offerings to the parents. Chase chose not to consider what type of animal protein was inside the lumpy cookies.

As expected, the team of all-stars ran the score up early, and each wave of subs did just as much damage as their starters. Shots that didn't find net gonged off the cross-bar, and their forwards charged the rebounds again and again. Chase had all eleven players back defending against a scoring frenzy. His goalie and fullbacks were hanging their heads each time the ref whistled a goal and walked the ball to midfield for another kick-off.

Across the field, parents were cowering away from Mitra's father, giving plenty of room to the lunatic shouting what must be vulgar threats in a strange language. Chase thanked god the man reverted to his mother tongue when drunk or distraught. Mitra was doing her best to calm him.

It was six to zero as the whistle blew for halftime. The teenage referee jogged over to their sideline. "It's okay if you guys wanna quit."

The boy glanced over his shoulder toward the crazy man in the white lab coat, obviously hoping they'd pack him up and cart him away as fast as possible.

"We don't quit," Tylea told the referee, and then looked around at her teammates for agreement.

"My wife will keep him under control," Chase said, stepping

away from the huddle with the boy. "Look, I understand if you have to call the game off. It's his birthday and he wanted to come. But I want the girls to finish."

"If he's swearing, I'm supposed to have him removed."

"He's from a country where they cut things off the losers," Chase said, but that didn't seem to reassure the boy. "If she can't settle him down, just blow the whistle and the game's over. Fair enough?"

Chase went back to his girls, who were drinking water and resting in the wet grass. Some were crying, and others sulked. He told them the score didn't matter; there were no standings, no record of wins or losses in their league. What counted was trying to win the ball each play, not trying to win the game. He told them he didn't care how many goals the opposition scored, but to take this chance to show courage and demand respect.

As halftime ended, they circled up and put their hands in the middle.

"We can beat them, Coach," Tylea said, and her teammates murmured agreement.

Chase knew they couldn't win, but that they could try.

A few minutes into the second half, Chase's center-midfielder dribbled past two defenders, then found her right wing open deep. Brianna brought the ball into the penalty area and sent a hopeful crossing pass to Tylea, who was cutting toward the goal on a diagonal run. It was a terrific play, but the defender was just too big. She easily out-jumped the little striker to head the ball out of the box to a teammate, who collected the pass and brought the ball safely over midfield.

Tylea and her teammates hustled back to help on defense. They fought for every ball despite being down by six goals. They charged each loose ball, challenged every forward run and made desperate clears from in front of their own goal. Against a team of all-stars, they had stopped sulking and played as if it were a scoreless tie.

Chase saw Doctor Bam sitting quietly in the mud on the far sideline, brooding, lab coat spread around him showing a constellation of brown freckles on his chest. He looked for Mitra, understanding for the first time what it must have been like for her as a child. Sure, she'd been raised to believe that life was meant to be spent hunched over in a laboratory, time frozen and practically meaningless; the father/daughter relationship a slight variance on that of professor and student. But that day Chase glimpsed something new—her father's inability to understand something so fundamental in his world as a coach. The simple concept of teaching kids to have fun whether they were winning or losing.

With less than ten minutes remaining, Tylea was charging after a loose ball at midfield when she was tackled from behind, bouncing hard and sliding face-first. The referee whistled for a stoppage and gave a yellow card. Chase ran out to kneel next to his daughter as she battled back tears, her face muddy and scraped. She writhed silently on the sloppy ground, clasping one knee in both hands. He cupped her head away from the wet grass and waited to see if the initial sharp pain would pass, as the trainer was radioed to come from another field.

Chase glanced beyond his little girl to where Mitra was holding back her father. He had risen from the mud, red-faced, eyes filled with murderous rage. The young referee witnessed this, too, was keeping Chase between him and the crazy old foreigner.

"I'm okay," Tylea finally croaked to the circle of hovering teammates. "It's okay." She rolled onto her knees in the muck, slowly rising to her wobbly legs. Slinging her arms over the shoulders of two teammates, she limped to the sideline. Once she was facing away from the other team, she let the tears flow quietly, in muddy rivulets onto her golden uniform.

With two minutes to go and the score unchanged, Tylea dropped her icepack and stood next to her father on the sideline. They watched the long clearing balls, as the other team's defense hunkered down and played everything safe to preserve the shutout. Chase was sure Tylea noticed the same open space about thirty yards in front of the opposition goal being left undefended. Their centerback was exhausted, hanging out at midfield, waiting for the clock to run out.

"Let me try it," his little captain said, bending and flexing her knee, which had begun turning a deep shade of purple. "I can score."

Chase called for a sub on the next throw-in.

Chapter 22

T HEY WERE IN their favorite spot along the wall in the deep
end of the pool.

"Push me to the bottom!" Tylea would happily screech,
over and over, as she took a deep breath and held her hands
tight against her sides, legs together and toes pointed down, as
straight as a pencil. She'd begin to sink, and Chase would put
his hand on the top of her head and push, leveraging against
the side of the pool with his other. Done just right, she would
swoosh downward, cutting through the water like a knife,
propelled to the bottom of the ten-foot pool. She'd flatten her
feet out, squat and then push off the bottom, thrusting herself
back to the surface.

They'd played this game a hundred times under the summer
sun, surrounded by laughing and screaming children of
families who lived here or rented by the season.

The pool dream first crept into Chase's sleep later that
summer. It started out vague, hard to remember, just bits and
pieces. But each recurrence was more vivid, usually invading
his subconscious in the hours just before dawn. It always began

innocently enough, just him and Tylea spending an afternoon along the wall in the deep end.

In the dream, she wouldn't stop at the bottom because there suddenly was no bottom. Just before disappearing into the cloudy blue depths she'd look back up at him and cry out, "No, Daddy!" He'd try to tell her not to speak, that she had to keep holding her breath. But all the air streamed out of her lungs in a long line of tiny bubbles which he recognized as trapped sobs. He could hear her crying as they popped all around him.

The dream changed toward the end of the summer. He began catching glimpses of something that had grabbed her from below and was dragging her down into the bottomless depths. Yes, he'd pushed his little girl, but something snagged her and wouldn't let go. He saw the white knuckles of a hand encircling Tylea's ankle, and the pale arm that was pulling and pulling. One night, he saw the face of Mitra.

The woman he'd loved and married was drawing Tylea down into the abyss, wrenching the precious air out of his child, stealing her away to a place impossibly out of reach.

But it wasn't the Mitra he knew. He could tell from a glimpse of her eyes it was someone very different, a stranger.

It was a woman he'd never met.

Chapter 23

T HE ASSIGNMENT WAS murder.
  An encrypted email from DB6 appeared in Chase's inbox during the first cool days of October. He hadn't seen it right away, only checking when he went online for something else. It had been the weather this time. The extended forecast, a look at the radar, then over to his inbox as an afterthought. It was a message marked urgent, an assignment to kill a man and grab a laptop computer. Make and model, the guy's name, address, and brief physical description went along with the death sentence.

Chase came close to clicking the delete button, forgetting he'd read the message. It would have been so easy and made so much sense the way his life was going. Nightmares? Everyone had a few nightmares here and there. Had something changed between Mitra and him? He supposed they were still recuperating from what had happened in Bernie's bedroom. Better to let it fade, the way things faded at the bottom of a deep swimming pool.

Richard Holeva's home was on a narrow road that wound through small towns in Northern New Jersey. Towns with familiar names Chase knew from growing up in the next county. He'd played soccer and baseball on some of their high school fields.

Holeva had no immediate neighbors, just an old, non-working farm across the street, its owners selling pints of raspberries from an honor-system table out front. A hand-printed sign read THREE DOLLARS. According to township records, Holeva had a pair of licensed dogs, which would be an issue. But his house was surrounded by woods and there was a row of pine trees in front for easy cover. No alarm services were available in the area and the local township police only had three full-time officers, according to their website.

He should have been given more information. Married, arrest record, military record, gun permits—things that could provide a heads-up. Even something easy like the occupation listed on his tax returns. Gun store owner? Hazardous chemical engineer?

There was a single exterior light at the end of a hundred-foot driveway, then plenty of shadows and unkempt shrubs in front of the ranch-style house. There was the front door and eight windows for possible entrance, and an attached two-car garage on the right side with probable access to the kitchen. The slope of the yard fell away, so the rear of the house was actually two stories. A deck ran the length of the top floor in back, but that's all Chase could tell from slow drive-bys.

He stashed his Jeep less than a quarter mile down the road, behind the guts of a new-home construction site. Lifting the hood, he used a wrench to loosen one battery cable. It would look like a drywaller's broken-down vehicle, just in case this was a routine spot for the cops to check. With a third of the soccer season remaining—and a lifetime with his little girl—it was no time to be sloppy. And he already had a bad feeling about this job.

It was dark when Chase walked away from his Jeep and followed the beam of his small flashlight. He stopped at the road to listen for cars, then turned and jogged toward Holeva's house. The road was lined by thick trees to the last fifty yards, but no cars came. He stepped onto Holeva's property, found a spot with a good view and waited.

Holeva arrived at six forty-five, using an automatic garage door opener to pull his Ford Explorer into one of the two parking spots. He left the door open and went inside to let out his dogs—two yellow Labs. The dogs pissed on half a dozen bushes before clamoring back into the garage for bowls of dry kibble. Holeva stayed with them, tinkering while they finished. The dogs then came back outside to crap along the narrow lawn, off to the right of the house.

Holeva was dressed casually in jeans and a long-sleeved button-down shirt. He wore running shoes and didn't have a visible cellphone.

With a short scope, Chase could have dropped him from where he watched with a single shot, snatched the computer and put distance between him and this place in a matter of minutes. But he wasn't a hit man, he was a reporter slash spy, and didn't have an arsenal of high-power rifles. The feeling that something was very wrong about this job grew stronger, wouldn't let his heart and breathing recover after the short jog. Chase stood on the dark carpet of pine needles and newly fallen leaves, certain it was his last job for DB6. He didn't sign on to be an assassin. Exactly what would they do if he simply stopped reading his emails? Would they send someone to try and convince him to keep working? Or had the screw-up in Vermont changed things? Was being sent here to kill a man part of that change?

When the dogs were inside and settled, Chase walked across the front lawn right up to the front left corner of the house. He could hear music and Holeva's voice as he sang along; he smelled roasting meat. The shower turned on. At eight, Holeva saved Chase the trouble of searching for the laptop by pulling a case from inside the closet door of his small, front bedroom office. Chase moved right up to the window—black cap and sweater absorbing the light through the glass—and watched Holeva power up and click open the browser. Holeva opened a mail server that looked vaguely familiar from across the room.

Chase backed away, slipped off his dark cotton cap and pulled the white shirt collar to expose it at the neckline of his sweater. He removed his PPK from its shoulder holster, checked the indicator pin to confirm the round in the chamber, and clicked off the safety. He made three unhurried, polite knocks on the front door. Nothing urgent sounding that might cause an adult male to first dial the cops, even out in these suburbs at this time of night.

Both dogs barked, sounding curious rather than angry.

"I'm so sorry." Chase was congenial over the dog racket, as the front door was unlocked and swung partly open. "I'm coming from my mother's home, and can't believe I ran out of gas." He gestured out toward the road, shaking his head apologetically.

"Oh, sure, okay," Holeva began, adjusting his bathrobe and trying to usher both large dogs out of the way. "Sorry, they'll lick you to death before …"

Chase's gun pressed to the side of the man's head.

"Put them in the garage." Chase's voice was slow and firm. *No need to make this all crazy. Just keep things calm*, he thought. But what was he waiting for? Leaving his Jeep exposed wasn't a huge risk, but any risk was bad. Risks had a cumulative effect. Half of him wanted to pop the man right there, just do the hit and get out. But something was wrong with this situation. The dead silence from DB6, then a domestic job so close by? Chase was hired as a spy, not a cold-blooded murderer. And DB6 knew this. They had to expect him to have apprehensions. They would have told Chase if this guy was plotting to import black-market radioactive materials from Russia. They'd have justified the hit for his benefit.

Or would they?

"Slow and easy." Chase followed Holeva through to the kitchen to shut the dogs in the garage. His finger tight on the trigger, he let Holeva turn and face him after closing off the dogs, who'd begun to whine at the stranger. Chase took a step back.

"I know who you are," Holeva said, and reached up to casually run both hands through his damp hair. "And I'd feel a whole lot more comfortable if you'd lighten your grip on that trigger."

"You have ten seconds to live, so you might want to talk fast," Chase said, without meaning it at all. Somehow, from somewhere deep inside his brain, he suddenly knew the swimming pool nightmare he'd been having was in some way real.

"Limp Shockley was my recruiter," Holeva said. "Your assignment to kill me didn't come from DB6 or the CIA, it came from the outside."

"What do you mean the outside?" Chase asked, but he already knew. He knew it in his heart and in his legs, which now threatened to collapse.

"Your wife, Chase, is one of the bad guys. I have a file for you to read on my computer." Holeva pushed past him, brushed the gun out of his face. He'd called him Chase.

"Stop," Chase said, but there was no stopping.

"She's an Iranian agent," Holeva called over his shoulder, and Chase's finger very nearly pulled the trigger.

Instead of reading the file about his wife, Chase slipped out the front door. He didn't need to read it. It fit together like the last pieces of a jigsaw puzzle. It took him over three hours to get home, but he wouldn't remember the drive. He just drove and drove, parked his Jeep when he got to the house and headed inside. He climbed out of his clothes, shoved his holstered gun on top of the bookshelf, and slid into bed next to Mitra, who had fallen asleep reading, as usual. He carefully pulled off her glasses and set them on the nightstand, along with her book.

Chase woke up just as the sky was transitioning from black to purple and quietly wandered into Tylea's room. She was surrounded by dozens of stuffed animals, sleeping on her belly with her hands tucked underneath. Her little kid breath still sweet in her sleep, Chase kissed her soft cheek and told her he loved her. She'd laid her book and glasses on the nightstand.

He went back to bed and fell asleep again. The nightmare didn't come.

Hours later, Mitra's car door woke him. She was loading Tylea in the back seat for school, just outside their bedroom window. He sat up in the shadowy room, waiting for her car to start, but something was different from the normal routine. No car engine, only low music from her speakers, and then the crunch of footsteps in the crushed gravel leading back to the kitchen door.

He glanced up at the high bookshelf where his gun should have been. The open end of the thin leather holster was facing him, and even in the bad light he could see it was empty. The kitchen door opened and closed, and there were light steps on the carpet outside their bedroom. The door pushed open. Mitra stood there a moment, momentarily silhouetted, before stepping inside and closing the door behind her.

Chase was grateful she wasn't smiling. He really wanted to believe she was regretting having to do this.

"I love you," he told her.

"I love you, too." She squeezed the trigger.

Chapter 24

CHASE HOPED THE song wouldn't be disco.

He could hear the cranky old CD changer's inner mechanisms struggling with the next disc. The distinct clicking and snapping echoed inside their small, high-ceilinged house in the hills, making its way through the open kitchen door to where he lay bleeding. The player hadn't been cleaned in years—if ever—and would sometimes skip past disc after disc before some glob of dust particles dislodged from the special eye on its own, bringing life back to music.

Disco would have added insult to injury. It was as if a KC and the Sunshine Band brotherhood existed among Third World dictators and drug lords he'd encountered. He needed something peaceful, encouraging.

Stoney had accused him of always worrying too much, sweating the details beyond what any sane person cared about. Chase recognized the irony in how he seemed to have missed so many of the details that had led him to his current state of affairs. And it left quite a bit more to worry over. But those worries could wait. Instead of his wife's Ultra Disco Dance Fever workout CD, the air was filled with the most beautiful song in the world. Bob Marley was how he put his little angel to sleep every night. Even a terrible singer like Chase gets the job done when the words mean so much to a little girl who's had a long, hard day.

And, boy, did Chase need a lullaby at that very moment.

The words told him not to worry, that it would turn out all right.

God, he was so cold and so hot, life suddenly complicated by paradox. His head felt like it was floating, yet filled with lead. He was trying not to fall asleep; it wasn't quite time to die. He wanted to hear the song one last time.

Blood seeped from the corner of his mouth, drop by drop, urged on by his heart's rhythm. It splashed on his shoulder and raced down his bicep and forearm, pooling in the cup of an upturned palm. He watched the flood level rise until it spilled over, some of it marking a path along his index finger where, like a tiny ruby waterfall, the drops cascaded one after the other into the goldfish pond.

Drip. Drip. Drip. Maybe it was a mixture of the soothing music and the hypnotic sound of the dripping making him so very, very tired.

Yes, his fat, overfed goldfish with gigantic eyes were sure going to miss him. There they were, hoping for a morning snack, making big Os with their mouths pressed right up to the air. Big "Feed me now" Os. But Chase had been lucky to get this far, having stumbled out of the bedroom, along the hall, and through the kitchen door. He had staggered down the deck stairs, finally collapsing on the large flat boulder at the edge of the small pond he'd dug and lined with heavy plastic after they'd bought the house.

All the blood … he was sure he'd made an absolute mess of the carpet, but the linoleum would be just fine. How long since they'd water-sealed the deck? The wood boards should be okay after a quick power-wash. No need for sanding and re-staining.

His daughter had named each and every one of the of the twenty-three surviving fish—a raccoon family had come through and eaten half the population—but he wasn't sure which of them took a taste of his blood before backing up, shaking its head disapprovingly, then bolting into the murky depths. *Sorry guys.* He really hated to disappoint them, but their bright orange can of flakes in the shed might just as well have been on Pluto.

And thirsty? The kind of thirst you get from trying to swallow a handful of baby powder. His tongue seemed to creak like an old stair as he willed it forward, hopelessly far from the surface of the water.

This was dying: being dreadfully tired and everything beyond your grasp.

Bob Marley was still telling him not to worry …

Chase had never been very good at managing worries. When you abandoned people you loved—like your best friend and your mother and father—a dark space formed in your mind. Chase imagined the space as a tumor-like black hole, surviving and growing as it ate away at the good things. But he also knew he wasn't special, that everyone had holes. He giggled painfully when it dawned on him that he'd recently acquired a brand new hole, thank you very much, Mitra. God, laughing was no good; it burned and twisted his guts.

As the minutes passed and the blood dripped, the pain from the hole punched somewhere in his stomach receded. It seemed that dying wasn't particularly excruciating once you got past the initial blast, which hurt like an absolute motherfucker. And he'd barked his right shin on the coffee table during the uneven journey out of the house. But then it was okay and the pain became manageable—as long as you kept from laughing. Chase was exhausted, and the rock was cold and not so comfortable, but nothing hurt anymore.

Chase decided that dying was mostly just melancholy. Despite some pretty big issues he'd had with Mitra, it was mighty sad to think of the lonely darkness he was headed for. He would miss dancing with her, especially those crazy weekend nights before Tylea and before her disco fad started. His petite biochemist turned small town librarian had been an amazing sight under the flashing lights. Floating among the Mohawk-headed, industrial punk boys, and the black-lipped goth girls with hulking shoulders, Mitra had been his little leather-clad pinball. If conjuring up images is something humans are able to pass time with in the hereafter, then those are the snippets he'd use to recall his wife.

Tylea? His funny little genius who'd made the newspaper as one of the rare children accepted into American Mensa. The reporter described her as a tiny, shy, bespectacled girl, politely quizzing the journalist on Occam's razor and the superstring theory during the interview.

His little girl would be crying herself to sleep an awful lot, and only because her father had screwed up and not seen this coming.

Tears burned his dry eyes, blurred the world. He remembered the look on Tylea's face when she'd scored her first goal. After three seasons and dozens of games against girls and boys who always seemed to tower over her, after being elbowed and knocked down and even laughed at by a couple of mean kids, after hundreds of hours of drills and juggling, of one-touch passes and shots, she had finally scored. And it was what they called a skill goal, as opposed to a lucky shot or just firing a blast from fifteen yards. Coach Chase's little striker dribbled through two fullbacks and chipped a soft shot over the diving goalie. Tiny Tylea Rain Allen looked at her coach with nothing more than surprise. Then she sprinted back to midfield for the kick off, ready to do it again.

Soccer is so beautiful. She is so beautiful.

Chase wondered if you could still love someone after you were dead.

And he prayed Tylea wouldn't be the one to find his body,

although she'd long since ditched her goldfish feeding chore. It was just too sad for her after the raccoon family incident. Christ, what would this incident do to her?

At some point, a new Marley song had begun. Chase thought he might have drifted in and out of sleep, in and out of consciousness, maybe.

The Rasta told him to rise up …

He'd had a great run, for sure. The nature of his job wouldn't let him show them off to the neighbors, but he was proud of the souvenirs collected over the years. A leper's right index finger he'd received as a present, his gun—the one used to shoot him, Adolph Hitler's favorite—the quarter he'd flipped in his dorm room that Stoney had finally found. All were treasures.

The reggae raised his energy level a bit and his eyes stopped tearing. He could see the blood more clearly as it began pouring into the pond, rather than dripping. Minutes passed and his arms began to tingle, seemed to go to sleep. He was no doctor, but could feel his pulse changing, becoming erratic, as though his heart was confused. By then a crap-load of blood had found its way into the pond.

"I gotta move, boys," Chase told his fish, not sure his tongue made the words, but pretty sure they wouldn't understand anyway. And without food flakes, he was just a huge disappointment. He struggled mightily, clenching his teeth in case any pain decided to return, as he rocked back and forth, side to side. With a final thrust, he managed to roll onto his back.

His new view showed exactly why they'd picked this house, with the tall skinny trees soaring upward. These trees couldn't be worried about wasting energy on lower branches. Their early lives had been purely a race to the sunshine, where they could finally spread out, grow leaves and sway mightily in the wind.

In a strong breeze, the canopy of trees waved like a field of wheat, tiny snatches of sunshine peeking through like flashes of lightning. Their chalet-style home faced the woods beyond the fish pond. It had two sets of sliding glass doors, with four huge panes of glass above. It was a struggle to heat in the winter, but he had loved feeling so immersed in nature, even when Tylea snuggled in next to him on the couch and stole the TV remote.

His little princess, Tylea.

His tiny, shy, bespectacled girl. He'd put the newspaper clipping in his journal.

Chase knew it broke one of the primary rules in the Spy Handbook—if there was such a thing—but he had his reasons for keeping a journal. Originally, he'd expected to one day burn it after having quit the business once and for all—one final grand gesture before setting out on a new life, with new adventures. Or maybe it was more like burning a mortgage after mailing off the last payment, a demonstration to say good riddance to that monthly burden.

Come to think of it, if his bosses ever found a journal containing details of his missions he could have been shot for treason. He laughed and it hurt again. And then the cold and heat came back hard and deep. His world blurred. It broke his heart to abandon Tylea like this. Even after she'd graduated from her big-kid booster seat, he had never left her alone in the Jeep, not even to run into the store or Post Office for just a second. Not even if he could still see her from inside. No way, not even when she begged him to go by himself so she could finish her book. He would never leave her alone.

Until now.

God, he was tired.

Why hadn't he seen this coming? He wanted her to know it didn't hurt in the end. When he'd started all this crap, he was just a stupid college kid, all jazzed-up about making a difference in the world. It had seemed so exciting. But his priorities all changed when Tylea came along. The best moments in his life were with her. Yes, and with her mom. He wanted to tell her not to be mad at him for dying and definitely not to take it out on her mother. None of it was Mom's fault. She had a job to do. And he could tell Tylea for a fact that even the worst wounds eventually stopped hurting. The pain slipped away and you forgot why you were crying.

The things we can't change, we just need to learn to accept.

There was silence. But it wasn't because Chase was dead. He could still turn his head and see two little orange guys, again looking hopeful, staring up at the gigantic, shadowy thing that used to bring food.

Click.

Chase knew the familiar sound. It was the CD player when it turned off completely and all the green and red lights winked out. The quiet was too much. After a few small test breaths he swallowed a big gulp of fresh air, intent on filling the void. Okay, he had a lousy voice, but it was time for a lullaby.

Chase began to sing.

Chapter 25

WEBSTER JON WIDGY streaked down the left sideline, waving his good arm, shouting for the soccer ball. He was clearly offside by twenty yards should the ball be passed to him, but this referee was not heartless enough to whistle the infraction. They'd never ask for it, but a team with four young lepers already down by a dozen goals catches a break every once in a while.

A twelve goal deficit was still pretty close for Chase's team, all things considered.

His own little white ghost—his Little Zonbi—was pushing the ball up over the smudged chalk at midfield. Two tall boys marked her tightly, but they were no match. She stopped the ball with the sole of her right cleat, pulled it back to draw both defenders even closer, then flicked the ball forward between both their sets of legs and sprinted around them to receive her own pass.

"Dooble nutmeg!" screamed the delighted mothers who lined the dusty field. The women danced in the same spot the cheerleading lepers had twitched and murmured approval years earlier. Chase supposed most of those lepers were dead, and new drugs were helping to end the cycle of misery.

These cheerleaders were much more animated. Except for the tattered rag dresses and thick accents, these were the same mothers as on American fields, screeching at their kids, unsure of the rules but often swearing at the refs anyway. Chase's Haitian Creole was progressing slowly, so practices were a mix of languages, but soccer was more a game of show than tell. And in a land accustomed to so much anguish, Chase tried to be careful with words. His soccer moms began assigning nicknames during the first day of official practice: Difom, Kakas, Kochma, and Maldyok, which roughly translated to Deformed, Carcass, Nightmare, and Bad Eye.

He made a new rule regarding nicknames.

Chase had suffered his own hurtful nickname early on, when first disassembling the pot farm. Moreau's ranch had still been protected by hundreds of dead bodies when Chase took it over, claimed it for their home. He would hear the word Malveyan— or Evildoer—while picking up supplies in Port-au-Prince. But once all the bodies were laid to rest as carefully as someone not terribly familiar with the controls of a front-end loader could manage, curiosity began replacing suspicion.

"Lion is okay," he'd told the mothers, who believed nicknames were critical to the sport. "Nicknames should be positive. Like Tig, or Rebel, but, *silvouple*, nothing about missing body parts."

Zonbi stuck for Tylea and Jeneral was sometimes his.

The soccer dads were a different matter. The Catholic priests, responsible for the property and many of the children, had recently voted to ban all the fathers who hadn't already been killed in the recent coup d'état, maybe for the rest of the season. Following a questionable call, two of them had brandished machetes and chased a referee off the field and down a narrow street. It was tough enough to get decent refs without crap like that.

The moms, though, had hearts in the right places. They were slowly learning proper etiquette and no longer cheered wildly when opposing players were injured. Getting them to stop bringing rotten fruit and cloudy water for halftime nourishment was another matter. Chase was still a stranger in a very strange land.

Tylea continued her magic on the soccer field. She dribbled past a chasing fullback who was unusually tall and bony as a skeleton. She did her step-over trick, faking a move toward the goal, and then dribbled into the penalty area to set up her right foot.

Webster Jon was now at the far post, unmarked because the other team knew he had only one working eye and often ran the wrong way when someone tried to pass to him; his depth perception had been wrecked by Hansen's Disease. The boy's breathing was wet and raspy because much of his nose was gone. Opposing players didn't like to cover him for a number of reasons, even though all the lepers had the proper medical slips proving they'd been on Dapsone for at least two weeks and were not contagious.

"Zonbi, here I am!" He jumped up and down like a spastic pogo stick on his good right leg. Paralyzed small muscles in his left foot had turned his toes into claws and he couldn't tie that cleat. He hopped and hopped, his beautiful new uniform—Chase had bought them for the whole team—dancing as if on a string.

Tylea had a plan from the moment she'd stolen the ball deep in her team's own end. She wasn't captain just because Chase was coach; she'd earned it through her leadership, despite being the tiniest player on their dirt field. Her wonderful skills were from long summers of hard work and her love for the game, easily making up for any lack of muscle and size.

"Now, now, Zonbi girl!" Webster Jon called, and Tylea took one more quick dribble before chipping a crossing pass over the charging goalie. She hadn't struck the ball hard, just enough to send it floating across the goal mouth. Chase's left wing, Webster Jon, stopped his crazy hopping and tried to get a focus on the ball's gentle arc toward him, the wide open net waiting for an easy header.

The mothers also froze. Their cheers stopped, and Chase could almost hear them draw in a deep, collective breath. All their teammates stopped to watch this pass, this gentle strike that seemed to travel in slow motion, first climbing out of reach of the goalie, then the lunging head of the last fullback. It had a slight backspin as it reached its apex then began its downward path toward Webster Jon's grimy forehead. Poor Webster Jon couldn't safely practice headers because of all the havoc his condition had wreaked on his face. Chase wouldn't allow it. He had to look out for all the players, but some more than others. Webster Jon's own mom wasn't here to cheer, having left him as a baby at one of the countless Port-au-Prince orphanages.

But in a world that seemed to be trying its absolute best to run over or drag under an innocent, already damaged boy, Chase's Little Zonbi refused to relinquish hope. She recognized the opening, the possibility of this fleeting chance for a kid which life had already been mauled pretty good.

CHASE HAD SPENT two weeks recovering from a single bullet wound to the abdomen, while Mitra's father tried his best to look after his granddaughter. Her inconsolable crying, the accusing CIA interrogations, and the apparent loss of his only child had left the man withered and hollow-eyed by the time the hospital set Chase free.

"You take care of this little scientist," he'd said, hugging Tylea hard on his front step. Chase's belly ached, but he knew Doctor Bam's heart was broken. Chase had never seen him cry before. "It is hard being both mother and father. Very, very hard."

In a bag of medicines and bandages given to him on his last day in the hospital, Chase found an envelope with a cashier's check for five thousand dollars. It included instructions to disappear from the country.

So he gathered up his little girl and escaped to the bottom of his nightmare pool, a place where life was heavily cloaked in thick layers of despair. He chose a destination where even the slightest glimmer of hope would be hard to miss, even for him. Tylea's mother was likely adjusting after a long debriefing process in Tehran, as the newly emancipated duo were settling in at an abandoned marijuana ranch on Montagne Terrible. The Jeep ride up was done after nightfall on purpose. Sometimes there really are monsters in the dark.

Haiti is a place so wrecked by wars and brutality that the last threads of hope remain only in hidden places. Fear is insidious, while love and compassion have been poisoned like the dying earth, the scorched and barren countryside, and the oily water. Nothing grows for very long, except maybe in secret places, where there were once great green fields of marijuana; where shiploads of guano and truckloads of nutritious eggs shells brought the dead soil back to life. A place that could one day feed whole villages, with a little hard work and a lot of hope.

Tylea didn't leave her new room those first weeks. She'd drawn pictures or read one of her books for a while but mostly wanted to be alone, unless it was night. In the dark, she never let her dad wander farther than the bathroom, or to get a glass of water. Chase knew she could feel what was out in the dark, those real monsters.

And so he began cleaning up the death in the immediate area, tying a rope to Moreau's guardian zombies, dragging their leathery corpses out into the nearest field. It was hard labor in the incredible heat and he'd shower off the stench a half-dozen times a day.

Each day, Tylea read a little more and began writing a journal. Chase felt more at ease, leaving her for a couple of hours at a time, but the same feeling of dread would return on the walk back up to the house after he was done zombie wrangling. His heart would be racing as he opened the front door, always imagining the worst as he went straight to her room. But there she would be, looking up at him from the middle of her bed curiously, her eyes puffy and red from recent tears.

Chase used the heavy equipment to dig a trench, a mass grave. He'd found a few young men from the valley who were desperate enough for money to help drag the lost souls to the edge of the pit, then send them rolling down to their final peace. At least he'd hoped it would be.

And then one day, Chase heard an unfamiliar noise when returning to the house to check on Tylea, a slapping sound echoing out of the open windows. He ran, throwing open the big heavy door and racing to her room.

"I'm sorry!" She was frightened and cradling something in her arms—a soccer ball found in one of the boxes in the hallway. She'd been juggling in her room, kicking the ball off one wall.

"Sweetheart." He grabbed her close, hugging her with the ball squeezed between them.

"I love you, Daddy."

"I love you, too."

"I miss Mommy so much." She buried her head in his chest.

"I do, too."

After the last of their supplies ran out, Tylea ventured into Port-au-Prince with him, bringing her soccer ball for comfort in this strange, crazy place. She carried her ball into the market like a Teddy bear as he gathered canned goods and powdered drink mixes. But as he was packing the groceries in the back of their truck, she'd dropped the ball to her feet, slowly dribbling over to a group of young boys in a corner of the dirt parking lot. One boy tried picking the ball up, but the oldest scolded him. Tylea motioned them into a circle and they passed the ball across and around, performing one of her team's drills. There was laughter.

Some of the laughter came from his little girl.

She sat staring out the window on the long drive back up the mountain and he could tell she was working on a plan.

"There are a lot of kids just hanging around, aren't there?"

On the next supply trip into Port-au-Prince, Tylea forced him to stop at an orphanage and then at the two Catholic churches within a few blocks of the market. Either directly or through an interpreter, she explained her plan, asking for the blessing of the adults in charge. Chase knew it was her smile and her hope that made them agree to her proposal.

Their soccer league had been formed with enough kids for six teams. And the teams were picked in the classic American playground style, where the oldest or best kids were divided up, then took turns choosing players. These older players were also going to be responsible for finding a parent, priest, or some local drunk to act as their coach and stand on the sidelines. Those were the rules.

Stepping forward, Tylea made it clear she wanted to be one of the six kids to pick a team. The drafting began, one by one, with the next best player going as the first pick, and so on. Tylea, who had sixth choice, pointed to a small group of boys huddled in the back, boys who didn't have their hands raised and weren't crying out, "*Souple, souple, souple!*" or, "Please, please, please!"

"*Ou!*" Tylea said, pointing to the most agile looking leper of the four—a tall young boy holding a deflated soccer ball under one arm. The boy limped away from his friends to get in line behind his new captain.

"You dumb, *blanc!*"

"*Aveg!*" another said, which was the word for blind, and the boys all laughed.

"*Asasen,*" Tylea said in a dramatic voice, shrugging toward the leper over her shoulder—who was cowering, crowding close—but the other, older boys stopped laughing. *Asasen* meant assassin in Creole.

"Okay, *blanc,* my turn." One of the older boys began the next round of picks, continuing until every child had a team.

Tylea had chosen all four available lepers.

"They are secret weapons," she told her father. "Nobody will cover a boy with leprosy."

But Chase knew she was kidding. She had picked the children who needed the most hope.

Tylea led her teammates in quiet ways. When it was especially hot, and some were dropping back and about to give up and walk the last lap during practice, she'd drop back, too, say a few things to them and match their stride. Those strides might be labored, but would never slow to a walk or a stop. They would always finish the run, and although Chase didn't think they ever came out and thanked her, he could tell by their looks it was what they meant to say. It seemed more than enough for her. This leadership made her a real captain.

Sometimes his little girl was ten, and sometimes she was much older and wiser than her father who'd run away with her to this place.

"You are different," the boys would say to her, touching the incredibly white skin of her forearm as they sat in a group, sipping water in the shade after practice.

"No, not different, you stupid boy," she'd say back, touching his uniform and hers at the same time. "We're the same team. We're the same."

And, like nearly all these children of poverty and war-ravaged Haiti, his little girl came from a broken home. Sometimes, late at night, she would cry inconsolably for her mom.

Chase did everything he could, although there was no way to replace a mother. And yet, even a man with a lousy singing voice could soften the sharp pain of the world, especially when the words meant so much to a little girl who's had a long, hard day.

He sang Bob Marley's song, the one that comforted him as he lay dying, assuring him that it would all work out.

When the tears finally stopped and she'd fallen asleep in her soft bed, in their new life, he'd kiss her pale cheek and head to the ebony writing desk in his bedroom to draw up some new plays, trying to figure out how to win a game, or at least come a little closer to winning.

No matter how much they have lost, everyone needs to feel there is still hope.

BACK UNDER THE glaring sun, Webster Jon Widgy moved the wrong way at the last second. The perfectly placed pass from Tylea somehow missed his dirty forehead by a foot, bounding harmlessly across the endline for a goal kick by the other team.

The moms began to cheer anyway. Tylea and Webster Jon ran back to their positions to defend, to try again. There was still plenty of time on the clock.

Hope was alive and well on their dirt field.

Discussion Questions for Book Groups

1. Chase Allen witnesses the slaughter of homeless boys during a college-sponsored aid program in Haiti. How does that incident affect his world view? Had you heard about such horrors before reading this account? Did this passage, along with other perspectives of life in Haiti presented in this novel, affect the way you regard that area now?

2. Chase has to decide whether to waste his summer smoking pot or take an internship with a local newspaper. What do you think leads him to make the responsible choice? What constitutes a fork in the road of life? Can you recall such a time in your own past? Did you recognize it as a turning point when it was happening?

3. Love and betrayal are major themes in this story. Chase is betrayed by his wife, but by keeping his true mission a secret, he is also a betrayer. Is he as much at fault as his wife, Mitra? Is he right to forgive her?

4. Another large theme in this novel is Loyalty to Country vs. Loyalty to Family. How does the cost of their missions affect Mitra and Chase's lives?

5. Chases encounters lepers at several points in this story, including the beginning and end. What does leprosy symbolize in this book? Does the leper finger represent

something other than the old woman's escape from her terrible existence?

6.   What do you think lies in store for Little Zonbi? Will she be able to escape her mother's legacy?

COLE ALPAUGH IS a former journalist, having worked at daily newspapers along the East Coast, as well as spending several years as a war correspondent in numerous hot-spots around the world for Manhattan-based news agencies. His work has appeared in dozens of magazines, as well as most newspapers in America. He was nominated by Gannett News Service for a 1991 Pulitzer Prize. Cole is currently a freelance photographer and writer living in Northeast Pennsylvania, where he also coaches his daughter's soccer kick-arounds. You can find him online at www.colealpaugh.com.

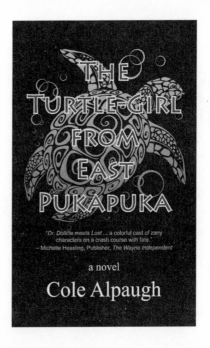

"*Dr. Dolittle* meets *Lost* ... a colorful cast of zany
characters on a crash course with fate."
— Michelle Hessling, Publisher, *The Wayne Independent*

a novel

Cole Alpaugh

THE ISLAND OF East Pukapuka lies in the path of a tsunami that will leave only one survivor...

BUTTER, a little girl more worried about the lives of the injured animals she cares for than her own. She is rescued by...

A LOGGERHEAD SEA TURTLE, who carries her away on his back. As she and her exhausted savior begin to sink, the girl is plucked out of the sea by...

JESUS DOBBY the boozy owner of a salvage boat who is thrilled, at first, to have found a genuine "turtle-girl" hybrid. Meanwhile...

DANTE WHEELER, a downhill racer, "dies" in a terrible skiing accident and revives in a twilight state, his memories of his former life gone forever. When he finally heals enough to leave the rehab facility, Dante heads to Polynesia, where he has found a new home in his dreams. There he enlists the help of...

OPHELIA, a beautiful blond policewoman who reluctantly agrees to transport him to East Pukapuka, where they will encounter…

JOPE AND RATU, a pair of bumbling pirates, who have stolen a vessel supplied with a mother lode of cocaine. They are soon hotly pursued by the drug-runners' hit man…

ALBINO PAUL, the descendent of cannibals, whose goal is to reclaim his heritage.

As in Alpaugh's beloved first novel, T*he Bear in a Muddy Tutu*, fate pokes its fickle finger in the lives of these hapless souls with as much clear intention as a three-year-old in a sandbox. Even the gods are incompetent. Alpaugh's world offers no lessons in morality. His characters are fatally flawed, hilarious, and heartbreakingly human.

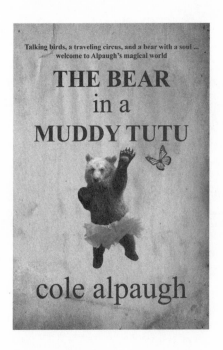

Talking birds, a traveling circus, and a bear with a soul ...
welcome to Alpaugh's magical world

THE BEAR
in a
MUDDY TUTU

cole alpaugh

WHAT BETTER PLACE FOR MISFITS
THAN A TRAVELING CIRCUS?

NEWSPAPER MAN LENNON BAGG is mourning the loss of his job and the abduction of his daughter by his ex-wife. Lennon rescues...

GRACEFUL GRACIE THE RUNAWAY BEAR, and helps her rejoin her trainer at...

A TRAVELING CIRCUS, which has illegally pitched its tents on a small island on the Jersey Shore. Their self-proclaimed shepherd is...

BILLY WAYNE, a wannabe cult leader, but when Lennon arrives, he is the one they turn to. Unbeknownst to Lennon, his daughter...

MORGAN is in Bermuda, having been told that her father is dead. Believing that dead people become birds, she is convinced that one day he will fly to her. Meanwhile...

LENNON AND BILLY have hatched a plan to save the circus. Lennon boards a plane headed into the Bermuda Triangle, along with a man who holds the record for being struck by lightning. And it's starting to cloud up...

IN THE BEAR IN A MUDDY TUTU, HOPE IS SOMETHING VIGOROUSLY AVOIDED BECAUSE IT USUALLY MEANS SOMEONE IS ABOUT TO BE RUN OVER BY A SPEEDING CAR.

THE POISON APPLES

LILY ARCHER

SQUARE
FISH

SQUARE
FISH

An Imprint of Macmillan

Square Fish and the Square Fish logo are trademarks of Macmillan
and are used by Feiwel and Friends under license from Macmillan.

Library of Congress Cataloging-in-Publication Data

Archer, Lily.
The Poison Apples / by Lily Archer.
p. cm.
Summary: At an elite Massachusetts boarding school, three fifteen-year-old
girls of very different backgrounds discover a common
bond and form a club to plot revenge against their evil stepmothers.
ISBN-13: 978-0-312-53596-4   ISBN-10: 0-312-53596-1
[1. Stepmothers—Fiction.   2. Boarding schools—Fiction.   3. Schools—Fiction.
4. Revenge—Fiction.   5. Best friends—Fiction.   6. Friendship—Fiction.
7. Massachusetts—Fiction.]   I. Title.   PZ7.A67466Poi 2007   [Fic]—dc22
2007032634

Originally published in the United States by Feiwel and Friends
Square Fish logo designed by Filomena Tuosto
First Square Fish Edition: January 2009
10 9 8 7 6 5 4 3 2 1
www.squarefishbooks.com

For my mother,
who is also my best friend
And for my best friends,
who are also my family

Prologue

Dear Stepmothers of the World:

As you probably know, more than 50 percent of marriages in America end in divorce. And more than 75 percent of divorced men end up remarrying. That means there are thousands—millions!—of stepmothers out there. Stepmothers in North Dakota. Stepmothers in Florida. Thin stepmothers and fat stepmothers. Rich stepmothers and poor stepmothers. Beautiful stepmothers and ugly stepmothers. Good stepmothers and bad stepmothers.

This book is not about the good stepmothers.

We're not saying good stepmothers don't exist. We know they do. We have faith. We know somewhere out there are stepmothers who love and care about their stepdaughters, stepmothers who give good advice and make goofy jokes and play Monopoly and rent slapstick comedies and take their stepdaughters out for Ethiopian food. In fact, there are probably *thousands* of girls out there with *really stellar* stepmothers.

Those girls are welcome to write a book about how great their stepmothers are.

We are not those girls.

We are the Poison Apples.

We all happen to have Incredibly Evil Stepmothers.

So. To any stepmothers who may feel that the stepmother population is unfairly represented in our book: We don't know what to say to you. Sorry? Honestly we have no idea why we ended up with such horrible stepmothers. Fate? Karma? Bad luck? In any case, we had enough good fate/karma/luck to meet one another at boarding school and form a family. Because the existence of the Poison Apples helped us realize something: You have to take your fate/karma/luck into your own hands. You cannot let the evil stepmother win.

This is our story.

To the good stepmothers: Keep on keepin' on. We hope to meet you someday.

To the bad stepmothers: You have been warned.

Signed,
The Poison Apples

PART
ONE

Alice Bingley-Beckerman

R. seemed okay at first. She invited me and Dad over for dinner at her apartment on the Upper West Side, and we spent most of the evening just standing around and watching her cook. R. was mesmerizing: she swept around the kitchen in her silk robe and purple eye shadow, stirring bubbling pots of marinara sauce and bending down every few seconds to kiss Godot, her Yorkshire terrier. I could tell Dad was charmed by her. She was beautiful and funny and she kept singing lines from different musicals. Dad would say, "*The Pajama Game*, right?" and she'd shriek, "YES! EXACTLY!" and then he'd sip his beer in this pleased-with-himself way. And it was nice she'd invited me. I guess it was like their first date, so it was a pretty cool move for her to say, "Why don't you bring your daughter?" It made her seem easygoing, sweet, kid-loving. Not at all like a crazy, jealous psychopath, right?

Wrong.

Dad and I were so innocent and unsuspecting. Probably because it was the first date Dad had been on since Mom died. We had no idea that R. Klausenhook—Tony Award–winning actress and darling of the New York theater scene—would turn out to be a bona fide Evil Person. Actually I think Dad still has no idea that R. is a bona fide Evil Person.

Hence the tragedy of my story.

The whole never-ending suckfest (that's what my friend Reena calls it—you'll hear about her later) started two years before, when I was thirteen and my mom died. She had cancer. It was pretty much the worst year of my life. Afterward I had to deal with all my classmates saying: "Oh my God, I'm so sorry. My great-grandmother died last year and it was really hard for me. I totally know what you're going through." I'd want to scream, *Your great-grandmother was ninety-five and living in a nursing home and you saw her three times a year, how could you possibly know what I'm going through—my MOTHER died, you idiot*, but instead I'd smile and nod. Because I make a point of not picking fights with people. I'm Alice. I'm the quiet girl in the funky clothes. Everyone likes me. Kind of. I'm everyone's third-best friend. This is what the entire school wrote in my junior high yearbook: "It was great knowing you! You are the sweetest!" Or: "You seem really really sweet! Have a great summer!" Or: "Thanks for being so sweet! You go, girl!" Eventually I realized that "sweet" meant no one knew me, and that (so far) I hadn't done anything to tick off anybody.

I did have it pretty good for my first thirteen years. I was an only child and I lived in this awesome brownstone in Brooklyn with my mom and dad. They were both writers. Pretty famous writers, actually. My dad is Nelson Bingley and

4

my mom is (was) Susan Beckerman. Maybe you've heard of them. They both wrote novels that got a lot of attention before I was born. Once I tried to read one of my mother's books, but it was way too weird. The first sentence had like three words in it that I didn't even know existed. But having two writers as my parents was really nice. They were at home a lot, typing away in their studies, and they always had these bizarro friends staying with us, like famous painters and musicians and movie directors. I still have this real glass eye that an Italian sculptor gave me as a birthday present. Other kids would come over to my house, shake their heads enviously, and say things like: "Your parents are the coolest." Yup, I was that kid. I had the cool parents.

But then one day I just had one cool parent.

It was rough for a while. Our house felt really big and empty, and there was a lot of me and Dad sitting silently in our dark living room every night and watching stupid TV programs that Mom would have hated. It also took me a whole year to stop myself from thinking, *Wait till Mom hears this*, whenever something interesting or cool happened. But then the day I stopped thinking, *Wait till Mom hears this*, was pretty horrible, too. Because there's forgetting your mother is dead, and then there's realizing that you're used to your mother being dead. The second feeling is actually worse.

Things went on like this for about a year and a half, until Dad wrote a play. It was his first play, and it was about a woman dying of cancer. Big surprise, right? But everyone *loved* it. Dad's agent called in the middle of the night and said she couldn't finish reading it because she was crying so hard. Three weeks later a Broadway theater picked it up and R. Klausenhook—the best actress in the city, the actress who

5

guaranteed sold-out houses and Tony Awards—wanted to star in it. Six weeks after that, it opened and *The New York Times* gave it a rave review, and Dad was smiling in a way he hadn't smiled since, well, since Mom, and three weeks after that, R. Klausenhook invited us over to her apartment for dinner. And I was happy for Dad. I truly was. I thought that maybe if he stopped being so sad all the time, I would stop being so sad all the time.

Dumb theory.

Anyway, R. really laid on the charm that first night. And the woman was an incredible cook. She made endive salad and garlic-roasted hen and baked eggs with tomato and basil sauce and this amazing raspberry tart sprinkled with fudge. Dad and I totally pigged out.

"Mmrf," Dad said, wiping his mouth with a napkin. "This is the best meal I've had in I don't know how long. Alice and I usually just microwave frozen fish sticks for dinner."

Now this is true. Dad and I did eat a lot of fish sticks. But somehow Dad's saying this to R. Klausenhook made me feel just a wee bit defensive. We were trying, you know? We were doing okay for ourselves.

"Oh no," said R. "That's awful. Food is unbelievably important to me. I believe that every meal should be its own sensual experience."

I didn't really know what she was talking about, but Dad listened intently and nodded his head like three times in a row.

R. reached across the table and placed her bejeweled fingers over mine. "What about you, Alice?" she asked. "What are your passions?"

"Um . . . ," I said. I looked to Dad for help. He just smiled blankly at me.

"You know," said R. "My passions are acting and food. And sex, of course. What are yours?"

I almost choked on my mouthful of baked eggs. "Uh . . ."

Dad jumped in. "Alice really loves snowboarding. Don't you, Alice?"

I nodded, relieved. "Yeah. Sure. I like snowboarding."

The truth was, I'd snowboarded about twice in my entire life. But okay. You could call it my passion. Whatever. I would have *liked* sex to be one of my passions, but I hadn't been given the opportunity to have it yet. I'd made out once with Keaton Church (this jerko senior) at a party on the Lower East Side during my freshman year, but he was just using me to make his ex-girlfriend jealous (they got back together the next day). That was the range of my experience. The only person who seemed interested in me was my second-cousin Joey Wasserman. Joey lived in Philadelphia and had a beard and smoked like six joints a day and tried to mack on me every Thanksgiving.

As Reena would say, my life was a real suckfest. I was fifteen, my mom had been dead for almost two years, and I'd never even had a boyfriend.

But things were about to get a lot worse.

Dad and I took a cab home that night after dinner at R.'s place, and he couldn't stop smiling. We didn't say anything for a while as we cruised down Madison Avenue, past all those fancy stores with their glowing storefronts. I breathed on the cab window and then absentmindedly drew a little *R* in the fogged-up glass.

"What does R. stand for?" I asked.

"Rachel," Dad said, this moony grin still plastered across his face.

7

"Then why doesn't she just call herself Rachel?"

He put his arm around me and kissed the top of my head. "I really like this woman, Alice. In addition to being wonderfully talented, she's very sweet and giving. She's not crazy like most of the actresses I meet."

I nodded. There was an awkward pause. Dad cleared his throat.

"Did you like her?" he asked.

Looking back on that evening, it probably wouldn't have made any difference if I'd said, "No, Dad, I didn't." Things probably would have turned out the same. But I still think about it a lot. Because back then I just wanted Dad to be happy, and not miserable like he'd been since Mom died, and I wanted to be a good daughter, and R. seemed nice enough, even if she was a little . . . eccentric.

So I looked Dad in the eye and said: "She was fantastic."

And, to tell you the truth, he looked so thrilled and relieved that I felt like it would have been cruel to say anything else.

Before long the two of them were Officially Dating. It started with Dad coming home late a couple of times a week with red wine on his breath, humming songs from different musicals. Then one Saturday morning I stumbled out of bed, walked into our kitchen, and there was R. in a purple satin bathrobe, flipping pancakes on the stove.

"Hello, darling!" she sang out, and gave me a perfumed kiss on the cheek.

Let me remind you that the last woman who'd stood at our kitchen stove flipping pancakes was my mother, Susan Beckerman. And Susan Beckerman is—was—not the type of woman who wore satin bathrobes and called people "darling." Mom liked sweatpants and her nickname for me was "Crinkle." Her nickname for Dad was "Gherkin."

Dad walked into the kitchen and sat down at the table in his pajamas, smiling bashfully. All of a sudden it seemed like the three of us were a *family*. And the truth was, I didn't know R. at all. I just knew that her passions were food, acting, and sex, and that she played a cancer patient in my father's Broadway show. Also she wore a lot of perfume in the morning. But what was I going to do? Things were out of my control.

"Those pancakes smell great," I said, and sat down at the table. Dad reached over and squeezed my hand.

A *couple of months* went by. It was the spring of my freshman year. I wanted a boyfriend, and I didn't get one, and I wanted a best friend, and I didn't get one (I only had *kind-of* best friends, girls who considered me their *second-* or *third*-best friend after their *real* best friend), and I wasn't chosen to sing a solo in our school's April Chorale Concert. Dad and R. kept seeing more of each other, and I was invited along less and less. Sometimes R. would come over and cook us dinner, but more often I'd come home from school and there'd be a note stuck to the microwave saying: "*Went to movie with R. Back before 11.*" Sometimes I heard them giggling in Dad's bedroom at night. Once I even heard bedsprings squeak, at which point I shoved my fingers in my ears, covered my head with five different pillows, and hummed the national anthem. Still, Dad was happy, and I was glad he was happy.

Then came the Announcement.

One afternoon I came home from school and there was a bottle of champagne on the coffee table in the living room.

9

R. danced out of the kitchen and embraced me even more enthusiastically than usual.

"HELLO MY DARLING," she bellowed.

"Hey, R.," I said. "What's the champagne for?"

She widened her eyes, her spiky eyelashes almost reaching her eyebrows, and put a finger to her lips. "Wait until your father comes in," she whispered.

A second later, Dad came in from the kitchen. "Hey, baby," he said.

"Hi," I said. Then I realized he was talking to R.

"Hey, baby," she murmured, and they put their arms around each other and kissed. I didn't even bother to look away. In the beginning I would turn around when they kissed in an attempt to seem respectful (also it was gross to watch), but eventually I realized that they didn't even care. Or notice. Finally Dad broke away from R.'s embrace.

"Hi, Alice," he said. "We have a very exciting announcement."

I tried to smile. This little voice inside my head piped up: *What if they get married?* but I quickly told it to shut up, that was absurd, they'd only been dating for three months.

Dad and R. sat down on the couch and held hands. "Alice," said Dad, "R. and I are getting married."

I blinked. I swallowed. I pinched the inside of my palm to make sure I wasn't dreaming.

"What do you think?" asked R. "Are you happy?"

That was an interesting question. Am. I. Happy? I didn't even know how to begin to form an answer. No, R., I'm not happy. My mom is dead, and you're sleeping with my father and filling the house with your perfume, and the longer you're around the less interested you seem in me, and you've only been around three months.

"You've only been around three months!" I blurted out.

The smiles on their faces kind of wobbled and disappeared. I could tell they were shocked. Why? Because I'm Alice. I'd been nothing but *sweet* and *nice*. I'd been nothing but *supportive* and *wonderful*. But no. Not anymore. Marriage? After three months? That was crazy. Mom and Dad had dated for six years before they got married.

"Alice," said Dad, "try to sound at least a little excited."

"I'm not excited," I said. "I'm infuriated and irate." (I'd been studying vocabulary words for the PSATs.)

"Why?" asked R. "It's very hurtful of you to say that, Alice. Your father and I are in love."

"I DON'T EVEN KNOW YOU!" I yelled.

Then I burst into tears and ran upstairs.

Okay, I admit it. Not the most mature response. But I'd reached the end of my rope. Where had being nice gotten me? I threw myself onto my bed, sobbed into my pillow, and waited for Dad to come upstairs to talk to me. I would reason with him. I would say: "Dad, I'm not saying break up with her, I'm just saying give it a little more time. What's the rush to get married?" We'd hug and he'd stroke my hair.

I kept crying into my pillow. A few minutes went by. I cried a little louder. More time went by. I wailed. I beat the wall with my fists. I looked at my clock. I tiptoed down the staircase and peeked into the living room.

They were gone. Their coats were missing from the foyer. I couldn't believe it. They hadn't even left a note.

I felt pretty bad for myself that afternoon.

11

But I didn't even know that things were about to get much, much worse.

Have you ever had a nightmare where someone in your life like turns on you? When I was really little, I had these recurring dreams about my mom and dad turning into evil ogres who wanted to eat me. Whenever I woke up I'd feel this flood of relief, like: *Thank God. It was all a dream. My parents are actually not evil ogres who want to eat me.*

After I failed to be Ultra-Supportive and Excited about Dad and R.'s upcoming wedding, R. basically turned into an evil ogre who wanted to eat me.

And I never got to wake up.

It's hard to describe. But the woman hated me. *Hated* me. You could see it in her eyes. Maybe she'd hated me the whole time, but in that case my little tantrum gave her permission to hate me openly. I tried to apologize the next day over breakfast ("Um? You guys? Sorry for freaking out yesterday...."), but she totally ignored me and started babbling at Dad about wedding plans. Dad thanked me with his eyes, but the two of them just talked about chocolate versus lemon wedding cakes until they left the table.

I thought maybe R. would only be mad at me for a couple of days, but instead it only seemed to get worse. She'd walk right by me in the living room without saying hello. She refused to make eye contact at meals. Dad would try to initiate conversation between us, but it never really worked. Sometimes it just made things even more horrible.

"I've been thinking about what kind of bridesmaid dress you'd like to wear at the wedding, Alice," Dad said over dinner one night, smiling at me across the table.

Before I could even answer, R. shot Dad a death glare. "Alice isn't going to be a bridesmaid, Nelson," she said sharply.

"She isn't?" Dad asked.

"No. Ruth and Pammy are my bridesmaids. Remember? I want Alice to be the flower girl."

I looked up in shock. "Wait, what? Isn't the flower girl supposed to be, like, a child?" The second after I said it I regretted it.

"You are a child," R. said, looking directly at me for the first time in, like, a week. But this time it was an uncomfortable, creepy, piercing stare.

"I'm fifteen."

"That doesn't sound very old to me. And it's not like you've exhibited the most mature behavior in the world, have you?" She smiled at me triumphantly over her wineglass.

I opened my mouth. I looked to Dad for help. He was staring down at his plate. Coward.

"I just don't know why I can't be a bridesmaid, too," I finally said.

"Because my sister and my best friend are going to be my bridesmaids," R. said calmly, "and I need a flower girl."

I closed my eyes. It wasn't so much the bridesmaid thing as the fact that R. now obviously hated my guts and was totally happy to let me know just how much she hated my guts in whatever way possible. So sitting there at the table, silently, with my eyes closed, I did something I'd never really done before. I prayed.

To whom or what, I'm not sure. My mom? God? I prayed that something would save me from this situation. I prayed that this wasn't actually my life. I prayed the same prayer as that girl at the beginning of *Forrest Gump* (okay, I didn't have a lot of prayer references to draw from. My parents were never that religious): *Let me be a bird and fly far, far away from here.*

That prayer was another bad idea. Where was I going to fly?

The answer turned out to be rural Massachusetts.

Because a few weeks later there was another Announcement.

I was sitting on the couch after school, reading a celebrity gossip magazine (Dad disapproved of all celebrity gossip magazines). It was early June. The wedding was scheduled for early July. Our house had been overrun with florists and caterers and planners, all displaying photo albums and ribbon cuttings and bouquets for R. to choose from. I usually skulked around the background, waiting for someone to ask my opinion.

No one ever did.

Anyway, this was a particularly quiet afternoon. R. was out tasting hors d'oeuvres at some catering place in Manhattan. I'd taken the opportunity to sprawl out on the couch and just . . . vegetate. To my surprise, Dad came out of his study, walked into the living room, and sat down next to me.

"Hey, kiddo," he said, putting his arm around me.

"Hey, Dad," I said, and got this nice warm feeling all over my body. It felt like the old days. The old depressing Mom-is-dead days, but at least not the terrifying, nightmarish, Mom-is-dead-and-R.-is-going-to-become-my-stepmother days.

"What're you reading?" Dad asked.

"Nothing," I said, grinning, and tucked the celeb mag into the couch pillows.

"I want to talk to you about something," Dad said tentatively.

14

I sighed, relieved. Maybe we were going to figure something out. Maybe R. didn't hate me after all. Or maybe they were going to postpone the wedding for a while. Or maybe—at the very least—they'd decided I didn't have to be flower girl.

"Go ahead," I said.

"Well," Dad said. "This is kind of interesting. I didn't think this was going to happen, but R. feels very strongly about it, and . . . it might be for the best."

The warm feeling was slowly melting away from my body. Was this *more* bad news? Was more bad news possible? I actually couldn't even come up with a worst-case scenario in my head.

I sat up very straight and looked at Dad. "Okay," I said. "What is it?"

"We're going to move," he said.

"Out of this house?"

"Yes."

My body went numb. Okay. Right. The house I grew up in. The living room with the chocolate milk stain on the carpet. The kitchen with the sun coming in through the ivy plants. Mom's shabby study with all her old books. The red staircase with the creaky step. My bedroom with the little stained-glass window. The glow-in-the-dark stars on my ceiling. Our front stoop. Our backyard. The Fernandez family across the street. Images of my life were flashing in front of my eyes like memories, even though I was still sitting in the middle of the living room.

I breathed deeply. *Act mature*, I told myself. "Okay," I said. "Where are we moving? Are we staying in Brooklyn?"

"Uh, no," Dad said. He seemed to be having a hard time getting the words out. "We're moving to Manhattan."

Okay. Right. No more Brooklyn. More images flashed before my eyes. No more brownstones and cute little streets. No more Brooklyn Heights. No more Park Slope. No more Phil's Diner. No more walking along the East River. No more sledding in Prospect Park. No more Junior's cheesecake. No more living five blocks away from school. Wait. School. I'd been going to the same Brooklyn Heights Montessori school for my entire life. I knew everyone there. I didn't *love* everyone, but I knew everyone. I was supposed to graduate in three years. We'd already started raising money for our senior class trip.

"I can still go to Montessori, right?" I asked Dad, trying to stop my voice from trembling. "It'll just be a longer commute, right? Where are we going to live in Manhattan? Will we be close?"

"Well, that's the thing," Dad said. He turned away and stared out the window. "That's the thing, Alice. We're moving into R.'s apartment."

"But that's on the Upper West Side. That's really far away from school."

"I know."

"R.'s apartment is also really small."

"Yes. It is."

I reached out and shakily grabbed hold of Dad's shoulder. He winced.

"Dad?" I asked. *Act mature act mature act mature act mature.* "Um. I . . . where am I going to sleep if we live in R.'s apartment?"

Dad finally turned to face me. His eyes were red. He looked guilty and scared. He looked like he'd just done something really bad. Like murdered a kitten.

"It's okay, Dad," I said weakly. "It's gonna be okay. I'll be okay sleeping in the living room. Or the study. Doesn't she have a study? If I can fit my bed in then I can—"

"Alice," Dad said suddenly. "You're not going to live with me and R. It doesn't make sense. There's not enough room, and you'd have to switch schools, anyway. In the fall you're going to attend a boarding school in Massachusetts."

There was a long, excruciating pause. I tried to think of everything I could say to Dad. I tried to think of what might make him change his mind. *I don't want to go. I refuse to go. I love New York City. I don't want to go to Massachusetts. I don't want to go boarding school. I'll be good. I'll live in R.'s bathroom. I'll sleep in a tent. I'll live with friends. I'll live with the Fernandez family. I'll be a bag lady in Central Park.* Anything.

"It's actually an incredible opportunity," Dad said. "I showed them your transcript and they were very impressed. They were willing to let you in even though the admissions deadline had passed. You'll get a great education. And it has a beautiful campus."

Massachusetts. Wasn't Massachusetts supposed to be cold? And boring? I remembered driving through Massachusetts on our way to a vacation house in Maine when I was little. It had lots of pine trees and gray highways. And fruit stands. And weird farmers with missing teeth.

I stared into Dad's eyes. *Dad,* I tried to silently implore him. *I don't want to freak out right now. I don't want to give R. another reason to hate me. I don't want you to think I'm a bad daughter. Just. Please. Don't. Make. Me. Go.*

The weird thing was, I could tell that Dad was also trying to tell me something with his eyes. He was silently begging me to be okay with this. To not make him guilty. To not make him feel like he was marrying a psychopath who wanted him to send his daughter away to boarding school.

Although he actually was marrying a psychopath who wanted him to send his daughter away to boarding school.

"Well?" Dad said, his voice cracking. "That's the plan. How does it sound to you?"

I broke away from his gaze and stared into the kitchen. I looked at the little crystal hanging in the window above the sink. Mom had bought that crystal when I was in elementary school, and we'd strung it up together in the window with dental floss.

"It sounds..." I said. I took a deep breath. "It sounds fantastic."

The New Y

Klausenhook/Bingley

Renowned stage actress Rachel Klausenhook was married yesterday to writer Nelson Bingley at Cipriani 42nd Street before a crowd of more than five hundred guests. The ceremony culminated in musical performances by some of Broadway's brightest stars. An interfaith minister officiated.

The bride is best known for her Tony Award–winning portrayal of Masha in Andre Blackmun's 1987 revival of *The Three Sisters*, and her original star-making turn as Debbie in the original cast for the 1975 hit musical *Say Yes.*

The bridegroom is an acclaimed novelist and two-time winner of the National Book Award. He was previously married (wife deceased), and has a fifteen-year-old daughter, Alice.

The couple met during rehearsals for Bingley's first-produced Broadway drama, *School of Luminism.*

"I knew right away," Klausenhook confided during the reception, radiant in a crimson Donna Karan gown and elbow-length white gloves. "Nelson walked into the rehearsal room, and I thought: 'That's the one.'"

Roses seemed to be the wedding's theme—red roses lined the walls and banquet tables, and each guest received a pink damask rose inside a glass box. The flower girl, Bingley's daughter, Alice (dressed in all black), threw white rose petals across the aisle just before Klausenhook made her way toward the altar.

The bride is keeping her name.

TWO

Reena Paruchuri

I hate yoga. I've always hated yoga. I mean, come on. Who wants to stand still for ten minutes with one leg lifted in the air? Who wants to lie on the ground twisted up like a pretzel while some lady in velvet stirrup pants tells you to "relax"?

White chicks, I guess.

Apparently yoga was originally an Indian thing. Ha. That's hilarious. I'm Indian, and everyone in my family is Indian, and if you asked any of us to get into a downward dog or child's pose position, we'd laugh in your face. And whenever I drive by a yoga studio (there are like ten billion here in Beverly Hills) and look through the windows at the crowds of skinny young women in short-shorts, contorting themselves into freaky positions, they're all white. White as white can be. Lily white. Wonder Bread white. Snow white.

Hmm. Speaking of Snow White. Actually, wait. More about how I hate yoga first.

I really, really, really hate yoga.

Don't get me wrong. Exercise is cool. I love running. I love dancing. I love *moving*. I'm just not interested in staying still, or relaxing, or being aware of my breath. Why relax? There are Things to Do! There are People to Meet! There are Plans to Make!

My older brother Pradeep says I sometimes remind him of a small, hyperactive dog.

He is such a jerk.

Anyway. I should probably be honest with myself and admit that maybe a teensy-weensy part of the reason I hate yoga so much is Shanti Shruti.

Shanti Shruti is a yoga teacher at the Beverly Hills Integrated Living Iyengar Yoga Body Arts Center. She is white, skinny, blond, blue eyed, and twenty-five years old.

She is also my stepmother.

Let's do some math. Shanti Shruti is twenty-five. I, Reena Paruchuri, am fifteen. My father, the distinguished heart surgeon Rashul Paruchuri, is fifty-three. Shanti Shruti is ten years older than me, and twenty-eight years younger than my dad. I'm not exactly sure what that means (that *I* should marry Shanti Shruti?), but I know that it's not a good thing. Trust me.

You may be thinking: Shanti Shruti! What an interesting name! Is it Hindi? Was Shanti Shruti born in India? Is she from Bangalore? Bombay?

Um, no. Shanti Shruti was born in Skokie, Illinois, and she was raised outside of San Francisco. And oh yeah: her name isn't really Shanti Shruti. It's Amanda Weed. She was raised by Charles and Mary Weed, inheritors of the Weed Breez-ee Air Conditioner fortune. Amanda Weed only became Shanti Shruti after she studied abroad in India during college and decided that even though on the surface she appears to be the

Whitest Chick in the World, she is, deep in her soul, an Indian woman. An Indian woman who wears skin-tight, pink T-shirts with the word *Om* stenciled across the boobs.

I first met Shanti Shruti a year and a half ago. In yoga class.

At that point I didn't know I hated yoga. I'd never done it before. My best friend Katie persuaded me to go with her. She was all, like, "It's so relaxing," and "It tones your butt." (My best friend Katie is a white chick. So, you know. You can't blame her for liking yoga. It's just a weakness that all white chicks have.)

So I went with her. Once. To try it.

And therefore, as Pradeep is fond of telling me, I am entirely to blame for our parents' divorce.

"Shruti," Shanti Shruti explained to us that first day of class, facing the mirror while neatly folding herself into the lotus position, "means 'what is heard' in Sanskrit. It represents divine knowledge. Shanti means 'tranquility,' or 'inner peace.'"

I glanced at Katie and pretended to strangle myself. Katie giggled. Shanti Shruti looked at us in the mirror and blinked her big blue eyes disapprovingly. Then she twisted herself out of the lotus position and shimmied upward into a standing pose. She stretched her arms out parallel to the floor and tucked her right foot behind her left thigh.

"Imagine yourself," she whispered, "as an ancient tree. You have deep roots. You have branches that stretch out into the sky. You are grounded. But you also can fly."

The twenty white chicks in the class and I attempted to

imitate the pose. A bunch of them balanced perfectly and did kind of look like trees. I took a deep breath. I put my right foot behind my left knee. I started to wobble. I steadied myself. And wobbled again. And then steadied myself. And then wobbled again. I concentrated hard and finally steadied myself. For a good ten seconds. Until I toppled over and crashed to the floor.

"Oh my God!" Katie shrieked.

Shanti Shruti rushed over and helped me up.

"I'm okay," I said. "It's fine."

"Take a deep breath," she instructed me. "Find your center."

"I'm fine," I said loudly.

She backed off.

I spent the rest of the class counting the minutes until I could get out of there. The hour seemed to stretch on forever. We lay on our backs with our legs in the air (painfulpainfulpainful) while Shanti Shruti told us to think about "nothing." Instead I thought about (in the following order): Peanut M&M's, Katie's mysterious dislike of Peanut M&M's, thong underwear (pros and cons), the third Harry Potter movie, the fifth Harry Potter book, geometry proofs, my dead grandfather, how visible the faint mustache above my lip is when I'm standing in the sun, how visible the faint mustache above my lip is when I'm not standing in the sun, whether I should return the cardigan I just bought at Nordstrom, and, finally, whether James Yonus-Good, the most gorgeous and inaccessible senior at Beverly Hills High, had maybe—just maybe—glanced at me the other day while buying Ring Dings in the cafeteria.

And then class was over.

"Stay calm," Shanti Shruti told us as we rolled up our sticky mats. "Don't forget to let yourself blossom."

I was going to blossom my way out of there and never come back.

My father was waiting for me and Katie, leaning in the door frame in the yoga studio, hands in his pockets, looking amused. I made a beeline for him.

"Get us out of here, Dad," I whispered.

"This is interesting," he said, grinning. "You like this yoga?"

I started to say, "Are you kidding me?" when Katie nudged me and tilted her head toward Shanti Shruti, who was standing behind us, getting ready to leave. Shanti smiled sweetly at all three of us.

"Is this your daughter?" she asked my father.

"This is my Reena," he said, putting a hand on my shoulder.

"She's a wonderful student," said Shanti.

I was probably the worst student she'd ever had.

"Reena is good at everything she does," my father said proudly.

Also a lie.

"Where are you from? Originally?" Shanti asked him.

I rolled my eyes at Katie. My father has a really obvious accent, and people are constantly asking him Where He's From. It's the first thing they say when they meet him, and it always drives him crazy. He'll be in the middle of open-heart surgery and one of the nurses will say: "What an interesting accent. Where are you from?"

I looked at my father to see how annoyed he was. But the weird thing was, he actually looked kind of pleased. And . . . nervous? No. Impossible.

24

"I'm from a university town in northern India," he said. "It's called Santiniketan. The poet Tagore founded a famous school there."

Shanti gasped. "I love Tagore!" she said. "He's my favorite poet ever!"

"You know Tagore?" asked my father.

"Of course," said Shanti, nodding solemnly.

"It's rare I meet an American woman who knows about Tagore," he said.

"I use him in class all the time," Shanti said. "You know what my favorite Tagore line is? 'Everything comes to us that belongs to us, if we create the capacity to receive it.'"

There was a long pause.

"Beautiful," my father said softly. "I had forgotten about that poem."

"Oookay," I said. "We should probably drive Katie home now."

"Yes, of course," he said, shaking his head as if to clear his thoughts. "Of course."

And so we bid Shanti Shruti good-bye (forever, I thought), piled into Dad's car, and drove away.

It was a long time before I thought about yoga—or Shanti Shruti—again.

Almost a year later, I walked into our house on a sunny Saturday afternoon and found my mother lying on the kitchen floor in a heap, sobbing and yelling incomprehensibly.

"Did someone die?" I asked. It was the first thing that came into my mind.

25

She looked up at me, her eyes bloodshot.

"Worse," she whispered. "Your father is leaving me."

"That's not worse than someone dying," I said. (Okay. Not the most supportive thing to say. But I'd gone totally numb with shock.)

My mother burst into a new round of sobs. "I'm *going to die*," she moaned.

"No, Mom," I said. I was trying my best not to start screaming and crying myself. I knelt down on the floor and put my arms around her. She wept into my shoulder. "You're not going to die. You're not going to die. You're going to be okay."

But what I was really thinking was: She is *so* not going to be okay.

My mom and dad got married in India when they were eighteen. They were one of those couples where you couldn't imagine one without the other. It's not like they had the same personality (my dad is kind of quiet and serious and critical of everyone, and my mom is loud and hilarious and accepting of everyone), but it was as if they each had the personality they did because of the other person. Does that make sense?

Everyone always said: "Your mom and dad are just so perfect for each other." They were one of those Great Couples. Parmita and Rashul. And they'd moved to America together, and my mom had raised us and worked as a waitress while my father went to medical school, and she was by his side when he got his first job as a surgeon, and together they'd moved out of our tiny apartment in the Valley and into our big beautiful white mansion with the big green lawn in Beverly Hills. If it weren't for my mom, my father would never have achieved everything he'd achieved. And if it weren't for my father, my mother would never have been able to finally relax and live in a beautiful house in a beautiful neighborhood after all the hard work she'd done.

Back to my mom sobbing on the floor:

"This must be some kind of misunderstanding," I said. "Where's Dad?"

"Gone!" she shrieked. "Gone!"

At this point Pradeep came in through the back door. He froze in his tracks and stared at the two of us crying on the kitchen floor.

"I'm assuming this is girl stuff," he said. "Am I allowed to leave?"

"Yes, leave!" my mother screamed, collapsing into my arms again. "Leave! Like father, like son! Abandon me! Abandon me forever!"

My brother looked aghast.

"Don't leave," I mouthed to him over my mother's shoulder. He nodded, his face drained of its color.

Eventually my mom calmed down enough to show Pradeep and me the e-mail (that's right, e-mail) that she'd just received from my father an hour before:

from: Rashul Paruchuri rparuch@ucmedcenter.com
to: Parmita Paruchuri parmeepatch@hotmail.com

Hello, Par:

Please do not forget to buy the soy milk for Reena when you go shopping this afternoon as I am quite concerned about her lactose intolerance and she is so stubborn about taking care of it herself.

Also I would like to let you know that I have fallen in love with someone else. It would be very difficult for me to tell you this in person. You have a terrible temper and I have various problems with confrontation as you know.

From tonight on I will be staying at a hotel or a different place of my choosing. Please tell Reenie and Pradeep that I will be contacting them shortly to explain in full.

I have a great deal of affection for you but think that it will be best to end our marriage in as civil a fashion as possible.

With regards,
Rashul Paruchuri, MD

It was finally starting to sink in.

My father was leaving my mother.

"I hate him," Pradeep whispered, the printed-out e-mail trembling in his hands. "I hate Dad."

"Don't say that," I said, and immediately started to cry.

My mother sat down on the floor again, her head in her hands. "I have no heart," she announced. "My heart is extinct."

"I don't think you mean 'extinct,' Mom," I said. My mother's English is pretty good, but sometimes she'll come up with these weird words and phrases that don't really make sense. "I think maybe you mean 'broken.'"

"Stop picking on her," Pradeep said.

"I'm not picking on her!" I said.

"My heart is extinct," said my mother again.

"Your heart can't be extinct," I said. "That's impossible. Wooly mammoths are extinct."

"Stop it, Reen," Pradeep said.

"YOU STOP IT!" I shouted. "GO SCREW YOURSELF!"

28

There was a long pause.

"If either of you see or speak to your father after today," my mother said softly, "I will never forgive you."

Dad smiled nervously and tucked his napkin into his lap.

"Well," he said.

Pradeep and I were silent. I looked around at the faces of all the other people in the restaurant. What were they thinking? Were their lives falling apart, too?

"Are you two going to say anything?" Dad asked.

Pradeep glowered into his plate. I bit my lip.

"Well, you should at least order some food," Dad said. "This is a very nice restaurant. Only the best for my children." He reached over and attempted to pat Pradeep's hand. Pradeep snatched it away.

"What's her name?" Pradeep demanded.

"Now, now," Dad said.

"Tell us her name," said Pradeep, "or we'll leave the restaurant."

I glanced at Pradeep, impressed. It was exactly a week since the e-mail and Mom's breakdown. We'd agreed to go out to dinner with Dad because . . . well, he was our dad, after all. He had the last word. He was like our boss. If he said he was taking us out to dinner, he was taking us out to dinner. Even if it did make Mom threaten to disown us (and she was always making threats she couldn't stick to). But now Pradeep was acting differently than I'd ever seen him act before. He was acting like, well, like his *own* boss.

"Her name," said Dad, clearing his throat after a long pause, "is Shanti Shruti."

The lump that had already been in my throat for the past week transformed itself into a giant boulder.

Pradeep frowned. "Is she Indian?"

"Well," Dad began.

"No," I croaked. "She's not."

Pradeep turned to me. "How would you know?"

"She's ... she's ... she's like my age," I whispered.

Dad slammed his fist down on the table, making the plates clatter. "She is NOT your age, Reena. Have some respect."

"I have no idea what's going on," Pradeep said. "Would somebody please tell me what's going on?"

I turned to my brother. "She's a white chick. She was my yoga teacher. She's half Dad's age. Happy?"

Pradeep opened his mouth and then closed it again.

"Dad," I said, looking my father in the eyes, "I don't think you understand what you're doing. Do you understand what you're doing?"

"Don't talk to me like a child, Reena," he said.

Tears sprang to my eyes. "Mom is a mess," I told him. "You've ruined her life."

"Your mother is going to be okay."

"You're wrong."

My father sighed. "Reena," he said. "I'm in love. What do you want me to do about it?"

Pradeep, still speechless, buried his face in his hands.

"I don't understand how you even got to know Shankee Shmooti," I said.

"It's Shanti Shruti," Dad said, giving me a withering look. "And we were friends at first. Then we eventually realized that our feelings had grown stronger and we had to—"

"ENOUGH," Pradeep shrieked.

The restaurant fell silent. You could hear the sound of a single spoon scraping against a dessert plate.

Dad cleared his throat. "Pradeep—"

"I ACTUALLY DON'T WANT TO HEAR ABOUT IT," Pradeep yelled. A tear rolled down his cheek and into the corner of his mouth. "I'M NOT INTERESTED."

"Okay," Dad said quietly. "Okay."

No one said anything for a little while.

"Listen," Dad said finally. "I want to make you both an offer."

We looked up.

"Things are going to become very difficult," he said, "between your mother and myself. We are both hiring lawyers. There is some question as to who will get the house, and—"

"Mom should get it," Pradeep interrupted. "Mom isn't having an affair with a yoga teacher."

Dad sighed. "These things are complicated."

"Where's Mom going to live if you get the house?" I asked.

"Let me finish my thought," Dad said. "Things will be messy. There is also the question of alimony. It is my suggestion—and this is only if you wish to go, of course—that you both leave LA and attend boarding school this fall. That way you will not have to be around such difficulties."

"You're trying to get rid of us," I said.

"That is not true," my father said. "I'm trying to give you another option. That is all. We all know how unstable your mother can be in times of conflict. But it is your choice."

He pulled a glossy brochure out of his pocket and put it on the table in front of us. Pradeep and I stared at it. There was a picture of a hillside covered in snow with a brick cathedral on top of it. The words *Putnam Mount McKinsey* were written across the top of the brochure.

"It's in Massachusetts," Dad said. "It's one of the best schools in the country. Shanti actually went there. Think about it. I know you're both angry with me, but trust me. It is a gift."

Pradeep and I looked at each other. Then we looked back at Dad.

"Mom needs us," I said. "You have a white chick yoga teacher. But she has nobody."

"Well, think about it," said Dad.

We all sat there in silence.

"Oh, and Reena?" Dad said after a while. "Please do not refer to Shanti as a 'white chick yoga teacher.' You and Pradeep are very important to me, but you're going to have to accept the woman I love. That woman is Shanti Shruti."

"Do you have the long underwear we bought?" my mom asked, wringing her hands.

I nodded.

"Which suitcase?" she said.

I shrugged.

"Probably suitcase number eleven," Pradeep said, chortling. "Or maybe twelve."

"Shut up," I said. It was true. I had no idea I owned so much stuff until I tried to pack it all into a single pink luggage set. Turned out I actually needed three pink luggage sets.

The three of us were sitting on plastic airport chairs, holding hands. A woman announced over the loudspeaker that our flight was going to board in five minutes. My mother quietly started to cry. Tears streamed down her face and onto her light green sari.

"We don't have to go," I told her.

"Go, go," she said. "I'll be all right. I will. Pria will take care of me."

Pria is my mother's older sister. She never married—she isn't the easiest woman in the world to get along with—but the second she found out my parents were getting a divorce, she insisted that my mother move in with her. "Don't stay in that house," she told my mother. "That house is poisoned." Pria had a nice—but small—bungalow in West LA. With only one extra bedroom. As the summer progressed, it became obvious that if Pradeep and I left for boarding school it would probably be the best thing for everyone. We didn't want to live with my dad and Shanti Shruti, but we knew that living with my mother would mean she'd have to support us, at least until the alimony was settled. And my mother didn't have a source of income. Her job, after all, had been raising us.

Also, to tell you the truth, Pradeep and I had been fantasizing about going to an East Coast boarding school since we were little kids. Boarding school just always seemed so... magical. Skiing. Sledding. Pine trees. Cute boys in earmuffs. We'd tried to convince our mom and dad to send us to boarding school when I was in seventh grade and Pradeep was in eighth, but they'd refused. No, at the time it was really important to them that Family stick together, and that Pradeep and I pass our teenage years spending quality time with the Family. So it was pretty ironic that boarding school was now the place they sent us when the Family completely fell apart.

And in a weird way I was happy to leave Los Angeles. I'd felt sort of numb ever since the afternoon I walked in and saw Mom crying on the kitchen floor. Kind of like I was living in a dream. Sometimes I'd even wake up in the morning and genuinely believe it *was* all a dream for a good twenty seconds. My life just didn't seem like my life anymore. All summer I hung out with my friends, and cracked jokes, and went shopping, and lay on the beach talking about cute guys, and anyone watching me would have said that I was Doing Just Fine, Considering. But it felt like the real Reena Paruchuri had been replaced by an identical robot version of Reena Paruchuri who didn't have any actual thoughts and feelings.

"Flight 1191 to Boston boarding now," a woman intoned on the loud speaker. "Flight 1191 to Boston boarding now."

My mother stood up and smiled bravely at us, the corners of her mouth trembling.

"Make me proud," she said.

"You're going to be okay, Mom," I said.

She shrugged, tears brimming out of her eyes.

"Dad is a jerk," Pradeep said loudly. "Don't waste time thinking about him."

"Pradeep," I warned.

"He is," said Pradeep.

"Go," Mom said. "Just go."

She put her hands on our backs and pushed us gently toward the gate. My heart skipped a beat. For a second, the real Reena Paruchuri flooded back into my body. And the last thing she wanted to do was get on that plane. The real Reena Paruchuri wanted to curl up like a baby, bury her face in her mother's lap, and cry forever. But it was too late. I took a deep breath, shouldered my duffel bag, and followed my brother into the buzzing white tunnel that led to our plane.

I didn't look back.

Los Angeles T

JULY 10,

Shruti/Paruchuri

When twenty-five-year-old yoga instructor Shanti Shruti told her friends she was dating a much older man, initially they were concerned.

"I thought, 'Oh no, there goes Shanti again, pursuing someone totally wrong for her,'" said Cindy Kallo, a close friend of Ms. Shruti's. "But then she introduced me to Rashul and it all made sense. Both of them are such calm, spiritual people. It's a match made in the stars."

Rashul Paruchuri, 53, is no ordinary "older gentleman." He is one of Los Angeles's most well-respected heart surgeons, and a warm, friendly man with a distinctive halo of gray hair. Also—despite the fact that he hails from northern India—he is not a practicing Hindu.

What, then, did guests make of the three-day-long traditional Indian celebration that took place this past weekend in Malibu, complete with *pithi*, a ceremony in which the bride and groom are covered in yellow paste the day before the wedding and rubbed down in order to "produce a healthy glow"?

"It's all Shanti," Kallo said. "She's always dreamed of an Indian wedding."

One might not immediately expect that from Shruti, a tall, lanky blonde. But the bride looked radiant in her traditional garb and headdress, and the happy couple performed their final vows on a cliff above the beach, standing in front of a "sacred fire," which they circled four times, signaling the four basic human goals of dharma, artha, kama, and moksha.

"I've never been very interested in traditional ceremonies," said the groom, who has been married once before. "But whatever makes Shanti happy makes me happy."

After the couple was showered with rice and rose petals, a *Saubhagyavati* ritual concluded the ceremony.

Normally seven married friends of the bride are asked to whisper blessings in her ear, but since none of Shruti's friends are married (some of them are still in college), Paruchuri's two children by his first marriage, Reena and Pradeep, were brought forward to administer the blessings.

"Have fun on your honeymoon," said Pradeep, the elder sibling, who was wearing a decidedly un-traditional tuxedo.

"Don't get food poisoning," added Reena, decked out in sixties-style minidress.

Then the happy couple exited—on horseback—and rode down a rocky beach path to a long white limousine that was waiting to take them back to Paruchuri's spacious Beverly Hills mansion.

The bride is keeping her name, although, Kallo confided, "It's not the one she was born with."

THREE

Molly Miller

"You are not taking the entire Oxford English Dictionary to boarding school," Candy Lamb said. She stood in the driveway, hands on her hips, squinting at me in the late summer sunlight. She wore an oversized sweatshirt that said, I'M NOT FAT, I'M PREGNANT WITH ICE CREAM'S BABY.

"Um," I said, "yes, I am."

"Everyone will make fun of you."

"I don't care."

"You'll seem like a big nerd."

I smiled pleasantly at her. "I am a big nerd," I said, and lifted Volume VI, P–Q, into the trunk of my father's station wagon. Then I started walking back toward the house, my feet crunching on the gravel. Only fourteen more volumes to go.

"You're not gonna wear that skirt, are you?" Candy hollered after me from the bottom of the driveway.

I ignored her.

Candy Lamb is my stepmother. She has short, bleached,

spiky hair. She has capped white teeth. She has a fondness for paisley leggings and blue mascara and gigantic sweatshirts with abrasive comments written across the front. She never tires of reminding me that she was BOTH prom queen and homecoming queen BOTH junior and senior year at North Forest High School. She feels that this makes her an authority on two extremely important subjects: Fashion and General Coolness.

When it comes to these subjects, I am a huge disappointment to her.

My name is Molly Miller. My father is Herb Miller, owner of Herb's Diner, the only restaurant in our hometown of North Forest, Massachusetts. My mother is Patsy Miller, associate manager of Shear Bliss, the only hair salon in North Forest. My little sister is Spencer Miller, the youngest North Forest baton twirler ever to win a blue ribbon at the Chesterton County Fair.

Something that's important to know about me: I'm not really that interested in Fashion and General Coolness. Or baton twirling, for that matter.

I am, however, interested in the Oxford English Dictionary.

People don't spend enough time talking about the OED. It is amazing. It's like a normal dictionary (it gives you a definition of every word in the English language), but then it goes way beyond the call of duty and gives you like the complete history of the word you're looking up. Where it originated, what country and language it's taken from, who first wrote it down, and how the word has changed over time. Each word gets its own little section of quotes that demonstrate all the different ways it can be used, and the quotes are from famous books and authors, and . . .

Yeah. You're already bored. I can tell. That's okay. Everyone thinks it's boring. I'm probably the only person in the world who thinks the Oxford English Dictionary is the greatest thing since sliced bread. But I do. And I plan to work there someday. The head offices of the OED are in Oxford, England. I've never been to England, but I know I'd love it. After all, everyone there speaks with an English accent. And I love English accents. I also imagine that everyone in England reads books and drinks tea and quotes poetry and goes apple picking. Oh, they also all own horses. And walk with little white umbrellas. And play croquet.

I guess I imagine England to be the polar opposite of North Forest. Because if you're someone who enjoys reading the dictionary and you also happen to be nearsighted and have frizzy hair and weirdly pale white legs that never change color no matter how long you lie out in your backyard every summer (they turn blotchy red for like twelve hours, and then go back to pale white), and you don't really like parties or baton twirling or prom queens or homecoming queens or outdoor sports or television, North Forest is a really, really, really terrible place to live. Especially if your ten-year-old sister is gorgeous, mysteriously tan, and adored by the entire town population (2,333 people, to be exact).

I've lived in North Forest my entire life.

So have my parents. So has Candy Lamb.

For some reason they all seem to think it's great.

Sometimes I pretend that I was actually born to a bespectacled, pale-legged, croquet-playing British couple, and that I was accidentally switched at birth with the real elder daughter of Herb and Patsy Miller. But then I realize: What in God's name would a bespectacled, pale-legged, croquet-playing British

39

couple be doing at the local hospital in North Forest, Massachusetts?

North Forest is basically one diner (my dad's), one hair salon (my mom's), one general store, one gas station, one post office, and one really terrible and underfunded public school, North Forest High. Oh, and a whole lot of maple trees.

The most important annual event in North Forest is the Fourth of July pork roast. The second most important annual event is the high school's February pancake breakfast. In the months between the pork roast and the pancake breakfast, people spend their leisure time watching television, drinking beer, shoveling the snow off their front walk and then watching a new coat of snow fall on it two hours later, playing poker, gossiping, watching more television, and drinking more beer. What else? North Forest is incredibly cold in the winter and incredibly hot in the summer. In the late spring all the trees get infested with gypsy moths, and everyone freaks out and congregates in the general store to try to come up with a solution (they never do). In the autumn everyone rakes their leaves to the curb and puts them in orange jack-o'-lantern trash bags, and if you forget to rake your leaves to the curb and put them in an orange jack-o'-lantern trash bag, you receive a very sad and betrayed-sounding note from the postman in your mailbox. (This happened to our family once, and it was my fault, and my mother never forgave me for it.)

Candy Lamb says I have a bad attitude when it comes to North Forest. She says that North Forest is an amazing place in which to grow up. Everyone knows everyone, and it's like one big family, and there's barely any crime (if you don't count the shaving cream felonies committed by the senior class every June), and the surrounding nature is so beautiful, and on a clear day you can see, off in the distance, the glori-ous peak of Mount McKinsey. . . .

The thing is, until very recently, just the mention of Mount McKinsey made weird, resentful chills run up and down my spine. Why? Because in the shadow of Mount Mc-Kinsey, just twenty miles away from boring, claustrophobic North Forest, lies paradise.

Perfect, unattainable, even-better-than-England paradise.

While I was growing up, sometimes, seemingly out of nowhere, a group of incredibly attractive, well-dressed teenagers would appear in the center of North Forest, buying penny candy from the general store or squeezing into a booth at my dad's diner and gigglingly ordering ice cream floats.

"Who are those people?" I would whisper, breathless, peeping out from behind the diner counter.

And my father would roll his eyes and say: "Probably Put-nam Mount McKinsey students. Spoiled brats."

I wasn't sure what he meant. But I remember gazing at one of them, a gorgeous boy in a pink shirt who was gobbling down his sundae and making all the girls at his table laugh, and I remember thinking: *What I wouldn't give to be a spoiled brat.* Then, later, when their little group got up to leave, I no-ticed a paperback book sticking out of the boy's back pocket, and managed to catch a glimpse of its title just before his per-fect denim-coated bottom sashayed out of my father's diner. The title was *The Collected Poems of Emily Dickinson.*

I'd never seen a guy that handsome walking around with a volume of poetry in his pocket. And I'd certainly never seen a guy that handsome who had read—or had even heard of— Emily Dickinson. I adored Emily Dickinson. I'd found a book of her poems at a thrift store when I was eight and had fallen in love with her. She was this reclusive Massachusetts poet from the nineteenth century who never married and stayed in her little room all day and wrote poems about death and loneliness and . . .

Okay. You're bored again. Sorry. The point is, I suddenly realized that there was a school within twenty miles of my house where handsome boys in pink shirts walked around with books of Emily Dickinson poems sticking out of their back pockets. It seemed impossible. But I'd *seen* one of them. I'd seen him with my own eyes. So I casually attempted to ask my father one night over dinner how a person could go about attending this school he'd mentioned, this "Putnam Mount McKinsey."

He coughed on his food, shook his head, took a gulp of his beer, and sighed. "How do you think, Mol?"

"Uh . . . I don't know. That's why I am asking."

"You know how much it costs for one year of school at Putnam Mount McKinsey?"

"It costs money?" I was surprised. I was twelve at the time. I'd attended public school my entire life. It had never occurred to me that other people paid to go to school.

My father looked at me sadly. "Mol, I'd send you there in a second if I could. God knows you're smart enough. But the place costs thirty thousand dollars a year."

I gaped at him. "You're kidding."

"It's a school full of rich kids, honey. Brats from New York City and Beverly Hills. Kids with private jets and boats who spend their summers doing nothing in Europe. You wouldn't want to be friends with them anyway. They're probably all little jerks."

I tried to nod and look like I understood. But all I could

think was *jerks from New York City and Beverly Hills with private jets and boats who READ EMILY DICKINSON.*

From that moment on, the existence of Putnam Mount McKinsey tormented me. I mean, I'd never been crazy about the North Forest school system. The teachers weren't great (my sixth grade teacher was fond of saying I was "too smart for my own good") and everyone called me Nerd and Brown Noser and Goody Two-Shoes. Oh, and Four Eyes. And Rabbit Teeth. And Big Mouth. And Molly Miller the Puppy Killer (I could never figure that one out. I used to weep and yell, "BUT I'VE NEVER KILLED A PUPPY!" and for some reason that just made everyone laugh harder). Still, I always thought that school was like that for everyone. But now I knew that within a half-an-hour drive of my house there was a school so wonderful that people paid to attend it. And my family just didn't have the money to send me there. Actually they didn't have a fraction of a fraction of the money to send me there. And it wasn't because my parents didn't work hard. It was because life—I was starting to realize—was Totally and Utterly Unfair.

Then high school started, and Candy Lamb entered our lives, and I decided that life was not only Totally and Utterly Unfair, it was also Cruel, Sadistic, Stupid, and Pointless.

Candy Lamb was one of the waitresses at my father's diner. I'd known her for years. She was always extra-friendly and extra-sweet whenever Spencer and I came in, and she'd sneak us free slices of key lime pie when my parents weren't looking. She always seemed a little fake, like maybe she was trying too hard to make people like her, but I didn't care. She was just part of the Herb's Diner staff. There were way weirder people who worked at the diner, like Gus, the prep cook, who had one eye and claimed to be a former pirate.

But then something strange happened. One day, out of nowhere, my parents stopped fighting.

This was actually much more surreal than it sounds. The background noise of my childhood was either Spencer, tutu-clad, screeching "The Star-Spangled Banner" into a plastic toy microphone, or my parents screaming at each other in the kitchen. Actually sometimes they would scream at each other in our driveway. Or our living room. Or the upstairs hallway. They were usually screaming at each other about money. Sometimes they were screaming at each other about how my father watched too much television. Or how my mother spent too much time talking to her friends on the phone. I would hear one of them threaten divorce, and then the other would climb into the car and screech out of the driveway, but eventually, by dinnertime, we were all sitting around the table and acting normal again. I guess I trusted that no matter how bad things got, they'd never split up. Even though it sometimes seemed like they hated each other, I always assumed that that was what marriage was like for everyone. Sort of like how I'd once assumed all schools were like the crappy public schools in North Forest.

Anyway, on this particular day I was lying on the couch reading the OED entry for *punctilious* (it originally comes from the Latin for "to prick," if you're interested) and I suddenly realized that it had been more than a week since I'd heard my parents screaming at each other. I put down the OED and looked around our living room. Both of them were home. My mother was peeling potatoes in the kitchen and my father was repairing our bathroom cabinet. Spencer was at Lassie League practice. So why weren't they yelling? I started to feel nervous. I'd always hated their fighting. But now its absence was eerie. Foreboding. Like what they say about the silence before a storm.

That night at dinner, my mother—with exquisite politeness—asked my father if he would please pass her the potatoes. My father said that he would be delighted to. And would she be willing to pour him another glass of water? My mother said it would be her pleasure.

I was starting to feel ill. I tried to make eye contact with Spencer, but she was too focused on building a castle out of her mashed potatoes and humming a song under her breath.

We all finished eating and I cleared the dishes off the table and brought them into the kitchen. I came back into the dining room and sat down. My mother and father smiled pleasantly at us.

"What's going on?" I asked.

My mother's smile got wider. And creepier. Her eyes were glittering like they were behind a mask.

Spencer finally stopped humming and looked up. "What?" she asked, as if we were all waiting for her to do something.

My father cleared his throat. "Your mother and I are separating," he said.

There was a stunned silence. My mother's face looked like it was going to fall off.

"Why?" I asked.

"We don't love each other anymore," my mother said. She was still smiling.

"You *don't?*" Spencer squealed.

"We haven't loved each other for a long time," said my father.

"Oh," said Spencer. Her voice sounded so small that I almost didn't recognize it.

"I'm moving in with Candy Lamb," my father said. "You remember Candy."

Spencer shot me a pleading you're-the-older-sister-do-something! look.

But I had no idea what I was supposed to do.

"Candy is a very nice woman," my mother added.

My father nodded. I could hear the clock ticking in the other room.

"Well," I said, "I think this is dumb. I think the two of you are really dumb."

"It has nothing to do with you guys," my mother said. "You know that, right? It has nothing to do with you."

There was a long silence.

"I'm going to go do my homework," I announced. I pushed my chair back and stood up.

"Do you want to talk about anything, Mol?" my mother asked. Her eyes were still gleaming desperately.

"No," I said. "I just think you're both stupid jerks."

I walked out of the room, up the stairs, and into my bedroom. I sat down at my desk and pulled out my English textbook. A single tear dropped out of my eye and onto the page. It landed on the word *until* and made the black letters blur on the white page.

I stared at the textbook for a long time, not reading, just letting my eyes pass over the same sentences over and over again. I felt like my entire chest had been hollowed out. But the same thought kept running through my brain, over and over again. Eventually I said it out loud.

"Got to get out of this stupid, stupid town," I whispered.

46

Downstairs I could hear the sounds of my mother and father washing the dishes and cleaning up the kitchen. They weren't saying anything. Then I heard Spencer stomp up the staircase and slam her bedroom door. Outside my window, the crickets seemed to be chirping louder than they'd ever chirped before.

I didn't tell anyone that I was applying to Putnam Mount McKinsey, except for the two teachers I needed to ask for recommendations. While I was filling out application forms, I just checked yes when the school asked if I wanted to be considered for financial aid. I got a copy of my transcript from the principal's office. I forged my mother's signature. I put the entire application into a large manila envelope and put it in the mailbox downtown. Then I made a conscious decision to forget that I'd ever applied at all. After all, if they let me in—and why would they?—we'd never be able to afford it, even if they did give me some financial aid. It was unclear why I'd applied at all. But I just felt like I had to.

It was my first year at North Forest High. I'd never gotten along with my classmates, but somehow things got even worse once we all entered ninth grade. The last of my fellow awkward female students grew into themselves and got contacts and straightened their hair and started wearing pink workout pants and refused to do their homework. Suddenly everyone was only interested in talking about cheerleading tryouts and the homecoming game. Girls I'd known for years were suddenly dating red-faced senior boys with bulging muscles. Boys I'd known for years were wearing white baseball caps and studiously ignoring me when I tried to say hello to them in the hallways. I was used to being teased and laughed at, but I wasn't used to . . . not existing. I mean, it's hard not to exist in a small town.

And yet somehow I managed it.

Meanwhile, my father had moved out of our house and in with Candy Lamb, who lived on the edge of town in a tiny house with her seven-year-old twin daughters, Randie and Sandie. I barely ever saw him. Since Spencer was always off doing a thousand extracurricular activities (one, she confessed to me late one night, was kissing boys) . . . there is nothing more humiliating than having your younger sibling kiss someone for the first time before you do . . . I spent most of my time home alone with my mother, who had undergone such a significant personality change since the separation that some days I barely recognized her. For most of my life, my mother had been a huge presence in North Forest. She was loud and social and constantly chatting with her friends on the phone or organizing huge poker parties for all the women who worked at Shear Bliss. Now she was more interested in watching television or cooking by herself in the kitchen. The phone would ring and she'd refuse to answer it. Our dinner conversations consisted mostly of silence. I'd ask her how she was doing and she'd say, "Fine, honey, just great," but then I'd see that same glittering desperate look in her eyes. Our house started to get really messy. I left a bunch of dirty dishes in the sink as an experiment (my mother always *hated* dirty dishes) and she never scolded me or even reminded me that they were there.

One afternoon I came home from school and my father was sitting on our couch. I hadn't seen him in weeks.

"Hi, Mol," he said.

"Hi, Dad," I said. I put on my best fake smile. "How are Sandie and Randie?"

He sighed. "Fine."

"Where's Mom?" I asked.

"Your mom," he said, and then paused. "Your mom is having a hard time, Molly."

"What does that mean?"

"She, uh... she checked in to Silverwood this morning. She, uh, called me and asked me to drive her there."

Silverwood was a small complex of white wooden buildings off the highway about two towns away. I'd always pressed my face to the car window and gaped at it when we drove by on our family trips. It was, for lack of a better phrase, a mental hospital.

I stared at my father. *There's a point,* I thought, *where life gets so unfair that you stop even caring.*

"You and Spence are gonna come stay with me and Candy for a while," he said. "Okay?"

"Stupid," I said. The word just came out of my mouth.

My father gazed at me. "What's stupid?" he asked.

"Everything."

He smiled sadly. "You say the word *stupid* a lot, Mol. You've been saying it for years. But I'm never exactly sure what you mean."

"I mean stupid," I said. "I mean dumb. I mean idiotic."

He sighed. "Why don't you go up to your room and start packing up your stuff? I'm going to go pick Spencer up at her dance class and then we'll all drive to my place."

I turned and started walking toward the staircase.

"Oh," my father said, "one more thing."

I turned around. He held out a thick white envelope.

49

"This came for you," he said. "But I think they might have the wrong person. It's from Putnam Mount McKinsey."

I heaved the last volume of the OED into the trunk of the car, took a step back, and checked my watch. We were leaving in ten minutes. Ten minutes until I embarked on the road to paradise.

I felt a small hand tugging at my skirt. It was Sandie. I looked down at her and was reminded once again of how she resembled a tiny vampire.

"Hi, Sandie," I said.

"Are you happy to leave us?" she asked. Her mouth and cheeks were streaked with red Popsicle stains.

I smiled down at her. *No*, I thought, *of course not! Why would I be happy to leave a stupid town, a stupid high school, a stupid absent mother, a stupid emotionless father, a stupid stepmother who openly states that she wishes I were "prettier," two tiny stupid stepsisters who just spent the summer short-sheeting my bed, and a stupid traitorous younger sister who actually seems to like our new life on the edge of town with Candy and Randie and Sandie? Who actually seems to get along with them and enjoy their company?*

"No, Sandie," I said. "Of course I'm not happy to leave. But they gave me a full scholarship and stipend. It'll save us money if I go."

She squinted at me suspiciously.

"I'll come back to visit all the time," I reassured her, and crossed my fingers behind my back.

Candy Lamb came out of the house, banging the front door behind her. Randie followed close behind, clutching a bedraggled Barbie doll.

50

"You sure you don't want to change that skirt?" Candy asked.

I grinned at her. Nothing could make me feel bad now. Nothing.

"I'm sure," I said.

"HERB!" Candy shrieked.

My father emerged from the backyard, brushing the dirt off his pants. "Yep?" he asked.

"Don't you think Molly looks like a librarian in that skirt?"

He gazed at me. "Huh," he said. "I don't know. What does a librarian look like?"

Candy sighed. "Just go," she told me. "I don't care if you make a bad first impression."

"Where's Spencer?" I asked.

"SPENCER!" Candy bellowed. I winced. Candy's favorite activity seemed to be screaming the names of her new family members at the top of her lungs.

The screen door creaked open, and Spencer's blond head peeped out.

"Aren't you gonna give me a hug good-bye?" I said.

She reluctantly stepped outside and made her way toward me, teetering in a pair of enormous high heels.

"What are you doing in those ridiculous shoes?" I demanded.

Spencer's bright blue eyes flickered in Candy's direction. "Candy let me try them on."

I turned to Candy. "You're letting her traipse around in a pair of trashy high heels?"

"Excuse me, young lady," Candy snapped, "they are not trashy. And what business is it of yours if—"

"Let's just go, Dad," I said, shaking my head.

51

My father obediently took out his keys, and the two of us squeezed into the front seat, wedging ourselves between the piles of books I'd stacked on the floor. My father turned on the car. Just the sound of the engine purring filled my heart with excitement. Candy and Spencer and Sandie and Randie stood in the yard and watched us pull out of the driveway. Randie waved her Barbie back and forth. Sandie did a little dance. Candy still looked angry about my skirt. Spencer stared at the ground, her arms folded.

I rolled down the window. "If Mom calls, you'll give her my new number?" I called out.

"Okay," said Candy. "Yeah."

"I LOVE YOU!" Sandie yelled.

I looked at her in surprise. Neither she nor Randie had ever said anything like that before.

"I love you, too," I said slowly.

Sandie nodded and wiped her nose, smearing more red Popsicle juice across her face.

"Ready?" my father asked me.

"Ready," I said, and he put his foot on the gas.

It was nearly a half an hour later—when we were just a few minutes from my new home—when I remembered that I'd forgotten to hug Spencer good-bye.

NORTH FORE

Section C2

Miller/Lamb

Longtime North Forest residents Herbert A. Miller and Candy P. Lamb were married this Saturday at the Moody Street Church of Christ.

The couple has known each other since high school, when the bride was North Forest High's head cheerleader and the groom was the football team's star quarterback. Still, it's taken Herb and Candy more than twenty-five years and a marriage to other people to finally, as Candy puts it, "get our act together."

Candy is known throughout North Forest for her sunny personality and commanding presence at PTA and town hall meetings. Herb, a quieter but equally beloved figure in the community, is the owner and manager of the North Forest institution Herb's Diner.

The ring bearers were Candy's adorable twin girls, Randie and Sandie Lamb, and the flower girl was Herb's beaming daughter Spencer (recently awarded a blue ribbon for her baton twirling at the Chesterton County Fair). His older daughter, Molly, was the maid of honor.

The couple plans to honeymoon "somewhere in Florida."

The bride will be taking Miller's name.

FOUR

Alice

There are a lot of graveyards in western Massachusetts. Our van passed by dozens of them on its way to Putnam Mount McKinsey. There were old shady graveyards with paper-thin tombstones covered in ivy. There were new graveyards with the sun beating down and little American flags whipping in the wind. There were graveyards on the sides of mountains. There were graveyards in the center of each tiny town.

"I guess people in Massachusetts die a lot," I said to the boy sitting on my right. He ignored me.

I was smushed into a big, weird-smelling van with ten other kids who had also flown into Boston from New York. They were all returning students who already knew one another (there had been about twenty minutes of squealing and hugging at the airport), except for the one guy on my right. When we piled into the van, he'd reluctantly introduced himself to me as "Judah Lipston the Third." Then he proceeded to bury his face in a comic book for the rest of the drive.

So I had nothing to do but stare out the window at grave-yards for the next two hours.

At first we were driving through the suburbs of Boston. Then we were driving through medium-size towns. Then we were driving through small towns. Then we were driving through tiny towns. Then we were driving through places that weren't towns at all, just expanses of farmland with the occasional dot of a house off in the distance, followed by a graveyard, followed by another expanse of farmland, followed by another tiny house dot.

At this point someone yelled: "There's Mount McKinsey!"

I squinted into the distance and saw the outline of something jagged and gray in the sky.

"I cannot *wait* until Mount McKinsey weekend," one girl murmured. She wiggled her eyebrows, and everyone laughed.

"The Essence Game," another girl said. "We have to remember to play the Essence Game."

"You are sooo sadistic!" shrieked her friend.

It was like they were speaking a foreign language. I glanced at Judah Lipston the Third for help, but he was staring fixedly into his comic book at a picture of a purple alien with boobs getting blown to pieces by a small boy.

We eventually turned onto a gravel road, and then a dirt road, and then we drove past a carved red-and-gold sign that said PUTNAM MOUNT MCKINSEY. Everyone cheered. I muttered a halfhearted "yay."

Then, suddenly, I absorbed the fact that we were *there*. This would be the setting for the next three years of my life. (That summer I had gotten in the weird habit of thinking about my life as if it were a movie. Every time R. scowled at me, or Dad ignored me, or I had to say a final good-bye to a friend or neighbor, I would just pretend I was watching a sad movie about girl named Alice. I would even imagine the musical score—when there would be cheerful trumpets, when there would be sad strings. It was kind of sick. But I couldn't stop.)

I stared out the window. The new set for *Alice the Depressing Movie* was . . .

Unbelievably beautiful.

First of all, the campus was the greenest place I'd ever seen. I didn't know a place could be that green. There were dark green swaying pines and bright green maples and light green grass and old brick buildings with green-shingled roofs. And then there was the *light*. It was magical. The late summer sun was starting to set, and it was like the air was filled with shimmering gold. Gold light fell in patterns across the pavement in front of the buildings. Gold light shone through the branches of the trees. Gold light filled our van and made the faces of my gossiping, makeup-y future classmates look positively . . . angelic.

"This is the most beautiful place in the world," I whispered.

Judah Lipston the Third briefly glanced up from his comic book.

"Middleton Dorm," the van driver bellowed, and we came to a stop.

I took a crumpled slip of paper out of my pocket and looked at it. It said: Alice Bingley-Beckerman, Transfer Sophomore, Middleton Dorm, Room 201.

"That's me," I said, and started gathering my bags.

"Ooh," someone said, giggling. "She got the bad dorm."

I swallowed, pretended not to hear, and squeezed out of the van. It drove away and left me standing in the middle of a gravel path, surrounded by my suitcases.

I looked up at my future home.

It was, for lack of a better way to put it, a huge zit on the otherwise perfect face of Putnam Mount McKinsey.

Whereas every other building we'd driven by had been made out of beautiful, vine-covered brick, this building was made out of beige stucco. Whereas every other building we'd driven by looked like it was built in 1870, this building looked like it was built in 1970. It was dirty. It was rectangular. The windows were thin slits. It kind of looked like a prison.

It was obviously the dorm for the new students who didn't know any better.

A paper banner sagged in front of the main entrance. It said: WELCOME ALL. A bored-looking girl sat on the steps, smoking a cigarette. Filled with dread, I limped up the gravel path toward her, weighed down by my suitcases. The girl gazed at me apathetically. She had bright pink hair tied up in a ponytail on top of her head. She wore a T-shirt that was slashed open across the shoulder. She had a lip ring. She had about twelve bracelets on each arm. Most impressively, she had a long silver chain that connected a stud in her left nostril to a stud in her left ear.

I stood in front of her and tried to smile.

"Hi," she said.

"Hi," I said.

"I'm Agnes," she said.

"I'm Alice," I said.

She nodded tiredly, and stood up.

"I'm your RA," she informed me, and then she picked up one of my suitcases and started trudging into the dorm.

"Cool!" I said, and immediately hated myself for saying the

word. Somehow saying "cool" in front of someone so much cooler than me felt degrading.

I followed her inside, through a dank, carpeted lobby lined with empty bulletin boards, past some kind of lounge filled with orange furniture, and up a dark stairwell.

"You're the first one here," she said as we clomped up the stairs, "which sucks for you."

"That's okay," I said, even though my heart was sinking in my chest, "I can just hang out."

Agnes stopped abruptly in the middle of the stairs, turned around, and stared at me. "You're not going to be, like, clingy, are you?" she asked.

"What?" I said. "Clingy? I . . . no."

"Good," she said. "I'm your RA, but I'm not like your mom or anything."

"Of course," I said. Just the word *mom* made the back of my eyeballs prick with tears. I prayed she couldn't tell.

"Don't come crying to me or anything."

I nodded.

She cocked her head to one side and looked me up and down. "You're wearing all black," she commented. "That's kind of weird."

I nodded. I *was* wearing all black (I was even wearing black underwear, but Agnes didn't know that). I'd always been a pretty creative dresser, but ever since my dad and R.'s wedding that summer, the only color that appealed to me was black. So I was letting myself wear black. Every day. Why not? I was in mourning, after all. Not only for my mother, but also for the loss of my old, carefree, idyllic life.

"Why?" Agnes asked, her eyes narrowed. "Are you, like, goth? Because you don't seem goth."

"Um," I said, "No, I guess I'm not goth. I'm just—"

"Whatever," Agnes interrupted, already bored with whatever explanation I was going to give. "We're all good."

Then she turned around and started walking up the stairs again.

I had been lying facedown on my new bed for three hours when my roommate finally arrived. I heard the knob rattle, then the door open, and then all of a sudden a beautiful Indian girl was inside my room, dragging a pink suitcase behind her and screeching into her cell phone.

"It's so *dirty*!" she exclaimed.

I could hear the muffled voice of the person on the other end of the phone responding.

"Like *really* dirty," the beautiful girl shouted. "There's this, like, gray carpeting? And fluorescent lighting?"

I sat up in bed and looked at her, hoping that my face didn't look too bloated and tear streaked. The girl shot me a brief but blinding smile, and then kept talking into the phone.

"Yeah," she said, nodding and chomping on her gum. "Yeah. Totally."

Still nodding, she lugged another pink suitcase into the room. And then another. And then another. I eventually ended up counting more than ten. Still on the phone, she began to unpack them. I watched her in disbelief. Was she even going to introduce herself to me?

"No, totally," she murmured into the phone while she dragged what looked like a sequined ball gown out of one suitcase. "Totally, totally. I know. I feel the same way. Yeah. It's totally lame."

I studied her. She was wearing short-shorts, a tube top, and a pair of tiny blue high heels. A pair of sunglasses rested on top of her head. Her shiny jet-black hair curled perfectly around her shoulders. Although she and Agnes the RA couldn't have looked more different, I had a hard time deciding who was more terrifying.

The girl took a shoe box out of one bag and opened it. It was full of magazine cutouts.

"Mm-hm," she said. "Mm-hm. Blond. Mm-hm."

Was she talking about me?

"Of course not!" she shrieked into the phone. "I would never!"

She carefully unfolded a picture of a muscled male model in a tiny red swimsuit and tacked it onto the wall, wedging the cell phone between her shoulder and chin. Then she unfolded another picture of a tanned, half-naked male model. Then another one. Then another one. They all grinned at me across the room, flashing their white teeth.

I wondered if this girl was going to talk on her phone for the rest of the school year. I decided it was a strong possibility. I sat there and waited a few more minutes while she "uh-huh"-ed and "mm"-ed. Then I gave up and lay back down, pressing my face into the pillow.

"Katie," the girl said, "I gotta go. Yeah. You, too. You are such a lame ass. Yes. You. Okay. I love you. Swizzle sticks. Bye."

There was a small beeping sound as she hung up the phone. Then there was a long silence. I could hear the birds chirping outside our window.

"Hey," the girl said.

"Mmrf," I said into my pillow.

"I'm Reena."

I was suddenly terrified that if I lifted my face up and exposed it to my new roommate, I would start crying. So I attempted to speak without moving at all.

"I'm Alice," I said muffledly.

"Where are you from?"

"Brooklyn."

"Brooklyn? Like New York City Brooklyn?"

"Mm hm."

There was a long pause.

"I'm from Los Angeles," she said finally.

"Cool," I said. That *word* again. I had to stop saying that word. I also had to stop constantly being on the verge of crying. People could probably sense it in my voice. They could sense I was lonely and pathetic and nervous and scared.

"Want a Blow Pop?" Reena asked after a horrible pause. "I have cherry, and uh ... grape?"

"No, thanks," I mumbled, and then turned my face to the wall.

After a minute I heard her start unpacking again, and the two of us didn't speak until Agnes knocked on our door and told us to head down to the lounge for orientation.

The expectant faces of thirty teenage girls turned in my direction.

"My name is Alice," I said slowly, "and I like ... um, apples."

"Someone already said apples," said the girl sitting across from me.

Everyone giggled.

"Oh," I said. "Okay. Um. My name is Alice and I like . . ."

My mind was going blank. I liked eggplant. I liked chocolate. I liked peanut butter. I liked raspberries. Were the any words in existence that began with A besides *apple*?

"I like . . ." My mouth was dry. I blinked. I swallowed. A wave of laughter made its way around the circle.

"Do you like artichokes?" whispered the girl on my right. I looked at her, surprised. She was tiny, with thick glasses and a smattering of pimples across her nose. She looked about twelve. I exhaled, relieved.

"My name is Alice and I like artichokes," I announced to the group.

That was a big lie. I hated artichokes. But I would have said I liked eating dog to get through my turn.

Then it was time for Reena to speak. She was sitting to my left. The two of us had been conscientiously ignoring each other ever since we left our dorm room.

I couldn't believe that my new roommate already hated me. And that I hated her.

But I only hated her because she so obviously hated me.

"My name is Reena," Reena said, with enough apathy in her voice to make it clear to everyone that she thought the game was dumb, "and I like radicchio."

"What's radicchio?" asked the bespectacled girl on my right.

Reena gasped. "You don't know what *radicchio* is?"

The girl shrugged.

"It's like this really, really delicious vegetable that they put in salads."

"Oh," said the girl with the glasses. "I guess I've never had it."

"Well, they serve it in all the best restaurants."

"Oookay," said Agnes, who was sitting in the middle of the circle. "I think that's everyone. Do you all know each other's names now?"

I looked around the circle at the faces of the other girls in my dorm. I couldn't remember any of them. They all looked the same: high ponytail, tank top, flip-flops, and sunglasses on top of their heads. They also all looked way more confident than I felt.

Except for the tiny girl with glasses on my right who didn't know what radicchio was.

She just seemed kind of . . . pathetic.

"All right," yawned Agnes. "What's next?"

She took a piece of paper out of her pocket and inspected it.

"Dinnertime," she announced.

And then, like a dam had broke, everyone rose to their feet and streamed out of the room. I was left sitting on the dirty orange rug all by myself.

Why, I wondered, am I *this* person? What's wrong with me? Why am I invisible? Why am I the one who never gets swept up in the crowd? And why does my own roommate already think that I'm totally boring and lame?

Is it because I actually *am* boring and lame?

Or is it because everyone thinks I'm goth?

I shakily got to my feet and walked out of the lounge and into the cafeteria.

It was chaos.

My fellow new students had already been absorbed into what seemed like a crowd of hundreds. Everyone was squeezed around a table and talking, or yelling across the room to one another, or standing in line, or circling the salad bar and chatting. I scanned the room for one girl, just one girl, who looked alone and out of place. But everyone had already found someone. Everyone had already found *five* other someones. Even the tiny girl with glasses and zits was cheerfully conversing with a cafeteria lady.

I stood in the middle of the dinner hall, my head throbbing. *Someone come talk to me,* I prayed.

I waited around ten seconds and was suddenly jostled by a beautiful girl with red hair, holding a cafeteria tray.

"Excuse me," she said. Her violet eyes sparkled while she looked me up and down.

"Sorry," I said. "Um ..."

Say something, I told myself. *Say something.*

I could barely choke the words out. "Um, my name is ..."

But someone was already whispering in the beautiful girl's ear, and the beautiful girl was already staring at me and giggling.

"Reena," she exclaimed to the person next to her. "You are *so bad!*"

Then the two of them walked away, arms linked and heads bowed together, their shoulders shaking with laughter.

I held my tears back just long enough to grab a handful of croutons from the salad bar, sprint up the stairs to my room, and fall face-first onto my pillow.

FIVE

Reena

Okay, so boarding school wasn't exactly what I expected.

Is it wrong that I hoped my dorm room would have wood floors? and a fireplace? and maybe the stuffed head of a mountain lion hanging over the mantelpiece?

Instead I got dirty gray carpeting, streaky walls, a buzzing fluorescent light, and not much else.

And is it wrong that I hoped my roommate might be a nice, normal, friendly person with whom I could hold an actual conversation? Maybe even a cool East Coast girl who could teach me how to roast chestnuts and make really good hot chocolate?

Instead I got a sulky blond chick wearing all black who looked exactly like a younger version of Shanti Shruti. And even that would have been okay, if she had deigned to talk to me. Instead Miss Cooler Than Thou lay on her bed and ignored me for hours while I unpacked. Well, fine. I didn't need her. I could make friends on my own while she sat around and looked down her nose at everybody. And it made total sense when she said she was from New York City. New York City kids—I'd always imagined—were ten times more sophisticated than everyone else. But Alice Bingley-Beckerman was sophisticated in a bad way. I could tell that she thought I was immature and dumb.

Point is, I already had one snotty blond woman in my life making me feel bad. I didn't need another.

Which is not to say I wasn't seized by terror when I walked into the cafeteria that first night and realized that I was going to have find someone else to talk to. And somewhere to sit.

I picked up a plastic tray and made my way toward the hot food line. I waited as the line moved forward, trying to keep a nonchalant expression on my face. *Show no weakness, Reenie,* my father had told me on my first day of school in Beverly Hills, right after we'd saved up enough money to move there. *The key is to never let anyone know you feel bad.*

I stared over the heads of my new classmates so it looked like I was spacing out and thinking about something incredibly important.

"Ew," someone behind me in line said.

I turned around. The someone was a frighteningly perfect-looking girl with shiny red hair and porcelain skin. She was wearing a purple minidress and purple eyeliner. Her pink lip gloss was flawlessly applied. Was she talking to me?

"What *is* that smell?" she asked, her lips pursed in distaste. Our eyes connected. Okay. She was talking to me. I had to say something witty in return. Something cool. Something disaffected. I assumed she was talking about the smell in the hot

66

food line, which, to be honest, was not as bad as it could have been. But there was something else my father liked to say to me: *Pick your battles, Reenie. Pick your battles.*

"It smells kind of like homeless man," I said thoughtfully. "Combined with old cheese. And nail polish. And my grandmother's sweat."

The girl shrieked with pleasure. "That is, like, the grossest thing I've ever heard!"

I grinned. "You haven't heard anything yet." It was true. I was famous at my high school for my disgusting sense of humor.

"I'm Kristen," the girl said. She held out her hand. I shook it.

"I'm Reena," I said.

"Reena? What is that?"

I wasn't sure exactly what she meant. "Um. It's Indian?"

"Oh. Cool." Her eyes flickered up and down my face, then up and down my body. "I like your shoes."

"Thanks."

"Are you new here?"

I rolled my eyes. "Unfortunately, yes."

"Me, too."

"Where are you from?"

Kristen tugged on the edge of her purple dress. For a split second, it looked like she felt uncomfortable. Then the look evaporated. I wasn't sure what had happened. She tossed her shiny red hair behind her shoulder.

"Westport, Connecticut," she said.

"Oh. Cool." I'd never even heard of it, but it sounded nice. Connecticut. I pictured thousands of red-haired Kristen clones, all living in perfect white houses with perfect green yards.

"Where are you from?" Kristen asked.

"Los Angeles."

"Agggh!" she yelled. "I hate you! That's where I want to move when I grow up!"

"Oh. Yeah. It's okay."

"Okay?" she said while cafeteria ladies spooned shapeless lumps of chicken and sauce onto our plates. "I want more information. Do you, like, know any movie stars?"

"Nah," I said, as we moved out of line into the dining hall. "I mean, except for the fact that some of them work out at my gym."

"You're kidding me."

"Uh, no. But that's not a big deal or anything. I mean, you see celebrities all the time. On the street and stuff. It's really not that exciting."

Kristen sighed. "I *totally* hate you."

We were standing in the middle of the dining hall, balancing our dinner trays on our palms. I cleared my throat nervously.

"We might as well sit together," Kristen said after a long pause.

"Yeah," I said. "Might as well."

I could have kissed her.

We made our way through the crowd, looking for an empty table. Suddenly I saw Alice Bingley-Beckerman. She was standing alone in her black skirt and T-shirt, looking around the cafeteria with an expression of utter terror on her face. For a second, I felt bad for her. But then I realized that what looked to me like fear was probably classic New Yorker disdain. She was just thinking about how uncool all her fellow classmates were.

Another nugget of gold from Rashul Paruchuri: *Be nice, Reenie. Just not too nice.*

Kristen and Alice bumped right into each other, and I saw Alice's face light up. *Oh no,* I thought. *I'm not cool enough for her, but Kristen is!* Before either of them could say anything, I leaned over to Kristen and whispered the first thing that popped into mind.

"I have to get out of here and smoke a cigarette," I hissed.

Kristen stared at me, delighted.

"You are so bad!" she shrieked, and the two of us headed off toward the exit, leaving Alice Bingley-Beckerman in our wake.

At first I felt a wave of relief. Then, slowly, I started to realize what I'd just said, and my stomach dropped.

I have this terrible habit of . . . well, you wouldn't call it pathologically *lying,* because I never mean to *lie,* but I have this habit of sometimes just saying things that, well, In No Way Correspond to Reality.

For example: My father once threw this party for all the surgeons at his hospital, and we were all standing around and mingling with champagne glasses when this one old guy said to me: "You know, I actually attended Woodstock in 1969." And, without even thinking about it, I nodded enthusiastically and said: "That's so funny! So did I!"

I was born decades after Woodstock.

The problem is, I can't control it. I don't even know that I've lied—I mean, said something that's not exactly true—until after I've already said it.

So when I leaned over and told Kristen that I needed to go outside and have a cigarette, I didn't anticipate that I'd actually have to go outside and . . . have a cigarette. I mean, I don't

69

smoke. I took one puff at a party in seventh grade and almost hacked up a lung.

But all of a sudden Kristen was leading me out of the building and over to a shady tree next to our dorm.

"We can eat here while you smoke," she said cheerfully, and plunked her tray down onto the grass.

I patted my pockets. I think I was half-praying that a pack of cigarettes would mysteriously appear inside of them.

"Aw geez," I said, "I'm out. I'm out of cigarettes."

"Oh no!" she said, a concerned look on her face.

"Yeah. It's okay. I can survive."

"Well, you must be *dying* for one."

"Um, well—"

"I mean, you must be, like, totally addicted, right?"

I nodded, my stomach churning. "Yeah. I guess I am."

She stared at me.

"Um," I said. I looked around the lawn. Agnes, my extremely weird Residential Advisor, was lying on the grass about twenty feet away, chatting with a guy wearing leather pants. I peered over at them. The guy was holding something small and white in his hands.

"Hold on a minute," I said to Kristen, and marched purposefully across the lawn toward them.

"Hi, Agnes," I said.

Agnes squinted up at me in the sunlight, her arms crossed behind her head. A slice of her stomach was exposed, and I saw that the skin below her bellybutton was pierced with a small silver barbell.

"Hey, Nina," she said.

"It's Reena."

"Right. Reena."

70

I swallowed and smiled at Agnes and her leather pants–wearing friend. "Um, I was just wondering...do you...do either of you have a cigarette?"

The guy raised his eyebrows at Agnes. Agnes sat up.

"You smoke?" she asked, staring at me.

"Uh, yeah."

"No," she said. "No way. Not you." Her eyes seemed to penetrate into my very soul.

"Oh, yes," I said.

Agnes sighed and turned to her male companion. "God. Smoking doesn't mean anything anymore, does it?"

I had no idea what she was talking about. Neither did he apparently. He shrugged, withdrew a red pack of cigarettes from his pocket, and held them out to me. I took one, tentatively held it between my thumb and forefinger, and stared at it. One end was light brown. The other end was white. Which part did you put in your mouth?

"Cool, thanks," I said to the guy in leather pants.

"You need a light?" he asked.

"Uh, sure," I said.

I held out the cigarette. Agnes chortled.

"You put it in your *mouth* first," she said. "Are you *sure* you're a smoker?"

I nodded, and looked across the lawn at Kristen. She waved at me. I waved back.

"Yup," I said. "We just, uh, do it a little differently in California."

"Like, *how* differently?"

I pretended not to hear. I put the white part of the cigarette in my mouth.

"WRONG END!" shrieked Agnes, and then she fell back

onto the grass, laughing hysterically. I prayed that Kristen couldn't hear.

I put the brown end in my mouth. The guy in leather pants held out his silver lighter. A blue flame leapt up. I put the cigarette in my mouth, leaned over, and dipped it into the flame. What next? I glanced up at the guy. It looked like he was wearing mascara.

"Inhale," he whispered.

I inhaled.

What felt like a brush fire went through the cigarette, into my mouth, and down my throat. I started choking. Some kind of phlegm rose up in my throat. Before I even knew what was happening, I'd spat out the cigarette onto the grass and was crouched over on the ground, hacking. Agnes wailed with laughter. The guy in leather pants was shaking his head.

"Thanks, anyway," I whispered, my eyes burning with tears, and jogged back across the lawn toward Kristen.

It felt like small demon was running around inside my throat, setting fire to my tonsils.

"What happened?" Kristen asked.

I was planning on just giving up and telling her the truth. I really was.

But then That Thing happened again.

"Those *cigarettes*," I said. "That guy had the worst cigarettes."

"Oh, really?"

"Yeah. I'm, like, extremely picky about the cigarettes I smoke. And those were really gross. Blech."

"What kind of cigarettes do you normally smoke?"

"Um. This really expensive French kind."

I wanted to punch myself in the face.

"I guess we'll go buy some later," Kristen decided, and patted a spot on the ground next to her. "Now tell me more about LA."

I sighed with relief.

I had a friend.

Now I just had to make sure not to compulsively lie to her.

"LIGHTS OUT!" Agnes bellowed, running up and down the hallway. "LIGHTS OUT, YOU LITTLE SUCKERS!"

Another big surprise about Putnam Mount McKinsey: It felt a little, just a little, like a prison.

All freshman and sophomores, Agnes informed us during our orientation meeting, had dinner at 7:00 PM, study period from 8:00 to 10:00 PM, and then lights out at 10:30.

I couldn't believe it.

In LA, I went bed at midnight. At the earliest.

Alice Bingley-Beckerman and I sat on the edge of our parallel twin beds, waiting for Agnes to knock on our door. Alice was wearing a beautiful black satin nightgown, and her blond hair rippled down her back.

I was wearing a pair of Pradeep's old boxer shorts and a tank top.

We were ignoring each other.

I felt ugly.

Even worse, I was starting to get this weird stomachache. I tried to remember another time I'd felt this way, and the only thing I could think of was this summer vacation Pradeep and I took when I was ten. We'd never met our mother's parents before and so they sent the two of us to Bangalore, India, to meet them. After a sixteen-hour plane trip, we spent two weeks in a tiny, hot house outside of the city, listening to a grandmother we'd never met before lecture us on how we were leading pointless, immoral lives in America. Between lectures, she'd chew dates and spit the pits into the palm of her hand.

There were also servants we weren't allowed to touch.

And one night I was forced to eat goat.

Anyway, the whole time we were in Bangalore, I had a stomachache. Maybe it goat-induced indigestion, but mostly I think it was homesickness. I missed my mom. I missed my dad. I missed my friends. I missed my dolls. I missed running in and out of the sprinkler in our backyard.

And the second I got back to LA and was folded into my mother's warm, rose-scented bosom, the stomachache went away.

Now I was sitting in a strange little room at this strange little boarding school in Massachusetts, next to a snotty blond girl who was ignoring me, waiting to be checked on by a scary older girl who seemed to be the only parental figure around, and it was that same feeling again. That same stomachache. That same feeling of homesickness.

And then I realized something even scarier: I wasn't even sure what I was homesick *for*.

I didn't want to go live with my mother and Pria.

I definitely didn't want to go live with my father and Shanti Shruti.

I was missing something that didn't exist.

I was missing the past.

I was pastsick.

There was a loud knock on our door.

"Yes?" Alice murmured.

Agnes threw open the door. "Yo," she said. "Just making sure you're both here."

"Yo," I said sadly.

She peered at me. "You know you can't smoke in the dorm rooms, right?"

Alice whipped her head around and stared at me. "You *smoke*?" she asked.

It was the first sentence she'd spoken to me all evening.

"Er," I said, "Yeah. I guess."

Agnes laughed in her horrible condescending way, and shut the door.

There was a long pause. I glanced in Alice's direction. She was bent over, her chin cupped in her hand, and her hair fell across her face.

"I guess I'll turn the lights out," I said.

She nodded.

I stood up, flicked off the light switch, and the room was plunged into total darkness.

"Good night," I said.

"Good night," Alice whispered, and I groped my way toward my bed, holding my hands out in front of me and trying to see its outline in the darkness. I felt the edge of my mattress with my knee, and touched my pillow with my finger. Then I let my body collapse onto my new, hard, cold, and unfamiliar bed.

I listened to the sound of my breath. I listened to the sound of Alice's breath. Someone had left a single glow-in-the-dark star sticker on the ceiling. I stared at it for a long time.

Then my cell phone rang.

Alice bolted upright.

"Sorry, sorry!" I yelped, and reached down to the floor to fish it out of my purse. Pradeep's name appeared on the screen. I took the phone and burrowed under my covers.

"Hello?" I whispered.

I heard Alice exhale in disgust.

"REEN!" Pradeep yelled into my ear. I could hear music playing and people talking in the background.

"Quieter, please," I murmured.

"REEN!"

"What?"

"IT'S AWESOME HERE!"

I didn't know what to say. Was he kidding?

"Aren't you in bed?" I asked.

"Aw, no way! Our RA is awesome! He's letting us stay up and party!"

"Oh."

"Are you okay?" Pradeep asked.

I sighed. "Um. I guess."

"Do you like your roommate? Mine is awesome. He's from *Nova Scotia*. Isn't that crazy? He, like, goes moose hunting for fun!"

In the background I could hear hooting and laughter.

"I don't know," I whispered.

"Wait. What? You don't know what?"

I sighed, exasperated.

"What are you talking about?" he asked again.

"Pradeep."

"What?"

"I have to go."

76

"Oh. Okay. Cool, cool."

"I'll see you tomorrow."

We hung up. I stared at the ceiling. I had never felt more alone in my life.

And it was all Shanti Shruti's fault.

SIX

Molly

Radicchio.

I couldn't believe it. My first day at boarding school and there was already a *word* I didn't *know.*

An unprecedented event.

Right after dinner I ran upstairs to my dorm room and looked up *radicchio* in the OED.

"A variety of chicory," I whispered out loud.

The door opened and then slammed shut. I looked up from my bed. My new roommate was standing in front of me, hands on her hips. Her violet eyes blazed with anger.

"Is this what it's going to be like?" she demanded.

"Hi, Kristen," I said.

She pursed her lips and stared at me for a long time.

"Is this what *what's* going to be like?" I finally asked.

"Living together. Are you always going to be in here, like, reading?"

"Um, no. But I do like to read."

She sighed and flounced down onto her bed. My heart did a terrified little leap. My roommate—Miss Kristen Diamond of Westport, Connecticut—uncannily reminded me of the popular girls at North Forest High. Except with more money. And more rage.

I had sort of thought everyone at Putnam Mount McKinsey was going to be thoughtful and nerdy and quiet and friendly. Like me.

Kristen kicked off her flip-flops and lay on her back. I tried to focus on the OED and listen to the whirring of the window fan.

"Do you have a boyfriend?" she finally asked.

I chortled, not taking my eyes off the dictionary.

"What's so funny?"

"I've never had a boyfriend."

"Never?"

"Nope."

"Have you ever been on a date?"

"No."

"God. That is tragic."

I stared at the OED entry. *Radicchio. From the Italian.*

"I've had, like, ten different boyfriends," Kristen announced.

"Good for you."

"Are you being sarcastic or something?"

"Nope. Not at all."

Normally having reddish purple, white-veined leaves. Not used in the English language until 1978. So I'd never had a boyfriend. Big deal. Not that I didn't want one. It was just that . . . no guy had ever really expressed an interest in me. And I'd never met a guy I thought was that great.

Except for that one guy in the pink shirt, the one I'd seen

years before in my father's diner. The Putnam Mount McKin-sey student with the book of Emily Dickinson poems sticking out of his pocket. He was perfect.

That guy had probably already graduated.

Kristen snapped me out of my reverie. "...sex," she was saying. "I've only had sex four times. But I plan to get a lot more practice here."

I nodded numbly.

"I've already seen a bunch of really cute guys."

There was no way I was going to be able to focus on my reading. I put down the OED and lay on my back while Kris-ten chattered away about her ex-boyfriends. My heart thumping quietly, I stared at the ceiling and thought about my new life. Everything had changed so quickly. Putnam Mount McKinsey was nothing like what I thought it would be, and my memories from that very morning—Spencer standing in the driveway in those terrible high heels—seemed incredibly far away. I didn't miss North Forest yet, not at all, and yet I couldn't really comprehend the fact that I didn't live there anymore. It was kind of hard to believe that I could climb in a car and just *drive away* from the place I'd hated my whole life.

But could I?

Because I was still thinking about it. I was thinking about my mom at Silverwood, sitting by the window in her rocking chair, staring out at the sinking sun. I was thinking about Candy kissing my father good night and making another snide comment about my skirt. I was thinking about Sandie and Randie squatting together under a tree and digging for earth-worms.

I was just . . . living somewhere else now.

Kristen kept chattering away, and I kept nodding and saying, "Mmhm," even though I'd stopped listening.

Where were the people who were going to become part of My New and Better Life?

I wanted to meet them. As soon as possible.

Early the next morning, I stood outside the student union with my fellow transfer classmates and listened to a psychotically cheerful junior scream into a megaphone.

"STUDENT LIFE AT PUTNAM MOUNT MCKINSEY IS ALL ABOUT TRUST!" she yelled.

A couple of people snickered. Kristen, who had made a point of standing as far away from me as possible, nudged a beautiful Indian girl who was standing next to her and winked at her.

Even though Kristen was my new Least Favorite Person Ever, I felt a twinge of jealousy. I wanted someone to wink at me.

"YOU HAVE TO TRULY TRUST YOUR FELLOW CLASSMATES TO CREATE A PRODUCTIVE AND HARMONIOUS ENVIRONMENT," the girl bellowed. "SO WE'RE GOING TO DO A FEW EXERCISES TO GET EVERYONE FEELING COMFORTABLE AND OPEN!"

At least fifteen kids groaned.

"COUNT OFF IN TENS!"

A halfhearted muttering passed through the crowd. I barely heard the girl next to me whisper, "Five."

"Six!" I said loudly.

Someone nearby burst out laughing.

"OKAY," the junior announced. "ONES, OVER THERE. TWOS, OVER THERE. THREES, OVER THERE . . ."

When she got to the sixes, she pointed vaguely at a patch of shady grass off in the distance, and I trudged toward it. Kristen was already standing there, tapping her foot impatiently. She looked at me in horror.

"Oh, God," she said. "You're kidding me."

"Nope," I said.

"Is it just the two of us?" she asked. "Because if it is—"

I never found out what she was going to say. A smiling boy had suddenly stepped into our little patch of shade. Kristen and I fell silent.

"Hey," he said, his hand outstretched, "I'm Pradeep."

Kristen and I both stared at him, speechless. Then, for some miraculous reason, I recovered my composure.

"I'm Molly," I said, and shook his hand. He grinned at me.

"What up, Molly?" he said.

He had thick black hair and skin the color of maple syrup. He had a gap between his two front teeth. He had hazel eyes. He had a crooked grin. He had ears that were just a little too big for his head. He had a gorgeous lips. He had the tiniest bit of chest hair poking out from underneath the neck of his V-neck T-shirt. He had bony wrists. He had a pronounced Adam's Apple that throbbed slightly when he smiled. He had—

"I'm Kristen," said Kristen. She stepped forward, her red hair falling across half of her face, and delicately offered him her hand.

The boy blinked. I watched his hazel eyes take in Kristen's perfect skin, her perfect hair, her perfect dress, her perfect body. *No!* I tried to telepathically communicate to him, *don't!*

"It's weird that you shake people's hands," Kristen said to him, raising one eyebrow.

He tilted his head to one side and stared at her, mock serious. "You got a problem with that?" he asked.

"Yeah," she said, her lips thrumming with a half-concealed smile. "I do."

They grinned at each other.

Great. Just great.

"OKAY, EVERYONE!" screamed the megaphone girl. "I WANT TWO PEOPLE IN EVERY GROUP TO PAIR OFF!"

"Well, I'm definitely not pairing off with you," Pradeep said to Kristen.

"You neither," she giggled, and they moved toward each other as if by magnetic force.

"Oookay," I said. "I guess you guys are the pair."

They ignored me.

"NOW!" the girl said. "THIRD PERSON, FACE AWAY FROM THE PAIR!"

I sighed and faced away from Kristen and Pradeep. I could see a Japanese-style pond in the distance, with tall reeds and stone benches. I pictured sitting on one of the benches with Pradeep and whispering word origins in his ear. *You're so smart,* he'd murmur, and then our fingers would touch.

"FALL BACK!" the girl yelled into the megaphone, interrupting my fantasy.

My heart froze. I turned around to face Kristen and Pradeep.

"What'd she say?" I asked.

Kristen stared at me, already annoyed. "She said fall back. Fall back and we'll catch you."

"Um," I said. "I don't want to."

"It's okay," said Pradeep. "You can trust us."

I looked at him for a long time. He smiled reassuringly at me, and I watched his amazing Adam's apple bob up and down. What would it be like to touch his neck?

"For God's sakes, Molly," Kristen said. "Fall."

"Okay, okay," I said, and turned back to face the Japanese garden. I paused. I didn't want to fall. Why was this a necessary part of boarding school orientation? What did this have to do with math and English class?

"FALL!" I heard through the megaphone. "FALL!"

I closed my eyes. The sun shone through my closed lids and made everything a pulsing orange color. I smelled the new-cut grass and the sunscreen on people's skin. Okay. I had to do it. I had to take risks. This was my new life. Everything was different now.

I took a deep breath. I rocked back on my ankles. Once. Twice. A third time. And then, my body rigid, my hands pressed against my side, I fell.

For a while everything went black.

I woke to find a bright buzzing light shining into my eyes. I squinted. My head hurt.

"She's awake!" someone whispered, and then a head floated into my line of vision.

It was Pradeep. I smiled groggily at him and assumed I was dreaming.

"Uh, hey," he said. "Molly? That's your name, right?"

"Mmhm," I murmured, and his beautiful eyes swam in and out of focus.

"I'm really sorry, dude," he whispered.

Unable to help myself, I kept grinning at him.

"Can you understand me?" he asked.

I bobbled my head around, trying to nod.

"It was really lame, what happened," he said. "We just . . . we were talking, and we forgot, and it was a total accident, but it was . . ."

I wasn't sure what he was talking about, but I didn't like the words he was using. Lame. Accident. *We.*

"Where am I?" I whispered.

"Oh, dude," he said. "You must be really out of it. You're at the nurse's office."

A stern-looking woman's face appeared above me. "You have to leave now," the face told Pradeep.

He nodded, and his head floated away.

My forehead suddenly throbbed with pain. I winced. I heard the door click as Pradeep left the room. The woman stared down at me.

"You, my dear," she said, "have a concussion."

"Nope," I said. "That's impossible."

"It is the very opposite of impossible," she said. "It's fact. Your friends forgot to catch you and your head hit the concrete."

I felt a stinging sensation in the back of my eyes.

Of course.

This was the kind of thing that could only, only happen to me. This particular brand of pathetic humiliation was Classic Molly Miller.

"They're not my friends," I whispered.

"What did you say, sweetheart?" she asked.

"They're not my friends!" I said, and then burst into hot, burning tears.

I drifted in and out of sleep. A day passed. Maybe two. I awoke to a ray of midafternoon sun streaming in through the window and falling across my legs. I could see thousands of dust particles in the air, fluttering in the beam of light like little insects.

"Molly," someone said.

The voice sent a chill down my spine. I recognized it but couldn't place it.

A hand reached out and shook my wrist.

"*Molly,*" the voice said again.

I raised my head up, painfully. Candy was sitting in a chair across from my bed, her hands folded across her lap.

It took all of my strength to stop myself from groaning out loud.

"How are you feeling," Candy said. She said it like a statement, not a question.

"I'm okay," I murmured. "Where's Dad?"

"At home with Sandie and Randie."

"Why aren't *you* at home with Sandie and Randie?"

"Do not mouth off to me, missy."

"Okay, okay."

There was a long pause.

"I want you to come back to North Forest," Candy said.

I shot up in bed. Pain seared through my skull. "*What?*" I yelped.

"You should come home."

"Why?"

"We need your help."

I stared at her. Her face was expressionless. Her mouth formed a tight little line. Her blue eyes looked dull and blank.

"You need my help doing what?"

"Your father and I are both working full-time. Spencer is practicing for the statewide twirling competition. Sandie and Randie need someone to—"

"No." My head throbbed. My whole body was trembling. My fingers clutched at the edges of the sheet. I made direct eye contact with Candy. "I will not come home."

"You don't belong here, Molly."

"Yes I do."

"Look at you. You get a, a *concussion* within twenty-four hours of—"

"Shut up!" I yelled.

Candy shook her head. "You're being irresponsible," she said after a while. "Your father and I need someone else to help out. The fact that you think you can just abandon your family and—"

"You're not my family," I told her.

"Excuse me?"

"You're not my family."

"Oh, yeah? Then who's your family?"

My stomach sank.

Candy gave me a rueful smile. "The rest of your family is checked into the loony bin."

"It's a residential treatment facility."

She laughed. "Right. Whatever."

"I'm never going back to North Forest," I said, trying to sound full of conviction.

"You're abandoning your sisters."

Spencer's face flashed through my mind. I shook my head and tried to push it away. "I'm not leaving."

"We'll see how you feel after first semester."

"No. No. No."

She stood up and folded her purse into her chest. "Well," she said, gazing down at me, "you might not have a choice."

And then, her high heels clicking neatly across the linoleum floor, she was gone.

SEVEN

Alice

It was a pleasant, breezy morning. The sun was peeking through streaks of gauzy white clouds. The bells of Putnam chapel were ringing.

I was miserable.

It was the first official day of classes. I had managed to get through three days of orientation without making a single friend, and now I was walking up a grassy hill toward the humanities building, toward my first class, all by myself. Surrounding me were clumps and pairs of my fellow students, giggling and talking and swinging their book bags by their side.

I walked through a set of big double doors and stopped in the lobby. It was a beautiful old building, with wooden floors and beams of light shining through stained-glass windows. I squinted at a sign with little arrows indicating classroom numbers and locations and then walked down a narrow hallway. My mouth was dry. I was worried nothing would come out if I tried to talk.

"Hi, Alice," a high, nasal voice piped up next to me.

I turned and looked. It was the same shrimpy girl with glasses from the first night of school. Except this time she had a white band of gauze wrapped around her head.

"Hi," I croaked, and kept walking down the hall.

She trotted alongside me. "You like artichokes, right?"

"What?"

She giggled. "Remember? From the name game? You couldn't think of a word that started with A?"

Great. Even the nerdy girl thought I was a loser.

"I'm Molly Miller, by the way," she added.

"Oh. Right." I glanced up and down the hall, trying to find an escape route.

"I like the all-black thing," she said. "It's very Hamlet. Have you read *Hamlet*?"

I shook my head.

"You have to. By Shakespeare? It's my favorite play. Hopefully we'll get to read it sometime this year. Are you in Humanities 101?" she continued brightly.

"Um, yeah."

"Me, too!"

"Oh. Cool."

"Hey!" she exclaimed, and stopped in her tracks. "This is our classroom!"

She flung open a door on our right and held it out for me like a bellhop.

I sighed. Maybe this made me a Bad Person, but I really didn't want to walk into class at the same time as Molly Miller. She was kind of a . . . dork. And I wanted to make friends.

People who looked like Molly Miller didn't usually have friends.

I entered the classroom with my head ducked down and slid into a seat. I could see my classmates talking and laughing out of the corner of my eye. I was too freaked out to look at any of them directly. Molly immediately plunked herself down in the desk next to me and leaned over, propping her chin in her hands.

"English is my favorite subject," she said in a loud whisper. "By *far*."

I nodded.

"I wonder what's gonna be on the reading list."

I nodded again. The last thing on my mind was the reading list.

Someone cleared his throat, and the classroom fell silent. I looked up. A young man—he was probably in his late twenties—was leaning against the desk at the front of the classroom, his arms folded. He was small and compact, with sparkling eyes, and his black hair was streaked with gray.

"Hi, everyone," he said.

There was a general murmuring in response.

"My name is David Newman," he said. "Welcome to Humanities 101. I'll be your teacher for the entire school year. So here's hoping we don't all hate each other."

There were a couple of chuckles. Molly let out a burst of high-pitched laughter. I winced.

"In this class," David Newman began, moving behind his desk and sitting down, "we're going to spend most our time studying the Greats. *Gilgamesh. The Odyssey. Henry the Fifth.* Wharton's *House of Mirth.*"

I could see Molly Miller nodding vigorously to the right of me. I had no idea what he was talking about.

"But," he continued, "I'm going to start us off with a

piece of twentieth-century literature. This is a fantastic work by a contemporary novelist, and it synthesizes many of the disparate themes and works we'll be discussing this fall."

My brain was somehow unable to absorb anything this guy said. I looked around the classroom desperately. Could anyone else understand him?

He reached into his desk, pulled out a book, and held it up in the air. I couldn't see the title, but it somehow looked familiar. Something about its color and the blurry illustration on the cover . . .

"This is *Zen Ventura*," he announced. "Has anyone heard of it?"

My heart stopped.

Molly Miller's hand shot up into the air. Slowly I raised mine, too. David Newman glanced in our direction.

"Okay. Two of you. Well, this was a seminal book in 1978. Just about everyone read it and was influenced by it. Nelson Bingley is one of the great writers in the post-1950 generation of—"

His words starting blending into each other. *Zen Ventura.* My father's first and most famous novel. The one I never bothered to read because it looked too thick and boring.

Now we were talking about it on the first day of school.

It had never occurred to me that this could happen.

I glanced over at Molly Miller. She was in the middle of talking.

"—one of my most favorite authors," she finished, her cheeks flushed with excitement.

"I'm so glad," David said. He nodded in my direction. "And what about you? When did you read it?"

I tried to swallow. My tongue was glued to the roof of my mouth.

"Um," I said. There was a long pause. Everyone in the class turned to look at me. I stared into the sea of their blank, disinterested faces. "Uh . . . I actually haven't read it. I've just . . . ah . . ." I trailed off.

"Heard of it?" asked David.

Another attempt at swallowing. "Yeah."

"Okay. Well. That's fine." He turned to the rest of the class. I breathed a sigh of relief. "There should be twenty-five copies waiting for you guys at the school store. By this time next week everyone should have read the first three chapters. Okay?"

General shuffling and nodding and whispering.

"Okay." He smiled at all of us. "So I guess that's it. I see no point in keeping you guys. I'm here to talk to you about literature, and since you haven't done the reading yet . . . we have nothing to say to each other."

Molly Miller let out another high-decibel squeal of laughter. Everyone rose to their feet and started trudging out of the classroom. I saw my roommate, Reena, and her new red-haired best friend whispering to each other and glancing over their shoulders as they walked out the door.

I sighed. They were probably talking about what a big loser I was. Reena had managed to ignore me for the past three days, except in the middle of our second night when she'd reached across the gap between our beds, poked my shoulder, and yelled: "YOU'RE SNORING!"

"Sorry," I'd muttered, my cheeks hot with embarrassment, and then I'd spent the rest of that night and the one after lying awake, paralyzed with fear.

So I was also pretty tired.

"Alice!" someone yelled.

I looked up. Molly Miller was standing in front of me, clasping her book bag to her chest. Except for us, the classroom was empty.

"I can't believe you like Nelson Bingley, too!" she said, and shook her head in happy bewilderment.

I buried my head in my hands.

"Alice?"

I didn't respond.

"Alice. Are you okay?"

I lifted up my face and gazed out the window. Green leaves shimmered in the sunlight. It was amazing how you could be in such a beautiful place and still feel miserable. I looked back at Molly Miller. She was staring at me. The gauze bandage around her forehead was starting to come undone. God, was she dorky.

"Why are you wearing a bandage on your head?" I asked. My voice sounded so cold and distant. Hearing it made me wince.

Her cheeks flushed. "Um . . . I fell."

"You fell? How?"

She looked down at the ground. "I actually don't want to talk about it."

There was a long pause. I stood up, slung my bag over my shoulder, and started walking out of the classroom.

"Hey, Alice?"

She was relentless. I turned around. "What?"

"You're really not at all interested in talking about Nelson Bingley? He's, like, one of the greatest writers in the—"

I couldn't stand it anymore. I threw my bag down on the ground.

"No. I don't want to talk about Nelson Bingley. You know why? Because he's my dad. And he's a huge traitor. You think I want to be here at this school? Well, I don't. But my mom died and he married a crazy person, so here I am."

Molly stared at me, her mouth open.

"Happy?" I asked. "That's what I have to say about Nelson Bingley."

I picked up my bag and walked out of the classroom, my heart pounding in my ears. I strode through the long hallway, burst out through the double doors into the sunlight, and stopped on the pavement. I squinted up at the treetops and bit my lip to stop myself from crying.

A small shadow approached me from behind.

"Please go away," I said.

There was a long silence.

"Mine is named Candy Lamb," Molly whispered.

"I have no idea what you're talking about."

"Her name is Candy Lamb."

"Who—whose name is Candy Lamb?"

"My evil stepmother."

I turned and looked at her.

"I have one, too," she said quietly.

And then dorky little Molly Miller did the strangest thing. She held out her arms.

So I fell into them. And cried harder than I'd cried in a long time.

"There are like a million stars!" I exclaimed. The wet grass prickled the back of my neck.

"This is nothing," Molly said.

"You can see, like, *three* in New York City. On a good night."

"Oh, you should see them from the top of Mount Austin in North Forest. It'll blow your mind."

I breathed in the crisp night air. The two of us were lying on our backs on the lawn in front of our dorm. For the first time in four days I didn't feel terrible.

"Show me Orion again," I said.

Her pale hand rose above our heads into the black air. "See those three little stars? In the diagonal line?"

"Uh-huh."

"That's his belt."

"And see that big one?"

"Mm-hm."

"That's his knee."

"Cool!"

The chapel bells rang out from the top of the hill. Molly sat up. "Oh, my God. I totally forgot. It's the fall commencement ceremony. We have to go."

I yawned. "Let's skip it."

"Are you kidding me?"

"Nah. That kind of thing is stupid."

Molly's little face hovered indignantly over mine. "You are such a cynical brat."

I laughed.

"Come on. Seriously. All the seniors come in wearing robes and candles. I think it sounds magical."

"It sounds dumb."

"*Alice* . . ."

"Okay, okay."

She held out her hand and I grabbed it. She hauled me up,

giggling, and the two of us ran up the hill toward the chapel, holding hands.

So . . . okay. Maybe Molly Miller was a huge dork. Actually I knew Molly Miller was a huge dork. Not only did she have all the outward signs of dorkiness—huge glasses, a squeaky voice, pimples, frizzy hair—but over the course of the evening, she'd informed me that her favorite book—besides *Zen Ventura*—was the dictionary. ("And not just the dictionary," she'd said pointedly. "The *Oxford English* Dictionary.")

But I was kind of starting to like her anyway.

And it wasn't just because she had a cold, distant father and a crazy, daughter-hating stepmother and a mother in an insane asylum.

I mean, that helped. We'd spent the entire afternoon talking about our horrible family situations.

But I was starting to realize that Molly Miller was also—in her own, bizarre way—kind of fun.

We ran up to the chapel, and it did look pretty beautiful. Its stained-glass windows glowed in the night sky, and crowds of students were pouring inside, their voices echoing as they made their way up the stone steps.

Molly clutched my hand tighter. I looked at her. Her eyes were shining. It was weird. She was totally into the, like, romance of boarding school.

It was kind of infectious.

The two of us filed into the chapel, and squeezed into a pew near the back. The place was packed. An old woman with a shock of white hair was softly playing the organ, and a middle-aged man with glasses and a big red beard was standing at the podium, shuffling through a pile of papers.

"That's Headmaster Oates," Molly whispered.

"*Him?*"

The guy definitely didn't look like a headmaster. He looked more like . . . an organic vegetable farmer.

"He's a former PMM student himself," Molly said reverently.

She'd clearly read the entire school brochure and transfer welcome packet from front to back.

The old lady started playing a slower, grander melody on the organ. The chapel was filled with the sounds of shuffling and breathing while everyone turned around in their seats and looked toward the front entrance.

The first senior walked through the door in a white robe, cupping a small votive candle in her palm. She was followed by another robed student, and then another . . . I pleasantly zoned out and watched the lights from the candles bob and blur while the organ played and the senior class filed in one by one and made their way toward the podium.

Until I saw him.

And then I'm not exactly sure what happened.

My heart stopped for a second and then started again. A little voice inside my head said: *Uh-oh.* Then I felt like a bucket of cold water had been dumped over my head. Followed by a bucket of hot water. Followed by another bucket of cold water.

He was walking near me, just next to me (his candle's flame seemed to burn more brightly and sorrowfully than any flame I'd ever seen before), and then he moved past me. He was gone.

I blinked. I swallowed. My brain started and stopped, like a car engine trying to rev to life.

"*Who,*" I whispered to Molly, "*was that?*"

She looked at me, puzzled. "Who was who?"

I couldn't believe it. She hadn't noticed him?

"That," I said hoarsely. "That *person*. That *guy*."

"Which guy?"

"The, uh . . ." I lifted my hand up and pointed, trying not to be too obvious. "He just walked by."

"A hundred guys just walked by. Are you talking about the one with the earring?"

I shook my head numbly.

"Alice. Are you okay?"

I shook my head again.

"Oh, my God. Are you breathing?"

I shrugged. The organ song came to a dramatic end.

"What's going on? You look like you saw a ghost or something!"

A girl sitting in our row leaned over. *"Shhh!"* she hissed.

Molly rolled her eyes. I turned toward the front of the chapel, trying to will my vision into focus. The hundred or so entering seniors were all standing in front of the podium, shifting their weight from foot to foot and cupping their little candles. Headmaster Oates looked up at all of us and smiled nervously.

"Hello?" he said into his microphone, and it shrieked and hissed in response. Everyone in the audience moaned and put their hands to their ears. Except me. I was still looking for . . . him.

"Oops," said Headmaster Oates, chuckling. "Sorry about that, guys."

And then there he was. His face was half-obscured by a tall girl with a blond ponytail, but I could see his gorgeous left eye . . . and his gorgeous left shoulder . . . the gorgeous left corner of his mouth . . .

I'd never reacted like this before. To anyone.

"Welcome," Headmaster Oates said. He beamed out at all of us. "Welcome, new students. Welcome back, old students. This fall is going to be an exciting one. We've hired some incredible teachers, built a new science building, and we're introducing an intramural Frisbee league that I'm sure will—"

His voice faded away. I stared at what I could see of the Guy, and my imagination was starting to run away with me. I pictured the two of us walking over the Brooklyn Bridge at sunset, the silvery East River gleaming below us. I pictured the two of us sitting across from each other at a romantic Italian restaurant. I pictured what it would be like to be the votive candle cupped inside his palm. What did his palms smell like? What did his sweat smell like? What words did he whisper in his sleep? What was his preferred brand of toothpaste? What was his favorite movie? What did he look like in a tuxedo? What was the name of his third grade teacher?

"Oh, no," Molly murmured.

I turned to her. "What?"

"No, no, *no*."

"What's wrong?"

She nodded toward Headmaster Oates.

"—a chance for parents and teachers to interact," he was saying. "And a chance for parents to be incorporated into extracurricular and dorm life. We're a family here at Putnam Mount McKinsey, but we also care about the families you came from."

"Parents Weekend," whispered Molly. "Apparently it's the week after next."

My brain snapped back into focus.

If my dad came by himself, it might be okay. Or ... not.

Because then everyone in my English class would know my father was Nelson Bingley. Which would be weird and... humiliating. But if my dad came with R., it would be even worse. She'd find a way to ruin whatever life I'd already established here. She would traipse around campus in her purple pashmina shawl, charming the pants off of everyone or freaking them out, depending on what mood she happened to be in. ("I thought you said your stepmother was evil," Molly would say, hypnotized, her pupils forming tiny concentric spinning circles. "But R. Klausenhook is *lovely*!")

And what would Miss Perfect Paruchuri think about my totally weird and dysfunctional family? It would only give her new reasons to make fun of me and talk about me behind my back.

I had to find a way to make sure my Dad and R. weren't coming.

I also had to find out the name of the Guy.

EIGHT

Reena

These were the cool kids.

Jamie Vanderheep, crouched in the corner of his dorm room, riffling through his pile of old records, a cigarette dangling out of his mouth.

Rebecca Saperstein, sprawled across Jamie's couch, idly drawing on her big toenail with a purple Magic Marker.

Jules Squarebrigs-Farroway, sitting at my feet, playing a video game and hooting whenever his character blew somebody up onscreen.

And Kristen Diamond. My new best friend. Laughing, lying next to me on the bed, her head in my lap while I ran my fingers through her long red hair.

I was In.

I'd always been pretty good at finding my way In. When we moved to Beverly Hills in the middle of my seventh-grade year, it took me exactly two weeks to befriend

Samantha Foote, the most popular girl in my grade, and then only two more weeks to make out with Frankie Olevsky, the most popular guy in my grade. I didn't even like Frankie Olevsky; I just knew that he and Samantha were my ticket In.

It always happened the same way, whether it was at a new school or summer camp—there was that first paralyzing moment of fear: the what-if-I-don't-make-it moment. But that was always quickly followed by the triumphant I-made-it-after-all moment; the moment right after I'd cracked everyone up, or caught the cutest boy in the room glancing at me as I walked by.

So I guess it went the same way at Putnam Mount McKinsey: one brief bout of fear, one brief bout of embarrassment (I blushed whenever I thought about the cigarette incident—and I was still constructing elaborate lies to convince Kristen I was a smoker), but finally, three days after I arrived, I received an invitation to a post-fall-ceremony-hanging-out session in Jamie Vanderheep's dorm room. And the deal was sealed.

"*You . . . are . . . hilarious,*" choked out Rebecca Saperstein. She lay curled up on the couch, shaking with laughter. I'd just done a spot-on imitation of Headmaster Oates, and now I was basking in the warmth of everyone's response. Kristen, her head still in my lap, grinned up at me. The two of us were the only sophomores in the room. Jamie and Rebecca were both seniors, and Jules Squarebrigs-Farroway was a junior. (You know you're really, truly In when you're not only hanging with the cool kids in your grade, you're also hanging out with the cool kids who are two grades above you.)

So I should have been happy.

I wasn't.

For one thing, I kept obsessing about my roommate, Alice. There was something about her that drove me crazy. For one thing, why did she hate me? And why did it seem like she was one of those people whose life was just ... perfect? like nothing had ever gone wrong for her?

And then I kept wondering what I was going to do about Jamie Vanderheep. He kept crawling over to me on the floor and showing me these old jazz records he'd bought over Christmas break in Pittsburgh. "Oh, man!" he kept saying, shaking his head and snapping his fingers. "You gotta hear this! The trombone, like, *sings!*"

Obviously he wanted to make out with me.

And he was cute—he really was. He had big blue eyes and sandy brown hair that curled around his ears and he was wearing a really awesome threadbare Jane's Addiction T-shirt from, he claimed, "like 1992." He was popular. He was a senior. He was co-captain of the Ultimate Frisbee team. He was known to walk around campus followed by a wide-eyed group of drooling junior girls.

But I couldn't stop thinking about David Newman.

I was completely, horribly, utterly, devastatingly, crushed out.

"How old do you think David is?" I asked Kristen, absentmindedly weaving a little braid into her hair.

"David who?"

"David Newman, dummy."

"Oh. God. *Old.*"

"Like over thirty?"

"Maybe."

104

Jamie Vanderheep spasmed on the floor, listening to a record he'd just put on. "The bass!" he cried out in ecstasy.

Kristen squinted up at me. "Wait, why do you care?" she asked.

"Oh. I was just wondering."

"Do you have a—"

My phone rang. I snatched it out of my bag, relieved, and looked at it.

"Who is it?" Kristen said.

"Ah, nobody. Just my brother, Pradeep."

Kristen sat straight up and looked at me. "Wait. Pradeep?"

"Yeah."

"Does he go here?"

"Yeah. He just transferred with me. He's a junior. He—"

She clapped a hand over her mouth. "Oh, my God. I *met* him the other day."

"Really?"

"He's adorable."

I winced.

"I mean, I don't mean that in a weird way . . ."

"Uh-huh . . ." Girls always went nuts over Pradeep. It really grossed me out, especially when they were my friends. One thing I loved about my friend Katie in LA was that she always thought Pradeep was—as she put it—"a total doofus."

"Are you gonna answer your phone?"

I sighed and looked at it.

"You should totally invite him over!"

"Okay, okay." I pressed Talk and put the phone to my ear. "Hey, Deep."

"*Deep,*" Kristen whispered. "That's so cute."

105

Ew.

"Hey," said Pradeep. His voice sounded drained of all emotion.

"What's wrong?" I asked.

"I need to talk to you. In person."

"Do you want to come over? I'm in East Dorm."

There was a pause. Then: "That's a boys' dorm, Reen."

"Yeah. I know. I snuck in."

Another pause.

"There are lots of people here," I added. "Not just boys. You should come over."

Kristen nodded eagerly, listening.

"I want to see you alone," he said. "Can you meet in front of the horse?"

There was an enormous bronze statue of a rearing horse in the center of campus, right near a grove of pine trees. According to Jules Squarebrigs-Farroway, it was *the* clandestine meeting spot for fights, make-out sessions, and drug deals.

And, apparently, brother-sister crisis counseling.

"Fine," I sighed. Then I hung up the phone. "Sorry," I told Kristen. "Apparently this is family only."

She smiled at me, her eyes glazed over. "God. Do you, like, love him?"

"Uh. Well. He's my brother."

"He must be, like, the best brother ever."

"I don't know about that."

"He's, like, really really funny."

I nodded and got to my feet, slinging my purse over my shoulder. "Thanks for having me over," I told Jamie, who was curled up in a fetal position on the floor, playing air trombone. "It was fun."

He blinked up at me. "You're leaving?"

"Family emergency."

"Well, you should come back sometime." He propped himself up on his elbow and gazed at me with his big blue eyes. "We can hang out, just the two of us."

I smiled feebly. "Yeah. Sure. Of course."

I reached out to put my hand on the doorknob.

"Wait!" Jamie screeched. "Stop!"

I turned around. "What?"

"You can't leave now. My RA is doing the rounds. You'll get caught."

"You're gonna have to climb out the window," commented Jules Squarebrigs-Farroway, not taking his eyes off the TV screen.

I stared at them. "Are you kidding me?"

"There's a maple tree right outside. You just climb out and slide down the big branch, and then you—"

"No. No way. I am not climbing down a tree in *this*." I grabbed hold of my pink angora miniskirt and raised my eyebrows threateningly. Everyone looked unimpressed.

"Don't be a baby, Reena," said Kristen from the bed. Suddenly there was a weird, urgent look in her eyes—a you-better-not-screw-this-up-for-us look.

"*Fine*," I said, exasperated, and marched over to the window. I wrenched it open. A late summer breeze came wafting into the room. I stared out into the night. The biggest branch of the maple tree was a long, long leap away.

"It's easier than it looks," Jamie said, standing behind me.

"Yeah, right," I said. A flurry of tiny butterflies released itself inside my gut.

He shrugged. "Just, like, sling your legs over, and then if you reach out, like, really far, you can actually grab hold of it."

"Just do it," piped up Kristen from the bed.

Painfully, awkwardly, I slung one leg out the window.

"Ack," I said. "I'm stuck."

Jamie grabbed hold of my other (bare, I might add) leg and lifted it up and out. One of his hands briefly grazed my thigh.

"Get your hands off me," I hissed.

"Chill out," he whispered, and then, suddenly, I was sitting on the windowsill, my legs hanging out above the twenty-foot drop.

"I can't do this," I announced.

"Just reach forward and grab hold of the branch."

"Impossible."

And then Jamie Vanderheep did something unforgivable. He shoved me.

For a second I was nowhere. The night air rushed around my ears. Time slowed down. I pictured myself falling for hours, days, months. Then I realized I'd stopped falling. My hands were grasping—precariously—the tree branch.

"See?" called out Jamie from the window. "It's easy! Now just put your feet on the branch underneath!"

I breathed in and out, shakily, but I still had the feeling of falling in my body. The sensation was terrifying. It chilled me to the bone.

"HEY!" Jamie yelled again. "ARE YOU OKAY?"

I took another breath, placed my feet on the branch below, and then dropped neatly onto the ground.

"Hey! Reena! Are you all right?"

I looked up at his little lit-up window,.

"GO SCREW YOURSELF, VANDERHEEP!" I yelled.

Then I ran away into the night, my heart pounding.

Maybe, just maybe, I was done being In.

At first I couldn't find him. Then I saw a pair of New Balance sneakers poking out from underneath a fir tree. A few seconds later, I heard the faint sound of rustling plastic.

Pradeep was always—without fail—eating some horrible form of junk food.

"Yo," I whispered. "Butthead."

The sound of rustling plastic got louder. Then a hand extended itself out from underneath the branches. I grabbed it, and it pulled me into a little dark cave hollowed out in the center of the tree.

Pradeep's round face faced mine, illuminated only by a slice of moon peeping through the branches.

"Wanna honey-roasted cashew?" he asked.

"Ew. Gross."

"Actually, buttface, they're delicious."

"You're disgusting. What is this place?"

"It's cool, right? Jamal showed it to me."

"Who's Jamal?"

"My friend. Don't you have any friends yet, buttface?"

"Shut up, butthead. I have plenty of friends. Care to tell me why I'm here?"

Pradeep stared at me ominously, chewing away on his cashews.

"Pradeep."

He swallowed and cleared his throat. "Okay. It's about Shanti."

"What about Shanti?"

"She's, um, nuts."

There was a long pause while I waited for him continue. He giggled, somewhat hysterically.

"Okay, I don't understand. Why is this funny?"

Pradeep bent over and pressed his face into his knees. His shoulders trembled with laughter.

"What the hell is going on?"

He could barely get the words out. "I'm . . . sorry . . . it's . . . it's just . . . that—"

"It's just what?"

He lifted his face up, wiped the tears from his eyes, and then let out a high-pitched chuckle. "It's just . . . everything is just, like, *so* screwed."

"Oh, come on, Deep. It could totally be worse."

He nodded. "Yeah, yeah, I know . . . it's just . . . uh . . . well, I talked to Mom tonight, and, um . . . she's, like, freaking out."

"Why?"

"Ah . . . she's living with Pria, you know, but she's running out of cash, and she's saying she's gonna have to sell her clothes and stop going to that really fancy hairdresser on Wilshire and—"

"Is that such a big deal?" I interrupted.

"Well, to Mom it is. You know her. She's used to a certain lifestyle." His eyes narrowed. "And you should talk, Miss Marc Jacobs Shoes."

I glanced self-consciously down at my pink high heels (now covered in dirt and pine needles).

"Why isn't Dad just giving her a little money to tide her over?" I asked.

Pradeep started giggling again.

"Deep. This is really annoying."

"I'm sorry. I'm sorry. It's just, uh, it's like I'm so upset I'm not even upset anymore, you know?"

I actually did know. So I nodded.

"The reason," Pradeep finally said, "that Dad is not giving Mom a little money to tide her over . . . at least, according to Dad, whom I also talked with tonight . . . is that he doesn't have any extra money to give. I mean, aside from the money he's putting toward his crazy divorce lawyers."

"That makes no sense," I said. "Dad is rich."

"Yeah. Well. He was. Until . . ." Another insane-sounding giggle. "Until Shanti decided . . . that she . . . that she, um, wanted a penguin."

I stared at him.

He continued: "You know that documentary that came out last year? About all the penguins and, like, how they have babies and—"

"Yeah . . ."

"Well, Shanti saw it, and she decided that she wanted, ah, a baby penguin. So apparently Dad made a bunch of calls—"

"You're kidding me. You have to be kidding me."

He shook his head no, his eyes gleaming white in the moonlight. "Apparently Dad called a bunch of places, like zoos and stuff, and this one zoo in Colorado had an extra penguin. It's not a baby, but—"

"Pradeep. Please tell me this is a joke."

"No. So Shanti is adopting this penguin, but it needs, like, a really cold, like *arctic* environment...so they're building an addition on the house, this, like, special terrarium or something with ice and water...and it's costing Dad like a million dollars...so," he finished, almost out of breath, "Dad doesn't want to cut Mom a break and just hand her some cash because he, um, needs all the cash he can get for Shanti's penguin's... home."

We looked at each other for a long time. I felt the edges of my mouth start to tremble.

"See?" Pradeep whispered. "It's so bad it's *funny*."

And then we both started laughing. Hysterically. I actually fell over and hit my head on a root. Pradeep spilled his cashews everywhere.

"Oh," he choked out, while I was convulsing with laughter on the ground, "and one more horrible thing—they're coming."

"Who? Where?"

"Dad and Shanti. They're coming for Parents Weekend."

I sat up with a bolt. "No."

"Yes."

"They can't be."

"Wait a second. This is upsetting you more than Mom having a nervous breakdown? That's really weird, man."

"It's just...they can't come. They can't. It'll ruin my life."

"Um, Reen? It sucks that they're coming, but it will definitely not ruin your life."

But I was thinking about Alice Bingley-Beckerman. I was thinking about her smug little face, and her perfectly combed hair, and her perfect New York City parents with their perfect little faces and blond hair, and I was picturing all three of them standing in the middle of our dorm room and laughing at me. Me and my crazy family.

And suddenly the situation wasn't very funny at all.

NINE

Molly

The thing that really broke my heart was the stuffed animal sitting on her pillow. It was this white bear with beady eyes, and it was holding a plush red heart that said, GET WELL SOON.

It made me feel like she was a little kid or something.

Spencer and I sat with her next to the window and watched the cars drive in and out of the parking lot. The leaves were starting to change their color, and this one tiny maple tree had already turned already bright orange. I held Mom's hand and pointed in its direction.

"Isn't that pretty?" I asked.

It was kind of a dumb question.

But I was having a hard time thinking of smart questions.

She smiled at me with what seemed like great effort. I smiled back and stroked her soft, knobbly hands. My mom has the softest hands in the world. It's weird how soft they are.

"The food is terrible here," she announced after a long pause. I nodded eagerly.

Spencer, who'd barely said anything since we arrived, began humming under her breath and tapping her fingers against her chair.

It was the Saturday after the first few days of classes. I'd been friends with Alice Bingley-Beckerman for less than a week, but it had made me realize how important it was, having someone to talk to. It had made me think about my mom sitting all by herself in a white room for months on end. So I'd telephoned Spencer and demanded that she meet me outside Silverwood on Saturday morning. I'd called a cab and Spencer had taken the free bus that lumbered between the small Chesterton County towns at about five miles an hour.

It was the first time either of us had seen Mom since the spring.

All summer, Dad had discouraged us from going— apparently Mom wasn't been "ready" for visitors. But when I asked him to phone the hospital during the past week, they'd said that she was "slowly on her way to recovery" and willing to see guests.

I looked out the window again. A young couple was leaning against their station wagon in the parking lot and kissing. Suddenly I was filled with anger. Why were these people being gushy in the parking lot of a mental institution? Why were they being gushy, period? Life was way too screwed-up to allow for gushiness. I stared at the couple. They looked so small from Mom's third-story window. It made me feel like I could reach out and just . . . crush them between my thumb and forefinger.

"How are you, Mol?" Mom asked.

I snapped out of my reverie. "Oh. Um ..."

"How's school?"

"It's okay. I mean, I'm having a little trouble adjusting, but ... it's good. I mean, it'll get better. And the classes are really good."

Her eyes wrinkled happily. "I'm so glad. And what about you, Spencer?"

Spencer kept staring at the window.

"Spencer," I said.

She tore her eyes away from the couple in the parking lot. "What?"

"Mom just asked you a question."

"Oh." Spencer's eyes flickered guiltily in Mom's direction.

"How are you, darling?" Mom repeated.

Spencer shrugged. "I'm okay. School is dumb. But cheerleading is awesome. And jazz dance. Oh, and baton. Candy is teaching me all these cool new moves."

I winced. Did she have to mention Candy?

"Did you know," Spencer continued, growing more cheerful, "that Candy was actually a twirling champion herself in—"

"Okay, enough," I said loudly.

There was an awful silence. Spencer went back to looking out the window. Mom stared down at her hands.

"Mom?" I finally asked.

"Yes, honey?" she whispered.

"When do you think ... when do you think you're gonna get out of here?"

We looked at each other. Her eyes seemed to dull and fade.

116

Almost like my question had made a little part of her go to sleep. I tried to backtrack.

"I mean . . . not that you know yet . . . I just thought *if* you knew . . ."

"I'm not sure, Molly," she said.

"That's fine. Of course. That's fine." I stared down at my lap. "It's just . . . next weekend is Parents Weekend. I was thinking that if you did happen to be—"

Mom stood up abruptly. Her white hospital gown was all wrinkly. She started smoothing it down nervously with her hands.

"Definitely not by next weekend, okay?" She walked over to her nightstand and started fiddling with the dials on the radio.

I swallowed. "Okay. Yeah. Sorry. Sorry for asking."

She stopped playing with the radio dials and started fingering the leaves of this little green plant next to her bed. Then she started pacing all over the room and touching everything—the knobs on the closet door; the TV antennae; our jackets hanging on the wall.

"Mom?"

"I'm fine." Now she was rubbing the wallpaper with her forefinger, her brow furrowed, like she wanted to see if it would rub off.

"Are you sure?"

She whirled around to face us. "Yes," she snapped. "But can you stop breathing down my neck for *one* minute?"

I stared at her. I stared at this new, unfamiliar person, standing in front of me in a white gown, hair disheveled, face red with anger.

117

There was a loud knock on the door.

"Lunch!" called someone gaily from the hallway.

Mom looked at us.

"I think," she said after a long pause, "that I probably should eat alone."

Spencer bolted up out of her chair and ran out of the room. Mom sighed. Then she moved toward me and embraced my neck with her soft, bony arms. Her cheek pressed against mine.

"Come back next Saturday, okay?" she said.

I extricated myself from her arms and turned away.

"Good-bye, Mom," I whispered, and hurried out the door, brushing past a smiling woman in a white uniform carrying a steaming tray of food.

Spencer and I stood at the bottom of the long driveway that led to Silverwood and waited for the Chesterton County bus in silence. When it finally came, Spencer immediately dropped down into a seat, took out her new nano iPod (a birthday present from Candy, she'd informed me), and stared out the window. I couldn't see the nano itself, just its little white wires extending out from under her head of blond hair and into the pocket of her jeans.

I took out my worn copy of *Zen Ventura* and tried to start reading it for the fourth time.

But I couldn't really focus.

I looked over at Spencer. The trees we passed along the side of the highway made an orange-and-red stream behind her head.

"Spence," I said. I wasn't sure she could hear me.

"Leave me alone," she muttered.

"Why are you ignoring me?" I asked

"You think you're so much better than us," she murmured, still not looking at me.

"What?" I exclaimed. "I do not! Better than who?"

The bus pulled into the parking lot of the North Forest post office. Spencer tore off her nano and started putting on her jacket.

"There's Candy," she said, and pointed through the bus's dirty window at a little figure in a huge pink ski jacket waiting next to our Dad's old Chevy.

Just the sight of her made me shiver involuntarily.

The bus cranked to a stop and Spencer ran down the aisle (cutting in front of several old ladies) and down the steps. I peered through the window and watched her bound over to Candy and embrace her. The two of them started gabbing immediately. Spencer said something into Candy's ear and then pointed in the direction of the bus. Candy started laughing.

Great. My little sister, who'd always seemed somewhat foreign to me, even when she was baby, had now officially gone over to the Dark Side.

Sighing, I gathered up my things and disembarked. It was Saturday. I'd agreed to spend the night in North Forest before returning to Putnam Mount McKinsey. But suddenly twenty-four hours seemed like an unbelievably long amount of time.

"Hi, Molly," said Candy as I trudged over to the car, slouching under the weight of my backpack.

"Hi," I said.

We gave each other long, stony stares while Spencer did a little dance, shifting her weight back and forth between her right and left feet.

119

"I'm cold!" she yelped. "Let's go home!"

I spent the car ride sitting silently in the backseat while Spencer and Candy discussed the junior high's new cheerleading uniforms.

Candy didn't ask either of us how the trip to visit Mom had gone.

What actually bugged me more was that Spencer didn't seem to mind.

We pulled into the driveway. Spencer immediately leapt out of the car and disappeared into the house. Sandie and Randie were running through the front yard, waving strange yellow foam swords around in the early evening light. The second I stepped out of the car they descended upon me and started stabbing random parts of my body.

"Agh," I said, and tried to push them away as gently as possible.

"Your stepsisters are happy to see you, Molly," said Candy pointedly.

"Mmhm," I muttered, and tried to wrench Randie free from my knee, which she had managed to wrap herself around.

"Stupid sister!" yelled Sandie, and shook a marker-stained forefinger in my direction.

Candy laughed. "They just missed you a lot."

"I'm not stupid," I informed Sandie.

She seemed to consider this possibility, then shouted: "You're made of poop!"

This made Randie laugh so hard that she loosened her grip on my knee, and I managed to wiggle free of both of them and run toward the back door.

Dad was standing in the kitchen, stirring a boiling pot of

pasta. When the door banged behind me, he lifted his eyes up and gazed at me, a vague, pleasant smile on his face.

"Hi, Dad," I said.

"Hi, sweetheart," he said, and then went back to stirring the pot.

I moved toward him, stood on my tiptoes, and awkwardly kissed his grizzled cheek.

"That's nice," he murmured.

"How are you?" I asked.

"Fine. Just fine."

I leaned against the refrigerator and waited for him to ask me how I was. He didn't. There was just the sound of his spoon scraping against the bottom of the aluminum pot.

"I really, really like Putnam Mount McKinsey," I announced.

"Aw, that's great."

"It's like: I never want to leave!"

I watched him carefully to see his response. I don't even know what kind of response I wanted, to be honest. I think maybe I wanted him to wish I would come home—but because he missed me, not because Candy needed a caretaker for Sandie and Randie. And even though I wanted him to wish that I would come home, I didn't want him to make me come home.

My feelings were kind of complicated.

But I got no response from him at all. He just stared down at the stove, moving the spoon around in concentric circles.

Candy and Sandie and Randie all came crowding in through the back door, and Randie scored one final sword jab in the small of my back.

"WASH UP FOR DINNER!" yelled Candy, and after they skittered out of the room she moved behind my father and put her arms around his waist.

"Mmm," she murmured. "Cuddle-duds."

Involuntarily I snickered.

Her arms still around Dad, Candy whipped her face in my direction.

"What's funny?" she asked.

"Nothing," I said.

"I'm glad you think you're so much better than your family already, Molly. That's nice. That's really nice."

"I don't think I'm better than anyone. I just thought I heard you say, 'Cuddle-duds.' But apparently I was mistaken." I smiled triumphantly at her. Saying "but apparently I was mistaken" made me feel smart. Like I had the upper hand.

"Cuddle-duds is my nickname for your father."

"Uh-huh..."

"What's so funny about that?"

"Okay, okay," my father finally said, and turned around to frown at us. His glasses were all steamed up from the pasta. "Quit it, you two."

"You two?" asked Candy incredulously. Her eyes suddenly filled up with tears, and covering her face with her hands, she ran out of the room.

My father sighed and looked at me.

"What?" I asked. "I didn't do anything."

"Be nice to Candy, Molly. Please. Okay? She's having a hard time."

"I'm having a hard time, too, you know!"

He sighed. "You get to live at your fancy boarding school and do whatever you want, and Candy has to—"

"You think that's what it's like? I get to do whatever I want? You don't think I work hard or—"

"That's not what I'm saying. Just . . . please. Be sensitive, okay?"

I couldn't believe it. He was even crazier than Mom. At least she knew she was crazy.

"Mol?"

I rolled my eyes. "Sure. Okay. I'll be sensitive. Whatever that means."

He turned back to the stove. "Will you set the table? We don't need knives. Just forks and spoons tonight."

I gazed at his stooped shoulders and the fuzzy gray nape of his neck. It was strange. I missed him terribly, even though he was standing right in front of me.

"Yeah, fine," I said. "Whatever."

I grabbed a handful of forks and spoons from the silverware drawer and headed out into the little dining room, where Sandie and Randie were already sitting at the table, drinking juice from plastic glasses decorated with pictures of Scooby-Doo.

"Hey, dudes," I said, trying to sound cheerful, and plunked down the silverware in front of them.

"Mom is crying," announced Sandie.

"Yeah, yeah," I said. "I know, I know."

"She's sick," said Randie.

I looked at her. "Sick?" I asked. "What kind of sick?"

"No," said Sandie, shaking her head emphatically. "Not sick. Prenant."

A spoon fell from my hands and clattered down on the table. "What?"

"Prenant."

"Pregnant?" I desperately tried to think of another word that sounded like "prenant," but couldn't. Where was the OED when I needed it?

Sandie nodded. "Yup."

"Yup in a cup," added Randie, and they both giggled.

I pulled out a chair and sat down in it with a thud.

"Great," I told my stepsisters. "Now *I* feel sick."

Spencer walked into the room, her nano firmly lodged in her ears, and slunk into a chair at the table, her eyes lowered.

A minute later Dad came into the room carrying a big bowl of pasta, and Candy came in from the other room, wiping her eyes and sniffling. They both sat down at the table and looked at me.

"Um," I said, "I'm sorry I laughed at you, Candy."

Somehow Sandie and Randie found this hilarious and started laughing themselves.

"Shh!" hissed Candy. They fell silent.

We all started to spoon out the pasta and pour drinks. I was barely able to form a coherent thought in my mind.

Pregnant?

Impossible.

"So does this food seem pretty boring to you, Molly?" asked Candy after a long silence. "Since you get to eat fancy gourmet food at boarding school?"

"Um," I said, "I actually don't to get to eat fancy gourmet food at boarding school. I get to eat really disgusting Sloppy Joes and this totally gross vegetable mush they recycle every night. This is much better," I added, and tried to smile.

Candy smirked. "So now she's complaining about boarding school," she commented to my father across the table.

"I'm not complaining!" I said.

"Do you want them to serve you champagne in teacups or something?" asked Candy. "Filet mignon?"

Spencer giggled.

"That's not what I meant," I said. I glowered down at my plate and thought about what it would be like to punch my fist through the bay window in the hallway.

Pregnant?

"Have you thought any more about what we discussed at the nurse's office, Molly?" Candy asked.

"I don't know what you mean."

"Oh, come on. Yes, you do."

"I don't." Without being too obvious, I tried to glance under the table to see if her stomach was bulging beneath her stirrup pants. It was kind of hard to tell.

"We discussed the fact that your father and I would like you to come back home and start helping out a little."

I looked at my father. He looked out the window.

"Oh," I said finally. "Yeah. I have thought about it. Not a chance."

Candy stood up. My father reached out and grabbed her arm.

"Candy . . . ," he said.

"Ungrateful," she said to me. "You're ungrateful."

"And you're crazy."

Randie started crying, softly.

"Tell her," Candy said to my father. "Tell her now."

My father sighed and rubbed his temples with his fingers.

"What?" I said. "Tell me what? That you're pregnant?"

They both stared at me, shocked.

"How did you know?" Candy asked. "Did Spencer tell you?"

"I didn't say a word!" shouted Spencer, and she pushed back her chair and ran upstairs.

Candy's eyes slid accusatorily in Sandie and Randie's direction. They both became very interested in eating their vegetables. Randie sniffed back her tears.

"I could just tell," I said.

Candy sat back down in her chair, patted her hair nervously, and gazed at me. "Are you happy about it?" she asked.

I sighed. "Sure," I said. The truth was, I was absolutely terrified.

"Doesn't that make you want to move back in?" Candy asked.

"No," I said. "It doesn't."

"Herb," said Candy, the color rising in her cheeks, "tell her she *has* to. We need the extra set of hands."

My father opened his mouth to speak, but before he could, I rose from my seat and ran out of the dining room and into the kitchen. The door swung behind me. I stopped at the sink and stood there, breathing heavily, trying to figure out what to do next.

"MOLLY!" bellowed my father from the dining room. "GET BACK IN HERE! WE NEED TO FINISH THIS CONVERSATION!"

Quickly I considered every possible outcome to the conversation in my mind. And then I realized there was just one thing I had to do.

Never come home again.

"MOLLY!" my father yelled again.

I snatched my jacket off the coat hook, flung the back door open, and started running. I figured that if I ran until I reached the highway, and then hitched a ride, I could be back in time for Agnes and lights out.

126

As I sprinted past the dimly lit-up houses of North Forest, the chilly autumn wind blowing my hair back and the dried leaves skittering around my feet, I felt a smile spread across my face for the first time all day.

TEN

Alice

We were both standing by the WELCOME, PARENTS sign, waiting. He looked as anxious as I felt.

Did he even realize I was there?

At first there had been about a hundred of us waiting around near the entrance to campus, chatting among ourselves, peering over one another's heads to see if the station wagon approaching was the station wagon that contained our parents.

Except Dad and R. didn't drive a station wagon. They drove a 1956 gold Cadillac, a gift from Andre Blackmun, the famous theater director who had taken R. under his wing when she was just seventeen.

Anyway. Station wagon after station wagon drove onto campus, and normal-looking, ruddy-cheeked parents leapt out and embraced their normal-looking, ruddy-cheeked children, and then everyone piled back into their cars to go get ice cream before the afternoon's activities began. The crowd of students began to dwindle. After a while, there were about thirty of us.

Then a dozen. Then five. Then Judah Lipston the Third, my silent friend from the Boston van ride, fell sobbing into the arms of a plump middle-aged woman and a tall emaciated man (I could only assume he was Judah Lipston the Second), who had just emerged from a parked car, and suddenly it was just me.

Me and the Guy.

I hadn't seen him since the night of the fall commencement ceremony.

I was pretending to find the grass at my feet extremely fascinating.

It was strange. I'd been thinking about him for almost a month. His face—or what I could recall of his face—had been my constant companion. It floated above me when I lay in bed at night. It stared back at me when I looked at my reflection in the mirror. It hovered between the peaks of distant hills when I sat with Molly Miller outside Middleton and watched the sun set every evening.

Now he was standing right in front of me, in the flesh, and I couldn't even bear to look at him.

In fact, his presence was so overwhelming that I forgot—briefly—how much I was dreading seeing R. again. Although, all things considered, I was pretty lucky; that morning Reena had brusquely informed me that she was meeting her parents in the town of Putnam itself for lunch. That meant that she wouldn't be waiting at the station wagon parade with me. And that meant maybe, just maybe, I could successfully avoid having her see or meet my father and R., period. The goal was to show them my dorm room when I was sure she wouldn't be there, quickly usher them out, and then avoid her and her functional family for the rest of the weekend.

"She's late," the Guy said.

I nearly jumped a foot in the air. Then I turned and looked at him. His hands were stuffed into his pockets, and he was staring off into the distance.

"Yeah," I said.

I prayed that I would think of something else to say. But nothing came to me. So I closed my eyes against the mid-afternoon sunshine and just...waited.

"She's always late," he said. "My mother, I mean."

"What about your father?" I asked, and then instantly regretted it. I sounded too curious.

I felt him turn and look at me. After a second, I turned and looked at him. I wanted to faint. It felt like his brown eyes were boring a hole into my forehead. But I forced myself to keep making eye contact. And there was something about him that made me want to tell him...everything.

"My dad is gone," he said.

"My mom is dead," I blurted out.

He looked shocked. I clapped a hand to my mouth.

"Aw, man," he said. "I'm sorry."

"Jamal?" someone asked.

I whirled around. A petite woman in sweatpants and a Yankees baseball cap was standing in front of us.

"Mom!" said the Guy, and then he and the little woman embraced each other. I tried not to stare.

"I got lost," she said, "and then I parked in the wrong lot, and then—"

"Don't worry about it," he said. "Let's go get lunch."

They slung their arms around each other and started to walk away. He glanced over his shoulder at me, smiled, mouthed, "Good luck," and then turned back to his mother

130

and began talking to her. Something he said made her giggle, and then they rounded a bend and were gone.

I took a deep breath.

His name was Jamal.

Jamaljamaljamaljamal.

We had actually spoken to each other.

He knew my mother was dead.

He was a Yankees fan.

I was a die-hard Mets fan.

It was like Romeo and Juliet.

Suddenly I heard the whirring and clanking of an ancient engine. I squinted into the sunshine, and saw R.'s gold Cadillac come rushing in my direction. It was unclear whether or not she could see me. In fact, as the car approached, it kind of looked like she was going to run me over. I waved my hands in the air and yelled. When it was about two feet away from me, the Cadillac screeched to a dramatic stop.

My family had arrived.

"It's so *windy*," R. moaned.

The three of us were sitting on a picnic bench in front of the ice cream stand in Putnam's town center. There was a pleasant breeze wafting through the branches of the trees and rustling the red and yellow leaves.

R. was clutching the edges of her silk shawl and shivering dramatically. She was also wearing a tiny hat with a peacock feather sticking out of its center. "It's so interesting," she informed me. "You're only three hours north of New York City, but there really is a huge difference in temperature."

131

As if I'd chosen to leave New York and move up to a tiny cold town in the mountains.

Dad and R. had only been in town for fifteen minutes, and I was already feeling lonelier than I had since arriving at Putnam Mount McKinsey. Sitting in your room doing homework alone is one thing; feeling alone in the presence of your only living parent and his wife is another. The first thing R. had told me—before we even said hello—was that she was making "a huge sacrifice" by coming to Parents Weekend (as if I wanted her there at all). Rehearsals had just started for her new play, a Broadway revival of *The Cherry Orchard*, and she was missing two of them by coming to Putnam.

Now the sixty-degree weather was making her miserable.

I clearly was The World's Most Evil and Unreasonable Stepdaughter.

Dad was sitting off to the side, wearing a wrinkled pinstriped suit and scratching absentmindedly at the surface of the bench with his thumbnail. Both Dad and R. looked—to put it mildly—out of place in rural Massachusetts.

"So, how are you?" Dad asked. "How's your roommate?"

"Oh. Yeah. Reena. She's okay."

"I'm looking forward to meeting her."

"Well. Yeah. Actually, I think she's pretty busy for most of the weekend."

R. let out a high-pitched shriek as another cool breeze wafted over us. "Are we *really* staying here until Sunday?" she asked Dad. "Because I'm going to get frostbite if we do."

There was a long pause.

"Hey, Dad," I said finally. "Guess what? We're reading *Zen Ventura* in English class this semester."

Dad looked up and blinked. "You're kidding me."

"Nope."

He shook his head. "That's absurd."

"Why is it absurd?"

He sighed. "Because, Alice. It's not *Johnny Tremain*. It's not an easy book."

"It's a very complicated text," R. added eagerly.

"Well," I said, "Mr. Newman is actually a really good teacher."

Dad guffawed. "I'm sure." Then he turned and gazed at R., pushing back a tendril of her hair. "Those kids are going to bludgeon my book to death, darling," he said.

I was horrified. He was actually starting to talk like her.

I stood up, abruptly. "Can we go now?"

"What's the hurry?" R. asked.

"I want to show you guys my dorm room before...," I trailed off.

"Before what?"

"Before the Welcome Dinner." What I really meant was *before Reena Paruchuri and her parents come back to campus and witness how totally bizarre you are.*

We climbed back in R.'s Cadillac and drove to campus. On the road next to the student union, I thought I spotted Reena's black hair and light blue headband. I ducked my head below my window before I could see who was walking with her.

"What are you doing?" asked Dad.

I held my breath until we were a safe distance away, and then I sat up again. "Oh. Nothing. I thought I saw some gum on the floor."

We parked next to Middleton and got out of the car. R. stared up at my dorm, shielding her eyes from the sun with her ring-bedecked fingers.

133

"Oh," she said. I could sense the disapproval in her voice.

"Yeah, yeah," I said. "I know. I got the ugly dorm."

"Uck," she said. "It's just that late sixties architecture . . . I hate it." She shuddered and flailed her arms, as if the cootie-infested goo of late sixties architecture had actually rubbed off on her body.

"Let's go inside," I said. I wanted to get this over with as quickly as possible.

They followed me into the dark, carpeted dorm lounge ("Eeek!" shrieked R. when a poster from the bulletin brushed against her shoulder), and up the flight of stairs to the second floor. I opened the door from the stairwell to the hallway, and almost knocked over . . .

"Alice!" said Molly. "Hey! What a surprise!"

"Hey, Mol," I said. "What are you doing on my floor?"

Molly and Kristen Diamond (who, Molly and I had decided together, after an evening of carefully tallying up their offenses, was an even worse roommate than Reena Paruchuri) lived on the fourth floor.

"Um . . . I was just dropping something off." She pushed up her glasses, and her eyes flitted to the right and behind me, where Dad and R. were standing.

"Oh," I said, and stepped aside. "Dad and R., meet my friend Molly. Molly, meet my father and, um, stepmother."

Molly smiled so widely that I thought her face was going to fall off. I also noticed that she had a tiny piece of spinach between her two front teeth. She thrust out her hand and forced my surprised-looking father to shake it.

"Mr. Bingley," she said. "A pleasure. An total and absolute pleasure."

I stared at her.

And then it hit me. I had completely forgotten.

Molly Miller was obsessed with my father.

"Yes," my father responded, looking a little uncomfortable. "Uh, likewise."

R., never one to be left out, offered up her hand. "I'm R. Klausenhook," she said. "You must be one of Alice's little friends."

Molly shook R.'s hand limply, not taking her eyes off my father's face.

"Yes," Molly said with great reverence. "We just love Alice here at Putnam Mount McKinsey."

We? Who was she talking about?

"Mmhm," said my father, and shot me a get-me-out-of-here look.

"What are your plans for the weekend, Mr. Bingley?" Molly asked brightly. "Hiking? Swimming? Skiing?"

"Skiing?" I echoed. She was really starting to freak me out. "It hasn't even snowed yet."

Molly blushed. "Well. Um. Of course. I mean . . ."

"Mol," I said, "you'll have to excuse us, but I wanted to show Dad and R. my dorm room before the Welcome Dinner starts, and—"

"Of course, of course!" Molly cried, and moved aside.

"I'll see you later tonight," I told her. "Maybe—"

"I'm sorry, Alice," Molly said loudly, interrupting me. "But could I maybe just ask you and your wonderful family for one favor?"

Dad and R. stopped in their tracks, chagrined. I stared at Molly.

"Um, what?" I said.

Molly looked at my father. Her eyes shone with pathos.

"Unfortunately," she said, "no one in my family was able to make it to Parents Weekend. My mother is in a mental institute, and my father and I have had a kind of . . . well, falling out."

My jaw dropped. Why was she telling my father this? Did she think he was some kind of god or something?

"I'm so sorry," my father murmured, although he didn't look sorry at all. He looked bored.

"So I was wondering," Molly continued, "if maybe I could accompany your family on some of this weekend's activities?"

I briefly closed my eyes.

"If," she added, turning to face me for the first time, "it's all right with Alice, of course."

"It's all right with me if it's all right with Alice," my father said tiredly.

Molly stared at me with gigantic, pleading eyes.

I groaned. "Fine, Molly. Whatever."

Molly clapped her hands with joy, and then darted down the second-floor hallway, beckoning my father and R. to follow her.

"Just you wait until you see the inside of Putnam Chapel," she told them, already taking on the role of official tour guide. "The stained-glass panels go all the way back to the nineteenth century, and they're going to change your life. . . ."

I followed, lagging a few feet behind.

It was just my luck.

My only friend at boarding school was already more interested in my father than she was in me.

"HA HA HA," Molly bellowed, and heartily slapped her own knee.

I couldn't believe it. I had no idea that people actually slapped their own knees in real life—it always just seemed like a cliché in books. But here was my new best friend, sitting to the left of me in the dorm cafeteria, and she was actually doing it.

"You have *got* to be kidding me!" she said to my father.

He smiled modestly and toyed with his silverware.

The four of us were having dinner in the dorm, surrounding by other kids and their parents. Although my dad had initially seemed somewhat horrified by Molly Miller, it had taken him less than ten minutes to realize that she was, in fact, his favorite thing in the whole world: a fan. A fan who thought everything he said was fascinating, and every story he told hilarious. Now he was eating up the attention, and R. and I first were staring off in to the distance, bored out of our skulls.

"That just seems so unlike Sam Shepard," Molly said, shaking her head.

"We writers are rarely who you readers think us to be," answered my father, raising his eyebrows.

"When you were writing your first novel," said Molly, putting her elbows on the table and propping her chin up with her hands, "how did you have the strength to keep going? How were you not totally consumed by self-doubt and anxiety?"

My father nodded. "I *was* totally consumed by self-doubt and anxiety. But I kept telling myself to just finish it, and then I could start tearing it apart. Writing is a delicate process."

"Mm*hm*," said Molly adamantly, as if she, too, had bravely plowed her way through a first novel.

"Also," my father said, after a hesitating for a second, "my wife—my wife at the time, Susan—Alice's mother..."

I froze. I hadn't heard Dad mention Mom...since I could remember. At least since before he met R. I also felt R. freeze, across the table from me, and I watched her eyes slide slowly in Dad's direction.

Dad cleared his throat. "Susan was a novelist, too, and although she was already an established writer at the time, she was incredibly encouraging. She really believed in me, and I trusted her opinion. So that...that helped." He nervously glanced over in R.'s direction. She shot him a tight-lipped smile.

Molly, in the meanwhile, had turned white. "Hold on," she said, and turned to me for the first time since dinner started. "Your mom's name is Susan...and you're Alice Bingley-Beckerman...."

I frowned at her. What was she getting at? "Uh-huh...," I said.

"So your mom is—was—Susan Beckerman?"

I sighed. "Yes, Molly."

"*The* Susan Beckerman?"

"Um, Susan Beckerman the writer, yes."

Molly put a hand to her heart. "Oh my God. I cannot believe you didn't tell me that."

"I told you that I had a mom, and that she—"

"But you didn't tell me who she was!"

I looked at Molly. "I'm sorry," I said, aware of the iciness in my voice, "I thought I had."

And then, refusing to look at her again, I went back to eating my horrible cafeteria meat loaf. Dad and R., in the meantime, had fallen into a traumatized silence. I could only imagine the fight that would erupt between them later that night in their hotel room.

Molly continued talking, not noticing the pall she had cast across the entire table. "That's just so weird. Because you'd think with your parents—I mean, your parents are like two of the greatest writers in the latter half of the twentieth century—you'd think that you, Alice, would be some kind of like crazy genius or something."

I kept staring at my meat loaf, my cheeks hot with anger.

My father chuckled. "How do you know Alice isn't a genius, Molly?"

"Well—"

I stood up. "Excuse me," I said. "I'm going to go get some dessert."

I marched away from the table, gripping my tray so hard that my knuckles turned white.

Clearly Molly Miller wasn't my friend at all.

She was just a brown-nosing fan.

Now I had zero friends. Zero friends and no real family to speak of.

"Hey, Alice," someone said.

I looked up. Of course. It was Reena, standing at the salad bar, looking stunning in a yellow off-the-shoulder top.

"Hi," I said sullenly.

"Are those your parents?" she asked, pointing in the direction of my table. I looked. Molly was still chatting away, R. looked like she was going to kill somebody, and Dad was staring uncomfortably into his lap.

"Oh," I said. "Um, no. Those are, um, Molly Miller's parents."

She squinted. "Really? That isn't how I imagined them."

I laughed uncomfortably. "Yeah. I know. It's strange. They're, like, really weird people. Kind of crazy."

She looked at me, and for a second it looked like a wave of insecurity passed over her face, although I had no idea why.

"Yeah," she said finally. "Crazy. Sure."

"Where are your parents?" I asked. This was maybe the longest conversation we'd ever had with each other. Somehow we'd manage to communicate entirely through disdainful grunts whenever we were alone in our room together.

She flushed. "Um. Oh. I . . ."

Suddenly, for no particular reason, her cafeteria tray slipped out of her grasp, and her plastic cup went clattering to the ground. Apple juice started spreading in a puddle across the linoleum floor. I bent down and began mopping it up with my napkin. Reena squatted down, too, and distractedly dabbed at the spill with a tissue.

"They're not here," she said.

"Who?"

"My parents. They . . . went out to dinner."

We both stood up.

"Why didn't you go with them?" I asked.

Her face dropped. "Oh. I . . . I wanted to eat with Kristen."

Without even thinking, I looked around the cafeteria, trying to spot Kristen's distinctive red hair.

"She's outside!" blurted Reena. "She's outside! I actually have to meet her there right now!"

And, putting her tray down on the salad bar and just leaving it there, she scurried out of the cafeteria.

I stared after her, and for a minute I was distracted enough to forget about my horrible family and the traitorous Molly Miller.

There was definitely something weird going on with Reena Paruchuri.

And I wanted to find out what it was.

ELEVEN

Reena

She was wearing a sari.

Even worse, it wasn't a real sari. It was the kind of sari
middle-age white ladies buy at their local "exotic goods" shop.
You know—those shops that sell incense and mood rings and
wind chimes and books telling you about whether your astrological sign is compatible with someone else's astrological sign.
And random "foreign" objects, like vests covered in mirrors
and tablecloths with little African elephants all over them.

Saris, in case you didn't know, are the traditional garment
worn by Indian women. They're basically like this long rectangle of fabric that goes down to your feet, and you wrap it
around your waist and sling it over your shoulder. I've only
worn a sari a few times in my life, like whenever there's a
wedding thrown by any of my more traditional cousins or
family friends. But my mother wears one almost every day.
And, you know—I hate to admit it—because they're like the
opposite of what you're supposed to wear if you're a cool

Los Angeles high school student—saris can actually look kind of sexy.

Obviously Shanti Shruti had figured this out.

Her sari was hot pink, and made out of this cheesy shiny synthetic fabric (my mother wore saris made only from cotton or silk). It had little sparkly beads sewn around the hem, and it made this horrible swishy, chime-y sound when she walked.

So when she and my father entered the pizza parlor on the edge of town (a meeting spot that Pradeep and I had come up with together, hoping to avoid as many of our peers as possible), my jaw dropped. Then I turned and looked at Pradeep, who was sitting next to me, and saw that he was shaking his head back and forth in disbelief.

"Hello, my dears," said my father.

He looked exactly the same. Big white hair, big white beard, gray suit jacket, pot belly, khaki pants.

"Hi, Dad," I said, and I awkwardly stood up and kissed him on the cheek.

Pradeep didn't stand up. After a silent standoff—he and my father stared at each other for what seemed like a full minute, unblinking, each Paruchuri man refusing to back down—my father grabbed Pradeep's shoulder and shook it. Then he tousled Pradeep's hair.

"Hello, son," my father said.

"Mmrf," said Pradeep. He bent over and shoveled half of his pizza slice into his mouth.

Shanti stepped forward and tucked a long strand of blond hair behind her ear, smiling nervously. Then she threw her arms around me. We were exactly the same height.

"You look *so* beautiful," Shanti whispered.

I broke out of the hug, and she held me out at arm's length.

"Wow," she said, "I am totally intimidated by how beautiful you look."

Ew. Gross. First of all, I didn't believe her. Shanti looked like an almost impossible mix of a Barbie doll, Gywneth Paltrow, and a swan. Second of all, I didn't look any different than I had during the summer. Third, she was my stepmother. She was supposed to be old and wise and kind, not intimidated by how beautiful I was.

But maybe that was unavoidable. After all, she was barely out of college.

Shanti turned away from me and looked at Pradeep.

"Hi, Pradeep," she said sweetly.

Pradeep picked up a jar of oregano and began sprinkling it over his pizza slice. He didn't look up.

"Pradeep," my father said.

Pradeep put down the jar of oregano. "Nice sari," he said, still avoiding eye contact.

I watched Shanti's face flush red. "Um, thanks," she said. She leaned against my father and rested her head on his shoulder. He stroked her hair.

We all paused there for a minute, silent: Pradeep sitting at the table, me and Dad and Shanti standing up, no one sure what to do next.

I actually heard the guy behind the counter flip a piece of dough up into the air and catch it.

"It is nice to see both of you," my father said stiffly.

Pradeep coughed into his hand. It seemed like a fake cough, but I wasn't sure.

"You, too, Dad," I said.

Pradeep peered up at me resentfully.

"I would like to see where you two live," my father said to us.

I winced. There was a good chance Alice Bingley-Beckerman's parents wanted to do the same thing. And I really, really, *really* didn't want them—or Alice—to see or meet or even come within a hundred of miles of my father and Shanti Shruti.

I tried to sound casual. "Oh, the dorm isn't that interesting. Just little rooms, you know, and bunk beds . . . Wouldn't you rather just go out to dinner or something?"

Shanti shook her head. "No, no," she said. "I'm dying to see the inside of Middleton Dorm again."

I blinked. "Again?" I asked.

"I lived in Middleton *my* first year," she told me excitedly. "Remember? I'm a PMM alum."

Oh, yeah. That was how I'd ended up in freezing-cold Massachusetts in the first place. I nodded. Then she leaned forward and grabbed my arm. "I'll show you how to sneak boys into your room," she whispered, "if you haven't figured it out yet."

"Shanti!" exclaimed my father.

"What?" she asked, and giggled again in her horrible way. Then she and my father gazed at each other, their eyes dancing. Shanti reached out and toyed flirtatiously with my father's hairy earlobe.

Barf.

An idea dawned on me. I looked at my watch. It was 4:30 PM. The Welcoming Ceremony was at 7:00 PM. Most of the kids and their parents would probably be there, including Alice and her parents. If we could all go see Pradeep's room now, and then eat an early dinner, and then skip the

145

ceremony, and go up to my room when no one was going to be there . . .

I proposed my ingenious plan.

"That way," I finished, "you guys don't have to sit through Headmaster Oates's really boring welcome speech. It'll put you to sleep."

My father looked dubious.

"Dad. Seriously. Trust me."

He shrugged. "Fine. I don't care."

"I don't care either," said Shanti, "as long as I get to see Middleton at some point before I go."

Pradeep looked at me like I was crazy.

"Trust me," I mouthed to him.

Pradeep sighed. "Whatever Reena wants," he said grouchily.

My plan was working.

Maybe I was going to get through Parents Weekend after all.

Two hours later, I stood out on the green lawn in front of the cafeteria, panting.

I had just narrowly avoided another Alice Bingley-Beckerman-meeting-my-parents disaster.

I stared up at the darkening sky and tried to calm down.

First of all, why did Alice Bingley-Beckerman also have to be in the cafeteria eating an early dinner?

But more important, why was she eating an early dinner with Molly Miller's family? Where were her parents?

I had just told Alice that I was meeting Kristen outside and had basically just made a run for it.

But Kristen was in Connecticut for the weekend. What if Alice knew that?

Once again, I was starting to drown in an ocean of my own lies.

My family was still inside the cafeteria, waiting for me to come back from the salad bar. But I couldn't come back. Not until I was sure that Alice Bingley-Beckerman had left the building.

Shivering—I'd left my jacket inside—I leaned against the trunk of a big maple tree and waited. And waited. After a few minutes, my cell phone rang. I took it out of my pocket and answered without looking at it.

"Hello?" I asked.

There was a long pause. Then, in a barely audible whisper: "Is she there?"

"Mom?"

An exasperated sigh. "Yes, it's me. I'm asking you a question. *Is. She. There?*"

"Shanti?"

"REENA!" she shrieked in horror.

I laughed. "She's not here, Mom. She's inside the dorm with Dad and Pradeep."

There was a sigh of relief. Then, suspiciously: "Where are you?"

"I'm waiting outside. For someone. I'm ... it's a long story."

"A boy?"

"No, no."

"Do you have a crush on a boy, Reenie?"

I paused for a second too long.

"You do!" she crowed.

"Oh, God, Mom. Leave me alone."

"What's his name?"

"Some other time, okay?"

147

"Fine." She returned to her original topic. "So, tell me what she's wearing."

I giggled. "You're not going to believe this."

"What?"

"A pink sari."

"You're kidding."

"I'm not."

For some reason I'd thought that my mother would think this was funny. Instead there was an ominous silence.

"Mom?"

"Does she look pretty?" she asked quietly.

"Oh, Mom."

"She does, doesn't she?" I heard a muffled sob.

"Oh, God. No. She doesn't. She looks really really dumb. Trust me."

"Has your father mentioned anything about money?"

"Uh, no."

"I had to sell the Blahniks, Reenie."

"The what?"

"The Manolo Blahniks! My favorite high heels!" She erupted into a fresh round of tears.

"Mom. I have to call you back later."

There was a short, high-pitched moan, and then the phone clicked off.

Great.

I'd just made my mother cry.

I was almost as bad as Shanti herself.

Suddenly I spotted a blond head of hair moving down the steps of the dorm and onto the grass. I darted behind the tree and peeked out. It was Alice. Walking with . . . Molly Miller's parents. With Molly Miller nowhere in sight. Weird.

148

Something fishy was going on.

I waited until Molly Miller's parents and Alice were a safe distance away, and then I darted up the stairs, into the dorm, into the cafeteria, and back to my family's table. Pradeep was staring at his plate. My dad and Shanti had their arms draped around each other's shoulders. Was it possible for them to stop touching for more than a second?

They all looked up at me.

"Where were you?" asked Pradeep.

"I, uh, ran into a teacher."

Pradeep burst into a wicked grin. "That David guy?"

I shot him a death glare. "No."

Shanti clapped her hands. "David? David who?"

"No one," I said. I sat back down at the table and stepped on Pradeep's sneaker with the heel of my stiletto boot. He yelped. Dad and Shanti looked at us, confused. Pradeep and I both gave them big, fake smiles.

"It is *so* weird to be back here," Shanti said, and stared dreamily around the cafeteria. "Everything looks the same."

"How's your penguin?" Pradeep suddenly asked.

I blushed, but Shanti didn't seem bothered by the question at all.

"His name is Ganesh," she said "And he's the sweetest thing in the world."

Pradeep nodded vigorously in a way that I recognized to be a complete mockery of everything Shanti was saying. But she didn't seem to catch on.

"He is just *so* cute, Reena," she told me. "You would die."

"Isn't he lonely without any other penguins around?" I asked.

She blinked. "Um. No. I don't think so. He has me, after all."

"How much does it cost to maintain his, uh, environment?" Pradeep asked.

Shanti suddenly looked uncomfortable. "Um . . . I'm not sure. . . ." Her eyes darted over to my father.

"That's an inappropriate question, Pradeep," my father said.

"Why?" asked Pradeep.

"Because—"

"Because it's money Mom should be getting but instead it's going toward an enslaved penguin?" Pradeep said, his voice icy cold.

Shanti's eyes widened and filled with tears. "Ganesh is *not* enslaved."

Pradeep burst out laughing.

"Pradeep," my father hissed, "if you don't stop right now, I promise you you will be sorry."

Pradeep stood up and pushed his tray forward. "I'm actually done," he announced, "with this delicious cafeteria dinner. I propose we go upstairs and see Reena's room. All in favor say aye."

Shanti sniffed. My father put a protective arm around her waist. I shrugged. Alice was safely out of the building. Now was as good a time as any.

"Aye," I said.

We trudged down the long, dimly lit second-floor hallway, Pradeep and I taking the lead, Dad and Shanti trailing behind us, holding hands.

"Wow!" exclaimed Shanti. "This dorm hasn't changed at all!"

"Yeah," I said. "Exactly. It could really use a renovation."

150

I peeled a piece of plaster off the wall and showed it to her while we walked.

We reached my door.

"Welcome," I said grandly, "to the Paruchuri abode."

Pradeep snickered. I threw the door open.

And then I heard someone scream. From inside the room.

I shrieked in response and fell back against the door.

"What in God's name is going on?" my father asked.

I took a deep breath and peeked inside.

Alice Bingley-Beckerman was standing in the middle of our room. With . . . Molly Miller's parents. She looked as pale as a ghost.

"Reena," she said. "Um . . . I didn't think you'd . . ."

"Hi," I said. "Yeah . . . I thought . . ."

We were unable to finish our sentences.

"I left my purse behind!" said Molly Miller's mother cheerfully. She was a tiny, beautiful woman, but her eyes seemed to gleam with a kind of psychotic rage. She was also wearing way too much makeup.

"Um . . . ," said Alice. Her mouth was moving, but no words were coming out. She seemed to be in some kind of physical pain. "Um," she said again. "Reena, I'd like you to meet my father and my stepmother." Her cheeks flushed, and she refused to look me.

I frowned. "Wait. I thought you said—"

She suddenly looked up, her blue eyes connecting with mine, and I suddenly saw that she was pleading, *begging* with me not to finish my sentence.

And for some reason—even though Alice Bingley-Beckerman had officially been my nemesis for the past three weeks—I didn't.

And then I thought: *Stepmother?*

"Hello," the woman said, and she glided forward and offered me her miniscule, jewel-encrusted hand. "My name is R. Klausenhook."

"Nice to meet you," I said. I had no idea what was happening. Why had Alice told me that this was Molly Miller's mother?

"I'm Nelson, Alice's father," said the tall, stern-looking man at her side, and instead of shaking hands he gave me a little nod.

"Reena?" asked a sugary sweet voice from behind me. "Aren't you going to introduce us?"

My heart fell. In the shocking moment of discovery that Alice Bingley-Beckerman, Miss Perfect, was the possessor of a stepmother, and weird-seeming one at that, I'd forgotten that I had one, too.

"Oh, yes," I said, and stepped aside. "Alice, this is my father and, um, stepmother." Now I was the one who couldn't look anyone in the eye.

"I'm Shanti Shruti," said Shanti Shruti loudly. I winced. Did she have to say her last name, too? The fake Indian-ness was too absurd for words. I glanced at Alice, who now looked as surprised as I'd felt a minute before.

"Hello," Alice said, and I saw her eyes move up and down Shanti Shruti's body, taking in her blond hair, her tanned skin, her lithe, young body, and her . . . sari.

"I'm Rashul," boomed my father, and for the next minute everyone shook hands with everyone else. Even Pradeep, who was sulking near the doorway, eventually introduced himself and offered out a limp hand to Alice and her father and stepmother.

"Well," said Shanti, beaming at Alice. "I'm so glad we got to meet you. It actually seemed like Reena was trying to hide you from us."

I closed my eyes, chagrined. But when I opened them I saw that Alice was looking at me and ... smiling.

"No, no," she told Shanti. "Not at all. If anyone's been hiding, it's me."

And to my surprise, I found myself smiling back.

TWELVE

Molly

All around me were teenagers trying, valiantly, not to cry.

It was Sunday afternoon, and Parents Weekend was finally over. And it was funniest thing: My fellow students had looked so miserable and self-conscious for all of Friday and Saturday, like they were just dying for their families to leave. Even the most popular and frightening kids on campus—the gorgeous Jamie Vanderheep, the icy Rebecca Saperstein—were rendered sulky and uncomfortable in the company of their plump, cheerful, fanny-pack-toting parents. The look on everyone's face, for all of Parents Weekend, was *Get these people away from me*.

But now the parents were taking off, piling into their cars and driving away, everyone was feeling the inevitable pang you feel when your parents finally do go, no matter how annoyed you've felt with them: suddenly you experience a strange, sinking, *oh my God don't leave me* sensation. Even the most bulky and imposing football player on campus was sitting alone and cross-legged near me on the student union green, toying with a dandelion and gulping back what looked like sobs of genuine loneliness and woe.

I just felt relieved.

I'd been one of the only kids on campus who didn't have a single family member visiting all weekend, and it had made me feel more like a freak than ever. I hadn't been in touch with my father and Candy since the night I ran away from their house—my father had phoned my dorm room repeatedly, I'd refused to return his calls, and then they'd finally just petered out—and there was no way my mom was going to be able to come. I'd called Silverwood a few days before and the staff had informed me that she wasn't even taking visitors for the next few weeks. Clearly things had gone downhill. I was trying not to think about it.

But it was hard. For forty-eight hours I'd been surrounded by hundreds of smiling, well-meaning families, and hundreds of kids not appreciating how lucky they were just to have one.

Alice Bingley-Beckerman, for example.

She'd spent the past month complaining to me about how evil her stepmother was (and, after meeting R. Klausenhook, I kind of had to agree—she was pretty awful), but her father was *Nelson Bingley*. One of the twentieth century's great geniuses. I couldn't even imagine what it would have been like to grow up with an intellectual, educated, perceptive father. Let alone the fact that her mother had been Susan Beckerman, another great novelist. Alice's childhood in Brooklyn Heights sounded idyllic. And hanging out with her father was like an honor in itself.

So I couldn't understand why shortly after dinner on Friday night, Alice had abruptly informed me that she needed some "alone time" with her father and R.

And then that "alone time" had extended itself to . . . the rest of the weekend.

Didn't she understand that I had no one to visit with, and nowhere to go?

Alice was supposed to be my new best friend. But during the past two days she had already hurt my feelings beyond belief. I'd spent the entire weekend alone in my room, lying under my covers and reading the Oxford English Dictionary. And even the fascinating discovery that the word *stepmother* has existed in some form in the English language since the year AD 725 didn't really make me feel any better.

Now I was lying on my stomach on the student union green, rereading *Zen Ventura* for Newman's humanities class, and hoping that Alice—now that her father and R. had most likely taken off—would come and find me.

I was mad and hurt, but I still wanted to see her.

A mosquito started flying around my head. I batted it away, annoyed. Every year in Massachusetts it seemed like the mosquitoes were around just a little longer than they should be. After all, it was already October. The mosquito buzzed closer to my ear. I could hear its wheedling, whingeing little voice get louder and louder. Suddenly I felt like it was actually flying around inside my brain.

"*Aaa!*" I yelped. I sat up and slapped the side of my head.

Then I heard giggles coming from a short distance away.

Assuming that the laughter was coming from the smirking mouths of kids like Vanderheep and Saperstein, I tried not to look in their direction. But then my eyes slid to the side in embarrassment, and I suddenly recognized the bright yellow head of hair.

It was Alice.

She was sitting with—could it be?—Reena Paruchuri.

The two of them were talking. And laughing. In fact, given all the solitary, red-eyed teenagers sitting by themselves on the green, Alice and Reena seemed almost inappropriately happy.

Without even thinking about it, I stood up. "Alice!" I called out.

Her bright blue eyes flashed in my direction, and then dulled at the sight of me. "Oh, hi, Molly," she said. Her voice sounded flat.

Reena, who had been in the middle of saying something, glanced up at me distractedly and then looked away.

I walked over toward them. My legs felt numb.

"Hey," I said, smiling at Alice.

She didn't say anything in response. I shielded my eyes from the sun with my hand and tried to keep smiling.

"How was the rest of your weekend?" I asked.

"Fine."

A long silence.

"What about you, Reena?" I queried hopefully.

Reena Paruchuri and I had never even really spoken to each other before. She and Kristen would sometimes hang out in our dorm room, but Kristen made a point—and it seemed like she told all her friends to make a point—of pretending I didn't exist.

"Terrible," Reena said, and sighed. "I hate my stepmother."

My mouth dropped open. "*You* have a stepmother?"

"Yeah. An evil one. Alice and I have totally bonded over our mutual bad luck."

"I have one, too!" I exclaimed.

Reena suddenly looked at me with interest. "Really?"

Alice cleared her throat and stood up. "Reen, let's get back to our room. I want to show you something."

"But Molly was saying—"

"But I really, *really* want to show you something."

"What?"

"Just . . ." Alice shot Reena an imploring look that I probably wasn't supposed to notice. "Please."

"Okay, okay." Reena hauled herself to her feet. "See ya later, Molly."

Alice grabbed Reena's arm and yanked her away. Stunned, I watched the two of them walk together across the green and back across the road toward Middleton.

I couldn't believe it.

What had gone wrong?

I suddenly felt myself turn into Molly Miller at Age Eight again, standing on the playground at North Forest Elementary and watching my (I thought at the time) best friend Suzanne get beckoned over to the crowd of "popular kids" standing next to the jungle gym. *"I'll just be gone a minute,"* she'd whispered to me.

But Suzanne had never come back. Not that day, or the next one, or the one after that. Years later, I would still see her huddled in some impenetrable corner of the North Forest Junior High School parking lot, smoking cigarettes, laughing, and pretending not to recognize me while I trudged by with my oversized backpack.

Now it was happening all over again.

But somehow it made even less sense this time.

Alice was smart. Alice and I had genuinely liked each other.

Was the attraction of someone like Reena Paruchuri—beautiful, fashionable, witty, friends with Jamie Vanderheep—really that strong?

I shook my head and tried to fight back tears. I'd thought better of Alice. I really had. But, I reminded myself, the world was a cruel, stupid place. My short-lived friendship with Alice Bingley-Beckerman had just made me momentarily forget that. Now I was in touch with reality again.

Suddenly I felt something thwack against my right shoulder. A shooting pain made its way down through my entire arm. A Frisbee thudded off my body and crashed onto the ground.

"Sorry!" I heard a guy call out.

That did it. Hot tears started dripping down my cheeks. Dizzy with anger, I picked up the Frisbee and hurled it off into the distance, far away from the green and toward the road.

"*Hey!*" I heard the same person say.

I turned around and realized, to my utter dismay, that it was Pradeep Paruchuri, looking confused and standing with another boy in a golden patch of sunlight.

A sob rose out of my stomach. Bending my head down in shame, praying he wouldn't recognize me, I ran away as fast as I could, back toward the familiar loneliness—and relative safety—of my little overheated dorm room.

But I had forgotten that Kristen was coming back.

Her absence had been the one nice thing about Parents Weekend. It was unclear why she'd gone back to Connecticut, instead of having her parents come to Putnam Mount McKinsey, but I, for one, certainly wasn't going to ask. I'd just felt relieved to have forty-eight hours away from her. Now it was Sunday evening and the time of her inevitable return.

I smelled Kristen even before I saw her. Her signature scent washed over me the second I opened the door to our room: a combination of artificial berry lip gloss, artificial berry shampoo, and artificial berry perfume.

Then I heard the muffled thumping of dance music coming out of the tiny speakers on her desktop computer.

Luckily, all these signs of Kristen gave me time to wipe the tears from my eyes and clear my throat before she actually saw me.

Then I stepped inside the room and took a deep breath. Kristen was unpacking her little leather suitcase and hanging her clothes back up in the closet. Her red ponytail swung back and forth as she bopped her head to her music.

"Hey," I said.

"Hey," she said, barely glancing in my direction.

I held my breath. No snide comment? No underhanded insult?

Kristen hummed cheerfully under her breath as she unfolded a pink silk skirt and smoothed it out with her hand.

Apparently not.

I was almost disappointed.

I plopped down on my bed, stared at the ceiling for a little while, and then reached into my bag and took out *Zen Ventura*. I stared at the cover. It had been my favorite novel since I was in sixth grade. So rereading should have made me feel better.

But now I kept flipping it over and looking at the author's photo on the back cover. There he was. Nelson Bingley. Alice had his clear, blue eyes, and long, straight nose. Her lips were different, though, and her cheekbones—

I shook my head. I didn't want to be thinking about Alice. Or her family. After all, she'd totally just rejected me. Maybe Nelson and R. thought I was stupid and uneducated. Maybe they could tell I wasn't from New York or some other snooty city. I began to stew in my own anger. I was just as smart as anyone! Smarter, in fact! I was *years* ahead of everyone else in Newman's humanities class, even though all the other students had attended snooty private schools their entire lives. Newman himself had said in our one-on-one conference that I was reading and writing at a college level. So who did the Bingleys think they were? Just because I wasn't a Beverly Hills fashionista like Reena or a New York intellectual like—

There was a knock on the door.

"I'll get it," said Kristen.

She delicately tiptoed her way toward the door through the mass of clothing strewn across our floor. I opened *Zen Ventura* and pretended to be deeply involved in it.

"Hey!" I heard Kristen exclaim.

My heart sank. A part of me had been hoping it was Alice, coming over to make peace. *Don't be so naïve,* I chided myself, and I went back to pretend-reading.

"What?" I heard Kristen ask. "You do?"

I peeked around the pages of my book. Reena Paruchuri was standing in the doorway, talking softly to Kristen. Just the sight of her made me angry, so I quickly turned on my side and faced the wall. A few seconds later, I heard the door shut, and Kristen stepped back inside the room.

"Molly," Kristen said.

"What?" I replied, not moving.

"Um ... I have no idea why, but Reena wants you to come talk to her."

I sat up, shocked. "What? Where?"

"She said to tell you that she'll be waiting for you in the third-floor lounge." Kristen looked annoyed. She folded her arms, pursed her perfect pink lips, and stared out of our window.

"What I don't understand," she said finally, "is why she wants to hang out with you before she even asked me about . . ." her voice trailed off, and she seemed to space out for a few seconds before whirling around and staring at me accusatorily. "Well, aren't you going to go talk to her?"

"Uh . . . yeah. I guess so." I stood up, pushed my glasses up with one finger, and started walking toward the door.

"I mean, did you guys, like, become best friends over the weekend or something?" Kristen suddenly asked, just as I was about to step into the hallway.

I turned around and looked at her.

"No," I said slowly, "not at all."

Kristen's violet eyes widened in relief, and then, within seconds—it was almost miraculous—shifted back to their normal condescending glare. "I didn't think so," she said, and then turned around and started folding her clothes again.

When I got to the third-floor lounge, I found Reena, sitting cross-legged on an old beat-up beige couch and eating a bag of microwave popcorn.

I stood on the stained gray carpet and eyed her warily.

"Want some?" she asked, and held out the still-steaming, grease-stained bag.

I shook my head.

"It's so weird," she said, "I eat more microwave popcorn in a week here than I did during, like, five years in LA."

I didn't respond. I actually felt the same way—in fact, I

felt like our entire dorm had permanently absorbed the smell of Orville Redenbacher and emitted its fumes even when no one was actually making popcorn—*but now,* I thought to myself, *is not the time to be agreeing with Reena Paruchuri.*

After all, she'd just stolen my best friend.

"Sit down," Reena said, and patted the saggy couch cushion next to her.

I sat.

We looked at each other.

"You and I are very different, Molly," Reena said.

I nodded. What was she getting at?

"But," she said, pressing a well-manicured fingertip thoughtfully against her chin, "I think we also have a lot in common."

I stared at her.

"Don't you think so?" asked Reena.

"Um," I said, "I don't think I understand what you're talking about."

She smiled. "You will." Then she reached into her pocket, pulled out a small white envelope, and gave it to me. Written across it in calligraphy was

Molly

I stared at it. "What is this?"

"It's an invitation. Don't open it yet. Just promise me one thing."

"What?"

"You won't tell Alice about it."

I stared at her. "Reena. For reasons that are beyond me,

163

Alice is not, like, even speaking to me anymore. So I don't think you have to worry."

She nodded. "Okay. Yeah. Good. Just . . . don't tell her."

I hesitated, then swallowed. "Do you happen to know why she's not talking to me?"

Reena suddenly stood up. "I gotta go, Molly."

"Wait. I . . ."

"Seriously. I, uh, I have a lot of homework." She tossed the popcorn bag in a trash can and made a beeline for the door. Then she stopped and turned around. "Just remember: Don't tell Alice. Or anybody, for that matter."

"I don't even . . . tell anybody what?"

She grinned. "You'll see."

And then she was gone.

I sighed and sank back on the dingy couch. Alone again. I could hear sounds of kids talking and laughing from down the hall. I looked down at the little white envelope in my hands. I wondered if it was some kind of practical joke. Then I ripped it open. Inside was a small blue card, and written across it in the same calligraphic script was the following:

> *You are invited to the first meeting of*
> ## *The Poison Apples*
> *To Be Held on the Roof of*
> *Middleton Dorm,*
> *October 17th, Midnight*
> *Invitation Only*
> *RSVP Unnecessary*

I read the card about five times, trying to decipher its meaning. But I couldn't. Reena Paruchuri was definitely a lot weirder than I'd given her credit for.

Who were the Poison Apples?

And why couldn't I tell Alice?

I stood up and stuffed the card in my pocket. Maybe it was some kind of practical joke, concocted by Reena and her horrible popular friends. Maybe Kristen was involved. *I should probably forget about it and not show up at all*, I told myself.

But somewhere inside of me I knew that I was going to find a way to sneak out of my room, climb out onto the roof, and see what Reena Paruchuri was all about. After all, today was October 17th, and midnight was only five hours away. Despite the risk of humiliating myself at the hands of the evil and more popular, I had to admit it: I was intrigued.

THIRTEEN

Alice

"I don't get it," I said. "Who else is gonna be there?"

"No asking questions," Reena said. She stepped onto her bed, her high heels sinking into the mattress. One of the many pictures of steroidal male models on her wall was starting to sag, and—with her tongue sticking out between her teeth in concentration—she was reaffixing it with a roll of Scotch Tape.

"What does 'Poison Apple' even mean?" I asked.

She turned around and mock frowned at me. "Just shut up," she said affectionately. "Okay?"

I couldn't help but smile back. My life had completely turned around in the past twenty-four hours.

Reena Paruchuri and I were friends.

Our friendship had started as quickly as our enmity had. Two nights before, after we'd bumped into each other in our room with our respective parents and stepparents, everything had changed. After Dad and R. left for their bed-and-breakfast,

I walked back to the room and found Reena standing in the middle of room, her arms folded, grinning.

"Hi," I said.

"You didn't tell me," she said, her grin getting even bigger.

"Tell you what?"

"About your stepmother."

Then it was my turn to grin. "Well, you didn't tell me about yours."

And we'd both burst out laughing.

Because it was like the big balloon of tension that had filled up the room since the first day we moved had suddenly . . . popped.

Now it was Sunday evening, and Reena (my roommate! my friend!) was handing me some kind of strange invitation with the words *Poison Apples* on it and insisting that I show up on the roof of Middleton at midnight.

She refused to go into any more specifics, and I eventually gave up asking.

I set the alarm for 11:50, went to bed at 10:30, and tried to sleep as much as I could in the time between. But Reena was snoring in the bed next to me, and some kind of weird owl was hooting in the elm tree outside our window. I also couldn't stop mulling the weekend over—how Dad had changed even more in the month I'd been gone than in the whole two years that passed after Mom's death. And how R. acted as if there was nothing weird about me being three hundred miles away at boarding school. As if it was perfectly natural. As if she'd had nothing to do with it.

Reena said Shanti Shruti had done the same thing: just acted as if nothing was wrong. That way if she, Reena, had thrown some sort of temper tantrum or been anything less than 100 percent friendly, she would have seemed crazy.

The thing was, acting friendly and normal sometimes seemed like the craziest thing of all.

A loud beeping sound interrupted my thoughts. It was the alarm. Reena rolled over in bed and groaned.

"Go ahead without me," she said.

"But you're the one who invited me."

"I'll be there in a few minutes."

I had a feeling she was just going to go back to sleep.

I hauled myself out of bed, slipped on my winter coat over my pajamas, and tiptoed out into the hallway. I had to be careful. Agnes the RA seemed to have the uncanny ability to smell freshman and sophomores who were sneaking out of their rooms at night.

I found my way to the stairwell in the semidarkness and walked up the winding staircase to the roof, wincing whenever I made the old wooden steps creak. I reached the top and stared up at the tiny metal ladder above my head. I'd never been up on the Middleton roof before. Agnes had informed us, time and time again, that it was strictly off-limits.

I stepped onto the ladder, the metal cold against my bare feet, and attempted to wrench open the door. I was sure that some kind of alarm was going to go off. But the door opened, and I didn't hear anything except the wind whistling up above me. I climbed up and hauled myself clumsily over the ledge and onto the slanted, shingled roof. The cold air blew against my face. A million stars shone above my head.

"Hi, Alice," someone said.

I turned around. Molly Miller was sitting right next to the chimney, wrapped in a blanket and shivering.

"What are you doing here?" I blurted out.

She shot me a resentful glare. "I could ask you the same question."

"Reena invited me."

"Good for you, big shot. She invited me, too."

I felt a gust of wind lift my hair up above my head. "I don't believe you."

Molly stood up, wobbled a little, and grabbed onto the chimney for balance. "What is that supposed to...," she spluttered. "What is wrong with you?"

"What is wrong with *you*?" I retorted. "I thought you were my friend!"

"What are you talking about? You were the one who—"

"SILENCE," a voice boomed out.

Molly and I both froze, then slowly turned around.

Someone was standing behind us.

And it took me a few seconds to realize that someone was Reena Paruchuri.

First of all, she was carrying a huge flashlight (she must have stolen it from the janitor's closet) that she was holding below her chin and shining up into her face. The bluish light made her look absolutely terrifying. Secondly, she was draped in some kind of enormous cloth that made her look floating and shapeless, like a ghost. Thirdly, she seemed to be wearing some sort of ... crown.

"Reena?" I whispered.

"SILENCE, MORTAL," the draped figure shouted. Then she burst into giggles, and her crown fell off. "Sorry, sorry," she said. She picked it up and put it back on again.

"Is that a Burger King crown?" asked Molly from her perch next to the chimney.

"NO QUESTIONS," Reena bellowed.

Molly sighed.

"What are we doing here, Reen?" I said.

Reena cleared her throat. "We are attending the first meeting of the Poison Apples."

"And what's that?"

"Please, please," Reena said, and held out her hand, palm forward. "Patience. As founder and president of the Poison Apples, I insist that before initiation we—"

"*Initiation?*" asked Molly, laughing.

The whites of Reena's eyes gleamed indignantly in the moonlight. "Yes, Molly Miller. Initiation. But I insist that before initiation begins we resolve any existing disputes between members."

Molly and I stared at her.

Reena sighed. "I believe there is a dispute between the two of you."

"Me and Alice?" Molly said.

"No," Reena said, "You and the other blond girl standing on this roof." There was a long pause, after which she tittered quietly at her own joke.

"Well," Molly said, "I'll be honest. I'm confused. I wasn't aware that there was a dispute between me and Ms. Bingley-Beckerman until this afternoon when she started totally ignoring me and acting like a jerk."

"And I wasn't aware until Friday evening," I added, "that Ms. Miller is only interested in being friends with me because my father is her favorite writer."

"Excuse me?" shrieked Molly.

Reena clapped her shawl-covered hands. "Good, good. Get it all out in the open."

Molly stood up and walked over to me, stepping carefully around the shingles. She faced me and put her hands on her hips. The moon reflected in big white circles off her glasses.

"I was never interested in being friends with you because of your father," she said, her voice trembling. "What made you think that?"

"Because," I said, trying hard to make sure that my own voice didn't tremble, "you basically ignored me and only talked to him. And then you made a big deal about my mom being famous, like that even matters . . ." (Oh, no. It was happening. My voice was shaking and tears were starting to well up in my throat. I continued anyway.) ". . . like that even matters . . . when she's dead."

There was a long silence. The wind blew a high-pitched song above our heads.

"Oh, Alice," Molly said.

"That's good," whispered Reena from behind us. " 'Oh, Alice' is good. That's what I imagined you'd say."

"Shut up, Reen," I said, turning around.

Reena nodded obediently.

Molly and I looked at each other.

"I'm sorry," Molly said. "You have to believe me . . . that's not why I became friends with you. I became friends with you because you're smart and funny and weird."

"I'm not weird," I said, slightly offended.

"Yes, you are," Molly said. "In the best way. You're extremely weird. And I acted dumb around your dad because he *is* my favorite writer. But that has nothing to do with me liking you for the wrong reasons. And . . ." Molly hesitated.

"Don't hold back!" piped up Reena.

"I was hurt that you didn't let me spend more time with you guys. Because even though you have a crazy family, at least they *came*. I didn't have anyone to complain about, because no one was even *around*."

She took off her tear-streaked glasses and wiped them with the edge of her shirt.

"I'm sorry, Mol," I said. "I was really hurt."

There was a long silence.

"This," announced Reena, "is exactly what I was talking about. Resolving existing disputes. Not as hard as it sounds."

Molly and I looked over at Reena. Her paper crown was sitting crookedly on top of her head, and the flashlight, now tucked under her arm, was illuminating her left earlobe. She looked thrilled.

"Reena," I asked, "why are we here?"

"Okay," she said. "Good question. Now that the existing dispute has been resolved . . ." She paused for a second. "Wait. It's been resolved, right? Do you guys agree that it's been resolved?"

Molly and I looked at each other.

"Yeah," I said finally.

"Yeah," said Molly.

My stomach flooded with unexpected relief.

"Okay. Good. Now we can begin. Please be seated."

Molly and I sat down on the cold shingles. We crossed our legs and looked up at Reena. She cleared her throat ceremoniously.

"Welcome," she said.

We nodded impatiently.

Reena reached underneath her enormous shawl and removed something. "Please step back," she said.

Since we were already sitting, we scooted back on our butts.

"Behold," she said, and held out her hand. "The Poison Apple."

It was pretty dark, but it looked like Reena was just holding a regular red apple.

"Is that a Red Delicious from the cafeteria?" asked Molly.

"No," Reena snapped. "It's a Honey Crisp. I bought it at the fruit stand next to the highway. It's much ... crisper. And more expensive."

Molly and I giggled until Reena gave us both the evil eye.

"So why is it a *poison* apple?" I asked.

"This apple," said Reena, "is symbolic. Don't you guys remember Snow White?"

Molly gasped. "Oh, my God. *The Poison Apple.* I'd forgotten."

"What about it?" I asked. "I don't remember a poison apple."

Molly turned to me, excited puffs of fog coming out of her mouth. "Yes, you do. You have to. Snow White is hiding out with the Seven Dwarfs and then her, um, her evil stepmother ..."

Reena nodded encouragingly.

"... Her evil stepmother dresses up as an old woman and comes to the house and, like, offers Snow White an apple. But it's poisoned, and Snow White falls asleep, or, like, dies or something, until the Prince comes along and kisses her and she wakes up."

Just the mention of kissing made Jamal flash through my mind. I blushed. Luckily, neither of them could tell in the dark.

"So ...." Molly stopped and frowned. "Wait, I'm confused."

"We're the Poison Apples!" Reena declared. "We're a society of mistreated stepdaughters! And we're coming together to take revenge!"

Revenge.

The word sent shivers down my spine.

But I didn't know if they were bad shivers or good shivers.

"But it's the evil queen who gives the apple to Snow White," Molly pointed out. "Not the other way around."

"Okay, Miss English Lit," Reena said. "But think about symbolism. Hasn't Newman taught you anything? The apple represents our unlucky fates. It represents our stepmothers' plots to ruin our lives. So we're reclaiming the apple. It's *ours* now. Two can play that game."

"What game?" I asked.

"The game of . . ." she trailed off for a second.

"The game of power," Molly finished for her.

Reena nodded. "Exactly. If they can be our evil stepmothers, we can be their evil stepdaughters. Right?"

"Right!" shouted Molly.

"Do we really want to be *evil* . . . ?" I started to ask, but Reena had already taken a chomp out of the apple and was handing it to Molly.

"We'll each take a bite," Reena said, "as a gesture of our loyalty and camaraderie. We are a group of unlucky heroines. And we are going to take action. We are going to take our lives back."

Molly sunk her teeth into the apple and then chewed on her piece. "Mm," she said. "You're right. This *is* better than the cafeteria apples."

"Your turn, Alice," Reena said. Molly held out the apple.

I stared at it. It gleamed red and yellow in the moonlight.

Okay. Reena had just said that the apple symbolized our fates. But, if I understood the fairy tale correctly, it also symbolized evil. And deceit. And trickery.

On the other hand, a society of mistreated stepdaughters sounded pretty great. It sounded kind of like a . . . family.

"Take a bite!" barked Reena. "We don't have all night!"

"That rhymed," said Molly, and giggled.

"Fine," I said. I took the apple out of her hands and bit into it. I let the sweet, slightly sour juice sit in my mouth for a minute, and then I swallowed and handed the apple back to Reena. She held it aloft.

"They cannot poison us!" Reena yelled. "We will fight back!"

She drew her arm back and pitched the apple out into the night sky. I watched it sail past the stars for a few glorious seconds, and then it fell, invisibly, down to the dark earth below.

PART
TWO

ONE

Reena

David Newman was looking at me.

I mean, he was looking at everyone. But he was looking at me just a little *more*. His eyes would move around the classroom, come to rest on my face, flicker a little, and then move on again.

He is so cute, I scrawled on a piece of scrap paper. I passed it to Molly, who was sitting at the desk to my right. She read it and rolled her eyes.

I guess she wasn't mature enough to recognize real love when she saw it.

It was the middle of November. Everyone at Putnam Mount McKinsey was waiting for the first big snowfall. A few days before, a few lonely flakes had drifted down out of the white sky while Pradeep and I were taking a walk, and the two of us had whooped and leapt around and shouted at the clouds to give us MORE, MORE, but nothing happened.

Now it was the Wednesday before Mount McKinsey Weekend, and the bored-sounding man on the radio that morning had predicted that we'd be in the middle of a full-fledged snowstorm by nighttime. David Newman's entire Humanities class was fidgeting excitedly in their seats and turning around every five seconds to look out the window. I was pretty much the only person in the room who wasn't interested in looking at anything but the seemingly endless depths of Newman's eyes.

Halfway through his lecture about the "culture of rebellion" surrounding the characters in *Zen Ventura* (which, by the way, although I wasn't going to admit it to Alice, I thought was totally boring), Newman pushed back his chair, stepped out from behind his desk, and howled in frustration.

Everyone snapped to attention.

"What is this about?" he demanded. "Why is everyone except Reena Paruchuri staring out the window?"

I blushed.

"There's going to be a snowstorm," Judah Lipston the Third announced sulkily from his desk.

"Ah," said Newman. "I should have realized." He stepped forward and stood in front of my desk. "And Ms. Paruchuri—why are you superhumanly able to focus on your class work when your fellow students are thinking about sledding?"

"Snowboarding, actually," Judah Lipston the Third said.

I shrugged. Molly snorted into her hand.

"Please," Newman said to the class, "it's Wednesday. You've got a three-day weekend coming up and a big trip to Mount McKinsey. Try to focus a little before Friday, when you'll cease to remember that Humanities class even exists."

I would never forget, I tried to telepathically communicate to him.

The bell rang. Everyone leapt out of their seats.

180

"Finish the book by tomorrow!" Newman hollered.

"I finished it a week ago," Molly whispered triumphantly, "for the fourth time."

"Oh, shut up, Mol," said Alice, who was sitting to my left. She stood up and started gathering up her things. "You're such a Goody Two-Shoes."

"Reena's the one who's 'superhuman,' remember?" Molly said, and poked me in the ribs.

Alice shook her head and stuffed her copy of *Zen Ventura* into her backpack. "I just don't think Newman gives us enough time to do all the reading. I mean, doesn't he know we have homework for our other classes?"

I studied Alice as she bent over her bag, her blond hair falling in strands across her pink cheeks. "Are you okay, Alice?"

"I'm fine," she snapped, and disappeared into the crowd of students filing out of the classroom.

"Whoa," I said.

Molly shook her head. "Don't take it personally. She's just upset that she can't get through the novel."

"What do you mean?"

Molly pushed her glasses up her nose and leaned in confidentially. "We were studying together in the library yesterday and she had *Zen Ventura* sitting in front of her for like two hours. You know how many times she turned the pages? Three."

"Well, maybe she was distracted."

"Maybe. But it looked like she was trying pretty hard." Molly held up her own well-worn copy of *Zen Ventura* and pointed to the author's photo on the back. "It must be tough to have a hard time getting through your own father's book."

I shrugged. The book wasn't hard for me to understand, but I did think it was pretty dull. The plot consisted of a bunch of New York intellectuals sitting around in living rooms, drinking wine, discussing politics, and occasionally deciding to get divorced.

By this time the classroom had pretty much emptied out. Newman approached me and Molly. My heart began to palpitate wildly.

"How do the two of you like the book?" he asked. Molly opened her mouth to speak, but then he shook his head. "Scratch that, Miller. I know you love it. How many times have you read it? Three?"

"Four," she said happily.

"What do you think, Paruchuri?" Newman asked, his head cocked to one side.

I found myself unable to look him in the face, so I gazed down at my hands and picked furiously at one of my cuticles. "It's okay."

"Okay?" he asked, and laughed. "Okay means you hate it."

I looked up. Our eyes connected. "Well," I began reluctantly, "I guess I just think everyone in it is kind of a . . . jerk."

Molly gasped in indignation. Grinning, Newman put up a hand to shush her. "Interesting. Why is everyone a jerk?"

"Well, they just talk about their problems all the time. They're so self-involved. They never get up and actually do anything."

Newman smiled. "Well, exactly. You've just articulated my favorite thing about the book."

I frowned. "*What's* your favorite thing?"

"That sense of stasis. These sad people sitting around

wanting to do things differently, but they're never actually able to get off the couch and change their lives."

I tried to nod, but the real world was fading around me. I was drowning in the shiny black pools of David Newman's pupils.

"And it's so realistic," Molly added, waking me from my dream state by shaking my elbow. "I mean, *Zen Ventura* is showing us what real people are actually like."

"Yes," Newman nodded. "It's all so painfully real and human."

I shook my head. "I don't think it's realistic," I said, "I'm not like that. I don't sit around and complain like those people. I get things done."

Newman smiled, beautiful crinkles springing up around the corners of his eyes. "Oh, really?" He turned to Molly. "Is that true, Miller? Does Paruchuri get off the couch and get things done?"

She considered this, chewing on her chapped bottom lip. "Yeah," she said after a pause, "I guess she does."

I could have kissed her.

Newman rocked back on his heels and observed me, his head still cocked to the side in that mischievous way. "I'm impressed, Paruchuri. And jealous. I'm definitely just a good-for-nothing *Zen Ventura* kind of guy." He picked up his big leather bag, which was stuffed full of our term papers, and nodded to us. Then he walked out of the room.

I sighed, closed my eyes, and pressed a palm to my burning forehead. Molly scrutinized me.

"Ew, gross," she said.

"What?"

"He's way too old for you."

"Love knows no bounds, Mol."

"Oh, my God. Don't make me retch all over myself."

We walked out of the building together and stood outside on the pavement, shivering and staring up at the sky. Gray clouds were floating ominously overhead.

"Okay, hold on," I said. "Newman just said that he was a *Zen Ventura* kind of guy. Do you think he was trying to, like, communicate something to me?"

Molly scrunched up her red nose. "What are you talking about?"

"Well, he's shy. He can't 'get off the couch.'"

Molly's mouth hung open as she stared at me, uncomprehending.

I sighed in exasperation. "He was telling me to make the first move!"

Molly shook her head. "No. No."

"Don't be so quick to—"

"I'm sorry, Reena, but you have completely lost your mind." She pulled on her wool cap and mittens and started walking back toward the dorm. "Come on. Let's go find Alice and eat lunch."

I refused to move from my spot on the pavement. "I don't think you understand."

"I do understand. You've gone berserk. Newman is not trying to subtly communicate to you that you should make a move. He's like forty."

"Thirty-two," I corrected her.

"Whatever." Her frizzy hair stuck out goofily from beneath her cap and her glasses were half-steamed up from her breath. "Let's go."

I wasn't done yet. I had to make her understand. I'd grown to love Molly in the past few weeks, but sometimes she acted so . . . immature.

"I know that the idea of dating an older man is difficult for you to comprehend, Mol," I said. "But you and I are very different."

"Oh, yeah? How?"

"Well, I don't think you understand romance in quite the same . . ." I trailed off. It was hard to explain. "I mean, it just seems like you don't think about boys that much. You don't even have a crush on anyone, and you—"

"How do you know?" Molly snapped.

I raised my eyebrows. "You have a crush on someone?"

Her face turned bright red. "No, I just . . . I just . . ."

"Who?"

She folded her arms against her bulky jacket and stared at the ground. "No one. Never mind."

"See?" I said. "I just don't think you know what it's like to have really, really strong feelings for someone."

Molly pulled her cap farther down over her ears and refused to look at me. "You know what? Do whatever you want. I don't care."

"Thank you."

I walked over, linked arms with her, and the two of us started heading back toward the dorm. Molly kept staring at the ground. She was clearly brooding about something.

"Don't worry, Mol," I said. "You'll find someone eventually."

She didn't respond.

"I mean, who knows—maybe you'll even meet a guy during Mount McKinsey weekend!" I added hopefully.

Molly nodded. Suddenly I noticed a few specks of white falling on the collar of her jacket.

"Oh, my God," I gasped. "I think it's . . ."

We stopped in our tracks and looked up. Cascading out of the sky toward our upturned faces were thousands of snowflakes. One landed in my eye and dripped down my face. I yelped happily and did a little dance, sticking my tongue out into the cold air.

"My first snowfall!" I yelled.

Molly nodded and held out her mittened hand, watching clusters of snowflakes form in her palm. "Funny," she said. "I think I've seen about a thousand of these."

It was Friday, and Mount McKinsey weekend had finally arrived. The storm had—to the delight of the entire school—lasted for all of Wednesday night and most of Thursday. We'd gotten almost a foot and half of snow. I'd basically spent the last two days staring out of our dorm window and whispering: "*Amazing.*"

Now every Middleton resident was standing on the snowy walkway outside the dorm, waiting for the bus that was going to take us thirty miles north to the top of Mount McKinsey. Everyone was talking and laughing so loud that I could barely hear myself think. So I just looked down at the snow and admired my hot pink galoshes.

I looked pretty good in them.

A yellow bus came rumbling up the road and screeched to a halt in front of us.

"No more than two in a seat!" shrieked Agnes the RA, but

186

she was drowned out by the sound of fifty girls all jostling one another to get on the bus first.

I pushed my way into line behind Alice and Molly, but then suddenly felt a hand on my arm. I turned around. It was Kristen.

"Hey," she said. "Long time no see."

I nodded, feeling guilty. I'd been kind of avoiding Kristen for the past few weeks. Well, not kind of avoiding. Definitely avoiding.

The thing was, I really, really liked Alice and Molly. I liked them because they were smart and interesting and, most important, they made me feel comfortable. Like I could be myself. And ever since that night in Jamie Vanderheep's dorm room, I'd been wondering why hanging out with the cool kids had always mattered so much to me in the past. My friend Katie in LA was one thing; she was popular and well-dressed, but she was also really nice to everyone. But making my way into the cool crowd so effortlessly at Putnam Mount McKinsey made me reevaluate why being part of the cool crowd was, in itself, so important. Kristen, in particular, had started to drive me crazy, even before I became friends with Alice during Parents Weekend. For one thing, Kristen was never into talking about our families. It seemed like she had a perfect life, and judged anyone who didn't. Her favorite activity was sitting around, painting her toenails, and talking about who needed to get a decent haircut and start dressing better (Molly's name would come up frequently).

So, slowly, I'd started to pull away from her. And after Parents Weekend and the first official meeting of the Poison Apples (which made me happier than I'd been in a long, long time), I'd pretty much decided that I didn't really want to be friends with Kristen anymore. At all.

But she was having a hard time picking up on my cues. In her defense, I think it was the first time anyone had ever stopped wanting to be friends with her. She was clearly one of those people who had, since her first day at preschool, radiated power and popularity.

"Where have you been?" she demanded, a weird, aggressive smile plastered across her face. "You didn't come to Rebecca's party the other night!"

"Yeah," I said, digging a little hole in the snow with the tip of my pink boot. "I know. I had a lot of homework. Sorry." The truth was, I'd stayed up late with Alice that night drawing goofy self-portraits of ourselves and laughing.

"We had an amazing time," Kristen said. The line to get on the bus moved forward, and I saw, to my chagrin, Alice and Molly get lost in the swarm of students.

I nodded. "Yeah. It sounded really cool."

There was a pause, and I saw a wave of insecurity wash over Kristen's face. She looked amazing—her long red hair was streaming out beneath a green cashmere cap that perfectly matched her green woolen peacoat and her short green-and-blue skirt and leggings—so seeing her turn pale with self-doubt was sort of incredible. It was like she'd never experienced rejection before, on any level, and so the feeling of rejection didn't come naturally to her. It clashed with her outfit. It clashed with her perfectly made-up face.

"Well . . ." Kristen hesitated. "Are you, like . . . okay?"

I was kind of touched. Kristen had never ever asked me if I was okay before. Her normal way of greeting me was grabbing my elbow and whispering something mean about the girl across the table in my ear.

"Yeah," I said. "I'm actually doing great."

She looked completely baffled.

"How are you?" I added.

"Um," she said. "Oh. Yeah. I'm fine. I'm fine. Yup. Fine."

"Good."

The line moved forward, and I climbed up the steps to the bus, Kristen right behind me. Sitting in the third row of seats were Alice and Molly. Together. Of course. I mean, why wouldn't they sit together? I'd lagged behind.

"Hey guys," I said, relieved to just see them again, and started to squeeze into the seat with them.

"Um, Reen," Molly whispered, "it's just two to a seat."

I blanched. "Oh."

"Sorry," she said, and looked at Alice for help. Alice shrugged and made a what-are-we-supposed-to-about-it? face.

I felt a hand grabbing my arm again.

"Reena," Kristen said from behind me. "We're sitting together, right?"

"Oh," I said. "Um . . . yeah. Sure."

"Vanderheep and Saperstein are going on the second bus. Which sucks. Because," and she leaned forward to whisper this last part loudly in my ear, "that means we're stuck with all the dorks."

I glanced at Molly, who had clearly heard everything Kristen said.

"Well," I began, trying to think of a way to defend my friends without getting into some kind of weird argument, but Kristen had already yanked me down into the seat right behind Molly and Alice and was pulling celebrity magazines out of her purse.

"You *have* to see this picture," she said, and started flipping through the latest issue of *People*.

I nodded weakly.

Hopefully the bus ride—which, I saw now, was going to be excruciating—wouldn't be representative of the entire weekend on Mount McKinsey.

After all, I had three extremely important goals for the trip:

1. Relax and have fun.
2. Conduct the second official meeting of the Poison Apples.
3. Kiss David Newman for the first time.

And, I told myself as the bus pulled out of the Putnam Mount McKinsey campus and onto the snowy highway, using the very words my father had said to me before taking his medical boards fifteen years before: *A Paruchuri Always, Always Achieves His (or Her, in this case) Goals.*

TWO

Molly

The sun was setting when we arrived at Mount McKinsey Lodge, and the silhouette of its roof made a sharp black triangle against the burning orange sky. As the bus came to a halt, we all fell silent, amazed.

It was a gigantic, sprawling old building, with three chimneys and two verandahs and a huge stained-glass window above the front entrance that—with the glow of the setting sun shining through it—cast strange, otherworldly shapes onto the floor of the lobby, where the entire school stood, agog, with our suitcases.

"MIDDLETON GIRLS!" Agnes yelled, and we all clustered around her.

She began handing out room assignments. I unfolded mine, ran over to Alice and Reena, and asked: "Room 405? Room 405?" They looked at their assignments, squealed with delight, and the three of us slapped five.

"Did I hear someone say Room 405?" a familiar voice inquired from behind us.

I turned around, horrified. It was Kristen.

"Yes," I said slowly. "Is that—"

Kristen pushed me aside and hugged Reena. "We're roomies!"

Reena bugged her eyes at me over Kristen's shoulder in a help-me expression. I ignored her. I wasn't going to feel bad for someone whom Kristen actually *liked*. And I was the one who had to deal with being her roommate all the time.

The four of us hauled our suitcases up four flights of creaky, windy stairs and were panting by the time we reached Room 405.

Reena turned the key in the latch and flung open the door. We all gasped.

"It's like we're in the nineteenth century," Alice said dreamily.

"More like the thirteenth century," said Kristen. She bent down, touched the floor with her forefinger, and then showed it to us. "Gross. Everything is covered in dust. Doesn't anyone ever clean this place?"

"Who cares?" I said. "It's beautiful."

The ceiling was slanted and crisscrossed with wooden beams. There were four single beds, each one with its own individual red velvet canopy and a tiny, tasseled, red lamp beside it. There were even four tiny desks and four wooden rocking chairs. I walked over to the one of the dusty oval windows and stared out at the winter landscape. There were the snowy bluffs of Mount McKinsey, then miles of evergreen forest, then the thin gray line of the highway, and then a little cluster of buildings that was probably the town of Putnam. I squinted even farther out into the distance, and thought I saw, nestled between snow-covered hills in the distance, a dark spot that might have been North Forest. Or maybe I was just imagining it.

North Forest. The thought of my hometown sent shivers down my spine.

I hadn't spoken to either of my parents in almost a month.

"Molly!" said Alice. "Can you hear me?"

I spun around. "Yeah. Sorry. I spaced out. What?"

"Are you coming down to dinner?"

"She's always like this," Kristen commented from the door, where she was waiting with Reena. "She's always staring into space, thinking about something nerdy."

I stared at Kristen. Nerdy. Right. The disintegration of my family was nerdy. "You're right," I said to her, my voice icy with rage, "I should be spending my time the way you do, coming up with ways to get Jamie Vanderheep to pay attention to me."

Kristen blushed a little, but then put her hands on her hips and tried to look nonchalant. "And what's wrong with that?"

"It's just a little pathetic when he so obviously has a crush on Reena."

Reena gasped. "Molly!"

"What? It's true."

Kristen's face had crumpled involuntarily, but now she was twirling a piece of red hair around her forefinger and clearly trying to come up with a comeback. Still—for once—it looked like I rendered her speechless. After a few awful seconds, she turned and left the room. We all stood there for a minute and listened to her high-heeled boots clatter down the hallway.

"Molly," Alice whispered, "that was really mean."

"Mean?" I asked. "You're calling me mean? That girl is the Queen Bee of Mean."

"Yeah, but two wrongs don't make a—"

"Alice," I said, "do not finish that sentence."

Reena, still standing in the doorway, giggled softly, covering her mouth with her hand.

"You think this is funny?" Alice asked. "Kristen looked like she was gonna start crying."

"I'm just impressed, that's all," Reena said. "Miller has guts."

"That's a strange thing to say," Alice informed her, "for someone who's totally unable to say no to Kristen, like, ever."

"I can say no!" Reena retorted. "And maybe you're just jealous because she doesn't even notice—"

"Okay, okay," I said, walking forward and linking arms with both of them. "Let's not fight. Who cares about Kristen? This trip is about the Poison Apples."

"You're right," Reena said as the three of us walked down the hallway and started descending the spiral staircase toward the sounds of our classmates chattering in the dining room. "We need to have our second meeting sometime this weekend."

Just as we were about to enter the lobby, Alice froze in her tracks, her foot hovering in the air between the last step and the floor. "Act normal," she whispered. "Just . . . act normal."

"Are we not acting normal?" Reena asked, confused.

"*Shhh,*" Alice hissed.

A cluster of PMM seniors passed by us, talking and laughing. A vaguely familiar-looking African American boy lagged behind for a second and smiled at us. "Hey, Alice," he said.

Because her arm was still linked in mine, I actually felt the goose bumps spring up on Alice's skin. Her temperature also seemed to drop about thirty degrees. Her eyes widened and she looked like she was about to faint.

"Um, what?" she asked the boy.

He frowned. "Wait, what?"

"I . . ." Alice hesitated for a second. "What?"

I could see Reena out of the corner of my eye, biting her lip to keep from laughing.

"I, uh . . . I just said hello," the boy said, looking uncomfortable. "But I should probably go, uh, catch up with my friends."

Alice nodded vigorously. "Yeah. Yeah. Of course."

He raised his hand, gave an embarrassed half-wave to me and Reena, and then dashed away.

For the next few seconds, Alice remained absolutely still. I watched her delicate nostrils flare as she attempted to inhale and exhale. Reena and I sent each other what-do-we-do-now? looks. Finally Alice whispered something inaudible.

"What did you say?" Reena asked.

"Kill me now," Alice muttered. "Just . . . kill me."

"It wasn't that bad," I told her, trying to sound positive. "You were both just a little . . . awkward. What's the big deal?"

"He's pretty cute," Reena said.

Alice turned to her, her face drained of all color. "Jamal Chapman is more than cute. He's the most beautiful boy in the world."

Nope, I corrected her in my mind, *Pradeep Paruchuri is the most beautiful boy in the world.* But I had to be careful to never, ever say that out loud. Reena would never let me live it down. And she'd probably run and tell Pradeep within five minutes.

"Oh my God," gasped Reena. "You totally have a crush on

him! I can't believe you didn't tell your own roommate about this!"

Alice shook her head back and forth. "I refuse to talk about it. Later. Right now I just feel like I'm going to die."

With Alice trembling between us, Reena and I proceeded to the dining room, where the sounds of silverware clinking against plates echoed like music off the tall cathedral ceilings. The windows were almost twenty feet tall, and they opened onto long, snow-covered verandahs. The sun had just set, and the sky outside was light violet. Ornate, sparkling chandeliers hung from the ceiling. There were dozens of round tables, each one covered in red cloth. Our PMM classmates, usually so raucous and obnoxious, seemed to have absorbed the dignity of the room they were sitting in, and were conversing softly—even laughing—in an uncharacteristically grown-up manner.

"I want to live in Mount McKinsey Lodge," I whispered, as we surveyed the room for a place to sit.

"They say it's haunted," Reena whispered back.

That was the first thing that distracted Alice from her stupor of humiliation. Her eyes widened. "Haunted?" she said. "Don't say that. Come on. You're kidding."

"I'm just repeating what I heard."

I groaned. "You guys are acting like little kids."

We found an empty table and sat down.

"I'll save our seats while you guys go to the buffet table," I told Alice and Reena. "Then I'll go by myself." I just wanted to sit and absorb the atmosphere for a while. I'd never been anywhere this elegant in my life.

They nodded and left, and I leaned back in my chair and

gazed up at the ceiling contentedly. There was something about Mount McKinsey Lodge that fit perfectly into fantasies I'd had when I was little girl. Everything about it was so old-fashioned and refined. There were even pictures in the lobby of all the famous writers who had stayed there when it was a working hotel. Being at the lodge made me feel like a totally different person. Instead of Molly Miller from North Forest, Massachusetts, I was Molly Miller from Paris, France. Molly Miller from Zurich, Switzerland. Molly Miller from Venice, Italy. Actually—even better—I was a world-traveling high-society woman from Monaco. I wore long white gloves and a single gleaming magnolia behind my ear. I went to masked balls and sat at the roulette table in Monte Cristo casinos, laughing and smiling and whispering sweet nothings into the ears of handsome men. At night I slept between silk sheets. I lived in a thousand different hotels, always arriving by steamer and carrying a golden birdcage that contained a single green parakeet named—

"Pradeep."

I gasped and jolted forward in the chair that I'd been absentmindedly tipping backward.

Pradeep Paruchuri had just sat down across from me at the table.

"Pradeep," he repeated. "That's my name. Do you remember me from Orientation Week?"

Did I remember him from Orientation Week? Was he trying to be funny?

I nodded. "I remember."

"Molly, right?"

"Uh-huh."

"My sister keeps telling me all these great things about you."

Something in my chest burst into flame, traveled up my throat, and burned my cheeks. I lowered my head and stared at the tablecloth.

"Well, Reena is great, too," I whispered.

"I just wanted to say again that I'm sorry about what happened during that—"

"It's okay," I interrupted him.

"During that orientation activity? Dropping you and all? I felt horrible about that."

"Pradeep," I heard myself saying, with uncharacteristic firmness, "please stop apologizing. The whole thing becomes exponentially more humiliating every time you say you're sorry."

His smile turned into a huge grin. "Ha. Reena was right. You are funny."

This left me completely speechless, and luckily Alice and Reena showed up at that moment and plunked their trays of food down on the table.

"You've got to get some of this," Reena informed me. "It's like real food. So much better than at school." Then she turned to her brother. "What are you doing here?"

"Talking to your friend. Is that such a big deal? Or am I not allowed to sit with you guys?"

Reena rolled her eyes. "Do whatever you want to do, butthead. Actually you and Molly should talk to each other. You're both big nerds."

"What is that supposed to mean?" Pradeep asked.

"You both spend all your time with your faces buried in books."

"Oh, yeah?" Pradeep gazed at me curiously. "Who are your favorite authors?"

I took a deep breath. *You are a nineteenth-century lady from Monaco,* I told myself. *You wear white gloves. You are charming. You think nothing of talking about books with a handsome young man.*

I propped my chin in my hand, trying to look casual and thoughtful at the same time. The author that always came to mind was Nelson Bingley, but I had to be careful these days not to freak Alice out.

"Emily Dickinson," I said. "Um . . . also Walt Whitman. I guess those are both poets. In terms of novelists, I really love Dickens. Especially *David Copperfield.* Um. I also really like—"

"*DAVID COPPERFIELD* IS MY ALL-TIME FAVORITE BOOK!" Pradeep shouted.

Reena buried her face in her hands. "Geez, Pradeep. Make sure the whole cafeteria hears how nerdy you are."

"It's really your favorite book?" I asked. My nervousness was ebbing away and actual curiosity was taking over.

"Yeah. I've read it like seven times. And I *love* Walt Whitman."

I looked straight into his eyes and smiled. "Weird."

Suddenly he leapt up out of his seat. "Shoot. I forgot to give Jamal back his iPod. I gotta go." He kissed Reena on top of her head, eliciting an indignant "ew!" and then he darted away.

Even though I felt as if I'd just been inside a dream, I attempted to act normal. "I didn't know your brother was a big reader," I told Reena.

"Yeah, yeah. He's always—"

"Did he say *Jamal*?" Alice interrupted.

"Oh. Yeah."

"Pradeep is friends with Jamal Chapman?"

"I guess."

Alice stared at Reena, her mouth open. "You didn't tell me."

Reena's fork clattered down to the table. "You are such a psychopath! I didn't know until *five minutes ago* that you had a crush on Jamal Chapman!"

"Shh!" Alice shrieked.

I stood up. We were all starting to go a little crazy. Maybe the high altitude was affecting our brain chemistry. I headed over to the buffet table and started spooning steaming lumps of roast beef and potatoes onto my plate. I looked to my right. There was Pradeep again. Helping himself to a generous portion of butterscotch pudding.

"Dessert for dinner," he commented.

"Mm-hm." I nodded and, wielding a pair of silver tongs, attempted to pick up some Brussels sprouts and deposit them on my plate. They fell onto the white tablecloth, making a horrible little thump.

"You gonna be at the dance tonight, Miller?" Pradeep asked. He pointed to a banner hanging above the entrance to the dining hall. WINTER WONDERLAND BALL, it read, FRIDAY NIGHT, 9:00 PM.

I nodded. "Um. Right. The dance. Uh . . . well . . . I'm not like a really big dancer or anything."

He shrugged. "Well, me neither. But it'd be nice to see you there." He awkwardly patted me on the shoulder and then walked away, joining a table of laughing juniors and seniors.

It'd be nice to see you there. I kept repeating that to myself while I stood, frozen in place, over the steaming tray of Brussels sprouts.

Was it the high altitude?

Or was Pradeep Paruchuri interested in me?

The three of us lay on our three red beds, swinging our socked feet off the edges of our beds and staring at the ceiling.

"Dances are stupid," Reena said finally. "They're so . . . adolescent."

There was a long pause.

"But we *are* adolescents," Alice said.

"I just wish they could have come up with a more grown-up activity."

"Like what?" I asked.

Reena crossed her foot over her knee, tucked her hands behind her head, and thought for a while. "Fine," she said after a while. "I don't know. We'll go to the stupid dance."

Alice sat up and clapped her hands. "Yay! It'll be so much fun! We'll all dress up!"

My stomach sank. I didn't have anything to wear. Well, that wasn't true. I'd brought the awful orange maid-of-honor dress Candy had made me wear to the wedding.

And Volume XI of the Oxford English Dictionary.

But you can't wear the OED to a dance.

Alice peered over at me from her bed. "What are you gonna wear, Mol?"

"Uh . . . just this, like, hideous orange puffy thing."

"You don't like it?

I shook my head. "Whatever. I'm fine." A complete and total lie.

Alice gave me a long look. "Hmm. Hold on a sec . . ." She

leapt off the bed and ran over to her suitcase. "Just try something on for me, okay?"

An hour later, the three of us were standing in front of the mirror, our arms around one another's shoulders.

Reena was wearing a crimson red strapless minidress with matching high heels and lipstick. Her hair was swept up in a messy bun, and she'd sprinkled—to my shock and awe—tiny bits of red glitter over her entire head, so in certain lights her black hair literally sparkled.

In keeping with her all-black-clothing-all-the-time theme, Alice was wearing a black peasant dress with embroidered flowers around the collar and little embroidered vines around the cap sleeves. She wore pale pink lip gloss and a shimmering of gray powder over her eyes.

And then there was me.

Alice had lent me one of her mother's old dresses. It was maybe the nicest thing anyone had ever done for me. Alice had saved it from her mother's closet just before her dad and R. cleaned out the brownstone in Brooklyn Heights and threw everything away. "This was her favorite dress," Alice told me. "She always wore it when I was a kid. It reminds me of her."

The dress did fit me perfectly. It reached my calves, so I didn't look dowdy or like I was trying too hard. It was made out of a soft, simple cotton, but leading up to the high collar was a line of tiny brass buttons—"Very neo-Victorian," Reena had informed me. The sleeves were ever-so-slightly puffed, and they tapered out just before my elbows, making my arms look unusually slender.

I made eye contact with my reflection and then, not able to help myself, I smiled. Reena had insisted on applying "just a touch" of mauve shadow to my eyelids, and wielding a beige stick of foundation, Alice had pinned me to the bed and covered up a few of my worst pimples.

I looked good.

"We look good," Reena announced.

Alice blushed and grinned, then looked around the room. "Wait a second. Where's Kristen? I haven't seen her in like three hours."

Reena shrugged. "Who cares? The dance already started. Let's go now."

We descended the stairs. The dining room had been completely transformed in the two hours that had passed since dinner. Tinsel and glass icicles hung from the chandeliers, and mountains of cotton were piled up in the corners, simulating snowdrifts. The lights were dimmed to a low, pinkish hue that reminded me of the times when I'd wake up in the middle of the night in North Forest and know, just from looking at the color of the sky out of my bedroom window, that there'd been a snowstorm. A dozen or so people had started slow dancing, but most of the students were lined up against the walls, murmuring nervously to one another.

"Ew," Reena commented as we paused in the doorway. "So cheesy."

Clearly this was nothing compared with the dances at Beverly Hills High. On the other hand, it was the most beautiful dance I'd ever been to. The North Forest High dances were always held in the gymnasium under a broken disco ball and usually involved shaving cream attacks on underclassman.

Alice and Reena and I made our way over to an empty section of wall and tried to look like we weren't obsessively scoping everyone else out. Or at least Alice and I did. Reena, confident as always, let her eyes pass critically over the room, and then narrated her impressions to us while we leaned against the wall and stared at our hands.

"Oh my God. Look at Millie Fitch. *Look* at her."

Alice and I refused to look at her.

"Her dress is so short you can see her butt, I swear to God. Oh, no. Judah Lipston is wearing a purple tie. And I think it's a clip-on . . . wow. Rebecca Saperstein must have spent like three thousand dollars on her dress and she still looks incredibly strange. Sad. But . . . but . . . you guys . . . Jules Squarebrigs-Farroway is walking over to her. I think he's gonna ask her to dance. Yup. It's happening. Man. She's had a crush on that guy since their sophomore year, apparently. Well, good for her. Wow. They're actually dancing. *So* awkward. Anyway."

Abruptly Reena stopped her monologue.

"Keep going," Alice whispered.

Reena shook her head. "I can't."

We both looked at her. Tears were brimming around the edges of her perfectly made-up eyes.

"Reen?" I asked. "Are you . . . ?" I couldn't even say the word. I'd never seen Reena cry before. Or even come close to crying.

Reena wiped the tears from her eyes with her red fingernails. "I'm fine. I'm fine. I just realized . . . um . . ."

Alice rested her palm on Reena's shoulder. We waited for her to continue.

"I just realized," she said, gulping a little, "that I'm always, like, standing on the sidelines and criticizing everybody."

"That's okay," I said, "that's what great artists do."

"But I'm not an artist."

She had a point.

"It's just..." She tucked a tendril of hair behind her ear and sighed shakily. "I just... I've never had a boyfriend. Like, I've kissed people, but I've never had a boyfriend."

"Well, neither have we," Alice said. "We're all in the same boat here."

"I've never even kissed anyone," I said cheerfully.

Reena gawked at me. "Oh, my God. That's terrible."

"Reen," Alice chided her.

"Sorry," Reena said. "I just wonder if... like, if I'm really honest with myself... if sometimes I make fun of people who make me jealous. It's just... look." She gestured toward the dance floor. "My instinct is to make fun of all those people, but the truth is, they really look like they're having a good time."

We all looked. She was right. Couples were swaying together, smiling together, whispering to each other, putting their heads on each other's shoulders. Rebecca Saperstein looked like she was in seventh heaven. And it all just seemed so foreign and unattainable. Like all those people knew something I didn't—like they'd learned some secret language or code used to communicate desire, mutual attraction, and romance. I didn't understand how you could like someone, how they could like you back, and then how one of you could work up the guts to tell the other one. It just seemed like a confluence of statistical impossibilities.

Alice slung her arms around our shoulders and sighed. "Romance," she said, "is just something that happens to Other People. Never me."

Reena and I nodded.

"Totally," I said. "That's just what I was thinking. And another weird thing is that—"

"Alice?" someone inquired.

Alice's arms slowly slipped from our shoulders to her sides, and I felt her temperature fall again.

Jamal Chapman was standing in front of us, wearing a gray pin-striped suit. He wore a white flower in his lapel and he looked . . . spectacular. He also seemed (and I couldn't understand this, since he was a senior and incredibly popular) nervous.

"Hi, Jamal," Alice said. At least she was able to form a sentence this time.

"Would you like to dance?" he inquired.

I couldn't believe it. It was like I was inside some kind of dream. Or like I was inside one of Alice's dreams.

"Um, sure," Alice said, blushing.

Jamal held his hand out and she took it. Then the two of them walked slowly out into the center of the dance floor. Alice put her hand on his shoulder, Jamal put his hand on her waist, and then it was just . . . *happening*. Like that. They were dancing. Alice had left my reality and entered the reality of Other People. All within ten seconds. I shook my head, stunned.

"Did that just happen?" I asked Reena, not taking my eyes off Jamal and Alice.

There was no response.

"Reen?"

I turned to my right. She was gone.

Confused, I spun around in a circle, looking for her. But she was nowhere to be found.

I was completely alone.

My heart thumping in my chest, I started walking around the dance floor, trying to find Reena. I pushed past crowds of my classmates, dancing, talking, drinking punch. I asked people if they'd seen her and was rewarded with apathetic shrugs. I kept going. I waded through piles of cotton balls. I grazed my head on a low-hanging fake icicle. I was starting to feel insane. Both of my friends had just disappeared. One for a boy, and one for . . . no reason at all. My face felt hot, and I cast my eyes around the room desperately.

"Miller? Are you okay?" Pradeep Paruchuri was standing in front of me in a blue shirt and a silky black tie.

"Pradeep." I stopped, put my hands on my hips, and tried to catch my breath. "Um. Yeah. I'm okay. I'm just looking for Reena."

"My sister?" He squinted out onto the dance floor. "I haven't seen her anywhere. Are you sure she's even here? She hates dances."

"Yes, I'm sure." I was trying to sound calm, but my voice cracked a little. "We came here together."

"Weird. Yeah, sorry. I have no idea." He smiled at me. "But I'm glad we ran into each other again. I wanted to talk to you."

I stared into his big hazel eyes. "Um, yeah. Definitely."

"It's just really nice to find someone else here at this school who actually reads for fun. It's, like, most people I know read because they have to for, like, school, not because they actually enjoy it."

I couldn't believe it. Was Mount McKinsey Lodge a magical place? Were we all living in some kind of surreal dream? Was Pradeep Paruchuri really cornering me at the Winter Wonderland Ball and telling me he wanted to talk about books? I crossed my hands behind my back and pinched the soft part of my palm.

It hurt.

Was he going to ask me to dance?

"Anyway," Pradeep continued, "another thing I wanted to say about *David Copperfield* was—"

He stopped short.

"What?" I said, trying to smile encouragingly.

"Um . . . ," his voice was fading out, and his eyes were fixed on something above and behind my right shoulder. "I . . . um . . ."

I turned around.

Kristen Diamond was walking toward us. As mysteriously as Reena had left, Kristen had appeared, and she was wearing a short dress made entirely out of tiny white feathers. Her red hair was in sausage curls that fell down her impressive chest and stopped just above her miniscule waist. Her skin glowed, her lips were parted, and her violet eyes were fixed, determinedly, on some point in the distance.

It only took me a few seconds to realize that that point was Pradeep.

And then she was upon us.

"Hi, Molly," she said sweetly. "Hi, Pradeep."

Pradeep and I stared at her, mutually agog.

"Pradeep?" she asked. "Would you like to dance?"

I felt as if someone very far away, very tiny and sitting inside a cave inside a mountain inside an uninhabited country in a remote part of the world, was screaming, *Noooooooooo!* But because the voice came from such a great distance, it registered as a tiny, terrible tremor, and then faded away.

I blinked.

"Sure," Pradeep said, grinning nervously. "I would love to."

It was like I had completely ceased to exist for Pradeep the minute Kristen entered the room. On the other hand, the acknowledgment he was about to give me felt so humiliating that I found myself wishing I *had* ceased to exist.

"Stay cool, Miller," Pradeep called over his shoulder as Kristen led him away.

And then she turned around herself and shot me a blinding and triumphant smile.

"Yeah," she echoed, her white teeth gleaming, "stay cool."

THREE

Alice

You spend a good part of your childhood lying in bed at night and thinking about the future. You're picturing what kind of job you'll have; what kind of person you'll be; what you'll look like. When you're in third grade you try to picture what sixth grade will be like. When you're in sixth grade you try to picture what ninth grade will be like. And one of the great, eternal questions you ask yourself during those long years of anticipation is:

When will I meet my first boyfriend?

What will he look like, how will he sound, what will he wear, and, most important, *what will it feel like to kiss him?*

I'd been asking myself those questions for as long as I could remember. And as I got older and older, and all the girls I knew met their first boyfriend, kissed him, broke up with him, met their second boyfriend, kissed him, broke up with him, and had already moved onto their third boyfriend before I'd even had a boyfriend at all, I started to worry that I would still be asking myself those questions when I was a fifty-five-year-old woman with chin hairs and pink curlers.

"You're crazy, Alice," my friends at the Brooklyn Montessori School would tell me. "It'll happen eventually, and then you'll stop worrying."

But it didn't happen...and it didn't happen...and it didn't happen...

And then, on a Friday night in November, at the Winter Wonderland Ball on top of Mount McKinsey, it did.

Everything happened so fast. Jamal Chapman asked me to dance, and then we were dancing, and smiling at each other, and his hand was resting on the small of my back, and then he rested his head on my shoulder, and then I rested my head on his shoulder, and then after a few songs he pulled away from me—my heart froze in fear—Was this the end? Would I ever see him again?—and asked if I wanted to take a walk.

Holding hands, we walked off the dance floor (I caught a glimpse of half the girls in the room staring at me with utter hatred) and out into the cavernous lobby.

Jamal took a deep breath. "It's nice to get some air."

I nodded. My heart was beating so hard that I was sure he could hear it.

Our hands still clasped, we walked up the length of the lobby and right up to the big bay windows facing the snowy bank that lay right behind the lodge.

Then we stood there for a while in silence, staring out at the night.

"It's weird," Jamal said, "I really don't know you at all, Alice."

I nodded again, gulping.

"But I kind of feel like I do. I have no idea why. It's creepy."

"I feel the same way," I admitted. "What's weird is that it's, like, mutual."

There was another silence.

"I want to know everything about your life," he said finally. "But I don't know where to begin, I guess."

Everything? No one had ever said anything like that to me before. What sprang into my mind were visions of my childhood. Sitting with my mother in Prospect Park in the springtime, drinking soup from a thermos. My mother and father setting a birthday cake in front me, candles ablaze. Walking by myself to school for the first time, my feet crunching over piles of autumn leaves, my backpack thumping on my shoulders. My mother kneeling in the doorway, opening her arms as I clambered up the steps of our front stoop in the sunshine . . .

Jamal was looking at me quizzically.

"Sorry," I said. "I kind of spaced out. Um . . . I had a pretty good childhood, I guess. Until my mom died. Then my dad married a psychopath and she sent me off to Putnam Mount McKinsey and so . . . here I am."

It was unbelievable. Something about this guy just made the truth fly out of my mouth. I had no control over it.

Luckily he started laughing. "Wow," he said, leaning forward and pressing his forehead against the windowpane. "That was an incredible summary."

I blushed. "I mean, it's more complicated than that."

He laughed even harder. "I would assume so. But I love the way you just *say* everything."

"Usually I don't. Usually I don't say anything."

We looked at each other. Whenever our eyes met, I felt like I was being sucked through a black hole into some kind of alternate universe. It was definitely a scary sensation. But I liked the way that alternate universe of me-and-Jamal felt. Things made more sense in it. Suddenly all the bad things that had happened to me in the past three years didn't seem as bad. And I did feel a weird freedom around him—like I could say whatever I wanted. Like all the fear and anxiety I normally walked around with had the potential to just . . . ebb away.

"What about you?" I asked.

"What about me?"

"Tell me everything." I giggled.

"Oh, man. I don't know if I can sum it up as well as you did."

Feeling suddenly bold, I reached out and touched his arm. "Try."

He gazed out the window. "Well . . . I grew up with my mom."

"Yeah. I saw her. That first day of Parents Weekend."

He nodded. "I remember. Let's see. The two of us are really close. Um . . . she raised me all by herself. I'm an only child. I grew up in Washington Heights, which is in the northern part of Manhattan."

"I know that," I said. "I'm from Brooklyn."

His face lit up. "You're kidding!"

I shook my head.

"I assumed you were this really rich girl from the suburbs of Connecticut or, like, southern California. That's so cool!"

My stomach fell a little. I was kind of a rich girl. After all, I'd gone to private school my whole life.

"Where in Brooklyn?" he asked.

I cleared my throat nervously. "Um . . . Brooklyn Heights."

"Oh."

"Yeah."

He cocked his head and looked at me. "So you *are* a rich girl."

I nodded. "Yup."

And then we both started laughing.

"Wow," said Jamal a minute later, wiping the tears from his eyes, "this is funny. This is really funny. I've never had a conversation like this with anyone. No tact. No tact whatsoever."

And that made us laugh even harder.

"Wait," I said, holding my aching sides. "What about your dad? I remember you said that he was gone. What does that mean?"

The smile seemed to literally fall off his face. "It means he's gone."

I wasn't sure how to respond to that. "Oh."

He rubbed his temples with his hands. "Sorry. That didn't make sense. Uh . . . he ran away when I was baby. So basically I never had a dad."

"Did you ever meet him?"

He smiled tensely. "Wow. Huh. Okay. Well, I guess I got myself into this, didn't I? I was the one who said I wanted to know everything."

"You don't have to talk about it," I reassured him. "It's okay. I don't need to—"

"No," he said. "It's good. It's probably good for me. I never talk about this stuff with anyone except my mom."

There was a pause.

"I grew up hating my dad," he said. "I mean, *hating* him. I'd never met him. All I knew was that he'd gotten my mom pregnant, and that the second he found out, he took off. Then when I was thirteen we got this postcard from him the mail. He was living somewhere in Queens and he wanted to meet me. The guy had been living in New York City and it had taken him thirteen years to get in contact with me! At first I refused to see him. Then I thought about how much I wanted to tell him off, in person. I wanted to tell him what a jerk he was, and how he'd left my mom penniless, and how she'd had to work three jobs until I was six. All of that stuff. I wanted him to, like, realize what he'd done."

I nodded. "That makes sense." Not only that, it reminded me of how I felt about R.

"So one afternoon I took the train all the way to Queens. I got off the train and I walked over to his apartment. Then the whole time I was walking up his stairs I was thinking about all the mean things I was going to say to him. Words were running through my mind. *Scumbag. Loser. Jerk.* My heart was beating so fast. And when he finally opened his door . . ." Jamal paused.

"What happened next?" I demanded.

"Look," he said, pointing out the window. "It's snowing."

Fine, glittery snow was shimmering down from the black sky and dusting the ground.

"Please, please finish," I said. For some reason I felt like my life depended on hearing the end of his story. *I really like this guy,* I thought to myself. *Actually, I like him so much it's terrifying.*

"Sorry. Okay. So he opens the door, then there's just this person standing in front of me. And that completely shocked me."

I stared at him. "Wait. I don't get it."

"I mean, I don't know what I was expecting. Some kind of powerful . . . demon or something? I don't know. Maybe I just was so scared and angry that I forgot he was a real person."

"Who cares?" I said. "He totally screwed you over."

Jamal pressed a finger to the fogged-up windowpane and began drawing something. "I guess my point is that he was pathetic. And sad. And I realized that I wouldn't want to know him or be him, not in a million years. I mean, being mad at someone gives them power. And this was the least powerful man I'd ever met." He took a deep breath in, then let it out. "Wow. I can't believe I just told you all of that."

I stared out at the falling snow. Something about his story made me want to cry. I bit my lip.

"Is everything okay, Alice?" he asked gently.

I nodded and turned to face him. "Jamal?" I asked.

"Yeah?" He reached out and touched my shoulder. I don't think I'd ever realized how many pleasurable nerve endings were in my shoulder before that moment.

"You're amazing," I said.

He smiled, and then, his hand still on my shoulder, he leaned toward me.

Suddenly I froze. This was what I'd been wanting for years. This was the person I'd been waiting years and years to meet. And yet when his face started coming closer and closer to mine, his eyes shut, his lips parted, I was overwhelmed by fear and anxiety.

"Wait!" I yelled.

Jamal's eyes flew open, and he backed away. "Oh, my God. I'm so sorry. I thought—"

"No, no!" I said, my cheeks aflame. "I just . . ."

He looked at me. I could see insecurity flooding across his face. Oh, no. I'd ruined it. I'd ruined everything. *Get it together, Alice,* I told myself. *Don't let your fears push this guy away.*

"Jamal," I managed to say, trying desperately to articulate

what I was feeling, "I really, really want to kiss you. But I've only kissed one other guy in my life, and I didn't . . ."

Oh, God. What was I admitting to?

"I didn't even like him," I finished. "So I'm scared. I wanted to let you know that I'm scared. Because . . . I really, really like you."

He grinned. "Me, too. I'm totally terrified."

I gaped at him. "You are?"

"Yeah. I'm, like, totally worried you're gonna think I'm a bad kisser, or annoying, or dumb, or—"

"No!" I said. "I would never!"

His grin got even bigger. "You know what?"

"What?"

"I think *you're* amazing, Alice Bingley-Beckerman."

And then, suddenly filled with a totally unfamiliar feeling of security and joy, I grabbed Jamal Chapman's cheeks with both hands, brought his face toward mine, and kissed him.

And he kissed me back.

His lips were soft. And warm. And strangely familiar and unfamiliar at the same time.

We kept kissing.

I'm not sure how much time passed.

Maybe an hour. Maybe two.

Eventually someone—was it Pradeep Paruchuri?—shouted, "Chapman!" from the other end of the hallway.

"Oh, God," Jamal muttered, his mouth against my neck.

"We should go," I whispered, "I think it's way past curfew."

He nodded. "See you tomorrow morning," he said in my ear. "I can't wait."

"Me neither."

He planted a small kiss on each of my eyelids, and then darted away into the darkness.

I sighed, my lips aching, my heart bursting with happiness, and gazed out the window at the huge, perfectly round moon.

It was at that moment that I finally saw what Jamal had written on the fogged-up pane with the tip of his finger:

J loves A
(helplessly)

FOUR

Reena

I slammed the door to our bedroom shut and stood there, panting and praying that no one had seen me leave the ball.

It was time to execute my Master Plan.

I ran over to my suitcase and started pawing through my clothes. I had to focus. Still, I kept picturing Jamal Chapman asking Alice to dance, and it distracted me from the task at hand. I wanted the best for Alice—I genuinely did—and yet there was something about the timing of her good luck that startled me. I was forced to stand there and watch her, without warning, cross from the land of childhood into the land of adulthood, and I wasn't prepared. One second the three of us were standing there in the corner, comrades in loneliness, and the next second she was off dancing with one of the cutest guys in school. Just some kind of warning would have been nice. Because right when she took Jamal's hand and stepped away from my side I got this sinking feeling that made me feel like I was a little kid getting left behind by my mother.

I took a deep breath. *Focus,* I told myself. Tonight was going to be a lucky night for me, too. Tonight I would move out of the world of fantasy and into the world of mature, adult romance.

Tonight I was going to kiss David Newman for the first time.

I unearthed a long, white satin nightgown that Katie had given me for my fifteenth birthday. I scrutinized it. Risky. But gorgeous. And Katie had always said that it made my skinny body look more curvaceous than it actually was.

I slipped out of my red party dress and into the nightgown. I unwound my bun and let my hair tumble down my shoulders. Then I stared at myself in the mirror.

I was disappointed by what I saw.

I looked pretty—there was no doubt about that—but I looked *young.* Younger than I imagined. Whenever I pictured myself kissing David Newman, I pictured a sophisticated, older version of myself, maybe with a throaty voice and reading glasses perched on the end of my nose.

The person in the mirror looked . . . well, she looked fifteen.

I sighed and threw back my shoulders. There was nothing I could do about it. I had to Keep My Eyes on the Prize. I had to Stay Goal Oriented. After all, things were already working out pretty well—I hadn't wanted Alice and Molly to know about my Master Plan (they would have laughed at me or given me a long, serious lecture about teacher-student relationships), and Jamal asking Alice to dance had been the perfect opportunity for me to make a getaway upstairs. And then there was the conversation I'd overheard earlier that day between David and one of the other teachers—I'd distinctly overheard him say that he was going to spend the evening correcting papers in his room instead of chaperoning the dance.

That only made me love him more. He hated dances, too!

I squirted a little jasmine perfume on the back of my neck, and smeared the black eyeliner I'd been wearing so it looked like I'd been taking a nap. (I had to have some kind of excuse for wearing a nightgown.)

I brushed my teeth three times in a row, and then I sat on the edge of my bed and maniacally sucked a cherry Jolly Rancher. After all, I wanted my breath to smell clean, but not too clean.

And then I was ready.

I hadn't realized how nervous I was until I quietly exited our room and started padding in my bare feet down the hallway toward the teachers' wing. At one point I was so overcome with fear that I considered just turning around. But I kept going. *Paruchuris do not give up,* I kept telling myself.

I reached his door. 422. I only knew it was David's because I'd snuck a peek over Agnes's shoulder while she was reading the room assignments out loud. I stood there for a while, breathless, listening to hear if there were any sounds coming from inside. At one point I thought I heard the creak of a chair. I leaned in a little closer and tried pressing my ear to the door. I thought that I could hear someone turning the page of a book.

And then the door flew open.

I gasped.

David Newman was standing in front of me, wearing a rumpled flannel shirt and sweatpants. He was holding *Zen Ventura* in one hand and the door handle in the other.

"Reena?" he asked disbelievingly, as if he couldn't quite believe I was standing there.

"I was going to knock!" I yelped.

He furrowed his brow. "What are you doing here?"

"Um . . ." I cleared my throat and smoothed out my night-gown with my hands. For some reason I wasn't been expecting that question. I thought that when David Newman saw me, and saw the smoldering Look in my eyes (although now I was so mortified I was staring at my bare feet), he would just fold me into his arms and . . .

"Why aren't you at the dance?" he asked. He actually sounded a little annoyed.

"I . . . um . . ." I finally looked up at him and made eye contact. I put my hands on my hips and attempted to appear confident. "I thought you might want to see me."

"Do you have a question about the final?"

I blinked. "What?"

"Do you have a question about the Humanities final?"

"Um . . . no."

There was a long pause.

"I just thought the two of us could hang out and get to know each other," I whispered. Although wasn't it obvious? I was standing in front of him in a white satin nightgown. Why wasn't he inviting me in, sitting me in front of the fire, and pouring me a glass of burgundy?

Now David was staring at me, his eyes filled with something that I can only describe as . . . pity.

It made me feel about two years old.

"Reena," he said softly, "what are you doing? And why are you wearing that nightgown?"

Why? *Why?* Because it was *sexy*.

"Um," I said. I couldn't stop saying "um." But maybe he still didn't understand? Maybe I needed to make things absolutely one-hundred-percent clear.

"I really like you," I added. "And you said that you're not, like, a get-off-the-couch type of person, and I thought maybe you wanted me to—"

He interrupted me. "*What?* When did I say that?"

"When we were talking about *Zen Ventura*? After class . . . ?" My voice was starting to falter.

David closed his eyes and began kneading the space between his eyes with his thumb and forefinger. "Oh, Reena."

The "Oh, Reena" did me in. It was like a death sentence. It was like the cherry on top of the worst year of my life. Even though I hadn't cried all semester at Putnam Mount McKinsey, my eyes started filling with tears for the second time that night.

"Reena," David said slowly, "I have no interest in you. You're fifteen. You're a great kid. But I . . . I have a girlfriend, and even if I didn't . . . you are way, way too young for—"

"My stepmother is twenty-eight years younger than my dad!" I yelled. Then I froze, shocked. I hadn't even been thinking about my dad and Shanti Shruti. But suddenly the words just flew out of my mouth.

David reached out and put a hand on my shoulder. The warmth from his palm coursed through my body. "I'm so sorry, Reena," he said. "I didn't know."

"And they're married," I finished feebly.

"I'm so sorry," he said again.

Then I couldn't stand it anymore. His pity, the comfort of his hand on my shoulder, his sad eyes, his rumpled shirt . . . all I wanted to do was crawl into his lap and scream and cry for hours. *I don't even want to kiss David Newman,* I slowly realized. *I just want him to hold me and tell me everything is okay.*

And since he couldn't, and since I'd just humiliated myself more totally and completely than I'd ever humiliated myself before, I covered my face with my hands and ran down the creaky wooden hallway, back to my empty room.

"Reena?"

Molly's voice sounded like it was coming from a great distance.

Probably because I was lying in a fetal position under one sleeping bag, three blankets, and an oversized pillow.

"All the lights are out," I heard her say. "Are you there? This is creeping me out. . . ."

I made a small, moaning noise, just to let her know it was me, but it must have frightened her, because she screamed and flipped on the lights.

I lay still underneath my snowdrift of blankets. I heard Molly's feet tiptoe in my direction, and then a hand reached forward and ripped back the pile of bedding in one swift motion. I shivered and squinted in the cold, bright light.

"It is you!" Molly yelled. "You abandoned me, you jerk!"

I grabbed a piece of my tangled, sweaty hair and covered my face with it.

"Reena!"

"Please leave me alone," I croaked.

"No, I will not leave you alone! You totally betrayed me out there on the dance floor! You left me high and dry!"

I began to snuffle and sob again, still shivering. Then I lifted up the hem of my nightgown and blew my nose into it.

"Oh my God!" Molly shrieked. "Ew! You are disgusting!"

I didn't respond.

After an exasperated silence, I heard her unzip my suitcase and paw through my clothes.

"Here," I heard her say, "lift up your legs."

I lifted up my legs. She slid a pair of flannel pajama bottoms onto my body.

"And put this on." She tossed me a soft, worn-out Polartec vest. "It's mine. You can wear it. It's really warm."

I finally sat up and put on the vest. I tucked my hair behind my ears and stared at Molly through my gooey, tear-filled eyes.

"You look pretty," I whispered.

With a resounding thump, Molly collapsed next to me on my bed and smushed her face into the pile of blankets. "I want to die," she murmured.

I shook my head. "No. I want to die."

"No. Me."

"No, Mol. There is no way you possibly, possibly humiliated yourself as badly as I just did."

She shook her head, her face still muffled. "You're wrong."

I reached over and grabbed her shoulder, flipping her onto her back.

"Did you just appear at the door of your teacher's room in a skimpy nightgown because you thought he wanted you to make the first move?" I demanded.

Her eyes widened behind her thick glasses.

"That's right," I told her, "top that."

"Oh, Reena," Molly said, and covered her mouth with her hand.

"No. No. I don't ever want anyone to say 'Oh, Reena' ever again. Worst phrase in the English language."

Molly propped herself up on one elbow and gazed thoughtfully up at the ceiling. "Well, the name Reena isn't technically a *word* in the English language, so it can't really be a phrase or else you'd—"

I pushed her and she toppled back down again.

We lay on our backs and stared at the ceiling for a while.

"Reen?" asked Molly after a long pause.

"Yeah?"

"Can I tell you something?"

"Sure. Anything."

Another long pause.

"I'm in love with your brother," she said.

It took me a few seconds to absorb the information she'd just communicated to me. At first I was shocked. Then, strangely, I felt a little grossed out and offended. As if Molly had just told me that she'd been using my toothbrush for the past two months, or wearing my underwear. But a few seconds later I thought: *Of course she's in love with Pradeep.* And a few seconds after that, I thought (and I felt like my heart might break right after I thought it): *There's no way he's in love with her.*

"Do you hate me?" Molly whispered.

I turned on my side and looked at her. Her blue eyes were swimming around anxiously behind her glasses. I reached over and pushed a tendril of hair back from her forehead.

"Of course I don't hate you," I said. "But I have to warn you, Mol, Pradeep is very weird when it comes to—"

She shook her head. "You don't have to say anything. He's dancing with Kristen Diamond right now. I'm an idiot."

I stared at her. "Kristen?"

"Yep. She's wearing some kind of swan dress. I don't want to think about it."

I shook my head. The tragedy of it all—of existence—was really starting to get to me. I hadn't understood it when I was younger. Life was easy then. My parents were married, we all lived together in one big house, I'd known my friends for years, school wasn't that hard yet . . . but now I was starting to get it. Life was about bad luck. Bad luck and mistakes. Other people mucked up things around you, and then you went and mucked up things once they were done.

Molly was clearly thinking similar thoughts, because after we lay there and stared at the ceiling for a while she announced: "Everyone is in love with the wrong person."

I nodded. "I guess so."

A second later we said in unison: "Except Alice."

"Except Alice," Molly repeated. "Gosh darn Alice. She must be doing something right."

We lay there for a while, brooding. Then—as if jolted by an electric shock—I leapt to my feet.

"Molly!" I shrieked. "What are we doing? We're being passive! We're not taking fate into our own hands!"

Still lying on her back, Molly cocked an eyebrow. "I don't know. You put on a satin nightgown and marched right up to fate's door. And look where it got you."

Slightly wounded by that remark, I plowed on anyway. "No. I'm not talking about romance. I'm talking about the Poison Apples. I mean, think about it. When did your life start going to pieces?"

Molly thought. "I guess . . . I guess when—"

"When Candy Lamb came into your life, right?"

"Yeah. I guess."

"And my life started going to pieces the day I met Shanti Shruti at that stupid yoga class."

"So what are you saying?"

"I'm saying our stepmothers are the root of the problem! That's why I formed the Poison Apples in the first place, right?"

Molly sat up on my bed and cupped her chin in her palm.

227

"Yeah. I have to say, though, Reen, I'm really glad David Newman didn't want to kiss you. No offense, but I think that would have been pretty creepy."

This remark also hurt my feelings, although now, in the harsh cold light of After the Fact, she kind of—*sort of*—had a point.

"Anyway," I continued, waving my hands in the air to dismiss that particular topic, "screw boys! We need to reclaim our lives!"

I was happy to see that Molly was nodding. Then she actually got to her feet and started pacing up and down the room.

"Okay," she muttered. "You're right. This is a war. But how do we win the war?"

"What do you mean, how do we win the war? We haven't even gone into battle yet!" My cheeks were flushed with excitement. I was starting to feel a little bit better.

"Okay, so . . . what? What do we do now?"

"We go to battle! We get revenge!"

"How?" She stopped pacing. "Seriously. How?"

I put my hands on my hips. "Um . . ."

Molly stroked her chin. "Well, okay. Let's think about it. Like what revolutionaries have done in the past. The Boston Tea Party, for instance. That was really effective."

I sat down on the bed, embarrassed. "Um. I kind of forget what the Boston Tea Party is."

"The Americans threw all the tea into the ocean. The tea that belonged to the British people."

I wasn't quite getting it. "Okay . . ."

"They took the thing that was most important to the British, and then they just . . . trashed it."

It was starting to make sense to me. Weird sense. But sense.

"So," Molly continued, "one way to wage war, or initiate war, or whatever, is to, like, take the thing that's most important to the person . . . and, like, throw it away."

We looked at each other.

"Molly Miller," I said. "I think you've got it."

"Get out some paper and pen," she instructed me, pushing up her glasses with her forefinger like she always did when she got excited, "and take notes."

Revenge—A Comprehensive Plan
(calligraphy by Mlle. Paruchuri)

The Enemies:
R. Klausenhook, actress/evil stepmother

Shanti Shruti, yoga instructor/evil stepmother

Candy Lamb, pregnant housewife/waitress/evil stepmother

The Heroines:
Alice Bingley-Beckerman, student/wronged stepdaughter

Reena Paruchuri, student/wronged stepdaughter

Molly Miller, student/wronged stepdaughter/lexicography expert

The Goal:
1. Destroy what is dearest to the enemy.
2. Get away with it.

The Time Frame:
Thanksgiving vacation.

Plan 1:
R. Klausenhook
What R. Klausenhook holds dearest: her acting career.

Instructions for A. Bingley-Beckerman: Destroy Acting
    Career.

Plan 2:
Shanti Shruti
What Shanti Shruti holds dearest: her penguin.

Instructions for R. Paruchuri: Destroy Penguin.

Plan 3:
Candy Lamb
What Candy Lamb holds dearest: her harmonious relationship
    with Spencer.

Instructions for M. Miller: Destroy the Relationship.

FIVE

Molly

"Destroy Spencer?" Alice gasped.

"No, no, not Spencer," Reena said. "The Poison Apples is a nonviolent organization. Destroy Candy Lamb's *relationship* with Spencer."

Alice drew a blanket around her shoulders and shivered. It was Sunday night and we'd just arrived back at Putnam Mount McKinsey, but Reena had insisted—on tiny slips of paper that had mysteriously made their way into our suitcases that morning—*Mandatory Poison Apples Meeting Tonight*—that we all meet on the roof of Middleton right after curfew. Reena had just unfurled the Revenge Plan and read it out loud to us.

"I don't get it," Alice said, shaking her head. "When did you guys come up with this plan? When did you make this list?"

Reena stood up, exasperated. She was wearing a bathrobe and slippers, and her hair was standing up in messy chunks. She actually looked kind of insane, with the stars and the night sky behind her and the full moon illuminating her profile. And she'd been acting a little insane, too. Almost as if to compensate for the great disappointment that turned out to be David Newman, she'd become maniacally focused on the Poison Apples and our Thanksgiving revenge plan.

"We made this list," barked Reena, "while you were making out on a bobsled with Jamal Chapman!"

Alice ducked her face behind her hair and waved her hands in the air. "Okay, okay."

"Show a little appreciation!"

"I appreciate it, I appreciate it. I'm just ... I'm not quite sure how we're going to, um, *execute* the plan."

"That's up to each of us, individually. Thanksgiving is this coming Thursday. I'm going back to LA, you're going back to New York, and Mol is going back to ... um ... North Flywood."

"North Forest," I said.

"Right, right."

I shook my head. "Wow, Reena. You really do have zero interest in any place that isn't a major city."

Reena smiled. "That's correct."

"So let me get this straight," Alice said. "Before Thursday, I have to find a way to sabotage R.'s career, Molly has to find a way to, um, find a nonviolent way of ruining Candy's relationship with Spencer, and you have to ... steal a penguin?"

Reena nodded. "Yup."

"And what will happen once we've completed these near-impossible tasks?"

"We'll have power," Reena said grandly. "Negotiating power."

"We'll be the ones holding the poison apple," I said, feeling poetic.

Reena looked at me, her eyes glinting. "Exactly," she said. "And they'll be the ones eating the poison."

This time no one was waiting for me when I got off the bus in North Forest. Not even Spencer. I shouldn't have been surprised—no one knew I was coming—and yet I still felt sad and lonely standing alone in the middle of the snow-covered parking lot next to the Savings Bank.

I don't belong here anymore, I thought.

But then I thought: *Did I ever really belong here?*

I trudged along Main Street, past the post office, past the American Legion, past the gas station, and, finally, past my mother's boarded-up hair salon. A light snow began to fall, and I stared at the streetlamps through the wet flakes that had landed on my lashes. The round yellow lights pulsed and beamed in all directions like stars.

I felt like a ghost. The town center was totally empty—it was the day before Thanksgiving—and the muffled silence of the falling snow made it feel like North Forest had been abandoned years and years ago. The sun had just set, and the sky was a deep indigo.

I was started to get cold. Really, really cold.

And I still hadn't figured out how to execute Revenge Plan 3.

Reena had made it explicitly clear: Spencer was my bargaining tool. But what did that mean? And what exactly was I trying to bargain for?

Maybe (and it was painful for me to realize it) I wanted

to be able to see my father again. To have dinner with him occasionally and still feel like I had a home. And I wanted to be able to do that without Candy threatening to pull me out of Putnam Mount McKinsey and make her her live-in maid.

I wanted North Forest to be a place I could go back to, and not the place where I lived.

Was that selfish of me?

I shook my head to clear my thoughts. ("No time for doubts!" Reena had instructed me. "No time for feeling guilty!") I continued walking down Main Street and then turned right, up the unplowed road that led to Candy's house. My old house—empty for over six months now—was on the other side of Main Street, and down a hill. I tried not to picture my bedroom, dark and cold and dusty. I tried not to picture the mice that were probably skittering over the floors, up and down the stairs—I always used to hear them moving inside the walls as I was lying in bed at night. Now they were probably having the time of their lives.

I continued up the side of the road, wading through the deep snow, shielding my face with my hand whenever a car swung its bright headlights around a bend. My boots were leaking, and my toes were starting to go numb.

Eventually I was standing in front of Candy's house. Or now, I reminded myself—my father and Spencer had been living there for more than six months, after all—it was my family's house.

Their car was in the driveway, and almost all the lights were on.

I stepped into the front yard. The top layer of the snow

had iced over, and my boots made a horrible crunching noise. I winced. I couldn't afford for anybody to see or hear me. I stepped behind a tree, then leaned out and peered through the dining room window.

They were all there.

Framed in the picture window, lit up by the yellow glow of a lamp. And—like a movie—they were all laughing. Even my dad, who almost never laughed. At one point Candy reached over and touched Spencer's hair. They were sitting around the table and passing around food and pouring drinks and they looked so . . . happy.

And instead of feeling angry, or left out, or abandoned—all the feelings I'd been having since the summer, all the feelings I'd ordinarily expect to have—I experienced a different sensation. At first I couldn't tell what it was, exactly. It was a slight stirring in my stomach, an impalpable feeling of longing. I didn't want to be inside with my father and Candy and Spencer and Sandie and Randie—I wasn't longing for *that*. After all, I wasn't part of that family.

And then I realized what the feeling was.

I missed my mother.

So then why was I standing by the side of the road, covered with slush, staring at them like some kind of crazy stalker, when my mother was sitting alone at Silverwood less than five miles away? So what if she was bonkers? She was my mother. And she needed me. Just like I needed her.

My heart surged with joy, and I stepped backward in the snow, away from the house. My boots made another loud cracking sound as they broke through the ice, and this time I saw Candy stop talking and turn toward the window.

She'd heard me.

Praying I wouldn't slip and fall, I turned and ran, sloshing through gray puddles of freezing slush.

I ran and ran and ran.

I stopped briefly just before I reached the highway, to catch my breath and take out my cell phone with cold, trembling hands. I quickly sent Reena a text message: PLAN 3 ABORTED.

Then I started running again.

When I reached the big wrought-iron gates of Silverwood, I bent over, put my head between my legs, and almost started hyperventilating. I couldn't feel my feet or my hands or my ears or my face, just the icy-cold air I kept gulping into my lungs. A minute later, my heart still pounding in my chest, I pulled open the heavy gates and started walking up the long driveway to the Silverwood's reception center.

"Oh my God," the woman at the desk said when she saw me.

I could barely see anything, because my glasses had steamed up the second I stepped inside the overheated building. I took them off to wipe them on my jacket, but then I realized that my jacket was soaking wet. Along with my shirt. And my pants. And my boots. And my hair.

"Hi," I said. My entire body was shaking.

The woman rose out of her chair and came out from behind the desk. She had a puffy gray halo of hair, and a pin shaped like a turkey affixed to her turtleneck sweater. "Are you okay?" she asked me.

I nodded, my teeth chattering. "Yeah," I said. "I'm okay."

"Do you need a change of clothes?"

"No. I'm . . . I'm okay. I'm actually here to see my mother."

She frowned. "Your mother? She's a patient here?"

I rubbed my hands together to try to get some feeling back in my fingers. "Yes. Patsy Miller. Is she still in Room 152? I'd like to visit her."

The woman suddenly took a step back, and her hand flew up, almost protectively, to touch her turkey pin. "Patsy Miller?"

"Yeah. I'm her daughter."

She closed her eyes, revealing a shaky blue line drawn across each of her eyelids. "Oh, dear."

There was a sharp, throbbing pain in my feet. "What . . . is something wrong?"

"Oh, dear," she repeated. "Oh, dear."

"Please just tell me what's going on," I said, trying to sound calm.

She took my elbow and led me over to one of the orange plastic chairs near the desk. "Have a seat first."

I sat. She stood in front of me, wringing her hands and moving her lips around, as if she were trying to find the right words.

"Patsy . . . ," she began, "your mother . . ."

"Yes?"

"She . . . no one told you?"

A cold drop of water ran down my cheek. The pile of snow that had collected on top of my head was starting to melt. "No one told me *what*?"

The woman folded her arms over her chest. "Your mother disappeared two weeks ago."

I stared at her.

"I'm sorry that I'm the one to tell you this. We told her husband—I'm sorry, ex-husband—and we assumed he'd let the rest of the family know."

I rose up out of my chair so fast that the woman backed away from me, her fingers still fluttering nervously.

"I don't understand," I told her. "I'm sorry. What does 'disappear' mean?"

The woman took another step backward. "It means that when the nurses showed up with her breakfast in the morning she was gone."

"I don't understand how that could happen."

"She was doing quite well, and we put her in a less closely watched wing of the building. We think she just . . . climbed out the window in the middle of the night."

There was a long pause.

"I'm so sorry," she whispered.

Melted snow dripped down my forehead onto my nose, and from my nose onto my chin. I didn't say anything.

"Let me get you some dry clothes," she said gently.

I shook my head, still speechless. She reached out to help me take off my jacket, and I jerked away from her.

"Are the police"—I couldn't even believe the words that were coming out of my mouth—"are the police looking for her?"

"Yes," she said. "Of course. But they haven't had much luck."

I nodded numbly, then turned around and started walking out the door.

"Wait!" she called out. "You can't go back out in this weather!"

I wrenched open the big glass doors, stepped out into the dark night, and started to make my way back down the long, slippery driveway.

It was snowing harder now, half sleeting, and the sky was

a mottled, churning shade of black and gray. The wind whipped against my face and I could feel my wet hair freezing into long icy strips.

I didn't care.

My mother was gone.

And it was all my fault.

This time there was no point running. After all, I didn't have anywhere to go. I took my cell phone out of my pocket and looked at it. Reena hadn't responded to my text message. Of course. She was probably furious with me. Now she and Alice were going to refuse to be my friend, due to my failure as a member of the Poison Apples.

I was alone in the universe.

I'd never known despair like this. It obliterated everything. It made the bleakness of the world around me—the storm, the night, the wind, the cars whizzing past me on the highway—seem insignificant. The hopelessness rising inside my stomach and taking hold of my heart was much, much scarier than any blizzard.

Walking along the edge of the road, I turned my face up to the sky and let the hail and snow pelt my cheeks and eyelids.

"I GIVE UP!" I screamed. "DO YOU HEAR ME? I GIVE UP TRYING TO CHANGE MY FATE! LUCK IS LUCK AND I'M JUST UNLUCKY!"

A car screeched to a stop next to me.

Now I was going to be murdered by an axe-wielding serial killer.

I wasn't even sure if I cared.

Someone rolled down the passenger-side window.

"Molly?" a voice asked.

I tried to squint into the car, but I could barely see through my soaked glasses and all the snow flying in front me.

"Oh, my God! It is you! Molly Miller, get in the car right now!"

The car door opened.

It was Candy.

Maybe the last person on the planet I wanted to see.

"No," I said. "I will not get in the car."

"I can't hear you! Get in the car!"

"No," I whispered.

I heard an exasperated sigh, and then a plump arm reached out of the car door and yanked me inside. A second later I was sitting silently in a puddle in the passenger seat, shivering and refusing to look up.

"What in God's name are you doing out here?" Candy shrieked.

I peered into the backseat. Spencer was sitting in the darkness, staring at me, her eyes wide with fear.

"I was trying to visit Mom," I muttered into my lap.

"Were you standing in our front yard an hour ago?" Candy demanded.

I nodded, sinking my head deeper into the neck of my soaking wet jacket.

"I thought so! We've been driving all over town looking for you! Why didn't you knock on the door?"

I shrugged. The misery inside my chest was deepening and thickening.

"Molly! Say something!"

I finally turned and looked at Candy. What I saw actually

surprised me. Her face looked pale and drawn. She looked . . . worried. And sad.

"Why didn't you tell me about Mom?" I asked her. My voice cracked.

She shook her head. "I . . . I can't believe this." The edges of her mouth started trembling. "I *told* your father that we owed you a phone call."

"Then why didn't you?" I asked, my voice getting louder and angrier. "Why didn't you?"

"He didn't think you wanted to talk to us. And he didn't want to hurt your schoolwork or disrupt your—"

"She's my mother!" I screamed. I couldn't tell whether it was melted snow or tears running down my cheeks. "For God's sake! She's my mother!"

"Oh, Molly." Candy held out her arms. "Come here."

I recoiled and threw myself against the car door, pressing my face into the window. "No!"

And then with the same surprising strength with which she'd yanked me into the car, Candy reached over, grabbed my shoulders, and pulled my body against hers. My freezing-cold face was smushed against her warm chest. Her round arms laced tightly around my back.

"Let go of me!" I said muffledly into her sweater, but I wasn't even sure if she could hear me.

"Molly Miller," she told me, "you are coming home with us."

I shook my head, still contained in her warm vise grip.

"Yes," she said. "You are."

I succeeded in wrenching my face far enough away from her bosom to make myself heard. "I don't want to have to leave Putnam Mount McKinsey," I bawled. "I like it there. You and dad are going to make me—"

"We won't make you do anything."

I stared at her. She stared back at me, her eyes still filled with that new, unfamiliar sadness.

"We won't make you do anything, okay?" she said again.

It was the strangest thing. I hadn't executed my revenge plan. I hadn't destroyed her relationship with Spencer. I hadn't done anything.

But the words I'd been wanting to hear all semester were coming out of Candy Lamb's mouth.

So even though I was still miserable, and full of despair, and terribly, terribly lonely, I pressed my face into the warmth of Candy's chest and cried. And she let me cry for what felt like a long time. Until Spencer piped up from the backseat: "Hey! When are we going home?"

I turned around in my seat. "Hey," I said, wiping my eyes, "Spencer."

"What?" she said, staring at me suspiciously.

"I'm sorry if I haven't been around that much this fall. I love you, you know. You're my sister."

She turned and gazed thoughtfully out the window. I was kind of expecting her to respond with *I love you, too, Mol*. Instead, after a long silence, she said: "Well, the twirling finals are next weekend. You can come see me then if you really want."

I smiled weakly. "Okay," I said, "that sounds great. Can I bring my friends Reena and Alice?"

She nodded.

"Awesome," I said. "I'll be there."

A small, almost imperceptible smile crossed my sister's face.

I sat back and fastened my seat belt. Candy cleared her throat, started the ignition, did a three-point turn in the middle of the empty highway, and started driving back to the center of North Forest.

Halfway home a small beeping noise came from the pocket of my jacket.

Reena had sent me a text message.

Alice

Port Authority Bus Terminal.

The embodiment of everything wonderful and horrible about New York City.

I stepped off the bus into the dimly lit building, and I breathed in a smell that I'd almost forgotten existed during my three months at Putnam Mount McKinsey.

That signature smell—the smell of midtown Manhattan and its seething bus and train stations—can be only described as a combination of car exhaust, urine, garbage, and roasting peanuts.

Strange to say, it is not entirely unpleasant.

I was so busy inhaling and exhaling, filling my nose with the scent of the city I'd missed so much, that I almost forgot about Jamal, standing next to me with his duffel bag, shifting nervously from foot to foot.

We'd taken the bus all the way from Massachusetts to Manhattan together, sharing a seat, holding hands, and listening to the same iPod (he got the right earpiece, I got the left).

Now it was time to say good-bye.

He had to take the A train to 175th Street in Washington Heights. I had to take the Number 2 train to R.'s apartment on the Upper West Side.

I threw my arms around his shoulder and buried my face in the nook behind his ear. That nook was my favorite thing about Jamal Chapman. Well, I had a lot of favorite things about Jamal Chapman. But the nook ranked pretty high. It was soft and tender and always smelled incredible.

He pulled away and looked me in the eyes. "Are you gonna be okay?"

I frowned. "What is that supposed to mean?"

"I don't know. Seeing your Dad and R. again. I don't want them . . ." He looked away, embarrassed. "I don't know what I'm talking about."

"Oh, Jamal." I reached out and touched his cheek. "It's okay. I'm okay. I mean . . . ," I trailed off. I'd just gone blank in the head. "Have a good vacation. That's what I mean."

He nodded, still looking worried, and then hoisted his duffel bag over his shoulders and trudged away under the flickering Port Authority lights.

"The Yankees suck!" I called after him.

"The Mets blow!" he yelled, not turning around.

And then he rounded a corner and was gone.

I sighed.

I had made a point of not telling Jamal about the Poison Apples' Revenge Plot, even though he'd asked me during the bus ride what my specific plans were for each day of vacation. And I'd told him about most of my plans: Thanksgiving dinner with my dad and R. on Thursday, the opening of R.'s new play (a highly anticipated revival of Chekhov's *The Cherry Orchard*) on Friday, and then a dentist appointment on Saturday morning.

Not only had I failed to mention the Revenge Plot, but I'd also failed—in the two weeks we'd been dating—to bring up the existence of Poison Apples at all.

Jamal knew that Reena and Molly were my best friends, and that we all had crazy stepmothers. He just didn't know anything about our clandestine meetings on the roof of Middleton. Or our plot to avenge and overthrow our respective stepmothers and reclaim our fates.

I'd like to say that I didn't mention the Poison Apples to Jamal because, as Reena had informed us that first night, the existence of the Poison Apples was Top Secret, Never To Be Mentioned to a Soul.

But the truth was, I secretly believed there was a chance Jamal would disapprove.

I lifted up my bag and started hauling it up the stairs towards the Number 2 train. *Jamal Chapman may be one of the best things that has ever happened to me*, I told myself, *but it won't do me any harm to forget about him for the next four days.*

After all, revenge plot aside, I had the world's craziest stepmother to deal with.

"THE TURKEY IS BURNING!"

R.'s voice pierced the air like a clarion call. I leapt up from the couch where I'd planned on just taking a minute to sit and flip through old issues of *The New Yorker*. Instead I'd dozed off.

I rushed into the kitchen and found R. standing in front of the stove, a potholder covering each hand, waving her arms in the air and fanning smoke.

"It's ruined!" she wailed. Then she turned to me, dagger-eyed. "How could you mess up the *one* thing you were in charge of?"

I sighed, yanked open the door to the oven, and, pulling my shirtsleeves down over my hands, took out the tray, and slammed it down on the counter. Huge billows of smoke rose up into my face. I started coughing.

"I can't breathe!" R. shrieked, and ran out of the room.

Alone in the kitchen, I surveyed the disaster that was going to be Thanksgiving dinner.

R. had announced to both me and my father the day before that she was going to cook the entire meal herself. From scratch.

"Really?" Dad had asked mildly as we all sat over breakfast. "I had assumed we were just going to order takeout."

R. had shook her head, her earrings a-jangle, her eyes shining. "I'm going to do it all."

"But opening night is the day after tomorrow," Dad reminded her. "Maybe we should all just hunker down and take it easy."

"Don't rain on my parade, Nelson!" she snapped at him, and then her eyes immediately slid in my direction, challenging me to speak up.

Now I'd ruined the whole thing. R. had instructed me to take the turkey out of the oven precisely at 5:00 PM, and now it was 5:30, and sitting in front of me on the counter was a . . . charred black mess. It didn't even look like a bird anymore.

R. stormed back into the kitchen, a silk handkerchief wrapped around her mouth like a bandit.

"Mmr dmmr in yer," she informed me through the cloth.

"I can't hear you," I said.

She lifted the handkerchief up for a second. "I am very disappointed in you," she announced, and then folded it back down.

I didn't answer. Instead I just gazed out the kitchen window. Our old kitchen window—the window in our Brooklyn house—looked out on a backyard, and the swaying leaves of a dogwood tree and a London plane would brush against the glass whenever there was a breeze. R.'s kitchen window faced the wall of another looming, gray, twenty-story apartment building and part of an air shaft.

I couldn't wrap my mind around why they wanted to live here.

By 7:00 PM, the three of us were sitting in a booth at Rick's Luncheonette, a dingy, fluorescent-lit diner around the corner from Dad and R.'s apartment.

I chewed morosely on a French fry while we all sat in silence.

R. had refused to order anything. Dad was eating some kind of horrible cole slaw.

"You know," Dad said after a while, "this isn't so bad. We could always be starving, you know. Or homeless."

I glanced at R. hopefully. But I think Dad's comment only made her angrier.

"What I was trying to do," she informed Dad coldly, "was cook a nice Thanksgiving meal for your daughter." Then she turned to me. "And you don't seem very thankful, young lady. You know, if you weren't here, your father and I would have made reservations at that great French restaurant across the park weeks ago. But now it's too late. Now we're stuck with"— she gestured around the diner in disgust—"*Rick's.*"

Don't freak out, I told myself.

"I would have been fine with a French restaurant," I said quietly.

She slammed her glass of water down on the table. "Great," R. said. "That's really sweet, Alice. You know, it would be nice if once in a while you tried to be a tiny bit less spoiled. But apparently that's impossible for you."

I gaped at her. A million retorts sprang to my lips. But I stopped myself: *Wait. Don't ruin Revenge Plot Number One. By tomorrow night, R. will have her comeuppance. Stay cool.*

A few hours later, I was lying on the air mattress Dad had set up for me on the floor of R.'s study and staring at the ceiling, my head swimming with anger.

Any guilt or hesitation I'd had the day before about executing Revenge Plot Number One was completely gone.

Screw Thanksgiving.

Screw my dad.

Screw Jamal and his Goody Two-Shoes view of the universe.

R. Klausenhook was going down.

I was going to take what was dearest to her and ruin it, irrevocably and forever.

I was supposed to meet Dad in front of the theater at 7:30, and the curtains opened on *The Cherry Orchard* at 8:00. The New York theater community had been anticipating this night for months.

I couldn't have cared less.

And yet it was only 4:00 PM and I was skulking around outside the stage door, shivering in my thin winter coat.

Why?

Because I was going to infiltrate the production.

And then destroy R's career.

I'd been thinking for days about the best way to get inside the theater, and that morning it had struck me: of course. How obvious. How did everyone else in the production get in and out of the theater?

The stage door.

The cast and crew had keys, of course. But all I had to do was wait around, look unassuming, and then when someone entered or exited, just follow behind as if that was the most normal thing in the universe to do.

So I waited. And waited. I knew the actors—R. included—wouldn't be arriving until 6:00, so I had plenty of time. Still, it was cold outside. And the street I was standing on was pretty loud, with cars honking and garbage trucks coughing up coffee grinds and turkey carcasses.

Finally, at 4:30, a woman with a baseball cap and glasses hurried up to the stage door and unlocked it. This was my chance. I jumped forward just as she opened the door and tried to follow her inside.

The woman stopped, turned around, and squinted at me.

"Who are you?" she asked.

I wasn't expecting that.

"Um...I'm..." The truth—that I was R. Klausenhook's stepdaughter—would have probably gotten me in. But I didn't want to leave a recognizable trail. "I'm...the assistant stage manager."

She glared at me. "That's impossible."

"Why?" I asked, trying to sound confident.

"Because *I'm* the assistant stage manager." Then she stepped all the way inside the building and, pointedly, slammed the door in my face.

Shoot.

I walked back over to my spot on the brick wall next to the theater and went back to waiting. This time, though, I was more nervous. What if I couldn't get inside? Or what if the woman caught me once I *was* in the theater and reported me? What if I was arrested? What if the police—

The door was opening.

But this time from the inside.

I darted forward and held it just as a sweaty, overweight man in overalls exited, pushing a cart full of two-by-fours.

He looked at me, surprised. "Thank you, miss."

I smiled. "No problem." Then the next sentence just popped out of my mouth. "Everyone in a production should help everyone else out, right?"

He looked confused. "You're in the production?"

I looked at him, temporarily flummoxed. Then something amazing happened. Without even deciding to, I became R. I lifted my chin. I flared my nostrils. I batted my lashes. I looked simultaneously contemptuous and sympathetic.

"Darling," I said to the man, "I'm the *star*."

He blinked. "Oh. Sorry."

I waved my hands in the air, picturing myself with long, purple fingernails. "No matter," I said airily.

Then I stepped inside the darkened theater.

The door slammed behind me.

I took a deep breath, taking in the smell of must and sawdust. Then I lowered my head and walked down the first hallway I saw.

I had to get to the dressing rooms without anyone noticing me.

Luckily, it seemed like almost no one was there. I could hear a few people moving around scenery onstage, but otherwise the theater was silent. I tiptoed down the hallway, checking the sign on every door: PROP ROOM. BOILER ROOM. COSTUME CLOSET.

That last one made me catch my breath. Reena would love me forever if I brought her back some kind of 1920s boa. And a pair of cool Victorian boots for Molly . . .

I made myself keep walking.

BATHROOM. TECHNICAL SUPPLIES. DRESSING ROOM.

I came to a halt.

DRESSING ROOM. Did all the actors share a single dressing room? It hadn't occurred to me. If that was true, my plan was in trouble. I took a few steps down the hallway just in case, and peeked at the sign on the next door:

DRESSING ROOM-KLAUSENHOOK.

Perfect. Of course R. would demand her own dressing room. How could I have expected anything less of her?

I pressed my ear to the door, and holding my breath, listened for any sounds inside.

Nothing.

I reached into my jacket and felt for the little pouch I'd been storing inside my pocket. That morning I'd gone to my old favorite toy store in Brooklyn Heights and walked straight back to the jokes-and-gags section. There it was, in its pink package with a cartoon on it of a man scratching himself wildly, his eyes bugging out in pain.

FRANKIE'S EXTRA-POWERFUL SUPER LONG-LASTING ITCHING POWDER.

I'd never bought it as a kid, just stared at it with curious longing. But now Frankie's itching powder was going to serve a real purpose in my life.

It was going to ruin R.'s career.

I was going to sneak into her dressing room and pour it in her shoes. In her dress. In her pantyhose. In the Russian shawl she'd been wearing around the house so as not to "break character."

There was no way that R. was going to be able to turn in the kind of awe-inspiring, life-changing, breathtaking performance that all the theater critics in all the New York newspapers had been anticipating. Not if her skin was on fire. That was the definition of breaking character. And—as she'd made a point of telling me and Dad five times over breakfast—everyone who was anyone was going to be at opening night. The reviews would come out the next morning.

I opened the door and stepped into the dressing room.

And there she was.

Sitting in front of the dressing room mirror on a stool. Hunched over, wrapped in her shawl.

Crying.

My jaw dropped. I stood there, trying to decide whether or not I should just run out of the room without offering an explanation.

R. slowly lifted her head up and stared at me, mascara streaks running down her face. "Alice?" she croaked.

I nodded.

"You came," she wept. "You came to see me. That's so nice."

She put her head in her hands and cried even harder.

I took a tiny step toward her. "What's—" I started to say.

"Your father called and told you?" she asked through her sobs.

"I . . ."

"I just . . . I can't imagine going on tonight. I can't do it. I can't go on." Her shoulders started shaking.

What was happening? I was living in some kind of alternate universe. One in which R. wanted to sabotage her own career.

"Why can't you go on?" I asked.

She looked at me indignantly, even more makeup started to drip off her eyelashes and eyelids. "Would you have been able to go onstage and play Ranevskaya right after your mother died?"

My mouth opened and then closed.

R.'s mother had died?

I'd seen R. at lunch and everything had seemed just fine.

"Um," I said. And then after a pause: "No. No, I wouldn't have."

R. flung herself onto the dressing room cabinet and moaned. Weirdly enough, she was actually reminding me of a real person for the first time in the entire year I'd known her.

"I'm so sorry," I said softly. "I know how awful it feels."

"They called twenty minutes ago," she sobbed. "A heart attack. She was perfectly . . . the last time I talked to her she seemed fine."

"Where does—where did she live?" I asked.

"Cleveland, Ohio."

I was shocked. "That's where you're from?"

She nodded. I'd had no idea. I had always just assumed

that R. was born and raised in Manhattan. Or at least Paris. Or London. Maybe—although it was a stretch—Madrid.

Definitely not Cleveland.

I pulled up a stool and sat down next to her. After a second, I reached out and touched her shoulder. She didn't pull away, so I started stroking it, making a small circle with the tips of my fingers. Just like my mom used to do when I was a kid.

She began breathing in big, heaving gulps.

Watching her, it was all coming back to me. The call from the hospital in the middle of the night. Dad and I had stayed there until midnight and then took a cab back to the house to get a few hours of sleep before we went back to visit Mom in the morning. And then the phone rang at 4:00 AM, and from my bed I had heard Dad let out a strange yell . . . a totally new and unfamiliar sound. . . .

Tears were starting to spring into my eyes. I tried to blink them back.

"Listen," I told R. firmly. "You have to go on tonight."

She shook her head. "I can't."

"Do you have an understudy?"

"No." She sniffed. "This show is all about my performance."

Of course.

"Just get through it," I said helplessly.

"I can't. I'm not in character. I feel . . ." She burst into a fresh round of choking sobs. "I feel like I'm five years old."

I kept rubbing her shoulder, unsure of what to say or do next. "I'm sorry, R. I understand what it's like, and it's horrible."

She nodded. "I know you do," she murmured.

255

I was shocked. There was no sarcasm in her tone, no irony. We'd just communicated for the first time.

"Oh, God," she bawled. "I'm going to ruin my career. I can't do it. I can't go on."

I sighed. "Listen. Two days after my mom died I had an English final. And I was sure I couldn't do it. I couldn't even get out of bed or speak to anyone. But I knew that if I missed the final, I'd have to make it up a week later. And I probably wasn't going to be feeling any better a week later. I was maybe gonna be feeling worse, because in a week my mom would still be dead, and the realization would just be sinking in even more. Then I realized that if I didn't take the test at all, I wouldn't be able to finish eighth grade."

She blinked at me through her tear-encrusted eyelashes. "What did you do?"

"I woke up the morning of the test and I thought: I can't do this. There is no way I can get out of bed and take a shower and put on my clothes and go to school. It is physically impossible."

R. stared at me, her mouth open, a small droplet of snot hanging from the tip of her nose. "And?"

"And then I got out of bed and put on my clothes and went to school and took the test." I started to giggle, remembering. "I refused to take a shower, though. I don't know why. Somehow taking a shower still seemed impossible."

R. cracked a tiny smile. "That makes sense."

We were silent for a while.

"I can't believe you did that," she said finally. "I can't believe you took an English test right after your mother died."

"I got a C-minus," I admitted.

She shook her head. "It doesn't matter. It's still a miracle."

I thought about it. "Well, you know what? I was just performing. That morning I was just pretending to be someone whose mother hadn't just died."

R. nodded. "You took your fate into your own hands."

I stared at her. Reclaiming your life. Taking your fate into your own hands. That was the goal of the Poison Apples.

But had I *already* reclaimed my own life without even realizing it?

R. stood up shakily and pulled the shawl around her shoulders. She faced the dressing mirror and slowly began wiping the makeup stains off her face. "I'll go to Cleveland on Monday," she said softly. "That's when we have the day off."

I stood up, too. "Good for you, R."

She turned and faced me. Her green eyes pierced into mine. "Thank you, Alice."

"You don't have to thank me."

She bit her lip. "Listen. I'm sorry if I . . ."

I held my breath. I'd never even heard the words *I'm sorry* come out of R.'s mouth before. What was she going to apologize for? Sending me off to boarding school? Selling the brownstone? Making me a flower girl instead of a bridesmaid? Screaming at me at least once an hour? Trying in every way possible to ruin my life?

After a long pause, she shook her head. "Never mind."

Then she turned back to the mirror and started pulling her hair back with her hands.

I tried to look like I didn't care. "Okay," I said, taking a step back toward the dressing room door, "I'm gonna go now."

She nodded, not taking her eyes off her own reflection. "I'll see you after the show."

"Cool."

I opened the door and was about to leave when she called after me: "Alice?"

I whirled around. Maybe the apology was coming after all.

She was looking at me curiously, her head tilted, her hands on her hips. "How did you get here ten minutes after I called your father and told him about my mother?"

I shrugged helplessly.

"The commute from the Upper West Side is at least twenty minutes," she said.

"Um..." I said.

We looked at each other.

"It was a Thanksgiving miracle," I blurted out. Then I turned and ran as fast as I could, down the hallway, out the stage door, and onto the crowded, smelly street.

SEVEN

Reena

It was our old house. Or at least it looked like our old house, from the outside. Same marble white mansion, same green lawn, same puny dying palm tree next the driveway that Pradeep had always refused to let us chop down. (He had a tendency to get attached to random nonhuman objects and attribute them with human traits. "That tree is a good tree!" he would scream at us. "It knows right from wrong!")

So when Dad pulled up to the house after picking us up from the airport in his brand-new red Audi, I was relieved to see that the tree (or "Palmy," as Pradeep was fond of calling it when he was younger) was still there. I wasn't sure how Pradeep would've reacted if they'd chopped it down.

And then we stepped inside.

It's hard to describe what we encountered in the foyer of what used to be our normal, all-American home. I guess it was the twenty-foot-tall wooden statue of Vishnu that caught my attention first. And I only found out it was Vishnu because I gasped and said, "What is *that*?"

"Vishnu," Shanti said, gliding out of the kitchen and smiling at us. "Don't you recognize Vishnu? He's one of the most famous Hindu gods."

I shook my head. "I don't know any Hindu gods."

Pradeep tugged at my sleeve and pointed. "Forget Vishnu. Look at that."

There was a huge golden fountain right next to the entrance to the living room, with a gigantic leaping golden fish spitting an arc of water out of its mouth.

I shook my head in disbelief.

"And *that*." Pradeep pointed to the right. There was a tapestry hanging on the wall next to the staircase. Set against a forest background, it was an intricately embroidered picture of a blue man intertwined with a red woman.

"Oh, my God!" Pradeep shouted. "Are they having sex?!"

Dad, who was standing behind us, placed his hands on our shoulders. "Okay, you two. Calm down. The house is decorated differently now. No reason to go crazy."

"I repeat the question," Pradeep said, not taking his eyes off the tapestry. "Are they having—"

"ENOUGH!" Dad boomed.

We fell silent.

I gazed around the foyer, then walked over and peeked into the living room. Then I opened the kitchen door, looked inside, swallowed a gasp, and walked back into the foyer.

"Wow," I said to Dad and Shanti. "It's very . . ."

"Different!" she said cheerfully.

I nodded. "Also . . . Indian. It's very Indian."

Dad shot me a warning glance.

"Yep," Pradeep piped up. "It's, like, more Indian than it was when four Indian people were living here."

"Pradeep . . . ," Dad said.

"Which makes me think," Pradeep said thoughtfully, "is it actually Indian at all? Or is it just a white person's version of—"

"OKAY!" Dad yelled. "I'm taking your bags upstairs! Follow me!"

We followed him. Reluctantly.

"Rash!" Shanti called up after us. "Don't forget! The landscapers are coming this afternoon!"

We turned around at the landing and peered down at her.

"Why are the landscapers coming?" Pradeep asked suspiciously.

"Forget it," Dad said.

But Shanti didn't hear him. "To cut down that tree!" she yelled gaily up to us. "The horrible little one next to the driveway!"

I can't even really put into words the look that passed across my brother's face.

But I will never forget it.

"Why don't you come see me tonight?" My mother's voice was buzzing plaintively in my ear. Sort of like a mosquito.

I transferred my cell phone from one side of my face to the other and propped my legs up on the windowsill. I was sitting in my bedroom, which—it was hard to believe—looked pretty much the same as it did before.

Except for a tiny decal of a many-armed Hindu goddess stuck onto the windowpane.

But I was okay with that.

"I'll come visit you and Pria tomorrow, Mommy, okay?"

"I don't understand. I don't understand why your father and . . ." Her voice shook. ". . . and That Woman get to see you first."

I sighed. "You don't understand. I have something I have to do here tonight."

"What?"

"I can't tell you."

"Why?"

She sighed. "I sold the flat-screen TV. Did I already tell you that?"

"Yes." My mother had taken up the habit of calling me and telling me which luxury items she was being forced to sell, post-divorce. So far she'd mourned the loss of her Manolo Blahnik high heels, her television, her visits to her favorite five-hundred-dollar-an-hour hairdresser, and her jet skis. (There was no way she was giving up her Porsche or her personal trainer or her monthly visit to the Golden Door Spa. Or the lawyer she'd hired to sue my father within an inch of his life.)

"So what are you doing tonight? Are you doing something fun with That Woman?"

"No. They're not even home. They went to some kind of fund-raiser." The second I said it I realized it was a mistake.

My mother gasped in indignation. "You're choosing to be home alone tonight when your poor mother is—"

Without even thinking, I pressed End on my cell phone and snapped it shut.

Then I stared at it, horrified. I'd never hung up on my mother before.

She was going to kill me when she finally did see me on Thanksgiving. But I had no choice. This was the one night Dad and Shanti Shruti were guaranteed to be out of the house. And Pradeep was hanging out at a friend's house down the street.

I had a mission to accomplish.

And I had to do it all by myself.

I crept out of my bedroom and into the hallway.

"Hello?" I called out.

I wanted to make sure no one was home.

"HELLO?"

Still no answer.

I walked down the hallway, past some kind of wrathful wooden mask hanging on the wall, and then I descended the staircase.

I had to find the penguin.

Dad and Shanti Shruti had both pointedly avoided the subject when showing us around the house, and I didn't want to ask, in case they got suspicious.

But there was a million-dollar arctic terrarium somewhere inside the mansion. And I was going to find it.

First I walked around the kitchen. Besides the fifty new paintings hanging on the wall (illustrations from the great Indian epic, the *Ramayana*, Shanti had informed me), everything was the same. Then I walked around the living room. Then the dining room. Then the foyer. Then Dad's study (I almost puked when I saw the framed picture of Shanti in her pink sari on his desk). Then I ran back upstairs and, starting to get frustrated, checked everyone's bedroom.

Nothing.

Where was Ganesh the penguin?

263

I walked back inside my bedroom and, exhausted, collapsed on my bed and stared out the window. I'd always loved the view out my bedroom window. Our house was on top of a small hill, and my window faced the sloping green of the backyard. In the nighttime, everything was black except for a few twinkling lights in the distance that made up the small cluster of skyscrapers in downtown LA.

But this time there was something different.

A small white light was pulsing in the darkness of the backyard.

I sat up and stared at the source of it.

It looked like a little barn, with a single, brightly lit-up window.

I leapt out of bed, ran downstairs, through the kitchen, out the back door, and stood in front of the small building.

I reached out and opened the metal door in front of me. It made a suctioned slurp, like the sound of a refrigerator opening. Then a gust of freezing-cold air blasted my face.

Bingo.

I shielded my face, hugged my sweatshirt close to my body, and walked inside. The door shut behind me.

What I saw once I was in nearly took my breath away.

It was like I was back on top of Mount McKinsey. In the middle of Beverly Hills.

Snow crunched under my feet. Snowdrifts lay piled against the walls. A bright white light shone down from the ceiling, so it suddenly seemed like midday.

There was even a small blue pool of half-iced-over water in the center of the room.

And then I saw Ganesh himself. Paddling slowly through

the miniature lake. Leaping out of the water and skidding onto his stomach against the snow.

I yelped in delight and clapped my hands. "You are so cute!" I exclaimed.

He looked my way, terrified, and flapped away behind a snowdrift.

I tiptoed after him, crooning, "Good Ganesh, good Ganesh." I peeked around the snowdrift, and he angrily waddled away again.

If I could just pick him up—and then make sure he didn't squirm his wet little penguin body out of my grasp—I could get him out of his little habitat and then just...leave him somewhere. The side of a highway? Next to the ocean? No. That would be too cruel. I would take my old childhood bicycle out of the garage, put Ganesh in the basket, and then deposit him at the gates of the Los Angeles Zoo.

Then Shanti Shruti would learn her lesson.

"Ganeshy," I murmured. "Come here, Ganeshy."

He was standing by the pool again. I leapt forward, my arms outstretched. He jumped into the water. I groaned and watched as he swam in anxious little circles.

I reached into the water and winced. It was, as I should've expected, painfully cold. I trailed him in the water with my hands for a few seconds, and then, gritting my teeth, grabbed his slippery little body and lifted it out of the water.

He writhed and squawked and almost successfully slid of out of my grasp, but I held on tight.

"Shh," I said, and brought his soaking-wet penguin body to my chest. "Shh."

He was still squirming.

For some reason I was starting to feel miserable. I wasn't sure why. *Maybe,* a little voice inside me said, *it's because you're kidnapping a penguin. What could be more depressing and pathetic?*

I grunted and made my way toward the door while Ganesh attempted to launch himself out of my arms. I couldn't wait to get out of there and just get the deed over with. I put my free hand on the metal doorknob and turned it to the right.

Or tried to turn it to the right.

It didn't budge.

I turned it to the left.

Still nothing.

"Oh, no," I breathed. "Please, God, no."

I tried pulling the door. I tried pushing the door. Ganesh squealed feebly and then attempted to peck me through my sweatshirt.

"NO!" I yelled, kicking the door.

Still nothing.

In one final burst of strength, Ganesh kicked his little penguin feet and flapped his little penguin arms and pushed his way out of my arms. He landed on the ground with a thump and skidded away into the outer regions of the room.

"I don't care," I shouted after him. "We're screwed anyway!"

I tried pushing and turning the doorknob at the same time. I tried pulling and turning it at the same time.

It was hopeless. I was locked inside.

I slid down along the ice-covered wall and sat down in a pile of snow, shaking. I was too cold to even start crying.

I'd left my cell phone inside my bedroom.

I was going to freeze to death unless someone came home

in the next two hours and, seeing I was gone, thought to look for me in . . . Ganesh's terrarium.

That was *so* not going to happen.

Oh, my God, I realized. *I'm going to die. I'm going to die because of Revenge Plot Number Two. I'm going to die because I tried to steal a penguin to get some kind of control over my life. Instead I locked myself inside a freezer. Now I'm not even going to live to age sixteen.*

Thoughts of my life, my beautiful life, flashed through my mind. The chapel on top of the hill at Putnam Mount McKinsey. The times Alice and I stood at the window of our dorm room and watched the sun set across the highway. Molly lecturing us on word derivations at the lunch table. David Newman and his gorgeous flashing eyes. Pradeep and the way he could always make me laugh, even when I was feeling horrible. My mother and the way she loved me, fiercely, so I never felt like a little piece of her wasn't with me. My crazy aunt Pria. Why hadn't I gone to see them tonight? Regret started welling up in my stomach. Why didn't I appreciate everything while it had lasted? A great brother. A great mother. Best friends. And even though things were terrible with my dad, at least he was alive. After all, Alice only had one parent.

I had the urge to cry again, but my tear ducts were frozen. My body was beginning to convulse and shake uncontrollably. I held my hands out in front of me and looked at my fingers. They were starting to turn purple.

Please, I prayed to the fluorescent white lights on the ceiling, *someone rescue me. I promise to start appreciating everyone in my life. I will be nicer to my mother. I will be nicer to the Putnam Mount McKinsey cafeteria ladies. I will be nicer to the nerdy kids who hit each other with foam swords on the student union green.*

I'll even be nicer to the mean popular kids like Jamie Vanderheep and Rebecca Saperstein and Jules Squarebrigs-Farroway and, okay, even Kristen Diamond, I will be nicer to Kristen Diamond, and, okay . . . I will try to be nicer to Shanti Shruti. I will never attempt to steal her stupid penguin again. I will—

The door flew open.

"YOU ARE SUCH AN IDIOT, REEN," someone yelled.

I looked up. My older brother was standing in the doorway in a pair of basketball shorts, staring at me with utter disgust.

We looked at each other for a long time.

"Hi," I finally managed to whisper.

"I repeat," he said. "You. Are. Such. An. Idiot."

"How did you find me?" I asked in a small voice.

But before he could even answer, I'd already thrown my arms around his legs and was sobbing hysterically onto his stained Adidas sneakers.

Apparently my tear ducts weren't frozen after all.

EIGHT

Molly

We all sat in silence for a while, stunned.

"Kristen?" asked Alice. "It was *Kristen*?"

Reena nodded and passed me the thermos of hot cocoa. "Yup. She was taking her own personal revenge, I guess. I must have really hurt her feelings on top of Mount McKinsey."

"What I don't understand," I said, "is why she thought Pradeep would rat you out."

Reena shrugged. "I think the girl doesn't understand the concept of loyalty."

"So, she was hiding in the room the whole time while we were coming up with the Revenge Plan?"

"Yup."

I shivered. It was the last day of November, and we'd just gotten back from vacation. It had made sense to call a meeting immediately, but the roof of Middleton was *freezing*.

"That girl is truly pathetic," said Alice, shaking her head.

"You know what's even more pathetic?" I said. "The fact

that I have to spend all of Christmas vacation taking care of Sandie and Randie and Spencer all by myself. My dad and Candy are going to Aruba. Can you believe it?"

Reena's jaw dropped. "You're kidding me. When did they break the news to you?"

"The second I was back inside the house in dry clothes. And they're not paying me a cent for the whole three weeks. Apparently, Candy wants to go on one last vacation before it's too late in her pregnancy. And she started bringing up how much help she could use around the house again."

"Wow," said Alice. "So, Candy was nice to you for—"

"All of three minutes," I finished.

"Yeah. R. was nice to me for like three *seconds* that afternoon."

We sighed.

"So, I guess this is the end," Reena said quietly. "No more Poison Apples."

"That's it?" I asked. "We're disbanding?"

"Wait a second," said Alice. "Just because our revenge plots failed? That doesn't mean the Poison Apples have to disband."

"Yeah, but then what good are we?" asked Reena.

"I thought the point of the apple is that we want to reclaim it," Alice said. "I mean, why do the Poison Apples have to be about getting back at people?"

"Well, we are called the *Poison* Apples," I pointed out.

"Yeah, but it's the evil stepmother who gives Snow White the apple, not the other way around. Maybe we can just be about reinventing the apple. Making it ours. We don't have to be evil in return. After all, two wrongs don't make a—"

"DON'T SAY IT!" I shrieked.

She grinned. "Fine. Sorry."

Reena stared pensively out at the night sky. "Yeah, I guess we do have a lot to be thankful for," she said. "I mean, we live in this beautiful place. We have each other. We—"

"Have to spend all of Christmas vacation taking care of our stepsisters," I moaned.

Reena looked at me, confused. "*That's* what you're upset about? I thought you'd be . . ." Her voice trailed off uncertainly.

I lowered my head. I knew what she was going to say. The problem was, I was just in denial when it came to thinking about my mom. No one had heard anything from her. Occasionally, I wondered if she were dead. Then the thought was too much to take and I just forced myself to focus on other things.

Alice came up to me and put her arm around my shoulder. "I have an idea," she whispered in my ear. "I *definitely* don't want to stay with my dad and R. for Christmas. Why don't I come back to North Forest with you and help out?"

I looked at her, amazed. "You would do that for me? What about Jamal? Weren't you guys gonna hang out over Christmas?"

"Well, you're just as important to me as he is. And he can come visit us, anyway."

I buried her face in her shoulder. "You're the best, Bingley-Beckerman."

"Hey," Reena barked. "What about me?"

We looked at her.

"You," I said finally, "are the world's worst penguin-napper."

She started laughing. "Well," she admitted, "even if the door hadn't locked behind me, that little sucker was much, much tougher than I expected."

Alice stepped back and frowned. "Wait a second. I just

thought of something. If Kristen was listening to that whole conversation on top of Mount McKinsey, then doesn't she know that we meet on the—"

Suddenly, the little door that opened onto the roof flew open.

We all gasped.

A few seconds later, Agnes's pale, tired-looking face peeked over the edge.

"Unbelievable," she drawled monotonously.

"Please, Agnes," Reena begged, "don't report us to Head-master Oates."

Agnes rolled her eyes. "Oh, please. You think I would do that? Then I would get in trouble for not knowing about this sooner."

"Thank you, Agnes," I said. "You're the best. You're—"

"Not so fast," she told me. "Don't think you guys are going to get off scot-free. All three of you are going to be doing my laundry for the next month."

We groaned.

"And," she added, grinning maliciously, "every night I expect someone to bring dinner up to my room."

"Oh, God," whispered Alice.

"Sweet dreams," Agnes said. "Be in your rooms in the next five minutes or I will personally murder you."

And she disappeared back down into stairwell.

"Well," said Reena finally. "Goes to show. There are evil stepmothers everywhere."

A *few minutes later*, I was tiptoeing through the darkness of my dorm room back to my bed. I groped around, then felt something on my pillow, where Kristen usually left my mail (when I got any at all). I held it in my hands. It felt like some kind of card.

I reached under my covers and pulled out my little flashlight. I crawled under my covers, pulled them over my head, and turned the flashlight on, squinting until my eyes adjusted.

It was a postcard.

And the handwriting was unmistakable.

It was from my mother.

My dear Molly, she'd scrawled. *I'm writing to let you know I'm okay. Don't tell anyone you got this. I am finding a new life. You and I will see each other at some point. Much love, Mom*

On the front of the postcard was a picture of the Grand Canyon. The word *Arizona* was printed across it in big red letters.

At first I felt incredible relief. My mom was alive. She was okay.

But a few seconds later, I was infuriated. We would see each other at "some point"? Didn't I have anyone I could rely on?

And then I realized I did.

I had two best friends.

My life was definitely a mess. But I wasn't alone.

It was a funny thing. I'd fantasized about Putnam Mount McKinsey for years, but it was always somehow related to boys in pink shirts reading Emily Dickinson. I definitely hadn't met any of them in the past three months. (Except for Pradeep Paruchuri, who was about as interested in me as Candy Lamb was in dictionaries.)

What had I gotten from boarding school was entirely unexpected: a new family.

Feeling a kind of bittersweet contentment, I pulled my blanket over my head and tried to focus on falling asleep.

And that's when I heard Kristen crying.

At first I couldn't believe it. It actually seemed . . . impossible. But then I listened harder. There were definitely muffled sobs coming from her bed.

Good, I thought triumphantly. *Whatever she's crying about, she probably deserves it.*

But a few minutes later, I found myself whispering: "Kristen?"

The crying stopped for a few seconds, then continued.

"Kristen."

She barely choked out her reply. "What?"

"What's wrong?"

A huge, honking sniffle. "Why do *you* care?"

"Um . . ." Why *did* I care? "I'm curious, that's all. You don't have to tell me."

"You hate me," she cried.

"I don't hate you." That was true. I didn't like her, but I didn't hate her. She'd made my first month at PMM hell, but that was the least of my problems.

There was a long silence, and then, from underneath her covers, I could hear her, just barely audible: "My parents are getting divorced."

I shot up in bed. "You're kidding."

A fresh round of sobs. "No," she wailed. "I'm not."

"Oh, my God. Kristen. I'm so sorry."

I was stunned. If there was anyone who seemed like she had a perfect life, it was Kristen Diamond. The wall above her bed was covered in glossy pictures of her and her father and mother, all of them unbelievably good-looking, leaning against Porsches and playing tennis and canoeing down rivers and waving from the windows of villas in Tuscany.

Her crying started to peter out. "I just can't believe it," she whispered. "They told me on Thanksgiving. On *Thanksgiving Day*. And my mom is ... oh, God. My mom is already dating her *golf* instructor. And they're acting like they're in love or something. Can you believe that?"

"Yes," I said. "I can. Family dysfunction never fails to shock me with how dysfunctional it is."

I held my breath. After a long pause, Kristen giggled.

Thank God.

The two of us lay there in the dark. After a few seconds she asked, "Molly?"

"Yeah?"

"Um ... I'm sorry."

I wasn't exactly sure what she was apologizing for. It could've been about a million different things.

"I've, um, had a really hard semester," Kristen said quietly.

"Yeah," I said. "Me, too."

"I know."

"Well," I said after a while, "thanks for apologizing."

She laughed, still sniffling a little. "You're welcome."

I pulled the covers over my head.

It was the weirdest thing.

Nobody was ever who she seemed to be. There was something very beautiful about that.

I pulled the covers off my head.

"Kristen," I said.

"Yeah?"

"Can I give you one piece of advice? For whatever happens with your parents during and after the divorce?"

"Sure."

"You are not them."

There was a long pause.

"I think I understand," she said.

"Just for the future," I said. "Remember it. It'll make you a lot happier. Your life is your life. Your fate is your fate."

"Okay," she said. "Thanks."

"You are not them," I repeated.

Then, a few minutes later, just as my eyes were starting to close, something occurred to me.

"Four apples instead of three," I muttered. "Would it work?"

"Did you say something?" asked Kristen.

And did evil *stepfathers* count? I would have to consult with Alice and Reena about that at the next meeting.

"Forget it, Kristen," I said. "I'll tell you later."

And I dropped off to sleep.

Acknowledgments

Many, many thanks to:

Jean Feiwel, who continues to surprise me with her intelligence, good humor, and uncanny knack for story and character.

Rich Deas, creative director/genius.

Melissa Flashman, phenomenal agent and dear friend.

RR, without whom my lifestyle is not bearable.

And B, my teammate and oldest friend. I hope we have meltdowns in front of each other for many, many years to come.

GOFISH

LILY ARCHER

What did you want to be when you grew up?
A writer. I always wanted to be a writer.

When did you realize you wanted to be a writer?
Since I can remember.

What's your first childhood memory?
Sucking on the ice in the frozen foods aisle at the supermarket and getting yelled at by my mother.

What's your most embarrassing childhood memory?
Once, I accidentally pulled down a boy's sweatpants. I swear it was an accident. I was just tugging on them to get his attention.

As a young person, who did you look up to most?
Francois Truffaut.

What was your worst subject in school?
Math.

What was your first job?
A cashier at a bakery.

How did you celebrate publishing your first book?
Sleeping a lot.

Where do you write your books?
In bed.

Where do you find inspiration for your writing?
Conversations with my mother.

Which of your characters is most like you?
Probably Molly.

When your finish a book, who reads it first?
My friend Rachel.

Are you a morning person or a night owl?
Night owl.

What's your idea of the best meal ever?
Potatoes and cheese.

Which do you like better: cats or dogs?
Dogs.

What do you value most in your friends?
A sense of humor.

Where do you go for peace and quiet?
My bathroom.

What makes you laugh out loud?
People ordering sandwiches at Subway.

What's your favorite song?
Oh, my God. Too many. I can't do it.

Who is your favorite fictional character?
Oblonsky.

What are you most afraid of?
Inadvertent cruelty.

What time of the year do you like best?
Fall.

What is your favorite TV show?
Mad Men.

If you were stranded on a desert island, who would you want for company?
My boyfriend.

If you could travel in time, where would you go?
Some place where I could wear a corset and do a galloping dance between two lines of other corseted people.

What's the best advice you have ever received about writing?
Forget everything you've been taught.

What do you want readers to remember about your books?
Weird little details.

What would you do if you ever stopped writing?
Write a dissertation. Oh, wait. That involves writing. Um. I guess I'd be an overenthusiastic tour guide.

What do you like best about yourself?
The fact that this question terrifies me.

What is your worst habit?
Crying.

What do you consider to be your greatest accomplishment?
My friends.

What do you wish you could do better?
Cleaning.

What would your readers be most surprised to learn about you?
I might have bedbugs.

You're The One That I Want

Also by Giovanna Fletcher

Billy and Me

St. Martins Press ❧ New York

You're
The One
That I Want

Giovanna Fletcher

YOU'RE THE ONE THAT I WANT. Copyright © 2014 by Giovanna Fletcher. All rights reserved. Printed in the United States of America. For information, address St. Martin's Press, 175 Fifth Avenue, New York, N.Y. 10010.

www.stmartins.com

The Library of Congress Cataloging-in-Publication Data is available upon request.

ISBN 978-1-250-07711-0 (hardcover)
ISBN 978-1-4668-8895-1 (e-book)

Our books may be purchased in bulk for promotional, educational, or business use. Please contact your local bookseller or the Macmillan Corporate and Premium Sales Department at 1-800-221-7945, extension 5442, or by e-mail at MacmillanSpecialMarkets@macmillan.com.

Originally published in Great Britain by Penguin Books, Ltd.

First U.S. Edition: April 2017

10 9 8 7 6 5 4 3 2 1

To Giorgina and Mario, for making my childhood
so much fun. Whether we were making up radio shows on
our brown Fisher-Price recorder, counting out a bag of marsh-
mallows to share (Giorgie, I know you always cheated and had
more), or jumping on the sofa as we sang along to *Grease*—
life was always great with you two by my side. Love you.

If this is love then love is easy,
It's the easiest thing to do.
If this is love then love completes me,
Because it feels like I've been missing you.
A simple equation,
With no complications to leave you confused.
If this is love, love, love,
Oh, it's the easiest thing to do.

—McFLY

Firstly, on behalf of my wife and I, I'd like to thank you all for being here. It means so much to be surrounded by our family and friends on what can only be described as the most important day of our lives.

Maddy

Only fifty-two feet stood between me and my husband-to-be. All that was left for me to complete the transformation from Miss Maddy Hurst to Mrs. Maddy Miles was to walk that fifty-two feet and say my vows. Then I'd be able to leave the past behind and look to the future with security, dignity, and the love of a good man, knowing that I deserved to be receiving it.

But even though I knew it was what I wanted, it was still the most difficult fifty-two feet I'd ever had to walk. I knew I was walking away from someone who had the potential to take me to new dizzying heights with his love—a love that was mine for the taking, but never truly within my reach. Perhaps if the circumstances were different we'd have had something magical. It pained me to be walking away from those feelings, from him, but I'd said all I needed to say. He knew I loved him and that my love for him was unconditional, as it had always been.

"Give Me Joy in My Heart" started playing inside the church, tearing me away from my wandering thoughts, and letting me know it was time for my entrance. One by one the bridesmaids calmly walked through the giant wooden archway. Pearl, the last of the bunch, turned to give me a big wink before following suit, the little train of her mint chiffon dress floating behind her.

"You ready?" asked my dad—who looked incredibly cute in his light gray suit and emerald-green tie—which I noticed was slightly wonky. His salt-and-pepper-colored hair was mostly covered up by a big top hat, which bizarrely made him appear shorter than usual, even though it gave him extra height. He looked as nervous as I did—something I wasn't prepared for!

I straightened his tie and gave him a little nod.

He checked over my veil in the way Mum had clearly instructed him to—so that it creased at the sides and not in front of my face. Then he stood beside me and lifted my arm before hooking it through his.

"You look beautiful, Maddy," he whispered.

"Thanks, Dad," I managed to say, the nerves seeming to have taken hold of me.

"Feeling nervous?"

Another nod.

"You'll feel better when you see him. Come on, grip hold of your old man. It's time for your groom to see his bride," he said, firmly squeezing my arm into his side.

At our cue, we started to walk at the steady pace we had agreed on—not so fast that we were almost running to the altar, but not so slow that people started yawning with boredom either. We'd practiced it that morning to ensure it wasn't a complete disaster.

I found myself clutching tightly on to Dad's arm as we turned into the church and walked through its doors. A sea of faces welcomed us—all of the congregation were on their feet, looking at me with the broadest smiles I'd ever seen. And there were so many of them! It was a wonder to think we even knew that many people.

During my wedding dress fittings I was told numerous times to enjoy that particular moment, to look at those faces, the ones of the people we both loved and admired, and bask in their warmth. Their love that day was for us. I'd been told to embrace it. But as I took in their faces, their happy smiles, filled with joy, they made the feeling that had been mounting in my chest for weeks tighten further.

That was it.

There was no going back.

A surge of happiness bolted through me as I spotted him, staring back at me from the altar, looking simply divine. My wonderful man, Robert Miles—strong, reliable and loving. My best friend. I pursed my lips as my cheeks rose and tears sprang to my eyes at the very sight of him, looking more handsome than ever in his gray suit. His tall muscular frame visibly relaxed as his dazzling green eyes found mine, his luscious lips breaking into a smile that I couldn't help but respond to.

And then I stole a glance to the right of Robert, to see my other love, Ben Gilbert—kind, generous and able to make my heart melt with just one look. But he wasn't looking back at me. Instead, he had his head bowed and was concentrating on the floor in front of him; all I could see was the back of his waxed brown hair—the smooth olive skin of his face and his chocolate-dipped eyes were turned away.

His hesitance to look up struck a chord within me, momentarily making me wobble on my decision.

Suddenly, something within me urged him to look at me. Part of me wanted him to stop the wedding, to show me exactly how much he cared. Wanted him to stop me from making a terrible mistake . . . but is that what I thought I was actually making? A terrible mistake?

I loved Robert, but I loved Ben too. Both men had known me for seventeen years—each of them had seen me at my worst, picked me up when I'd been caught in despair, been my shoulders to cry on when I'd needed to sob. They were my rocks. Plural. Not singular.

Yes, I'd made my decision. I'd accepted Robert's proposal, I'd worn the big white dress and walked up the aisle—however, if Ben had spoken up, if he'd even coughed suggestively, then there's a possibility I'd have stopped the wedding.

Even at that point.

But, as the service got underway, as the congregation was asked for any reasons why we should not have been joined in matrimony without a peep from Ben, it started to sink in that he was not about to start fighting.

He was letting me go . . .

Maddy caught my attention on the very first day I clapped eyes on her. She looked adorable with her scruffily wild bob and red cheeks. She also looked as though she was going to burst into tears at any minute. I'm not sure what she made of me and my wingman, with our chubby faces and overly keen ways—well, actually, I think she was pretty terrified. But we won her over eventually. We're still not sure how we managed to pull that one off...

Ben

It was during the arduous task of deciding whether a red or green felt-tip pen was best for the snake hair of my Medusa drawing (a very important decision and not one to have been made lightly) that I noticed her—looking around the class with her big blue eyes. Her cheeks and nose were rosy from her walk to school in the frosty February air and the ends of her not-so-perfect auburn bob flicked in and out uncontrollably in a careless fashion. Her school uniform, the same as every other girl in the class (which was the same as us boys, but we wore trousers)—grey pleated skirt, white T-shirt, and green jumper with our school logo of the local church—was far too big for her. The skirt hung way past her knees and the sleeves of the jumper were gathered at her elbows to stop them from covering her hands, both of which were clutching hold of her green book bag so tightly that her knuckles appeared to whiten with the strain. Her lips were clasped together as though she was trying to stop herself from crying. She was visibly squirming in her new surroundings— which wasn't too surprising seeing as the majority of us had stopped what we were doing and were gawping at her.

Our form teacher, Mr. Watson, who always looked like he was in a foul mood as he glared at us through his wire-rimmed spectacles, took her to her new desk. It was the spot none of us had wanted—facing the wall and the class toilet—a double whammy of depressiveness. Not only did you have to sit looking at the sick-colored wall that was thirty centimeters away from your face, but every now and then, if someone decided to go for a number two in the loo, you'd get a whiff of it—occasionally the smell lingered for a couple of hours too. It was pretty gross.

I'd wanted to go to her then. I wanted to make her feel welcome so that she didn't feel so alone. But nine-year-old boys didn't do things like that. So I resisted the urge. I just continued to sit and stare like everyone else who'd spotted her.

"Have you got the green pen?" asked Robert, my best friend who sat to my right every day. We were inseparable. Had been since our mums met in the local park when we were still in our prams and sucking on dummies—prompting them to meet up daily for tea, biscuits and some light relief from baby chatter. They'd revelled in having another adult to talk to after months of just Robert or me for company while our dads were out at work. According to my mum, Robert handed me a single raisin from his Sun-Maid box on that first day, and that was it—firm buddies for life. Well, they say it's the simple things . . .

Sitting at our desk, I flustered at his question—I hadn't decided which color to use for the snakes yet, but ended up handing him the green pen anyway. It no longer mattered—I was more focused on the new arrival. Medusa could wait.

"What you staring at?" Robert asked, brushing his blond hair out of his eyes.

I said nothing but his beady green eyes followed the direction of my gaze.

"Oooooh . . . nice," he giggled.

Robert lowered the newly acquired felt-tip pen back onto our desk and joined me in staring at the newbie. We didn't say a word. We just sat and watched. She really did look quite nice, I decided, agreeing with Robert.

"Okay, everyone," boomed Mr. Watson, scratching the side of his rounded tummy that threatened to spill out from beneath his white shirt, as he demanded our attention. "I'd like you to say a warm good morning to your new classmate, Maddy. She has just moved to the area from London."

"Good morning, Maddy. Good morning, everyone," we all chorused together in unison—a trick we'd been trained to do since our first day there at Peaswood Primary School. I wonder when, as a society, we grow out of things like that—you don't get grown-ups barking at you in the same manner when you start new jobs. If I walked into a new place of work and had everyone turn to me and shout, "Good morning, Ben Gilbert," with sickly sweet smiles, I think I'd run a mile. It's quite cult-like. But, I have to say, I thoroughly enjoyed saying good morning to Maddy Hurst on her first day.

I watched as she looked up while we chorused in her direction, and was left stunned when her eyes found mine for a tiny second. My cheeks suddenly sprang to life and I felt them lift into a huge goofy grin. She smiled briefly before her gaze fell next to me for a second and then back down to the ground—her cheeks pinking further. I turned to Robert to see that he was wearing the same silly grin as I was. He looked up at me and let out a second giggle.

Robert never giggled. He laughed, but never giggled. The new girlish squeal he'd been unable to hold in was quite amusing.

At lunchtime Robert and I wasted no time in going over to Maddy and saying hello. We took her to the dinner hall (where we tucked into potato croquettes, dinosaur-shaped breaded turkey, and baked beans—food back then was awesome) and gathered as much information as we could about the girl we'd decided would be our new friend.

Our hearts almost exploded when she revealed she lived around the corner from our homes—we both looked at her with open-mouthed grins, not believing our luck, as we wondered how soon we'd be able to knock for her to play outside with us.

It would be fair to say we became instantly aware that Maddy possessed something different to any other girl we'd ever met—something that had us spellbound from our first glimpse of her nervous frame as the class's new girl. She just had this air about her, this inexplicable quality that drew us in like two obedient puppy dogs.

Not a single part of me wanted to fight against that attraction.

I was happily won over.

Immediately smitten.

Maddy

I wasn't very happy when Mum and Dad announced we were moving "to the sticks"—even if they said it was for a "better way of life." In my head I imagined we were going to be living in a wooden shack with no one else around us for miles and miles, surrounded by fields of hay and smelly chickens—like something from *Little House on the Prairie*. But actually, it wasn't so bad in Peaswood—our house was made of brick for a start, we had neighbors, and there wasn't a chicken in sight. There was a bustling High Street, which was within walking distance no matter where you lived in the village, filled with shops and pubs (there were four pubs—a tad excessive for such a small place), and a big community center at one end. The local Church of England church stood in the middle of the busy street, flanked by the florist and the baker's—the smell of freshly baked bread and cakes making tummies rumble as people knelt and prayed.

I had been nervous about starting a new school and making new friends. It wasn't like I was the popular kid in my previous class, but I had a nice bunch of mates who I was sad to say good-bye to when we moved. Like any girl at that age, all I'd wanted was for my new classmates to like me.

On my first day I was feeling extremely nervous and flustered as Mr. Watson brought me to everyone's attention in his brisk manner.

It's mind-boggling that teachers don't realize how stressful and awkward that moment is for a kid—knowing that everyone's sizing you up and deciding whether they're interested in making you their new BFF or whether you'll be doomed to be the class loser forever more. It's excruciating. I felt my face redden and my bladder weaken in seconds—it took every ounce of self-control to stop myself peeing on the spot. That would have been a great start.

Spotting Robert and Ben, once I'd finally plucked up enough courage to look up from the thinning brown carpet at my feet, both sending the cheesiest smiles in my direction, had made me feel much more relaxed. My inner turmoil momentarily gave way, enabling me to flash them a smile before, once again, looking down at the brown below.

Even though we'd exchanged smiles, I was still surprised they were the first to come over to talk to me. I thought the girls of the class would be. I assumed one of them would be happy to have someone new to hang out with, but it appeared not. None of them bothered with me at all on my first day. Instead, it was the two boys who took an interest.

I can remember thinking they were a funny pair, Robert and Ben. Robert, who I noticed was clearly the more confident of the two, wore his strawlike blond hair in straight silky curtains that ran either side of his face, down to his cheekbones. His sparkly green eyes, splattered with flecks of gold, never seemed too alert—it was like he was half asleep with two little slits on his lightly freckled face. Ben was painfully shy, but reminded me of Bambi—his chestnut hair was gelled into perfect spikes and he had these humungous brown eyes, which appeared all the richer due to his olive skin.

Thanks to their ridiculously big smiles and kind manners when taking me to lunch, I quickly felt my worry at being in a new school melt away. I was also thankful not to have been completely rejected by my new classmates.

Although, saying that, I was more than surprised when the pair turned up at my door that night, asking if I could go out to play as they both sat on their matching blue BMX bikes, using the tips of their trainers to rock forward and backward on their wheels. I couldn't help but smile back excitedly at them. It was the first time anybody had ever stood at my door asking after me.

Unfortunately, Mum decided it was too soon for me to be wandering the streets of Peaswood with two boys she didn't know. So as a compromise she invited them inside to play instead—once they'd called their mums and told them of their whereabouts, of course. The boys gleefully accepted the offer and discarded their bikes in our front garden without a moment's hesitation. I can remember looking down at their bikes and smiling to myself at the thought of how safe our new neighborhood must be, before shutting the door and joining my new friends inside. I'd felt wanted and included.

My relationship with the boys kickstarted with great gusto and enthusiasm, whereas trying to strike up a friendship with the girls in my class was much more problematic. They were a tight bunch, made all the cosier by the fact that they (Laura the ringleader, Michelle, Becky, and Nicola) had a special name for themselves—the Pink Dreamers. A name that was also used for the girl band they were in. I can't express how much I wanted to be included when I heard that, but it seemed the friendships I'd already sparked up with the boys were going to put my chances of primary-school popstardom and any friendship with the girls in jeopardy. Yes, even at nine years old, social politics were rife.

They hated the fact that I hung around with the boys and would tell me so while asking if I fancied one of them or had kissed them. It was horrible to feel so interrogated and like such an outsider. Unfortunately, when my brain was taken over by some crazy acceptance-needing twerp, I decided the best thing for me to do would be to cut all ties with Robert and Ben. I'm ashamed to say I ignored them, sat away from them at lunchtimes, ran away from them at breaktimes—I figured it was the only way to make the Pink Dreamers (I can't believe I cared so much for a bunch of girls who called themselves that) want me to be a part of their group.

And I thought I'd succeeded at one point.

One day at lunch I was called over by Laura to join the girls. At last, I thought, I'm in.

Oh what a foolish girl I was.

The whole thing was a set-up.

I sat on the spare plastic orange chair, ready to enjoy my first lunch with my new BFFs, only to feel the chair give way beneath me. I flew backward through the air with an almighty screech and landed on my back with my legs in the air—white cotton knickers on display, my dignity splattered alongside me on the floor. I'd never felt so humiliated.

Off I ran to the toilets, riddled with humiliation, only to be followed by Robert and Ben. Bless them, they even came *into* the girls' loos to see if I was okay. Not many little boys would venture into such formidable territory, without caring whether they were caught by our peers or not.

In that little loo our friendship was restored. We pinkie promised that I'd never be such a loser again and that the three of us would stick together as a threesome until the end of time. It was a deliciously cute moment and one that firmly cemented us as a united force.

I had my boys, I needed nothing more.

Ben

It wasn't long after that uplifting moment of friendship that my dad walked out on me and my mum. He just upped and left with no explanation, no apology, and no emotional farewell. It seemed easy for him to sever his family ties and start a new life elsewhere. Not caring that he may never see the innocent little boy who worshipped the ground he walked on, ever again.

He'd found another woman. Someone he worked with in the police force—another officer. I don't think she was younger than my mum, as is the usual stereotype. I don't even think she was prettier, nicer, or more intelligent—but then, I wouldn't, would I? I've always thought of my mum as beautiful with her short raven bob and dark brown eyes, her tiny frame making her seem delicate and breakable—but, in actual fact, her bones were made of steel, something I learned over the years. She was tough enough to take a few knocks from life. Perhaps the new woman in Dad's life understood the pressures of the job better than my mum had, but then I don't want to justify what he did by admitting that.

The thing that hurt me most was that she had a kid of her own, this new woman. A son named George who was a couple of years younger than me. Dad took him on as his own—as though he was a replacement for the son he'd left behind. It was that easy, it seemed.

Obviously, we didn't know any of that information when it first happened, we just heard bits of gossip from my nan and aunts as time went by. They weren't meant to tell us, of course, but it slipped out occasionally. Little nuggets of information that I managed to piece together.

You know, he didn't even leave a note to inform us that he'd left. We only knew because most of his stuff had disappeared. He'd done it when I was at school and Mum was at work. What a coward of a man.

When Mum collected me from school that afternoon I asked if Robert could come over for dinner (Maddy was busy doing something, I can't remember what), and not knowing the void that was waiting for us at home, she happily said yes, as usual. Robert was always welcome.

We knew that something was wrong as soon as we walked through the front door. It felt colder, or as though something was missing. The same feeling that might be aroused if you were to come home and find you'd been burgled. It was unsettling and different.

Mum sighed. That was her reaction to the whole thing, to sigh as if she knew it was coming. Knew that the waste of space she called a husband would desert us in such a loveless manner after thirteen years of marriage.

"Boys, do you want to play out in the garden while I put dinner on?" she asked, managing to keep her voice strong and steady.

"Should I get changed out of my school stuff?" I asked. I was never allowed to play in my uniform, usually my T-shirt was in the wash as soon as I'd taken it off—Mum ran a tight ship.

"No, you're all right, love."

She wanted to stop me from going upstairs in case Dad's getaway was apparent—wardrobes left open with no clothes in, empty hangers splayed across the room carelessly as he made his quick escape. She'd wanted to save me from that hurt, that embarrassment.

I knew, of course. They always say kids have a sixth sense about those sorts of things, and I certainly did.

I nodded and shuffled outside with Robert. Silently, we went down to the bottom of the garden, away from the house, and climbed up into my treehouse. Dad had assembled it as a present on my previous birthday, the last one he was ever around for. It was a four-foot-by-four-foot square of timber, completed with a flat roof and small window looking back at our home—Mum had offered to put curtains in it at one point, but I thought that would take away the boyness of it all. Hanging from the roof, through a hole in its base and to the ground below, was a thick, knotted blue rope—perfect for me to scramble in and out of my new den. Dad had told me I was big enough at nine years old to have my own bit of space—although Mum was always fretting about my safety, unable to cope with her little boy being capable of climbing up and down freely with confidence.

While we sat up there on that bleak afternoon, I turned and looked at Robert. I noticed that he was anxiously pulling his bottom lip through his teeth and it dawned on me that he knew too.

"I think my dad's gone," I said quietly. It felt odd to say it out loud. Hearing the words come from my mouth forced me to see the truth of the matter, allowing the sadness to creep in and grip firmly around my heart. I felt so . . . disappointed.

"Yeah . . ." Robert said, looking at me with concern.

We sat in silence for a while, side by side, looking up at my family home. Until that moment it had always been a place of safety, but it quickly and violently became a place of uncertainty. Of course, we'd all heard about parents getting divorced; I wasn't the first one in my year it had happened to. One girl in our class hadn't even met her dad, he'd buggered off before she was born, so, yes, we knew about it, and we feared it. Every time there was a squabble at the kitchen table or a disagreement in the car about bad directions, we'd feel the worry tiptoe in. For me, in that moment, the nightmare had turned into a reality. Millions of questions floated around my brain as I wondered why he'd left, if I'd done something wrong to upset him, if we'd have to move house and leave Peaswood, if I'd ever see him again, and whether he still loved me.

I thought about that morning with my dad, the last time I ever saw him, and searched it for clues—a task I repeated over the years whenever he made an unwelcome appearance in my thoughts. I wondered whether he had done anything to suggest he was anxious about the big decision he was about to make, whether he showed me any more affection than normal or if he seemed sorry to leave me. As far as I could tell there was nothing. No looks or strange utterings to decipher. Just the normal morning routine—breakfast while he read the newspaper, then off he went to work.

"You'll be okay," Robert eventually said with a nod.

"Yeah . . ."

"You'll always have me."

"Thank you," I managed before bursting into tears, no longer able to keep the sadness in.

Robert put his arm around me and firmly held me, silently becoming my anchor of support as I crumbled.

We sat like that for the next thirty minutes.

Nothing more was said.

We never talked of my tears once I'd finished, but that afternoon had altered things between us. We'd been exposed to something our fragile young minds weren't ready for, a grief that, in an ideal world, we should have been protected from. My dad had left me, discarded me like a worn and used jumper. He'd done nothing to try and save me from the pain of his leaving—in fact, Robert, at just nine years old, did more to comfort me than my own dad had. How pitiful. It was the vulnerability that the situation provoked in us both which caused a firmer alliance to be built between us. From that moment Robert had turned from my best friend to my rock, and I worshipped him for it.

Maddy

Two years after stepping through the doors of Peaswood Primary School I was happily settled thanks to my two bestest buds, Robert and Ben. We went everywhere and did everything together. It was rare to see one of us without the other two in tow. This was helped by the fact that our parents had become close too, meaning that while they had their grown-up dinner parties and weekly Friday nights at the community club, we were allowed to wander off and play. On top of that, hardly a day went by without us doing something together after school. Our mums would come and collect us at the school gates, take us to our individual homes, and within minutes one of us would be knocking on the others' front doors, asking if they wanted to play out.

Thankfully, things had changed in class—mostly because I no longer had any desire to become a Pink Dreamer, although it wasn't an easy conclusion for me to come to. After various spats, I suddenly saw sense—much to the boys' relief. In turn, because I stopped caring so much, Laura and company stopped picking on me. Thankfully we'd come to some sort of truce.

On May 15, in our final year at primary school, our whole class was stood at the bottom of the school playing field in the spring sunshine, next to the great big fir trees, waiting to watch Becky Davies (one of the nicer girls in the Pink Dreamers) and Greg Reed (the most popular boy in class) do a very grown-up thing . . . get married. It was all taken very seriously with Laura as the priest and the rest of her gang playing the bridesmaids (hardly a surprise).

"I don't understand why we have to watch this," huffed Robert from my right.

"Because! It's romantic!" I said back.

"It's stupid."

I didn't respond any further to his moaning because I was pretty sure that Robert had a bit of a soft spot for Becky. That was the real reason for him thinking the whole thing was ridiculous. He was jealous.

"I like it . . ." said Ben from my left with a beaming smile.

"Really?" questioned Robert in disgust, flicking the ends of his hair out of his eyes with irritation.

"Yes," Ben nodded, eagerly.

Laura was standing beside Greg in what was our childish make-shift version of a romantic spot to get married in—a collection of sticks, daisies, bluebells, and dandelions had been arranged into a circle, like a little love nest.

We edged a little nearer to them when the ceremony was about to start, much to Robert's annoyance.

"Please welcome the bride and her bridesmaids," Laura shouted, as she theatrically swept her hand in the air toward the incoming group of girls, who'd been hiding behind a few of the trees.

Nicola and Michelle, the other two Pink Dreamers, walked up to the circle carrying small bunches of daisies, as they hummed "Here Comes the Bride" with great enthusiasm. Behind them walked Becky wearing a big white shiny dress over her school uniform.

Laughter came from my right.

I turned to see Robert with his hand covering his reddening face as he failed to suppress more mocking laughter.

I elbowed him in the ribs.

"Ouch."

"Ladies and gentlemen, boys and girls," Laura boomed louder, her voice sounding more serious and grown up than normal. "Thank you all for joining us here today. Becky and Greg are delighted to be sharing this wonderful moment with their friends."

Robert sighed next to me, unable to hide his irritation.

"Marriage is about two people saying they like each other very much and showing it to the world," she said to the crowd. "It's them saying they love each other more than anyone else they know. That they are happy to be there for each other from now until the day they die."

I couldn't help smiling as I glanced at Robert, who was flicking bits of grass around with his foot in boredom, and then at Ben, who was paying close attention—his expression full of awe as he soaked up the meaning of the words.

Once Laura had come to the end of her speech and the bride and groom had finished repeating Laura's words, she came to the finale of the service. "Becky and Greg, by the power in me, I now call you man and wife . . . Greg, you may now kiss the bride."

We all watched in stunned silence as Greg placed his hands on Becky's cheeks, pulled her into him and kissed her straight on the lips. It was, and still is, the friskiest first kiss I've ever experienced at a wedding. It lasted a couple of seconds and was followed by a big grin from the newly married couple as the gathered crowd erupted in whoops and cheers.

"That was a bit much," huffed Robert, rolling his eyes.

While the crowd continued to go crazy, a warm and clammy hand found its way into mine. It was Ben's. He gave my hand three little squeezes before pulling his hand away.

I looked up at his face as he flashed me a bashful smile.

Ben

I.
LOVE.
YOU.

That was what I'd wanted to say in those three little squeezes.

I knew I meant it.

I really did . . .

Being in that setting, with the emphasis of the occasion one of love and happiness, it was hard to escape the intense desire that took hold of me—making it impossible to ignore. I had an overwhelming urge to open my mouth and say the words out loud, but I couldn't. Instead I found another way to express what I was undoubtedly sure I felt. The words pulsed through my body and out of my hands into hers, the one I loved inexplicably.

Of course, it would be easy to brush the whole thing off and insist it was a crush, a silly little case of puppy love, but it wasn't. It was far more than that.

From the moment I saw Maddy she'd captured me. She had me completely gripped. I was fascinated with everything about her—the way she looked with her firelike hair and flushed cheeks, the way her heart-shaped lips spoke with a softness and warmth, and the way she appeared so vulnerable as she exposed her caring heart. I adored her—it was that simple.

With Maddy in my life I felt whole. She added a magical sparkle that I'd never want to live without. And so I told her, with those three little squeezes. I had no agenda, no hidden plan or desire for anything to change between us—my only thought was to relieve myself of those feelings by communicating them in the only way I felt I could.

Three squeezes of love.

From me.

To her.

Being friends with two boys wasn't always the easiest thing for Maddy to have to put up with. There were times when just being friends with us cost her more than a few tears and heartache. Especially since, as everyone knows, girls and boys can't be just friends. But we liked to think of ourselves as an exception to that rule. And when the shit hit the fan, which inevitably it did, we decided—over a pinkie promise, if I remember rightly—to stick together like glue. It was a symbol that we would always be there for each other and that we'd never waver on that promise, no matter what life threw our way. Of course, as soon as puberty struck, our teen years were filled with wild misdemeanor. Well, hanging from trees counts, right? But, for Maddy and me, a school trip to Paris was where our story really started. Whether there had been something between us all along, or whether the city of love cast a spell and claimed our hearts, it's hard to say. All I knew was that things would never be the same again . . .

Ben

"What do you think of Maddy?" I asked Robert as we kicked a football around his garden. It was a Saturday afternoon in mid-June, but a cool, cloudy day. Maddy wasn't about, she'd gone to visit her nan, who still lived in Harrow, so it was just us two for a change. Football wasn't really her thing, so we made the most of having a kick-around when we could do—without being grumbled at. I took the opportunity to talk to Robert about something that had been playing on my mind. Maddy.

"What do you mean?" he asked, confused by my vague question. He rolled the ball back on to his toe and flicked it upward so that it landed on his knee, enabling him to bounce it from one to the other, on to his chest and then back over to me with considerable control. Robert was ridiculously talented with a ball—in fact, he was great at any sport, ball or no ball. He always won, no matter what the game—something that was helped by his competitive streak. He liked being the best, whereas I was too laid-back to care. Perhaps that's why we worked so well together.

"I dunno . . ." I shrugged, putting my foot on top of the ball to stop it before slowly passing it back in his direction as I struggled to formulate my words. "She's not like the other girls in our class . . ."

We'd been attending Peaswood High for the past four years. It was a lot bigger than our primary school, with loads more children, but all three of us had managed to get into the same form class—thanks to us begging our parents to ask the headmaster. So nothing much had changed when it came to our friendship. We still lived in each others' pockets and were as tight as ever. Occasionally one of us would get close to another kid and they'd join us for a bit—but they'd wander off eventually, put off by how close we all were, I reckon. So the three of us had stuck together, as we'd promised we would. We'd even come up with our own group name—"The Tripod." Yeah, it was only mildly better than Laura and her Pink Dreamers, but it meant something. The name came from our first science lesson with Mrs. Fellows—an extremely strict teacher with an irritatingly high-pitched nasal voice. One of the kids in class had been playing with his tripod, instead of listening to her riveting lesson on the periodic table, and bent one of its metal legs. The teacher made him stand on his chair as punishment and, as if that wasn't embarrassing enough, proceeded to give him a massive lecture on respecting school equipment before detailing the important qualities of the tripod. She said, "Tripods have three legs. They rely on each other for support. If they stand together they are strong and united. BUT if one breaks, they are all rendered useless . . ." We turned to each other with little smirks, all thinking the same thing—yeah, we're a fricking tripod!

"What's made you ask, anyway?" Robert probed as he flicked the ball in the air and headed it repeatedly, continuously keeping an eye on it as he jerked his body around to wherever the ball was headed—always a step ahead and ready to tap it skywards.

"Nothing . . . It's just I heard Antony and John talking about her," I shrugged.

"Yeah? What did they say?" he asked with a frown, catching the ball in his hands and looking at me—my revelation grabbing his full attention.

"That they thought she was fit."

"Really?" He raised both his eyebrows and puffed out his cheeks as he mulled over the comment.

Going to "big school" and mixing with people from outside of Peaswood (they all arrived on coaches every morning—streamed in by their hundreds), we suddenly discovered how sheltered our lives were. Our idea of a fun night was riding around on our bikes down our road and grabbing some penny sweets or collectible stickers from the newsagents, but in those first few years at secondary school we were shocked as we heard many tales of raunchy things happening at under-eighteen discos. Even the school discos or birthday parties we went to were eye-opening—kids would go around snogging as many people as they could, tallying them up in some sort of tongue-wagging competition. The three of us would be awkwardly stood on the dance floor, getting our groove on to "Cotton Eye Joe," as we tried to stop ourselves from gawping at the sight of it all. Before going to Peaswood High, that kiss between Greg and Becky was the rudest thing we'd ever seen and that was nothing to our new classmates. Even four years in we struggled to keep up—we were too busy being the children we were supposed to be. Some of the other kids were simply much more advanced than us—kids like Anthony and John, who we knew had both been "all the way" with various girls in our year. Knowing that they were now talking about Maddy in that way, that she was on their radar, made me feel really protective of her. And irritated.

"Well, she's not ugly . . ."

"Definitely not."

"In fact, yeah, she is cute, I guess," shrugged Robert, his face returning to its earlier frown as he contemplated our best friend in a way he clearly hadn't before.

Robert had been flirting with a girl in our class called Daniella that week. They both knew they fancied each other and that they'd be snogging each other's faces off at the next party, it was only a matter of time. I think his own concerns for our female friend were fueled with the knowledge of the racy thoughts that had been going through his teenage mind about his looming first sexual encounter with Daniella.

"It's strange to hear that said about her, though, you know?" he added.

"Yeah, that's what I thought."

"Makes me feel weird."

"Same . . ." I nodded.

"Do you think Maddy likes one of them?"

The question threw me. It was toe-curling enough thinking of them fancying her, but I hadn't even thought about Maddy fancying one of them. We didn't really talk about that sort of stuff with her—she could ask us any questions she liked, for instance she'd been quizzing Rob no end about him fancying Daniella, but we'd never probed her on the topic of the opposite sex. Well, I didn't anyway.

"I dunno . . ." I muttered.

"Maybe you should ask her."

"Do you reckon?"

"Why not? I bet she'd like hearing that they called her fit," he grinned.

Standing there, just the two of us, in the safety of his back garden, I thought about telling him how I felt—confessing that I thought Maddy was more than fit, that I thought she was the most amazing girl ever to have graced the planet, but I didn't. I'd been feeling that way for so long and our friendship, the one the three of us shared, stopped me from saying anything, like it had done in the past whenever the words were on the tip of my tongue. We were a tripod. We stuck together to help each other through whatever dramas life chucked our way, we weren't meant to be creating them or making things complicated between each other. I'd always thought that if I were to tell Maddy how I really felt it would have caused things to change between the three of us. It could have ruined everything and driven a humongous wedge between us that we'd never be able to get rid of. I never wanted that to happen to us. I carried those fears with me and they kept my heart in check—stopping me from blurting out declarations of love that, for all I knew, I could have ended up regretting.

Anthony and John paying her attention had got my back up, perhaps because they had the freedom to say what they felt and more of
a chance with her than I did—and I knew they'd use that chance to
get as far with her as they could. They'd have no respect for the kind
and wonderful girl I knew her to be. They were teenage boys with
one thing in mind. Sex. I couldn't stand it.

Our morning routine had been set on our first day at Peaswood
High—Maddy walked round to mine, then we'd both continue
round to pick up Robert before heading into school. It had originally
started with our mums taking us in convoy, but within a month we'd
managed to persuade them that we were fine to do the five-minute
walk alone. So, on the Monday morning after speaking to Robert,
as soon as I'd closed my front door and taken one of the pink
peardrop sweets she was offering me, I decided to bring up the conversation.

"Erm . . . I heard Anthony and John talking about you the other
day," I said, popping the sweet into my mouth, my eyes instantly
watering at the sweetness of it.

"Those two idiots," she sighed, rolling her eyes. "What were they
saying?"

"They called you fit."

"Haaa!" she shrieked, as she grabbed hold of my arm and stopped
on the pavement. Shaking with laughter, she tilted her head back,
covering her face with her hands to quieten the sound.

"What's so funny?"

"Anthony Burke and John Martin?" she giggled.

I shrugged—not understanding her apparent aversion to them.

"Pass me a bucket!"

She laughed the whole way into school.

I couldn't help but smile. She wasn't about to start dating one of
them if that was what she thought of them . . .

Or so I'd thought.

It's possible that my little chat with Maddy had resulted in her mind being awoken to the possibility of fancying John—the dim-witted yet more pleasant of the two rogues. Such is the fickle nature of a teenager's heart, what wasn't there one minute had grown into a colossal flirtation the next. At least, that's what it felt like for me—and the change came suddenly. That very same day, when we were in afternoon registration, John walked over and whispered something to Maddy. I have no idea what was said, but was surprised to witness her cheeks pinking as she pouted out her lips into a smile before tapping him gently on the arm. She was visibly flirting. And I knew that was the case because she couldn't look at me for several minutes afterward—no doubt she could sense my unbelieving eyes staring at her incredulously, questioning her behavior.

It simmered along in that playful manner for a few weeks, suggestive gazes and whisperings going back and forth, until Julia Hicks's birthday party. On that night of childish antics, not only did Rob go off to snog Daniella, but Maddy ended up tucked away in a dark corner of the room playing tonsil tennis with John.

The never-ending stream of cocktail sausages at the buffet table were my only comfort that night.

I wouldn't say I was happy a week later when John decided Maddy wasn't his type after all. Watching her become deflated and embarrassed at being carelessly dumped was certainly uncomfortable, but I definitely felt relieved that their coquettish behavior had come to an end. I selfishly found it reassuring and comforting to have things go back to normal. Well, almost back to normal—John may not have taken his relationship with Maddy much further, but Robert and Daniella had become an official item. This was a pairing I didn't mind so much. It didn't leave me seething and depressed; in fact, it was almost the opposite. I enjoyed having Maddy to myself a little more when Rob's attention had been diverted away from us. I liked us becoming a twosome.

Maddy

The summer before going into year eleven was a glorious one. Every day seemed to be spent running around in the sweltering sunshine with careless abandon. The long days stretched the daylight hours, increasing the time we had to explore and play. More than any other summer holiday I can remember, that one was gay and merry—our last chance to be proper kids before heading back to school, turning sixteen, and starting the grueling lead-up to our GCSE exams. For the last time in our lives we were free from worries, responsibilities, and expectations. It was a summer filled with smiles of contentment . . . for the most part, anyway.

We were that little bit older by then and our mums felt at ease about us going out independently, allowing us to go into the village on our own—as long as we promised to stay together and headed home before it got dark. They implied they were doing us a favor but, let's face it, we were a handful and it was a relief for them to get rid of us for a few hours when they could. There was only so much they could take of us being under their feet after they had been used to sending us off to school each day. With us out of their hair they were left to enjoy the peace that had only existed before we came into the world kicking and screaming.

Robert and Daniella (the school's current golden couple) had frequently been found snogging each other's faces off whenever they had the chance during term time. Despite their keenness, though, they hadn't actually managed to see each other so far during that summer break. Instead they had been texting almost every day and spent an hour every night on MSN. Much to Ben's and my disdain.

Our local park, to which we'd become regular visitors, had a variety of trees lining the pathways and clustered around its edges, most of which we'd succeeded in climbing. The boys had developed a little routine when it came to tackling their vertical beams, one that was aggravating to say the least. Essentially, they would clamber up as quickly as they could, perch from up high and grin down at me, heckling for me to start climbing. I had no doubt that Robert and Ben never saw my being a girl as something that made me a lesser human being, but when it came to climbing trees I was slower and more fearful—something that amused them. Now, I wasn't a girlie girl, I wasn't scared of getting grubby. I just wasn't overly keen on heights! Usually I overcame my fear and cautiously ascended, taking care not to look down until I was on a sturdy branch but, occasionally, if the tree just seemed too big and freaked me out, I'd decline the challenge and remain grounded, much to the boys' annoyance. I'd lie beneath the tree, basking in the gorgeous sunshine, ignoring the leaves and twigs that they playfully threw down at me until they got bored and descended, joining me at ground level.

Three weeks into our six weeks of freedom we were once again in the park, toward its back end, with the boys deciding what tree to take on.

"This one!" shouted Ben as he approached a sparse-looking beech tree, and started to fly up it with ease.

Robert followed suit. Only once they were both dangling from its branches, swinging with youthful serenity, did they look down at me, Ben grinning manically, while Robert simply raised his eyebrows, daring me to join them.

"Come on," called Ben. "Hurry up!"

"Don't rush me," I warned in a huff as I placed my baby blue rucksack next to the base of the tree, took out a bottle of Coke and downed a big gulp of it, the fizz burning my insides in my haste.

"I don't understand what takes you so long."

"I'm just getting ready."

"You've climbed bigger!" encouraged Ben.

"I know, I know . . ." I faltered, peering up at the pair of them, each in their grubby army-like camouflage shorts and khaki-green T-shirts. Their look was certainly Action Man inspired, my own was a touch more Sporty Spice, with dark blue Adidas trackie bottoms that had three florescent orange stripes running down each leg. Stupidly I'd put on a white T-shirt that day, and there was no way it would still be gleaming white by the time I got home, so I knew I'd get a telling off from Mum for getting it dirty.

"It's an easy one!" Ben encouraged.

"Get up here!" yelled Robert, taking a more forceful approach. After a heavy pause he slowly, and teasingly, added, "Don't be such a girl, Maddy."

Well, that was enough to get me out of my mood and up the tree instantly. Talk about succumbing to peer pressure. Ben was right, it wasn't as hard as some of the others they'd forced me up and, as long as I looked up it and not down at my feet, the height didn't seem so bad. I just took my time.

"I knew that would get you up here," Robert laughed with a cheeky wink, once I'd joined them on the steady branch they were both perched on.

"Very clever," I smiled, looking out at the rest of the park.

Putting my fears aside, there was nothing like being up high in a tree with Robert and Ben. Even though we were realistically only seven or eight feet in the air, to us that seemed ginormous—we might as well have been at the top of the Empire State Building, it would have evoked the same feeling of wonder. The air seemed different up there, cooler and fresher, and the view more beautiful than when we were grounded. We could see the whole park. There was also something about becoming invisible to others as we hid behind the tree's leaves and branches that felt magical. I completely understood why the boys loved being up there so much. An overwhelming sense of peace would take over us for a moment or two when we first sat there, as though we'd entered a new world.

Inevitably, at some point, the peace and tranquility we'd marveled over would descend into chaos with the boys shaking the branches and trying to do forward rolls on them. I'd clamp my arms and legs onto the branch and scream my head off at them to stop, scared that we were on the verge of falling and breaking all of our bones. They never listened to me, they just cackled, finding my fears hilarious.

Getting down was always fun too . . . NOT. The boys would courageously swing and leap to the ground, landing with ease, whereas I'd painstakingly hold on for as long as I could while the boys shouted at me to jump—occasionally pulling at one of my legs if they got really bored of waiting for me.

That's how it had been on that day in the middle of our summer holidays—the boys had teased me just as much to get down the tree as they had to get up it. That's why, as we were walking back through the park heading home, I decided it was time to get my own back on the overly confident duo. I hated being the weaker one. It was time for them to squirm instead. And so, as we walked toward a tree we'd nicknamed "The Big Green," a monster of an oak tree that had been too difficult for any of us to master with its wide girth and sporadic branches, an idea popped into my head.

"Go on, then," I said to them both, pointing toward the giant feat, feeling pleased with myself for thinking up such a great plan. "I dare you."

"What?" shrieked Ben, laughing at the ridiculousness of what I'd suggested, shaking his head so vigorously that his cheeks wobbled. "No chance."

"Why not?" I demanded.

"Because!"

"That's not a proper answer," I said.

"It's dinner time. We have to get back," he replied, his voice becoming shrill with panic.

"Don't be such a wimp."

"I'm not being a wimp."

"You are," I goaded.

"I'm not!"

"Are."

"Not."

"Are!"

"Not!"

"I'll do it," Robert said calmly, breaking in on our bickering, causing Ben and I to whip our heads round to face him.

"Really?" Ben asked, clearly as shocked as I was by his bravery. Or stupidity.

"Of course," he shrugged, as though it was nothing.

I was impressed, although sure he'd change his mind as we made our way closer to the Big Green; after all, the nearer we got, the more of a monster it became. Just standing beneath it and looking up at its expansiveness was enough to make me nervous and dizzy, even though I wasn't the one about to climb it. There's no questioning the fact that Robert was the most confident of the three of us—that was something we'd always been aware of—but surely even he had his limits! I'd expected the pair of them to quake at the very thought of it—not for one of them to give it a go!

"You sure?" I gulped.

"Yep," he barked, without the slightest quiver in his voice.

And off he went, up the tree, hugging it as he pulled himself higher and higher. His legs and arms were strong as he scrambled up to near where its branches began to poke out.

Ben and I stood below, gawping at him as he kept going higher and higher, inch by inch.

"Whoa!" I muttered.

"I know," he whispered.

Within seconds that wonder turned into panic. Maybe it was

because he was getting cocky from our admiration and trying to show off, making him less careful, or perhaps the challenge was simply too great for him after all.

Somehow Robert's left foot slipped, the rubber of his Hi-Tec trainers grinding along the bark to make a terrifying scraping sound as it did so. He tried, with a giant reach, to grasp hold of the tree, of its branches, of anything he could, but failed. Instead, his hands grabbed at the air as he fell backward, legs and arms flailing around helplessly, before landing on the ground next to us with a thud and an almighty crack. He writhed in pain, clutching hold of his thigh, his face distorted with agony.

"Argh!" he screamed.

Ben rushed to his side first and knelt down beside him, placing a hand on his shoulder to comfort him. Once the shock allowed me to move again I joined him, taking hold of one of Robert's hands. It was the only thing I could think of that might soothe him in some way. He gripped it tightly. So tightly it caused me to clench my jaw to steady myself.

"Rob, you okay?" Ben asked. "Where does it hurt?"

"My leg!" he yelped, the torturous pain causing him to roll from side to side on his back.

Looking at his leg we could clearly see he'd broken it. A bone was sticking out in a grotesque manner. I couldn't help but wince at the sight of it.

I looked up at Ben as panic started to rise within me. Surprisingly, for the boy who was eager to be led rather than followed, he looked calm and composed as he took control and decided what we had to do.

"You stay here. I'll go to get help," he said, looking from me to our injured friend, firmly gripping him on the shoulder. "I won't be long, Robbie."

"Quick!" he screamed, before inhaling sharply between his teeth.

"You gonna be okay?" Ben asked me, getting to his feet and grabbing for my hand, which he squeezed three times as though he was pumping courage and strength through his touch.

I nodded and watched as he turned away from me and sprinted across the park. My heart ached as I looked down at Robert and saw his face scrunched up as he battled with the pain, groaning as he held on to my hand a little tighter, his breathing becoming erratic and forced.

"Shh . . ." I breathed, trying to keep myself from bursting into tears as I attempted to comfort him. Not only was I horrified at seeing my best friend in such pain, and lost over how to help him, but I also felt enormously guilty. I was the one who'd sent him up that ridiculous tree, after all. I'd only wanted to show them that we all had limitations and that I shouldn't have been given such a hard time for my own. I hadn't expected Robert to climb it and I certainly didn't think he'd break something as a result.

"I'm so sorry," I sobbed eventually, after watching his suffering for a few minutes, unable to keep in my shame any longer. Robert was the strong one of the three of us, and I'd reduced him to a vulnerable mess with my stupidity.

"What are you crying for, you loser?" he croaked.

"Because it's my fault."

"What?"

"I told you to go up there. This wouldn't have happened if I hadn't done that . . ."

"Don't be such a girl, Maddy," he groaned, flinching in pain as laughter trickled out of him.

I stopped crying and just stared at him open mouthed, wondering how he could possibly use that line on me when he was in such a state himself.

"*Me* being a girl? What about *you*?" I teased, giving his shoulder a gentle shove.

"Huh?"

"If Daniella saw you now she'd think you were the biggest girl she's ever seen," I continued. "I mean, she'd probably dump you on the spot," I shrugged.

"Maddy . . ."

"What? At least I *am* a girl! What's your excuse?"

"Really? You're choosing this moment to verbally abuse me?"

"You started it."

"I fell out of a tree and broke my leg," he said incredulously, his face still twisted in agony at the pain. "Please, just . . . be nice!" he exhaled.

He laughed then. Laughed so hysterically that I couldn't tell if he was laughing or crying for a moment or two. Perhaps it was a mixture of both as they battled against each other, but the laughter eventually won. His chuckle filled the air around us as he leaned back and closed his eyes, bringing his free hand up to cover his crinkled face.

Looking at him, at the ridiculousness of the situation, at our bickering, I couldn't help but dissolve into a fit of giggles myself. My body doubled over, causing my forehead to gently rest on Rob's chest before I rolled off on to my back. With our heads and shoulders touching, and hands still gripping hold of each other, we laughed uncontrollably side by side as our cackles drifted skywards and entwined into the leaves of the Big Green.

It was a perfect moment, born from something horrific and shocking, that briefly brought us closer than we'd ever ventured before.

By the time Ben came back with Robert's dad, we had tears streaming down our faces and couldn't stop smiling. Ben looked at us not only as though we'd gone mad, but also with a bemused sadness, as though he was troubled to be left out of whatever was going on. He quizzed us both eagerly, asked what we were laughing about, but his confused face, and the fact that we were effectively being giddy over nothing, made me laugh harder—so hard that my body convulsed once more with laughter, moving me on to my side so that my mouth was nuzzled into Rob's neck, as I tried to calm myself down.

It was when Robert's dad started to inspect his injury that he yelped out in pain again, stopping the moment in its tracks and sobering us instantly.

A quick dash to the hospital told us that, as predicted, Robert's leg was broken. Thanks to me, he spent the first few weeks of life in year eleven on crutches with a massive bright orange cast on his wounded leg—which we all signed and put rude messages on. He might have been temporarily disabled, but he rarely complained. That's mainly because it guaranteed him ample attention from everyone—the football team who missed him, the girls who cooed after him like he was a poorly puppy, and the teachers who gave him preferential treatment. He got out of lessons early to avoid getting crushed by the crowds in the crammed corridors and was granted access to the front of the dinner queue . . . Well, as far as silver linings go, his wasn't bad.

The only thing it didn't help was his relationship with Daniella. She'd started going ice-skating every Saturday with her mates. Rob couldn't exactly go along and, as a result, she met Russell. He was one of those more capable skaters who rushed around the ring as though he was about to knock everyone over with his menacing speed, putting the fear of God into all the nervous skaters on the ice. Evidently Daniella liked that sort of thing.

She dumped Robert by text.

Nice.

That had been my first experience of Robert having a girlfriend, and I hadn't liked it one bit—especially after the incident under the tree. I teased him about his relationship and jibed him for being "under the thumb" whenever her name popped up in conversation. That probably makes me sound like a spoiled brat, longing for his attention, but I just had this urge to get under his skin on the topic and to make sure I wasn't being forgotten about.

With much guilt (although I don't think it's a surprising confession), I'll admit that I was relieved Robert was no longer spending hours at his computer sending Daniella soppy messages. Being dumped hadn't fazed him at all—he was as funny, witty, and charming as ever.

I was thrilled to have him back!

Ben

Robert's new-found single status meant that he was back with me and Maddy once more. I was chuffed to have him with us again, obviously, but it meant I wasn't getting as much alone time with Maddy as I had since the start of the autumn term—and I can't hide the fact that I'd been enjoying it. I'll even admit that I felt deflated somehow at having to "share" her again. It was the first time I'd become what can only be described as possessive over her.

Being a threesome again led me to feel a bit paranoid, and that irritating feeling had started to creep in even before Rob got dumped. The day he fell and broke his leg, I'd left a shaken Maddy and pain-stricken Robert beneath that tree to go and get help. I thought I was being heroic . . . taking control and being the leader for once. But when I got back, I was taken aback to find them wrapped up in each other looking like they hadn't a care in the world—laughing and taking pleasure in each other's silliness. I felt like I was intruding on something, and that was an unfamiliar and uncomfortable sensation.

If it weren't for the bone visibly protruding from his leg, I'd have thought I'd dreamed Robert falling and needing my help.

It irked me, even though I told myself it was nothing, reasoned with myself that Robert was with Daniella and didn't see Maddy in the same way that I did.

I was being hypersensitive . . . a douchebag! Still, it took a while for those feelings to simmer down and disappear and for me to feel like everything was normal between the three of us—between the two of them.

That summer changed my outlook on my own feelings, and not just because of the way I'd found them underneath the Big Green. I'd been to see *Pearl Harbor* at the cinema (I'd taken my mum out for her birthday), and was left feeling as though my heart had been ripped out. It might sound pathetic, but the message was clear—seize the day, love like there's no tomorrow, and declare your feelings before it's too late. That's how I'd come to realize that I could no longer bottle things inside. What, I wondered, was I trying to prove by living in the torturous barricade of my own heart? I'd let myself be tormented by what I hadn't said, rather than what I had . . . paranoid about what others might be feeling, rather than just asking outright. Yes, I'd decided to take control, to put my feelings out there to be reciprocated or rebuffed. Either way, *something* was better than nothing.

With a trip planned in year eleven to the most romantic city in the world, I decided to bite my tongue a little longer. It was only a few months, I told myself, and I wanted the moment I finally decided to lift my silence and speak up to be memorable. And so, for months I thought of nothing but Paris. Vivid images filled my mind—of us together at the top of the Eiffel Tower, surrounded by the romantic view, and the look of adoration on Maddy's face as I opened my mouth to utter my love confession. It fueled my sleepless nights that summer and gave me a giddy feeling of excitement in my gut.

It felt as though Paris had become, in many ways, the pinnacle of my very existence. Nights were spent plowing through information on the Web to formulate my plan, hours were spent with a pen and paper writing out what I was going to say when the moment of truth finally came. It was as though years of wonder and desire had led me to that point and to that precise spot I needed to reach at the top of the Eiffel Tower. I wanted, more than anything, for it to go right. It had to be perfect.

Maddy

The best thing about taking Art as a GCSE was that you got to go on an art trip to Paris in year eleven. A week away from parents, exam stress, and schoolwork, traipsing around the millions of museums and eating trillions of crêpes and macaroons, understandably sounded very tempting. And that was why the three of us all decided to take up art when it came to filling out our options for the years ahead— yes, we all sat down and had a big chat about certain subjects we should all go for so that we'd get time together. Along with our compulsory subjects, we all opted for French over Spanish, Art over Drama, and History over Religious Education. I however went for Food, while Robert went for Physical Education and Ben went for Graphic Design—something he was insanely good at. Our plans did backfire a little bit when it turned out that each year group was separated into new class sets for the mandatory core subjects as well as those we'd optioned, but we found ourselves together in Art, and at least we all got most of the same homework to plow through together.

In the weeks leading up to that art trip I felt an endless wave of apprehension. No, I wasn't worried about being stranded in the capital (that would have simply been an adventure) and I wasn't worried I'd get homesick (I couldn't wait to get out of the house) . . . Nope, I was nervous because of a feeling that had been brewing inside during the previous months. Those feelings had nothing to do with Paris, but everything to do with Robert. A fact I was struggling to comprehend.

As a result of that afternoon underneath the Big Green, I was drawn to him like a piece of flimsy metal to a powerful magnet—there was no way of avoiding its strength. No way to resist. That unspeakable energy tingled away beneath the surface, giving me a surge of something unidentifiable every time I thought of him. It felt like we were on the cusp of a momentous change, but I wasn't sure how I felt about it.

Robert treated me as he always had—like one of the boys he could have a laugh with, or, at times, a little sister he was fiercely over-protective of. He was always draping an arm over my shoulder, or gently mocking me for something I'd said or done. It was how we'd always been. So, was I the only one looking further into every touch shared? Every gaze he placed in my direction? Embarrassingly, it seemed so.

Robert's enchanting ways (which had naturally transpired from his confident role as our group's leader) continued to capture more girls' hearts than ever. He'd always been a charmer (his flirty and confi-dent ways had been buried deep within his gorgeous exterior), but seeing him tease or fool around with any other girl after that moment under the tree was excruciating. Each suggestive glance, wink, and mutter that he flung in another girl's direction stung my teenage heart—a fact that confused me beyond belief. Then there was the gossip that lingered around him—girls speculating over who he'd end up snogging while we were away. For obvious reasons I was never even suggested, but for once, that omission left me feeling jealous. Envious not to be seen as having a chance . . .

Of course I knew what those alien emotions meant, but I also knew that I wasn't going to be the one to act on them. I wasn't going to show Robert that I'd succumbed to his charms and found myself plonked in the middle of his fan club with tens of other girls. Oh yes, he really did have a fan club. The girls in our year, in fact our whole school, swooned over him relentlessly—more so when he'd broken his leg! Huddles of girls would frantically walk around the school to find him on his lunch break, they'd giggle as he passed them on the stairway, dribble at the smallest glimpse of him in the corridor, and if there was ever any accidental body contact, like arms brushing as he walked past, there'd be a near-fainting situation . . . It was mind-boggling and quite sickening to watch, but Robert loved the attention from his adoring fans and often played up to them, much to their delight. Due to their lovesick nature, his admirers continuously treated me with caution—I was, after all, a girl with unlimited access to Robert. It was something they could only dream of. I wasn't too bothered by their occasional evil glances. In fact, I found the whole thing funny. Yes, I knew Robert up close and personal—but that didn't just mean I got to see his handsome (there's no disputing his good looks) face on a regular basis behind closed doors, but I also got to see him scratching his arse, popping his hand down between his boxers and trousers for a quick squeeze (as though to check his bits were still intact), and a million other little idiosyncrasies that would leave others' minds boggled. The Robert they saw, the charming, suave, and well-groomed prince, was a tad different to my grubby friend Rob—and I loved it that way.

I had a secret piece of him.

Did I really want to give up that piece and turn into every other girl looking at him through rose-tinted glasses? Sadly, it seemed it was way out of my control. That's what led me to be full of nervousness about going to Paris. If something *was* going to happen between us, then it was sure to occur there when we were cocooned in a bubble of holiday abandon. Right?

And if it didn't?

If he ended up kissing someone else right in front of me?

Well, I just wanted to get on that trip so I could witness which of the two scenarios would win out. At least then the anxiety of not knowing could be put to rest.

On the morning we left for the trip, I experienced a rush of excitement as I wheeled my suitcase through the school gates and saw the green coach waiting to take us all across the English Channel. Instead of walking into school with Robert or Ben, my mum had decided to go with me. Partly because of the early start—it was six o'clock in the morning and still dark thanks to it being November—but mostly because it was my first-ever trip abroad without her and my dad and she wanted to see me off safely. I could already see the tears of concern threatening to spill in her eyes and had to stop myself from rolling my eyes at her—horrified that she was on the verge of embarrassing me with an emotional good-bye.

"You just make sure you stick with the group, okay?"

"Yes, Mum," I said, trying to stop her from worrying—although it was no use, she'd had her knickers in a twist ever since she and Dad got the first letter about the trip at the start of the school year. Honestly, you would have thought she'd be happy to have me, her premenstrual-screaming-raging-teenage-daughter-who-is-lovely-to-everyone-else-but-the-actual-devil-at-home, out of the house for a little bit. But it appeared *not* having me at home caused her just as much stress as having me there did.

"And listen to everything that your teacher says . . ."

"Mum, it's going to be fine!" I said for the umpteenth time. "I'm not a kid!"

"Don't you take that tone with me, madam!"

Luckily, Robert started walking toward us. Not only did a pang of nerves shoot through me, but it also stopped Mum in her scolding as she planted a welcoming smile on her face.

"Hello, Robbie!" Mum beamed, opening her arms and giving him a big hug. She was always delighted to see him.

When we were nine years old Robert and Ben melted Mum's heart as they sat on their bikes at our front door asking for me to play outside—seven years later and they still had the same effect on her, although their relationships varied. Robert had my mum wrapped around his little finger. He was incredibly cheeky with her, always winding her up or telling naughty jokes—she couldn't help but laugh at his funny ways. As for Ben, she was always going on about how respectful and polite he was whenever he came over. The first thing he used to do in our house was ask Mum if she wanted him to make her a cup of tea or if he could help with whatever she was doing, like dinner if she was cooking, or the gardening if she was weeding on the patio. Their glowing personalities made them look like angels and me look like a hormonal brat, although I think that was just the joy of having a teenage daughter—gone was the little princess she'd dressed up in frilly outfits, replaced by an adolescent who huffed and puffed her way through home life. With that in mind, it's unsurprising that Mum treated the boys as though they were her own delightful kids—the sons she never had. It was clearly a case of wishful thinking.

At sixteen years old, Robert had changed a considerable amount since I'd first met him. I'm pretty sure that, back when we were nine, we were roughly the same height. Not any more. During the summer the year before he'd shot up and become over six feet tall—the difference was astounding. The only trouble was that his body had put so much effort into growing upward that it had forgotten to grow a little bit outward too. He was incredibly lanky and clumsy with these long limbs that he'd miraculously accumulated overnight, but there was clearly something endearing about him as females swooned in his presence.

"You excited?" Mum asked Robert.

"Yeah! Can't wait. Have you got your camera?" he asked me.

"Of course!"

"I've only let her take three disposable ones," Mum informed him. "That way she won't have to worry if she loses them. You know what she's like . . . careless."

"Thanks for clarifying that, Mum," I grumbled.

"Have you forgotten what you did with your dad's binoculars when you went to Dorset?"

I rolled my eyes. Here we go again, I thought to myself. She'd revel in any excuse to bring up how useless I was.

"Yes, you brought them back covered in cow pat, and then you didn't even bother to wash them—you just placed them back in the cupboard, where they waited for me and your dad to find them a month later. The smell, Robbie, was atrocious."

Robert grinned at me as he shook his head.

Other people might have worried about their parents speaking to them, and treating them, like a child in public, but Robert and Ben had seen my mum talk to me in that way countless times, in fact she'd even spoken to them in that tone on numerous occasions (like the time we'd played tag in the garden and ruined some of her newly bloomed flowers—big mistake), so they found it amusing rather than embarrassing. A good thing when my mum was around.

"So you've only let her have *three* cameras?" Robert asked my mum with a smirk.

"Is it a bit much?" she frowned. "You know she likes to take an account of every little detail."

"You're telling me. I'm surprised her face hasn't morphed into a camera after covering her face with one for so long."

"Oh, Robbie," my mum giggled in response.

After badgering my parents endlessly, I'd been given a top-of-the-range camera for Christmas the previous year. They probably thought I'd get bored of it and discard it like every other present I'd begged for in the past, but instead I took it everywhere I went. It was irritating that I wasn't allowed to take it to Paris with me, the disposable cameras would be crap in comparison, but I also didn't want anything to happen to my most prized possession, so I didn't put up too much of a fight when they insisted I left it behind. Not that I'd have let them know that—such is the prerogative of a teenage daughter. I thought I was meant to argue against every boundary they set.

"I was just wondering how on earth she'll be able to annoy us when those three films have run out," continued Robert with a playful shrug.

"Oi," I shrieked, acting insulted.

"Come on," Robert laughed, grabbing for my suitcase. "I'll take it round."

"You're such a gent," Mum beamed.

"I try," Rob smiled back before gesturing to the other side of the bus. "My mum's over there talking to Ben and June."

"Oh, I didn't realize your mums were coming too," said Mum, clearly happy not to be the only one that'd shown up.

"What? When there's a chance to embarrass us? Of course they're here."

"You cheeky little monkey," Mum laughed. "I'll tell your mum you said that."

"What have you got in this?" Robert asked me as he tried to do the macho lift with my suitcase, rather than drag it along on its wheels like a girl.

"Stuff," I shrugged. I'd definitely overpacked. I hadn't had a clue what to take with me so had ended up bunging in loads of extra clothes that morning, even though I knew I wouldn't end up wearing half of it.

"We're only going for a week . . ."

"Yeah, yeah . . . it has wheels, you know. Just use them if your muscles haven't fully developed yet," I teased.

With this he lifted the whole suitcase up onto his shoulder and walked off to put it on the bus.

"Show off!" I called after him.

He turned and gave me a wink. I knew the hearts of other girls would have melted at the gesture, but I grimaced back to make him think mine hadn't. Although, as soon as his back was turned, I couldn't help a small smile forming on my lips—the nervous excitement bubbling away once again, no matter how much I tried to squash it.

As we walked around the bus we spotted Robert's mum, Carol, and Ben and his mum, June, huddled together in a small group and headed toward them.

Like Robert, Ben had also changed a lot over the years—he'd

grown a good couple of feet as well, but he wasn't quite as tall. Instead, his body had stayed in proportion as it *did* manage to grow outward at the same time, giving him a much sturdier appearance. Much to Ben's annoyance, though, he'd also kept hold of some of his puppy fat—that's not to say he was fat, there was just a little more of him. Yes, I would have described Robert as a long stick and Ben as a round ball that you just want to squidge. He was soft and cuddly. And his dark facial features had maintained the cuteness that they'd always had. He might not have got the same sort of attention from the ladies as Robert did, but he was well loved by them all nonetheless . . . they were more likely to go to him for advice (or a squeeze—he was the best hugger, he really held you tight) than to flirt. I don't think that bothered Ben as he never really seemed into any of the girls that he talked to. My dad had actually asked me at dinner one night if he "batted for the other team." I almost choked on my cottage pie. I told Ben what Dad had said on our way to school the next morning and he'd almost choked on the sweet he'd been sucking . . . Choking was obviously the standard reaction when questioning Ben's sexuality. It put an end to that little query, anyway. He was straight, he liked girls, but seemed too laid-back to want to do anything about it.

As we were nearing our group, Ben let out a huge yawn—one that he didn't bother to cover up with his hands. It seemed to go on forever, highlighting just how tired he was.

"Bit early for you, love?" Mum laughed.

"Just a tad."

"Well, you should've seen him jump out of bed this morning," said June, pointing her thumb sideways in Ben's direction. "I've not seen him like that in a while. Anyone would think he couldn't wait to get away."

Ben shrugged in innocence with a sheepish grin, wrapped his arm around her and rested his head on hers—he was at least a foot taller than her. I always loved seeing little moments like that pass between Ben and June. Unlike Robert and me, who both went through stages of being embarrassed by our mums (or declaring we hated them), Ben hadn't. He worshipped her and gladly showed that in public.

"You would not believe how hard it was to get her up today," tutted Mum, giving me a gentle poke in the ribs and making me yelp in shock.

"Ooh, quick photo of our leaving party before we go?" I pleaded, pulling one of the cardboard-covered cameras from my coat pocket and winding the film along.

"Do we have to?" moaned Mum.

"Yes."

"But I haven't even got my face on yet . . . here, give me the ruddy thing. I'll get one of you and Ben instead," she demanded, grabbing the camera off me before I managed to get a quick picture of her makeup free.

I wrapped my arms around Ben's neck and smiled, but just before Mum captured our pose Robert jumped on us from behind—turning it into a laughing picture of the three of us.

"I see she's started already then?" Rob jokingly asked Ben while frowning at my camera.

"Only just," Ben laughed. "Hope you've been practicing your fake smiles."

"Yes, my speciality. Well, now that's done . . . Miss James is about to let everyone on the bus. Quick!" Robert whispered. "Bye, Mum," he added with a cheeky grin and a wave before turning on his heels and running back around to the door of the bus.

Ben and I instantly sprang to life, the race for the back seat was on. Yes, the downside to being a threesome was that, on coaches, one of us had to sit on our own unless we managed to bagsy the back seat. It wasn't an easy task when there were so many other groups of friends wanting to get it too—it took some cleverly planned timing and for one of your team to be as quick as a bullet! With Robert first in line, he made the prospect of us getting our desired seats highly likely.

Robert's mum was close on his heels.

"If he thinks he's going to get away with saying a crappy good-bye like that without giving me a proper kiss, when he's leaving me for a bloody week, he's got another think coming," tutted Carol, as she shook her head and wandered off after him, causing us all to laugh.

"Bye, Mum," Ben said, leaning down and hugging June tightly before giving her a peck on the cheek.

"Oh, come here," said Mum as she took me in her arms for my own cuddle good-bye, which I happily entered into. Despite my huffy appearance, I was nervous about the week away and I knew I'd miss my mum and her crazy ways.

Ben

The excitement on the bus, even at that time in the morning, was sky high. We were getting away from school life, from exam stress and from our parents for a whole week. We were off to chill with our friends in Paris, to marvel at some wonderful art while sketching it (badly) into our workbooks, eat loads of crêpes, and to test out our French on actual French people—it was time to see whether we'd actually learned anything in our lessons. I wasn't holding my breath on that score and had packed my mini French phrase book, just in case—so had Robert and Maddy. For some reason I was doubtful that the one French phrase that stuck in my head, *"Où est la piscine?"* (where is the swimming pool?) was going to get me very far.

Once Miss James had called the register and found everybody had made it on board, even though it was frightfully early, we were free. Maddy, Robert, and I squished up against the window at the back of the bus, and waved good-bye to our mums—all of whom were teary-eyed and rubbing each other's backs in support. We couldn't help but laugh at them, making them giggle back at the stupidity of their emotional outbursts. We were only going away for a week—you'd have thought we were moving to the other side of the world indefinitely the way they were carrying on.

As the coach started moving, carrying us away from our mums, away from the school and away from Peaswood, I experienced an un-expected lull—as though reality had hit, causing me to abandon my joyfulness momentarily. I worried about my mum. I shouldn't have, I knew she was far tougher than I was and could cope with far more than me, but it was the thought of her in that empty house on her own, without me there for company. The other mums had their husbands to rely on, but she obviously didn't. Dad leaving had made us closer than ever—we looked after each other, made sure we didn't dwell too heavily, and moved each other into the light any time his absence hit us hard. It worried me that she'd have no one to do that for her without me there.

I looked up at the others to find Robert looking back at me. He winked and gave me an encouraging nod. He knew what was on my mind even though I hadn't said it, and I knew what he was saying even if the words hadn't worked their way out of his mouth. Mum would be fine. Everything would be okay.

But as soon as my thoughts of Mum had subsided a different feeling arose from the pit of my stomach. This is it, I thought to myself, this is the trip I've been waiting for, the trip that will change my future and hopefully give me the girl of my dreams. I took a deep breath to steady the nerves building up inside.

"You okay?" Maddy asked to the right of me, her hand resting on my arm.

"Yeah! Knackered . . ."

"Me too," she smiled, before taking my hand in hers, resting her head on my shoulder and nuzzling her body into mine.

It felt lovely.

I couldn't help but smile as I intuitively squeezed her hand. Three times. "I love you," I declared in what I hoped was the last time I'd have to do so in my coded way. Paris was going to give me the freedom to verbalize it, at last.

"I love the way you always do that," she smiled, rubbing my arm in response to my gesture, clueless as to what it actually meant. "Three squeezes. It's your thing."

"Is it?"

"Yeah," she laughed. "You must be aware that you're doing it?"

I stared at her with this gormless expression on my face, but before I could respond she started talking again.

"Did you see Lauren and Daniel getting on the bus?"

"I think they're here somewhere," I said with relief, stretching my back and craning my neck to see over the tops of the seats in front of us.

"No," she giggled, pulling me back into my seat. "I mean, did you see the way he asked her if she wanted to sit next to him?"

"Oh. No. Why?"

"It was a bit . . . odd."

"Was it?"

"I don't even think I've ever seen them talk before." She was trying to talk as quietly as she could, but her eyes were practically popping out of her head as she willed me to grasp whatever it was she was saying.

I looked at her blankly. It was too early for guessing games.

"I think he likes her," she eventually spelled out.

"Really?"

"What's this you're whispering about?" asked Robert, leaning across both our laps so that his face was right in front of ours. He was so close I found it hard to focus on him.

"Lauren and Daniel," Maddy mouthed, smiling.

"Yup. Spotted it," he nodded knowingly, pursing his lips.

"Really?" asked Maddy, excited at having a little gossip, especially as it was on the topic of love. She wasn't a girlie girl, but she was certainly a romantic. "Do you think they'll get it on?"

"Don't see why not," shrugged Robert.

"Anyone else you think might?" Maddy asked, her eyes widening in delight.

"Let's see," Robert said, taking a quick peek around at the rest of our classmates on the bus, as though to remind himself of who else had joined us on the trip.

"I think Aaron has a thing for Jessica."

"Yeah, but she wouldn't go near him," Maddy protested, shaking her head. "Rebecca would, though."

"Obviously. She'd have anyone who gave her a chance. So what about you?" Rob asked her. "Anyone you've got your eye on?"

"Nooo . . ." she blushed, visibly embarrassed by the question.

"Well, I wonder if anyone has theirs on you . . ."

"Doubt it," she muttered, nibbling on her lip.

"Jackson? Williams? Tipper? Mr. Brown?" he offered, listing the surnames of some of the guys on the bus, his eyebrows rising more with each suggestion given.

Maddy screwed up her face in reply.

"Might be your lucky trip, Maddy Hurst. I bet someone's got their eye on you," he grinned.

"Doubt it. We can't all be as popular as you," she teased.

"It's quality that matters, not quantity, Maddy."

"Is that right?"

"Yep."

"If your fan club could hear you now."

"I'm not being ungrateful!" he protested with his eyes wide. "They're all lovely, but . . ."

"What?"

"Well, I'm just waiting to be swept off my feet by the right girl."

"And you think you'll find her in Paris?"

"It's a nice place to start looking."

I stayed quiet. In fact, I think I may have even stopped listening (and breathing). I couldn't look at them. We were all seated so close together, Robert was still lying across us. I felt wedged in with no escape. I panicked that the conversation was going to be turned around to me and who *I* fancied. I had no idea what I'd have said. All I could think about was my plan being messed up if I so much as uttered the wrong thing. I zoned in and out of their conversation, a bead of sweat appearing on my upper lip as I continued to freak out.

But the conversation just ended.

Just like that.

Robert sat upright and dived into his rucksack, chucking out a chocolate Curly Wurly bar for us each and that was it.

The only thing remaining of the exchange was Maddy's pink-stained cheeks.

The moment had clearly been forgotten by Robert who, instead, decided to unload the rest of his bag and impress us by revealing its contents—a mountain of treats: biscuits, crisps, chocolate, and sweets. A staple diet for any growing teenager.

"No way I'm eating frog's legs or snails!" he declared, with a cheeky grin.

"Yuck!" chorused Maddy and I, pulling disgusted faces.

Yes, shamefully we all believed the stereotype that, at some point on that trip, we'd be forced to eat such dishes—something we were all terrified of. But for a few minutes, as we sat back in our seats and started to munch on the chewy caramel chocolate, our fears melted away.

Even though I was relieved that the conversation had quickly moved on, I didn't fail to notice Maddy's eyes twinkling as they roamed along our classmates and visibly continued to dream up different possibilities and matches in her head.

I wondered if she was thinking about her own chance of romance . . . and if she was thinking of me.

"You're so lucky that you get to share a rooooom!" whined Maddy as she stomped her way through our hotel room door and plonked herself on my bed.

The room was pretty basic but better than we imagined. Our twin room had two single beds (made up with cream-colored sheets and blankets rather than a comfy duvet—our first Parisian grumble) along opposite walls with a wooden bedside table placed between them. The walls were off-white and blue curtains hung at the windows, which looked out at a brick wall of the building next door rather than a breathtaking view of the city. The most wonderful thing about our room was the en-suite, which was exciting enough, but it also had a shower in it. We only had a bath at home back then. What a luxury!

"I have to share with Kelly Sinclair—I don't even know her! Why can't I be in here with you?" Maddy continued, her face all screwed up as she moaned.

"You know why," shrugged Robert, a cheeky smile appearing— the one he always used before saying something naughty. "The teachers know you wouldn't be able to keep your hands off me if you slept in here."

I was used to Rob winding Maddy up in this way, but never had he said something quite so sexually suggestive. It shocked me. To my horror, I started to wonder if I wasn't the only one to harbor feelings for our best friend—although, if that was that case, I wondered if Rob would really choose to be so blatant about it. Surely he was just winding her up, I hoped. Nevertheless, my paranoia started to return.

A second or two seemed to pass with me gawping at the two of them while Maddy widened her eyes at a smirking Robert in disbelief.

"Argh, you're so gross!" she eventually whined, much to my relief, as she pulled one of my pillows from the bed and flung it at him. "What's this?" she asked, holding up a scruffy stuffed toy rabbit by its ears. I'd brought it with me and quickly hidden it under there when Robert had gone to the loo earlier. I didn't expect Maddy to come in and find it mere moments later.

"Erm . . ." I hesitated.

"Wait, I recognize it," she said, as she brought it round to face her, ruffling its shabby lilac hair. "I got you it for your birthday. Years ago."

"Yeah . . ." I raised my eyebrows and sighed, shaking my head and acting as though I was as confused by its appearance in our Parisian hotel room as she was.

Maddy had given it to me on my tenth birthday and at that time it was the most precious thing I owned. It's not like I went to bed with it every night or anything, I'd only done that for the first year, but when I was packing to go away I saw it sitting glumly on my bed-side table and thought it might be a nice thing to have with me—my lucky mascot, if you will. I wrongly thought it would go unnoticed.

"I've no idea what it's doing here. Mum must've put it in my bag. You know what she's like," I said with a quick shake of the head and a roll of my eyes.

"Yes, I do."

"Nutter . . ." I added without much gusto. I wasn't used to talk-ing badly of Mum.

"And who put it under your pillow?" she asked after a pause.

"What?"

"Your pillow?"

"Huh?" I heard her the first time and knew exactly what she was getting at.

"It was under your pillow, so somehow it hopped out of your suit-case and dived into your bed before either of you noticed . . ."

I looked at her with my mouth wide open, willing my brain to form some sort of an explanation. Nothing came. Suddenly *I* was the rabbit, caught in the big flaming headlights of embarrassment.

"Leave him alone!" yelled Robert, coming to my aid and throw-ing the pillow back in Maddy's direction. "Are you trying to tell us that you've not brought one yourself?"

Maddy covered her face with her hands, unable to stop a girlish giggle from escaping.

Later on that night, once Maddy had left to go to her own room and we were lying in our beds, one topic whirled around inside my head: Maddy and Robert.

"Do you fancy Maddy?" I asked, much to my own surprise. I couldn't stop my mouth from opening and the question firing out as the overriding urge to quiz Robert fought against my brain's resistance.

"Huh?" he questioned, sounding half asleep, even though we'd only just turned the lights off.

"Maddy?" I couldn't face asking the whole question again, so I hoped he'd heard the majority of it, and opted to just repeat her name instead. I was so thankful that I'd waited until the lights were out—I could feel my face burning up, making me feel flustered.

"Oh . . . not that I'm aware of," he laughed, sounding more awake. "Why?"

"You were being quite flirty with her earlier."

"Was I?" he asked.

"More than normal," I said, in what I hoped was a laidback tone of voice.

"You know what she's like," he sighed. "She gets so uptight and bashful, I was just winding her up."

"That's what I thought . . ." I nodded to myself.

"Did I take it too far?"

"Maybe . . ."

"I hope I didn't offend her." He sounded genuinely worried at the idea.

"I'm sure you didn't," I reasoned, mentally bashing myself around the head for having said anything in the first place—one thing I'd started to understand about love was that it made me feel more suspicious than anything else ever had. It was torturous.

"Still, I'll apologize tomorrow. I was only messing around . . . it's nice that you're protective over her," he added after a brief pause.

"You are too."

"I guess we can't help it."

The conversation ended there. I wasn't sure if Robert had simply fallen back to sleep or whether he, like me, was lying there thinking of Maddy.

I hoped it was the former.

The next morning we were forced out of bed ridiculously early (which probably wasn't that early, but seeing as none of us had bothered to move our watches forward an hour it seemed like it was still the middle of the night). We might have thought we were on holiday, but our teachers were hell-bent on getting us out of bed and on to the streets of Paris as soon as they could. We'd mumbled good mornings to each other at the breakfast table as we slumped into our seats.

"Okay, sleepyheads," welcomed Miss James with a smile before handing around printed worksheets. "Here's a rough itinerary for the next few days and the work I expect you to do in each museum or place we visit."

"Work?" queried Robert. "But I thought the idea was just to look at the art, Miss. Surely that's what the artists would want."

"Nice try, Mr. Miles."

I swear I saw her blush.

I quickly skimmed my way through the itinerary and longed for the words to pop from the page, but I didn't see them.

"Miss? Where's the Eiffel Tower?" I asked, unable to hide the panic in my voice. "Surely we're going to go there . . . ?"

To my relief a few of the others grumbled their own protests at the omission.

"I was planning on talking to you all about that. I thought it might be a nice thing to do the morning we leave to go home—a splendid way to round off what I'm sure will be a great trip. Although that does mean getting up very early, and getting on the bus to go straight back home from there, rather than going from here. Does that sound okay with you lot?"

There was a split reaction from the group—the girls all nodded in approval, beaming great big smiles at the thought of gracing the super romantic spot, and the boys grunted—either because they weren't as bothered or because it was still too early. Needless to say I was with the girls on this one. Going there on the last day would be all right, I decided. I'd have preferred to go there straight away and get the whole thing over with as soon as I could, rather than having to wait for the entire trip and agonizing over what was to come, but the important thing was we *were* going there. All I had to do was hold it together until then.

Gazing over the plans for our busy week, we tried to eat the crusty rolls and slices of ham and cheese given to us (none of us were too impressed with that continental malarkey), and then our crazy week of cramming in every tourist attraction Paris had to offer commenced. We gazed up at Notre Dame cathedral while singing the songs from the Disney classic, which included a lonely hunchback (then had to stop ourselves from continuing to sing when we were inside the holy building—although I'm pretty sure I heard Robert humming along to himself). We explored the Rodin Museum and copied the moody pose of *The Thinker*, walked around the Picasso Museum and debated whether he was a genius or just off his rocker. Got dragged through Père-Lachaise cemetery as Miss James listed details of a load of dead people we didn't know—actually we had heard of Jim Morrison and Oscar Wilde, but even then it was hardly riveting stuff—they're dead! Plus, it was freezing cold and standing around bored was irritating. We marveled over work in the Musée Marmottan Monet, complained how small the *Mona Lisa* was in the Louvre (after queuing for ages to see her—plus the glass case in front of her was dirty), and questioned the respectability of almost every piece in the Pompidou Center ("How can *that* be art?")—all the while making notes and scribbling sketches in our notebooks so that our teachers would think we were actually doing some work, but more so that we had something to show our parents when we got home, giving them the satisfaction that their money had been well spent. Hardly any crêpes were eaten—one of my biggest disappointments of the trip when it came to experiencing the joys of Paris. Well, that and the fact that our trip to the Eiffel Tower never felt like it was getting any closer.

The days crawled by at a snail's pace, as if they were purposefully trying to torment my lovesick heart. However, every now and then, in the distance over a bridge or from a viewing platform at one of the museums, I'd catch a glimpse of that metallic beacon of beauty and romance and feel a surge of happiness ping through my heart. Every day, every minute, and every second inched me closer and closer to its magic, reminding me that my plan was still intact, that the trip's grand finale was just around the corner. I had no doubt that the Parisian air had the power to propel us into something new. Something different that would change our lives forever.

In many ways, I was right.

Maddy

It was our last night in Paris and, as a treat, Miss James and the other chaperones decided to take us out to a little French restaurant for dinner. While we were getting ready and putting on our makeup, my roommate, Kelly Sinclair (one of the cooler kids from our year who always looked perfect with her dark smoldering eye makeup and long tousled brown hair) turned to me—her head leaning to one side as she squinted her eyes at me suspiciously.

"You and Robert were looking close on the way back today."

Her comment was nothing new, I was used to being quizzed in such a manner when it came to me and the boys. Sometimes it was Ben and I cuddling that got people talking, other times it was the playful banter between Rob and I that caught their attention. I could usually brush it off, insisting that I didn't believe in the assumption that girls and boys could never be *just* friends, but on that trip I'd become even more aware of things shifting. Everything between us felt more charged, like we were both just waiting for something to happen. Like the chat on the bus about him waiting for the right girl—was that a hint? And was he questioning me about other guys in our class to suss out my reaction?

I was more than embarrassed when he lay there and mocked my supposed inability to keep my hands off him—I wondered if he could sense what was going on in my head. And if he could, well, that was just humiliating. He apologized for that, actually. The morning after the hands-off incident he'd gone out of his way to pull me to one side and say sorry, but not in a macho can't-believe-I'm-doing-this way. It contained real concern as he placed his hands on the tops of my arms and held my gaze while he made sure he hadn't upset me. It did nothing to ease the growing feeling inside—instead it put it on high alert. If I were to be quizzed on Robert's whereabouts at any point on the whole of that trip, I'd have been able to answer straight away. I was in a permanent state of awareness. Although, funnily enough, there was one moment at the Rodin Museum when I was lost in thought sketching the great bronze statue of *The Thinker*. I must have been sitting on the bench, hidden in the museum's gardens, concentrating for quite some time (it was the only piece of work I'd almost managed to complete). Being the main attraction of the museum, many people came, saw, replicated for a photo, and left— there was a constant buzz around the piece. Once I was nearly finished I looked to the person on my right (they'd been sat there for a while) and found Robert staring at me.

"Did you know you bite your lip when you're concentrating?" he asked with a frown.

"Do I?"

"You've been doing it for the last half an hour."

"You've been sat there that long?"

He nodded keenly.

"Just staring at me like a nutter?"

"Oh no, I drew you too."

"What?"

Before I had a chance to be amazed by his revelation, he turned his sketchbook round to face me. He'd opted for the "stick man" approach. The only part of me that he'd gone into any detail with was my hair—for which he'd used the color red to draw an aggressive-looking bird's nest on top of my head. The windy air was clearly doing me no favors.

"Nice," I muttered, raising my hand to smooth down my wild hair.

"Don't," he insisted as he took my hand and placed it back on my lap. "It's cute."

I raised an eyebrow at him, questioning his comment.

"I think I've captured you perfectly," he smiled proudly down at his work. "I've called it My Red-headed Thinker."

The use of the word *my* did not go unnoticed by my hammering heart.

The day Kelly chose to question me there had definitely been another moment between us as we made our way back from the Louvre.

This time I'd started it.

As we walked side by side to the hotel a silence had fallen between us. It wasn't an uncomfortable one, but nonetheless, I felt the need to fill it with something to stop my wandering thoughts. So I playfully pinched his thick blue scarf and wrapped it around my own neck. I hadn't expected it to escalate into him grappling me to the ground in the middle of the sanded pathway in the Jardin des Tuileries and me being tickled into hysteria until I handed it back.

It was more than just the two of us mucking around as normal—this time it was physical. It was feisty and intense. However, Kelly pointing it out made me feel protective over the whole thing. I didn't want to be asked about it. I wanted her to butt out.

I shook my head and rolled my eyes as I pinched in my cheeks and swept on some pink Rimmel blusher.

"Oh really," I sighed nonchalantly, hoping Kelly would get the hint that it was a topic I was bored of explaining.

"You were flirting," she continued.

"No, we weren't," I protested, my voice hitting slightly higher notes than I wanted it to.

"You were jumping all over each other."

"No. It was flipping freezing so I nicked his scarf. He was trying to grab it back off me. That's all."

"It was classic flirting."

"Kelly . . ." I flustered, shaking my head.

"I think he likes you."

"Don't be silly. He's my friend and that's all there is to it," I said matter-of-factly, trying to end the conversation there.

"Yes, I know. But you're not kids any more, Maddy. You must be able to see the way he looks at you and the fact that there's shitloads of chemistry between you."

"There really isn't," I said firmly, almost losing my patience in a way I never had on the topic.

"Right . . ." she sighed, gazing back at her reflection in the mirror. I thought she'd finally relented, but then she added, "He is so fricking hot."

"I don't see it . . ." I lied with a shrug, watching her as she expertly applied purple eyeshadow to her already dark eyes, wishing I knew how to do the same to mine. No matter how hard I tried I knew I never matched up to the other girls in the way they took care to groom themselves to perfection—perhaps it was the only downside to being friends with boys over girls. We spent our time in trackies outside, taking on new adventures, while girls experimented with makeup and learned to make the best of what was given to them. I was years behind and it showed. I'd never known what to do with my fair skin—fake tan made me look like an Oompa-Loompa, and I'd acquired far too many freckles to cover up with foundation. My red hair was the only thing I liked—it was thick and manageable, although it was usually thrown up in a ponytail to keep it off my face (even then, wispy bits always broke free and created a frizzy ring around my face—as Rob had nicely pointed out in his drawing). Why would Robert be attracted to someone boyish like me, I wondered, when he could have someone beautiful like Kelly? As soon as I heard the question bounce around the walls of my inner mind, I knew I was in more trouble than I cared to admit. Self-doubt just wasn't in my nature. Well, not over a boy anyway.

"You don't see that Robert is the fittest guy in our year? Really?" Kelly asked further, looking at me in disbelief.

"Yes, really!" I shrugged.

"Perhaps you should start looking then . . ."

I smiled at her as I picked up my mascara and unscrewed the wand.

"Because I've got to say, if you don't look, I might be forced to make him look in my direction instead," she said with a saucy wink.

All at once I started to feel nauseous.

I felt extremely awkward when I joined Robert and Ben in the lobby half an hour later. All I could think about was what Kelly had said, and the realization that I'd definitely developed ulterior feelings for my best friend. I felt irritated by how self-conscious it made me feel— for instance, I was aware of every part of myself, which made me feel like an inexperienced Bambi walking on ice as I approached them. The way Robert looked me up and down with a delirious expression on his face didn't help (it made my insides flip inside themselves), and neither did the pair of them wolf-whistling at me as I approached.

"Cut it out," I hissed, giving them both a firm shove on the shoulder.

Yes, being with Kelly had prompted me to make a bit more effort than usual—I was wearing more blusher and eyeshadow than my mum would have liked, along with an emerald mini-dress, tights, and heels—Kelly's heels, not mine. I'd felt good as I left my room, sexy and mature, but now their gaze was on me I felt silly and exposed.

"What? You look hot," laughed Ben, smiling at me as he took my hand and gave me his usual comforting three squeezes.

"Ouch," said Robert as he cheekily rubbed the opposite shoulder to the one I'd pushed, giving me a smirk. He was always trying to treat me like a feeble girl, simply because he knew it wound me up. Or was he flirting, I wondered. And, if so, had he always been?

"I'll do it harder if you like," I warned, perhaps with a bit more gusto than I'd meant.

"Promise?"

I couldn't fail to spot the glisten in his eye as he raised an eyebrow at me, tilted his head ever so slightly, and licked his lips as they formed a smile. The action had me transfixed and I literally had to pinch myself to pull myself away from the magnetic force of his whole being. It was more than him being his usual cocky and suggestive self, and that knowledge caused a rush of excitement to whizz through my body. I could feel my cheeks beginning to blush at the unexpected sensation.

As I turned away from them both and busied myself with putting my gloves on, I cursed Kelly for putting the thoughts I'd been grappling with into the forefront of my mind. Pull yourself together, I told myself, you do not fancy Robert and he certainly does not fancy you . . . you silly, silly girl.

Well, there's nothing like trying to fool yourself into believing something that's a blatant lie.

We were taken to La Ferme des Beauvais—a little Parisian restaurant on the corner of one of the side streets north of the Louvre. Windows covered the breadth of the external walls, displaying its name in silver-framed red lettering that curved like a rainbow on each pane of glass. Inside, the wooden tables were lined in rows to make the most of the limited space and covered with red cloth, tealights and a single red rose on each one. On the walls were photographs of Paris taken throughout the years, all in black and white. There was no doubt it was a cheap place to eat, we were on a school trip after all, but it was these little touches that helped make the place more atmospheric and inviting.

The majority of the group opted to eat pasta on our final night, as we had most nights. It was always the safest option—although it was washed down with pieces of French bread, so it did at least have something traditionally French about it.

As our feast was being gobbled up, Kelly turned to Miss James, who was in deep conversation with Miss Stokes, another teacher. We'd never been taught by her before and she'd been very quiet the whole trip—we'd almost forgotten she was there.

"Miss James," Kelly called from beside me.

"Yes?" she shouted back.

"Seeing as we're in France and we've been good all week, can we have a glass of wine each?" she tried with a cheeky shrug.

Miss James cackled at the request.

"Come on," pushed Robert, hoping his charm would help win her over. "We're eating anyway, it's not like we're going to get drunk. It'll just wash it down nicely."

"Nice try," she smiled. "As lovely and good as you all are there's no way I'm letting any of you drink alcohol."

"You're having some," stated Kelly.

"I'm an adult."

"Oh, go on," she pleaded.

"I'm afraid there'll be no underage drinking on my watch," she finished, turning back to the conversation that had been interrupted.

"That's what she thinks," Kelly whispered, winking at Robert before slinking off to the toilet. When she came back she discreetly pulled a bottle of vodka out from underneath her jumper.

"Where'd you get that?" I squeaked in shock.

Ben's eyes, like my own, widened with surprise. Robert looked impressed—something that didn't go unnoticed by me.

"Never you mind," she laughed, before winking over at one of the waiters at the bar. "Pass us your glasses." As we did so, she quickly added the alcohol into our Cokes before carefully passing the bottle along to the next table. "There's more where that came from too . . ." she teased with a wicked smirk.

I was never one to break the rules, not really, but on that occasion, as I watched Kelly, Ben, and Robert grin at each other as they picked up their glasses and gulped away, I certainly didn't want to be the only person not involved. After just a few mouthfuls the worry I'd been feeling earlier that evening started to slide away, leaving me to feel giddily free and naughty—a feeling that was increased when I lowered my glass to find Robert winking at me. God, I fancy you, I thought, with such clarity that I stunned myself.

Once dinner was finished the tables were cleared away, and cheesy pop songs started blaring from the restaurant speakers, replacing the sounds of Edith Piaf that we'd endured throughout dinner. Miss James had organized a surprise mini disco for us to round off what had already been an amazing trip. None of us needed any encouragement to dance (probably thanks to a certain tipple lubricating our inhibitions), we were up on our feet as soon as the first intro started. Thankfully we were the only diners in the dimly lit restaurant, so we didn't have to worry about us teenagers upsetting anyone with our dizzy behavior. We could just be carelessly joyful and silly as we danced along to the nineties classics being played. Hits by artists like Sugar Ray, Madonna, and No Doubt boomed through the room, putting us on even more of a high. Robert, Ben, and I were pulling the craziest moves we could muster, singing raucously and making each other laugh hysterically. It felt incredibly liberating.

At some point toward the end of the night, Hanson's "Mmmbop" started blaring out of the speakers, putting us all into more of a childish frenzy. We jumped around, making even sillier shapes with our bodies, waving our hands in the air, and shaking our heads to the music. We might not have looked cool, but it was so much fun we didn't care.

"I'm just off to the loo!" Ben shouted at us as he hopped his way through the excited group, continuing with his wacky moves as he went.

As we carried on singing along to the music, Robert grabbed my hand and thrust it up in the air, gesturing for me to spin under it. I did so. He then threw me around, spinning and twirling, several times with dizzying speed, causing me to get light-headed. I ended up laughing manically as I fell into his chest to steady myself.

As the song came to an end and the next song started playing, the mood suddenly changed.

The familiar piano intro to K-Ci and JoJo's "All My Life" filled the air, replacing the childlike mood with an intense one, laden with sentiment and emotion . . . and a whole heap of sexual tension.

As my head was already on his chest and my body close to his, Robert gently placed a hand on my lower back, holding me securely into him, before picking up my hand and cradling it in his. With his head bowed, he rested his cheek on the side of my head.

I closed my eyes and savored every detail of the delicious moment.

I could feel his heart pumping through his chest.

I could feel his hot breath in my ear.

I was aware of every single movement and spasm that our bodies were involuntarily making as we swayed to the music—his hand as it slowly moved across my back, his thumb as it rubbed up and down mine, and the fact that I'd almost stopped breathing.

Understandably, we were nervous. We'd never been this close before. This intimate. I willed it to continue—I didn't want Robert to change his mind and stop. My whole body was in a state of suspense, waiting for him to make the next move—it had to come from him, there was no way I could have instigated anything. I had to know I hadn't been stupidly making up the whole thing in my head.

He lowered his head further. With my eyes closed, I could feel the corner of his mouth rest at the side of my face. He stayed there for a few seconds before slowly sliding further down my cheek, his lips causing my body to tingle as they tantalizingly brushed my skin. I knew what was coming and I held my breath, waiting for it to happen. Willing it to.

He kissed me.

Actually kissed me.

Robert's big juicy lips were on mine, as his hands roamed up and down my back, and in that moment I completely melted. I devoured the new sensations of heat and electricity running between us both, knowing there was nowhere else I'd rather be.

Okay, I told myself, you're right—you do fancy Robert. But, not only that—it would seem that he flipping well fancies you too.

Ben

I stood frozen in the middle of the crowd as I watched the tender moment between my two best friends. My heart ached as it understood its significance and a feeling of sadness swelled through me. I felt lost—unsure of what to do with myself. Should I have gone over and made a joke of their locking lips, ruining whatever magic was passing between them? Should I have retreated back to the loos and come back out a bit later, pretending I hadn't seen anything? Well, that's what I wanted to do, but before I had a chance to do anything the song was over, they'd pulled apart and noticed me—both of them looking at me with great big grins on their faces, insanely happy with themselves.

I had no choice but to grab the nearest girl to me, who just happened to be Maddy's roommate on that trip, Kelly, and give her a quick snog. It was horrible and sloppy, we even banged teeth in my haste, but at least I didn't have to look at their elated faces, I thought. At least I didn't have to talk to them.

It had been the last song of the night and as soon as it was over Miss James was ushering people to get their coats on and head outside. I managed to keep my distance from Maddy and Robert by diving in, getting my stuff, and walking outside before they'd even moved from their romantic spot in the middle of the makeshift dance floor.

I trailed behind at the back of the group as we walked to the hotel, aware of the irritatingly joyous chatter going on in front of me. Everyone was talking animatedly about how much fun the night had been and how wonderful they'd found the whole trip—I didn't give a flying crap. I would have given anything to be able to teleport home and get far away from Paris and every single one of them.

Even though there were at least sixteen people between us, I could see that my two best friends were still holding hands. I was so inexplicably angry; angry at them for kissing, angry at them for thinking it was all jolly and fun and that there wouldn't be any consequences, angry at Robert for kissing Maddy when he could have picked any other girl at school—but most of all I felt sorry for myself, because I'd missed out. My hopes and desires for that trip came tumbling down around me. I'd been a mere twelve hours or less from standing at the top of the Eiffel Tower and telling Maddy how I felt, but I'd been beaten to it. Accusing questions formed in my head as I started to beat myself up over my mammoth disappointment. Why did I think I needed some romantic gesture or setting to go along with my declaration of love? Why didn't I just tell her months earlier when I first thought of doing so? Why did I allow time to get in the way and steal her from me?

It quickly dawned on me that I'd lost her. Either way, whether things continued between Maddy and Robert or not, there'd be no chance for us. Maddy, the girl who glittered beautifully, who carried an indescribable magic in her very being, would never be in my grasp. I was heartbroken.

When we got to the hotel I scampered off to our room with great speed, but not before I painfully caught a glimpse of Robert and Maddy kissing once more as they said goodnight.

I got to our room, stripped off, and got straight into bed, trying to hide myself in the hope that Robert wouldn't want to talk when he came in. I was wrong, of course. Even though I was feigning sleep he sauntered in and started talking loudly as soon as he walked through the door.

"There you are," he said, standing in the middle of the room with the biggest grin on his face. "What a night that was."

"Yeah," I muttered, pretending to be half asleep.

"I tell you what, I wasn't expecting that to happen when we went out tonight. I mean, it's Maddy! Maddy!" he practically squealed, puffing air from his cheeks as he mulled it over. "Maddy and me! Who'd have thought."

Not me, that's for sure. Well, I had, but I'd been talked out of thinking such paranoid thoughts. How ironic.

"Why did you say you didn't like her in that way?"

I was annoyed with myself as soon as I'd said it. Not only had I dropped the whole tired guise, I'd also asked him a question, prompting him to talk about the whole thing further. I'd given him the encouragement he'd needed to cheerily talk his head off about it.

"Mate, I wasn't sure how I felt. Until I could understand it myself, I thought I'd best stay quiet about the whole thing," he exclaimed, coming over and sitting on the edge of my bed, happiness irritatingly radiating all around him. "I don't even know what happened tonight—we were just dancing stupidly, you were there, you saw that. And then, that song came on and it got really . . . I dunno, heated. Seriously, it was weird. I had this urge. Well, actually, I've had that urge for a while, but tonight—I couldn't stop myself," he shrugged in amazement as bewilderment flickered across his face.

I wondered whether he was already replaying the little moments between them—the gazes, the feel of her lips on his, her taste. The very thought crushed me.

"I know she's our best friend and all that, but, my God, Ben! I mean, it was electric. *She* is electric. How on earth have we not noticed that before?"

His face had become dopey, full of surprise and wonder at the night's events. I'd never seen him like that. The more I looked at him, the sadder I felt. It seemed I wasn't the only one who'd fallen for Maddy's charms.

I'd had years to make some sort of sense of my overwhelming

feelings so that I could tell her exactly how I felt, but I hadn't. I'd hesitated and allowed life to get in the way—because of that I knew I had no right to be angry with either of them. They didn't know that she was my world. That I'd loved her since the day she walked into class with her manic bob and cute red nose. I was a coward for keeping those feelings to myself and foolish for not realizing that I had to act on them sooner. I was gutted for myself that Robert's confidence had led him where I desperately wanted to be—with Maddy.

I didn't sleep that night. Instead, I repeated their embrace in my mind again and again, as though it was some kind of mystery that needed to be solved. When I left them they were busting their stupidest dance moves to a bloody Hanson track and then—one pee stop later, that had changed into a lovers' clinch. It didn't make sense to me.

Confusion whizzed around in my brain as I tried to process how it had all happened and what would happen next. I dreaded them becoming an official item, I wasn't sure how I'd cope seeing what I saw that night all day, every day. It was like I was trapped in some sort of nightmare. I wanted it to stop. I longed to wake up.

My only flutter of relief came when it dawned on me that if Robert was what Maddy was after, then I'd have had no chance anyway. In fact, the timing had done me a favor and saved me from a bitterly embarrassing situation. Like I said, it was only a "flutter" of relief. It didn't make it hurt any less.

Maddy

I was deliriously giddy and couldn't remove the smirk from my face as I kissed Robert goodnight. I hadn't wanted to leave him, I could have easily stood in the hotel lobby and kissed him all night long, but Miss James wouldn't have allowed it. Instead she sent us off in separate directions to our rooms, much to our dismay.

"So you don't fancy Robert, then?" laughed Kelly, as we walked away from him and headed up to our room.

"No, definitely not," I giggled, suddenly feeling like the biggest girl in the world as a strange feeling danced around in my tummy. Yes, you guessed it, butterflies. Robert Miles—my best friend of seven years, had given me butterflies. I loved the sensation.

"Can you believe you kissed him?"

"I really can't," I said, shaking my head at the madness of it all.

"Did it feel weird? Was it anything like kissing a brother?" she asked with a perplexed look. "That's the one thing I was worried about with you guys."

"Definitely not brotherly, no."

"Good! That could've been really awkward."

"You know what, it just felt right. We fit together."

"You lucky bitch," she howled.

I didn't even bother trying to sleep that night—I couldn't, someone had to stay awake and keep an eye on the grin that had exploded onto my face and refused to leave. Instead I spent the night looking at the ceiling, thinking of Robert. I wondered what thoughts were in his head at that moment, whether, like me, he was feeling lightheaded from it all, or whether he'd regretted it as soon as he'd left me. I was sure it wouldn't have been the latter, not so soon afterward anyway. The whole thing had been too delicious to think negatively on.

Ben

Dread filled me as I woke up on the last morning in Paris and realized we were still going to be taking a group trip to the Eiffel Tower. It was the last place I wanted to go—I didn't want to be anywhere near it. It was hard enough knowing that my plan had failed, I couldn't have faced Robert and Maddy canoodling up there in front of me and soaking up all the romance I thought would be there for me.

It seemed, for once, my prayers were answered.

As soon as our suitcases were packed and closed there was a knock on the door from Miss James, coming to tell us that due to torrential rain, she thought it best if we canceled our Eiffel Tower trip, although she did promise to get the bus to drive right by it so that we could take some snaps.

I didn't grumble or moan.

I was relieved.

Due to Maddy and Robert being busy sucking each other's faces off as they said good morning, I was put in charge of getting us the back row of the coach on the way home. I purposefully failed to get it, which thankfully meant we had to sit apart. I managed to smile at them both as I suggested they sit together, telling them I was knackered and would probably sleep the whole way anyway. They agreed and found a spot toward the back of the bus, obviously away from Miss James in case they wanted to continue to lock lips. Deciding to go toward the front of the bus, I sat facing the window, glumly watching the world pass me by.

I didn't look when Miss James announced we were approaching the Eiffel Tower, with the warning to get our cameras out . . . I closed my eyes and tried my best to ignore the gasps of admiration coming from everyone else around me.

It was remarkable how differently I felt about the place within the space of just a few hours. Before that trip it had been the iconic objectification of love, as it was and is to millions of people around the world, but on that cold, wet, and miserable morning, it became the symbol of devastation and despair—a representation of a lost love, of a squandered hope.

I couldn't bear to be so close as it highlighted my failure and mocked me callously.

I was ready to pretend the whole thing hadn't happened. I was hoping (rather foolishly) that Maddy and Robert would denounce it as some crazy holiday fling spurred on by the romantic setting, which they'd come to regret once we were home. But it didn't happen.

The following Monday, when Maddy knocked for me on the way to school, I noticed there was something different about her. I couldn't quite pinpoint it at first, I just noticed she looked glossier and more glammed up. Turns out she was wearing more makeup than usual. Not loads, the school would never have allowed that, but her cheeks were rosier from blusher, her lips were smoother from balm and, to complete her look, her hair was perfectly placed, gliding over her shoulders in silky auburn waves.

"You look nice," I offered.

She looked at the ground coyly, unable to stop a smile from forming.

It was for Robert, I realized with sickening clarity.

As we walked together in silence I could tell she was nervous about seeing him. Unless they'd met up without telling me, that morning was their first encounter following their Parisian love affair. I loathed having to be there for it, and wished I could have had the foresight to pull a sicky that day instead.

Once we knocked for him, they held hands straight away, confirming their couple status as Maddy bashfully smiled in my direction. I had no choice but to smile brightly back at her, like some crazily overenthusiastic kid's entertainer, before we silently continued our journey.

Once at school it was impossible to avoid the situation; even if they weren't with me, it was all anybody wanted to talk about. Those who were in Paris wanted to share what they'd seen like it was some modern-day mythical tale, and those who weren't wanted to know all about it—drinking up the details with surprise and awe as though it was the most romantic thing they'd ever heard.

Unsurprisingly, when I was with them it was worse. Walking around the school you could hear the whisperings of gossip as we passed—that and the sound of teenage hearts being crushed as they realized their heartthrob, Robert Miles, was off the market.

As soon as I walked through my front door that night, my mum was there, quizzing me about what had happened in Paris. She didn't even give me time to take my school shoes off before words excitedly flew from her mouth.

"Oi, you! Why didn't you tell me about Robert and Maddy?" she demanded. "Her mum called today and was saying how Maddy's been nonstop talking about him since she got back—Carol said that Robert's been the same!"

"Oh, I just . . ." I started with a shrug, leaning down under the pretense of undoing my shoelaces, but actually trying to hide my face, unable to keep up the cheery façade any longer. I had to let the smile that had been frozen to my cheeks all day drop. I was exhausted.

"Who'd have thought it. I mean, I didn't see it coming. I expect they look cute together, though . . ."

I burst out crying then, failed to hold it back any longer. Sobbed into my worn-out leather shoes as my mum awkwardly hugged me from above, letting every ounce of emotion I'd held inside me since their first kiss, the regret and sorrow, spill its way out of me. I couldn't remember ever crying in that way before; even when my dad upped and left, it wasn't as bad as that. It was like I'd lost all control.

Mum said nothing for a good five minutes. It must have shocked her to see her teenage son in such a fragile state, so different from the jovial, carefree child she thought of me as. She just held me tightly into her skinny body, rocking me from side to side, shushing me whenever a fresh sob bubbled out of me. How ridiculous.

"Sorry, Mum . . ." I mumbled, slowly uncurling myself, leaning against the hallway wall for support.

"Don't be daft. Want to talk about it?" she asked, gently rubbing my arm.

"It's nothing. It's just . . ." I sighed as fresh tears sprang to my eyes, the loss of restraint irritating me. "I'm such a dick."

"Oi!" she reprimanded, gently slapping me on the arm.

"Sorry," I mumbled.

"I get it, Benny," she said, placing her hand under my chin and raising my face so that I was looking at her. "You guys have been friends since you were little—three peas in a pod. You're worried that if them two get together you'll be left out. Or, if things go pear-shaped, like they did with me and your dad, that you might lose one of them."

I hadn't even thought of it like that, but I didn't want to tell Mum the truth. I didn't want to tell her that the possible love of my life had kissed our mutual best friend, and that because they had kissed it meant I was unlikely to have my own chance with her.

"It'll be okay, darling. You'll see."

"Will it, though?"

"Ben, sometimes life chucks these things in your way and you just have to go for it. No questions asked."

"Isn't that what Dad did? Act on his feelings and not give a toss about us?"

"Robert and Maddy aren't your dad," she said calmly, not showing any sign that my words had hurt her, but that was Mum all over. She was, hands down, the strongest woman I'd ever known. She didn't crumble when the love of her life walked out on her, she just got on with it. It's only growing up that I realized she wasn't really left with any other choice, she couldn't give up—she had me to look after. "They're two young people, without any baggage, who've discovered they like each other," she continued. "Do you realize how brave it is of those two to do this?"

I looked down at the red rug on the floor, concentrating on the loose bits of fabric the cat had scratched up, willing the conversation to end so that I could go up to my room and sulk.

"What they really need from you right now is your support, Ben," she sighed. "They don't need you going all weird and making things harder."

"I wouldn't do that . . ."

"I know, I know," she said, grabbing my hand. "Just never doubt their love for you, because that'll never change."

I nodded my head and gave Mum a little smile. What else could I have done?

"You're coming with us tonight, right?" asked Robert later on that week at lunch.

We were stood in the school corridor in a raucous queue outside the canteen, waiting for Maddy to join us after her food tech class.

A group trip to the cinema had been planned for weeks. *Bridget Jones: The Edge of Reason* had just been released and Maddy was adamant that we all go and embrace our feminine sides with a girlie film, insisting it was payback for us always making her watch countless action and sci-fi films. Before Paris I was quite looking forward to it, but now, the idea of watching a rom-com with the new lovebirds made me feel queasy.

"Er . . ."

"You could bring Kelly?" he smirked, giving me a wink.

"Naaaah . . ."

"She really likes you."

"She's not my type," I replied dismissively, looking ahead at the queue, willing it to go faster.

"Didn't look that way in Paris . . . it could be a double date."

"Look, if you guys want to go on your own I'll totally understand," I offered, the words, "double date" ringing in my ears as visions of them smooching the whole way through the film filled my brain. If that evening's trip turned into being Robert and Maddy's first ever date then that was the last place I wanted to be, especially as we'd be watching a rom-com—proper date material.

"Don't be daft."

"Well, it's going to happen at some point—I can't be with you every single time you're alone together. I'll be a proper gooseberry."

"What are you two talking about?" asked Maddy, as she arrived and squeezed in between us.

"Tonight and the cinema," informed Robert, raising his eyebrows before pulling her into him and planting a kiss on her forehead.

"Ooh, have you asked him about Kelly?" she said with a grin on her face as she looked from Robert to me.

"Nothing's happening with Kelly," I said, irritated that the pair of them had clearly talked and decided to couple me off with someone.

"Why not? She's nice."

"She's not his type apparently—and, he was just about to bail on us."

"What? No way! You're coming!" she demanded.

"But—"

"I've been waiting for months to see this and haven't once moaned when you two have dragged me along to your boy films."

"It's a chick flick . . ." I protested.

"And?"

"And you guys are on a date."

"Do you want to sit in the middle?" she offered.

"Erm . . ." started Robert, a frown forming on his face at the very thought of it.

"No!"

"Because you can . . . if you want to."

"I don't want to."

"That's a relief," laughed Robert.

Maddy rolled her eyes at him, before smiling at me.

"Ben, tonight is not a date."

"It is," tried Robert.

"It's not," she repeated, shooting a warning look in his direction. "It's us three going to the cinema together as usual. Okay?"

"Fine," I said, caving in. There was no way I could get out of the night without upsetting her and, despite my urge to get out of it, I didn't want to do that.

"But, it still could be a date," smirked Robert. "If you brought Kelly . . . please bring Kelly!"

"Leave him alone," laughed Maddy, looping her arm through mine as we made our way into the canteen.

Maddy

Robert wasn't my first ever boyfriend (how I wish I could forget my brief, yet embarrassing, relationship with John Martin), but I instantly knew that he was going to be my first *proper* boyfriend. That we would be together for a long time, that he'd be the first boy I'd ever say "I love you" to and that our being a couple would have a huge effect on both our lives. I think knowing that was what had made me so aroused by the whole thing.

The night we got back from Paris, I was up in my room reliving the previous night, dreamily hugging my pillow, unable to wipe the smile from my face yet again. I'd only been home about ten minutes or so when Dad shouted up the stairs that Robert was on the phone.

I sprinted down the stairs.

"Hey . . ." he purred when I picked up.

"Hey, you," I said back as I curled myself into the corner of the hallway floor and coyly fiddled with the telephone cord, grinning to myself with giddiness.

"I can't stop thinking about you."

"You only saw me ten minutes ago," I laughed, relieved that I wasn't alone in my thoughts.

We hadn't really talked on the coach coming home, we were both shattered from our busy week and all the excitement on our last night.

Instead I'd tucked myself into Robert's toned chest (yes, what a delicious treat), and we'd both slept most of the way. Okay, there was some more kissing too . . . but my point is there was not a lot of talking.

"I miss you."

"Already?"

"Yep."

"I'm sorry, who is this? What have you done to Robert?"

A gentle laugh came from the other end of the line, making a smile spring to my cheeks.

It's surprising how content you can feel, even in a silence, and there was a lot of silence on that first phone call as a new sense of shyness fell over us both.

Eventually Robert attempted to get to the root of why he'd phoned, "I was calling because . . . I don't want you to feel like you're just . . . I dunno . . . just another girl . . . because, you know . . . you're not like anyone else," he sighed. "You know I think the world of you. I really like you . . ."

"Robert?"

"Yes?"

"What are you trying to say?"

"Do you want to be my girlfriend?" he blurted.

I cackled into the phone.

"You're not meant to laugh!"

"But it's you—you asking me that! Robert who's known me forever, one of my best mates!"

"And?"

"It's weird."

"Bad weird?"

"No!"

"What then?"

"What if it all goes wrong?"

"It won't."

"How do you know that?"

"Because I won't let it," he said quietly.

I smiled into the phone.

From the tone of his voice I could tell he was smiling too when he asked again, "So, will you be my girlfriend?"

How could I possibly refuse?

After years of poking fun at the hoards of girls who swooned at Robert's charms, I'd found myself giving up the fight and joining in. I was swooning, swooning bad! It was quite unsettling.

And so, as a result of that conversation and us becoming an official item, I knew the cinema trip had turned into our first date for Robert. At first I wanted it to be too, if I'm honest, but I was aware Ben was meant to be coming with us and that we couldn't just ditch him or make him feel unwanted because we'd hooked up. I also knew about his little breakdown—mums talk, after all. June phoned my mum the next day, unsure of what to do—it can't have been easy seeing her happy-go-lucky son crumble like that. I felt bad knowing about it, especially as I knew Ben would hate that I knew, but at least it meant I could try my best to make sure Ben wasn't feeling left out or made to feel uncomfortable. I didn't want him to feel like everything was changing. Our friendship group was always going to be the most important thing for me, and I didn't want him questioning that.

I knew Robert would understand why we had to tread carefully, but I decided not to tell him about Ben's breakdown. Perhaps I should have done, then they could have had some awkward lad conversation and talked it all through, but I thought it would be cruel to talk about him behind his back. I just hoped I could balance everything enough to keep them both happy.

Obviously, that night in the cinema was a bit tricky to start with, but I wasn't sure if that was because I kept looking for signs that Ben was uncomfortable. I thought he was at first—as he stood alongside us, waiting to buy tickets, he fixed his gaze on the surrounding posters of future films with an overly keen interest. I was sure he was doing it to avoid having to interact with us, but I couldn't be sure.

I might have been trying to play it cool, but Robert clearly wanted us to act like a couple; he was extremely touchy-feely. He barely let go of me, continuously placing a hand around my waist or taking my hand in his. It was difficult, I didn't want to just brush him off and leave him feeling rejected, that would have been a crap start to our relationship, but I didn't want the whole thing to be thrust in Ben's face either. I wanted it to feel normal.

"I'll get yours," Robert said as we got to the counter.

"Oh . . ."

"Thanks," joked Ben, managing a smile.

"Nice try."

"You don't have to get mine," I argued, putting my hand over the ten-pound note he was holding out to the cashier.

"Er, yeah I do," he said, gently pushing my hand away. "That's what boyfriends do. Get used to it."

I looked up at Ben and gave him a meek smile, which he winked back at before pulling out a fiver to pay for his own ticket.

The wink took me by surprise, it was confident and reassuring. After that he seemed to relax a little, although I wasn't entirely sure why. Despite his initial outburst to his mum, it seemed as though Ben was feeling calmer about the whole situation. He even managed to joke around with us when we were eventually sat in our seats, saying things like, "I can hear you," when we were kissing, and, "You promised it wasn't a date," which obviously killed the moment as it made us laugh, but I was thankful for the humor.

It was gorgeous being there with Robert, holding hands and kissing (when we could). I felt ridiculously comfortable and happy sat next to him, loving the new feelings passing between us and the warmth radiating from his body.

There was one awkward moment, though, which happened during the film—annoyingly, it could have easily been avoided if it wasn't for our teenage lust. Needless to say, things heated up between us in that darkened cinema room, which resulted in Robert and me getting a little carried away. We'd completely given up watching the film—exploring each other's mouths was far more in-teresting, as was Robert stroking my skin and his hand working its way up my top.

I'd wrongly assumed that Ben was preoccupied with the action onscreen.

He wasn't.

Our groping did not go unnoticed. Instead, rather embarrassingly, Ben leaned over and asked for the popcorn just as Robert's hand had finally cupped hold of my boob. Rob flapped around for a few sec-onds trying to free his hand (which had become trapped under my bra), before handing over the snack with a shameful look on his face.

I almost died on the spot. It was like being caught by my mum.

We were all sitting in my lounge the following day, watching *Friends* on repeat. The weather had turned bitterly cold, and none of us could be bothered to walk to the High Street. Instead, we set up camp in our comfies and splayed our homework around us, languidly mak-ing our way through it. Both boys were on the sofa, while I was on the floor cutting out pictures of different types of bread for my food-tech coursework, with little effort or thought put into it.

"I think I'm going to ask Kelly if she wants to go out with us all," said Ben coyly, as he wrote in his notepad.

"Really?" I squealed.

"Yeah."

"You mean on like a double date?" smirked Robert.

"Why not," Ben shrugged, still not looking at either of us.

"I knew you liked her," I said, pointing the tips of my scissors in his direction. "I can sense these things."

"You're just like Cilla Black," mocked Robert, grinning at me.

"Maybe we could go ice-skating or something?" I said, ignoring him. "We could go tomorrow?"

"Let's not rush things!" he said worriedly, looking up at me. "I'll have a chat with her on Monday and see if she wants to plan something for next weekend, yeah?"

"Spoilsport," I jokily pouted.

"She might not even want to!"

Bless him, I thought, he'd clearly not pursued things with her because he was worried about being rejected. I'd assumed that was what had stopped him from asking her to the cinema with us, and possibly part of his meltdown—Ben wasn't the most confident person when it came to the opposite sex.

"Oh . . . she'll want to," I said, grinning at him.

Kelly might have boldly told me on our last night away that she thought Robert was fit, but, as a result of Ben pouncing on her, she'd quickly switched the target of her affections. As soon as we got back to school on the Monday she was asking questions about him; what he was like, whether he'd mentioned their kiss, or whether I thought he liked her, etc. I knew he'd have no trouble getting her to go out with him, although the thought of them together petrified me—Ben was sure to be eaten alive by the foxy minx.

The upshot? Me and Robert would be free to go on an actual date without feeling awkward.

Ben

I had seen Robert's hand up Maddy's top in the cinema. In fact, I was ridiculously aware of every single movement the pair made; when they started to hold hands, when their legs entwined, when they first kissed—the film hadn't even started by that point; his tongue was down her throat before the lights had gone down. I couldn't help but stare at them in my peripheral vision. A couple of times I purposefully asked for the popcorn bucket, or interjected with some little remark, but that was only to gently remind them that I was there—and that they had promised it wasn't a date. The breast-touching hand beside me, though, suggested differently. God knows what happened to Bridget and that Mr. Darcy bloke, I wasn't paying the slightest bit of attention to what was going down on the massive screen in front of me. I was far too distracted.

Earlier on in the night I could tell she was panicking, she kept staring at me with this worried expression, paying close attention to my every move—I guessed my mum had spoken to hers about my tearful outburst. I knew that I had to man up. I had to put her mind at rest, otherwise I'd crack up under such scrutiny. Even though it killed me inside, I had to put on a brave face and act like I wasn't bothered by the changes going on.

The whole thing was a bit of a nightmare for me, and that was

why I agreed to ask Kelly out. At least it would keep my mind occupied when we were all out together and stop me from feeling like
the world's biggest pervert because, disturbingly, when I saw his hand
up there, the first thought that went through my head was, "I wonder what that feels like." My hand tingled as I contemplated it and a
hotness rushed through me, causing a stirring down below. Yes, the
first time I'd got an erection from thinking of Maddy in a sexual way
was when she was being fondled by my best friend. Up until then
my feelings had been mostly innocent. I couldn't be thinking thoughts
like that!

Inviting Kelly along seemed the most sensible thing to do, but as
Monday loomed and I realized I was going to have to approach her,
I couldn't help but feel queasy. I was such a wimp. It was ridiculous.
It didn't help that Robert and Maddy kept pulling faces at me the
whole way through our art class, gesturing for me to go over to her.
I never performed well under pressure. Still don't.

I seized the opportunity to have a quiet word with her when she
was over by the sink washing her brushes. I picked up one of mine
and casually strolled over.

"Hi, Kelly . . ." I smiled, as I stood alongside her, running my
brush underneath the warm flowing tap.

As she looked up and saw it was me, I noticed her deep red lips
push out into a pout. Kelly was one of the hot chicks in our year,
and she knew it. There was something about her that was danger-
ously sexy—she was wild and carefree, something her untamed long
hair and dark eyes helped to amplify.

It was at that point, while I was lingering next to her at the tap,
that I remembered our teeth bashing when I'd pulled her in for a snog
in Paris. I couldn't help but shrink into myself as I internally cringed
with embarrassment.

"Maddy and Robert, huh? What a shocker . . ." she laughed, blowing a loose strand of black hair out of her face.

"Tell me about it."

Kelly picked up a cloth and started to dry her clean brushes. I kept mine underneath the tap, thinking of different ways to approach the subject.

"You know, if you want," she started, releasing her words slowly as she gazed at me with her smoldering eyes. "I could always hang with you guys. I'd hate to see you feel left out when they're smooching each other's faces off."

I laughed in relief at not having to ask, she'd simply offered it.

"We can't let them have all the fun . . . can we?" she whispered wickedly as she leaned forward and took the brush from my hands in what can only be described as a suggestive manner—circling her fingers loosely around the end closest to me and slowly skimming her hold along the shaft before gripping completely at the end and pulling it off me. It was practically pornographic to my teenage mind.

And that was the start of my fling with Kelly.

I'm not going to say that I ever loved her in the same way I loved Maddy, I really didn't, but she moved me in a very different way. She excited me and kept me guessing. She awoke something new in me—the desire for physical connection. I hadn't really realized its significance until she came along.

Put frankly, she made me fucking horny.

I tried to bury my head in the sand, or, more accurately, in Kelly's massive tits, when it came to Maddy and Robert. It had been difficult to watch them get together in the first instance, but it was far worse watching them fall in love. That hurt more than anything. Every day they stayed together affirmed the notion that I'd never have a chance with Maddy. She would never be mine, never know how much I loved her. I wished I'd been brave enough to tell her my feelings before we'd gone to Paris. I wished I'd told her after telling her Anthony and John thought she was fit, or when her dad queried whether I was gay or not . . . or at that childish wedding back at primary school when I'd only had the guts to tell her with those three desperate squeezes that I constantly used throughout our childhood, hoping one day she'd suddenly hear me and understand their meaning. I was a coward and I hated myself for being that way.

Maddy

From the moment Robert and I kissed in Paris I knew I'd lose my virginity to him. I wasn't sure when it would occur—in a week's time, a month's time, six months, a year—I just knew it was going to happen. It was a thrillingly scary thought.

We'd talk about it, a lot. Of course we did. What teenage couple didn't talk about the possibility of having sex? But one thing Robert was brilliant at was reassuring me. He was in no rush to lose his V-card (it's what the cool kids were calling it), and neither was I. That was until he told me he loved me . . . from that point on I just wanted to do it more than anything. There was a desire that surged through me, threatening to cause an almighty explosion if something wasn't done sharpish.

It ended up happening over the Christmas holidays, just a month after we got back from Paris—yes, I'm aware that it would have been nice to wait a little longer, but there was no stopping our lascivious behavior once the cogs were in motion. Plus, we'd known each other since we were nine years old—we trusted each other unconditionally. So many qualities you'd hope to build in a new relationship already existed between us. I didn't feel the need to wait any longer.

It happened on a Tuesday.

Our parents were at work.

Ben had taken himself off somewhere for the day—I've no idea if this had been planned between the two boys, or if he'd arranged it himself not knowing what we were about to get up to.

I spent the morning making myself look and feel wonderful. I shaved my legs, armpits, and everywhere else I thought shouldn't have been displaying hair, put on some simple, but matching black underwear (it's not as though I had anything lacy or provocative at that age—my mum would have killed me), some makeup, a pair of black trousers, vest top and a red cropped jumper, and tidied my hair back in a pretty, loose fishtail plait. I hoped I looked effortlessly cozy and gorgeous—like the girl next door that all boys seem to want to sleep with.

On the short walk to his house I started to worry. What if I wasn't very good at it, I wondered. What if I was so bad Robert decided he never wanted to do it with me again?

My heart was beating so fast by the time Rob opened his front door—but one tiny smile from him brought back all the desire I'd experienced in the lead up; it was all the reassurance I needed. I was nervous, more nervous than I'd ever been about anything, but I knew it was what I wanted.

Robert took me by the hand and guided me over the threshold. As soon as the door was shut he cupped my face in his hands and kissed me, slowly and with such a pensive look on his face—I realized it wasn't just me who was nervous.

"Should we go upstairs?" I heard myself squeak.

He just nodded, took my hand, and led me to his room in silence.

Once we were in his blue box of a room with the door shut, he exhaled sharply and drew me into him for a hug—a tight, loving embrace. I felt it was to comfort not just me, but himself. All the cheekiness and cocky behavior Robert possessed was just a façade to win others over, I knew that, but it was still a surprise to see that front completely dropped—to have the vulnerable part of Robert stood in front of me feeling, perhaps, that he didn't want to be the leader for once. He needed to make sure it was what I wanted. That it was right.

Still held in his clasp, I took his fingers in mine and brought them to my lips, kissing each of them individually in what I hoped was a tantalizing manner, as I looked into Robert's eyes intently. They questioned me, asked if I was sure. In response I backed on to the bed away from him, before reaching my hand out and beckoning him over.

He didn't come. Instead he put his hands on his hips and stared at me in his newfound shy manner.

"Should I put some music on?" he mumbled, before turning to his stereo and playing with some buttons until he finally settled on a radio station playing cheesy love songs.

"Sounds good," I encouraged, willing him to stop acting so weird.

"Let me just shut the curtains . . ." he faffed, going over to the window. "There . . ." he declared once they were closed and the room was a little dimmer.

As soon as he was next to me on the bed, our lips about to kiss, something else popped into his brain and he was back on his feet once more.

"Candles. Shit, I forgot I bought candles," he said urgently, before practically falling from the bed in a clumsy manner as he reached for his rucksack. He pulled out a fifty-pack of vanilla-scented tealights from Ikea.

"You're not planning on lighting all of those, are you?" I asked, wondering how long it would take.

"Sorry . . . I was going to have it all done before you arrived but . . ." he said with a panic-stricken face, as he rested the bag on the bed.

"It doesn't matter," I insisted.

"It doesn't?"

"No."

"I just wanted it to be perfect, though."

"It's already perfect because I'm here with you, you big softie," I laughed, grabbing his hips and pulling him back on the bed with me.

He pouted at me, his perfect face still full of concern, before breaking into a little smile. "I'm being a girl . . ."

"You are," I smiled, loving that our old joke could still lighten the mood. I ran my fingers through his hair and pulled his head toward mine so that our lips found each other.

"I love you," he mumbled.

"Then that's all I need."

The first time we had sex I kept my eyes closed the whole way through, well, for at least the majority of it. I'd read somewhere that you should always kiss with your eyes closed, so it made sense to me to stick to that rule when doing that greater deed too. I'll admit that I did decide to sneak them open at one point but the look of intensity and determination on Rob's face surprised me, so I decided to shut them again for fear of getting nervous giggles.

Once it was over I felt relieved. So did Rob. Half an hour later we did it again. It lasted far longer and was much more pleasurable knowing what the unknown actually was. Gone were any remaining nerves, what was left was just . . . lovely.

Afterward, Robert brought up our lunch on a tray—chicken dippers, potato Alphabites, and spaghetti hoops. A feast to celebrate the day we both lost our virginity and moved onto the next, more serious stage of being a couple.

As we sat curled up in his bed, utterly naked, tucking into the sophisticated meal, I felt completely relaxed and content. Growing up, I'd heard of girls regretting their first times (they were drunk, it was too soon in a relationship, it was with someone they didn't really care for), but I felt an overwhelming sense of pride that it wasn't the case for me.

Robert was a natural leader, something that was apparent in our friendship group, but as a lover I'd discovered him to be even more caring and giving than I thought possible. My cheeky friend had the sweetest heart with the most gorgeous love to give—I felt blessed to be the one receiving it.

Dating someone who'd seen me at my worst, and who I'd seen at her worst, was a whole new experience for us both. We couldn't lie and pretend to be perfect like some couples do in those early days. We knew each other inside out. It changed things between us drastically, as you'd expect. There was no way I could pretend Maddy was one of the boys any more. Well, I certainly wasn't treating her like one of the boys any more, that's for sure. Something I'd like to apologize to our fellow tripod member, Ben, for. There were certainly a few moments in our younger years where Ben copped a load of something he shouldn't have.

Maddy

Ben and Kelly's relationship didn't last long. Well, they fooled around together for nine months before she left to go to college—but as we all stayed at Peaswood High in the sixth form to do our A-levels, their relationship came to an amicable resolve. But just because Ben and Kelly didn't last, it didn't mean that Ben was back to being on his own with us and looking like a tag-along. Kelly had given him a newfound confidence with the ladies, and so had losing his puppy fat. He'd become effortlessly slender and the way he Brylcreemed his hair back made him look like a Mediterranean Superman with his olive skin and dark eyes. He was popular, but he wasn't a womanizer—he didn't treat anyone badly or just use them for sex; it's simply that he was never short of female company. Years of being the perfect listener to many of the girls in our year, added to the fact that he'd grown some self-belief and learned how to flirt, had given him a tantalizing charm—made all the greater by the fact that he didn't realize what a catch he was.

I asked Robert if he was envious of him once.

"Why would I be?" he'd asked innocently.

"Because he gets to be with all these girls while you're stuck with me, that's why."

"It's never even crossed my mind," he muttered, pulling me into his chest and kissing the top of my head.

I had no doubt that Robert was happy with me, but the fact that their roles had almost been reversed must have had some sort of impact on him, even if he didn't want to admit it. After all, Ben, with his many admirers and string of dates, was leading the life all three of us would have predicted Robert, with his cheeky ways and army of fans, would have had, if it weren't for our relationship.

"You know what's funny?" he said into my hair.

"What?"

"I don't miss it at all."

"Being popular?"

"Ha!" he spat, pulling me closer and tickling me until I begged him to stop. "It never meant anything to me, but you? Now, you mean the world to me."

And just like that, my strong, loving, thoughtful boyfriend eradicated my fears . . . well, at least for the time being.

We'd come to the end of school life and our university days were looming around the corner, ready to take us on the next big journey of our lives. There was a huge chance that the three of us would end up at different places around the country, a fact we'd decided not to worry too much about until our results were collected and offers accepted—but the wait was agonizing, even if we didn't admit it.

We all had different universities down as our top choices, having decided to focus on different subjects. It meant that, if we all got the grades we'd been predicted, our friendship group would be separated for the first time in nine years. Robert, who had taken PE, Biology, and English Language A levels, was hoping to go to Nottingham Trent to study Sport and Exercise Science. Ben, who'd taken Graphic Design, Art, and English Language, was hoping to go up north to Northumbria to study Graphic Design. And I, having studied Art,

English Literature, and Psychology, wanted to go to Bristol and study Photography. If everything went to plan we'd be miles apart. It was a sobering thought.

A fry-up was the only way to start results day. Our grades, and our future fate, wouldn't be accessible until ten o'clock and, seeing as we knew we'd all be up anxiously pacing around our homes, we figured getting together would keep our brains occupied. A somber mood filled the kitchen in my house as we cooked in silence. Each of us lost in our own thoughts.

"How are we all feeling?" I asked, once we were seated and had started tucking in to our bacon, sausages, eggs, beans, and toast.

Two shrugs were given as answers. It was a gesture I was used to receiving, but on that particular day I'd expected more from them.

"I'm the only one crapping myself, then?" I huffed.

"Mad, there's no point worrying until we know what we're worrying about," said Ben with an appeasing smile.

"Well said," nodded Robert, although I could see the worry in his face, highlighted by the frown on his brow. Robert needed to get the highest marks of our group to get onto his chosen course—two As and one B. I knew he was feeling the pressure, even if he wanted to pretend that he was laid-back about the whole thing.

"Where are we going tonight, then?" asked Ben, changing the subject to something more jovial.

"Tonight? I think we should start straight away," Robert laughed, pulling three miniature bottles of Jack Daniels from his pocket and handing one to each of us. "To the tripod," he toasted, unscrewing the lid of his bottle and thrusting it in the air.

"To the tripod," Ben and I repeated, giggling as we knocked them back.

The school was in chaos when we arrived, with people running around screaming in delight or crying in despair—their future fate decided.

It caused a lump of nerves to form in my throat as we strolled to reception and picked up the awaiting white envelopes.

"Should we go somewhere quiet?" asked Robert. "Away from everyone?"

"Over here," I gestured, leading us away from the crowds and into an empty classroom.

"Here goes," sighed Robert.

"Moment of truth," I laughed weakly.

"On the count of three . . . ?" suggested Ben, to which we nodded. "One, two, three . . ."

We all hastily opened our envelopes, and took out the result papers, taking time to understand the meaning of them before any reactions were given.

"Three fucking As!" screamed Robert, fist pumping the air.

"One A and two Bs!" I squealed—it was more than I needed to get into Bristol. I threw myself on Robert in excitement, thrilled that everything was on track for us both.

But one of us wasn't celebrating. I turned to face Ben to see that he was still staring at his paper, looking disappointed.

"You all right, mate?" asked Robert, clamping a hand on his shoulder. "How did you do?"

He looked up and shook his head.

Ben had needed to get an A and two Bs to get into Northumbria, but instead he'd got three Bs.

"Fuck!" offered Robert.

"What are you going to do?"

"I'll phone up and see about clearing, I guess, but . . ."

"There's a 'but,' that's good!" encouraged Robert.

"Well, it's good enough for my second choice . . ." he said looking at me with an apprehensive smile. "Bristol."

"Ahhhh!" I screamed, running in for a hug. "Please come with me! Please!"

"I might not have a choice," he laughed, trying to struggle away from me.

"Oh great, so now I'm the only one who's going to be on my own. I'll be a loner!" moaned Robert.

"Oh, people will love you," I giggled. "You'll be the popular kid as usual!"

"You won't have us two geeks dragging you down," offered Ben.

"Well, when you put it like that," he chuckled, putting an arm around each of us. "I'll try not to have too much fun without you guys."

Leaving Peaswood High behind us, we wandered down to the local park—the same park that lent me, Robert, and Ben its trees to climb and play on when we were younger. We spent the majority of the afternoon in the sunshine, along with most of the upper sixth. We sat in several circles (with the majority of people sticking with their friends—even at the end people refrained from socializing too much with other peer groups), and drank our way through copious amounts of wine and beer while listening to indie music. Bands like the Kooks, the Zutons, and Kaiser Chiefs pumped from a portable stereo like we were at a mini music festival. Whether people had received good news or bad regarding their future, we were united in saying good-bye to the school that had been our home for the last seven years. Freedom and new beginnings were ahead of us—the world was our oyster. I can remember looking around at one point, seeing the sunshine beam down on everyone laughing and singing, and feeling like I'd entered a euphoric state. It felt warm, weightless, and hippy-like.

Those feelings stayed with us over the summer months before we headed off to university, endless summer evenings drifting by with ease. The daytimes were a different matter. With three months to kill there was no way our mums would have let us bum around aimlessly; we were forced to go into Tamsgate, our nearest town, and get jobs. I wound up in a department store called Magpies in the home department (relentlessly refolding towels all day long and sighing with frustration every time a customer carelessly came and messed them up), while Robert and Ben were both at Spin—a cool music shop—having a whale of a time. It was possibly one of the only times in our whole friendship that I felt left out and jealous, but seeing as Robert was going to have to put up with me and Ben being together for the next three years, I kept my petty grumbling thoughts to myself.

The plus side to them working in Spin was that they got me a massive discount on any CDs or DVDs that I wanted. We'd all started driving that year and nothing beat the feeling of cruising along (let's face it, we'd drive even when there was nowhere to go) with our windows down as great music pumped from the stereo. Thanks to the boys, all of our cars were filled with current albums.

In return I got us all a load of sheets and towels, which might sound pretty lame, but it came in really handy when we were getting ready for our new lives in student halls . . .

Ben

On my eighteenth birthday Robert found me perched in my tree-house at the bottom of my garden. I'd been sat in that spot for at least an hour and was in a grumpy, contemplative mood as I stared at an old photo of my dad and me together on my ninth birthday, taken after he'd led me outside into the garden to see his gift for me—that treehouse, built from scratch with his own bare hands. In that vintage and rare photo, my arms are wrapped around his neck with glee, excited that I had a cool den to play in. He's laughing at my reaction with his eyes closed, a lovely image of a dad getting a hug from his grateful child. There wasn't even a hint of the trauma that was to come just five months later. Perhaps leaving us wasn't even on his mind at that point.

"Happy birthday, mate," Rob grinned at me as he popped his head up through the floor of my wooden house and pulled himself inside.

I said nothing but tried my best to return the cheeky expression he was wearing. I clearly wasn't very good at it, though—he frowned at me straight away, sensing something wasn't quite right.

"What's up?" he asked, crouching his body in two as he made his way through the small structure to my side—it was a tight squeeze now we were on the verge of adulthood. "Oh," he pouted as he caught a glimpse of the picture I was holding.

"Yeah . . ." I nodded dejectedly.

Robert sighed and sat down next to me.

"Why doesn't he want anything to do with me?"

"Maybe he does . . ." Rob shrugged feebly.

"Dude, he knows where I live—it's the same place he tucked me into bed for almost ten years before he fucked off with some other family. He's got a replacement son and can't be arsed keeping in touch with his own blood. It doesn't bother him that I'm the product of his one singular winning sperm."

"Eurgh!" chuckled Robert, giving me a gentle nudge.

"I can't get my head around the fact that he's never been in touch," I exhaled. "Even today? All those birthdays he's missed out on over the years, but today stings the most. It's a special one."

"I get that."

"In theory, from this point forward, I'm an adult. He missed most of me being a kid, and now it looks like he's going to miss the rest of my life along with it."

My words lingered in the silence that fell upon us.

"So what?" he asked, matter-of-factly.

"Huh?"

"You have a great life. You're surrounded by people who love you, you've got a wicked relationship with your mum, and you're fucking talented. So why care about someone who hasn't taken the time to realize how awesome you are?"

I looked at the picture in my hands and said nothing, instead concentrating on nibbling at a tiny bit of loose skin on my bottom lip. It wasn't quite the reaction I'd been expecting from Robert—it was far more diplomatic than the bashing of my dad's crummy morals that I was after.

"Is someone who could walk out on you when you were just a kid really worth pining over? Is he really worth the energy or effort?"

"I wish it was that simple."

"Maybe it can be," he shrugged, turning to me with wide green eyes.

"But not having him makes me feel trapped and desperate," I confessed, feeling defeated at having to share my niggling thoughts. "Some days I come up here and I feel like that little nine-year-old all over again, wanting him to come back and apologize, to tell me and Mum he still loves us . . . I know it sounds ridiculous."

"No," Rob breathed, shaking his head.

"This place pulls me in, acts like a safe haven, and then reminds me of his betrayal," I added, as I took in the aging and weathered wood around us.

"Then why come up here?"

"It calls out to me. It's just too tempting not to. I spot it from the kitchen or from my bedroom window. I've always thought of it as a place to be closer to him—but I've been feeding myself a sack of shit. All it does is remind me of what I no longer have."

Rob puffed out his cheeks as he exhaled and ran his fingers through his hair, pulling the blond strands away from his eyes.

"I'll be back in a bit," he said quickly, as he shuffled along the floor, grabbed hold of the blue rope, and jumped down and out of the hole to the grass below. I watched him as he walked around the house and out of the side gate. When he returned ten minutes later he was carrying a bright yellow plastic toolbox.

"What's that for?" I yelled down, sitting up and trying to get a better view of what he was up to.

"Call it a special birthday present," he grinned, opening up the box and taking out a hammer and saw.

"What?"

"A few pieces of wood shouldn't make you query how loved you are—or taunt you about what might have been if your dad wasn't such a dick. Now, come down here, grab some tools and let's demolish the crap out of it."

"Seriously?"

"I want to free you of your chains," he smirked.

"I feel like Rapunzel," I joked as I hung out of the window of my childhood treehouse.

"That makes me your Prince Charming, then," Rob winked. "Are you coming down? Or do you want me to carry you?"

Eagerly, I made my way down from the treehouse for the last time. Adrenaline pumped through me as I took the saw from Robert and reached up to start hacking away at one of my hidden demons. We ripped, smashed, crushed, and split every piece of that wooden structure until there was nothing but a simple apple tree left behind. It must have taken less than half an hour, but I enjoyed every second—at one point I even threw the tools aside and just started pulling at it with my hands, yanking rusty nails away from their embedded homes. Never had I felt so pumped and full of energy.

"Now what?" I asked in my out-of-breath state as I stared at the treehouse's carcass in a heap on the ground.

"We burn it," he grinned, pulling out lighter blocks from the plastic box, along with a box of matches.

I'll admit that the whole thing had an air of teenage-girl drama about it. You know, girl gets ditched by asshole boyfriend and burns every picture of them together in some ritualistic voodoo cursing manner . . . but as I watched those pieces of wood go up in flames, and flicked that picture from the day it was created on top of the burning pile, I felt a sense of release.

I put my arm around Rob's shoulders and thanked him for giving me the best birthday present I could have asked for.

"Anything for you," he winked, ruffling my hair. "Now, let's go find that girlfriend of mine . . . I believe she's been making you a cake."

Maddy

And so, the time came to head for university. We were all leaving Peaswood on the same Saturday morning in early October. Gloriously warm sunshine beamed down on us as the sun dug its heels in and refused to give in to the winter weather that was heading our way.

Robert was to travel in his own car to Nottingham while his parents followed behind in theirs. You'd have thought that as he was the youngest of three boys, both of whom had previously been sent off to university, they'd be blasé about him going away, but he was still their baby, therefore they insisted on going with him and getting him settled. Much to his annoyance.

Me and Ben were going in separate cars, while our mums and my dad followed behind.

All three of us were going to have our cars with us, which we were hoping would make the miles between Bristol, Nottingham, and home appear more bearable. Plus driving still felt cool and gave us great freedom—we weren't too keen on giving that up so soon and relying on public transport.

As agreed, at eleven o'clock Ben, Robert, and the parents drove over to ours to say a final farewell. I'd said a proper good-bye to Robert the night before. He'd come over to help me pack, but he proved to be quite a distraction and kept picking me up and dragging me away from my suitcase. He'd always been athletic and strong, but in our last year at Peaswood High his pole-like frame had suddenly bulked up and become more manly, once again capturing the attention of not only the girls at school, but any female we passed on the street— occasionally males too. As ever, he liked to show off his strength, which was why he kept picking me up and plonking me back on my bed, no matter how much I protested.

As we lay on my bed, once I'd given up fighting back, he turned to me with a sad sigh.

"I can't believe you're going to Bristol and that Ben's going with you!"

"At least you'll have someone to keep an eye on me now."

"As if I needed that anyway," he said, pulling me closer.

"You never know, I might be swept off my feet by some arty type," I laughed.

"Don't even joke," he said with a pout.

"Oh, and there's not going to be a swarm of girls falling over themselves to get to you, Mr. Muscles?"

"I'm blind to everyone else . . . you know that."

"Yeah, just wait until you get to Freshers' Week and you see just how short the skirts are and just how high the boobs have been pushed up."

He raised his eyebrows at me and laughed, "How high are we talking?"

Prompting me to whack him on the head with a pillow, leading to a play fight.

Eventually, as we calmly snuggled in together once more, he whispered in my ear, "We'll be okay."

"We will, won't we?"

"Absolutely . . . there's only one girl for me and I love her with every beat of my heart."

"So cheesy."

"So true," he whispered, pulling me on top of him and kissing me

in a way we both knew would lead to some very naughty behavior—
even with my parents downstairs.

We fell asleep at some point, causing my mum to come in a couple
of hours later and shout her head off like a crazed madwoman as she
spotted my unpacked suitcase. Robert later snuck off home, after
more snuggling at the doorway, deciding it was about time he started
his own packing—although I was sure his mum would have done
the whole lot for him already.

There was nothing final about our good-bye that Saturday—even
though we were entering into new worlds and new lives, it was joyous rather than sad. Well, for us it was, but you wouldn't have thought
so if you looked at our mums, who were all sniffing into their tissues
before we'd even got into our cars.

The three of us stood in a huddle and hugged good-bye, Robert
holding me around the waist while Ben took my hand and squeezed
it three times in his ever-comforting way—I was thrilled that he'd be
going to Bristol with me, that I'd still have him for constant support.

"So, we'll see you next weekend or the one after, then?" I asked
Robert, as we broke away, bouncing my car keys in my hand in excitement and doing a little jig with my knees.

"Yes! We'll play it by ear. See what's planned for us all in our Freshers' Weeks."

"Watch out for those girls, Mr. Miles," I warned.

"How high did you say they were again?" he grinned, placing one
hand on his chest to mockingly measure the assumed Freshers'-Week-
Boob-Height, before putting his hands around my waist and pulling
me close.

"Oooh, you little monkey," I laughed.

He gave me a tender kiss before turning to give Ben an embrace,
slapping him on the back in that brotherly way guys do to each other.

"Look after her," I heard Robert say quietly.

"Of course," promised Ben with a nod.

It was a sweet moment between the two of them, even if they were acting as though I wasn't there and that I was some feeble girl who needed looking after. I had no doubt I would be fine—it was the boys I was worried about, after all, their mums did practically everything for them. I had no idea how they were going to cook and clean unaided. Not that I said as much.

After the three of us joined together for one final huddle, I got into my little red Ford Ka and manically waved good-bye. We beeped our horns the whole way to the motorway, excitedly starting the journeys to our futures.

I'd picked Bristol as my top choice for university mainly because of its beautiful location and scenic views—I'd been there years before with my family and had thought of it as a magical place ever since. Although, obviously, the photography course I'd be studying sounded great too. Ever since Mum and Dad had bought me that first camera, I'd never been able to shake off my love for the art. I knew Dad would have loved me to study something more solid, like business or English—something that offered more prospects once the degree was complete and would secure me a future, but he never tried to sway me from doing the course. At eighteen, I had no idea what I planned to do with a photography degree, but I figured something would pop up somewhere along the line. Taking pictures was what I loved doing. Plus, not to blow my own trumpet, I was good at it. Now I'm not saying that I thought I was about to become the new Mario Testino, or anything like that, but I was better at doing and creating rather than forcing my mind to think about mundane tasks and sums. A doer, not a thinker, perhaps.

Bristol was just as beautiful as I'd remembered it from my childhood. The area that had stuck in my mind most vividly was Totterdown, with its multicolored houses sitting all pretty in the hills. In my head I'd assumed I'd be living in one of them when I went to university there, so I was mildly disappointed to learn it wasn't a possibility. It was student halls for me. Although that didn't stop me over the years wandering down to Totterdown and pretending it was my neighborhood—I liked living in that little fantasy whenever I could.

The rest of Bristol itself was far from ugly with its historic-looking buildings at the heart of it; with the rivers winding their way through everything—the campus, shops, and houses—it felt like you were never far from the water. Plus, there were loads of beaches a cycle ride or a drive away (depending on how adventurous you felt), where we could sunbathe over ice cream, Dinky Doughnuts, or a bag a chips. Perfect. I knew I'd be spending most of my time inland in the busy part of the city, but it was lovely knowing that those views were only minutes away and easily accessible.

On the day I arrived there, once the cars were unpacked, my room was set up, and we'd met a few other students who were staying in the same halls, I finally managed to persuade Mum and Dad that it was okay for them to leave me in this strange place called Bristol.

As soon as I waved them off and returned to my room (after a million good-bye hugs and kisses), I found myself disturbed by the silence. It was eerie. I lay on my single bed and looked around my new home. The bland white walls were hardly warm and inviting, but I knew I could spruce it up with some photos from home Blu-tacked to them. Along one side there was a white wardrobe and a chest of drawers, which were already brimming with clothes—I'd had no idea what to pack, so decided to bring the majority of my wardrobe. Next to those was a wooden desk, on which I'd already lined up my course books as well as my new computer and camera. I was also given the gift of an en suite—something I was truly grateful for as it would spare me the awkwardness of half-naked encounters with strangers in the hallway after showers and, perhaps more importantly, the embarrassment of having to hide the smell of my number twos when going to the loo. Yes, I knew an en suite would make my life there much more comfortable.

I took in the new space around me and let out a sigh, suddenly feeling a bit empty—or perhaps it was boredom seeping in after such a hectic and thrilling day. It was, after all, fairly anti-climactic. I'd been so excited to get to Bristol and for university life to start, but we still had a whole thirty-eight hours to go until we walked through those university doors and officially became its students.

I picked up my phone and called Ben. His accommodation wasn't in the same block as mine, but was luckily only a couple of minutes' walk away.

"Hey," he said, picking up instantly.

"Are you unpacked?"

"Yeah, all done. Mum left ages ago. I've been helping some of the others bring their suitcases up the stairs and stuff."

"Very nice and sociable of you."

"I'm going to be living with them for a year—always good to make a good impression."

"Fair point," I answered, suddenly wondering what my new companions thought of me. I'd briefly met three students from my halls, Pearl, Jennifer, and Flo. They seemed nice enough, although we hadn't all got together and had a proper chat yet, we'd been too busy organizing our new rooms while our parents faffed around us. I thought about going in and getting to know one of them a bit better, kicking off one of those firm friendships that people always talked about creating at uni, but the comfort of having Ben there, who I knew so well already, drew me in. "What are you doing now?"

"Nothing. Just chilling in my room."

"Same here. Fancy going to the pub for one?"

"Yeah, why not."

One drink turned into two, turned into three, turned into four, turned into Ben having to carry me back to my place, only I couldn't for the life of me remember what floor I was on or what room I was in. It was funny for all of two minutes and then, as we were shattered and too drunk to care, we gave up trying to find my new bed and took a little walk to Ben's room instead. We curled up on the single bed and passed out instantly.

And so started our student life.

It didn't take me long to form firm friendships with the girls in my halls, which wasn't like me, but Pearl, Flo, and Jennifer were awesome. Pearl, from East London, was a proper cockney—tough and feisty. She might have been just a little over five feet, but she had some gob on her and was as blunt as anything—a quality that was alarming at first but equally refreshing. Flo was from the Wirral, and was our group's English rose. Her honey-like hair fell down in waves to just below her shoulders and her milky skin was flawless, not freckled like mine. She too had a boyfriend that she was separated from—he was a bricklayer and was staying up north—so I instantly felt drawn to her through our similar situations. Jennifer, an exotic-looking beauty with Indian roots on her mother's side, was, rather ironically, from Nottingham, making her an endless source of information when Robert started heading out to all these places that I'd never heard of.

The morning after the night I'd slept in Ben's bed instead of my own, I wandered in to find them all standing in the hallway, each leaning against their bedroom doors—Pearl's room was next to mine on the left, Jennifer's was adjacent to hers, and Flo's was directly opposite mine. They were all still in their pajamas, looking like they'd not long since woken up, gulping on mugs of tea. They were mid-conversation but stopped when they saw me walk in wearing my previous night's clothes, confirming that I hadn't just got home late and then ventured out first thing before they'd woken up—I'd slept out.

"There you are!" sighed Flo, sounding relieved, before eying up my clothes with a troubled look. "We've been worried!"

"Really?"

"Of course we have, Maddy," Jennifer added with a sympathetic smile. "We thought you might've got cold feet and decided to leave us already."

"So . . . where have you been?" asked Flo.

"God, I got so drunk . . ."

"Did you shag someone?" asked Pearl.

See? Where others might have been more restrained on a topic, she was always ready to wade in and get to the root of a matter without hesitation.

"What? No!"

"Oh! I was sure this was going to be our first walk of shame," she laughed with mock disappointment. "What a pity!"

"She's not stopped going on about it," added Jennifer, rolling her eyes.

"I have a boyfriend," I protested.

"Well, that doesn't stop some people!" smirked Pearl.

"I told her you weren't doing that," chimed in Flo almost to herself as she gazed into her mug, looking uncomfortable with the conversation—I had a feeling that she, like me, wasn't keen on any sort of confrontation.

"So where were you, then?" prodded Jennifer.

"With Ben," I shrugged.

"Your extremely fit BFF?" asked Jennifer, her dark brown eyes widening in surprise.

I nodded, prompting the girls to look at each other and giggle.

"What?"

"Oh, nothing . . . I just hope I find a hunky friend to share a bed with, at some point," laughed Pearl, twirling her brown hair through her fingertips.

"But it's not like that," I argued, getting ready to defend our boy/girl friendship once more, something I was very used to doing. Hoping that it wasn't going to be made into a massive issue. I liked these girls and didn't want there to be a question mark hanging over me and my loyalty every time I hung out with Ben. That's what had led me to feel judged and isolated in the past—and I didn't want history to start repeating itself yet again.

"Shush, you," broke in Jennifer, interrupting my frantic thoughts. "She's pulling your leg."

"Yep. I've seen a photo of your boyfriend . . . *Phwoar!*" Pearl growled.

"Thanks," I sighed.

"Any brothers I should know about?"

"Two!"

"Like heaven to my ears!" Pearl cackled.

"Want a cuppa?" asked Flo, moving toward our communal kitchen. "Kettle's just boiled."

"Sounds fab. I'll just go shower first, though." I felt stale and horrid from the previous night's overindulgence—I knew I still smelt of alcohol too, it hovered around me, prompting unexpected waves of nausea every time I caught a whiff of it.

I showered quickly and threw on a new pair of stripy purple and white pajamas (I'd bought them especially for uni), guessing the day was going to be written off in terms of exploring the city, and left my hair wet—I couldn't bear the thought of drying it in my hungover state, and didn't even care that it would dry frizzy and wild.

"Here you go, tea, two sugars," Flo beamed, handing me a mug as soon as I walked out of my room, back into the hallway.

"Feeling better?" asked Pearl, still standing in the same spot I'd left her.

"Much."

"Fancy a chocolate Hobnob?" she asked, pulling a massive packet from the pocket of her dark-blue dressing gown.

"That is just what I need!" I sighed, happily taking one.

"I've got two mega packs," she grinned, swinging out her hip and showing me another packet hiding in her other pocket.

"We've decided a girlie flick is in order," smiled Flo.

"Yes, come join us in my little boudoir. We're watching that new one with Billy Buskin in—*Halo*," Jennifer said, opening her bedroom door to reveal the den she'd created. Radiant red and aubergine-colored fabric was hanging from the walls, hiding the dull white-painted surfaces behind, and incense was burning, making it look like an Arabian haven. It was beautiful.

"How have you managed to make it look so cool?" I asked, mentally comparing it to my own bleak hideout. I thought I'd done a pretty good job personalizing it and making it my own, but Jennifer had shown me otherwise.

"Mum made me pack a whole bunch of saris, just in case the perfect Indian boy turned up on campus . . ." she chuckled. "I figured I might as well put them to good use instead, plus I was running out of space in my wardrobe."

"They look incredible!"

"I'll be frantically taking them down whenever she decides to come visit . . . and wearing them!" she laughed. "Right, grab a space, girls," she said, gesturing toward the bed as she switched on her television and located the chosen DVD.

We scrambled onto her neatly made bed, which was lavishly covered in red silk sheets and embroidered cream pillows, and nestled ourselves into comfortable positions with our cups of tea cradled in our hands and Pearl's chocolate Hobnobs temptingly placed out in front of us to nibble on.

That, at eighteen years old, was my first ever girlie afternoon. It's bizarre to think that I'd gone that long without one. As we sighed at the romantic storyline between Sid Quest and Scarlett James (cooing over Billy Buskin's charming ways), giggled awkwardly at the sex scenes (can anyone watch them in the company of others and not feel über weird?) and cried our eyes out uncontrollably at the ending (seriously, it's so sad—how could they leave it there?), I realized how fun it was going to be living with the girls and being part of a girlie friendship group for once. Now, being with the boys had always been effortlessly comfortable, and I knew nothing would ever replace or better that, but the new bond that I felt growing was a whole new experience for me, and I liked it.

Robert came to visit us for two nights the following weekend—
we didn't quite manage to last the two weeks apart we'd loosely
planned—something I was rather pleased about. It was nice to know
that he hadn't forgotten about me as soon as he got to Nottingham
and was out of reach. We'd all survived Freshers' Week and avoided
any disasters, other than gaining splitting headaches from our raging hangovers—students could drink!

"Just what I thought," Robert said, wandering into my room, nodding as he inspected the place. "It's basically the same as mine, but
with your added girlie touch."

"It's not girlie!"

"No, you're right," he said, picking up one of my floral pillowcases
from my bed as he sat on it—just to prove his point.

I wouldn't have normally gone in for the floral thing, I was the
least girlie person in the world, but I'd become obsessed with all the
colorful sheets and towels when working in Magpies that summer. I
don't know what had come over me.

"Compared to your boyish lair, which no doubt has nothing out
other than your weights, I think you mean it's more welcoming and
homely," I said, jumping on top of him and wrapping my arms around
his neck—I was so excited to have him there.

"Ah, yeah . . . that's totally what I meant," he said with a wink
before kissing me. "Your housemates seem fun."

"They're great. Love you already, I can tell."

"They seem like a nice bunch."

"They are."

"Make sure that Pearl doesn't lead you astray."

"What? How do you mean?" I asked, instantly feeling defensive
over my new friend.

"She's a wild one," he shrugged. "I bet she'll be getting you lot into
all sorts of trouble."

I thought back to the previous night—us girls and Ben had all gone to Castle Park to sit and relax on the green while taking in the gorgeous views of the castle and the river. We hadn't been there long before Pearl whipped out five plastic cups, a family-sized carton of Tropicana orange juice (with the bits), and a liter bottle of vodka. Remembering the sore head I'd woken up with that morning, I realized Robert might have had a point—not that I was going to tell him that.

"What makes you think I'm so easily led?" I bluffed. "You never know, I could be the ringleader."

Robert raised both eyebrows at me.

"Yeah, fair point," I giggled.

"I'm sure if you got your camera out right now there'd be all sorts of incriminating evidence."

I smiled and gave him an innocent shrug, remembering that, as was usually the case, the evening had been well documented—I was always snap happy, but more so when I'd had a bit to drink. I made a mental note to leave my camera at home on nights that might take a turn to the drunk-photos-are-never-a-good-idea zone.

"So, you've managed to find your way back here okay since your first-night adventures?"

"Yes!" I groaned. "Ben now has my room number memorized, so he's able to point me in the right direction and get me back safely."

"Ha! Just as well he's here with you. Can you imagine what would've happened if you were alone?"

"I'd have been fine . . . Well, I would have found my way eventually, I'm sure."

"Hmmm . . ."

"Although Ben's bed is actually far more comfortable than mine."

"Should I be worried?"

I rolled my eyes. "Yes, Robert. You should totally be worried that, due to the fact that he has a comfier bed, I'm going to run off with our mutual best friend."

"Why, you little . . ." he laughed at my cheekiness, squinting his eyes at me before placing his fingers on my ribs and tickling me, making me jerk around with laughter. He lifted me from his lap and swung me around so that we were lying next to each other, leaning in for a kiss with that look in his eyes that left no doubt as to where the moment was leading. His hand expertly found its way under my T-shirt to my skin, where it roamed around in a playfully teasing manner. God I missed having him with me every day, I thought.

"MATE!" Ben screamed, opening my unlocked door without knocking, and jumping on top of us with a diving hug, squandering our hopes of a quick fumble. "We've missed you, buddy!"

"So I see," Robert laughed, returning the hug.

"We're just so boring without you—it's like we've lost the ability to have fun," I joked.

"I bet."

"We're like Samson when he chopped off all his hair!"

"Well, unless Pearl's around," argued Ben. "Did you tell him about last night?"

I groaned.

Robert turned to me with a smile—what was it he'd been saying about Pearl? "No, she hasn't . . . spill!"

"She got us roaringly drunk. I only signed up for a chilled night with a couple of cans—but somehow we ended up skipping through the city center at four a.m. pretending we were animals from *Snow White*—no idea why."

"Sounds like quite a night."

"It was—she's crazy."

"What's the plan?" I asked Ben, changing the subject as I ignored the look Robert was throwing in my direction, clearly finding it funny that I'd been caught out. Yes, Pearl was a little on the wild side, but she was fun. It wasn't like I was going to go off and do something stupid just because someone jeered me on—I wasn't nine years old any more. Plus, I knew he'd have been getting up to the same drunken behavior in Nottingham, the only difference being that I didn't have a trusted friend there who'd spill the beans on him. Although, I'd no doubt that, with his new gang, he certainly would be the leader, just like he had always been with Ben and me. With us, it really had been a case of he jumped and we followed. Usually without hesitation.

"You tell me," shrugged Ben, in his usual carefree manner. "I'm up for anything."

"I thought we could go on a bike ride, give Rob a tour," I suggested. "We have ours here and Flo said there's a place you can rent one up the road. Fancy it?"

"Sounds good," Robert nodded, still smirking at me.

"I'm in!" agreed Ben, jumping up off the bed and heading out into the hallway, keen to get going straight away.

Getting up from the bed I gave Robert a playful shove, making him fall backward into my flowery pillows.

"What was that for?" he laughed.

"For being so smug!"

"Come here," he smiled, sitting on the edge of the bed and grabbing hold of my waist, looking up at me as he pulled me close. "I'm glad you've got a nice bunch of people around you."

"Good."

"I just worry."

"About what?"

"That you'll forget about me."

"Like that's gonna happen."

"Or that you'll end up like one of *those* girls."

"What girls?"

"You know, the ones with boobs up to here," he smiled, bringing his hand up to below his neck.

"Have you met many?"

"Several. It's been awful."

"You poor thing."

"I know," he pouted. "I'm mentally scarred."

"I'll tell you what," I purred, running my fingers through his hair. "I'll keep mine under lock and key tonight, to save you from further trauma."

"What?" he practically squeaked.

"I think it's for the best."

"Huh?"

"It's a shame really, I had a whole night of fun planned—special outfits and everything," I teased with a smile. "But, well, I don't want you to think I'm one of *those* girls . . ."

I winked and cackled wickedly, as I freed myself from his embrace and walked out the door.

The majority of trips to see each other during our uni years were Robert driving to us, rather than us going to him. We did go to Nottingham a few times, but seeing as there were two of us in Bristol, it seemed to make sense to do it that way round. As a result I never really got to know the people he lived with, the life he led there, or Nottingham itself. I did like it there, though, it felt steeped in history and the main part of the city was absolutely gorgeous with all its old buildings and the big water feature in the square.

I quite liked the fact that he was always coming to me. It felt like he really wanted to see me. Whenever I went there I felt a bit of a nuisance; it was very much a boys' place—as I'd predicted, the only things out on show in his room were his weights. Oh, and a framed picture of us from our sixth form ball which had been neatly placed on his nightstand. I couldn't help but smile when I first saw it.

We spoke to each other all the time—a few times every day in fact. He was the first person I spoke to in the mornings, and the last person I spoke to at night. There was not one part of me that queried his loyalty to me. Not one part that worried about him being out and getting drunk with other girls around. Not one part of me that feared he'd go off and cheat. Would it have changed anything if I had? Probably not.

I took for granted the fact that he was my one and that, one day, we'd get married, have babies, and grow old together. I didn't think anything would come along and jeopardize that. I'd never seriously worried about him being around *those* girls. Perhaps I should have.

Instead I was content with life. I loved my photography degree and happily snapped away whenever I could (not just when I was given coursework), had my wonderful boyfriend who visited me whenever he could (and was only a phone call away at other times), and a best friend who made me feel like I was back at home whenever he was around (which was most of the time). I knew my uni experience would have been very different if I hadn't had Ben there to share it with.

I loved how my life was shaping up. Everything seemed to be falling into place.

I should have realized it was all too good to be true.

Ben

I loved uni life—everything about it. The fact that we were suddenly in charge of our own lives; of feeding ourselves, washing our clothes, keeping ourselves occupied with no guidance from our parents, well, from my mum. It felt like anything was possible—if we wanted to go out until eight the following morning, we could. If we wanted to eat McDonald's for breakfast and Pot Noodles for dinner, we could. If we wanted to wear the same T-shirt three days in a row, we could (although Maddy would have told me off for that one). We were in control and, as long as we turned up for lectures ready to learn and got all our coursework in on time, we were left to our own devices. We'd been taken from our feeble existence in Peaswood and planted in the midst of university mayhem. What wasn't to love?

Bristol was incredible. At night we were your typical mischievous students, jumping from pubs to clubs, to house parties, and wandering back to our rooms when the sun had already started to rise. But daytimes were a stark contrast—the city offered hundreds of different things to keep us occupied when we weren't busy in lectures or studying. There was something therapeutic about the place. Bristol was inviting and vibrant and its leafy appearance made it seem more like a big town than an overbearing city. It also had more of a laid-back air to it rather than the fast pace found in most others—instantly making it friendlier.

I'm ashamed to admit that I loved it being just Maddy and me, too—a thought I kept berating myself for having as soon as it popped into my head. I just liked hanging out with her. For us it was just like before, except now we were in this little bubble—a bubble for two. It felt like we were sewn together, living in each other's pockets. Despite living in different halls, taking different courses, and having different lectures, we saw each other daily. We'd grab dinner together, go to the library and study together, go out and get drunk together. And, rather frequently, we'd just chill out together. We'd curl up under my duvet and whack on boxsets of some of our favorite shows—*Friends* (mutual choice), *24* (my choice), *Prison Break* (mine again), *Gossip Girl* (hers, totally hers), and *Dawson's Creek* (hers, but I have to say, it turned into my guilty pleasure). Hours of our time were spent like that and I loved it—it was even better than when Robert dated Daniella when we were fourteen, leaving us as a two. It just felt lovely . . .

That first instance of her sleeping in my room hadn't been a one-off, in fact it kicked off a regular occurrence—something that was never planned, but always a likelihood if she was too drunk, or if we stayed up late watching something on the television and she hadn't the energy to venture back to her own bed. It was easy and there was absolutely nothing sordid in it, certainly not from her part. As she lay beside me, gently snoring (she'd hate me saying that), it was almost weird to think that I wasn't her boyfriend. That she belonged to someone else . . . our other best friend.

It pained me to realize that the reason she was doing that with me was because she felt so comfortable, because she had no idea of the feelings lurking inside of me. The ones I'd been suppressing since the moment I met her. I'd often lie there wondering how she would react if I just blurted it out and told her. Would she freak out? Be angry that I'd kept it from her? Pity me? Love me back?

Even as I thought about it, I knew I'd never just come out and say it—because of Robert. Not just because she was with him, but because I knew he trusted me more than anything. There was no other guy in the world he'd trust to be in his girlfriend's life to the extent that I was. I've often wondered if he found it weird, us being together so much. He never voiced any aversion to it, so I assumed not.

For a large chunk of our lives, when they went off to uni together, Maddy saw Ben more than she saw me—something that worried me and pleased me in equal measure. I've known Ben my whole life, so I know what a great guy our best friend is. My worry was that she'd suddenly have an epiphany and realize she was with the wrong friend.

Ben

Our third year came along and chomped us on the arse with terrifying speed, leaving us with only a few months to figure out where we wanted to live once we'd finished and what we were actually going to do with our lives once we were handed our scrolled-up certificates and sent on our merry way into the big bad world of reality. On top of that we were craning our necks trying to complete dissertations and final assignments, as well as attending our normal lectures.

On April 16th, a Friday afternoon (I remember the date clearly for reasons you'll come to understand), I found myself free from lectures. Rather than sitting indoors and fretting over my remaining work, I'd decided to make the most of the freak springtime heatwave and go on a mammoth bike ride along the coast. I'd asked Maddy if she wanted to come but she'd declined, insisting she was too busy finishing off coursework—I pictured her sat on her bed, frantically editing her latest photographs, a worry line forming on her brow. She was such a perfectionist, but it paid off. Her work was always awesome. She had a natural eye for capturing little moments, even if photography was something she insisted she "fell into" through being clueless about her future plans.

So, there I was, enjoying the glorious weather and the salty wind blowing through my hair, when Robert called. Needless to say we still spoke on the phone daily, some days two or three times. Maddy always joked that I spoke to him more than she did; I think, back in those days, she could have been right. I pulled over and got off my bike before picking up, perching on a stony wall that was separating me from the sandy beach below.

"Mate!" I breathed into the phone, my lungs only just starting to recover. "You coming down tomorrow night?"

"Something's happened," he blurted, steamrolling my chatter with haste.

Everything inside me froze as I heard the fear in his voice. It was far from the calm and cheeky tone I was used to hearing—I knew it was something serious.

"What's happened? Are you okay?"

"No . . ."

"Rob, what is it?" I instantly thought the worst. I thought he was about to tell me something had happened to my mum.

"I've done something really stupid."

"What?"

"I've slept with someone . . ."

"You've what?"

To say I was shocked would be an understatement. I was hit by a wave of nausea as my surroundings slipped away from me, all my senses focusing on Robert's voice.

"You heard," he muttered, not wishing to repeat it.

"When?"

"Last night."

"Fuck!"

"Yeah . . . what a cock," he berated himself.

"But what about Maddy?"

"I know."

"What are you going to do?"

"I don't know."

"Have you told her?"

"No! I wanted to tell you first."

"Why? I'm not telling her for you," I stammered, not wanting to be the one to break her heart—he could do that himself.

"Of course not, I wasn't going to ask you to. I just wanted you to know so that you can be there, you know, when I do."

"Right, yeah. When you going to do that?"

"Now. When I get off the phone to you."

I thought of Maddy going about her day as usual, blissfully unaware that her boyfriend was about to drop the biggest bombshell on her. I couldn't believe Robert, the guy who we thought we knew so well, who was loyal and trustworthy, could do such a thing.

"Why'd you do it, Rob? Who is she?"

"I can't answer why, it just happened. She's just a girl. A random, stupid, girl."

"Fuck!"

Neither of us spoke for a few minutes—a million different thoughts raced through my head as I tried to make sense of it all.

"Look, I've got to phone Maddy. I've got to tell her."

"What are you going to say?"

"I don't know. I'm so confused by the whole thing."

"Right . . ."

"Look, just be there, okay?"

"Of course . . . aren't you going to come see her?"

"I think I should do it on the phone. Just get it over with. Get it out there."

"But—"

"I can't, Ben. I just can't," he said forcefully.

Anxiety took a hold of me as we said good-bye. I stayed there for a few minutes, perched on the wall looking out to sea, trying to calm myself down and compose myself as I watched the waves relentlessly crash and foam.

I was angry at Robert, angry that he'd messed up in such a huge way. Maddy wasn't just some girl he'd been dating for a few years, although that would have been bad enough, she was his best friend.

Our best friend. One of us. How could he be such an idiot? Why would he risk losing her for some random girl?

I felt helplessly sad for Maddy. She'd never been the jealous type, never uttered a word of worry to me about what Robert was up to in Nottingham without us to hang out with. I knew the news would crush her.

Cursing Robert for not having the guts to come and face up to his actions, I shakily jumped on my bike and started to make my way to hers, ready to pick up the pieces of her broken heart that my trusted friend had so thoughtlessly trampled on.

We'd moved out of our halls and into actual houses in our second year. Despite the fact that we spent almost all our free time together, we'd decided to stay living apart—mainly because we didn't want to start irritating each other with our bad habits (I was messy, she was a clean freak) but also because her flatmates, Flo, Pearl, and Jennifer, wanted to have some sort of all-female, spotlessly clean sorority house. The deal was sealed for Maddy when she discovered that the bedrooms had en suites—a luxury she was reluctant to let go of. We were still only a few minutes away from one another, both only a couple of miles from the center of town.

Maddy was in her room when I got to her house an hour later, after a hectic cycle back into town. I found her curled up on her bed in the fetal position, hugging her pillow, with a handful of snotty tissues in her palm. Her mascara had been smeared all over her cheeks thanks to her tears, and her face was blotchy and swollen. Her lips looked redder and fuller than ever as they pouted outward with misery.

I'd not seen her in such a state since primary school.

"Hey," I said softly, walking toward her. Suddenly feeling awkward in the space I knew so well and in front of the other person in my life I thought I knew inside out.

She sat up slightly, her big blue eyes looking at me in such a forlorn manner my heart dropped to the floor.

"Do you know?" she asked feebly.

"Yeah, he called a little while ago." I hated admitting that. Knowing before her made me feel like I was Robert's accomplice somehow, even if I had only known a few minutes before. It made me feel guilty by association, or like I'd been there and not stopped it from happening.

"Oh . . ." she said, nodding her head as she sighed. "What a twat."

She moved over onto one side of the single bed, and stretched out an arm to me, beckoning me to her. I took Maddy into my arms and gave her a squeeze, trying my best to comfort her.

"Why'd he do it?" she whimpered after a moment or two, shifting her body so that her head rested on my chest.

"I don't know."

"He's such a fucking dickhead."

"I think he's saying the same thing."

"He's not."

"What do you mean?"

"I think he wants a break . . ."

"He didn't tell me that."

"He said he needs time to think things through," she whispered with a quivering voice.

"Oh . . ."

I had thought it would be a broken Maddy splitting up with Robert when she heard what he'd done. I hadn't expected it to be him throwing in the towel instead. I'd assumed it was just a one-night thing, a drunken mistake; I wondered if there was more to it than I'd been told. Otherwise, Robert would surely be there fighting to stay with her—mopping up her tears as he begged for her forgiveness. It upset me that he wasn't. I couldn't help but feel disappointed with him as Maddy lay there heartbroken in my arms.

I tried not to think about how Robert's actions would affect the three of us, but I couldn't help worrying. After all, it wasn't just their lives that would be altered—it would be mine too. I knew a fracture within the group would change everything. I wasn't sure how we'd cope. Or, more to the point, how I'd cope if the two of them could no longer bear to be in each other's presence. They were my rocks, the other two legs of my tripod. The disorder felt, in many ways, worse than when my dad had left—at least back then I had my mum for support. I knew she wasn't going anywhere. But with Maddy and Robert, there was a possibility that there'd never be a sense of calm again. They were selfish thoughts, though, and, at least for that night, I knew I had to be there for Maddy, when Robert had decided he didn't want to be.

"Do you think he still loves me?" Maddy asked softly, after a heavy silence.

"Of course he does," I lied. I didn't know what was going on in his head and that was the alarming thing. I'd never felt so out of touch with the guy I'd thought of more as a brother than as a friend. His actions were so out of character. "But do you still love him? Could you forgive him?"

She let out a sigh before sobbing, "Oh Ben. Why on earth has this happened?"

We stayed curled up together on her bed for hours. I let her cry, moan, and shout angry words at our best friend—she really did call him every name under the sun. I'd never heard her swear so much, but heartbreak had unleashed a new side to her.

"Right, I'm done," she said dramatically, hours later, picking herself up off the bed and stretching her face as she swept her hands over her cheeks, shaking her body as though she was shaking the stress away. "No more tears, that's it. We're going out."

"Really?"

"Yes. He's not here, Ben. He hasn't realized his monumental mistake and arrived demanding to sort things out. Hell, he hasn't even called or texted since he told me," she said, picking up her phone and showing me the empty home screen.

"Well, I—"

"He doesn't give a crap," she said forcefully. "I'm not prepared to go all weak and helpless just because I've been dumped by the flipping love of my life."

As she said it I saw her lip wobble and her eyes glass over with fresh tears, belying the strength she was trying to convey.

"Mad, it's okay . . ."

"I'm fine," she said sternly, mostly to herself as she commanded the tears to back off. "Now, I'm going to chuck some fresh makeup on and then I'm going out to get wasted. Coming or not?"

I let out a nervous laugh, "Are you sure that's what you want to do?"

"Abso-fucking-lutely," she boomed.

Maddy

I took us to the nearest pub I could find. It wasn't one we'd ever been to before; we usually headed out to places that were nearer to campus where there would be loads of people we knew and a good vibe, but that night I didn't care for friends or atmosphere. I just wanted to get shitfaced. That's how we ended up in the Red Fox, a dingy little pub, only minutes away from mine. We must have walked passed it hundreds of times in our three years in Bristol, but never had any desire to venture through its doors. Outside, the pub's crest-shaped sign swung wildly in the breeze from one hook, rather than two, it's paintwork was flaky and peeling off, and burly men with "England 'til I Die" tattoos puffed on cigarettes while arguing about the football. Inside wasn't much better with its den-like appearance. A lack of windows made it dark and the little peach-colored lamps were near useless in their bid to brighten the place up. A pokey-sized place filled with wooden benches, covered in worn-down cushions, and sticky tables. It was uninviting, but I didn't care. It served alcohol and that was all I wanted.

It didn't take me long to accomplish my goal for the night, especially since I was ordering double Sambuca shots with every drink we ordered. Curled away in a dark corner of the pub, hidden from the locals, we drank, whined about everything that was wrong with life, and laughed at the stupidity of it all. The world was starting to turn into a blurry mess, and that was exactly what I wanted. I wanted to numb myself to the heartache Robert had caused, to distance myself from his infidelity. To forget. It didn't work; eventually I'd slip back into thinking about him, cursing myself as I did so. I couldn't help it. It was a pretty big deal to be dropped so carelessly by someone you'd loved for so long. And worse, for them to do so over the phone, telling you that not only did they mislay your trust but, perhaps, it would be best if they were to become a "free spirit" for now, while they were still young and devoid of responsibility. Yes. That was the terminology Robert used. Free spirit . . . he'd picked a fine time to turn into a hippy.

I hadn't seen it coming. Even though we lived miles apart, there was never a single time in those three years when I fretted about other girls, not seriously, nothing that was more than playful banter between the two of us. I'd trusted him, I thought I had no reason not to.

Hours into our heartbreak-drinking session, silence engulfed me as I stared into the bottom of my glass, hoping it would give me answers to the neverending stream of questions that bubbled away inside me, that threatened to make me blub once more.

"Penny for your thoughts," Ben smiled, pulling out a one-pence piece from his jeans pocket and placing it on the table in front of me. He couldn't help but laugh at his own joke.

"You know, I was just wondering why he'd do that to me."

"Oh Mad . . ." he said sadly, his face falling with concern.

"Am I not clever enough?"

"Don't be silly."

"Maybe she was one of his sporting pals, all trim and toned—am I not fit enough?"

"You're being ridiculous, there's nothing wrong with you."

"Maybe I should've joined you on more bike rides," I moaned sarcastically.

"Nah . . ."

"Am I not pretty enough?" I slurred.

"Of course you are," he said with exasperation.

"Am I not sexy enough?"

"Well, I—"

"I mean, I've changed a lot over the years—there he is looking like the bloody Hulk and here's me, always eating one or two chocolate Hobnobs more than I should."

"Why are you talking about chocolate Hobnobs?"

"Because they're always on my mind," I moaned. "See? Mr. Fitness Freak with little Miss Piggy was never going to work."

"You're not little Miss Piggy."

"Am I not good enough to be with him?" I continued. "He was the popular kid, what did I think I was doing. He's so out of my league."

"He really isn't."

"What did I do wrong, Ben?" I begged, persisting to badger him with my self-doubt, longing for my friend to tell me what I'd done to get myself into such a sorry mess.

"Nothing. You did nothing wrong," he said, reaching across the table to take my hand, which he firmly squeezed three times—for once it failed to comfort me.

"I must have," I shrugged. "He shacked up with someone else. Some floozy."

"You didn't do anything. You're absolutely perfect, Maddy."

"Hardly."

"No, you are. It's so annoying that you can't see that."

"Oh Ben, lovely Ben," I cooed, leaning into him and resting my head on his shoulder. "I can always rely on you to make me smile."

"You really can, Maddy . . . I'll always be here."

"If you were my boyfriend, I know you'd make me smile every day. You'd never give me any of this crap."

"I'd try my best to make you happy, that's for sure . . ."

"And you would!" I chirped over the top of him. "You'd never have done this to me—you're too kind and loving."

"You're not so bad yourself. As people go."

"Tell me, Ben. Tell me what else you would've done if you were Mr. Maddy Hurst," I said, sitting up and facing him, enjoying the silliness of the conversation.

"I'd have made sure you knew exactly how special you are and how much you meant to me," he said, smiling at me.

"And how would you have done that?"

He took a few seconds to think about his answer before saying, "I'd have started by telling you how much I've loved you since the very first day I saw you."

"Nice touch, bringing up our history—that's priceless. Not a soul can compete with a lifetime of memories."

He laughed before picking up his half-full pint of beer and downing its contents.

"You'd have been a lovely boyfriend," I said, placing a hand on his arm. "I totally picked the wrong best friend to snog in Paris."

"Cheers," he said quietly, playing with his empty glass before holding it up to show me it needed refilling. "Fancy another?"

"Do you even have to ask?" I cheekily grinned, as I held up my own depleted drink.

I watched him plod off to the bar and wait for the barmaid to come—it was quiet, even though it was a Friday night, but that didn't make her serve him any quicker, as she languidly continued to clean glasses while talking to one of her locals, oblivious to Ben standing there. Not that he was trying to get her attention, though. He wasn't even looking at her. Instead, he had his elbows up on the bar and was resting his head in his hands, rubbing his forehead. Something was clearly on his mind—he appeared agitated.

In my drunken state, it dawned on me that he'd spoken to Robert before I had, that he'd already confessed everything to Ben before calling me with the delightful news. I wondered if Robert had gone into more detail with him. Told him something that Ben felt uncomfortable knowing—perhaps also promising not to tell me. In the few minutes it had taken Ben to acquire the barmaid's attention and come back with our drinks, I had convinced myself that it was the case. He knew things I didn't, and I wanted to find out what they were.

"Out with it," I practically barked at him as soon as his bum was back on the cushioned bench.

"What?"

"There's something you're not telling me."

"No, there's not," he protested, but the reddening of his cheeks told me otherwise. They goaded me on, told me he was lying, that there was more he was keeping from me.

"I know you know something about Robert," I insisted.

"I don't."

"He told you something, didn't he?"

"No, he really didn't."

"Did he tell you not to tell me?"

"What is this? There's nothing to tell you, Mad," he said, his voice rising in panic at being put on the spot. His eyes were wider than ever as they proclaimed his innocence, but the clenching of his jaw and the guilty swallowing of bile fought against his claim.

"You can't keep a secret from me, Ben."

"There's no secret."

"There is. Don't lie."

"I'm not lying."

"Then why have you gone red?"

"Because you're being an idiot."

"I can't believe you're covering for him."

"Mad, I'm not," he sighed, looking more and more distressed.

"You're my best friend too, Ben. I know you two have this brotherly love thing going on, but you're meant to be looking out for me as well."

"I'm always looking out for you," he frowned, hurt by my accusation.

"Clearly not if you're willing to side with him and keep secrets from me. What has he told you? Was it more than one time? Different girls? Is it more than sex? Has he finished with me for her?

Because you might as well tell me, I'll find out sooner or later. I'll be seeing them together. It's better if it comes from you," I ranted, the alcohol and hurt causing me to push him further than I would normally.

"It's not about Robert," he blurted, looking shocked that the words had leaped from his mouth.

"So there is something?"

"Maddy. Please, just leave it," he groaned, looking around the pub as though he was looking for a way out of the very tight spot I had him trapped in.

"Ben, what is it?"

I was relieved it was nothing to do with Robert, but the way Ben was acting troubled me. He was acting all sketchy and weird—there was definitely something troubling him and I wanted to find out what.

"Ben, you can tell me. Whatever it is, I'm here for you."

"I can't."

"You can tell me anything . . ."

"You don't get it, do you?" he asked, his large Bambi-like eyes searching my face to see if I had even the smallest inkling of what he was hiding. I didn't. I hadn't the foggiest. He looked back down at the floor in despair.

"Get what?" I pleaded, taking his hand, my voice calmer than before. I hated seeing the torment on his face.

He took a deep breath to steady himself before he looked up and faced me, his eyes looking straight into mine.

"I love you."

"Of course you do. I love you too," I smiled, stupidly tapping him on the nose in a childish manner, a cringeworthy reaction to his words.

"No, not like that," he said, getting frustrated with himself, or perhaps at me. "Maddy, I mean it, I really love you."

I suddenly felt very sober as I watched my best friend literally spill his heart out. It was the last thing I expected to hear that day, but then again, I didn't expect to get a call from my boyfriend telling me he'd cheated as he promptly ended our relationship either. It was a day of surprises.

"But—"

"Yes, I know, I know. Things are how they are . . . but if I had to wait a lifetime to be with you I would, because you're the one I've always wanted to be with."

"You don't mean that, Ben."

"I do."

"You can't . . . you're just drunk." I tried to laugh but the seriousness of the situation caused it to bubble in my throat and wither away.

"I always have, though. You've always been the girl for me."

With that, he leaned forward and gently placed his hand on my cheek, his thumb brushing lightly against my skin. He paused and looked at me, really looked at me, inspecting my face with what could only be described as love and wonder. It was a look filled with meaning, the first time he was allowed to look at me with his heart open and the pretense dropped. The change and intensity enticed me. I could feel myself mirroring him, fascinated by the shift of emotion that felt strange yet familiar all at once—I knew that face, I knew him, but there was a new depth that I felt compelled to explore. It excited me. Thrilled me. Drew me in.

He edged his face closer to mine, focusing his eyes on my lips, that were just centimeters from his, and paused once more—something that wasn't done on purpose to add suspense, but because he was nervous. As was I.

"You okay?" he asked, looking back up at my eyes.

I nodded, knowing what was about to happen, not wanting to stop it.

"Good," he whispered, as he slowly leaned closer and kissed me. The touch sent an unexpected surge through my body. I pulled away and looked back into his eyes—noticing the love had been replaced by hunger. In that moment I felt like I wanted and needed him more than I'd ever wanted anything else.

The second time we kissed, it was me who leaned forward and cushioned my lips against his. As I pulled away I couldn't help but grin at him, making me shake my head and sigh into my hands.

"What is it?" he smiled.

"I can't believe we're doing this."

"Neither can I," he said softly, removing my hands from my face and kissing me back.

We sat at that corner table in the pub, gazing at each other with our newfound admiration and kissing like giddy love-struck teen-agers, until closing time. When we were eventually kicked out (the barmaid made no effort to disguise her haste to get home as she swooped up our half-finished drinks), we aimlessly wandered around Bristol holding hands as though it was the most natural thing for us to be doing.

Ben stopped when we got to the river and pulled me round so that my back was against the railings with him stood in front of me.

"You're so beautiful," he beamed.

I smiled, it was strange hearing him say that.

"I mean it. I've always thought so," he said, lowering his head for another kiss. "It feels so good to do that . . ." he grinned. "I can't tell you how long I've wanted to."

"Ben, why haven't you said anything before? I mean, if you've se-riously felt this way since we were kids, why did you keep it a secret?"

"I was scared it would ruin our friendship if you rejected me."

I couldn't help but laugh.

". . . and then you got with Robert."

"Oh . . ." Just the mention of his name caused a tug inside me. There's only so long you can live in a fantasy world before the reality comes along to sharply put you back in your place. I pushed those thoughts away. Reminding myself that he didn't want me, he'd slept with someone else. I didn't owe him anything, I thought, as I con-centrated on Ben—lovely Ben, who did want me and who I knew would never hurt me in the same way.

"You should've said something."

"Well, I've always told you I loved you, even if you didn't realize I was saying it," Ben smiled, managing to ignore the fact that Robert had been mentioned.

I looked up at him in confusion. "Telepathically?" I asked sardonically. "Because it really didn't work."

"Three squeezes," he laughed, taking my hand and squeezing it three times in the way I was so used to him doing.

I shrugged, not understanding the meaning.

"I," he said as he squeezed my hand, "love," with another squeeze, "you," he finished with the third squeeze.

I couldn't help but laugh as I recalled the number of times I'd been aware of him making that gesture, the first one being at the childish wedding in primary school—the last time being when we were sat in the bar, just moments before he said the words out loud for the first time. Ben had told me he loved me so many times, I just wasn't listening properly.

"You've been telling me you love me all that time?"

He shrugged and bit his lip as his cheeks blushed. With his eyes down he concentrated on my hands, really inspecting them, as his thumb made circular motions on my palm. "I know, it's stupid," he muttered.

"No, it's sweet . . . I can't believe I didn't twig."

His eyes flicked up at me before quickly looking back at our fondling hands. His expression changed to one filled with uncertainty.

"What are we doing?" he asked abruptly, a pensive look descending on his face as he slowly stepped backward, away from me. "We shouldn't be doing this."

"I know . . ."

"It's wrong. I shouldn't have said anything."

I watched as he walked a few feet away and stared out at the river, leaving his back to me.

I should have felt guilty by that point, or been hit by remorse—Ben backing away should have shocked some sense into me and made me question what I was doing. I'd been so angry at Robert for cheating, I'd spent the whole night slamming him for what he'd done, but my actions had made me just as bad, if not worse. We were his two best friends. Even as I realized that, I knew I wasn't prepared to let the feelings I'd discovered go. Not yet. I was enjoying it too much—all I felt was the desire to have Ben near.

"Ben, I know it shouldn't, but it just feels so right to me . . ." I said meekly, walking toward him and placing a hand on his shoulder blade, slowly running it up and down his back, trying to bring him back to me.

"Same here," he whispered.

"I don't want to stop."

"Neither do I," he said, slowly turning round to face me.

"Then let's not," I implored, pulling his face down to mine, allowing my body to melt into his as we kissed.

"Maddy . . ." he croaked, starting to shake his head.

"It's okay. I want this."

We stayed at his that night, but not before we walked for long enough to hear the birds singing and see the morning sky start to waken with orange light. It must have been about five o'clock by the time we got to his bedroom.

I'd become used to borrowing a T-shirt and sleeping in Ben's bed after a night out or if I couldn't be bothered to make the short walk back to mine—but this was different, suddenly everything was so electrified. As soon as the door was closed we just stood there and nervously stared at each other, each knowing what was about to happen, but wanting the other one to make the first move.

I started it.

I cautiously undid the buttons on my shirt-dress, aware that Ben's face looked full of nerves as I removed it from my shoulders and let it drop to the floor, leaving me in just my bra and knickers. The movement left me feeling exposed, but ridiculously sexy, something I was aware I hadn't felt in a long time—the thrill of being with someone new after years of being with the same guy, added to the way Ben hungrily looked at my body, as though he wanted to devour every inch of it.

Stepping toward him, I reached the bottom of his T-shirt and brought it over his head, instantly hugging his body into mine, enjoying its warmth, wanting every part of our naked bodies to connect. Expertly he unhooked my bra and ran his fingers over my breasts as he knelt in front of me, licking my nipples playfully before taking them into his mouth, causing me to let out a gasp of excitement as he nibbled gently.

Still on his knees, Ben inched down my knickers, removing them slowly as his eyes locked onto mine. I could hardly breathe at the suspense. Discarding my underwear, his hands reached behind me, sliding over my bum cheeks as he pulled me forward, his tongue tracing my hip bone, his lips brushing over my stomach, building my desire as his hands continued to feel their way around the contours of my body—everywhere but the place I longed for him the most. Back on his feet, his mouth made its way back up my body, past my breasts, along my neck, and sucked on my earlobe, his gentle moaning vibrating through my body, massively turning me on. I nibbled on his lobe with desire as I grabbed at his belt, undoing it with speed, unbuttoned his fly, and let his jeans drop to the ground.

To my surprise, Ben was commando.

He grabbed for my hands and held them out to our sides, stopping me from touching further, leaving us with just our mouths to roam and explore each other's bare skin, the bodies that we'd seen regularly but were only just discovering.

Putting force onto my palms, Ben guided me to shuffle backward onto his bed, which we clumsily climbed. Ben lay on top of me and slowed the pace as he stroked my hair away from my face.

"Are you sure?" he asked, searching my eyes with concern.

"Yes," I smiled. "You?"

He nodded, as he took a deep breath and looked away from me, brushing my arms with his fingertips, "I can't tell you how much I want this, Maddy . . ."

I took his head in my hands and pulled us together as I kissed him, excitement rising as I felt more of his body connect with mine.

"I love you so much," he whispered. "I completely love you, Maddy Hurst."

"And I completely and utterly love you, Ben Gilbert," I promised.

At those words he closed his eyes as though he was in physical pain, taking a gulp of air and drawing away so that his body moved away from mine. Draping the bedsheets over himself, he covered his face with his hands.

"I'm sorry . . ." he began.

"Ben? It's okay," I pleaded, moving toward him.

"It's not, Maddy. It's really not."

The firmness in his voice stopped me.

"What do you mean?"

"We can't do this!"

"What? Why?"

"It's . . ." he started, but couldn't finish. Instead he shook his head.

"Because you feel a sense of loyalty to Robert? Because he doesn't know the meaning of the word. I wouldn't worry about him." I ranted.

"No, well, partly, yes. He's like my brother . . ." he whimpered.

I stared at him, watching as he battled with his emotions once more.

"But mostly because I also don't want us to start out like this," he mumbled, unable to look at me. "If we're to be anything—which we don't know because we're still drunk and you're in the midst of heart-break, but if we were . . . I don't know. This moment is something I've dreamed about for years. Seriously, it is. I don't want it to be some quick drunken shag."

"It won't be."

"Look at us," he said, looking up at my face. "That's exactly what it would be. I don't want to be the guy you slept with to get over Robert, or worse, something you end up regretting. I want to be something more."

"But you said you love me."

I sounded like a child, but sitting there naked, opposite Ben, I felt stupid and exposed. My best friend told me he loved me, kissed me, got me naked, and then rejected me. How pitiful.

"I don't just love you, Maddy . . . I'm in love with you," he sighed. "There's a huge difference between those two things."

"I know."

"Do you?" he implored. "Loving someone is something you can do from afar, admiring someone and appreciating their existence in your life—but being in love's different. It's all-consuming to the point where being away from that person seems unbearable. There's no stopping that feeling . . . It's been so long and I've tried everything to stop feeling the way I do, but I can't. Do you see?"

"I think so."

In that moment, I knew I was experiencing a dangerous amount of lust, but I was also aware of the way my tummy whirled around chaotically, churning up new feelings of admiration. I reasoned with myself that if Ben had been feeling even a sliver of those emotions for all those years, then I owed it to him to make sure whatever we did, we did it right, on his terms. Feeling the way I did, I had no doubt that what we had together had the potential to grow into something more, that I could love Ben in a way I'd never experienced before—if that was what I wanted.

"Maddy, I just don't want to fuck things up. That's the reason why I've never said anything in the past. I'd rather have you in my life and not be with you than you not in my life at all. We have to take things slowly to make sure it's what you actually want . . ."

His words lingered between us.

"Wait until it's right?"

"Yes. Until we both know that there's nothing else clouding our judgment. No rushing in like drunken buffoons."

Stopping there was a wise move. We weren't bad people, we had morals despite our earlier flutter suggesting otherwise. Sleeping with each other in such a careless manner would have been a mistake. If a relationship were to blossom from that night, it would do better not to stem from the darkness.

"So what do we do now?"

"I don't know . . ." he said, reaching across for my hand, which he lovingly cradled in his own.

We each stared at our cupped hands in silence, deep in thought.

After a few minutes I watched Ben as he walked to his cupboard and pulled out a T-shirt, before picking up my discarded knickers and his boxers and bringing them back to the bed.

"Stand up," he said quietly.

I did as he said.

Ben bent down in front of me, picking up one leg at a time as he carefully placed my feet through the leg-holes of my knickers, before sliding the black-laced fabric up my legs, back to where they had sat half an hour before. Next he put on his own underwear before picking up the gray T-shirt, pulling it over my head and guiding my arms through the sleeves, slowly pulling it down to cover my boobs and stomach.

With our modesty protected, he stopped and looked down at me, pulled me toward him and hugged me close.

"If we do this, we do it properly," he sighed. "Believe me, this is taking a huge amount of restraint."

I couldn't help but laugh, "What a difference a day makes."

"Well, I certainly didn't think I'd have a naked Maddy Hurst in my room wanting to sleep with me when the day started."

"Kiss me . . ." I asked quietly, looking up at him, not sure if the request was out of bounds now that we had stopped proceedings.

He tilted his head down toward me.

"Gladly," he whispered, before he gently placed his lips on mine, his fingers running through my hair, down to the base of my neck.

At some point we decided to get back into bed under the covers, although this time the speedy need for sex was replaced by a little bubble of wonder—of nerves and excitement. Snuggling into each other's warm bodies, our arms and legs entwined, we took pleasure in the new feelings being shared between us—an intimacy that felt alarmingly natural.

"Tell me how you're feeling, in one word," he whispered, kissing my nose.

"Just one?" I smiled.

"Yes, that's the rule."

I said the first thing that came into my head, "Happy."

"That's a nice word."

"You?"

"Loved."

I closed my eyes and enjoyed the word, one I could have easily used too.

For those few hours I had no fear. I wasn't worried that things would become awkward, or that, at some point, we'd be forced back into reality and made to suffer the consequences of our actions. What we thought would become of us outside our cocoon, I really didn't know. It wasn't something I thought about in that room on that night. We didn't talk about life outside of that bed, by which I mean Robert wasn't mentioned again. Somehow I'd managed to cut myself off and detach myself from real life. It was unsettlingly easy to do, but Ben made me feel safe, secure, and loved, like I needed nothing else in that particular moment.

We didn't sleep a wink, preferring to talk about everything and nothing instead, smiling at each other like super-happy-psychotic Cheshire cats. Ben smiled at me in a way he'd never done before—wider, bigger, more doe-eyed and lovelier than I'd ever seen. It was like he'd saved that smile just to give to me on that special night. A secret smile, just for me. It filled my heart with an unbelievable joy to watch it spread so infectiously across his face. It was beautiful. As was he.

It pained me to leave him the following morning, but when I did it literally felt like I was walking on air. I know that's what people in movies say, "walking on air," and I agree that it's a saying that would ordinarily make me want to puke my guts up, but there's no other description for the light and giddy feeling that overtook me as I drifted (there was no way I walked, my feet didn't touch the ground once) from his to mine, recalling flashes of images from the previous night as I went—some innocent, some not.

Being with Ben was completely different to what I'd experienced before. It was tender and romantic—I felt special, sexy, and wonderful. Possibly the biggest surprise was that it was Ben who'd made me feel that way. Ben who I'd spent almost every day with for the previous twelve years of my life. How he'd managed to keep his feelings hidden I'd never know—they were threatening to spill out of me that morning at every opportunity. I passed strangers on the street and couldn't help but smile at them, or say good morning, as though I was bursting with kindness and a love for life.

What I wasn't expecting was to walk into my house and find Robert on my bed, looking like he'd been staring at the door for hours, waiting for me to return; his worried face puffy and wide-eyed from a lack of sleep, his hair manically pointing in all directions. I had visions of him running his fingers through his hair in panic at my absence, an action I knew he did whenever he was anxious.

We stood frozen. Staring at each other as though we didn't know who the other person was, we'd become strangers, but maybe that was just how I felt about him moments after being with Ben. After all, to him I was still his Maddy, the same girl I was before I kissed our best friend. He didn't know any different.

The floaty feeling I'd been experiencing just moments prior vanished. It deserted me and left me to drop to the ground with a terrifying speed. I felt heavy and trapped as I lingered in the doorway, not wanting to go inside.

"Hey . . ." he started, his face full of shame and regret. I'd almost forgotten he was carrying his own burden.

"Hi," I mumbled.

"Where have you been?"

"Out."

"I know that. With who?"

"Why does it matter?"

"Mad . . ." he sighed.

"Ben," I said sternly. "I was with Ben."

"That's a relief," he almost laughed, putting his hands through his ruffled hair. "I've been having all sorts go through my head. I thought you might have been, you know—with some random guy or something. Getting back at me. Not that I'd have blamed you, of course, I'd have deserved that."

"Right . . ." I said dryly, slowly walking in and shutting the door.

A faint smell of Ben's aftershave wafted off me as I moved, catching me off guard. It didn't soothe me. Instead, as I looked up at Robert and the guilt began to creep in, I was left irritated. I didn't want to feel ashamed, I didn't want to be regretful of my actions, I didn't want to feel like what I'd done was wrong, even though I knew it was. We might have stopped, but we didn't want to—we wanted to take it further, and that was the problem; as a result it wasn't just a physical connection we'd made, it was an emotional one too. We hadn't just had sex and woken up in the morning feeling embarrassed about what we'd done, looking for absolution as we awkwardly parted ways—we'd stayed up and developed something else. Standing there, in front of Robert, with a feeling of defiance over the previous night, I knew that what we'd done was worse.

"Why are you here?" I asked, unable to hide my annoyance, my voice surprisingly cold.

"To make things right."

"Why didn't you come yesterday?"

"I was confused. I wasn't thinking straight," he conceded.

"And now you are?"

He looked up at me with a sorrowful expression. "I sat at home for a few hours thinking about it all—not only what I did, but about what I said to you afterward. I drove over as soon as I'd talked some sense into myself. I've been here all night."

"So I see."

"I know I fucked up," he said exasperatedly, starting to get up off the bed. "I know I've been a complete dick, but we can get through this, Maddy. I know we—"

"What if I don't want to?" I interrupted.

The color drained from his face as it dawned on him that the situation wasn't as simple as he'd thought—he couldn't just waltz in and expect all to be forgiven.

"What do you mean, Mad?" he said.

"I'm going to have a shower," I said quickly, ducking away from him as he came closer, swiftly closing the bathroom door behind me before he had a chance to reach for me.

"I was wrong. I'm so sorry," he said through the door. "Please forgive me."

I stood and listened to him as he started to quietly sob. I hadn't heard Robert cry in years—not since he fell and he broke his leg, but even then he managed to maintain a certain amount of composure. A gentle bang as his head rested on the door and the sound of his hands brushing against the frame broke my heart further as I pictured him standing just inches away from me, caressing the wood as he tried to get to me, to bring me back to him. Ignorant to the fact that not only had he chucked my heart away, but that someone else had been there, ready to catch it when he had.

The awful thing was that although he was feeling sorry for his crime, I wasn't for mine—and that devastated me. Yes, he'd done wrong, but at least he was facing up to it. Thanks to Ben, I totally understood how quickly and easily something like cheating could happen. Yes, what I had done was far worse because I had an absolute lack of remorse. At least Robert had the human decency to show guilt.

"Please, Maddy. You have to forgive me . . ."

I was forced into feeling ashamed as I stood in my bathroom and listened to my woeful boyfriend. When I couldn't bear to hear any more I stripped off and got in the shower. Battling with my thoughts as I placed my head under its piping-hot water, sinking down to sit in the shower tray as the liquid continued to run over my body. Doubt seeped in as I became more and more unsure of what it was that I wanted—or, more importantly, who.

I wondered whether I should have come clean with Robert, and begged for forgiveness, just like he was doing, in the hope that we'd be able to start again and move forward. He did tell me that he thought we should go on a break; that he didn't know if he wanted to be with me any more. Would it really be that awful to say that I'd messed up too? Realistically I knew it was more than that. I also knew that if I did come clean, I wouldn't be able to tell him it was with Ben—that fact would destroy Robert, Ben, and me as a unit, ruining years of friendship and any chance of us getting back together. But then, I didn't even know if getting back with Robert was what I wanted. After being so brutally dropped I wasn't sure if I could just forgive and forget. Perhaps, as we'd grown up, we'd drifted apart. We'd been in different cities for the past three years, living completely separate lives . . . perhaps it would have come to a natural end at some point anyway. Although, something I couldn't quickly forget was that Robert, first and foremost, was one of my best friends. I'd no doubt that cutting him out of my life would be more painful that I cared to imagine.

My night with Ben continued to linger in my mind, making it impossible to just forget it had happened. If I stayed with Robert, would I able to blot out what I'd felt with him? I wasn't sure I could do that to Ben and his kind and loving heart. He'd put his feelings out there and opened up after years of keeping them a secret—I couldn't face the thought of rejecting him, after all, that fear was what had caused him to hide his love away.

I wondered whether Ben was worth the sacrifice—it would change everything, not just who I dated. It would affect our friendship group, our families—I was aware it would have a massive impact on them too.

My head had become cloudy and confused. Plagued by a million scenarios, concerns, and questions, it struggled to make sense of anything.

I was in the bathroom for far longer than necessary, trying to avoid facing Robert and having to make any sort of decision. When I finally opened the door, none the wiser over what to do, Robert shot up from the spot he'd been sitting in on the floor and frantically grabbed for me.

"Don't touch me, Robert. Please. Don't," I begged, pulling my arms around myself. I didn't want him near me, couldn't stand the thought of being held by those hands that had roamed over someone else's body.

"Maddy, please . . . I love you. It was a mistake; you've got to believe me. I don't even know the girl, and yes, I know that makes it worse in a way, that I'd do that and risk losing everything we have, I just . . . it was a split-second decision, Mad. I was a fucking prick," he ranted in desperation. "I don't expect you to understand why I did it, or what could possibly make me act out in that way . . . but if I could take it back, I would."

"It's not that simple, though, is it?" I snapped, his words touching a nerve.

Robert mutely shook his head, looking sheepish and scared.

"You talked about going on a break . . ."

"But, I don't want that, I don't need one," he said with urgency.

"What about wanting to be a 'free spirit?'"

"That was just nonsense. It wasn't even about you, it was more that I couldn't believe I could do that to you. That I had it in me to do that to the person I love, to you."

"And then you just snapped out of those thoughts?"

"I love you. I love you, Maddy. I want to be with you. We've almost finished uni—I want us to move in together. I want to give you everything you ever wanted, for us to grow old together and have loads of kids. I was wrong, I made a stupid mistake, but I know what I want now. It's what I've always wanted."

As the words tumbled from his mouth I stared at him in sadness and disbelief. If I'd have heard him say those words two days before I'd have been elated, but at that point I just felt pity, not just for him, for myself too. I was sad at the crappy situation we'd suddenly found ourselves in.

"I don't want you to want those things just because you're feeling guilty, Rob," I said calmly.

"I'm not!" He dropped to his knees and pulled me in to him so that his face was buried into my stomach, his hands grabbing me with desperation. This time I didn't back away from him. "Please, please, give me another chance. You know me! You know me better than anyone in the world. You get me. You know me."

"Which is why this is so hard!" I moaned.

"You have to forgive me, Maddy. Please."

"I don't know if I can . . ."

"But say you'll try . . ." he looked up at me and I saw a glimpse of the nine-year-old boy I first met, all bravado and cockiness evaporated. His little slit eyes were the widest I'd ever seen them as they desperately begged, literally begged. I was shocked to see him looking so broken. How on earth had we come to that? Our relationship had been so placid, so strong, so secure—referred to as perfect by others—and then, in the space of twenty-four tiny hours, all those years of togetherness had been blown apart. It didn't seem to have any logic to it.

I was so confused. All I knew in that moment was that I didn't want to hurt Robert. After years of being with him, I didn't want to crush him the way he'd crushed me. I loved him. I couldn't refuse him and break his heart. I couldn't be that cold.

I cupped his head and pulled it in to me, cradling it against my stomach. I couldn't find any words, but the gesture was enough for him.

"Thank you, Maddy. Thank you," he wept, squeezing his arms even tighter around my body. "I promise I'll never be such an idiot ever again. I never want to lose you."

I felt three tears roll down my cheeks as I thought of Ben.

That afternoon we sat next to each other on my floral bed and pretended to be fixated by the television screen. Four hours worth of *Come Dine with Me* was watched as though it was the most interesting thing to ever grace the airwaves. In reality, neither of us cared whether Moira from Hull's triple-baked cheese soufflés rose to the occasion or not, but focusing on it stopped us from having to focus on each other and the mess we were in. Although, it didn't stop Robert from trying his best to lift us out of the somber mood—trying to make light conversation (about Moira and her soufflés, "Oh no, they're going to collapse, poor woman"), or by offering to make us cups of tea every five minutes. I wasn't ready to pretend everything was normal and happy, but I didn't want to spend all afternoon talking about it either. I was tired, irritated and, I'd almost forgotten, hungover. I just wanted to sit in silence and avoid life for as long as I could.

Bodily contact between us was kept at a minimum, something which was unusual for us, as we were always snuggling up or at least holding hands. We were always connected in some way, but that afternoon we sat apart—Robert with his body facing mine (looking eager to lessen the distance between us in his remorseful way), me sat rigid, with my legs curled up, facing the telly straight on. It pains me to say it, but I basically ignored him as much as I could.

I told myself that once Robert had left for Nottingham I'd have time to think things through properly, maybe even talk to Pearl. I knew she was hard to shock, able to keep a secret and good with her advice. If I wanted to talk to any of the girls about it, she'd be the best to go to, definitely—especially as she wouldn't judge me or get all self-righteous. She was far from a saint herself—something Robert was right about.

I also wanted to talk to Ben, see what he was thinking or feeling. Up until that point, in the twelve years Robert and Ben had been in my life, not a single major decision had been made before talking to one or both of them. Now that it was all on my own head, I felt bewildered and panicked.

"These are awesome," Robert encouraged as he attempted to start up yet another meaningless conversation after coming back from the kitchen with yet another tea round. He was looking up at my latest photographs that I'd hung on the walls.

They were portraits of a whole mixture of people (students, teachers, shopkeepers, children, etc.), anyone I could rope into having their faces painted with an array of wild animals and walk through town— there was even a priest with a tiger guise, a shot I was particularly proud of. All of them were rather striking and meant to encapsulate the wild side in all humans that we keep hidden, the idea being that the animalistic side of us is still there somewhere deep inside—we've just learned to conform to what is socially acceptable.

Ben was one of my volunteers and I'd asked him to be a deer—it had been my one and only time to turn him into the Bambi I'd always thought of him as with his big brown eyes. As Robert pointed out the portraits and scanned the different faces, Ben's face seemed to be bigger than anyone else's. It grabbed my attention and made me feel paranoid as it looked back at me, teasing me as if the picture was about to tell Robert the truth. I knew it was my mind playing tricks on me, that all the portraits were identical in size, but that didn't stop it from freaking me out with its torment. It made me feel itchy.

"They're really great," he nodded with forced enthusiasm.

"Cheers . . ." I mumbled.

I watched him in my peripheral vision, biting his lip and running his fingers through his hair, and knew he was desperately searching for something else to say. Some new reason to talk and engage me in any way that wasn't instantly crushed by the sense of foreboding that we were clearly drowning in. It wasn't that he was deluded to hope for things to go back to normal instantly, more that the reality of the whole thing was too depressing for him to dwell on. He was a doer— put a problem in front of Rob and he tried his best to fix it. It was no doubt infuriating for him to be in a situation (one formed from his own doing) that couldn't be sorted so easily. Even by Rob.

"Do you want to go somewhere? Do something?" he endeavored, turning to me, clearly finding the day as agonizingly painful as I was. "We could call Ben. See if he wants to do something."

He looked back up to the picture on the wall. He had seen it. To some extent I was right, that glossy little print had screwed me over, but in reality I knew he was suggesting it in the hope of digging us out of the awkward hole we'd painfully dug ourselves into. He was suggesting anything he could think of in the hope that something would work to erase the unpleasant feeling in the room. Little did he know, he was making it worse.

"I'm sure he mentioned some work he has due in for Monday . . ." I lied.

"We could still ask. Knowing him, he's already done it anyway."

"You know what, I'm happy here," I shrugged, snuggling back into my pillows.

"It's a sunny day, Maddy, a bit of air would probably do us good," he said, reaching for his phone.

"We don't have to ask Ben along, though."

It was an odd thing for me to say to Robert, and I knew it. I'd never had a problem with asking Ben to join us before. In fact, it was usually me encouraging Robert to invite him. The comment didn't go unnoticed; Robert became shamefaced once more. His upbeat pretense dropped.

"Is everything okay? Is he mad at me?"

"No. I don't think so," I said, trying to hide the panic from my voice. I did not want to be talking about Ben to Robert. I also did not want to be in a situation where the three of us had to hang out together.

"Are you sure? I feel bad the way I put him in the middle like that. I shouldn't have. I didn't even think before phoning him. He no doubt thinks I'm a complete dick now. I would."

"Robert, I'm sure he's fine. He's just busy, that's all."

He looked from me down to his phone with hesitation. "You know what, I'll call him anyway. It would be good to just speak to him. He'll be worried."

My heart sank as Robert dialed, put the phone to his ear, and wandered out of my room. From the hallway I could hear him talking but he was back in the room within seconds.

"Answer machine," he muttered.

I felt relieved.

When the following evening finally came and it was time for Robert to head back to Nottingham, he didn't want to go. He put it off as late as possible, hating having to leave when everything felt so unresolved. He had tried his best to hold everything together, to bandage us back into one piece with his earnest attitude, but even he wasn't sure if he'd done enough. He couldn't take our mistakes away, no matter how hard he wished he could.

When it was time to say good-bye, he hugged me tighter than ever, still trying his best to knock down the barrier that had been built between us. It was futile to try so early. I needed time, space.

What am I saying?

I wasn't sure what I needed.

I just wanted him gone.

I hadn't been alone for more than fifteen minutes when a letter was slid through the crack at the bottom of my door. It was from Robert.

Maddy,

When we first kissed in Paris our love required a leap of faith. We didn't know what was going to become of those strange teenage emotions that had taken over. It was scary voyaging into the unknown but we had each other for support as we put aside our fears and trusted that our feelings would lead us to the place we were meant to be.

I've never regretted that moment, or doubted the love in our relationship, nor have I ever questioned our future together. I need you to know that what happened was not because I do not want to be with you, more that I'm a fool who made the most momentous mistake of his life.

I'm prepared to spend the rest of forever fighting to put things right—to make you see that I'm your Robert. The one you deservedly put so much trust in, and who promised to love you forever.

All I ask is that you take another leap of faith with me, like you did five years ago, although this time, I promise to never let you go.

Yours forever,
Robert xxx

In fact, I was pretty sure she did end up preferring his company to mine on occasions, but he brought her back to me in one piece once our university days were through, so I'd like to take this opportunity to say thank you to Ben, for that. Without him there, who knows what might have happened. She could have been whisked off her feet by an utter charmer and this day would never have happened.

Ben

TWENTY-ONE YEARS OLD . . .

"Hey, mate. Look, so sorry about all this. I shouldn't have phoned you first and put you in the middle like that. I'm over at Maddy's now. Wanted you to know everything's okay, we're just talking things through. Really want to see you before I go back. Give me a call. Oh, and thanks for looking after her last night. You're a true gent."

I was still in bed when he called. I'd been replaying little scenes from the previous night in my head, over and over again—I was still in disbelief that it had actually happened, that I hadn't just dreamed the whole thing. For years I'd held in my feelings and not told a soul about how I'd truly felt, too worried that I'd ruin the great thing we had going—worried that I'd be rejected if I confessed anything, not that I'd ever admitted that to myself. I'd told myself I would never get to tell her how I felt, too much time had gone by and then she was with Robert for years, so I was getting used to the fact that she'd never know the truth, that she'd never be attainable to me. I thought that ship had well and truly sailed, but then when she kept pushing me to tell her what was on my mind, pushing and pushing, I suddenly went for it. Put my cards on the table like a freshly opened deck, too tempting to ignore.

I told her everything, about how I loved her, about the three squeezes, it all came tumbling out . . . once I'd started I couldn't stop. I needed her to see its importance, understand that I wasn't just drunk. There she was, the love of my life, listening to my every word. Moved by what I was telling her. It was better than I'd ever imagined.

And when I kissed her? Wow. The way I felt, the emotion inside me, made everything so intense, so much better. Everything about her was as wonderful as I'd imagined; the softness of her milky-white skin, the sweetness of its taste as I ran my mouth over her body. Her voluptuous bum, her smooth breasts, her small blush nipples—I couldn't get it out of my mind. It had taken every ounce of self-control I had to stop myself from having sex with her. Something I was pleased with myself for. I didn't want her to wake up the next day regretting it. But also, I wasn't a total rogue, there was something nagging away inside of me. Typically known to all as my conscience. I couldn't stop Robert from popping up in my brain, reminding me what a tosser I was being to him, my best mate, the guy who'd do anything for me. That was his girlfriend that I was with, and whether they were technically still together or not was beside the point. I was being an asshole. They had not been apart more than a few hours before I'd swooped in. But then, as I sat there thinking about her plump pink lips, I wondered if he would care. After all, he'd discarded her, got with someone else, and talked about breaking up.

I was being ridiculous.

Of course he would care.

My blood ran cold as soon as I saw Robert's name pop up on my phone. I completely froze. I wasn't sure what to do. It was such a normal thing, him calling me, but suddenly it felt like the most alien and bizarre thing in the world to happen. My mind entered into a mad spin as I tried to work out why he could possibly be calling me.

I thought he might have found out and that was why he was phoning. I imagined maybe Maddy had called and told him everything as a way of getting back at him, or something. That made me feel really sick, which was pathetic—if anything were to happen with me and Maddy, which I was sure I wanted, then of course Robert was going to find out. We'd have to tell him. It was something I hadn't thought about until his name popped up. I would have to tell him and that could potentially ruin over twenty years of friendship. I could lose him. Is that what I wanted? I wondered if I loved Maddy that much. I'd always thought I would sacrifice everything for love, but the reality wasn't as clear-cut. I wasn't sure if I was ready to give up on Robert, but then, I couldn't be sure if it was loyalty or guilt making me feel that way.

If I'm honest, I wasn't sure where I saw me and Maddy going, and that hurt. It pained me that, after years of wanting her so badly, I wasn't sure what the future had in store for us. I'd spent years with her not knowing the truth, of plodding along with her and Robert as my best friends. Having her know the truth after so long was more complicated than I'd feared, leaving me to feel more confused than I thought I ever could over the possibility of being with Maddy.

With all those thoughts and worries whirling through my mind, I didn't pick up the phone to Robert. I knew I needed to speak to Maddy first—to find out exactly where we stood and what was going to happen next.

A loud bleep let me know he'd left a voicemail. I took a deep breath, reached for my phone and nervously held it to my ear as Robert's jolly voice boomed through the speaker.

I sat up in bed as I listened to the twenty-nine second message over and over again.

Everything was okay, he'd said.

He was with her.

They'd talked things through.

They were back on track.

Where the hell did that leave me, I wondered.

Somehow, in the mere hours since Maddy had left my room, she'd gone back to Robert. She'd forgiven him for his misdemeanor. I was just a pitstop along the way to her reaching that conclusion. The night rendered forgettable and meaningless—it hadn't been as special for her as it had for me. But then, what did I expect? They'd been a couple for years, shared a bond that could stand a few knocks. My pathetic few hours with her would never have been able to compete with that. I was foolish for thinking otherwise. Stupid for believing she could love me back in the same way.

The rejection hurt just as much as I feared it would.

I almost had her, and then Robert came back to reclaim her, pushing all thoughts of me and the night we'd shared out of her mind. Yes, Robert had caused me to have my own doubts, but all I'd needed to do was talk to Maddy, to try to decipher the complicated situation we were in. I hadn't expected her to move away from me so swiftly, to turn her back on our night together so coldly.

I sat in silence on my bed, looking around my room. Hours before, it had been a place of love and warmth, now it was bleak and barren. Deserted. I needed to get out, to be surrounded by noise.

I didn't even wash, I just chucked on a pair of jeans and a crumpled shirt and walked back to the Red Fox. I didn't care that it was dirty, I just liked the fact that I knew I'd be left to mope into my pint of Carling . . . of which I had several.

I was already fairly smashed when I got a call from Roger, a guy on my course, reminding me about a house party he was having that night and wondering where I was. In my inebriated state, going along sounded like a top idea.

When I turned up at his place, which was only meant to be a fifteen-minute walk away but took me half an hour to get to because I couldn't quite walk in a straight line—plus I got lost twice—it was rammed full of people, most of whom I didn't recognize. They cluttered up the narrow hallway, the stairs, and the kitchen, making it difficult to find Roger. I gave up looking for him fairly quickly, actually, and instead looked around the room and wondered where to place myself.

I decided to join a group of about ten people who were passionately playing drinking games around a dining-room table, boisterously cheering as their friends were made to neck various combinations of alcohol. I watched them finish their game of "Arrogance," essentially a dangerous game of heads or tails, before joining them to play "Finger in the middle"—a game where players pour a hefty amount of their own drink into the central cup, then have to guess how many people are going to leave their fingers on the rim of the cup after the count of three. It sounds boring but it becomes fascinatingly funny when you're drunk—which we all were.

Luckily for me, I won the first round—no idea how—and so just had to watch the others battle it out.

It was the loser of the game that caught my eye—a cute little thing with an enormous smile. I'd seen her around campus before and at a few parties. She was hard to miss with her elfin features and petite little body. I had no idea who she was, we'd never spoken, but in that moment she had my attention hooked on her.

I'd watched her as she giggled her way through the game, laughing playfully and covering her face with her hands every time she guessed wrong. Her joy quickly turned to dismay, though, as she lost and realized she'd have to down the entire contents of the half-full pint glass. She grimaced at its gray-colored liquid, which had curdled thanks to somebody adding Bailey's into the mix of beer, wine, and spirits. Every time she went to drink it she burst out laughing as the gathered crowd cheered in encouragement, "Down it, down it, down it."

"Do I have to?" she laughed.

"Yes," shouted back the excitable crowd, not giving her any allowances for being a girl—if you were in to play, you were in for the forfeit. That was the rule.

She looked over at me and I winked at her, the alcohol giving me more confidence than normal.

In return she flashed me a massively beautiful smile.

She pushed her long blonde hair back behind her ears and lifted the cup to her mouth, her hazel eyes flicking back in my direction before she downed the lot—causing the gathered crowd to cheer in approval before dispersing in search of more alcohol for their next game.

"Argh, that was awful," she said to me seconds afterward as she stumbled toward me, wiping her mouth in disgust. "I promised myself I wouldn't do that tonight."

"Oh really?"

"I'm a sucker for peer pressure," she giggled, grabbing my bottle of beer from me and taking a mouthful. "Sorry—trying to get rid of the taste."

"More alcohol is definitely what you need after that," I grinned.

"Tell me about it," she grimaced, handing me back my drink.

"So, what brings you here?" I asked.

"It's my house," she smiled.

"Ah . . ."

"You?"

"Doing Graphic Arts with Roger."

"Oh, I see. You're . . . ?"

"Ben."

"Ben," she smiled with a nod. "I'm Alice."

We laughed as we took hold of each other's hand and gave a formal businesslike handshake.

At that point the drinking-game group had come back into the room with new supplies. One of them, a short skinny guy with bushy hair that covered his eyes, had a row of drinks cradled in his arms, clearly stocking up for more than the one game. As he passed us he got pushed by one of his more robust mates, causing him to trip, knock into another mate, and spill his drinks over everyone standing around him. I was fairly unscathed, but Alice received the majority of the beer-based tidal wave.

"Sorry," the guy said evasively without looking at anyone in particular, picking up the now empty plastic cups from the floor before tottering off to the kitchen to refill them, the loss of alcohol causing him more concern than anyone's wet clothes.

"Oh crap," Alice moaned, wiping some of the foamy beer off her orange dress with the back of her hand, flicking the drips onto the floor.

"Should I go get you a cloth or something?" I offered, gesturing toward the kitchen.

"No, don't worry. It's only beer—I'm sure it'll come out in the wash," she sighed, looking down at the soggy material that had decided to cling to her toned body.

I couldn't help but notice her nipples which, thanks to the cold liquid, were standing to attention.

"Are you sure there's nothing I can do," I flustered. "You're soaking wet."

"Easy, tiger," she giggled.

I joined in, shaking my head at my unintended sexual innuendo.

"I'll just get changed," she shrugged, pulling the dress away from her body and giving it a little shake. "It's getting late now anyway— I'm sure no one will notice if I slip away to my room for a bit. Maybe get changed into my PJs instead . . ."

"Sweet," I nodded, looking around at the rest of the party, who seemed to be as drunk as I felt. The next round of drinking games had started, minus the bushy-haired guy who was still sourcing new drinks, Michael Jackson was blaring out of the stereo and a rowdy gaggle was attempting a comical dance-off, moonwalking around a few guys who'd passed out on the floor. Elsewhere in the room people were either in deep conversations or getting frisky with one another.

"Want to come up?" Alice leaned in and purred, tugging hold of my T-shirt in a playful manner that could only suggest one thing— she wasn't about to show me her PJ collection.

"Sure . . ."

We fought our way around the dance troopers, carefully avoided the gamers, passed the people still loitering on the stairs, and eventually made it to outside Alice's room. She removed one of her high-heeled shoes and fished out a key.

"The last thing you want at a house party is to go to bed and find it's already occupied," she smirked, unlocking the door and leading us into the darkness.

As soon as she'd shut the door behind us, Alice, who I'd assumed to be fairly sweet and innocent, turned into a complete vixen—tearing at my shirt, ripping open the buttons and pulling at my jeans, pushing me onto her bed like a crazed sex beast. She was all over me—had me in her mouth within seconds.

The sex was angry and quick, full of grabbing, biting, and slapping. It was a complete contrast to the loving nature of the night before, which was exactly what I needed. I couldn't stop Maddy from entering my thoughts, no matter how much I tried to push her away. I was so angry, so fucking angry. It was her that I thought about as I thrust deep inside Alice.

After I came, I cried, much to my embarrassment.

I was distraught that the only girl I'd ever loved didn't love me back, humiliated that I'd given such a huge part of my heart away to something that had only ever existed in my head, and ashamed of myself for betraying my best friend.

Without asking any questions, Alice took my head to her chest and ran her fingers through my sweaty hair, running her hand over my forehead until I fell asleep.

I was grateful for the company.

Thankful I didn't have to spend the night in my bed, on my own.

The following Tuesday, once my lectures were finished for the day, I took myself off to the library to study. I wasn't able to get any work done in my room, the sight of it reminding me of the weekend's activities, so I thought sitting alongside other students hard at work might inspire me. It turned out to be fairly quiet in there—although that wasn't too surprising seeing as the sun had decided to grace us with its presence. I'm sure most students had opted to "study" in the sunshine while they topped up their tans instead of sitting in the gloomy library, staring vacantly at a computer screen.

I was at a huge study desk on my own when Maddy came and sat down next to me. I didn't even have to look up to know it was her, the smell of her perfume, Ghost's Deep Night, gave her away, the sweet scent drifting in before she had. It was something that had always lifted my spirits, but on that occasion it made me squirm in my seat.

It was the first time we'd seen each other since she'd stayed at mine. It was going to be an awkward encounter, after all—I assumed she was about to break my heart and let me down gently as she told me she was back with Robert, so I braced myself.

What took me by surprise was her mood—I could tell she was pissed off at something. Her breathing was heavy, as though she was trying to keep herself calm. Her face was flushed with what appeared to be anger. She swung the chair around so that she was facing me.

I struggled to look back at her.

"Did you sleep with Roger's housemate?" she asked in a quiet voice, her eyes darting around the room to make sure no one could hear us.

I was stumped.

I knew we were in dire need of a serious chat and that being with her again was going to be gut-wrenching, but I hadn't expected that curveball to be thrown into the mix. I was thinking it would be more of an explanation from her as to what had happened after she'd left mine and ran back into Robert's arms, forgetting that I even existed, along with some kind of apology—or possibly even making sure I wasn't about to tell Robert about that night now that they were staying together, just in case the guilt ever got hold of me and made me want to confess all. Those were the two scenarios that had run through my head as possible first conversations post "that night." Alice hadn't factored into it at all.

"Erm . . ."

"No point denying it. I've just bumped into him."

"Who?"

"Roger."

"Right."

"Have you known her long?" she asked briskly, her tone thick with spite—I'd never heard her voice sound like that before, it was startling.

"No, I've just seen her around a few times. We've never actually spoken before," I shrugged, suddenly feeling like a kid being reprimanded by their mother.

"Good to know she's someone you really care about," she said sarcastically. "Do you remember texting me?"

"No."

"Well you did, telling me how much you loved me. Actually, I'm surprised you could bring yourself to tell me that while you were with her—I never knew you were such a multitasker," she cackled.

I shifted uncomfortably. I did remember contacting her. I was still in the pub at that point. I'd been in the middle of sending my fifth and final message when Roger had called. I probably wouldn't have answered the call otherwise, but I'd picked it up by accident. I could also remember the drunken voicemail I'd left as I stumbled through town on my way to his house. They were all messages declaring my love, but I'd been unable to hide my sorrow in them, or my disappointment—luckily I couldn't remember exactly what I'd said. I was embarrassed enough at having contacted her so desperately.

"At least I know why you've been ignoring my calls since," she added.

"Maddy, I'm sor—"

"And to think I actually believed you," she interrupted, her eyes squinting at me in disbelief.

"Stop it," I begged.

"That I told you I loved you, that we almost . . ." She hesitated as she once again glanced around the room. ". . . slept together. You told me you loved me."

"I do."

"So what happened?"

"What do you think happened?"

"Wow. I meant that much to you that within twenty-four hours you were sticking your cock into someone else."

"Maddy!" I was shocked by the vulgarity of her tone, the explicitness of her language, and the anger raging within her—wasn't I meant to be the angry one in that situation? Wasn't it me who had been royally screwed over by her?

"What happened? Once you got all those feelings out, you decided you didn't care as much as you thought you had? Or was I that much of a disappointment when you finally got me naked?" Her eyes bored into me, demanding a response. "Well?"

I had nothing to give—no reason and no excuse.

"You've made a fool of me, Ben."

"I haven't," I protested, shaking my head at her words.

"You've made me feel like a complete mug. There I was thinking about you, about us, thinking about how we might be able to make this work, while all the time you were in bed with—"

"No, there you were, reconciling with Robert, Maddy. Don't try and play the martyr here, because you're really not," I spat, taking the bait and allowing myself to be riled. "So let's talk about that, shall we? Let's talk about how hours after you left me in my bed you were patching things up with Robert."

She brought her hands up to her face in horror, her bullish façade slipping as tears sprang to her eyes. She shook her head profusely.

"I was trying to think things through," she said helplessly.

"By getting back with Robert?" I scoffed.

"I didn't know what to do."

"Seems like you made up your mind pretty quickly to me. It didn't take you long to forgive him."

"I didn't . . ."

I sat silently as she tried to piece together her words. I couldn't look her in the eye. Instead, I focused on her hands in her lap, her fingers wriggling in discomfort, wringing the loose material on her skirt. She looked lost. All I wanted to do was embrace her and take that feeling away. In all our years of friendship I'd never been the cause of

Maddy's tears, I'd always been the one to mop them up and make her feel better. It was agonizing to sit and watch her struggle.

"It's not that simple . . ." is all she managed before trailing off.

"From where I've sat, it really is," I said calmly.

"But I love you . . ." she mumbled as a tear escaped and fell onto her lap.

Her words gave me little pleasure.

"Did you tell him?"

"Of course not. I wouldn't . . ." she said, shaking her head, a sob rising from her mouth.

I took hold of her hand then, I couldn't resist it, my thumb rubbed the back of it.

In return she squeezed my hand.

Three times.

The gesture shocked me. Rebuked me into pulling my hands away.

"Maddy," I sighed, my patience wavering slightly. "I don't know what you want from me. You know how I feel. I opened up to you, finally told you everything I've ever wanted to say, but you're back with Robert. You clearly don't feel that love back."

"But I do!"

"You have a boyfriend."

"And?"

"That's a pretty big 'and' right there."

"Are you going to see her again?"

"Who? Alice? I dunno, I hadn't thought about it. I might. Why not?" I shrugged, confused as to why she was bringing up Alice—it seemed insignificant in the circumstances.

Defiantly, I wondered why there should even be a problem if I were to see Alice again. Maddy was back with Robert, leaving me on my own, once again. It seemed unfair that I'd be doomed to watching the two of them all loved up as though nothing had happened. Surely, I told myself, it was time for me to have someone of my own—someone to stop me from focusing on what I couldn't have.

"Right . . ."

"It makes no sense to just hang around, you know?"

"Yeah . . ."

"Now I know where I stand with you, that is," I said. I loitered on that sentence for a while, offering a spot for her to interject and protest, but she didn't. I plowed on. "To be honest, Maddy, for the sake of our friendship and for Robert, I kind of think we should just forget it ever happened. It was only one night after all. We can put it all down to the drink and heightened emotions."

The expression on her face as she looked up at me was one I'd never forget—one of shock, sorrow, and disbelief. As though my words had literally slapped her across the face and simultaneously ripped out her heart.

"If that's what you want . . ." she muttered, looking back down at her hands.

I shrugged in reply, hating myself as I did it, not fully understanding why I was pushing her away so viciously. It wasn't what I wanted at all.

"Oh . . ." she looked as though she was going to say more, but decided against it.

My heart ached as she got up and walked away from me.

If only falling out of love was as easy as falling in it.

If only being with the girl I loved was as easy as all the songs on the radio insisted.

A day later the e-mails began. All the things that weren't said, that maybe we couldn't say face to face, written in safety from behind a computer screen. Saving us from having to speak the words out loud that we wouldn't have had the courage to utter in person, although perhaps leading us to boldly say things that we otherwise wouldn't have—the keyboard allowing us too much honesty, giving us too much bravado, making us forget ourselves.

Maddy sent the first one:

Look, I know you probably don't want to talk, you made your feelings quite clear yesterday when you told me to just forget the whole thing, but I have to get some things off my chest. I want to talk about this, even if you apparently don't. You might feel like acting as though it never happened, but I can't just do that. Not straight away. I feel like I need to explain a few things first. I need you to understand me.

I want you to know how much the other night meant to me. Never in a million years did I think you'd tell me you loved me, that I'd hear I'd been so blind to what was going on in your head for so long. I thought I knew everything there was to know about you, but that was a pretty big secret you'd been keeping. One second you were my trusted friend and then the next—BAM—something more. You were offering me possibilities I never knew existed, a love that was more wholesome and honest than I'd ever thought possible—it felt enchanting. It felt right.

Because of the feelings you stirred in me, I was shocked when I found out about you and Alice. I felt like it lessened the importance of our night together and it made me feel a bit cheap and just another "almost" notch on your bedpost. Am I? I hope not. I just can't get my head around how you can say you feel one way but then sleep with someone else straight away after. As they say, actions speak louder than words. Perhaps it's a guy thing, but it's not like you to do something so shitty.

I know you said about me jumping back into bed with Robert, but deep down you must have realized that wasn't the case. I couldn't have done that. We didn't. We haven't. And the reason for that was because I've not been able to get you and me out of my head.

Ben, you know I love Robert. I've been with him for five years, and have known him for as long as I've known you. He completely fell apart in front of me, something I wasn't expecting (you know he's usually so strong) and that threw me. I was prepared to hate him for what he'd done but when he was stood in front of me like that I faltered. I couldn't hurt him further when I could see how much agony he was in. Even when he left I wasn't sure what I was going to do. It wasn't as simple as I forgave him, forgot about you and we moved on to a happy-ever-after existence. I was coming to find you the other day to talk it all through with you, to try and make things clearer in my head. For me, there was still a big chance of you and me being together, or at least of talking and seeing what the possibilities were. I'd thought about it, a lot. But then I bumped into Roger. I felt crushed.

After seeing you yesterday, and hearing what you had to say, I called Robert and told him I was ready to put what he'd done behind us and move on. I was surprised that I'd done it when I put the phone down, but, if I'm honest, I only did it because I was angry with you. I still don't know what I want. It's all so raw still.

You're saying you want to move forward as though nothing has happened between us. After years of hiding your feelings you're certainly being very quick to brush them aside, as though they weren't as important to you as you proclaimed. Why are you giving up so easily, Ben?

I really don't know what to say to make all this better. You're my best friend and a huge part of my life. Can we meet up and talk? Go for a drink, or a walk, or something? Anything?

Deflated. That would be my one word right now.

I love you, Ben. Always have, always will.

Maddy xoxo

I was in my bedroom working when the e-mail pinged through. Reading it caused me to drop everything I was doing, to get up, walk outside, and go for a mammoth bike ride. I was out for hours, trying to process my different thoughts and emotions—each of them conflicting with the next.

I waited a few days before I replied. Not because I was trying to hurt her or punish her in any way, I simply didn't know what to respond with. Parts of her e-mail angered me, while others made me sad.

None of it made me happy.

I sat in bed with my laptop on my knees trying to piece together some sort of response. All I wanted to tell her was that I loved her unconditionally, and that I would always be there waiting for her, but there was no point. She'd made her decision. Me harping on wasn't going to help matters. In the end I typed out a response in seconds and sent it before my heart had time to process its true feelings.

> There's nothing to sort out, Maddy. I love you, but you're with Robert. It's that simple. I'll always be your friend, you know that.

Even I was disappointed with myself and my seeming lack of effort.

She replied within minutes.

> It's not that simple and you know it! I love you too! I know some people don't believe that you can love two people at the same time—but I'm starting to think you can! You can and it's an awful feeling, because no matter what you decide to do about it you're always going to hurt someone.

And thanks for the short e-mail. What about everything else I said?

My fingers hastily ran away from me as I typed a response straight away, against my better judgment.

Maddy, what do you want from me? You and Robert have shared five years together as a couple—we've had one night. Therefore you chose him. There's nothing I can do to change those facts, all I can say is I get it. I understand. What more do you want? My blessing? If so, you have it. Being in love with two people? Perhaps you're just saying it to flatter me. As it's only been five days I hope you'll be able to fall out of love as quickly as you fell in it. That should clear you of your woes.

As for you being another notch on my bedpost—how many girls do you seriously think I've slept with? Do you honestly think I treat girls in that way? You know me better than anyone so I'll try my best not to be offended.

I got with Alice that night because I felt like it and because you didn't give me any other option. Actions speak louder than words—yes, you're right. They do. Which is why Robert and you being together on Saturday spoke volumes. Instead of kicking him out, he stayed there and you talked things through—leading to him calling me! You could've given me some warning. In many ways it was the catalyst for the rest of the night. If it appears that I've brushed away any feelings then it's because someone handed me the broom. Not that I'm trying to lay blame on anyone else.

My feelings for you haven't altered, but my outlook on the situation has. We're best friends. You and Robert are my rocks. I know everything will be fine. At some point everything will go back to the way it was and we'll move past this. I don't think meeting up to talk about any of it is going to help either of us. I'm a bit busy at the moment, so not really free to meet up anyway, but we'll definitely do something soon.

Ben x

As soon as I'd sent that one I wished I hadn't. I wanted to disconnect and make things easier for both of us, but instead I'd added coal to the fire and prodded it aggressively with a giant rod. I only ever had love for Maddy, but the situation made me hide that, made me show her an ugly side instead, one that I hated. I suppose the same must have been true for her. We became vicious and snappy—something we'd never been with each other before, even when we were young and thoughtless.

Handed you the broom? Are you kidding me? You say there's no one to blame, but that's blatantly pointing the finger at me. How dare you. You're the one who started all this. You felt a certain way and bottled it up inside for years. Why not keep it locked up? You were obviously good at keeping it a secret. Why put it out there so that I have to deal with it too? Why wait until I'm heartbroken and drunk? Or was that your plan all along? Have you been waiting all this time for Robert to slip up so that you could jump in and make yourself look like the hero?

After looking at the screen for an hour, not knowing how to respond, I decided, instead of e-mailing back with further malice that I didn't mean, to put my laptop away, pick up my phone, and call Alice. I'd been putting off doing so because my head and heart were still feeling fragile and bruised, but I came to the conclusion that what they actually needed was a bit of TLC.

"Hello, you . . . Long time no speak," she giggled, as she answered.

"Hey! Yes, I know. Appalling behavior on my part."

"Don't you know it's rude to leave a girl hanging like that?"

I couldn't help but laugh. "I'm sorry, it's been a manic week."

"I see . . . remind me, how long does it take to send a quick text these days?"

I could tell she was still smiling, even if there was honesty in her disappointment.

"I wanted to wait until I had time to call."

"Hmmm . . . I see."

"I was wondering if you fancied going out tonight? For dinner or something?" I said as I got up from my bed and paced around the room.

"Tonight? Are you really expecting me to drop all my important plans for you after you had sex with me and didn't call for a week?"

"Oh . . ." I suddenly felt stupid for having asked.

"Only joking," she cackled. "You'll only be saving me from a night in my PJs eating chocolate. Pick me up at seven."

"Deal."

I knew I needed to get Maddy out of my head and, as Alice came with no complications, she was a welcome distraction. That's what was appealing about her. That and the fact that she was ridiculously pretty and had a wicked personality to boot. If anyone was going to help me get over Maddy, I thought she would. Plus, let's not forget, I cried after having sex with the girl. I felt she deserved a little more respect than me never calling her again. A nice chilled-out dinner—I owed her that much.

When she answered the door at seven o'clock, we both stood there nervously, hesitant over how to greet one another. When I left her on the Sunday morning I'd kissed her good-bye—well, I had just slept with her, it would have been rude not to—but it would have seemed too forward to repeat the gesture then, when we were both totally sober and back to feeling like strangers again. So, instead, I stood there grinning at her.

She looked ridiculously cute with her hair bundled up in a high bun on the top of her head, her petite frame wearing a pale blue denim dress and with cream Converse on her feet, patterned with a design of dainty pink flowers. I towered above her, a fact I liked.

We didn't hold hands as we walked the short distance to the restaurant. In fact, we hardly spoke. Alice wasn't acting like the giggling girl I remembered her to be—instead she was suddenly demure and shy, with a preoccupied expression plastered on her face, making her seem wary. It troubled me.

For our date I'd picked a nice little Italian restaurant on the river—I'm ashamed to say it was a place I'd taken other girls previously. Antonio's had a great view, felt like an authentic Italian (the owner had the thickest accent to accompany his rather thick and dark mustache), and the food was delicious—much better than anything I could have knocked together. But best of all, it was relatively cheap—I was, after all, paying for it out of my student loan, or what I had left of it. Needless to say, I was on a tight budget.

As soon as we had sat down to dinner and ordered some wine, I decided to get to the root of what was going on with Alice.

"Are you okay?" I asked, taking the red cotton napkin from its fan-like position on the table and placing it over my lap.

Her eyes widened in embarrassment as she looked up at me.

"Yes!" she said slowly, picking up her own napkin and unfolding it. "It's just I'm aware that we've done all of this the wrong way round."

"Done what?"

"This," she said, waving her hand manically between us both, the napkin flapping around in the air. "You've seen me naked before even finding out my second name."

"Oh, right," I smiled, heartened by the sweetness of it all. "So what is it, your second name?"

"Turner," she said calmly, neatly placing the cloth over her thighs. "Alice Turner."

"And yours is Gilbert," she stated with a coy smile.

"Yes!"

"See, I knew that. Oh, I don't know," she sighed, as she put her head in her hands, seemingly embarrassed. "I made it so easy for you. I don't usually do that. You know, what happened the other night. I'm surprised you even called. I wouldn't have if I was you. What a tart."

I laughed, unsure how to respond. Alice was cute. Her girlie nerves made me feel protective—they made me want to reassure her. "Well, I did. Plus, and I really don't want to point this out, but, if you're a tart, that makes me a tart . . . so at least we're in good company with our tarty ways."

She let out one of her sweet giggles as she visibly started to relax.

Once the waiter, Antonio with his signature mustache, had poured us some wine and taken our orders—we'd both gone for spaghetti and meatballs, with a side of cheesy garlic bread—I focused my attention on finding out more about Alice Turner.

"So, come on, then. Out with it. I'm ready to find out everything about you."

"Everything?" she asked, raising her eyebrows as she sipped on her wine.

"Yes."

"That could take a while . . ."

"True. Good job we have time, then," I shrugged.

"And I'm not that interesting," she smiled.

"Maybe just some highlights into the world of Alice Turner, then. Give me five fun facts."

"Ooh, the pressure is on!"

"Make them good," I teased.

"How to make myself sound fun and desirable . . ." she pondered with a smile, as she rested her chin on the palms of her hands and tapped her fingers against her cheeks. "Okay, fact one, I study English Language and am in my third year, which, yes, means that we've been in the same city for three years and never actually spoken."

"How weird!"

"Not really. I've seen you around but you've usually been with a girl, a redhead, so I assumed you two were an item until Roger told me otherwise. Plus, I was dating this guy for most of that time—a loser. Unimportant," she said, waving her hand to dismiss him further with a grimace on her face.

"Ha! Carry on," I beckoned, wanting to swiftly move past the fact that Maddy had been brought up; something I didn't want us to dwell on for too long.

"Fact two, I grew up in Brentwood, Essex, with my mum, dad, and little brother, George."

"An Essex girl?"

"Why does everyone say it like that?" she said with a bemused frown.

"Like what?"

"You know."

"No . . ."

I did.

"Wipe that grin off your face, mister. Contrary to popular belief, us Essex girls do actually have brains—we're not all handbags and white stilettos."

"Clearly," I smiled, enjoying the glimpse of her feisty side.

"Fact three, I thought I was going to be a time traveler like Dr. Who when I grew up, until I found out that he was fictional and that it wasn't an actual job. So, now I want to be a journalist."

"You followed up your argument about having brains with admitting you wanted to be a time traveler?"

"Ha! Fair play, but I was young."

"Oh, forgiven, then," I nodded, enjoying teasing her. "So, what sort of journalist?"

"A features writer for some big, fat, glossy magazine!"

"Sounds great."

"Gosh, these were meant to be interesting facts!"

"They are!" I laughed.

We paused as the waiter came back over with a basket of bread and butter.

"Okay, fact four, I have a slight obsession with giraffes. Nothing major, but I do have a giraffe onesie that I like to chill out in . . ."

"Sounds delightful. You've talked a lot about your PJs."

"Have I?" she giggled. "I do love a good pair of pajamas! And fact number . . . oh, I've forgotten what fact I'm on. Fact whatever-this-is, I own, and wear in private, a pair of slippers."

"Is that it?"

"Oh no, these are not just any slippers. These are a pair of blue Little Miss Bossy slippers—they're like big cuddly toys that go on each foot. I can hardly walk around when I'm in them, they're so huge, but they keep my feet warm . . . I just can't get rid of them."

"Do you wear the slippers and the onesie at the same time?"

"Don't be ridiculous . . . I'd look stupid. Besides, they clash. Believe me, I've tried it," she laughed. "Now, that's enough about me, I want to know all about you!"

"Well, I'm really not interesting. I don't have an animal onesie for a start."

"But if you could pick an animal outfit to chill out in, what would it be?" she pushed.

"Ooh, that's a tough one."

"You have to think carefully."

"Maybe something like a koala? I imagine they'd be good to snuggle in."

"Mmm . . . good choice," she giggled.

The rest of the night flew by with ease. The hesitant start a distant memory by the time I dropped Alice off at her door hours later.

"It's been a great night," I said as we stopped outside.

"It has . . ." Alice smiled, rooting through her bag and pulling out her front door key.

Before she had a chance to put it in the lock, I put my arm around her waist and pulled her in for a kiss—our first that night.

She started giggling as soon as it was over.

"What?"

"I don't know," she smiled, looking up at me. "Are you coming in?"

"Not tonight."

"You're not?" she asked, sounding surprised, playing with the sleeve of my top with her fingers, her lips forming a little pout of disappointment.

"No . . . I usually save that until at least the third date, and I don't want you to get the wrong impression of me—or worry that I have the wrong impression of you."

"I see . . ." she pondered, nodding her head.

"Hmmm . . ." I playfully sighed as I fiddled with the strap of her dress on her shoulder, tempted to go against my own valiant words.

"So you think there's going to be a next time?" she asked, raising her eyebrows.

"I'd like to think so," I said, leaning in for another kiss. "And a time after that."

"If you're lucky," she giggled.

I got back to five e-mails from Maddy. The first continued with the same angry tone as before, the middle three were wondering where I was and the last was more like the Maddy I knew . . . calm and reasonable.

> I'm sorry. I'm just going to put it out there right now. I'm being a complete twat. Getting angry with you isn't going to help things. My head's a bit messed up. Well, I say a bit . . . really I mean a lot. Of course I don't wish you'd never said anything. That was a stupid and pathetic thing to say. I'd never want to take away what happened the other night. I'll never wish it didn't happen. It was beautiful.

I'm getting irate because I'm scared of losing you and I
don't want that to happen. You know how much you mean
to me. I know we'll be able to get through this—it'll just
take time.

Sorry for being a loser . . . and a crazy nutcase. Hope you don't
think less of me. In fact, please ignore all previous emails. Off
to seek professional help immediately. I believe they'll have a
straitjacket waiting for me upon arrival. Ha!

Let me know you're all right. x

I sighed as I closed my laptop and put it away, realizing that Maddy
was always going to have the ability to draw me in. It was the way
I'd conditioned myself to be over the years—my heart would always
belong to her. Knowing that irritated me after spending such a great
night with Alice, and, instead of it making me want to cool off things
with her—after all, I doubted anyone could level up to the unrealistic pedestal I'd put Maddy on—it made me want to make more of
an effort with her. I thought she deserved a chance.

Maddy and Robert were staying together, so I knew it would have
been painful for me to remain single and watch the two of them
together, acting as though nothing bad had ever happened between
them. I didn't want to be sat on the sidelines pining after Maddy, yet
again. No, I told myself, it was time to make some changes, and pursuing things with Alice was how to start. Plus, I imagined being
with her would ensure that I'd definitely keep my distance from
Maddy, stopping me from crossing boundaries once again. Not that
I thought I would, but having obtained something I'd desired for so
long, well, it increased my thirst rather than quenched it. The thought
of being with Maddy was more real than ever before, I knew what I
was missing, knew how we could be together, knew her body's secrets, the way it curved, the way it responded to my touch—they were

no longer just little thoughts I'd imagined in my head, instead they were very real.

I knew I needed to push those thoughts from my mind, and divert that energy onto something else, before I ruined things beyond repair.

Alice was my only hope, so I decided to give her my all.

Maddy

I'd known and seen Ben almost every day for the past twelve years, but, following our passionate love affair, when I thought of him I was bombarded with visions of his face that night. The way he'd nervously smiled as he confessed his feelings at the pub, the way he longingly looked at my lips before kissing me, or the way his mouth grazed my body. Just thinking of the latter would cause a tug on my insides and a wave of excitement in my knickers—something I'd instantly feel ashamed of.

I was angry with him for sleeping with Alice, but what did I expect? Of course I could see everything from his point of view. The situation was so messy. In a way he'd given me a get-out clause, given me reason to turn my back on him and his words, but I had an internal need to know that he loved me and cared. I didn't want to feel that what we'd shared wasn't real. I needed to know it was more than a lusty night. I wasn't the sort of girl to drop my knickers for anyone who came knocking, after all. For the first time in my life I'd done something completely reckless and I hated the fact that it made me a bad person.

I bumped into Ben down the street from his house. Which, yes, sounds suspiciously like I was stalking him and trying my best to run into him . . . that would be a correct assumption to make. I wasn't sure what else to do. He'd stopped answering my e-mails, calls, and texts when I'd turned a bit psycho in an e-mail to him. Okay, it was several e-mails in the space of a few hours, but I hadn't meant to, I was just so frustrated by the whole thing and emotionally drained. Seeing as Ben was the only person who knew the full extent of my life's current affairs (bad choice of words, but you know what I mean) it seemed like he was the only one I could vent to. I was taking every ounce of anger I'd been feeling out on Ben thanks to the guilt that had decided to rear its ugly head, making me unable to vent such frustrations at Robert—even though he'd started the whole thing. How pathetic does that sound?!

The way I'd acted toward Ben was unfair and I regretted the e-mails straight away. He eventually sent a lovely reply back—he didn't just leave me in silence to hate myself (although he didn't relieve me of my torment for a whole twenty-seven hours and nineteen minutes), saying he completely understood and that all he wanted was for us both to be happy. It was the few days of silence that he followed that up with that led me to engineer seeing him that morning! I knew he was avoiding me and it's fair to say it was starting to make me go a little mad. So, one Thursday morning, when I knew he'd be heading for a lecture, I accidentally-on-purpose made sure I was walking in the opposite direction and that we would inevitably collide into each other at some point. I spotted his bouncing walk from quite a distance; it created a wave of affection and brought a smile to my lips, something I wasn't prepared for. He noticed me a few hundred yards away and continued to walk toward me. I took that for a good sign. As he got nearer I saw he was smiling, and the butterflies inside me went berserk.

"Hey, you," he said casually as he got closer.

"Hey . . ."

Stopping when he was yards away from me, Ben rocked backward and forward on his feet in uncertainty, no doubt wondering what I was doing springing the surprise visit on him. Stupidly I hadn't planned what to do after bumping into him, which led to me looking like a complete idiot as I became tongue-tied. I knew he'd been ignoring me; I had just wanted to see him and check everything was okay. Force him into making some sort of interaction with me, but instead, I knew he felt cornered. Ben hated any kind of confrontation, always had.

The silence between us spoke volumes. It was one of those moments where subtext and body language said everything where words failed. I felt aware of every part of my body and ridiculously aware of his. The way he licked his upper lip with the tip of his tongue, ran his fingers through his thick hair and gave it a tousle, the way his eyes focused on mine briefly before looking down at the ground. The connection sent a bolt of unexpected pleasure through me as it instantly transported me back to his bedroom, back to his bed, back to the way he'd looked at me with fresh eyes—back to his secret smile.

Being so close to Ben was far more charged and awkward than I had expected, creating an astounding amount of conflict within me. I immediately wished I wasn't there and reprimanded myself for manipulating the ambush . . . but then, a large part of me wished I could just go up and kiss him. That it was my tongue licking his lips, my fingers running through his hair—and that we were back in his bed, picking up where we'd left off. I winced at those thoughts and wondered why my brain was so quick to betray Robert, the guy I was supposed to love with all my heart. The one I was trying to forgive.

"How have you been?" he asked, looking up at me properly for the first time, allowing his gaze to rest on mine for more than a split second.

"Fine," I answered, unable to resist smiling at him. "You?"

"Good. Really good."

"Great."

"Yeah . . ."

"You're looking good," I blurted.

"Really?" he laughed, looking down at himself. He was wearing his normal ripped baggy jeans, with a slim-fit stripy blue and white T-shirt. He looked the same as normal, but there was something different about him, and I don't think it was solely down to my raging hormones. "Must be the sunshine," he offered as he gestured upward.

"Yeah . . ."

An awkward silence fell upon us as we looked up at the blue sky above, as though we were inspecting the weather. We were far from relaxed together.

"Ben, is everything okay? With us?" I asked quickly, embarrassed to be even asking the question. It felt like such a silly and adolescent thing to ask. I wasn't used to speaking in that way to him. I'd never had the need to before.

His eyes rested on mine as he exhaled. "Of course."

"You've been avoiding me."

"I haven't," he shrugged.

"Are you really going to try and deny it?" I asked, raising my eyebrows at him.

"Okay, you're right," he sighed, tugging on the strap of his backpack as he jiggled uncomfortably on the spot. "I thought that it was for the best. Just for a little bit, mind. But I'm feeling better about everything now. You know?"

"I guess, but you could've given me some warning before you went MIA. I've been going mad with worry."

"Ha! Sorry about that. I feel like I've got my head screwed back on again now. All I needed was some time."

"But you're back now?"

"Yes! Definitely," he beamed as he gave me a squeeze on the arm.

The arm.

Not the hand.

Just one.

Not three.

I couldn't help but feel sad as I noticed the absence of the two extra pulses.

"Robert's worried about you," I said in a strained manner, aware that I was bringing up he-who-shall-not-be-named. "I said you've been busy with work and stuff, but he wants to see you when he's down at the weekend. He's even mentioned storming into your bedroom and dragging you away from your desk."

Ben laughed loudly.

"He thinks you're angry at him."

"Oh. I see. I'll give him a call later."

"Thanks."

"Actually, talking about work, I'd better be going," he said, pointing his thumb in the direction he was meant to be walking in.

"Yes, of course . . ."

"Where are you off to?"

"Oh, I was just . . . wandering around," I couldn't help but smile. I knew he knew I was there just to see him.

"Sounds great," he grinned, slapping his hands against the sides of his thighs. "Right, I'll speak to you later, Mad."

He grabbed hold of me and pulled me in for a hug then. I'm not sure if it was just a habit that he'd forgotten to break or whether it was an urge like the ones I'd been fighting that had led him into the embrace. He lifted me up slightly and ever so gently brushed my naked neck with his lips. The sudden intimacy led me to inhale deeply as his being took over my body, eradicating all rational thought. The bubble that we'd previously found ourselves in had come back to cocoon us once more, making everything around us disappear within seconds.

The way he released me abruptly, jumping back in shock and putting distance between us once more, suggested the action had caught him off guard too. But, whereas I'd welcomed it, he hadn't. It alarmed him and caused him to flee.

"Must dash!" he said nervously, his cheeks flaming red as he launched himself into a fast-paced power walk away from me.

As I watched him get further away, one word sprang to mind—FUCK! It dawned on me that the next few months were going to be incredibly hard if my mind so easily disintegrated in his company, if his touch could generate such a colossal reaction within me. I wasn't sure how I'd cope.

"I've finally spoken to Ben!" Robert said with relief on the phone that night.

His call had woken me up. I hadn't been sleeping well for obvious reasons, but had somehow crashed out on my bed early evening without meaning to when I was trying to get some work done. The sound of my phone ringing roused me with a shock, making me disorientated.

"What?" I croaked, unable to hide my irritation.

"Ben! I've just spoken to him."

"Oh really?" I asked, as I reached for the glass of water from my bedside table, trying to stop my head feeling so groggy.

"You okay?"

"Yeah, I was asleep."

"It's only nine o'clock!"

"Really? Blimey."

"So, like I was saying—I found Ben," Robert continued. "Turns out he wasn't busy with work like we thought, or joined a religious cult like I feared."

"Thank God for that," I laughed dryly.

"He's started seeing someone!"

"What?"

"Yeah, I know! What a dark horse. He goes missing for a couple of weeks and then comes back with a girlfriend. I'm surprised he didn't tell you about it."

I thought back to that morning, he had seemed happier and lighter—I'd commented on it, he'd said it was the sunshine, but it was actually because he had a girlfriend. Surely, I thought, after everything we'd been through, he'd have told me about something like that. Especially before mentioning it to Robert! I knew there was no way Ben wouldn't have known the impact it would have on me. I wondered, momentarily, whether it was Ben's way of getting back at me—showing me that he was fine, or highlighting the fact that he had options, lots more than I did. Even as I thought it, I doubted Ben would be so manipulative or calculating. It wasn't in his nature.

"We haven't really seen each other," I lied. "We've been busy."

"Oh, right. I said to him about us going out when I'm next over at yours."

"Yeah . . ." My mind was elsewhere, not paying much attention to what Robert was harping on about.

"I'll feel better once I see him," he said meaningfully, alluding to how concerned he'd been about not being able to get hold of him. I hadn't spoken to Rob a lot in those two weeks, not wanting to rush into too much too soon, but every time we spoke he'd mentioned how worried he was about Ben. I knew he felt it wasn't just me he'd let down—that he had to clear things up with him too. "Besides," he said with a gentle laugh, "I want to meet this girl he's left us for!"

"Already? He's only just started seeing her. Plus, I've got so much stuff on . . ." I said, trying to keep the panic from my voice. I did not want to go out with Ben and some girl he had just started dating. It was the worst idea I'd ever heard. I frantically tried to think of how to get out of it in a way that wouldn't make Robert suspicious, but nothing sprang to mind.

"Come on, we can double date like old times."

"Do you really think he likes her that much? Knowing Ben he'll have changed his mind within a week." I added a rather feeble laugh to try and make light of the subject and to dismiss the idea entirely. It didn't work.

"I don't think so. He seems really keen on Alice."

"Alice?" I questioned, remembering her name from an e-mail Ben had sent. Alice was Roger's housemate, the girl he'd slept with the night after being with me.

I couldn't quite get my head around that. From what Ben had said, he'd slept with her because he thought I was back with Robert, or because he was stupidly drunk. Whatever the reason, if Robert was right, the girl he'd vented those frustrations with had somehow become his girlfriend. I wondered how that had come about, what had urged Ben to turn a one-night stand into more.

It saddened me that he hadn't had the guts to tell me himself, that he felt it was okay for me to hear the information secondhand from Robert instead—that he had such disregard for me and my feelings.

It took every ounce of self-control to stop myself from calling Ben as soon as I got off the phone to Robert—which I did in a grumpy and flippant manner, in the fastest way possible. A part of me wanted Ben to know how much his indifference was hurting me, but then, what right did I have to be to hurt or angry at him? As far as he was concerned I'd made my choice, he was free to do as he wished. It dawned on me that all I really wanted was to know that he cared about me still, and that I wasn't so easily replaced. I couldn't help but feel I'd been pushed aside. I needed to know that I hadn't acted so appallingly and been unfaithful for something meaningless. I didn't want it to be a drunken fumble to be ashamed of. My needs were selfish, but it irritated me that he wasn't willing to fulfill them.

I was also, for the first time in my life, experiencing jealousy. I was jealous of Alice even though I'd never met her. I was envious of whatever qualities she had that had led to Ben moving on so swiftly after declaring his love to me. I also resented the fact that she would be able to have Ben adore her in such a carefree manner, when I knew I couldn't.

By that point I hadn't spoken to Pearl like I'd planned, I'd let it all fester inside me instead, and avoided the girls as much as I could. On hearing that Ben was seeing Alice, that he was developing actual feelings for her, I decided I needed to talk to someone. I tiptoed across the landing to her room and knocked on her bedroom door.

"Pearl?" I whispered.

"All right, darling," she growled. "Come in."

She was at her desk in her pajamas, with books and loose pieces of crumpled paper covered in handwritten notes surrounding her. Her hair was gathered in a crazy pineapple at the top of her head—her favorite way of keeping it out of her face while she worked.

"Revising?"

"Doing what I can, but I fear it's a case of too little too late," she said, swiveling in her chair and turning to face me.

I must have looked as troubled as I felt—as soon as she saw my face her own curled downward in a frown.

"Dude! What's up?" she asked, as she stood up, took me by the arm, and led me to her bed to sit down.

"I don't even know where to start, Pearl," I said, crossing my legs and picking up one of her pillows to hug, burying my face in it.

"Tell me. Is it all this stuff with Robert?"

"Yes and no," I said, looking up at her.

"Go on . . ."

"I kissed Ben."

Unshockable Pearl's jaw dropped. "What? When?"

It's one thing admitting to yourself that you've done something wrong, it's another when you've got to tell someone else how much of a plonker you've been. Pearl stayed uncharacteristically quiet as I told her everything. From Ben and me getting drunk, kissing, having a fumble, him sleeping with someone else, him saying to forget it ever happened, to having to go on a double date with him, Alice, and Robert.

"Hold on a minute. Rewind. You didn't sleep with him?" she said, holding her hand out and stopping me.

"No."

"You just cuddled?" she asked, raising her eyebrows.

"Not quite, but in the end, yes."

"Jeez, what are you even worrying for?" she sighed.

"It was more than that, Pearl. Cheating is cheating, whether it's a kiss or mind-blowing sex."

"It's really not. It's totally different," she argued, shaking her head dismissively.

"Is it, though?"

"Yes! Do you want me to go into detail to prove it? Remind you exactly what you could've done had you not stopped?"

"No, thanks," I squirmed, knowing Pearl would go into a graphic description that would make even pornstars blush.

"Shame," she sighed comically.

"It's not only that, though, I feel like I've fallen for him. That's got to be way worse than sleeping with someone."

Pearl looked at me with confusion as her face crinkled up in bewilderment.

"Mad, your boyfriend did a really shitty thing. In response, you got rat-faced and kissed someone. That's all it needs to be. Don't go turning it into something else, especially if that person's now gone off and started screwing this other bird."

"He said he loved me."

It was almost the same thing I'd said to Ben, the same argument that stopped me from being able to get past the whole thing and accept that being together wasn't even a possibility.

Pearl looked at me and sighed. "And then he did something even shittier than your boyfriend did in the first place."

I'd never thought of it like that. It seemed ridiculous to me that, even after he'd slept with Alice, I was the one running around after him, e-mailing him with heartfelt words (and crazy ones), placing myself somewhere that I knew he'd turn up. I couldn't explain what had led me to do those things, or say what I was hoping to gain.

"I think you've freaked yourself out," Pearl continued, standing up and pacing around the room, nodding her head as though she was agreeing with her own words. "You've acted in a way that's completely out of character—Maddy, you're the most loyal person I know. You've shocked yourself and now you're trying to give it a greater meaning to justify your behavior. Babe, you did wrong, but that one action doesn't define who you are." She grabbed my hand in hers and patted it sympathetically.

"I just don't know what to do," I said feebly.

"What to do about what exactly? It looks to me as though Ben is no longer an option," she said matter-of-factly, perching herself back on the bed. "You need to get him out of your mind, pronto."

"How?"

"Do you still love Robert?"

"Yes."

"Do you think you'll be able to forgive him?"

"I don't know. I think I might," I shrugged.

Robert's cheating was something I'd found difficult to think about. It wasn't that Ben filled my head and pushed aside all thoughts of Robert's wrongdoings, more that it upset me too much to think about what he'd done. He'd hurt me far more because he'd risked the years we'd been together and made me question our whole relationship. Yet, I still loved him—and that's what left me irritated, annoyed, and confused.

"Are you willing to try and work things out?"

Without much gusto, I nodded in reply.

"Maddy, a couple of weeks ago you two had your whole lives planned out together—take a leaf out of Ben's book. Pretend nothing has changed."

"I don't know if I can do that."

Pearl raised her eyebrows at me.

"Seriously? This is all over one night. Get a grip."

I knew Pearl was going to offer blunt advice, she was always to the point in every situation with the inability to filter what she thought—and that was why I went to her over Flo or Jennifer. The whole situation had already become over-romanticized in my head, I needed someone to knock a bit of sense into me. She was right, I had to stop thinking of Ben in that way; if he was moving forward, I had to too.

I couldn't explain what had made me focus so much on Ben at that point and not on saving my relationship with Robert. It was like my brain had been taken over by some alien being. I knew, like Pearl said, I needed to get my head out of the clouds and focus on what I did have. I needed to work on things with Robert and see if what we had was salvageable.

I had to forget about Ben . . . but if only doing were as easy as saying when it came to matters of the heart.

The double date had been arranged for the following weekend. Needless to say I had no part in the planning—I left Robert and Ben to do that, it was enough for me to just turn up on the night. It was happening, it was inevitable, I just had to get on with it.

Me being there was a classic case of "curiosity killed the cat." After all, I could have made a last-minute excuse, but the truth was I needed to meet Alice. I wanted to know everything about her, what she looked like, what her voice sounded like, how she laughed, where she'd grown up, what her likes and dislikes were, what her taste in music was like . . . morbid curiosity meant I needed to know what Ben saw in her. Perhaps to understand, or perhaps just to see how I measured up in comparison.

The boys had decided to go bowling. Robert and I were the first to arrive, which meant we were there when Ben and Alice came through the door hand in hand and giggling their heads off. To say I felt nauseous would be an understatement.

I'd built up images of Alice in my head—I expected her to be tall, dark, and modellike, but it was worse than that. She was extremely petite, around five foot two, with a beautifully dainty frame. Her long blond hair fell in waves around her shoulders and her hazel eyes had the most dazzling flecks of green in them. She was naturally beautiful. The kind of girl you knew would roll out of bed in the mornings and look amazing. She wore a floaty yellow dress which came down past her knees, its thin straps exposing her delicate shoulders and collarbone. Even in those first few seconds I knew there was something endearing about her, she radiated warmth.

"Here he is!" shouted Robert as he grabbed hold of Ben and gave him a manly hug and a bit of a wrestle, leaving me to smile in Alice's direction awkwardly, dubious as to how to greet her.

"Hi! I'm Alice!" She giggled, coming toward me for a hug. "You must be Maddy?"

"Yep. Don't worry, I won't be doing that to you," I smiled.

"Gosh, thank goodness," she laughed. "I've heard a lot about you."

I wondered what Ben had been telling her, causing my mind to falter momentarily.

"Sorry, got a bit carried away. I'm Robert," said Robert breathlessly, breaking away from Ben and giving Alice a kiss on the cheek.

Ben didn't really look at me before walking in my direction and giving me a klutzy hug. It was brief and as soon as it was done he turned to the others with a smile.

"Let's do this!" he laughed as he grabbed hold of Robert and they galloped over to the counter like overexcited kids.

"Here goes," I said, following them, feeling deflated that things were still on edge with Ben and me. But what had I expected? It wasn't as if we were seriously going to bounce back into being normal with each other after what we'd done, especially not with Robert around.

"Are we allowed to use the bumpers?" asked Alice next to me, pulling me from my thoughts.

"Oh . . . the boys don't usually let me, they tell me it's cheating."

When we were younger the three of us had gone bowling and they'd allowed me to have the bumpers up, as it was my first time. Miraculously I'd won even though my ball had rebounded off the side each time I bowled, occasionally even a few times in one throw, creating a pretty zigzag pattern as they made their way down to the pins. The boys were understandably livid and told me I'd won unfairly. I might have been their best friend, but they were still competitive, especially Robert who sulked the whole way home. From that point onward I was never allowed to use the bumpers again.

"Really? But I'm rubbish!" moaned Alice.

"Same here."

Even though I'd been forced to play without the aid of bumpers over the years I was still terrible at the game. My problem was that I didn't have the patience for it. I was a just-throw-it-and-see-how-it-goes girl. I couldn't be bothered with the whole lining it up and getting your elbow in the right position malarkey.

"We're having the bumpers up, right?" said Alice sweetly as we joined the boys in the line for our shoes. It was more of a leading question than anything else.

Both boys looked at her with their mouths open, unsure of how to say no nicely—they were both aware that they were meant to be making a good impression on her.

"*Erm* . . ." started Ben. "Oh, we didn't book a lane with them, I'm afraid."

"Yeah, and usually you have to ask," Robert answered, with an apologetic shrug.

"No, it's okay! They have those electric ones now . . . we just press the button on our control thingy and they pop out," she smiled. "I know how to do it too, so you don't need to worry about a thing. I'll do it."

Ben and Robert just stared at her. I couldn't help but laugh. She knew the boys were trying to fob her off, and that they'd be too polite to argue with her. She turned to me and raised her eyebrows, trying not to laugh as she changed the subject. "Are you going for laced or buckled shoes, Maddy?"

The boys needn't have worried, as even with the bumpers up, Alice and I were as crap as each other. We were lucky to get a couple of pins down each time. Clearly my win all those years ago had been more to do with beginner's luck than actual talent, and Alice couldn't help but laugh every time she took her turn, clearly feeling embarrassed by the whole thing. She'd go up full of gusto, line up her shot, and then keel over in a fit of giggles before she'd had the chance to throw it. Her giggle was infectious, though, and we couldn't help but laugh along with her.

Alice and Ben weren't as touchy-feely with each other as I'd feared they were going to be. They may have sat next to each other on the sofas throughout the game and looked deeply smitten, but they weren't there snogging each other's faces off, which was a big relief. In contrast, Robert and I were still distant from each other, or rather, I was avoiding having any sort of PDA with him with the aid of the whopping big barrier that I'd erected and had been unable, so far, to knock down. So, despite how hard he was trying to make things seem normal, they weren't.

At the end of the first game, which our sporting hero Robert obviously won, we stopped for some food. Burgers, fries, and milkshakes were brought over to us at the lane, which we greedily devoured while sat on the comfy red leather sofas.

"I've seen you around campus before, actually," said Alice to me as she popped a chip into her mouth.

"Oh, really?"

"Didn't Ben tell you? I thought you were his girlfriend," she giggled.

"Something you two want to tell me?" Robert jokingly accused, nudging me with his elbow and raising his eyebrows at Ben.

I felt like a rabbit caught in headlights, completely unsure what to say. So I just gormlessly looked from Alice to Robert.

"Oh don't worry," Alice laughed at Robert. "It's only because they were together that I thought that . . . there was clearly no chemistry whatsoever."

My eyes flicked up at Ben, who was looking at me for the first time that night. For a split second the guard he'd put up slipped away and I could see the real Ben exposed, full of love and honesty. It was as though a magnetic force had been switched on, drawing me to him, making it near impossible to look away. It was a dangerous look to share in public. I felt ashamed as my insides tingled at the connection. I had thought being in the company of others would stop that feeling arising, that we'd be able to lock it away. But it seemed the inappropriateness of it made it more intense, and left it to linger and grow like an unattended fire.

"At least he's keeping other prowling guys away for you, Robert," giggled Alice.

My eyes darted down to my food and stayed there, unable to look up. I felt Robert shamefully stiffen next to me and Ben, opposite us, shifted in his seat uncomfortably.

Not noticing the sudden change in mood, or the fact that we'd all ventured into silence, Alice continued to place her petite foot even further into her mouth, "That's what friends are for, though. Shame they haven't had someone returning the favor in Nottingham."

A weak "Ha" was all Robert could muster in reply. I almost felt sorry for him.

"Must be tough being away from these two, though," she smiled, turning to Ben and me. "From what I've heard you're quite the terrible threesome."

It was clear that Ben hadn't told Alice anything about recent events in our group. I suspect it was a case of where to start and at what point to stop. She'd meant nothing scathing by her comments, she was just trying to make friendly conversation.

"Life's been very different, that's for sure," I nodded.

"I bet Robert can't wait to get the crew back together."

"Yeah, you're right," he agreed, seeming to relax.

"So what are your plans? For after?"

"We haven't really talked about it yet," I said, purposely being vague to end the conversation there.

"What would you like?" Alice asked Robert.

"I'd love us all to move to London. Maybe get a little flat or something."

"Really?" I asked, in as bright a tone as I could muster, giving him a little warning look.

"Well, it's something we always talked about when we were younger, you know, moving in together as a trio . . ." he shrugged, trailing off, unable to hold eye contact with me.

"We haven't talked about that for years," laughed Ben nervously, clearly as thrown as I was. "I've no idea what I'll be doing . . ."

It was something that we had talked about a lot, but only when we were incredibly young—mostly before me and Robert had even started dating. It was a topic that, especially once we knew we were going to different universities, had been dropped. None of us knew realistically what the future was going to bring, we hadn't even talked about what came after our scrolls of paper were handed out at graduation.

Alice continued to push the idea, much to my discomfort.

"Are you telling me that if Rob found you all an awesome pad somewhere amazing you'd give up the opportunity to live with your two bestest buds? As if!" she laughed, looking at us as though we'd gone mad.

"I guess it depends on a few things, and besides, things change," I smiled, hoping that the conversation would be dropped. In the end I decided to turn the topic of our futures back onto her—it seemed the safest way to stop me losing my rag. "What about you, Alice? What are you going to do?"

"Well, I'm from Essex so I'll probably be heading back over that way. I've always fancied getting a place somewhere more central, though. Plus, most magazines and stuff are based in London, so it makes sense for me to be there."

I glanced over at Ben to see him nervously looking around the bowling alley.

"We should probably play the next game," he said, looking at his watch. "We've not got long left!"

"I'm gonna kick arse this time," giggled Alice. "I can tell!"

"Good luck with that," laughed Robert politely, clearly relieved to be getting back on his feet and away from the conversation.

As soon as we'd said good-bye to Ben and Alice and got into his car, Robert turned to me with his eyebrows raised.

"So, what do you think?" he asked, popping on his seatbelt.

"She's adorable."

I really meant it too, even if it was painful for me to admit. Alice was bubbly and sparkly—a pleasure to spend time with. I understood what Ben saw in her, although I'd been shocked to see how different she was to me. We weren't alike in any way—appearance or personality. It bothered me and I couldn't put my finger on why—I hadn't expected a carbon copy, but I had thought she'd have a least a few qualities in common with me. In reality, I felt decidedly average around her, which irked me after Ben had made me feel so special.

"Ben seems really happy," Robert added, starting the engine and pulling out of the parking space.

"Yeah."

"I was really nervous about seeing him."

"Really?"

"You know how protective he is over you—I half expected him to lamp me one."

"He wouldn't do that," I half laughed, half squeaked, in shock.

"You never know . . ."

"Things were fine, though, right?"

"I don't know. He seemed a little distant at first."

"What, when you guys were jumping all over each other like apes?" I tried to joke.

"No, after that. When we were stood at the counter, it was like he had something on his mind. Maybe that's just me reading too much into it, looking for signs that something was wrong," he frowned, nibbling on his lower lip.

"Must be," I muttered.

It was possible that, like me, Ben had struggled with us all being together and acting as though everything was normal. It was also likely that being stood next to Robert once again had reminded him of our betrayal.

"He didn't say much about us all moving in together, did he?"

"None of us did really . . ."

"Do you reckon he wants to?"

"We haven't even decided what we're doing yet."

"I know, but I assumed—"

"We've been through a lot lately, Rob," I snapped.

I hated myself for saying that, especially as I'd not said it purely because I was still angry at him, more because I wanted him to drop the subject, at least until I could figure out a good reason for us not to live together. There was, after all, no way I was going to be able to live with both Robert and Ben. Just the thought of us all under the same roof was enough to make me feel queasy. The idea was completely inconceivable.

"But we're fine now, aren't we?" Robert asked with sadness. We hadn't even made our way out of the car park yet, he was still trying to work his way around its one-way system.

I looked ahead as I thought about his question. "I hope we will be, but things take time. You can't just magic us back to normal. Too much has happened," I exhaled.

"Yeah," he nodded sadly, my words deflating him.

"Anyway, I'm sure Ben won't want to live with us when we're in the midst of coming through all of that," I reasoned.

"I guess so . . ."

He pulled over and turned to me, gently taking my hand in his.

"You know how sorry I am about the whole thing, Maddy," he said softly. His face was a picture of regret and sorrow, as his eyes searched mine. "I love you with my whole heart. It'll never ever happen again. No one else could hate me more than I do for it. I was an absolute jerk."

"It doesn't matter," I said dismissively, annoyed that we were talking about his mistake once more.

"It does because I hurt you. I was wrong," he persevered, lifting my hand to his lips and kissing it. "I want you and me to live together, Mad. It's that simple."

He pulled my hands into his chest and cradled my arms, causing my body to lean toward his. He kissed my lips softly.

It was the first time he'd kissed me since his confession, and the simple gesture made me feel overwhelmingly sad, reminding me of the love we'd shared and were close to throwing away. I knew there was something special, comfortable, and loving between us—I just had to allow him to work his way through that barrier I'd built so that I could start seeing it again.

Ben

After our interesting double date, I walked Alice the short distance back to hers. Her front door was already in view when she turned to me and asked me in.

"Is it wise?" I asked, not wanting to take advantage. Up until that point we'd still been trying to keep things respectable by going on dates and getting to know each other properly. Not only was Alice a welcome distraction from other things that were going on, she was also great to be around. She lightened my mood and made the world seem like a less complicated, happier place. I wouldn't say she made me forget, but she certainly made me think about the Maddy situation a lot less.

"I think, now that we're several dates in, we can resume where we started," she said with a cheeky grin.

"Oh, really?"

"Or, if you don't fancy that, we could chill on the sofa, watch a movie . . ." she teased.

"Your first offer was a bit more tempting, but I'll take either."

I excitedly followed her inside.

She'd been wonderful that afternoon, full of all the charm and warmth that had attracted me to her in the first place. I needed to see her like that around Robert and Maddy, I needed to see that I had someone of my own who was special at last.

"So, do you think they like me?" she asked, once we were in her room and lying on her bed, facing each other—one of her housemates that I didn't know was watching TV in the lounge, so we'd decided to go up to her room instead—well, that was our excuse, anyway, but we both knew that was where we preferred to be.

"They loved you."

That was definitely true of Robert, who wasted no time in leaning in and telling me how fit he thought she was, although later on he'd also winked at me whenever Alice did something funny or cute—she'd effortlessly won him over. As for Maddy, well, I'd watched her around Alice, I wanted to gauge her reaction for some reason—see how she responded to me being there with someone else. She seemed fascinated by her and watched her keenly for most of the afternoon with intrigue. I was surprised Alice had failed to notice.

"You sure?"

"What's not to love?"

"Whoa there, tiger, with the love talk!" she giggled.

Putting my hands on her hips, I pulled her on top of me and gave her a kiss.

"Before we get carried away . . . I have something for you," she said, untangling herself from me as she pulled a large present from the side of her bed, offering it to me with a smirk.

"What's this?" I asked her, looking at the neatly wrapped gift and juggling it around, trying to work out what it was—it was soft and made no sound when I shook it; I had no idea what she was giving me.

"It's only something small," she shrugged. "I just thought it would make you smile."

I tore apart the blue wrapping paper to find a koala onesie and couldn't stop myself from grinning as I kissed her once more to say thank you. It was the most thoughtful gift I'd ever received, I couldn't help but be blown away by the gesture.

"You really are the cutest little thing," I said, cupping her face with my hands.

"Why, thank you! Once you experience the joy of this onesie, I swear it'll be hard to get you out of it."

"Oh, but I hope you'll try."

"Ben!" she squealed with laughter, giving me a playful slap on the arm.

"I'm joking . . . sort of. Seriously, though, thank you. It's so sweet of you."

"Not really, it just gives me an excuse to wear my onesie around you and not feel stupid."

"Ooh, ulterior motives, Miss Turner?"

"Made sense for when you finally managed to make your way back into my bedroom."

"Crafty."

As we sat there grinning at each other a thought popped into my head. "Actually, Alice, I have to go home next weekend, for Maddy's dad's fiftieth. Fancy coming?"

If I'd spent a little more time thinking about it I'd probably have concluded it was a bad idea, but I hadn't. Sitting in front of her, basking in her sunshine, it seemed like a perfect idea.

"I can't just turn up uninvited."

"I'm inviting you."

"You can't do that."

"I can, I was given a plus one on the invite."

"But I don't know anyone."

"Alice, I'm trying to ask you to come home with me and meet my mum, would you not make it so difficult?"

"Oh! I forgot she'd be there," she giggled. "I'd love to."

Every social event, ever since Maddy and Robert had become an item, had turned into me being asked a million questions about my love life, which ultimately would turn into me being given sympathetic looks and told not to worry because "it'll happen" if I just "hang in there." That's a whole five years of being made to feel like I was on the reject pile when it came to love.

I wasn't prepared to receive the same treatment yet again, as I watched Maddy and Robert act all loved up, as though the past few weeks had never happened. I'd decided I was going to have someone wonderful on my arm to avoid the glum chat. To make me feel like an equal and, hopefully, to help me enjoy what would otherwise be a very dreary night.

I knew Maddy wouldn't be overjoyed, but hoped she'd be able to understand that I couldn't just watch her walk away from me. I had to occupy myself—keep my heart busy.

Maddy

The weekend after our double date, we all went back to Peaswood. It was my dad's fiftieth birthday and a big party had been planned to celebrate. The hall in our local community club had been booked, a mullet-coiffed DJ hired and a few dozen blue and silver helium balloons had been puffed up for decoration.

After all the drama of the previous weeks I had been thrilled to be going home, back to familiar surroundings where everything was once so simple. However, our calm little house had been taken over for the weekend and turned into chaotic madness. With distant relatives invading us to share in the celebrations, there was a battle over the bathrooms, hairdryers, and any tiny little space as we all fought to get ourselves ready for the party.

At seven twenty-five on the dot, once my hair was in a high bun and I'd managed to squeeze myself into my floor-length emerald dress, the taxis arrived. As the rest of the family cascaded into the waiting cars, Mum turned to me with her hand on her forehead.

"I completely miscalculated how many of us there were."

"Huh?" I frowned, slipping my feet into my heels. "I'll just squeeze in the back."

"No, the driver won't allow that. You wait here and I'll send someone back for you."

"But, Mum . . ." I whined, hating the idea of being left behind and having to turn up on my own.

"That way I can check everything's okay with the hall before everyone else arrives. Thanks, love," she flustered, before giving me a kiss on the cheek and running out the door.

Rather bemused, I sat on the stairs and waited.

After about five minutes, the doorbell rang. I opened it to find Robert, looking dashing in a gray suit, his blond hair slicked back into a stylish quiff. Somehow, despite all the recent events and how much he'd hurt me, he still managed to take my breath away.

"Did Mum send you?" I asked, reaching for my clutch bag.

"Not quite."

"What do you mean . . . did you ask her to leave me behind?"

"Maybe," he smiled, looking nervous, still wary of how I might act around him. "I just thought it would be nice to go together. We've not had a night out like this since, well, I think it was our sixth-form ball."

"I guess not."

"This is for you," he offered, pulling a corsage from behind his back. A thick row of gorgeous pearled beads made up the band, on to which was attached a deep red rose. "May I?" he asked, gesturing for my wrist.

I couldn't help but smile then. It was exactly the same as the corsage he'd given me on the night of our ball three years before, when he had, again, picked me up from my doorstep and escorted me.

"This is very nice," I smiled, appreciating the effort.

"Thank you," he said softly, looking bashful.

Once the house was locked up, I took hold of his arm and let him lead me to the taxi, where he opened and closed the door for me like a gentleman.

As the car started moving and we sat in silence with our hands entwined, I felt closer to Robert than I had in weeks. I shut my eyes and rested my head on his shoulder, allowing myself to enjoy the warmth I'll admit I'd begun to miss.

The car stopped sooner than I expected. To my dismay, I opened my eyes to find we were outside Ben's house. Not only was he walking toward the car, but so was Alice—something I was completely unprepared for.

The joy I'd been experiencing suddenly vanished, I was back to the same unsettled feeling I'd had before I'd come home. Despite the effort he was making, I instantly became angry at Robert for not realizing he should have just kept it as the two of us.

After a courteous hello to Ben and Alice, I stayed quiet for the rest of the ten-minute journey, I sulked in the corner, allowing my frustrations to rise dramatically.

Needless to say, Ben's arrival at the party with Alice managed to get dozens of tongues wagging as our families speculated over the significance of it. They cooed over whether she could she be "the one," like Ben's love life was some sort of prophecy to be fulfilled. It was all anyone wanted to talk about.

And they played quite the perfect couple. Ben had stuck by her side all night, taking care that she always had a drink in her hand, was introduced to everyone, and that they had fun on the dance floor—watching them slow dance together was excruciating. It felt as though Ben was flaunting his new relationship, letting me know that he was fine. He'd found someone else. Someone better. It hurt to be so easily and quickly replaced. And yes, I liked Alice. I thought she was a lovely girl, but I didn't want her perfectness to be rammed down my throat and to have all our parents talk about how great she was and how happy Ben looked.

Robert tried to continue being the gentleman he'd shown me at the start of the night, and was, to his credit, just as attentive as Ben was with Alice, but I rebuked and rebuffed every advance as I found fault with his every move. I became a grump for the rest of the night. I snapped at Robert more than was necessary, and generally walked around like I had a huge thunderous cloud above my head, threatening to strike him with a bolt of lightning whenever he irritated me. I'm surprised he remained by my side and didn't run for the door.

Unfortunately for me, when I snapped at him because he hadn't noticed his shoelace was undone (it seemed like a massive deal at the time), my mum overheard. She leaned over to me as though she was giving me a motherly embrace, but her hand clamped on my arm with a little too much pressure to be comforting.

"I don't know what's got into you, young lady, but snap out of it," she hissed through her teeth, continuing to smile at the other guests who were looking in our direction. They were unaware that Mum was telling off her twenty-one-year-old daughter who was, I'll confess, acting like a five-year-old . . . and a spoiled brat.

The rest of the night wasn't much of an improvement—my mood stayed dark and stroppy, something that wasn't helped by me watching Ben and Alice like a crazy, unhinged stalker. I tried my best to avoid any conversations with our family friends and relatives, preferring to sit in the dark festering in my self-pity.

I hated Robert for shagging some slutty stranger while blowing apart our version of perfect and for thinking so little of me as he did so.

I hated Ben for ripping open my heart and then leaving it to bleed while he gaily sauntered around with his new girlfriend.

But mostly, I hated myself for not having the answers to make everything better.

Needless to say, I wasn't in the jovial mood required for parties.

Unfortunately for me and my new friend, the-big-black-cloud-of-doom, my room had been given away to family for the night, with Mum and Carol planning for me to stay with Robert. For once I wished our mums were stricter about us sharing a bed at home.

As soon as we got back to his box room I got into my nightie, curled up under the sheets, and pretended to be fast sleep.

I'm not sure whether he knew I was faking or not, but after he'd got into bed and turned out the light, he faced me and let out a desperate sigh.

"I love you so much, Maddy," he whispered.

I said nothing, but kept my eyes clamped shut.

"All I wanted to do tonight was remind you of a happier time, before I screwed everything up . . . I guess I failed."

His breathing became erratic then. I'm not sure whether he had a lump in his throat or whether he was actually crying, but I wished he'd stop. It wasn't just him who'd failed us. I had too.

"I made a mistake. A stupid, horrible, mistake that I will regret for the rest of my life. I don't want to lose you. I couldn't bear that. You know, I'd do anything for you to forgive me, Mad. Just tell me how I can make that happen . . ."

It took a whole lot of stubbornness for me not to blub at his words. I was aware of how I was treating him and was annoyed at myself for being a complete cow as I tried to push him away—perhaps as a means to find atonement for my own mistakes. I still don't understand why Robert allowed me to treat him in the way I did, or why he didn't pull me up on my behavior and tell me I was being unfair. He was probably scared of what might have happened if he did. I can't blame him for that.

The morning after the party I made my way downstairs while Robert was still asleep, hoping to make a quick escape back to mine. Instead, I was stopped by Carol. She appeared from the kitchen as though she'd been waiting for me, looking like she'd been up for hours with her short blond hair perfectly set and her make-up reapplied.

"Want to come have a cuppa before you leave, Maddy?"

"Well, I really should be making a move, I've got to drive back today . . ."

"Come on, five minutes won't hurt. It would be good to sit and have a chat with you. I never get to see much of you any more."

Guilt-tripped into it, I agreed.

"But I really can't stay long," I warned.

Placed on the kitchen counter was a pot of tea, two mugs, a jug of milk, a bowl of sugar, and a basket of warm croissants and Danishes, confirming my earlier suspicion that she'd been waiting for me. Carol placed an apricot Danish (my favorite) on a plate and slid it in front of me before pouring us both some tea.

Feeling tentative, I pulled the pastry apart and nibbled on it slowly, anything to fill the silence that fell upon us. I could feel Carol looking at me, I knew she wanted to say something. I guessed she'd realized something was up with Robert and me and that she was trying to find out what. Carol was quite a nosy mum when she wanted to be—all our mums were. They always wanted to know exactly what was going on in our lives and to add their two pence worth to any situation, even if we hadn't asked for their advice. My plan was to act dumb, pretend she'd picked up on nothing, and to dismiss the whole thing.

"Robert told me about what's been going on lately," she sighed.

"Oh."

Well, that completely threw me. Robert was always a high-achiever, a child for his parents to be proud of. I was surprised he'd risked denting that wonderful reputation by confessing to his mum, a woman who had often been very vocal with her thoughts on married men who strayed. You should have heard her talk about Ben's dad—he might as well have been the devil himself the way she went on.

"I can't say I wasn't disappointed, but I'm glad he told me—that he's owning up to his mistake," she said, shaking her head before hesitantly continuing. "The thing is, Maddy, and I'm sorry to butt in like this . . ."

"What's wrong?"

"I saw the way you two were together last night. You and Robert."

"I was just drunk," I shrugged, with a lie. I hadn't touched a drop all night, it was the only way I could be sure I wouldn't say or do anything I'd end up regretting. It clearly hadn't worked, but I could only imagine the fall-out if I'd had a drink or two to boot.

"Were you?" she asked, busying herself by pouring two sugars into her tea and giving it a good stir.

I stared into my mug and longed for the chat to be over. Getting pulled up for my bad behavior by my own mum was bad enough, but having Robert's mum do it too was agony.

"I'm not saying you're wrong to punish him, not at all. What I'm thinking, Maddy, is that you have to either forgive him and move on, and try and make things work, or you don't."

"It's not that simple," I muttered.

Of course, Carol had told me off with the boys when we were younger for our general naughtiness, but that was always as a collective, I'd never been singled out. I knew she was talking to me in her kitchen because of the appalling way I'd been treating her son. I couldn't help but be sheepish. I didn't blame her for getting involved, though. After all, I'm sure any mum would be protective over their son. I knew she just wanted to help talk some sense into the situation.

"Oh, I know that. Believe me, every relationship goes through its testing times. It happens to the best of us."

I looked up to see Carol raising her eyebrows at me, giving me a precarious smile.

It was a rather unsubtle hint that something scandalous had happened between her and Richard at some point in their marriage, although she failed to give any further information on when, which of them, or who with. She knew she'd made her point just by alluding to it—even couples who might appear to be perfectly close and happy go through their fair share of troubles. It also explained, if Richard were the guilty party, why she had such a strong reaction to others who'd done the same.

"It's how you pull through it all, darling, that lets you know whether what you have is worth saving or not. But you've got to be willing to try, otherwise there's no point in putting either of you through further heartache."

"It's just difficult."

"Relationships are hard work," she nodded, agreeing with me. "And, sadly, getting into trouble and jeopardizing what you have is far too easy in comparison. But I know my son, Maddy. He's made his mistake. He won't be making another one. You've got to learn to trust him again."

"I just don't know how to begin to do that."

"Patience, love, and understanding will take you a long way."

I cried then. Again! Years of growing up with boys had meant crying was hardly ever an option, but in those couple of months it seemed I'd lost all control of my tear ducts. They wept freely.

As Carol walked around the counter and put her arms around me, I knew I had to release the anger that had been floating around inside of me. What was done was done. There was no going back and changing it. I had to move forward. Forgive Robert. Forgive myself.

The world had not decided to stop and grace me with some thinking time, it had, instead, pushed on and presented us with Alice. I knew that I had to move forward, I just needed to work out how. I needed to focus on what I did have, rather than what I didn't—just like I'd promised Pearl I would do the week before.

Robert wasn't Ben, but nor did I want him to be. He had a million of his own qualities that had made me happily fall in love with him all those years before. It became apparent in my mind that I needed to remind myself what they were, and be grateful for the amazing guy I had in my life.

Pearl was waiting for me on the sofa when I returned home that night, with a cup of tea and some much-needed chocolate Hobnobs. They made up a large part of her staple diet at university—I've no idea how she managed to maintain her size-ten figure with the number of packets she went through.

"How was it?" she asked, taking a biscuit out of the packet and dunking it in her tea. She pulled a grimace as she waited for my reply, rightly assuming that I wouldn't have had the best time of my life.

"Awful."

"Crap."

"I was a right bitch."

"Oh dear. Still confused?"

"Actually, no," I said with a smile, taking a gulp of my tea and reaching for the packet. "I think I'm on the verge of having a mental clear-out. I should be fine soon . . ."

"Glad to hear it," she smiled back. "I've been thinking while you've been gone. I understand, honestly I do. You three have been inseparable for years and now this guy you've loved as a friend speaks up and turns it into something else. He gave you another option when things had gone a bit shit. But face it, he led you to a fucking big crossroads and then walked off with the map."

"Ha! Great analogy."

Pearl winked at me, but continued with her line of thought.

"What you need to realize is that you don't need that map. You just have to decide which road you want to take . . ."

"What's this? Is my cockney east-Londoner going all sentimental on me?" I joked, giving her a playful shove on the shoulder.

"No chance . . ." she laughed. "All I'm saying is choose your love story and stick to it."

Choose my love story and stick to it . . . I liked that. I liked that a lot.

I'd also like to thank all of our parents, not just mine and Maddy's, but June—you too, you've certainly been a mum to us both over the years. So thanks to you all for helping the three of us out and for being there with your endless support and pearls of wisdom. Whether we've asked for your input or wanted to hear it is a different matter but... only joking. You guys have always known best, so, thank you.

Ben

TWENTY-FOUR YEARS OLD . . .

By the time my twenty-fourth birthday arrived I was living in a flat share in Bethnal Green with Alice, and had been for over a year. We'd found the place on Gumtree—a room in a two-bed flat, on the fourth floor. It was tiny and meant we'd had to leave the majority of our belongings in my mum's garage, but it would do. It was cheap and central. We shared the place with an IT consultant called Kevin, who seemed to be out drinking most nights, so we usually had the whole flat to ourselves.

Before that, straight after university, I'd gone back to my mum's in Peaswood. Robert wanted us all to get a place together, but, for obvious reasons, I wasn't keen on the idea. I excused myself, explaining that I needed to find a job and save before I could even think about renting a place. He sulked for a bit but decided not to put any more pressure on me, thankfully.

It was strange being back in my old room, squeezed in with all my old toys and memories, and having my mum fussing over me again—but luckily Alice had moved in with her sister near Brick Lane, so I was there a lot, escaping the motherly furore—she was excited and it came from the right place, it was just overbearing after years of total freedom.

Being a newbie freelance graphic designer was tough. I had no contacts, no experience, just my portfolio filled with coursework. In fact, I guess the good thing about living at home with Mum was that I could get some internships and work for free, building up relationships as I went, hoping that it would build into something more. It did. I eventually fell in with a film-production company, who employed me each time they were in production. Just that tiny chance opened up the doors to other great opportunities, and I was truly thankful. So, after a further two years at home, I was finally earning a regular-enough income to move out of home. I was thrilled—so was Alice when I asked her if she fancied living together. She was so unassuming and never tried to force me into thinking about the future and where we were headed—I liked that about her.

Robert and Maddy had moved home for the summer, as I had, but then quickly moved back out again. Robert had landed on his feet straight away and bagged himself a job as a PE teacher at a posh all-boys school in West London. As he was awarded a regular salary with twelve weeks *paid* holiday a year, they could afford to rent a pretty flat in Chiswick—a beautiful corner of the capital for yummy mummies and creative types. The picture-perfect couple fitted in nicely.

Maddy struggled to get paid work for her photography straight away, so, after years of studying decided to work in a local art shop instead—the plan was that she'd do that until something else popped up, but even after she started up her small, yet successful, business taking family portraits, she agreed to stay on there a few days a week. I think she liked the stability of knowing when she was going to have money coming in, plus they were lenient about her switching her days off if a shoot came up.

She still took her camera everywhere she went—eager to catch life at its best.

We all saw each other every Sunday, without fail, taking it in turns to travel across London to do so. They were still my bestest buds, although, by that point, Alice had been added to the mix, making us a neat little foursome.

Maddy had been right, things had got better over time. Not seeing her every day had certainly helped, although I'm gutted to admit that she never strayed far from my thoughts. The distance made me miss them both, but mostly her, and excited to see them each weekend as a result. The love I'd felt never faded, even though I was happy that a new love had blossomed with Alice—the sweetest girl I'd ever known.

I still visited my mum in Peaswood all the time. Yes, she did irritate me when I'd moved back home, but as soon as I moved out again I missed her terribly. My dad leaving when I was so young was an awful thing to deal with, but, by that point, I'd spent the majority of my life with it being just the two of us. I was used to it. I never forgot that, in many ways, I was her life. So despite me living elsewhere, I made sure I gave her as much time as I could so that she was never by herself for too long. Not that she minded being alone—she'd not had a man in her life since my dad left all those years ago, but I'd never heard her moan, making me wish I'd inherited some of her thick skin.

She spent most of her evenings either with, or on the phone to, Carol. Our mums were still as inseparable as they'd been all those years before when we were younger. It was great to know Mum had people around her when I wasn't there.

One Wednesday night, just after Christmas, I'd gone over to hers for dinner. Alice was covering an event for the magazine she worked for, so I was on my own. I knew something was up as soon as I walked through the door. She couldn't stop smiling, as though she knew something but wasn't allowed to say. I said nothing, just waited, knowing she'd tell me whatever it was if she wanted to—thinking it was probably something village-gossip-related that I wouldn't be too interested in anyway.

We sat down to dinner (I was stuffing my face with her delicious homemade steak pie), when she finally cracked.

"Okay, okay, okay," she said excitedly, waving her arms in the air, her grin getting bigger with each second that passed. "I'm not meant to say anything, but then, you probably know already so there's no point us both pretending we don't know when we do."

"What are you talking about?" I asked—I couldn't help but smile back, she was totally giddy over the news she'd been told, and I rarely saw her like that—like a naughty teenager, unable to keep a secret.

"Oh, give over," she said, tapping my arm across the table, as though I was playing with her. "You clearly know. I can see it on your face."

"I don't, Mum. Honestly."

"Why are you smiling like that, then?"

"Because I've never seen you act like this before, that's why."

"Oh . . ." she said, suddenly unsure whether she should carry on or not. "Well, perhaps I should keep it a secret, then. You don't want to hear it from me. Forget I said anything."

"Mum! Go on, you can't leave it there."

"Ah, it's just too exciting to keep from you, and there's no one else I can tell," she practically screamed, bursting with happiness. "Robert's gone and asked for permission."

"What sort of permission?"

"Don't be daft. To ask Maddy to marry him. He went over to see Kathryn and Greg yesterday—Carol told me this morning. They're all so excited."

I should have guessed it would happen one day. They'd been together since they were sixteen and had lived with each other for three years—it was the next step, we weren't kids any longer. The feelings it conjured shocked me—I was happy for them, but, mostly, I was sad. Sad that, if there was ever any doubt about the matter, Maddy and I would never have a chance of being together. It was a selfish thought, but it arose in me nonetheless, causing me to be annoyed at my heart for betraying me after all those years.

"Didn't he say anything to you?"

"No," I said, managing to smile at my mother's beaming face.

"I expect he wanted it to be a surprise for you too. Oh, it'll be a lovely day for all of you really, not just them two."

"Do you know when he's going to do it?"

"No idea, love. Next few weeks or months, though, I'd have thought. I don't think he has a ring yet."

"Wow."

"I know. Exciting, huh? Better get looking for a hat!" she beamed, unable to hide her excitement. "Ooh, and, well, I know Rob's got two brothers, but I'm sure you'll be best man. You'll have to do a speech and everything. We can go through the loft and dig out some old photos. I think we've even got some from when I first met Carol. Yes, some great ones of you two eating ice cream in your prams, it's all over your faces."

I played along with her joy, trying to ignore the panic stirring within me at the thought of losing Maddy, the girl I'd tried so hard not to love.

That Saturday night Alice and I were on our sofa watching *The Jonathan Ross Show*, tucking into an Indian takeaway—something we treated ourselves to more than we ought to. It was a bad habit that had lingered with us since our university days.

"Do you ever think about the future?" I asked, topping up our glasses of wine, of which we'd had quite a few—another bad habit that had carried over from student life.

"In what way?" she asked, mopping up some pilau rice that had escaped from her plate and fallen onto her lap.

"I dunno, what you think it'll be like?"

"Well, when I was six we were asked to draw a picture of what we thought the millenium would look like—I drew some elaborate flying car and a robotic dog. My teacher said I was unrealistic but imaginative . . . I guess I'm still waiting for my flying car to be invented," she shrugged with a giggle.

"Not like that. I mean, where do you see yourself in five or ten years' time?"

"Oh," she tutted, tapping her fork against the side of her plate as she thought of her answer. "Editor of my own glossy magazine, with my own office overlooking the river—a vast upgrade from the shambolic mess I currently work in . . ."

"Nice," I encouraged, watching her forehead crease as she contemplated her future.

"Living in a massive house with a swimming pool and a pink Ferrari on the swooping driveway."

"Pink? Not red?"

"This is my vision, not yours. Am I being unrealistic again? Was my teacher right?"

"Not at all," I laughed. "You can have your pink Ferrari."

"Good. I'll also be married to some charming man, whoever he may be," she chuckled. "And mum to a few delightful sprogs."

"Sounds wonderful."

"Doesn't it?" she laughed. "You?"

"Same," I nodded

"Editor of a magazine?"

"Obviously not, but the rest of it works."

"Marriage and kids? Most guys our age would run a mile at the very thought of it," she said, taken aback by the revelation as she raised her eyebrows.

"Not me."

As we sat there smiling at each other, over our chicken tikka masalas, the next words spurted from my mouth before I'd even had a chance to think them through properly.

"Will you marry me?"

It wasn't just me they'd surprised—Alice's wide-eyed look told me that I'd completely caught her off guard too. Just like me, she hadn't been expecting it.

We sat in silence, looking at each other with our mouths open in shock.

"What did you say?" she asked, her voice wavering with emotion.

"I think I just asked you to marry me," I laughed nervously.

"Did you mean it? There's still time to take it back, if not."

"Do you want me to take it back?"

"Not at all . . ."

We laughed then, broke down in giggles over the grown-up thing we were committing to.

"So, will you? Will you be my wife?"

"Of course I will. Yes!" she beamed.

It was the most unromantic proposal in the world. Unplanned, unnecessary, and done purely because I'd been scared of my own feelings. Petrified that I wasn't over Maddy and aware of just how much it was going to hurt watching her walk down the aisle toward someone else. I was in need of having my own future secured to give myself a little piece of armor, so that I'd be okay when that day finally came. It was the most selfish thing I'd ever done.

Maddy

It was Ben and Alice's turn to head out our way that Sunday and, rather than stick to the High Road, we decided to go down to the Old Ship—a pub that sat on the river with great scenic views of the city. We'd found it the previous summer and loved spending our warm nights under the twinkling fairy lights which hung over their wooden benches. It was just as heaving in the winter months, but luckily we'd booked a table. The place was rammed with people who'd gone for walks along the river only to find themselves in need of warming up after being frozen by the bitterly cold December air—families fooled into not wearing enough layers of clothing by the bright blue skies.

Robert and I were sitting in our window seats, people-watching the walking ice-pops, when Ben and Alice arrived, both looking rather pleased with themselves as they fought their way through the other diners. Hugs, squeezes (not that sort), and kisses were shared before they whipped off their jackets and sat in their seats. The drinks hadn't even been ordered by the time Alice leaned across, unable to contain her excitement any longer, and shrieked out their news.

"We're getting married! Ben asked me last night. You're the first people we're telling," she giggled, before looking at Ben with admiration. "We've not even told our parents yet."

There was an indisputable momentary hiatus, which probably shouldn't have occurred, as Robert and I looked to Ben for confirmation. I knew the cause of my own surprise, but not Robert's.

"It's true," Ben laughed, grabbing hold of her hand and beaming back at us.

They looked ridiculously happy and in love.

"Wow! Congratulations," I smiled.

"Brilliant, just brilliant," added Robert, with a slight edge to his voice.

It didn't take me long to notice the absence of a diamond ring, letting me assume the proposal had been a hasty decision on Ben's part. I wondered why. I'd thought Alice might have been pregnant, that Ben was keen to do the right thing by her and their unborn baby, but as Prosecco was ordered to toast their engagement and swiftly drunk by Alice, the idea was quickly erased. There was no baby. In fact, as the afternoon wore on, Ben revealed that he hadn't intended on asking the question, it popped out and surprised him just as much as it had Alice. Not that either of them seemed to mind its spontaneity; the fact that it was an off-the-cuff decision seemed, to them, to make the whole thing more romantic.

I liked Alice a lot. I even liked her and Ben together. Having her there, as a part of our group, had, in the end, made life easier for the pair of us. Everything was less awkward with her around. She made it easier to pretend certain feelings had never been an issue, that boundaries had never been crossed. I hadn't, however, expected Ben to ask her to marry him. Ever. The thought hadn't even crossed my mind.

I'd taken Pearl's advice all those years before, and reminded myself of her words regularly; that day was one of those times, as I realized I wasn't the only one who'd chosen their path and stuck to it. It occurred to me that, if Ben was willing to make such a grand gesture, prompted by the love he felt for Alice, I was far from his mind. I can't deny it, the truth stung probably more than it should have.

Alice radiated joy that afternoon, she had a real sparkle of happiness in her eyes—and talked nonstop. Clearly buzzing with elation as she reeled off endless possible ideas for their wedding, all the while smiling at Ben as though we weren't even there. The omission was probably a good thing, as neither of them seemed to notice the lull coming from our side of the table. Yes, I wasn't the only one dubious about the sudden announcement—Robert seemed off about it too. He acted strangely all afternoon, was quieter than usual and appeared agitated, not that he admitted to it.

"You okay?" I asked as we walked the short journey back to our house, holding hands through our matching black gloves. Even though we both had on our thick winter coats, mine mustard yellow, his black, the wind managed to work its way in and chill our bones wherever it could, causing my jaw to chatter uncomfortably as we talked.

"Yeah. Course," he frowned.

"Weird to think that one of us will be getting married," I laughed, trying to prompt him into a conversation.

"Yeah."

"I never thought it would be Ben going first, though."

"You're telling me," he answered glumly.

"They both seem really happy about it."

"Yeah."

"Wondered if she was pregnant at first."

"Me too."

"She's not, though."

"No."

"You sure you're okay, Rob?" I asked, getting irritated with his monosyllabic responses.

"What? Yeah. Just got a lot on," he sighed. "School stuff."

"Right."

I knew he was lying, but didn't want to push any conversation involving Ben. My guess was that he was just disgruntled because Ben, his bestest buddy, hadn't shared the news with him first—or given any warning that it might have been a possibility.

It was also possible that he could have been a bit sad to realize that they were about to become even more divided than ever. Before I'd come along they'd been an indivisible duo, by each other's side night and day, but since we were eighteen they'd become more and more separated—first by university, then by living apart. I wondered whether he was worried marriage would separate them even further. Robert might put on a tough exterior, but his friendship with Ben was something he always treasured and valued highly.

Sometimes men were more complex than women gave them credit for. I left him to his own thoughts, knowing that, if he wanted to share them, he'd do so in his own time.

He never did.

Ben

Robert had decided to tell Carol about me suddenly popping *the* question. I knew this because on Monday morning I woke up to find six missed calls from my mum. The fact she'd tried to call so many times did not bode well. I could envisage the steam from her ears increasing each time she hit the redial button, only for her call to be left unanswered.

Deciding to bite the bullet and get the conversation over with, I called her back straight away from under my duvet, closing my eyes in preparation for the bollocking I was about to receive. Following our conversation the previous week I knew, once my mum found out, I'd have to own up to being a prize idiot, or plead ignorance . . . whatever I said, there was no way she was going to let me act as though I'd done nothing wrong, or let me get away with it.

"What on earth have you gone and done?" she shouted down the phone. I was glad Alice had already left for work, otherwise she'd have definitely heard her shrieking tone, and I've no idea how I'd have explained that one.

"I thought you'd be pleased," I said. That was a lie. I knew Mum would be angry at me, I just hoped her anger would subside quick enough so that I could take Alice over to celebrate—the longer I left it, the more suspicious she'd become; I didn't want her thinking my mum didn't like her. That was why I'd said we should wait before telling our parents—suggesting it would be nicer to do it once we had the ring and could tell them face to face. Alice, who, unsurprisingly, liked the idea of getting her finger blinged up first needed little convincing.

"You said you liked Alice," I cheekily continued.

"Oh, I do, you know that," she said, thankfully losing a bit of the honking volume in her voice. "And, yes, I'm very pleased that Alice is going to be a Gilbert one day."

"Well, then . . ."

"That's really not the point, though, is it?" she continued.

"Isn't it?"

"No, and you know it, Ben," she said with exasperation. "I told you what Robert had planned."

"And?"

"And? And?!" she shouted. "Less than a week later you've gone and ruined it."

"How?"

"By getting in there first, that's how."

"Mum, it's not like that."

"Just tell me one thing, had the thought even crossed your mind before I told you about Robert asking Kathryn and Greg? Answer me honestly."

I screwed up my face before giving her my answer.

"No."

I couldn't lie about that, besides, it was more of a leading question than an actual inquiry—she knew what I was going to say before I said it.

"Oh, Ben," she groaned.

"What?"

"What have you done?"

"Nothing, Mum . . . it's not going to affect him doing it."

"Of course it is, he's not going to ask her now, is he? He'll have to wait—and not just weeks, months!"

I hadn't even thought of it like that, but Mum was obviously right. There was no way Robert would ask straight after I had—even if his own proposal was going to be properly thought through and planned. He wouldn't want his proposal to overshadow mine (he was gentlemanly like that) or, even worse, for it to look like he was only doing it because I had. Maddy would have hated the overlap of celebrations, and he knew it. I'd realized he was annoyed the day before—he'd been full of smiles when we first walked in but then hardly said a word after Alice told them, other than to mutter his congratulations. It occurred to me later that, having sought Maddy's parents' approval, I might have been next on his list of people to speak to about it—perhaps he'd have found a quiet moment at the pub to tell me—the idea made me feel like crap. I'd been so apprehensive about Maddy's response that I hadn't even thought about what might have been going through Rob's mind.

Maddy didn't even flinch at the news. A smile broke out on her face within seconds as she showered us with congratulations, seemingly delighted for us. It put into perspective how little past events must have meant to her, forcing me into focusing on Alice, basking in her smile as I reminded myself of all the things I loved about her, why marrying her was a good idea and why I didn't need Maddy.

"Sorry, Mum," I mumbled.

"A bit too late for that, isn't it?"

"I just didn't think."

"You're telling me."

"Okay, so I hadn't thought about asking before you mentioned it," I rambled, hating the fact that Mum was clearly disappointed with me. "But hearing that made me think about Alice and me, about our future and what I wanted. I admit, I stupidly got too excited about asking and it slipped out when I hadn't meant it to."

I was greeted with silence from the other end of the line.

"Mum?"

"If I wasn't so annoyed with you I'd almost find that romantic,

Benjamin Gilbert," she laughed, as it became apparent she'd been holding back her tears.

I was grateful to have won her over.

"I rang Maddy earlier," Alice told me that night, as she grabbed vegetables out of the fridge to go into the dinner. The chicken was already in the wok, so we were halfway toward sitting down with our stir-fry with sweet chilli sauce—I was ravenous, it already smelt amazing.

"Oh, really?"

Maddy and Alice talking on the phone wasn't something that happened all the time, but the two of them had managed to grow quite close over the years—hardly surprising seeing as we were all hanging out together every weekend. It would have been weird if they weren't friends.

"Yeah," she continued, plonking a pepper, a carrot, and some baby sweetcorn on the kitchen side to be chopped and sliced. "Well, I suddenly thought—remember that lovely shoot she did with that couple last year, when they got engaged?"

"Yeah . . ." I said slowly, concerned as to where the conversation was going.

I remembered the shoot—Maddy had taken the couple down to the river and snapped some great pictures of them together while they gazed lovingly into each other's eyes as though they hadn't a care in the world. I liked them. I thought Maddy had done a wonderful job. I mean, they were cheesy beyond belief, but I don't think it's possible to do such a shoot without a little bit of Cheddar being thrown in. All those lovey-dovey looks and smug faces as you congratulate each other on finding "the one"—it's definitely not for the cynics out there. That's for sure.

"Well," Alice grinned, looking pleased with herself. "I thought we could do that."

"Really?"

I was far too negative straight away, screwing my face up in horror. Alice was quite taken aback by the reaction, instantly becoming defensive.

"All right, not if you don't want to."

"Huh?"

"If you think it's a stupid idea then we won't," she huffed, picking up the pepper and aggressively chopping it into chunky rings before chucking them into the wok and stirring them in.

"I didn't say that."

"You're being all hesitant and weird," she said, brushing her fringe out of her eyes with the back of her hand.

"Am I?"

I was. I knew I was. I can't deny it.

"Yes. It doesn't matter if you don't want to do it," she said dismissively, picking up the carrot. "It was just a thought."

"Isn't it a bit cheesy?"

"You didn't think so when she showed us them, in fact you really liked them."

Like I said, I did. I couldn't argue with that.

"Won't it be weird having Maddy do it for us, though?" I suggested.

"She's your best friend, Ben. How many photos has she taken of us over the years?"

"True," I mumbled.

"I just thought it would be a nice thing to do. Give our parents some lovely pictures of us," she muttered, her face falling with disappointment. "It's no big deal."

"You're right," I nodded enthusiastically. "Let's do it." There was no way I could possibly get out of it and I didn't want to upset Alice if it was something she really wanted to do—it was only taking pictures, after all.

"Really? You mean it?"

"Yeah. Why not."

"Great," she smiled, banging on the kitchen side with delight.

"So, what did Maddy say?"

"She said she'd love to—she was in the middle of something when I called, but she said she'd get back to me later on with some dates."

"Marvelous."

Maddy

I was sitting on my backside in the rather dead art shop when Alice called. It wasn't manic and I wasn't busy. I just felt the sudden urge to get off the phone to her and call her back when I was mentally prepared.

Of course, I'd taken hundreds of photos of them before, they were all over my Facebook page, so it's not like I was averse to them being a couple or shied away from picturing them together. But taking photos of days out or when people are drunk and giddy is quite different to doing a shoot based on their love for each other. It's not that I felt I couldn't bear to see Ben and Alice together, or like I was worried feelings would start stirring in me again, more that I felt like I would be a big, fat fraud taking the photos for them. *That* was my problem.

I sat in the shop for the rest of the afternoon and glumly thought about the best thing to do. In the end, after much deliberation, I came to the conclusion that I was worrying over nothing. If Alice had asked it meant that she must have spoken to Ben first, and if he hadn't been bothered about it then perhaps I'd been overthinking it. Three years had passed since our one night together. I reasoned it was silly of me to keep thinking of it so highly and giving it such importance, especially as Ben was clearly so happy and in love . . . as was I.

I phoned Alice back later that night. Robert was watching the football in the other room and I'd just cleaned up after dinner. I sat at the kitchen counter, gulping on a large glass of rosé, while I waited for her to pick up.

"It's Maddy," I heard her whisper, presumably to Ben, as she brought the phone to her ear. "Hello, you."

"Hey, Alice. So sorry about earlier, there was a sudden mad rush. All of Chiswick's loyal art collectors must have dashed out at once to find something new."

"Not at all, don't worry," she laughed. "I should've called tonight when I knew you were at home. It just suddenly popped into my head and I got a bit excited about the idea."

"Honestly, it's no problem at all," I smiled, still finding her cheeriness as infectious as ever.

"So, what do you think? Are you up for doing something similar with us?"

"Yes, definitely. I think it'll be a lovely thing for you guys to do."

"Nothing mad, we don't need to go crazy with it—just some of us wrapped up all cozy and walking along somewhere pretty would be lovely. Something nice and chilled so that Ben doesn't feel like an idiot."

"That sounds doable," I nodded to myself.

"Are you sure it's okay?"

"Definitely. Consider it an engagement present from us," I offered.

"Oh, Maddy, thank you. That's so kind. We could even do it when we come to you next, if you like? Save you lugging all your equipment across London."

"Are you sure?"

"Yes! It makes sense."

"Perfect. Robert can be my assistant and then we'll go have dinner afterward."

"Brilliant. Thanks again, Maddy."

"It's a pleasure," I insisted, bringing the glass to my mouth and sloshing more wine down my gullet.

Two Sundays later we took a leisurely stroll down by the river in the wintry sunshine. Ben and Alice hand in hand, me running ahead with my camera up at my face and Robert running alongside me holding my tripod, light reflector, spare lenses, memory cards, and batteries, looking like a clueless (but enthusiastic) donkey. We snapped as we went, making most of the shots natural with Ben and Alice just talking and laughing with each other, looking all cozy beneath the mountains of layers they were wearing—Alice in a khaki fitted woolen coat, thick gray tights, and flat leather boots, Ben in a sheepskin coat, faded jeans, and chunky Timberlands. They did their best to ignore the fact that we were even there.

I was enjoying myself. I had my photographer's head on and had managed to detach myself completely from who I was photographing. My main focus was making sure the shots all looked good through the camera, that they were framed nicely by the sparse trees and river, and that I was positioning myself correctly so that I could capture them at their best. I was relieved to be finding it so easy.

Walking along we eventually came to a pretty bend in the river, offering a great view of London's skyline in the far distance. I instantly knew it would be a lovely spot to get a few more posed shots, if they were keen.

"Okay, shall we just stop here a second?" I called, getting out of the way of a nosy group of elderly people who had been trailing behind us, trying their best to see what we were up to.

"I was thinking you guys should rest against here," I said, tapping the barrier by the river. "It'll be great to get some close-up stills—I think we've nailed the whole romantic walking thing now. You're pros at that."

"What should we do?" asked Alice as she jumped into position, holding her arm out for Ben to walk into, eager to get going straight away.

"Pose like you're in love," joked Robert.

"Thank you," I said, shooting him a warning look to shut up, knowing his input would deter us from what was going on. "Just snuggle into each other a bit. We can do some of you looking at one another, away dreamily into the distance as you contemplate your lifetime of happiness together and then a few down the lens."

I ignored Robert as he scoffed next to me. That jargon usually worked for others, but I'd forgotten I had Mr. Romance-Is-For-Pansies stood by my side . . . although it probably was a bit much.

I raised my camera back to my face, ready to start shooting again. And that's where it all got a bit awkward. Whereas before Ben had looked comfortable, he'd suddenly become rigid and stiff, clumsily not knowing where to put his hands or where to look. He was far from relaxed. Seeing as he kept stealing glances in Robert's direction and cracking jokes it looked like it was just because he was embarrassed posing in the romantic way I was after.

After they'd burst out laughing for the fifth time, I lowered my camera and just raised my eyebrows at them both, willing them to stop.

"Guys!"

"What?" Robert asked innocently, trying his best to keep a straight face.

"Five more minutes then we're done. Can you save being idiots until then?"

"Just forget we're here," smirked Robert.

"It's a bit hard with that clicking going off," Ben moaned, pointing at the camera.

"Nothing I can do about that I'm afraid. It's the shutter," I shrugged, becoming impatient with the pair of them.

"This is just weird . . ." he grumbled uncharacteristically.

"Hey," Alice cooed, grabbing hold of Ben's coat and pulling him into her, dragging his attention away from what was bothering him. "Close your eyes."

Without saying a word he sighed and did as she said. I was sure he was going to burst out laughing again, but as Alice raised her head and rubbed her nose gently against his chin, his face started to soften.

"I love you," she whispered after a moment or two, smiling contentedly at him.

Ben opened his eyes slowly and looked at his beautiful wife-to-be, his eyes full of doe-eyed love as his face expanded in a smile.

His secret smile.

But that time, it was for her.

Not me.

That was it. As the sun reflected off the water's peaks to make enchanting shapes of light dance majestically behind them, adding to the dazzling beauty of the moment, I took one single shot.

It was the perfect picture of the perfect couple, full of admiration, devotion, and completeness. It was full of love—simple, pure, and uncomplicated.

Ben

I'd never been very spontaneous when it came to love. I'd also never been able to show myself off as much of a romantic either. I'd always had too many feelings that I'd had to lock away, to hide, to avoid indulging in or risk exposing a one-sided love. What I loved about being with Alice was that I could feel something and declare it straight away. I didn't have to think it through carefully or hold anything back—I'd feel it and I could say it. It was that easy. Unfortunately, as I realized too late, it led me to make big gestures, like proposing, before I'd had a chance to think it through properly.

It took me a few weeks to realize I'd made a terrible mistake by asking Alice to marry me. The more I thought about it, the more certain I became of its error.

There was no doubting that Alice was a wonderful woman. She came along and unknowingly saved my heart from utter torment— she gave me hope and made my world a little brighter each day she was in it. But I couldn't marry her. The heart she'd helped to mend wouldn't let me, no matter how much I tried to convince it otherwise.

It might have taken days for me to regret, but sadly, it took me six months to rectify. We had by that point already booked the church for the following summer, a little place in Essex near where she grew up, and Alice was on the verge of going out with her mum and best friend to find her wedding dress. It was at that point I decided I couldn't have her trying on those gowns knowing that I was doubtful about the whole thing and that, irrevocably, we weren't going to be getting married. There was no way I could ruin that special moment for her—I wanted her to be able to enjoy it one day in the future, when she did eventually marry someone who deserved her. Not someone who'd used her as some diversion tactic to get over his own hankering existence.

She was sitting on the sofa, looking through the bridal magazines that had littered our flat for the last six months, when I broke the news to her. I hovered in front of her for a few moments before the words found their way, from the loop they'd been circling in my head, out of my mouth.

"I don't want to get married," I said.

There was no way I could dress the issue up, or find an easier way to say it. I didn't want to be one of those guys who find faults in their relationships by blaming her for things she hadn't done as I pushed her away, or picking pointless fights in the hope that she would call the whole thing off. I knew Alice was perfect, and I'd meant it every time I told her I loved her, but that didn't change the fact that I didn't want to marry her. I couldn't marry her.

She froze.

She sat there, staring at the magazine as though she was trapped in its world of pretty dresses, blossoming flowers, and a forever love, the world I'd promised her months before, but was snatching away from her so abruptly.

"Did you hear me?" It was a stupid question. I knew she'd heard. I just wanted to fill the silence, to get the agonizing moment over with, to stop it from lingering any longer than necessary. "I don't want to get married."

A wave of heat worked its way up my back and to my cheeks, burning them as I waited for her to react.

"What do you mean?" she asked quietly, her eyes still on the page in front of her.

"What I said," I swallowed hard, forcing myself to stay strong. "I don't want to get married."

"Do you not like the church?" she asked feebly, her voice thin and panicked. "Because we can change that. Or if it's the cost, we can invite fewer people. I don't mind doing that. It doesn't have to be anything big, as long as it's you and m—"

"It's nothing to do with any of that," I said firmly and quickly, stopping her from coming up with more petty reasons for my sudden change of heart. Hating myself, I repeated the words—as though she hadn't heard it enough times already. "I just don't want to get married."

Slowly she closed the magazine, its pages fanning noisily in protest as their offerings were sent into darkness, banished from our lives and from the perished Gilbert/Turner wedding. Her hands moved to cover the face of the glowing bride on its cover, as though her gloating happiness mocked Alice in her misery.

"Then why did you ask me?"

"Because I thought I did. Then."

Her tiny frame seemed smaller and more fragile than ever as I watched my words smash away at her heart.

"What's changed?"

"I don't know."

"Tell me," she said, looking up, her glistening eyes boring into mine as tears made their escape, rolling down her cheeks. "What have I done since then to make you think otherwise?"

"Nothing."

"I must've done something."

"You haven't."

"Is it just marriage you're suddenly opposed to? Or is it a lifetime with me?"

"It's not like that."

"But you don't want to be with me."

It wasn't a question—it was a statement. I faltered at hearing her say it out loud. It sounded so cold, so final. For a moment I wanted to take it back, to retrieve what had been said, but I couldn't. I knew, whether I told her then or at the altar, I wouldn't be marrying Alice Turner. My heart wouldn't let me marry into a lie that I'd let fester for long enough already.

"Alice, I think the world of you. I love you."

"Don't say that. Please, Ben, don't you dare say that."

"But I do. It's true. There's nothing I wouldn't do for you."

"Except marry me," she jeered sadly, raising her eyebrows, defying me to contest her words. "Or be with me."

"Alice . . ."

"Is there someone else?" she asked curtly, cutting me off.

"Of course not."

"You sure? There's not some girl who's caught your attention at work? Made you think twice about being stuck with me?"

"No."

"Then why don't you want to marry me? If there's no one else and you love me, why don't you want to be with me any more?"

"Because it's not what I want."

"And what do you want?"

"I don't know."

"Why are you doing this to me?" she screamed, furious with my lack of substantial responses. She hurled the mocking magazine at me, the corner of its bind catching me on my forehead, cutting it and making it bleed.

"I'm so sorry, Alice," I shouted back.

"Sorry you ever asked?"

"No."

"Then what for?"

"For hurting you. I never wanted to do that."

"You saying that doesn't make it any less cruel," she spat. "You're still breaking my heart and making me look like a complete fool."

I hated that I'd turned the most happy, bubbly, and loving girl I'd ever met into such a ball of anger—it was yet another failure to add to my evergrowing list of mistakes.

Robert was the only one who'd known that I was calling my wedding off and ending things with Alice. I'd phoned him the morning I planned to do it.

I'd been in our bedroom, surrounded by her things and pictures of us together with giddy faces on various holidays, funny trips, and *that* picture, when I'd had an overwhelming urge to leave—to just walk out and avoid the confrontation as I broke her heart. The desire was so strong I knew I had no choice but to talk to her that night. Something had snapped inside me and I was worried that if I didn't act quickly my longing simply to flee would become a reality. I didn't want that.

Leaving our room, our home, I wandered into Victoria Park and walked round in circles for hours. Surprisingly, there weren't many thoughts spiraling around in my head, it seemed it had made its mind up. Instead it numbed my doubt and affirmed the end of our relationship.

At lunchtime, when I knew Robert would be at his desk and not in lessons, I sat on a bench by the vast lake at the bottom of the park, pulled out my phone, and called him.

I needed to hear the words said out loud, before I said them to Alice, and the only person in my life who would not judge me for saying them or for making the decision was Robert.

"Are you sure?" was the first thing he'd asked.

"Yes."

"Blimey," he puffed. "Have you been arguing?"

"No."

"Cheated?"

"No."

"Has she?"

"I hope not."

"Why, then?" he asked, sounding confused.

"It's just not right."

"Mate, it's not just prewedding jitters, is it? Because once you do this, there's no going back," he warned.

"I'm aware of that."

"I think you should give yourself some time before you do anything drastic. You might change your mind."

"I won't."

"How do you know? A few months ago you wanted to marry her. Maybe sit on it for a bit," he suggested. It wasn't like Robert to hand out rational advice, but by then my mind had been set far too long to adjust my plan and reconfigure my emotions.

"I don't need to."

"But you might wake up in the morning and regret it."

"I might, but I doubt it."

"I don't know what to say."

"There's nothing to say. It's shit."

"Yeah . . ."

Convinced that I couldn't be talked out of it, or persuaded to wait, Robert sighed.

"Stay at mine tonight."

"No, you don't want me there, moping around."

"Where else are you going to go?" he asked.

I hadn't thought of that. There was no way I could expect Alice to let me stay in the flat and sleep beside her, and I wasn't ready to go home and tell Mum. I didn't want to break two women's hearts in the one night.

"Please," Robert pushed. "Maddy's out with Pearl anyway—think of it as keeping me company."

"Okay."

Knowing it was just going to be us was all the convincing I needed. He was ready and waiting for me when I turned up on his doorstep at eleven o'clock that night, armed with two suitcases of my belongings—the upshot to living in a tiny rented bedroom was that I didn't have much to take with me when I left. Robert took me inside, handed me a beer, and sat with his arm firmly around me while I looked straight ahead, wondering how I'd managed to make such a pig's ear of everything.

I couldn't help but be reminded of sitting next to him in my treehouse all those years before, when we were just nine years old. It struck me that, all these years later, he was still there to be my anchor. I didn't even need to ask for the voiceless comfort—he was just there to console me in the way he knew I needed.

That's when I decided he deserved better than a shitty friend like me, and it wasn't just Alice I needed to get away from.

Maddy

Ben stayed on our sofa for a week following his split from Alice. He left it a few days before heading back to Peaswood to tell June there wasn't going to be a wedding. Robert went along with him for moral support. Unsurprisingly she took it well, praised him for realizing something wasn't right, and bravely acting on that rather than just going along with it because he was too scared to hurt Alice's feelings. He'd been anxious before seeing her, but once he had he seemed a little happier, as though he was ready to start moving forward.

Toward the end of his stay at ours, we were having dinner (I'd made us a Mexican feast) when Ben's future was brought up for discussion.

"So, any more thoughts, Ben? What's next?" asked Robert, before stuffing a taco into his mouth, taking care not to lose any of its filling. There was no tidy way of eating the dish—it was the only one he could eat like a slob and not have me moaning at him for it.

Ben sighed at the question, put down the taco he was eating and wiped his mouth with the side of his hand.

"Now there's a question," he smiled.

"There's no rush for you to leave here!" I explained, not wanting him to think we were hinting that he'd overstayed his welcome.

Robert and I had agreed that he was welcome to stay as long as he wanted, knowing he'd do the same for either of us if ever needed.

"That's lovely of you both, but, actually, I do have a plan."

"Oh, really? Do share."

"I've decided I'm going to go away for a bit."

"Great idea, a holiday would do you the world of good," Robert nodded, slapping him on the back in encouragement before turning his attention back to the food on his plate.

"Not quite a holiday, mate. I'm going to be away longer than that."

"What do you mean?"

"I'm going to go traveling."

"As in backpacking?" I squeaked in surprise.

"Ha, yes."

"But why?" asked Robert, a frown forming as he looked back up at him.

"Why not? You said it yourself, some time away will do me good."

"I meant a week in Tenerife, or somewhere slutty like Magaluf."

"How long will you be gone for?"

"I don't know. A year, two years, maybe."

"Two years? What? Why that long?" demanded Robert, unable to hide the disappointment of losing his friend for that long.

"Because there's a whole world to see."

"And you want to go on your own?" I asked, trying to ask a few sensible questions seeing as Robert was working himself up into some sort of hysteria.

"It'll be good for me," he shrugged. "Do a bit of soul searching."

"Soul searching? Ben, what's really going on? You suddenly got engaged, then broke it off and dumped the loveliest girl you've ever met for no apparent reason, and now you're going off? Leaving us? Why?"

"Robert," I warned, worried that he was being too hard on Ben after everything he'd been through.

"No, Maddy, I mean it," he said gruffly. "What's going on?"

"I need a change. Things weren't right with Alice, even though, yes—thank you for pointing it out—she was great," he sighed, casually picking up another taco from the table and filling it with sauce, as though he hadn't just dropped a massive bombshell on his two best friends and told us he was about to move thousands of miles away.

Robert looked at him as though he'd gone mad. I must admit that even I found the whole thing to be a rather dramatic way of getting over whatever had happened between him and Alice, but it wasn't for us to dictate what he did or where he went. We were only meant to be there for him—something that Robert, in his shock, had forgotten.

"I'm going to say this, and I don't want you to freak out on me," Robert said slowly, looking concerned. "Is it because of your dad?"

"What?"

"Are you worried that you're like him? That you'd wake up one day and decide to leave?" he asked, his hands to the heavens as he looked at Ben imploringly. "Because you're so far from ever being the coward he was. You're flipping amazing, Ben. You've got nothing to worry about."

"Thanks for the textbook analogy. But that's really not it. I know I'm nothing like him," he assured him, his spirits luckily not dampened by his words. "This is something I've always thought about doing at some point, I just wasn't sure when."

"You never told me," Robert shrugged.

"Because I was in a relationship and I guess it seemed like an unrealistic thing to do. After finishing things, it dawned on me that if I don't do it now then I never will."

"You can't just up and leave, you've got a good thing going here."

"Have I?" he questioned, pulling Robert up on his words.

"Yes, with work. Think about all the contacts you've worked hard to make."

"True, but I'm also twenty-four and still acting like a student."

"You're an artist," Robert declared passionately. "Aren't you meant to be all floppy-haired, wearing baggy clothes, and eating Pot Noodles?"

"Thanks. You're forgetting that, right now, I'm also homeless."

"You can just stay here," Robert pleaded, his arms waving in the air at the space around us.

"No, I can't do that."

"Why not?"

"Because it wouldn't be fair. Besides, it's something I really want to do," he insisted.

"When are you thinking of going?" I asked, interrupting them, having sat quietly listening to Ben continuously rebuke Robert's attempts at changing his mind for long enough. His rough approach wasn't working. Ben was set on his plan to travel; there was no way his decision was going to be swayed.

"Soon. In a few weeks. I've got to finish some bits on the film I'm working on and then I'll set off."

"Can you even afford it?"

"Rob, I'm flattered that you want me to stay, but cool it. I'm going," he said gently, leaning over and laying a hand on his arm. "And don't worry—I plan on meeting up with a few friends for some of it, seeing what work they can throw my way to make ends meet."

"You've really thought about it?" Robert asked sadly, sighing as he started to accept Ben's plans.

"I have."

"I'm really going to miss you, mate," he whispered glumly.

"You too."

It was rare to see the boys get emotional with each other like that. I just sat there and let the moment happen, touched by its potency.

Robert went up to bed soon after dinner—the joy of having to get up at six o'clock each morning meant he was always left shattered by ten at night. Having Ben there meant he tried to fight it for as long as possible, but that night, in the end, when he could hardly keep his eyes open any longer, he'd been forced to cave in and retire off to our bedroom.

Ben and I were left to tidy up the dirty plates, saucepans, and everything else I'd bashed around and used while making dinner that evening. Unfortunately, we didn't have the luxury of owning a dishwasher, which meant having to do the lot by hand.

"Are you honestly okay, Ben?" I asked, as we stood side by side at the kitchen sink, him washing, me drying.

"Yeah . . ." he sighed.

"Really?" I pushed, putting down the cream tea towel I'd been using and turning to look at him, scrutinizing his face for any flickers of betraying emotion. "Because it's okay to say, if you're not."

"Well, I'm not the best I've ever been. But I'll be fine," he smiled sadly, bowing his head as he distracted himself with the washing up, tackling the big silver saucepan I'd cooked the chilli con carne in with a scouring pad, trying to remove all the black burned bits from its edges.

"Your plans sound fun."

"Thanks."

"Not what I thought you'd be doing."

"Me neither. Especially not at my age."

"It's like a delayed gap year."

"Yes," he laughed. "But I'm hoping my days will be filled with more enlightenment than parties and cheap shots."

"Enlightenment?"

"Well," he shrugged. "I want to explore what's out there."

"Where will you go?"

"South America first, for six months or so—tour around Ecuador, Brazil, Argentina, Peru, anywhere and everywhere. There are places you can go that do crash courses in Spanish. They'll probably be useful, seeing as I'll be on my own."

"Let's hope you pick it up quicker than you did French."

"Oi!"

"I'm joking," I cackled.

"I'm pretty sure I was the only one of us three who could order a bottle of water over in Paris."

"If that was the extent of your French after studying it for five years, I'll stick to my earlier statement," I mocked.

"You cheeky monkey," he simpered, holding up a wet hand and flicking me with the water dripping from his fingertips.

"Have you heard from Alice?" I asked when I eventually stopped laughing and started drying the silver saucepan Ben had finished washing.

"No. It's weird. I thought I would, you know?"

"Really?"

"Yeah, I expected to get something from her—an angry text or a teary drunken phone call, but no. Nothing. She's far too dignified for that," he said sorrowfully, pulling the plug out of the sink and stepping backward to rest against the counter as the water noisily drained away. He crossed his arms over his chest and let out a sigh. "She must hate me."

"I'm sure she doesn't."

Even as I said it I knew I was lying. What girl wouldn't hate the guy who'd offered to make her his wife and then decided, without any apparent reason, that it wasn't what he wanted after all? But that wasn't what Ben needed to hear at that particular moment.

"Have you spoken to her?" he asked.

"Well, I've texted her a couple of times, but she's not really said much about anything."

It was something I wasn't sure I should do, but I felt compelled to. I'd needed to contact her. I knew Ben was my best friend and that it was our job to help him through their breakup, but I'd grown to like Alice. I'd wanted her to know that I was thinking of her. The thought of what she must have been feeling and going through was horrendous. Understandably she was still fairly cut up, although she'd gone to stay with her sister, so at least she wasn't alone with her grief.

"It's hard knowing I've hurt her so much."

"I bet it is."

"I was such a jerk."

"What really happened?" I asked. It was the one thing none of us had understood—even Robert.

He groaned gently and buried his head in his hands.

"It can't have been that bad," I pushed.

"Okay," he said slowly, fanning his fingers over his cheeks, stretching out the skin and pulling down on his jaw, as though to relieve some of the tension that had been building up. "I realized I was marrying her for the wrong reasons. It wasn't fair on her."

"Wrong reasons?"

"Yeah . . ." he murmured.

"What reasons were they?"

"I think it's best I don't go there."

"Why?"

"Let's just say nothing good can come of it."

I looked up to find him staring back at me, his cheeks bright red as a worried look fell on his face.

"Oh."

"Yeah . . ." he sighed. "That old chestnut."

Silence fell upon us as the meaning of what wasn't said took shape. It hadn't been what I was expecting. I'd seen him and Alice together, the way he'd looked at her with complete admiration and wonderment—in my mind he'd clearly loved her far more than he had ever loved me. It had been blatantly obvious. Hadn't it?

"You know," he said, abruptly standing up straight and making his way to the kitchen door, clapping as he did so to emphasize the end of the conversation. "I'm shattered too, actually. I'd better go get some sleep. Got a busy day of planning ahead of me tomorrow."

"Ben?"

He stopped, swiveled on the spot and faced me.

A sadness lingered between us as we took each other in.

There was so much I could have said, but in that moment none of those unsaid words leaped from my mouth. Instead, I stood there staring at him, my mind scrambled with confusion.

"Night, Maddy," he whispered. There was no hope in his voice, no longing. Just defeat.

"Night, Ben."

As I stood there, looking at the spot where Ben had been moments before, I was reminded of all the feelings I thought had long since disappeared. Rather than making me feel loved, they made me feel bereaved. I was standing in the kitchen of the home I shared with the man I loved, thinking of another man. I wasn't too keen on the type of woman that made me.

I felt for Ben and hurt because he hurt, but I couldn't allow what had passed to take hold of me. I loved Robert and the life we'd built together and I didn't want anything to come along and ruin it. I couldn't allow that to happen.

Ben

I sat on the sofa in the lounge with my head cradled in my hands, full of self-hatred. Unable to believe what I'd done, what I'd practically confessed. How stupid of me. How utterly vile of me to behave in that way when Robert had done so much for me. Even if that *was* the reason for my actions, there was absolutely no way I should have let it be known to Maddy. Ever. That hadn't been my intention when I'd agreed to stay round there. It hadn't even entered my head that it was a possibility. I was going away. I was purposefully freeing myself from the torment of the situation, so why on earth had I acted in that way?

The look she gave me, when she realized what I'd implied, I'll never forget. It was pitiful. She pitied me in that moment. There's no questioning that. Her jaw dropped and eyes widened at the crazy man standing in her kitchen who was clearly unable to move on from what had barely existed years before. She didn't need to say anything, the look said it all—she'd been mortified at my revelation. Bewildered.

The following day I moved to Mum's, telling Robert there was no point me sleeping on their sofa when I had a room of my own waiting for me back at Peaswood, along with a mum who I knew would be desperate to see as much as she could of me in the few weeks before I left.

I was gone before Maddy got home from work the next day, something I assumed she'd be pleased about.

Maddy

I hardly saw Ben again after that night. Not before he went off traveling, anyway. He went back to Peaswood and I faked a few social events when he and Robert met up. The only time I couldn't get out of it was the mini going-away party that June threw for him in their house. It would have been rather unfriendly for me not to go to that. But, seeing as all of our families were crammed into his mum's modest-sized lounge, there was no chance of us being alone together, which was a comforting thought.

It had been a lovely afternoon and wonderful to see how close our families still were after so many years of friendship. Our mums were continuously off gossiping with each other as they brought in more mountains of food (you'd have thought the whole village was coming—it was only us lot!), while the two dads lounged on the sofa and grunted about the football. Robert and Ben had everyone in stitches as they talked through stories of our childhood (tears, tantrums, and laughter), reminding the parents how much of a nuisance we all were. I sat quietly, pigging out on the sausage rolls and chicken nuggets, and listened, feeling lucky to be part of such a close-knit group—although sorry that things had become so complex that Ben had decided to leave. It didn't seem fair.

As we left I hugged Ben good-bye on his mum's driveway. It was the truest hug we'd had in years. Our guards were dropped. I felt an overwhelming pang of sadness knowing I'd not be seeing him for a long time. I squeezed him tightly and breathed him in, holding back the tears at having his arms wrapped around me, holding me securely.

I'm ashamed to say that I walked away from him feeling relieved at knowing he wasn't going to be around confusing my heart once more with his almost-confession.

I waited until he'd left, and was firmly on South American soil studying Spanish in Ecuador, before I decided to tell Pearl of our encounter in the kitchen. We'd been in the Roebuck, one of Chiswick's great gastro pubs on the High Road, for about an hour and had already scoffed our way through steak and chips (her), and bangers and mash (me). We were about to dive into the sticky toffee pudding and salted caramel ice cream, which we'd decided to share because we were so full (but cheekily asked for an extra scoop of ice cream to be added), when I told her that Ben had, quite possibly, insinuated that he'd finished with Alice because he still loved me. It was enough to make her take her eyes off our dessert, for a split second.

"Let me get this right," she said slowly as she pieced together the facts, waving her spoon in the air as she did so. "The first time he told you he loved you he slept with someone else—the girl he got engaged to."

"Yep."

"And the second time he told you he packed his bags and went traveling? Seriously?" She shook her head at the madness of it, before taking another mouthful of dessert.

"Well, he didn't actually say it this time."

"No chance you could've misread it?"

"None."

"What is he playing at?" she asked, screwing up her eyes suspiciously.

"Nothing, he's gone."

"Yes, and has left you behind, sat at home thinking of him. Crafty bugger."

"I don't think that was his plan. I don't think he had a plan. You know Ben's not like that. I think he was just confused, he's been through such a tough time, it hasn't been easy."

I stopped, knowing I was rambling in his defense.

"His plan certainly hasn't worked then," she smiled, putting the last piece of pudding smugly into her mouth.

She was wrong, I told myself. I knew Ben, and I knew it wasn't some manipulative plan to stir up trouble. He'd innocently alluded to things. That was all. I'd brought up the conversation, I'd asked the questions, he had just answered them. As a result he'd momentarily opened the door to those old feelings and given us a glimpse of what was . . . but he'd left it there and slammed the door firmly shut again by going away. If he had wanted anything from me after that revelation, he would have made it clear then, rather than moving thousands of miles away from me. He'd closed the conversation before there was any real declaration of love, making it obvious he wanted nothing from me in return. There was no point in me running my mind ragged over what was clearly a slip following his breakup. There was no need for clarification.

Once again, I had to focus on my love story, the one I'd chosen, and ignore the feeling of elation Ben had caused to rise in my chest.

I'd be the first to admit that I'm not the most romantic guy in the world. I don't buy Maddy flowers for no reason—only her birthday or anniversaries—I hardly ever run her hot baths of an evening, I probably don't even tell her enough how gorgeous she looks—which she does, all the time. Especially today, Maddy. You look incredible!

So, because of my lack of effort in everyday life, I knew I had to do something seriously wonderful when popping the question . . .

Maddy

Robert had asked me to take the Friday before our nine-year anniversary off work, but wouldn't let me know what he'd arranged, insisting that he wanted to surprise me. We'd never done much for our anniversaries in the past. I think that was possibly the only downside to being friends before we became a couple—it made all that lovey stuff seem weird, making us both prefer to do something fairly chilled, like curl up on the sofa with a pizza or something. It's because of that and the fact that he wasn't normally one for big romantic gestures, or planning ahead, that made me so excited to see what he'd organized.

The night before I'd come home to find him waiting for me in the kitchen, wearing one of my aprons over the top of his trackie bottoms and T-shirt (it was what he'd worn for school that day). In his ruffled but delicious attire, he was stirring the contents of a pot on the stove. Just by the smell I could tell he was cooking a pasta sauce—one of the only meals he'd learned to make at university that was actually quite tasty. Not only was he cooking, but the table had been laid and decorated with a dozen red roses in a vase and some glittery heart-shaped sequins were sprinkled on the cream cloth. Two glasses of wine had been poured out in preparation for my arrival. I couldn't help but smile at the effort.

"This is all very lovely," I grinned, putting down my coat and bag before walking over to him in the kitchen and inspecting the sauce he was concocting.

"You haven't seen anything yet," he teased, leaning over and giving me a kiss.

"Really?"

"Yep," he grinned. "You're in for quite a treat."

I let out a girlie giggle as I put my arms around his waist and gave him a kiss. "I love you."

"Good. Now, sit down, have some wine," he ordered, ushering me out of the kitchen and into the dining area. "Dinner won't be long."

Once we'd finished the scrummy meal and our tummies were protruding from the carb-fest overload—there'd been a massive slice of triple chocolate cheesecake for dessert (shop bought)—I decided to fish for more information on the next day's activities.

"So, what are you planning for tomorrow, then?" I asked coyly, tilting my head and batting my eyelashes in an effort to win him over. Hoping he wasn't going to keep me in the dark any longer.

"Ah, I can't tell you that, but take this," he said, handing me a red envelope.

"What is it?"

"Open it."

I tore it open to find an anniversary card with a handwritten poem inside:

> *For nine years you've made me smile by being by my side,*
> *I hope you know how much your love fills me with pride.*
> *For three days we'll go away, it'll just be you and me,*
> *So grab your coat and pack your bags, there's lots of things to see.*

"We're going away?" I shrieked excitedly, jumping up from my seat and standing in the middle of the room in surprise, unsure of what to do with all the giddiness twirling around inside me.

"Yep," he laughed.

"Where?"

"I'm not telling you that until tomorrow."

"Rob, please!" I begged, with a desperate laugh. "How will I know what clothes to pack?"

"Oh, hadn't thought of that." His face creased up as he pondered over an answer. "Just bring warm stuff that you feel comfortable in. But also nice bits. Maybe a dress?"

"What?!"

"Trust me," he said, standing up with a grin and kissing me before piling up the dirty dishes and walking them to the sink. "You go get started, I'll wash these and then come up."

"You're washing up too?"

"Of course. Oh, and bring your camera," he added over his shoulder.

I couldn't help smiling as I made my way up the stairs and pulled my empty suitcase from the airing cupboard. As I opened it on the bed and started making piles of possible clothing to take, I thought of my own anniversary gift to Robert with horror. Even with just the home-cooked meal he'd made that night, he'd already outdone my stupid picture book. I grabbed a pile of sexy underwear that I kept at the back of my knicker drawer for special occasions and packed them inside the suitcase first, thinking they'd go a long way in balancing things up.

At five thirty the following morning Robert's phone played out its irritating alarm tune. For once I didn't mind it. I slid to his side of the bed and nestled into his warm body, my own body perfectly fitting into the nook of his armpit, as I rested my head on his shoulder.

"Morning," I whispered, my hand sliding up his muscular chest.

"Morning," he replied sleepily, lifting his head and giving me a kiss.

"Am I allowed to know now?" I smirked.

"Nope," he teased, as he shook his head and pursed his lips together tightly, pretending to zip them up.

"But you said I'd find out today," I moaned, shifting so that my chin was resting on his chest, half of my body splayed on top of his.

"Yes, but not right now."

I pouted at him like a little child, hoping that would persuade him to tell me, but it didn't work—he was far too in-tune with my little feminine tricks and had clearly built up a protective shield against them over the years, rendering their power useless. I'd have to wait and find out whenever he was ready.

"It's so unfair," I moaned—my last attempt in persuading him.

"You're such a monkey," he smiled, craning his neck to give me another kiss.

"Please?"

"No!" he laughed, a smug smile forming at his mouth. "Right, let's get showered—taxi's going to be here soon."

"You mean, we're not driving?"

"No . . ." he teased.

My eyes widened with excitement. I'd no idea what Robert had planned, but the fact we weren't driving to wherever we were going was extremely intriguing. In fact, it blew any suspicions of what he had planned out of the water.

When, an hour and a half later, the cab dropped us off outside King's Cross Station, my head whipped round to Robert as a smile exploded onto my face.

"Are we . . . ?" I asked with surprise, unable to finish the question.

His face creased up as he laughed in response. Ignoring the swell of early morning commuters who tutted as they made their way around us and into the station, he clasped at the lapels of my coat and pulled me into him.

"I thought it might be nice to go back and see where this little love of ours blossomed," he winked, kissing me before pulling out two first-class Eurostar tickets from his pocket. "But, this time, I thought we'd steer away from a smelly coach."

"Paris!" I beamed in confirmation, throwing my arms around him and plastering his face with dozens of kisses.

"Although we'll probably still need these," he laughed, pulling away from me as he handed me two battered French phrase books. The same two we'd taken with us all those years before—they even had our names written in blue biro on the first page.

I couldn't believe my luck. It was the most thoughtfully romantic thing that Robert had ever done for me. I was astounded at the gesture.

I was still pinching myself as we pulled into Paris's grand Gare du Nord three hours later, *and* when we got in a taxi and took in the sights as we drove through the Parisian streets, *and* as we eventually pulled up outside our luxurious-looking accommodation, Hotel Vernet. A four-star boutique hotel, not far from the Arc de Triomphe, at the top of the Champs Elysées—the famous road lined with fabulous restaurants and expensive shops. Our hotel exterior was what you'd expect in Paris, its traditional stony cream surface patterned with horizontal lines, while at the bottom of its many windows sat intricately detailed black railings, woven with the green twigs of potted plants. Red canopies hung over each of them, giving the place an air of opulence, helped by its expansive glass entrance. It was a far cry from the shabby-looking place we'd stayed in before—it even had a lift, and a porter to take care of our bags as we checked in.

"This is amazing, Rob," I said, looking around our suite—yes, a suite no less! Not only did the room have a stonkingly massive bed with an army-load of pillows laid on top of it, but it also had another room with a large cream sofa, a massive flat-screen TV, and a desk—in case we felt the need to do any work while we were on our romantic trip. It was like nothing I'd ever stayed in before with its high ceilings and curtains that ran all the way up to them at the huge windows—there was even a box of Ladurée macaroons waiting for us on arrival. I took them to the bed and collapsed into the pillows while I popped a pink one into my mouth. Yum, strawberries and cream. I was in heaven.

"Glad you like it," Robert smiled.

"Ah, I could stay here all day."

"Oh really?" he said, climbing onto the bed and straddling me at my waist, taking a yellow macaroon and shoving it in his mouth whole, groaning at its deliciousness. "That sounds like a very tempting idea."

"Doesn't it . . ."

I pulled him down to me, hooking my arms around his neck as I licked his lips with the tip of my tongue.

"Maddy Hurst!"

"Yes?" I asked, widening my eyes innocently.

"You little minx," he growled, nibbling at my lip.

I hadn't even had time to unpack the frilly knickers I'd packed before we started greedily tearing each other's clothes off.

Once we'd managed to untangle ourselves and leave our gorgeous hotel room, we wrapped up warm and wandered leisurely, hand in hand, down the Champs Elysées, taking in the vastness of it as we went, and stopping to eat crêpes (filled with Nutella and banana) in one of Jardin des Tuileries' restaurants for lunch.

We had decided to revisit some of our favorite spots from our teenage trip—starting with the Louvre, which had become increasingly well known since our previous visit thanks to the book (and film) *The Da Vinci Code,* making its glass pyramid even more famous than before. Dozens of people stood queuing, just to have their photo taken next to it, each adopting the same thumbs-up pose.

That night Robert had booked us into a restaurant for dinner, telling me to wear the smartest outfit I'd brought with me. We looked quite the dashing pair as we checked ourselves over in the hotel mirror before we left. Robert had put on a brown fitted tweed suit for the occasion and had even put a cream hankie in his breast pocket (extra posh), and polished his best black shoes so much that they

gleamed. His short hair was waxed in a messy-yet-organized manner, finishing off the look nicely. Robert's slickly groomed appearance was hugely different from the sweaty state he would come home
in every night after a day of sports with the kids. He looked scrummy.
I'd decided (after lots of deliberation) on a tight black below-the-knee
dress that hugged my curves and showed just the right amount of
cleavage—enough to keep Robert entertained if I were to lean across
the table at dinner, but not too much that other men would ogle inappropriately. With my hair curled and pinned to the side so that it
hung over one shoulder, little silver hoops in my ears, and killer black
stilettos with silver heels on my feet, my look was complete. Yes, we
really did look dashing. I couldn't help but feel proud of how well
we'd scrubbed up.

My jaw practically dropped as the maître d' guided us through
the high-ceilinged restaurant. The chic room was covered in gold—
from the sparkly chandelier that hung from the center of the gold-
encrusted ceiling, to the candelabras placed on each table which
caused the glasswear to twinkle in the candlelight. The majestic feeling was taken further by classical background music being played
softly by a pianist and harpist in the corner. It was like nothing we'd
ever been to together before—it was so grand and sophisticated.

We were taken to a window seat, giving us a spectacular, uninterrupted view of the iconic Eiffel Tower.

Taking into account that we were in Paris, that it was our anniversary weekend, and that we'd just been given the best table in the
restaurant, it's not surprising that I suddenly assumed Robert was going to be getting down on one knee that night. It had always been a
topic I pondered over whenever we went away or celebrated a birthday or anniversary (or New Year's Eve, or Valentine's Day; anything
that had a name attached to it, really). I was always speculating over
when he might do it, but, sitting there among all that splendor, for
the first time it seemed like it was likely to become a reality.

For that reason, the excited butterflies in my tummy went berserk,
stopping me from eating or enjoying myself as I cheerfully watched

Robert like a hawk for any further signs—checking to see whether he was quieter than normal, nervous in some way or acting shifty. I saw nothing. Robert looked calm and relaxed as he talked nonstop, ate off my plate (apparently making the most of my lack of appetite), and guzzled down the red wine. Each time our dirty plates were taken off to the kitchen, and we were left to gaze at the view, I'd stop breathing, thinking that it could be the moment Robert had planned to ask.

Nothing came after our starters.

Nothing came after our mains.

Nothing came after our desserts.

Nothing came after our coffees.

Nothing.

Once the bill was paid and Robert stood up to leave, I stayed sitting at the table in a state of shock.

"Let's stand outside and get another look at the Tower before we get a taxi back," he winked.

My heart almost leaped into my throat at the wink, thinking it was him being suggestive—that the proposal was on its way. I gathered my bag and coat in haste, before grabbing his hand and following him outside.

Robert wrapped his arms around me from behind and gazed up at the Tower, its twinkling lights creating a magical atmosphere as they danced along the steel structure.

Stood there, in an embrace, I was again sure the moment would come.

I waited.

And waited.

And waited.

"It's nippier than I thought!" Robert eventually said in my ear. "Want to head back?"

He wasn't proposing. The realization made me sad.

"You okay?" he asked, as we walked back toward the main road to find a taxi. "Have you had a nice night?"

"It's been wonderful. Thank you," I smiled, trying to ward off the tears that had been threatening to spill.

I'd never been so disappointed.

The following night, Robert suggested we take a walk and just see where we found that was nice for dinner. I was happy with that suggestion. Knowing how expensive the previous night had been, I expected Robert would be on the lookout for somewhere cheap and cheerful.

We wandered back down the Champs Elysées and through the Jardin des Tuileries (our feet seemed to automatically take us that way after having walked the route so often).

Robert stopped before the Louvre.

"I'm getting hungry now. Want to walk up there and see if there's anything good?" he asked, casually pointing up one of the roads.

"Yeah," I shrugged, not too fussed.

I recognized La Ferme des Beauvais, the restaurant we'd visited with school, straight away. Perched on the corner with windows that covered the breadth of the external walls, displaying its name in silver-framed red lettering that curved like a rainbow on each pane of glass—although the lettering had started to peel at its corners.

"Are you sure that's it?" Robert asked with a frown, not looking too impressed with the place.

"Positive," I squealed.

"If you say so," he said dismissively.

"We have to eat in there."

"Really? I don't remember their food being the most amazing thing I'd ever eaten," he said, looking up the road and squinting at the other restaurants to find something better.

"I don't care. Come on," I said, as I pulled him inside.

It was exactly as I'd remembered—the same red tablecloths covered the tables, upon which were tealights and single red roses. Even the pictures on the walls were still the same.

"Surely you recognize it now?"

"Yeah, I guess. A bit," he shrugged.

I asked the waiter to seat us at the same table we were at before, causing Robert to laugh at me.

"What?"

"Nothing. You're cute," he said with a wink. "I like it when you're sentimental."

"I want us to order the same too."

"Really? You don't fancy trying snails?"

"Yuck, no," I protested, screwing up my face.

"Okay. I'm up for that."

"Although we are getting a dessert."

"Of course. And wine."

I gasped jokingly, "What would Miss James say?"

Spaghetti Bolognese was ordered and eaten, washed down with French bread and copious amounts of red wine. Needless to say, it wasn't to the same standard of fine dining we'd experienced the night before, but we didn't care. We were relaxed, talking and laughing, making the most of each other's company.

Once our plates had been cleared away and dessert ordered (I'd gone for a chocolate and hazelnut pastry), Robert started to stare at me with a gooey expression, his face softening and a loving smile appearing.

"What?" I asked, a little perturbed—he rarely looked at me like that.

"Nothing. You're just so beautiful."

It was at that point that the ever-familiar piano intro to "All My Life" started playing through the restaurant speakers, prompting Robert to stand up and turn to me, as he gestured for my hand.

"What?" I giggled.

"Can I have this dance?"

"Here? We can't, people are watching," I whispered, looking around at the handful of other couples who were enjoying their meals.

"I don't care," he smiled, pulling me out of my seat and into his arms.

We slow danced on the spot, turning in little circles as Robert put his mouth to my ear and sang along to the words K-Ci and JoJo were singing. I closed my eyes and enjoyed the moment, thinking it was the perfect way to spend our anniversary.

Once the song had come to an end Robert stepped away from me and knelt down on one knee. Using two hands, he held up a sparkling diamond ring that he'd fished out of his jeans pocket.

"What the—" I started in shock.

"I'm not done yet," Robert winked, stopping me from talking further. He blew out air from his cheeks, steeling himself before he continued. "As you know, nine years ago we shared our first kiss on this very spot. It was the start of everything for me. You've always been such a huge part of my life, and I seriously don't know what I'd have done without you over the years. So, here's the question . . . Maddy Hurst, will you marry me? Will you be my wife?"

"Yes!" I practically screamed, dragging him up from his knelt position so that I could kiss him. "Of course I will!"

A cheer rose from around us at my answer.

I was ecstatic.

I'm thrilled to say that in that moment no one else entered my head. My biggest fear over the years about when that moment eventually came was that Ben would pop into my thoughts and ruin it. That somehow, my heart would hijack the occasion and use it to turn against me. But as Robert said the words, I was touched by nothing other than my utter love for him. He was offering me my forever and I couldn't have been happier.

"Did you ask them to play that song then?" I asked, when we were back at our table, unable to keep from gushing manically.

"Yeees," he smiled.

"What? When I went to the loo?"

"Do you seriously still think we came here by accident?" He leaned his head backward as laughter spilled from his opened mouth.

"What?" I asked. "What is it?"

It suddenly dawned on me that the whole night had been planned—our feet hadn't just automatically walked up toward the Louvre, Robert had guided us.

"But you didn't even want to come in!"

"Yes, I did."

"It didn't look like it."

"I knew that if I'd told you I'd booked us in here you'd know I was going to propose."

He was right, as the previous night had shown—any bit of effort on his part would have led me to that conclusion.

"It would've ruined it," he added. "But I also knew that as soon as you saw this place you wouldn't be able to resist coming in."

"Very clever," I laughed.

"I know," he smiled, taking my newly ringed hand and admiring his handiwork.

The ring was absolutely stunning, but then, anything that sparkled would be. A single round diamond beautifully set in a dainty white-gold band. It was flawless.

"When are we going to tell everyone? Who already knows?"

"No one knows. I mean, I asked for permission last year and that was enough to get them all flapping around in a frenzy."

"Last year?"

"Yes. Long story," he grunted, rolling his eyes. "But, anyway, I didn't even tell them we were coming to Paris."

"No!"

I was shocked that he'd managed to keep the whole thing to himself—and plan it all on his own.

"One of them would've said something. Thought you'd enjoy going round and telling them ourselves."

"That's a great idea! We'll have to do it straight away, though, there's no way I'll be able to keep this whole thing a secret. I want the whole frigging world to know," I squealed.

"What about Ben?"

The question threw me.

"Huh?"

"When are we going to tell him?"

"Did he know you were asking?"

"No. I was going to tell him, but then all that shit with Alice happened. I didn't want to tell him before he left, thought it would be insensitive."

"But that was ages ago."

"Yeah, thought I'd let him settle. Figured we'd tell him together. Surprise him."

"Let's wait until after we tell our parents, though."

"Obviously." He lifted my ringed hand and took it to his lips, kissing it softly. "I love you so much."

"I love you too," I whispered.

I leaned forward and kissed him, forcing myself to focus on his lips, on the two of us together in Paris, and on the fact that Robert, who loved me so much, wanted me to be his wife. Our love was real. It had grown from the foundations laid in that very restaurant. It was offering me a future that I could depend on. I knew that I loved and trusted it.

Ben

I'd been in South America for five months, traveling from place to place. I started, as planned, in Ecuador at the Montanita Spanish School—it's surprising how quickly you can cut off from your previous existence when you're thousands of miles away, sitting on a beach in the sunshine with new friends who know nothing about you. Needless to say, I told no one of the brokenhearted girl I'd left behind and, although I did talk about Maddy and Robert, I'd decided to not tell anyone about my other feelings. No change there, then.

I'd gone from Ecuador to Colombia, Brazil, Paraguay, Uruguay, Argentina, Chile, and Bolivia, in that order. Catching buses and planes, or sometimes trekking if I was feeling super-adventurous. For the first time since university I felt liberated and carefree, ready to do anything or go anywhere that tickled my fancy—I fell in love with the sights again and again. Every day brought a new experience to treasure.

I listened to the thunder of the water at Iguazu Falls, Brazil, which was, quite awesomely, like something from *Jurassic Park*. Huge waterfalls splashed from every corner while I sat on a feeble-feeling viewing platform, unable to peel my eyes away—expecting a pterodactyl to fly overhead at any second. I was mildly disappointed when it didn't.

I soaked up the peaceful tranquility of Lake Titicaca, watching the sunset as it caused a vivid array of colors to reflect on the expansive lake. Oranges, reds, pinks, and purples swirled in the sky and in the water, making it appear otherworldly. Maddy would have loved it—the photographs I'd managed to take on just my bog-standard camera were insane.

Of everything I'd done on my trip by that point, sandboarding down the dunes at Huacachina, taking in the obscene view as I went, was definitely one of my highlights. Not only was I propelled off a sandy mountain at a ridiculously fast speed (it's a wonder I didn't scream like a girl all the way down), but the beauty of the world around me was breathtaking—massive sand dunes curved their way for miles around, eventually ending at the horizon where they were met by the deep-blue sky above. It was impossible not to feel in awe of it all.

The world was a big place with so much to offer, I was happy to greedily soak up as much as I could of it.

That day in November I'd arrived in Cusco, Peru. Getting off a long bus ride late-afternoon, I'd decided to chill in one of its town squares with a cold beer as I watched the locals around me going about their daily business. A group of old men, all wearing a mixture of gray and white trousers and shirts, had gathered on the adjacent bench to me, taking it in turns to talk passionately about something as the others keenly listened and nodded in agreement. I'd no idea what they were saying, but they were interesting to watch. Mothers wandered past, their babies barely visible beneath the multicolored blankets they were tied to their bodies with. All the while, at least a dozen stray dogs roamed around to different people, seeing if anyone would offer them scraps of whatever food they were eating.

It was while I sat there, in the Peruvian sun with my Peruvian beer, that I got a text from Robert asking if I was free for a Skype chat later that day. I hadn't spoken to him for a couple of weeks—it wasn't always easy to keep in touch, especially if I was off somewhere remote.

As a rarity, I'd treated myself to a private room in the hostel I was staying in for a few nights, knowing that I'd be camping a couple of days later when I joined the Inca Trail. I'd known I needed to get in as much decent sleep as I could before that. So rather than having a bunch of strangers around me as I tried to make the private call, it meant I was on my own, in my little single room, when the Skype call came through a couple of hours later.

When the image appeared onscreen, I was surprised to see Maddy as well as Robert. Even though I'd spoken to her a few times since I'd been away, Maddy had usually found an excuse to flit in and out as Robert talked—busying herself with making the dinner or doing the washing. Sometimes she'd miss the Skype chat altogether—insisting she'd e-mail me later on. Which she did, most of the time. I'd get the odd couple of vague lines about how everything over there was the same as ever, perhaps get updated on what the university lot or her parents were up to, but nothing really substantial or full of thought. I'd e-mail her back my photos—not of me, obviously, but of the places I'd been and seen. I liked to feel like there was still some communication running between us, that I hadn't managed to ruin everything.

I couldn't help but smile at the rare occurrence of having her join us.

"Mate!" boomed Robert, shifting the screen of his laptop, which he was resting on his knees, so that they were both nicely in view.

It may have been early evening for me, but it was late at night for them in England, and as a result the pair of them looked disheveled and sleepy as they leaned into each other, dressed in their pajamas and ready for bed. I noticed they were on their brown leather sofa in the lounge, the one I'd been staying on before I'd left.

"Hey, guys," I smiled back, waving with my free hand. It's a funny thing, I rarely waved hello at people when I greeted them in real life, but put a Skype call in front of me and it was the first thing I did. Always. Perhaps it was the novelty of being able to see people when they were miles across the other side of the world—I felt like I had to make the most of being seen, starting with that gesture.

They waved back, grinning manically at me as they did so.

I'd assumed they'd missed me.

"Nice to see you've still got your color," laughed Robert.

My olive skin had turned four shades darker on just my first day in Ecuador, something Robert was still shocked by every time we Skyped, continuously making it one of the first things he opted to talk about.

"Where are you?" asked Maddy.

"In Cusco, Peru."

"That's where Paddington Bear's from," she informed me with a knowing nod.

"Really?"

"Yep. What's it like?"

"Well, allow me to give you the guided tour of tonight's sleeping quarters," I said, turning my iPad to show them the bare white walls surrounding me.

"Looks great," laughed Robert. "I like what they've done with the place."

"Yeah, I know, very inspiring. I think they're worried that if they put anything up on the walls it'll get pinched."

"They know what you travelers are like," Rob winked. "Where are you off to next?"

"Inca Trail—four days of hiking before arriving at Machu Picchu."

"Sounds awesome."

"I can't wait."

I'd saved it until near the end of my stay in South America because it was one of the things I'd most wanted to see. I'd heard so many wonderful things about the ancient Inca city from other travelers who had been there—I knew I wasn't going to be disappointed.

"I've heard that's ultra spiritual," smiled Maddy.

"Here comes your awakening. You'll be a monk before you know it," laughed Robert.

I didn't bother correcting him that there weren't really monks in Machu Picchu. I didn't want to be an arse. Instead I just smiled and nodded.

"So, what's new with you two?"

At the question, something Maddy did caught my eye. I saw her eyes widen as she glanced at Robert, a flicker of panic crossing her face as she opened her mouth to speak before closing it abruptly and pursing her lips together. Stopping herself.

Robert, however, was giddily smiling. He placed his arm around Maddy, pulling her into him as he planted a kiss on her forehead.

I knew what was coming before it was said.

"I've asked Maddy to marry me!"

Maddy sprang her left hand up and flashed the sparkling ring as clarification.

I clenched my jaw while my lips formed something resembling a smile.

"Wow. When? How?" I fired.

I had to ask the questions to give me time to steady myself, but I wasn't too keen on hearing the answers. I zoned out as Robert started telling me about Paris and how he'd tricked Maddy into thinking he hadn't remembered the location of the restaurant we'd all been to. I must admit, from what I heard, it sounded romantic.

My heartache wasn't like before when we were sixteen years old and I hadn't known their romance was about to kick off. This time I'd known exactly what was coming—my mum had, after all, told me he was going to ask at the start of the year. Part of me had expected the news every time his name appeared on my phone screen, causing a wave of anxiety as I picked up. I felt a little soothed that the moment I'd feared had finally arrived, that I wouldn't feel that same nausea when he called in the future.

This time I wasn't going to sulk, or cry to my mum, and I wasn't going to go off and sleep with another girl in a ridiculous bid to prove the impossible to myself, because for once I realized that the moment wasn't about me. It was about the two people I loved declaring their love for one another. I had nothing to do with it.

Being far away from home had given me the time I needed to reflect on the years I'd loved Maddy, and on everything that had happened over the previous decade and a half. Talking to other travelers, and hearing their tales of heartache, helped to put everything into perspective. Yes, it hurt, and yes, that pain was all relative to me and was real because I was living it, but I wasn't the only one in the world to feel that way. The difference was that other people were able to come out of such times and move forward, creating happier memories, new lives. Even though I thought I was moving forward with my life before—I'd had a good job, I was engaged—deep down I was waiting, although I hadn't told myself what for. For Robert to stray again? For Maddy to leave him? To realize she loved me? Whatever it was, it had stopped me, and that was something I'd realized while I was away. But I was the only one whose life was hindered by me pointlessly holding back. I was spoiling life for myself.

Maddy was happy. I could see that as I looked at her on my screen that day. She was visibly glowing as she gazed at Robert.

He made her happy.

She wasn't waiting for me.

I wasn't the guy for her.

That was when I realized that I'd never allow myself to stand between them ever again. It was yet another affirmation that I was wrong to ever have spoken up and act on my feelings. They were always going to end up together. I should have known that from the start.

"That all sounds magical," I said as Robert came to the end of whatever he was saying.

"That's not all, actually," he grinned. "I was wondering if you'd be my best man."

Mum had predicted it. I'd shunned the idea.

I was speechless.

I couldn't think of anywhere better to go and ponder over a broken heart than Machu Picchu—a deserted city built for the Inca kings on the peak of a mountain.

I was taking on that adventure with a mixture of people that the tour company had bundled together—a few travelers who'd been to almost all the same places as I had, an older couple from Canada who'd decided, after years of working hard, to stop and go see the world, and an English family with two sons who were a little younger than me. Our trek guide was a short, tubby man called William, a local from Peru with limited English, meaning that, although he was eager to please, it wasn't always possible to get the information we craved. For instance, I'd heard many different theories about why Machu Picchu was built and who for and had loads of questions about it—but each time I queried him I ended up more confused. From what I understood, Machu Picchu had been built in the fifteenth century for the Incas to live in, a sacred place built by the people to show their devotion to their kings.

The walk getting there was mind-clearing enough. Even though our bags were carried by donkeys, it was still a struggle. The altitude made it difficult to walk more than five minutes before it swooped in and took your breath away, and when that wasn't an issue our legs occasionally went stiff from the number of stairs we had to scramble our way up. The plus side was that it forced us to stop and take a look at the surroundings.

I'd seen photos. I knew what Machu Picchu was going to look like, but as I climbed up the final uneven steps of the Inca trail and crossed through the Sun Gates to see it for the first time, I was overcome with emotion. Perhaps it was the exhaustion that made me feel that way, but I found myself having to walk away from the group to shed a few tears.

It was the first time in over five months that I felt part of a group and not a lone traveler. Yes, there were moments when I'd spend a few days with people here and there—but being on the Inca Trail gave the group a sense of unity. We were traveling toward something and did our best to help each other get there. It made me miss home. Miss Robert and Maddy and being a part of our team.

As I sat at the mountain's peak, overlooking the vast number of buildings that had been erected by worshippers who died to make their Inca kings happy, I thought of my two best friends. It hurt that Maddy had distanced herself so much from me and that I was becoming more of a stranger to her than someone she confided in. It was my own fault that things had become that way, but I missed her. I missed having her as a best friend to chat to every day. And as for Robert, I'd always felt like I owed him so much for always being there for me, but instead of repaying him I betrayed him. In many ways I'd started to wish that I could take the last few years back—transport us back to the days of innocence, when everything was far less complicated.

I was twenty-one when I drunkenly told Maddy I loved her. The way I acted following that showed my lack of maturity at the time. I should have talked to her and explained how I felt, not just acted out. I dread to think how I'd look back at the whole thing in my old age, with further years of worldly wisdom to draw upon. I wondered whether I'd cheer at myself for acting on impulse and seizing the moment, or reprimand myself for betraying a friend and acting so foolishly. I had a feeling it would be the latter.

I'd already known there was no way that I was ever going to get the girl, but hearing that she was getting married, that she'd be forever out of my reach, hurt. She'd agreed to marry Robert. No matter how she felt about me, the fact she'd said "yes" to being his wife told me everything I needed to know.

I needed to forgive myself for the things I could not change, and move forward in the hope of salvaging the best friendship and love I'd ever known.

I wanted my friends back.

Paris served us well once and, as you are sitting here now you will know that it served us well a second time. I can't tell you how honored I am to be married to the most wonderful woman in the world. Kathryn and Greg, I promise I'll take good care of her. And Maddy, I promise that from now on I will bring you home flowers for no reason at all, I will run you baths and I will tell you just how gorgeous you look.

So please, join me in raising a glass to my beautiful wife. The Bride.

Maddy

TWENTY-SIX YEARS OLD . . .

It's quite impossible to move forward and tell yourself that you're doing the right thing when everything seems to be making you question it. Weddings make you think for a start (and I'd been to two that year), as do love songs on the radio, romantic films, or crazy dreams full of wacky scenarios and flashbacks—highly unhelpful. I thought of Ben a lot in the lead-up to my wedding. More than I should have.

It upset me that he kept springing into my thoughts. I couldn't understand why, when I was so happy, his face kept coming into focus to contest that.

And I *was* happy. I was completely happy with my life with Robert. That's something I can't stress enough. He was my best friend, he made me laugh every day, he challenged me physically and mentally, he was my ultimate pillar of support, always there, always loving, always giving. There was no reason for me to look elsewhere or consider the possibility that we weren't right together. We were, I knew we were, had done since day one.

But what did Ben taking over my thoughts mean? That's what I kept asking myself. Was it the Universe's way of telling me to think wisely before getting married? Was it suggesting I was meant to choose Ben? Or was he simply on my mind because I'd put him there.

A couple of months before my wedding, after driving myself slightly loopy, I decided to write an e-mail to Ben, to get all my thoughts out in the hope that he'd be able to shed some light on the matter. I'm not entirely sure what I expected from him, but it helped to sit down and just blast out all my feelings. It helped me to organize them and see things more clearly.

That e-mail sat unsent in my drafts folder for weeks. I thought about sending it time and time again. I'd look at it and reword bits, making sure it made sense, and that it truly reflected how I felt. It did, but something stopped me from typing his name in the address bar and pressing the send button. I let it sit there for as long as I could.

The night before my wedding I was in my old bedroom trying to sleep, but wasn't having much luck. I had too much nervous energy bubbling away inside me. It didn't help that my gorgeous wedding gown was hanging from the door of my wardrobe, demanding my attention—doing its best to tempt me out of bed and squeeze into it ahead of schedule.

Lying in the bed from my childhood, I thought about everything that could possibly go wrong the following day—the normal bride worries—but I also thought about me and Robert, about how far we'd come since our first smile at nine years old, to our wedding day. Thinking of our future, I knew we'd have a lifetime of happiness together. I knew, for absolute certain, that it was what I wanted.

Suddenly I decided I'd waited long enough.

I needed Ben to know how I felt.

I picked up my laptop from the floor and went into the draft folder of my e-mails.

I typed in his e-mail address.

I clicked SEND.

Ben

Ben,

A few years ago I was told that, in order to stop my heart from being so torn, I had to choose my love story and stick to it. The thing is, I never really felt like I had a choice. You'd got with Alice and seemed perfectly happy, you never gave me cause to think otherwise. You also never fought for me or made me think that a future with you was a viable option. If I'm honest, it made me question if you'd ever really loved me at all. As a result I invested all my love and energy into Robert. I forgave him, and ended up loving him even more than I had before, because at that point I knew what it was like to be without him. I can't say I regret the decision or the years we've spent together. I'm incredibly happy and loved. As we both know, Robert is a wonderful man.

However, every now and then I think about you and what could have been. Not constantly, but it's been tugging away at me enough to keep you in my thoughts more than perhaps you ought to have been. For a while I thought I was having doubts— that it was my heart's way of saying it's you I love and should be with, but I've come to conclude that that is not the case. I DO love you, you can be certain of that, but I don't believe we're meant to be together, I don't think I'm meant to be with anyone. Instead that decision is one our hearts must make for themselves.

I know you didn't believe it when I told you I loved you all those years ago, but I honestly did, and still do. Completely and utterly. Just thinking of you makes me smile. I don't want to go through life without you there supporting me, and nor do I want you to be without my support and love.

Until now, I thought a part of me had been longing for you to come along and rescue me, but we both know I'm not in need of saving. Not in the slightest. There's nothing to save me from. I'm in love with someone we both think is amazing. I'll be full of happiness on the day of my wedding because I know that things are the way they should be.

So it's not because I don't love you that I'm marrying someone else, and it's not because you didn't love me that you stopped fighting for me or pursuing things. Instead, it's because we both have so much love for the one man who's been keeping us apart. He is OUR rock, OUR best friend, OUR Robert. It's not from a lack of love that we'll forever be apart, but too much.

You will always be in my heart and I know I'll love you forever.

Yours, Maddy

xoxox

Maddy

That was it.

There was no going back.

A surge of happiness bolted through me as I spotted him, staring back at me from the altar, looking simply divine. My wonderful man, Robert Miles—strong, reliable, and loving. My best friend. I pursed my lips as my cheeks rose and tears sprang to my eyes at the very sight of him, looking more handsome than ever in his gray suit. His tall muscular frame visibly relaxed as his dazzling green eyes found mine, his luscious lips breaking into a smile that I couldn't help but respond to.

And then I stole a glance to the right of Robert, to see my other love, Ben Gilbert—kind, generous, and able to make my heart melt with just one look. But he wasn't looking back at me. Instead, he had his head bowed and was concentrating on the floor in front of him; all I could see was the back of his waxed brown hair—the smooth olive skin of his face and his chocolate-dipped eyes were turned away.

His hesitance to look up struck a chord within me, momentarily making me wobble on my decision.

Suddenly, something within me urged him to look at me. Part of me wanted him to stop the wedding, to show me exactly how much he cared. Wanted him to stop me from making a terrible mistake . . . but is that what I thought I was actually making? A terrible mistake?

I loved Robert, but I loved Ben too. Both men had known me for seventeen years—each of them had seen me at my worst, picked me up when I'd been caught in despair, been my shoulders to cry on when I'd needed to sob. They were my rocks. Plural. Not singular.

Yes, I'd made my decision. I'd accepted Robert's proposal, I'd worn the big white dress and walked up the aisle—however, if Ben had spoken up, if he'd even coughed suggestively, then there's a possibility I'd have stopped the wedding.

Even at that point.

But, as the service got underway, as the congregation was asked for any reasons why we should not have been joined in matrimony without a peep from Ben, it started to sink in that he was not about to start fighting.

He was letting me go . . .

I did not stop the service.

I did not run off like the girls in films or books who decide at the last minute that their wavering hearts need to be with "the other guy," who had been patiently waiting in the wings since forever. I did not have a moment of realization and "put things right."

There was nothing dramatic, no big outing of my scandal. Nothing. Just me, standing in front of Robert, telling him that he had my heart, that I would love, honor, and obey him for the rest of my life. I declared my vows with love and determination, strength, and clarity. Looking into Robert's eyes and remembering everything we'd been through, how he had been there for me, stood by me, fought for me. All the while telling myself that I was doing the right thing. I was making the right choice—because there was no other choice.

Never before has the term "bittersweet" been truer. I was marrying my best friend, the guy who made me laugh more than anything in the world, the one who I knew would do anything for me, but I was also saying good-bye to the possibility of the alternative love story—the one I had never and, from that point, would never, allow to have a proper chance.

My love story had been chosen. It might not have been the one others might have picked, but it was the one I was more than happy to live with.

Once the ceremony was complete and the register signed, we wandered hand in hand back through our gathered family and friends, smiling as they all cheered in delight, welcoming the newly formed Mr. and Mrs. Miles into the world.

That evening, during an unexpected break before dinner and the speeches, I stood outside, catching some fresh air in a trancelike daydream. I looked out at the candles that were beautifully placed on the vast green that was encased by towering trees, the sort the three of us had spent our carefree childhood climbing.

What a day it's been, I thought to myself with a sigh.

I'd been there for a few minutes when I heard footsteps coming toward me. My breath caught in my throat as I took a quick glance and realized who was walking in my direction.

Ben.

"You okay?" he asked, his voice low and quiet.

I nodded in reply and turned back to the view.

He stood next to me.

Side by side we watched the candles' flames dance and flicker, matching the twinkling of the starry sky above.

Without saying anything more, he took my hand in his and I instantly knew what was coming—those infamous three little squeezes, those longed-for three little unvoiced words, in the way he'd told me since he was just eleven years old.

One.

A bolt surged through me.

Two.

My lip wobbled.

Three.

My tears started to fall.

"I always will," he leaned in and whispered, before slowly releasing my hand, turning around, and walking away.

Ben

I.
LOVE.
YOU.

That was what I'd wanted to say in those three little squeezes.

I knew I meant it.

I really did . . .

Being in that setting, with the emphasis of the occasion one of love and happiness, it was hard to escape the intense desire that took hold of me—making it impossible to ignore. I had an overwhelming urge to open my mouth and say the words out loud, but I couldn't. Instead I found another way to express what I was undoubtedly sure I felt. The words pulsed through my body and out of my hands into hers, the one I loved inexplicably.

Of course, it would be easy to brush the whole thing off and insist it was a crush, a silly little case of puppy love, but it wasn't. It was far more than that.

From the moment I saw Maddy she'd captured me. She had me completely gripped. I was fascinated with everything about her—the way she looked with her firelike hair and flushed cheeks, the way her heart-shaped lips spoke with a softness and warmth, and the way she appeared so vulnerable as she exposed her caring heart. I adored her—it was that simple.

With Maddy in my life I felt whole. She added a magical sparkle that I'd never wanted to live without. And so I told her, with those three little squeezes. I had no agenda, no hidden plan or desire for anything to change between us—my only thought was to relieve myself of those feelings by communicating them in the only way I felt I could.

Three squeezes of love.

From me.

To her.

It was enough to know that she felt the same way back. I couldn't have asked for anything more from her. I wanted Maddy and my best friend to have a lifetime of happiness together, knowing that I would always be there by her side, loving her unconditionally in return.

As I let her go, into the arms of the best man I'd ever known, I felt a sadness knowing the best man had won—it just wasn't this best man.

I'm pretty sure everyone here knows who I am, but just in case there's anyone here these guys happened to meet when I wasn't glued to their sides, I'm Ben. I'm the best friend, well, best man for today.

When I look back at my childhood it strikes me that it was always sunny. Literally, if I were to recall a single tale from that time you can guarantee that the sun would be there, perched in the sky with her hat firmly on as she flamboyantly sucked on an orange Capri Sun and nibbled on some Party Rings. As I get older and I witness more cloudy and murky days than beautiful blue skies, I can't help but think there's something slightly off-balance with the way I've stored all those days in my memory bank. But, thinking about it, they all had one thing in common—nearly every story from my childhood, at least all of the ones with the sun shining, also contained two very special people. So, perhaps, what I actually remember is a feeling of warmth radiating from a special bond, rather than an accurate account of the weather in the nineties and noughties.

Robert and Maddy are my sunshine. Without

either one of them I would be lost in a swarm
of rainy days. So, thank you, guys, for pushing
those dark clouds away and filling my days
with light and laughter...

Epilogue

BEN

As I dropped my son off for his first day of school, I watched with a swell of pride as he gaily ran into the playground and played with anyone who showed the slightest bit of interest—he wasn't picky, yet. A friend was simply someone who flashed a smile in his direction and included him in whatever they were doing. He had no reason to be cautious or wary of their intentions. I hoped he had many more years of that delectable innocence ahead of him—before the school politics kicked in and taught him otherwise.

I wasn't the only one to become overwhelmed at that momentous milestone in my son's life. His mother, my wife, hastily fished around inside her brown leather handbag—searching for a tissue to mop up her falling tears.

"Hey—you okay?" I asked, as I put my arm around her and pulled her into my chest for a hug, kissing the top of her head and taking comfort from the familiar smell of her shampoo.

"I'm being silly. Sorry . . ." she mumbled, shaking her head slightly at the emotion continuing to mount inside of her. Unable to regain control of her breathing, she allowed soft sobs to escape as she continued to talk. "He's just so grown up. Where did the time go?"

"He's still our little Scruff," I assured her, using the nickname we'd given him on account of the fact that no matter what we dressed him in, and no matter how much we scrubbed him clean, our little tyke always looked like he'd been on some great grubby endeavor. His rosy cheeks and unruly dark curly hair didn't help to make him look any smarter.

She pursed together her lips and gave a little nod of agreement before exhaling and pulling her golden-brown hair away from her face. "I just hope he likes it," she shrugged.

"He'll love it."

"But what if he misses us?" she frowned, turning to check on his whereabouts, her bottom lip pouting out in the same way our son's did—it was hard to decide which of them had picked up that little habit from the other. I wondered if she'd always pulled that expression, and whether it was just amplified now that I had two gorgeous faces showing their scrummy bottom lips whenever they were worried and looking for comfort. Either way, they both had the ability to melt my heart within seconds. I wanted more than anything to resolve their woes, for them to know I was there, with them unconditionally— that they'd always have me for support. I was never going to be a dad who upped and left, or a husband who deserted his wife without a second thought. But then, why would I when I knew the two of them brought out the best in me and that I had everything I'd ever need within the four walls of my family home? Nothing would ever tempt me into tearing our happy existence apart. I knew that unquestionably.

"Kate," I breathed, unable to stop a smile from spreading across my lips—she really was adorable. "We've been stood where he left us for the last five minutes and he hasn't looked round once to check if we're still here. He's far too excited about getting up those monkey bars and having a swing."

"True," she sighed, as she brought her crumpled tissue up to her hazel eyes once more.

"He'll be home in a matter of hours, chewing our ears off with every little detail."

With a nod, she smiled up at me, "I know. You're right. We'll never be able to shut him up."

"Exactly," I laughed, leaning forward and planting a kiss on her forehead.

"Nice to see my wife's not the only one who's an emotional wreck," Robert mockingly grunted before laughing, as he walked toward us with Maddy clinging on to his arm. Her face was as red and swollen as Kate's, leaving no doubt that she'd been finding the morning our little ones gained some independence just as tough.

"Shove off," she choked, nudging him with her elbow, before covering her face and dissolving into laughter herself.

"And to think you used to laugh at your mum for doing the same thing," I reminded her.

"God, I know. I'm an embarrassing mother already!" she sniffed, taking the tissue Kate was offering her and wiping her dewy face. "I swear I saw her roll her eyes at me this morning too. Such attitude! She's five!"

"And it's only the beginning," added Kate. "It'll be worse in ten years' time when they've got all those teenage emotions flying around."

"They probably won't even talk to us then," Maddy muttered sadly.

"Yep. And everything will be our fault," nodded Kate.

"Speak for yourself, I'm always going to be the cool dad," answered Robert with a grin and a wink in their direction.

"Of that we've got no doubt," Maddy replied with an eye roll. "Shit—did she get that from me?"

We all laughed at the shock on her face.

"Seriously, though, I wonder what they are going to be like . . ." I marveled aloud.

A silence fell upon the gathered group of adults, as we looked over at the children in the playground and started dreaming up different versions of the futures that lay ahead of us as we watched our babies grow and develop into fully functioning adults. What would become of us? But more importantly, what would become of them?

I was envious of my innocent little boy starting out on his first big adventure. Because school, no matter how insignificant and annoying it may seem as we get older and can't wait to get away, sets us on our life's path. It plants ideas for us to thrive upon, teaches us where we want to go, and who we want to be—feeding us the notion that our dreams are limitless, that we can do anything if we believe in it enough and truly set our minds to it. But best of all, it encourages us to seek the friendships of others, to learn to lean on them for support and to console them in return. After all, it's the people you meet along the way who really make a lasting impression and who will, if you're lucky, stick with you for the rest of your life.

"We could spend a lifetime standing here thinking about that," mused Robert, breaking the moment. "Want to come back to ours for some coffee instead?"

"We have biscuits!" grinned Maddy. "Chocolate ones!"

"Sold!" laughed Kate, looping her arm through my red-headed best friend's and nuzzling her head onto her shoulder.

The two mothers had become exceptionally close—probably because our children had become as inseparable as Robert and I had been at that age. It was a comfort to see how much each of them valued the other's friendship—and how far we'd all come.

Before any of us had even budged from our spot at the school gate, we all took a collective (and tentative) look into the playground, making one last check that all was calm and happy (and that our presence was still unrequired), before tearing ourselves away.

I left Isaac in the comfort of his new surroundings, but for the rest of that day, in fact, for many days, weeks, months, and years to come, I wondered what stamp school would end up leaving on his heart. I hoped with every ounce of my being that he would have the pleasure of knowing love and heartache in the way that I did. It might sound strange me wanting my five-year-old son to experience heartache, but without it I wouldn't have met his mother—a wonderful woman who taught me just how uncomplicated falling in love can be when it is with the right person, as well as highlighting the notion that timing is everything. If I had met her earlier in life I've no doubt that I'd have made a complete mess of the whole thing. I wouldn't have been ready to receive her love or to give the love I'd spent years accumulating. I was unaware that it had been building up so intensely inside of me, longing to be given and bursting to cherish another being in all its entirety. When Kate came along I knew I was ready to open my heart again, but was as surprised as she was to discover its magnitude and strength—love oozed out of me like an uncontrollable tidal wave, happy to be freed as it quickly enveloped her in a tight embrace—promising never to let go.

Without it I wouldn't have him—my biggest challenge, yet my greatest achievement. Nothing on earth could make me happier than watching my son discover the world. He fills each of my days with happiness and pride, a feeling I know I'll savor and never let go. Ever.

Without that love and heartache I also wouldn't have the unconditional friendships I have with his godparents Maddy and Robert. I couldn't even begin to imagine what my life would have been like without the two of them by my side—if I'd become friends with other kids and hadn't even known them. Without them, I wouldn't be me. That's something I can be sure of.

Nor would my little boy have such a close relationship with Emily Miles—the beautiful little redhead who's every inch as wonderful, magical, and spellbinding as her mum.

I tell myself that there's no significance in the way his eyes twinkle when he looks at her, that he talks about her nonstop, or the fact that he holds her hand whenever possible . . . but you never know.

Acknowledgments

Writing book one was easy—I didn't really have a deadline and was simply writing it for fun. Book two, however, was a whole other story thanks to the expectations I placed upon myself and the fact that life has gone a little bit crazy.

So, for keeping me sane I'd have to say a massive thank-you to my agent Hannah Ferguson. Not only for continuing to believe in me, but also for getting me to believe in myself again once the self-doubt had started to seep through. Apparently it was all part of something I like to call "Second Book Syndrome." *Phew.* A special thanks to everyone at The Marsh Agency (who work alongside Hannah), for looking after me and making everything so simple.

As *Billy and Me*'s editor Claire Pelly took some well-deserved time away from her MJ desk to look after baby Tara (she's so cute—I've seen photos), I was left in the capable hands of Celine Kelly. Thank you for your ideas and inspiring pieces of cake.

Katie Sheldrake, Kim Atkins, Fiona Brown, Beatrix McIntyre, and the wonderful PR, marketing, digital, and sales teams at MJ— thanks for being so enthusiastic about my books and being lovely, bubbly people.

Thank you to Kat Brzozowski, for introducing me to the team and Melanie Fried, and to Elizabeth Curione, Cheryl Mamaril, Anna

Gorovoy, Rowen Davis, Karen Masnica, Brittani Hilles, and Brant Janeway, for continuing to share my work with a new readership over in the States.

To everyone who's messaged me on Facebook, Twitter, and Tumblr demanding to know when they can get their hands on my next book—thank you for the support. I hope you enjoy it.

To all my wonderful friends—you rock my socks off!

Mum, Dad, Debbie B, Giorgina, Lee, Mario, Bob, Debbie F, and Carrie—thanks for being the best family on the planet . . . my life is a lot easier and happier with you guys in it!

Tom, thank you for inspiring me with your many talents and encouraging me to nurture some of my own.

Buzz and Buddy, you two are our everything. Thank you making your dad and me laugh every day. You inspire us beyond words.

Discover *Billy and Me*, Giovanna
Fletcher's gorgeously romantic debut
novel! Read on for an excerpt.

Me

When I was four years old, all I ever wanted was to have a peeing Tiny Tears doll. I'd never been into dolls really, but when my best friend was given one for her birthday I decided that a doll that cries actual tears and wets itself was exactly what my life lacked. After hassling my parents for a few weeks they eventually caved in—although, if I'm honest, it captured my attention for about a week and then the poor thing was left in a puddle of her own mess (oops!). I have no idea what became of her, but I'm guessing my mum sold her at a car boot sale or something similar.

When I was eight years old, all I ever wanted was to appear on Live and Kicking and dance with Mr. Blobby. There was something about that big dopey pink and yellow spotted blob that had me entranced for hours. Sadly, my desire never came true—but I still hold my Mr. Blobby cuddly toy as one of my most treasured possessions and he happily accompanies me to bed every night (despite his missing eye).

When I was ten years old, all I ever wanted was to be a Spice Girl. I used to drive my mum and dad crazy, running around the house, shouting out the lyrics to Wannabe while performing a little dance routine I'd made up. I was constantly putting my hand on my hip and swinging it out to the side, making a peace sign with my other hand and shouting "Girl power!" as loud as I could. I loved them so much that I even *named my goldfish Ginger after Geri—my favorite Spice. I was devastated when she decided to leave. The Spice Girls with no Ginger just wasn't the same, and so my passion to become one of them simply ended (after crying my eyes out for hours, of course).*

At some point that extrovert little girl who used to sing to anyone who would listen and dance without a care in the world, became painfully shy and bashful. I suddenly became less confident at school and around other people—preferring the company of a good book to an actual human. It's bizarre how everything changed; at primary school I was the girl everyone wanted to befriend, but by secondary school I had become awkward and tried my best to avoid everyone. I hated attention, people asking me questions or putting me in the spotlight; I preferred to blend into the background unnoticed. I felt safer that way. On the odd occasion that anyone would attempt to hold eye contact with me I'd usually end up shaking like a leaf or turning bright red, causing me to stare at the floor for the rest of the day. Actually, I did have one friend, Mary Lance, who was as socially inept as I was. I say we were friends—but in reality we hardly ever talked to each other, so I guess she was more like a silent partner. It was just nice to have someone by my side at lunchtimes or in class, someone who wouldn't pry into my life. I think we took comfort in the fact that we weren't alone.

At the end of my A levels, when the rest of my year had either secured a place at university (Mary went off to study dentistry at Sheffield) or planned to take a gap year so that they could travel the world, I was still unsure of what I wanted from life. I decided to join those taking a gap year, although not to travel. Wandering aimlessly around the globe and experiencing what the world had to offer did have its appeal, but I just wasn't quite ready to leave my home or my mum at that point. I was simply going to stay in my home village of Rosefont Hill, deep in the Kent countryside, and get a little job to tide me over until I decided what I wanted to do with my days.

I started my job hunt by dropping off my CV in the village shops—there weren't and aren't that many to target. We have a bank, a library, a post office, Budgens, a florist, a few clothes shops, a hardware store, a café, and a teashop . . . hardly the most riveting high street ever! The last place I entered was Tea-on-the-Hill, perched on the hill's peak, with great views over the rest of the village.

As I entered the teashop, my eyes wandered over the seven tables covered in mismatched floral print tablecloths, each surrounded by two or three chairs—all different shapes and designs. The cups, saucers, and teapots being used by the customers were also contrasting in their patterns. Absolutely nothing matched, but bizarrely it all fitted together perfectly. The smell of freshly baked scones filled my nostrils and 1950s jazz played softly in the background. I was staring at a secret little den for women—why had I never been in here before?

Flying around the room was a woman who I guessed was in her sixties. Her gray hair was set in a big rolled quiff at the front, with the rest of her curls held in underneath a net. I watched her dart between customers—taking orders, bringing out food, and stopping briefly for a little natter here and there. She continued to keep a calm smile on her face, even though it was clear that she was running the shop alone.

I stood at the counter and waited for her to come over, which she eventually did while wiping her hands dry on her pink floral apron, which covered a glamorous light blue dress underneath.

"Hello there, dearie. Sorry about the wait. What can I get you?" she asked, with a broad smile and kind blue eyes.

In the previous shops I'd walked into I had just wanted to throw my CV into the manager's hands and then bolt for the door, instantly feeling uncomfortable as panic started to consume me, but there was something about this woman that had me rooted to the spot. I even held her eye contact for a few brief moments and almost felt comfortable doing so.

"Actually, I came to drop off my CV," I said, as I fumbled through my bag and pulled out a freshly printed one. The lady took it from my hands and casually glanced over it.

"Have you ever worked in a shop before?" she asked, squinting at the paper.

"Yes, a florist's," I said quietly.

"So you already know how to greet customers with a friendly smile?"

I nodded politely as I felt her scrutinize me from head to toe, the smile still plastered on her heavily wrinkled face.

Perhaps I should have told her at this point that I'd spent most of my time there washing dirty buckets in the back room out of sight and not with the customers at all; but before I could speak up she'd moved on.

"How many hours are you looking for?" she asked.

I hadn't thought this far ahead, but one glimpse around the room told me that I'd gladly spend a lot of time here. "As many as you can give me."

"And—one last thing—do you like cake?"

"I love it," I said, giving her a nervous smile.

"Good to hear! You're hired. You've come in at a very good time actually, my last waitress unexpectedly quit yesterday—with no explanation!"

"Really?"

"Sadly, yes . . . although she was a grumpy chops so I'm not too bothered. I'm Molly, by the way."

"I'm Sophie." I offered my hand for her to shake but she looked at the hand, grabbed it, and pulled me in for a warm hug instead. I can remember actually gasping at the intimacy, as it wasn't something I was used to. At first I felt rigid and stiff but once the shock had subsided it became strangely calming and pleasant.

"Now, do you have any plans for the rest of the day?" she asked softly, releasing me from her embrace.

I shook my head and shrugged my shoulders.

"Great, let's class this as your first day, then." She slid a tray with a pot of tea and a cup and saucer in my direction. "Go take that to Mrs. Williams, the lady in the cream blouse with the purple rinse to the left—the one with her nose buried in Bella. I'll go dig you out an apron."

Picking up the tray, I made my way over to Mrs. Williams and carefully placed the pot of boiling tea in front of her. She lowered her magazine and peered up at me over the top of her glasses; I instantly recognized her from out and about in the village.

"You're new here," she stated.

"Yes, I've just started. Literally."

"You live in Willows Mews, don't you? Your mum's that lovely lady at the library."

"That's right," I nodded, shyly.

"Aw, she's ever so kind—always helps me take my books home. I've got greedy eyes when it comes to books, you see!" She let out a childlike chuckle and screwed her eyes shut. "Send her my love then, won't you, darling," she said, while pouring out a cup of tea and stirring in two sugars.

"Will do, Mrs. Williams," I said, as I walked back to Molly at the counter.

"You're Jane May's daughter?" Molly asked.

"That's right," I said, with a slight nod.

"I thought so. Well if you're anything like her then I'm lucky to have you on board," she said with a kind smile as she held out her hand and gave me an apron.

My first day working in the teashop whizzed by in a blur—there was one hairy moment when a plate managed to slip out of my hand, fly through the air, and smash rather loudly into a billion pieces, causing me to blub dramatically—but other than that it went quite smoothly.

My gap year flew by before I'd even had a chance to think about what I wanted to do next, and so I extended it to two years . . . then three years . . . then four, until I suddenly realized that I had no desire to go to university at all; I was happy where I was, and am still just as happy eight years later.

Although I'd started as a waitress, Molly put a lot of faith in me and taught me all she knew about baking cakes and service with a smile. Every day we bake fresh scones, muffins, and cakes, and experiment with new recipes, while putting the world to rights. At sixty-six years old, Molly is continually being told by her doctor that she should be *slowing down and starting to take things easy—but she's not one to listen.*

I didn't just find a passion and career path when I stumbled upon Tea-on-the-Hill that day; I also found a best friend. Looking back now, I know Molly had an inkling of who I was as soon as I walked into the shop. I also believe that, knowing who I was, there was no way she would turn me away without helping me, because it's in her nature to help those in need of healing; and I certainly needed some of that.